Acclaim for
Nelson DeMille's Novels

The Quest

"Nelson DeMille is at the absolute peak of his powers... This is adventure on the grandest of scales and richest of tapestries, Wilbur Smith and Fredrick Forsyth rolled into one with some Indiana Jones tossed in for good measure. A masterpiece fashioned by a storyteller who simply has no rival."

—*Providence Journal*

"...a thrilling story that deserved to be retold—and one that fans of both DeMille and Dan Brown will devour."

—*The City's Magazine* (Fort Worth, TX)

The Panther

"DeMille just gets better as the world gets scarier."

—*New York Daily News*

"He is the most entertaining fiction writer on the planet."

—John Lescroart, *Sacramento Bee*

"Gripping...DeMille gives you a great sense of the people, cultures, and emotions. Plus the writing is entertaining, insightful, and often funny."

—*San Jose Mercury News*

"A fast-paced thriller...DeMille offers a good number of gritty action scenes along with the snappy dialogue."

—*Washington Post*

THE
QUEST

Nelson DeMille

THE QUEST

CENTER STREET

NEW YORK   BOSTON   NASHVILLE

Center Street
Hachette Book Group
1290 Avenue of the Americas
New York, NY 10104
www.CenterStreet.com

Center Street is a division of Hachette Book Group, Inc.
The Center Street name and logo are trademarks of Hachette Book Group, Inc.

The Hachette Speakers Bureau provides a wide range of authors for speaking events. To find out more, go to www.hachettespeakersbureau.com or call (866) 376-6591.

The publisher is not responsible for websites (or their content) that are not owned by the publisher.

Printed in the United States of America

Originally published in hardcover by Hachette Book Group
First international mass market edition: September 2014
First U.S. mass market edition: December 2014

10 9 8 7 6 5 4 3 2 1
OPM

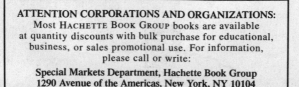

To My Three Creative Geniuses—
Lauren, Alex, & James

Author's Note

The Quest was first published as a paperback original in 1975, and if you were one of the very few people who read it then, you won't recognize it now. The original *Quest* was about 75,000 words in length, and this new edition is about 140,000 words—nearly double in size. Also, I did substantial rewrites on the original material in order to make it blend seamlessly into the new material. As an aside, the U.S. Copyright Office issued a new copyright for *The Quest* based on the extensive revisions and new material. In fact, under copyright law, I could have retitled the book, but I chose to present it as a rewrite in the interest of truth in marketing.

Also, I may have started a trend. A few other bestselling authors have brought or will be bringing back some of their best earlier works, many of which were paperback originals that had a very small audience when they were first published by these then-unknown authors. Their purpose, like mine, is to make these forgotten and out-of-print books available in all formats—hardcover, audio, and e-books—to their new and larger readership.

I can assure you that rewriting and expanding an

existing novel is a lot more difficult than starting from scratch, but it was all worth it. *The Quest* debuted at #2 on the *New York Times* bestsellers list, and reader mail through my website, www.NelsonDeMille.net, has been most favorable, with people thanking me for making *The Quest* available for a new generation.

I hope you agree, and I hope you'll enjoy *The Quest* as you'd enjoy an old Cecil B. DeMille epic that has been restored with enhanced sound and color, and with newly discovered scenes added.

PART I

Ethiopia, September 1974

"What is it?
The phantom of a Cup which comes and goes?"
"Nay, monk! What phantom?" answered Perceval.
"The Cup, the Cup itself, from which our Lord
Drank at the last sad supper with his own.
This, from the blessed land of Aromat…
Arimathaean Joseph, journeying brought
To Glastonbury…
And there awhile it bode; and if a man
Could touch or see it, he was heal'd at once,
By faith, of all his ills. But then the times
Grew to such evil that the Holy Cup
Was caught away to Heaven and disappear'd."

—Alfred, Lord Tennyson,
　　"The Holy Grail"

Chapter I

The elderly Italian priest crouched in the corner of his cell and covered himself with his straw pallet. Outside, screaming artillery shells exploded into the soft African earth, and shrapnel splattered off the stone walls of his prison. Now and then, a shell air-burst overhead and hot metal shards pierced the corrugated metal roof.

The old priest curled into a tighter ball and drew the pitifully thin pallet closer. The shelling stopped abruptly. The old man relaxed. He called out to his jailers, in Italian, "Why are they bombing us? Who is doing this thing?"

But he received no answer. The older Ethiopians, the ones who spoke Italian, had gradually disappeared over the years, and he heard less and less of his native tongue through the stone walls. In fact, he realized he hadn't heard a word of it in almost five years. He shouted in snatches of Amharic, then Tigregna. "What is it? What is happening?" But there was no answer. They never answered him. To them, he was more dead than the ripening bodies that lay in the courtyard. When you ask questions for forty years and no one answers, it can only mean that you are dead. But he knew they dared not answer. One had answered, once, when he first entered his cell. Was it forty years now? Perhaps it was less. The years were hard to follow. He could not even remember the man who had answered, except for the skull. His jailers had given him the skull of the one who had answered him. The skull was his cup. He remembered the man and his kindness each time he drank. And the jailers remembered when they filled his cup; they remembered not to speak to him. But he asked anyway. He called out again. "Why is there war? Will you release me?"

He stared at the iron door on the far wall. It had closed on a young man in 1936, when Ethiopia was an Italian colony, and the door had not opened since. Only the small pass-through at the bottom of the iron door was ever used. His sustenance came in and his waste went out once a day through that small portal. A window, no larger than a big book—really just a missing stone—above eye level, let in light, sounds, and air.

His only possessions in the cell, aside from his tattered *shamma*, were a washbasin, a pair of dull scissors that he used to cut his hair and nails, and a Holy Bible, written in Italian, which they had let him keep when he was first imprisoned. If it weren't for his Bible, he knew, he would have gone mad many years ago. He had read the holy book perhaps a hundred, two hundred times, and though his eyesight was growing weaker, he knew every word by heart. The Old and New Testaments brought him comfort and escape, and kept his mind from dying, and kept his soul nourished.

The old man thought of the young man who walked through the iron door in 1936. He knew every detail of the young man's face and every movement of his body. At night, he spoke to the young man and asked him many things about their native Sicily. And he knew the young man so well that he even knew what went on inside his mind and how he felt and where he went to school and the village he came from and how old his father was. The young man never got older, of course, and his stories were always the same. But his was the only face the old man knew well enough to remember. He had seen that young face in the mirror for the last time close to forty years ago and not again since, except in his mind's eye. He wept.

The old priest dried his tears on his dirty native *shamma* and lay back against his cell wall and breathed deeply. His mind eventually came back to the present.

Wars had ebbed and flowed around his small prison and he imagined that the world had changed considerably in his absence from it. Jailers got old and died. Young soldiers grew old as they paraded through the years in the courtyard of the small fortress outside. When he was younger, he was able to hang from the sill of the window much longer. But now he could no longer gather the energy to pull himself up for more than a few minutes a day.

The shelling had jarred loose many things in his mind. He knew that his imprisonment was at its end; if the explosions did not kill him, then the guards would, because he knew they had standing orders to kill him if they could no longer continue to guarantee his incarceration in this place. And now he could hear the sounds of fleeing garrison soldiers. And the jailers would soon open that never-opened door and do their duty. But he held nothing against them. Those were their orders and he forgave them. But it did not matter if they or the explosions killed him. His own body was failing him anyway. He was dying. There was famine in the land and the food had been poor for over a year. His lungs made a liquid sound when he coughed. Death was here. Inside his cell and outside his cell.

The old man's biggest regret, he thought, was that he would die in ignorance—that as a consequence of the two score years of being held in darkness, he knew less than the simplest peasant did about his world. He did not regret the dying—that held no special terror for him—but the thought of dying without knowing what the world had come to in his absence was a peculiarly sad thing. But then again, his calling was not of this world, but of the next, and it should have made no difference what the world had come to. Still, it would have been nice to know just a little something of the affairs of men. He could not help wondering about his friends, about his family, about the world leaders of his day.

He wrapped the *shamma* around himself more tightly. The sun was fading from his window and a chill wind blew down from the highlands. A small lizard, its tail partly severed by a piece of shrapnel, climbed awkwardly up the wall near his head. Outside in the stillness, he could hear the soldiers speaking in Amharic about who would have to kill him if it became necessary.

Like so many other imprisoned and condemned men and women, like the martyred saints, the thing that had sustained him through his ordeal was the very thing that had condemned him in the first place. And what had condemned *him* was his knowledge of a secret thing. And the knowledge of that secret thing comforted him and nourished him and he would gladly have traded forty more years of his life, if he had them to trade, for one more look at the thing that he had seen. Such was his faith. The years in prison saddened him because they meant that the world had not yet learned of this thing. For if the world knew, then there would be no more reason for his solitary confinement.

He often wished they had killed him then, and spared him this living death for forty years. But he was a priest, and those who had captured him, the monks, and those who had imprisoned him, the soldiers of the emperor, were Coptic Christians, and so they had spared his life. But the monks had warned the soldiers never to speak to the priest, for any reason, or death would come to them. The monks had also told the soldiers that they had leave to kill the priest if his imprisonment and silence could not be guaranteed. And now, he thought, that day had surely come. And he welcomed it. He would soon be with his heavenly father.

Suddenly the artillery began again. He could hear its thump and crash as it walked around the walls of the small fortress. Eventually the artillery spotter made his corrections, and the rounds began to land more accurately within the walls of the compound. The sounds of secondary explosions—stockpiled petrol and ammunition—drowned out the sounds of the incoming artillery. Outside his window, the old priest could hear men screaming in pain. A nearby explosion shook the tiny cell and the lizard lost its grip and fell beside him. The deafening explosions numbed his brain and blotted out every awareness except that of the lizard. The reptile was trying to coordinate its partially severed halves, thrashing around on the reverberating mud floor, and he felt sorry for the creature. And it occurred to him that the soldiers might abandon the garrison and leave him here to die of thirst and hunger.

A shock wave lifted a section of corrugated metal off the roof and sent it sailing into the purple twilight. A piece of spent shrapnel found him and slapped him hotly across his cheek, causing him to yell out in pain. The old man could hear the sounds of excited shouts outside his iron door. The door moved almost imperceptibly. The old man stared at it. It moved again. He could hear its rusty stubbornness over the roar of the fiery hell outside. But forty years was a long time and it would not yield. There were more shouts and then quiet. Slowly, the pass-through at the base of the unyielding cell door slid open. They were coming for him. He clutched his Bible to his chest.

A long, gaunt Ethiopian slithered through the pass-through onto the mud floor and the old man was reminded of the lizard. The Ethiopian rose to his feet, looked at him, then drew a curved sword from his belt. In the half-light, the old priest could see his fine features. He was undoubtedly an Amhara from Hamitic stock. His hooked nose and high cheekbones made him look almost Semitic, but the tight, black hair and dusky skin revealed him as a descendant of Ham. With his scimitar in his hand and his *shamma*, he looked very biblical, and the old priest thought that this was as it should be, although he could not say why.

The old priest rose, carrying his Bible, and his knees shook so badly he could barely stand. His mouth, he noticed, was quite dry now. He surprised the Ethiopian by deliberately walking across the small cell toward him. It was better to die quickly and to die well. A chase around the cell with upraised arms to ward off the blows of the scimitar would have been grotesque.

The Ethiopian hesitated, not wanting to do his duty in the final analysis and wondering now if perhaps he could circumvent it. But having drawn the short straw, he had become the executioner. What to do? The old priest knelt and crossed himself. The Ethiopian, a Christian of the ancient Coptic Church, began to shake. He spoke in bad Italian. "Father. Forgive me."

"Yes," said the old priest, and he prayed for both of them in snatches of long-forgotten Latin. Tears welled in his eyes as he kissed his Bible.

A shot rang out above the dwindling sounds of artillery outside and he heard a cry. Another shot, then the sounds of automatic rifle fire.

The soldier said in Italian, "The Gallas are here."

He sounded frightened, thought the old man, and well he should be. The priest remembered the Gallas, the tribal people who were as merciless as the ancient Huns. They mutilated their prisoners before they killed them.

The priest looked up at the soldier holding his scimitar and saw that he was shaking in fear. The old priest yelled at him, "Do it!"

But the soldier dropped his scimitar, then drew an ancient pistol from his belt and backed away toward the door, listening for sounds outside.

The soldier seemed indecisive, thought the priest, torn between staying in the relative safety of the cell or going out to be with his comrades, and to meet the Gallas, who were now within the fortress. The soldier was also torn between killing the old priest or letting him live, which could cost him his own life if his commander discovered what he had done—or failed to do.

The old priest decided that he preferred a quick and merciful death at the hands of this soldier; the Gallas would not be quick or merciful. He stood and said to the soldier in Amharic, "Do it. Quickly." He pointed to his heart.

The soldier stood frozen, but then raised his pistol. His hand shook so badly that when he fired, the bullet went high and splattered off the stone behind the old man's head.

The old priest had suffered enough, and the strange emotion of anger rose inside him. Here he was, after close to forty years in solitary imprisonment, and all he had wanted in his last moments was to die well and to die quickly, without losing his faith, like so many others did in those last seconds. But a well-meaning and inept executioner had prolonged his agony and he felt his faith slipping. He screamed, "Do it!"

He stared down the barrel of the gun and saw it spit another flame at him. And he thought of the thing that had condemned him. And the vision of that thing glowed like the fire from the gun, all golden and blinding— bright like the sun. Then everything went black.

He awoke to the miracle of being alive. The roof was mostly gone and he could see pinpoints of starlight against the sky. A bluish moon cast shadows across the floor, which was strewn with timbers and stone. Everything was unearthly still. Even the insects had abandoned the fortress.

He looked and felt around for his Bible, but could not find it in the rubble, and thought perhaps the soldier had taken it.

The old man crawled toward the door, then carefully out the pass-through. The soldier lay naked outside the door, and he saw that the man's genitals had been hacked off. The stripping, the mutilation; this was the mark of the Galla tribesmen. They might still be near.

The old man rose unsteadily. In the courtyard, naked bodies lay in the blue moonlight. His insides burned, but he felt well otherwise. It was hard to feel anything but well, walking now under the sky and taking more than five paces in any one direction.

A cool breeze picked up swirls of rubble dust, and he could smell the burned earth and the death around him. The damaged concrete buildings gleamed white in the moonlight like broken teeth. He shivered and tucked his arms in his *shamma*. His body was cold and clammy. He became aware that his *shamma* was caked with dried blood, sticking to his skin, and he moved more slowly so as not to open the wound.

It had been forty years, but he remembered the way and walked to the main gates. They lay open. He walked through them, as he'd done in dreams five thousand times, and he was free.

Chapter 2

The Jeep bounced slowly over the rutted track, and its filtered headlights picked out the path between the tight jungle growth. In the distance, artillery boomed and illuminated the black sky, like flashes of distant lightning.

Frank Purcell gripped the wheel and peered hard into the distorted shadows of gnarled trees and twisting vines. He hit the brakes, then shut off the hard-idling engine and killed the headlights. Henry Mercado, in the passenger seat, asked, "What's the matter?"

Purcell held up his hand for silence.

Mercado peered nervously into the encroaching jungle. Every shadow seemed to move. He cocked his silver-haired head and listened, then looked out of the corners of his eyes into the darkness, but he could see nothing.

From the back of the open-sided vehicle, on the floor among the supplies and photographic equipment, came a soft feminine voice. "Is everything all right?"

Mercado turned around in his seat. "Yes, fine."

"Then why are we stopped?"

"Good question." He whispered, "Why are we stopped, Frank?"

Purcell said nothing. He started the engine and threw the Jeep into gear. The four-wheel-drive dug into the track and they lurched forward. He moved the Jeep faster and the bouncing became rougher. Mercado held on to his seat. In the back, Vivian uncurled her slender body and sat up, grabbing on to whatever she could find in the dark.

They drove on for a few minutes. Suddenly, Purcell yanked the wheel to the right, and the Jeep crashed through a thicket of high brush and broke into a clearing.

Vivian said, "What the hell are you doing? Frank?"

In the middle of the clearing, gleaming white in the full-risen moon, were the ruins of an Italian mineral bath spa. A strange, anomalous legacy from the Italian occupation, the spa was built in ancient Roman style and sat crumbling like some Caesar's bath in another time and place.

Purcell pointed the Jeep toward the largest of the buildings and accelerated. The stuccoed structure grew bigger as the vehicle bounced across the field of high grass.

The Jeep hit the broad front steps of the building, found traction, and climbed. It sailed between two fluted columns, across the smooth stone portico, and through the front opening, coming to rest in the center of the main lobby of what had been the hotel part of the spa. Purcell cut the engine and headlights. Night creatures became quiet, then started their senseless, cacophonous noises again.

The moon shone blue-white through the destroyed vaulted ceiling and lit the pseudo-Roman chamber with an ethereal glow. Huge crumbling frescoes of classical bath scenes adorned every wall. Purcell wiped his face with his sweating palm.

Mercado caught his breath. "What was that all about?"

Purcell shrugged.

Vivian regained her composure and laughed mockingly from the back of the Jeep. "I think the brave man just lost his nerve in the dark jungle." Her accent was mostly British with a mixture of exotic pronunciations. Mercado had told him that her mother tongue was unknown and her ancestry was equally obscure, though she carried a Swiss passport with the surname of Smith. "A woman of mystery," Mercado had said to Purcell, who'd replied, "They're all a mystery."

Mercado jumped from the Jeep and stretched. "We're out of the jungle, but not out of the woods." Mercado's own voice had that curious mid-Atlantic accent, common to people who have traveled between the British Isles and North America all their lives. His mother was English and his father a Spaniard—thus the surname—though he'd spent most of his youth in boarding schools in Switzerland, and spoke French, German, and Italian like a native.

Frank Purcell cupped a cigarette in his hand and lit it. In the glow of the match he looked older than his thirty-odd years. Lines worked their way around his mouth and his brown-black eyes. Gray was sprinkled through his shaggy black hair and he looked tired. He slumped back in his seat and exhaled a long stream of smoke. "What is this place, exactly?"

Mercado was pacing around over the mosaic floor of the huge lobby. "Roman baths. What do they look like, old man?"

"Roman baths."

"Well, there you are, then. Bloody Fascists built

them as part of their civilizing mission back in '36. I did a story on them, as I recall. You'll find them in the most unlikely places. Come on, then. If the mineral springs are still flowing, we'll have a nice bath."

Purcell stepped stiffly out of the Jeep. "Keep your voice lower, Henry."

"Can't very well keep it low if I'm over here and you're over there, can I, Frank? Come along. Let's explore."

Vivian joined Mercado at the entrance of a colonnade that led to an interior courtyard. Purcell walked slowly over the rubble-strewn floor. Five years in Indochina as a war correspondent had expunged any fascination he might have once had for ruins. The last ruins he had gone out of his way to see were the ancient city of Angkor Wat in Cambodia, and that side trip had cost him a year in a Khmer Rouge prison camp. That year would remain a very big part of his life. He'd lost there, among other things, any illusions he might have had about his fellow man.

He joined Mercado and Vivian as they walked slowly down the moonlit colonnade. A statue of Neptune with upraised trident stood in the middle of the walkway and they had to go around him. The colonnade made a ninety-degree turn, and as they rounded the corner they could hear the gentle lapping of water.

"We're in luck," said Mercado. "I can smell the sulphur. The baths should be up ahead."

Vivian stepped onto a low marble bench and peered across the courtyard. "Yes, I see the steam. There, behind those trees."

They walked across the courtyard toward a line of

eucalyptus trees. The large expanse, once paved in white stone, was overgrown with lichens and grass. A two-faced Janus rose up out of a thicket of hedges and projected a monstrous moonshadow through which they passed quickly. The courtyard was surrounded by the colonnade, and vines had grown over most of the columns. Broken statuary of Roman gods and goddesses dotted the yard. The impression was of one of those fantasy paintings of Rome as it may have looked in the Dark Ages, with shepherds and flocks passing through great columned imperial buildings overgrown with vegetation.

They walked by a dry fountain in a melancholy garden and passed between two eucalyptus trees. In front of them was a stone balustrade that led to a curved staircase, and they descended the crumbling steps. At the bottom was a pool about forty meters square. Sulphurous fumes made the air almost unbreathable.

They approached the pool. It looked black, but the moon touched its gently moving ripples with highlights. A huge stone fish spit a never-ending supply of mineral water into the ever-demanding pool. The sound of the falling water echoed off the bathhouse on the far side of the pool.

"It stinks," announced Purcell.

"Oh," said Mercado. "You Yanks. Everything must smell like underarm deodorant to you. These baths are an ancient European tradition. These and the roads are the only good things Mussolini did for this country."

"The roads stink, too," said Purcell, stretching his muscular frame.

Vivian had peeled off her khakis. She stood naked at

the edge of the pool, her milk-white skin shining in the moonlight, like fine, rubbed alabaster.

Purcell regarded her for a few seconds. In the three-day cross-country jaunt out of Addis Ababa, he had seen her naked at every bath stop. At first he was taken aback by her lack of modesty, but she had insisted on being treated with no special considerations.

Mercado sat on a mossy marble bench and began to pull off his boots. Purcell sat next to him, his eyes darting toward Vivian from time to time. He reckoned her age at no more than twenty-five, so she had been only about sixteen when he was stepping off the plane into the maelstrom that was Saigon's Tan Son Nhut Airport in 1965. He felt old in her presence. Who was she? he wondered. Her features were mostly Caucasian and her skin was like milk, but her eyes were definitely almonds and her jet black hair was long, straight, and thick like an East Asian, or maybe a Native American. But those almond eyes—they were dark green. Purcell wondered if such a combination was genetically possible.

Vivian held up her arms and inhaled the fumes. "It does stink, though, Henry."

"It's refreshing and salubrious. Breathe it in."

She breathed. "Graviora quaedam sunt remedia periculis."

Purcell stared at Vivian. There was no mistaking that that was Latin. This was a new language in Vivian's repertoire. He asked Mercado, "What did she say?"

Mercado looked up from tugging at his boot. "Huh? Oh. 'The cure is worse than the disease,'" he answered as he pulled off his boot.

Purcell didn't respond.

Mercado said, "Don't go feeling all inadequate, old man. She doesn't know the language. Just a phrase or two. She's just showing off."

"For whom?"

"For me, of course."

Purcell pulled off his boots and looked at Vivian, who was sitting on her haunches and testing the water with her fingers.

She called out, "It's warm."

Mercado slipped off his shorts and padded toward the edge of the pool. His body, Purcell noticed, was showing the signs of age. How old could he be? He was here in Ethiopia during the Italian invasion in 1935, so he had to be at least sixty. Purcell looked at Vivian, then back at Mercado, wondering what their relationship was, if any. He slipped off his shorts and stood near Mercado.

Vivian, a few feet away, rose to her feet, stood on her toes, and stretched her arms in the air. She shouted to the sky, "There's hell, there's darkness, there is the sulphurous pit; burning, scalding, stench, consumption!" She fell forward and the black, warm mineral waters closed quietly around her.

Mercado hunched down and touched the water. "That was Shakespeare, Frank. King Lear's description of a vagina, actually."

"I hope that wasn't his pickup line."

Mercado laughed.

Purcell dove in and swam. The warm water smelled like rotten eggs, but it was not unpleasant after a time. He could feel the fatigue run out of his body, but the heat made his mind groggy.

Mercado lowered his big bulk into the water, then began to swim.

Purcell floated on his back and drifted. He felt good for the first time in days. Maybe weeks. He let the pool currents take him, and the rising steam lulled him. In the distance, he could hear Vivian cavorting, and her shrieks of animal joy echoed off the surrounding structures. Purcell wanted to tell her to be more quiet, but it didn't matter somehow. He noticed that his member was stiff. He rolled over and swam toward a stone platform in the middle of the pool. The platform was awash in a few inches of water, and he climbed onto it and lay on his back, then closed his eyes.

Mercado bobbed up beside him. "Are you alive, Frank?"

Purcell opened his eyes. He could see Mercado's face through the steam. "Tell her to pipe down," he said groggily. "She'll have every Galla in the province here."

"What? Oh. She's sleeping by the poolside, Frank. I told her before. Were you dreaming?"

He looked at his watch. A full hour had slipped by.

"Let's get back to the Jeep, old man. I'm worried about the gear."

"Right." Purcell turned and swam with steady even strokes toward the side of the sulphur pool and climbed out. He noticed Vivian sleeping, curled like a fetus by the edge of the pool. She was still naked.

Mercado looked around. "I'm sure there's a freshwater spring around somewhere. Probably in the bathhouse over there."

"I'd rather get out of here, Henry. We've taken enough chances."

"You're right, of course, but we smell."

Purcell sat on the lichen-covered marble bench and wiped himself with his bush jacket. Mercado sat next to him. The older man's close nakedness made Purcell uneasy.

Mercado pressed some water out of his thick gray hair, then nodded toward the naked, sleeping Vivian and asked, "Does she make you...uncomfortable?"

Purcell shrugged. Mercado had not offered to define his relationship with the young lady, and Purcell didn't know if he cared. But he *was* curious. He had the habitual and professional curiosity of a newsman, not the personal curiosity of a meddler. Back in Addis, he had agreed to drive Henry Mercado and Vivian Smith to the northwest where the civil war was the hottest, and he hadn't asked for much in return. But now he figured Mercado owed him. "Who is she?"

It was Mercado's turn to shrug. "Don't know, really."

"I thought she was your photographer."

"She is. But I met her only a few months ago. At the Hilton in Addis. Don't know if she can photograph or not. We've taken scads of pictures, but nothing's been developed yet. Don't even know if she uses film, to be honest with you." He laughed.

Purcell smiled. The moon was below the main building now and a pleasant darkness enveloped the spa. A soft evening breeze carried the scent of tropical flowers, and a feeling very near inner peace filled him. He wondered if he was getting Indochina out of his system. Apropos of that, he asked Mercado, "You were in jail, weren't you?"

"Not jail, old man. We political prisoners don't call it jail. If you're going to talk about it, use the correct term, for Christ's sake. The *camps*. Sounds better. More dignified."

"Still sounds like shit."

Mercado continued, "That it should have happened to me was more ironic, since I was a little pink in those days myself."

"What days?"

"After the war. The Russians grabbed me in East Berlin. January of 1946. All I was doing was photographing a damned food line. Never understood it. There were food lines all over Europe in the winter of 1946. But I guess there weren't supposed to be any in the workers' paradise. And the damned Russkies had been in charge there for only—what? About nine months? Hard to erect a Socialist paradise in only nine months. That's what I told them. Don't take it personally, chaps, I said. You beat the Huns fair and square. So what if they have to stand on bread lines? Good for the little Nazis. You see? But they didn't quite get my point."

Purcell nodded absently.

Mercado continued, "I had Reuters send all the press clippings I had written since the Spanish Civil War in 1936. All my best anti-Fascist stuff. I even had a lot of nice things to say about the brave Red Army in some of those pieces. I don't know if the bloody beggars even saw my articles. All I know is that I was bundled off to Siberia. Didn't get out until 1950 because of some prisoner exchange. And not so much as an apology, mind you. One day I was 168AM382. Next day I was Henry

Mercado again, Reuters correspondent, back in London, with a nice bit of back pay coming. Four years, Frank. And was it cold. Oh my, was it cold. Four years for snapping a picture. And me a nice pink Cambridge boy. Fabian Society and all that. Workers of the world, unite."

Again, Purcell did not respond.

Mercado asked, "How many years did you do, Frank? A year in Cambo? Well, we can't compare it in years alone, can we? Hell is hell, and when you're there, it's an eternity, isn't it? Especially with an open-ended sentence. You can't even count off the days you have left."

Purcell nodded.

Mercado asked rhetorically, "What are you to them? Nothing. Do they let you know that your wife has died? Certainly not. They don't even know themselves, probably, that you have a wife. They don't know anything about you, except that you are 168AM382, and that you must work. So what if your wife is dying of pneumonia and penicillin is like gold and a woman by herself can't—"

Mercado stopped abruptly, and a look of weariness came into his watery blue eyes. He said in a low, hoarse voice, "Bloody Reds. Bloody Nazis. Bloody politicians. Don't believe in any of them, Frank. That's good advice from an older man. They all want your body and your soul. The body's not important, but the soul is. And that belongs to God when He calls for it."

"Henry, no religion, please."

"Sorry. I'm a believer, you know. Those priests in the camps. The Russian Orthodox priests. Had a few

Baptist ministers, too. Some Catholic priests, some rabbis. I was in a camp with a lot of religious people. Some of them had been there since the 1920s. They kept me alive, Frank. They *had* something."

"Lizards and centipedes kept me alive in Cambodia." Purcell pulled on his pants and stood. "Let's get moving." He walked away from Henry Mercado.

Vivian had been awakened by their conversation, and she moved past Purcell in the darkness. He could hear the soft sounds of whispering as she spoke to Mercado. The words were lost, but the tone was soothing. Poor Henry, Purcell thought, the grizzled old newsman having a teary moment in front of a woman half his age.

They dressed and headed back toward the hotel lobby in the darkness. Mercado, who seemed to be feeling better, said, "I'll give this place three stars."

Suddenly the northern sky was illuminated so brightly that all three stopped in their tracks and crouched.

They looked up and could see star shells bursting in the night sky. An infantry attack had begun somewhere in the hills to the north and one side or the other had sent up these artificial suns to light the way. Automatic weapons fire could be heard now and green and red tracer rounds crisscrossed the hills. The deep, throaty sounds of muffled artillery rolled down into the spa complex, and explosions lit up the low mountain range like a thousand campfires.

Purcell stared at the close-by hills. He could see illumination flares pop and float to earth on their parachutes. Even after all the years in Indochina, the sights and sounds of battle awed him. He stood mesmerized as the hills lit up and sent a crescendo of sound through the night air. It was as though it were a light and sound show, a mixed-media symphony played only for him.

Mercado asked, "Who is killing whom tonight?"

"Does it matter?"

"No, I suppose not. As long as it isn't us." Mercado suggested, "We should stay here tonight."

Vivian agreed, and Purcell said, "All right. We've found the armies. In the morning we'll go see who won the battle."

They continued on and entered the main building. The Jeep stood in the middle of the lobby looking very exposed. Purcell glanced around for a place to move the vehicle and spend the night. He noticed that one corner of the roofless lobby remained dark when the illumination flares burst. Between the Jeep and the dark corner was some rubble from the ceiling, but it was not an impossible task to get the Jeep through it. He stepped up to the vehicle and began pushing, not wanting to start the engine and create noise. Vivian jumped behind the wheel and Mercado helped Purcell push.

As their Jeep approached the patch of blackness in the far corner, an illumination flare lit up the lobby, and they saw standing in front of them a man holding a skull.

Chapter 3

They laid him on a sleeping bag between the Jeep and the dark corner, and Vivian fed him cold soup out of a can. Purcell threw the skull out a window.

The man's *shamma* was in tatters, so they covered his shaking body with their only blanket. In the dark corner, they did not see the dried blood on the *shamma*.

They could not make out what or who he was. So many Ethiopians were light-skinned, with straight noses and Semitic-Hamitic features, and many wore beards like this man.

Mercado leaned over and asked in Amharic, "Who are you?"

He responded in Amharic, "Weha." Water.

Mercado gave him water from a canteen, then took a flashlight from the Jeep and shined it in the man's face. "He's not an Ethiopian. Not an Amhara, anyway. Maybe an Arab from Eritrea. I know a little—"

"Italiano," said the old man.

There was a long silence.

Mercado crouched next to him and spoke slowly in Italian. "Who are you? Where do you come from? Are you ill?"

The old man closed his eyes and did not respond.

Purcell took the flashlight from Mercado, knelt

beside the old man, and stared down at him. The man's beard was unkempt and his skin hadn't seen sunlight in years. Purcell took the old man's hand from under the blanket. The hand was filthy, but the skin was soft. "I think he's been locked away for a while."

Mercado nodded in the darkness.

The old man opened his eyes again, and Vivian spooned more soup into his toothless mouth. "He's in terrible shape, poor old man."

The old man was trying to speak, but his lips trembled and only small sounds came out. Finally, he spoke in slow Italian. Vivian sat close to Purcell and whispered the translation into his ear as she continued to spoon-feed him. "He says he is wounded in the stomach."

Purcell took the can and spoon from Vivian and laid them down. The old man protested. "Tell him he can't eat until we've seen the wound."

Mercado pulled down the blanket and tore aside the *shamma*. He turned on the flashlight again. A large mass of coagulated gore covered the man's stomach. He spoke to the old man. "How did this happen? What made this wound?"

The man made a small shrug. "A bullet, perhaps. Maybe the artillery."

Mercado said to Vivian and Purcell, "We'll have a look at it in the morning. There's nothing we can do now. Let him sleep."

Purcell thought a moment. "He may be dead in the morning, Henry. Then we'll never know. Talk to him."

"I can see why you were put up for a Pulitzer, Frank. Let the old duffer rest."

"There's all eternity for him to rest."

"Don't write him off like that," said Vivian.

The old man moved his head from side to side as if trying to follow the conversation.

Mercado looked at him. "He seems alert enough, doesn't he? Let's get his name and all that—just in case."

"Proceed," said Purcell.

Vivian moved next to Purcell again and put her head beside his.

Mercado began in Italian, "We cannot give you more to eat because of the stomach wound. Now you must rest and sleep. But first, tell us your name."

The old man nodded. A thin smile played across his lips. "You are good people." He asked, "Who are you?"

Mercado replied, "Journalists."

"Yes? You are here for the war?"

"Yes," Mercado replied, "for the war."

The old man asked, "Americano? Inglese?"

Mercado replied, "Both."

The old man smiled and said, "Good people."

Mercado laid his hand on the old man's arm and asked, "What is your name, please?"

"I am—I am Giuseppe Armano. I am a priest."

A long silence hung in the darkness. Outside, the sounds of battle died slowly, indicating that everyone was satisfied with the night's carnage. Occasionally a flare burst overhead and gently floated to earth, and as it fell, the crisscrossed steel reinforcing rods of the collapsed concrete ceiling cast their peculiar grid shadows over the floor, and the room was bathed in blue-white luminescence. But the small corner of the big chamber remained in shadow.

Mercado took the old priest's hand and squeezed it. "Father. What has happened to you?"

The old priest winced in pain and did not respond.

Mercado gripped the priest's hand tighter. "Father. Can you talk?"

"Yes . . . yes, I can. I must talk. I think I am dying."

"No. No. You're fine. You'll be—"

"Be still and let me speak." The old priestly authority came through his weak voice. "Put my head up." Mercado slid a piece of stone under the sleeping bag. "There. Good." The old priest knew when he was in the presence of a believer and again became the leader of the flock—a flock of one. Vivian moistened his lips with a wet handkerchief.

He drew a deep breath and began, "My name is Father Giuseppe Armano and I am a priest of the order of Saint Francis. My parish is in the village of Berini in Sicily. I have spent the last . . . I think, forty years, since 1936 . . . what year is this?"

"It is 1974, Father."

"Yes. Since 1936, almost forty years. I have been in a prison. To the east of here."

"Forty years?" Mercado exchanged a look with Purcell. "Forty years? Why? Why have you been in prison forty years?"

"They kept me from the world. To protect the secret. But they would not kill me because I, too, am a priest. But they are the old believers. The Copts. They have the sacred blood and the . . ." His voice trailed off and he lay still, staring up at the sky.

Mercado said to the priest, "Go on. Slowly. Go slowly."

"Yes . . . you must go to Berini and tell them what has

happened to me. Giuseppe Armano. They will remember. I have a family there. A brother. Two sisters. Could they be alive?" Tears welled up in the old priest's eyes, but he insisted on continuing. He spoke more quickly now. "I left my village in 1935. August. It was a hot day. A man came and said I was in the army. Il Duce needed priests for his army. So we went...some other priests, too...and many young boys. We walked in the sun and reached Alcamo. There was a train for us in Alcamo and then a boat from Palermo. I had never been on a train or boat and I was frightened of the train, but not so much of the boat. And the boys, peasants like myself, some were frightened, but most were excited. And we sailed in the boat to Reggio. And there was a train in Reggio and we went north to Rome..." He lay back and licked his dry lips. Vivian moistened them again as she translated for Purcell.

The old man smiled and nodded at the kindness. He again refused Mercado's offer to sleep. "I am very sick. You must let me finish. I feel the burning in my belly."

"It's just the food, Father. It has made the acid. You understand?"

"I understand that I am dying. Be silent. What is your name?"

"Henry Mercado."

"Henry...good. So we went to Rome, Henry. All my life, I wished to go to Rome. Now I was in Rome. What a city...have you seen it? Everyone should go to Rome before he dies...You are a Catholic, Henry?"

"Well, yes, sort of. Yes."

"Good." The priest stayed silent awhile, then continued. "We were taken to the Vatican...all the priests from Sicily...there were twelve of us, I remember...to the Vatican, some place in the Vatican. A small building near the Sistine Chapel. There was a cardinal there dressed all in white. He did not give his name and I remembered thinking that this was ill-mannered, but what was I going to say to a cardinal of the Sacred College? We sat in chairs of fine fabric and we listened. The cardinal told us we would go with Mussolini's army. Go to war in Ethiopia. We listened sadly, but no one spoke. The cardinal showed us an envelope, a beautiful envelope of hard paper, colored like butter. On the envelope was the seal of His Holiness...the ring of the fisherman..." The old priest stopped, and Vivian finished her translation.

Purcell thought he had passed out, but then he opened his eyes and asked, "Who sits on the throne of Saint Peter, now? How many since Pius?"

"Three, since Pius, Father," Mercado replied.

Purcell said to Mercado, "The guy is near dead and he wants to know who his boss is. Listen, Henry, he is going to ask you a thousand irrelevant questions. Get him back to the story, please."

"He is telling the story in his own way, Frank. The man has suffered. You and I know how he has suffered. These questions are important to him."

Vivian put her hand on Purcell's arm and said softly, "Let Henry handle it."

Purcell grunted. Mercado spoke again in Italian. "After Pius XI was Pius XII. Then John XXIII. You would have liked him, Father. A good man. He died eleven years ago. Now Paul VI sits on the throne of Saint Peter. A good man also," he added.

The old priest made noises that sounded like quiet weeping. When he spoke again, his voice was husky. "Yes. All good men, I am sure. And Il Duce? Is he still alive?"

Mercado replied, "There was a war. In Europe. Mussolini was killed. Europe is at peace now."

"Yes. A war. I could see it coming, even in Berini. We could see it."

Mercado asked, "Father, did you see what was in the envelope? The one the cardinal showed you?"

"The envelope...?" He paused. "Yes. There was an envelope for each priest. The cardinal told us we must keep the envelope in our possession always. Never, never must it leave our person...we were never to mention the envelope to anyone. Not even to the officers. The cardinal explained that when a priest dies in the army, all his possessions are given to another priest. So the envelope would always be in the hands of those who were sworn...we had to take an oath...sworn never to open it...but we would know when to open it. This cardinal with no name said that as a further precaution, the message on the inside was written in Latin, so if someone else should open it, he would have difficulty with the words. My Latin was bad and I remembered being ashamed of that. Latin is not used so much by a country priest. Only in the Mass. You understand? But the letter was in Latin, so that if it was opened by error, it would no doubt be taken to a priest for translation. This cardinal said that if we ever came upon the letter in that way, we were to say we had to take the letter and study it. Then we were to make a false translation on paper and burn the letter." The priest breathed heavily, then moaned.

Vivian finished translating for Purcell, then said, "This is getting interesting." She suggested, "Henry, push him just a little."

"In his own way," Mercado answered flatly. "He will get it all out."

The priest moaned again. Vivian put her hand on his sweaty forehead. "He has fever, Henry. Isn't there anything we can do?"

"I'm afraid not. If he holds out till morning, we can make Gondar in a few hours. There's an English missionary hospital there."

Purcell reminded them, "Prince Joshua's army and the Provisional government army are less than an hour away—in those hills. I wouldn't try it now, but in the morning, maybe. They should have a surgeon."

Mercado thought a moment, then replied, "I don't know. He is obviously a fugitive of some sort. When we find out from whom, then we can decide where to bring him."

"Right. But push him just a little, Henry," he said, mimicking Vivian's words.

Mercado turned his attention back to the priest and asked him, "Father? Can you continue?"

"Yes. What are you talking about? I cannot go to Gondar."

Mercado told him, "We will take you to an English hospital in the morning. Continue, if you feel—"

"Yes. I must finish it. The envelope...he told us that we were on no account to open it, unless, when we got to Ethiopia, we should see in the jungles a black monastery. Black like coal, made of black stone, he said. Hidden...in the jungles. There was none like it in all of Ethiopia, he said. It was the monastery of the old believers...the Coptics. And in this black monastery was a reliquary and within that reliquary was the relic of a saint, he told us. An important saint. A saint of the time of Jesus, he told us...The relic of the saint was so important that His Holiness himself wanted very much to have the relic carried back to Rome where it belonged, in the true church of Jesus Christ. In the Church of Saint Peter."

Vivian translated for Purcell, who commented, "Don't they have enough stuff in the Vatican?"

Mercado leaned closer to the priest. "Which saint? What kind of relic? A lock of hair? A bone? A piece of a garment?"

The priest laughed. "It was not the relic of a saint at all. Can you imagine such a thing? A cardinal of the Sacred College lying to a flock of rustic priests...Yes, we were well chosen to follow and serve with the Italian infantry. We asked no such questions as you ask now, Henry. We were simple country priests. We had strong legs and strong hearts and strong backs for the infantry. And we asked no questions of the cardinal who spoke to us in the shadow of the Basilica of Saint Peter, a man who had no name himself, but who spoke in the name of His Holiness. One priest, though, a young man... he asked why we should take a relic from a Christian country, even though it was not a Catholic country. It was a good question, was it not? But the cardinal said the relic belonged in Rome. That priest did not go to Ethiopia with us." The old priest laughed softly, then let out a long groan and lay back.

Purcell listened to Vivian's translation and said, "It

sounds to me like Father Armano actually saw this relic—or whatever it was."

Mercado nodded.

Purcell continued, "And probably tried to grab it for the pope, as per orders. And that's what got him in the slammer for forty years."

Again, Mercado nodded and said, "That's a possible explanation of what he's saying."

"There may be a good story here, Henry."

Mercado looked at the priest, who was now sleeping, or unconscious, and said, "This may be the end of the story."

"Wake him," suggested Purcell.

"No," said Vivian. "Let him sleep."

Purcell and Mercado exchanged glances, knowing that the priest might never wake up.

But Mercado said, "If it's meant to be that we should hear the rest of this man's story, then it will be."

"I envy you your faith, Henry," said Purcell.

Vivian looked at the priest and said, "He's traveled a long road to meet us and he'll finish his story when he awakens."

Purcell saw no way to argue with the illogic of Mercado's faith and Vivian's mysticism, so he nodded and said, "We'll post a watch to listen for Gallas and to see if the old man wakes up, or dies."

"You're a very practical man," observed Vivian. She added, "All brain and no heart."

"Thank you," said Purcell.

Mercado volunteered for the first watch, and Purcell and Vivian lay down on two sleeping bags.

The two armies in the hills seemed to have lost their

enthusiasm for the battle, though now and then a burst of machine-gun fire split the night air.

Purcell stared up at the black sky, thinking about the priest's story, and about Henry Mercado. Mercado, he thought, knew something or deduced something from what the priest had said.

Purcell also thought about Vivian, lying beside him, and he pictured her naked, standing beside the sulphur pool.

He thought back a few days to when he'd met her and Henry Mercado in the Hilton bar in Addis Ababa. It had seemed like a chance meeting, and maybe it was, just as meeting the priest in this godforsaken place was totally unexpected. And yet...well, Vivian would say it was fate and destiny, and Henry would say it was God's will.

A parachute flare burst overhead and lit up the sky. He stared at it awhile, then closed his eyes to preserve his night vision, and drifted off into a restless sleep.

Chapter 4

They took turns sitting up with the sleeping priest, listening for signs of death and sounds of danger.

At about three in the morning, Purcell woke Vivian and informed her that the priest was awake and wanted to speak.

She wondered if Purcell had woken the priest, and she said to him, "Let him rest."

"He wants to speak, Vivian."

She looked at Father Armano, who was awake and did seem to want to speak. She shook Mercado's shoulder and informed him, "Father Armano is awake."

Mercado moved toward the priest and knelt beside him. "How are you feeling, Father?"

"There is a burning in my belly. I need water."

"No. It is a wound of the stomach. You cannot have water."

Vivian said, "Give him a little, Henry. He'll die of dehydration otherwise, won't he?"

Mercado turned to Purcell in the darkness. "Frank?"

"She's right."

Vivian gave him a half canteen cup of water. The old priest spit up most of it, and Purcell saw it was tinged with red.

Purcell said, "It's going to be close. Talk to him, Henry."

"Yes, all right. Father, do you want to—?"

"Yes, I will continue." He took a deep breath and said, "In Rome...the cardinal...the relic..." He thought awhile, then spoke slowly. "So he told us to go with Il Duce's army. Go to Ethiopia, he said. There will be war in Ethiopia soon. And then he warned us—the black monastery was guarded by monks of the old believers. They had a military order...like the Knights of Malta, or the Templars. The cardinal did not know all there was to know of this. But he knew they would guard this relic with their lives. That much he knew."

Vivian translated for Purcell, who asked, "How can he remember this after forty years?"

Mercado replied, "He has thought of little else in that prison."

Purcell nodded, but said, "Still...he may be hallucinating or his memory has played tricks on him."

Vivian replied, "He sounds rational to me."

Mercado said to the priest, "Please go on, Father."

Father Armano nodded vigorously, as though he knew he was in a race with death, and he needed to unburden himself of this secret that burned in him like the fire in his stomach.

He said, "The cardinal told us to go carefully, to go only with soldiers, and if we should find this black monastery, go into it. Avoid bloodshed if you can, he told us. But you must move quickly, he said, because the monks would spirit the relic away through underground passages if they thought they were being overpowered. He spoke as if he knew something of this." Father Armano needed more water, and Purcell took the canteen and poured it slowly around his lips as Vivian translated.

The priest asked to be propped up so they sat him against the wall in the corner. He began talking without prompting. "So, a bold priest asked, 'How will we know what to look for and what to do when we enter the monastery?' And the cardinal said, 'The words of His Holiness are in the envelope, and if you should ever arrive at your destination, you will open the envelope and you will know all.'"

Father Armano paused, and a faraway look came into his eyes. At first Purcell thought he was dying, but the priest smiled and continued. "Then something happened which I will never forget. His Holiness himself came into the small room where we sat with the cardinal. He spoke with the cardinal and we could hear him address the cardinal by his Christian name. He called him Eugenio. So now the cardinal with no name had a name we could use in our heads when we thought of him. But we could not call him Eugenio, could we?" The priest asked for some time to rest.

Mercado seemed to be thinking, and Purcell asked him, "Do you know who this Cardinal Eugenio could be?"

"No..."

Purcell asked, "How many cardinals would there be living in Rome at that time? And how many do you think were named Eugenio?"

Mercado replied, "I wasn't a believer in those days and cared not at all for cardinals...but there was one who was secretary of state for Pius XI...Eugenio Pacelli."

"Sounds familiar for some reason."

"He assumed another name in 1939. Pius XII."

"That sounds more familiar."

Vivian pondered this information. "But we don't know for sure..."

"No," said Mercado. "We'll have to go to the Italian Library when we get back to Addis."

The old priest was following some words. Mercado turned to him. "If I showed you a picture of this cardinal as he looked in 1935, would you—"

"Yes. Of course. I could not forget that face."

Realizing that Father Armano might not live long enough to see a photograph, Mercado asked, "Was this cardinal tall, thin? Aquiline nose? Light-complexioned?" He added a few more details.

"That could be him. Yes."

Mercado leaned closer to Father Armano and asked, "And did His Holiness say anything to you?"

"Yes. He came right up to us. We were standing, of course. He seemed a kind man. He even tried to speak in the Sicilian dialect. He spoke it with a bad accent, but no one laughed, of course. He spoke of humility and obedience...he spoke of duty and he spoke of the Church, the true Church. He said we should treat the priests of the Ethiopian church with respect, but also with firmness...He did not mention the envelopes. The cardinal still had them on his person. His Holiness seemed not to know of the mission sometimes, but other times he seemed to know. The words were general. You understand? He blessed us and left. The cardinal then gave everyone an envelope and also we took an oath of secrecy. I am still bound by that oath, but I must tell you all that happened, so I am breaking my oath. It is of no importance after such a long time...And we made the oath under false..." His voice trailed off.

Mercado touched his arm and said, "It's all right, Father—"

"Yes. Yes. Let me finish. So, we were taken to the Piazza Venezia. There was a military procession there. Tanks, cannons, trucks. I had never seen such things. It seemed that all Italy was in uniform. And he was there, also. The new Caesar, Il Duce. He stood like Caesar on a balcony. I did not like that man. He was too much with guns and the talk of war. And the king was there too. Victor Emmanuel. A decent man. Is he...?"

"Dead. There are no more kings, Father. Go on."

"Yes. Dead. Everyone is dead. Forty years is a long time. Yes...I must finish. In the piazza they had the ceremony of the blessing of the guns. They put us to work, the priests from Sicily. We helped with the blessing. Then His Holiness arrived. He blessed the guns also. I did not like this. His Holiness stood with the king and Mussolini. Then came the cardinal, Eugenio. I was close to them. They spoke very intently. All the parade was going by for them, and the soldiers marched, but they paid no attention. I did not like the looks in their eyes. I was that close. Perhaps I imagined all this later...in the prison. The looks in their eyes, I mean. Perhaps they were talking about something else. Who knows? But I felt then, or maybe later, that they were talking about the thing..." His voice cracked and he stopped speaking.

Purcell picked up the canteen, but Mercado grabbed his arm. "You'll kill him, Frank."

"If he doesn't have a bad stomach wound, we're killing him with dehydration. If it's bad, then he's dead anyway. We can't get him to a doctor for hours."

Mercado nodded.

Purcell emptied the canteen over the old priest's mouth, saying to Mercado, "Keep him on track, Henry. The monastery."

Mercado said, "I'm starting to feel guilty about pushing a dying priest to stick to the facts and give us a good story."

Purcell replied, "The whole point of the Catholic religion is guilt."

Mercado ignored him and asked Father Armano, "Would you like to rest?"

"No. I must finish." Father Armano continued, "The next day I was brought to an infantry battalion. The soldiers were all peasants from my province in Sicily. We went to a boat and the boat sailed for many days. And we sailed through Egypt and we could see Egypt on both sides of the canal. The boat went to Masawa, in Eritrea. You know the place? This was the new Caesar's African empire. He called us his legions. 'Go to Africa,' he said, 'and make Ethiopia Italian.' In Masawa our engineers were building the harbor. Ships arrived with soldiers and tanks...there was going to be a war. A fool could see that. The army marched to Asmara. It rained every day. But then the dry season began...The governor of Eritrea assembled the army in front of his palace. He read us a telegram from Il Duce. 'Avanti! I order you to begin the advance.' Then a general—I cannot recall his name—he read a proclamation. He spoke of the new Fascist Italy and of sacrifice. The bishop of Asmara rang the church bells and everyone sang the Fascist anthem,

'Youth.' Everyone seemed happy on the outside. But on the inside, there was much sadness. I know this because the soldiers came to me and told me they were sad. We marched on Ethiopia. At first it was not so bad, except for the heat and the fatigue. In the early part of October we entered Adowa. There was little fighting. But then we marched out of Adowa and the army of the Ethiopians began to fight. So, this Ethiopian emperor was a brave man. Haile Selassie—they called him the King of Kings. The Conquering Lion of Judah. Descended from King Solomon and the Queen of Sheba, they said. A descendant of the House of David. A brave man. He led his army with his own person, while our new Caesar sat in Rome. I am sure this man is dead, no? He must have died in battle."

"No," said Mercado, "the emperor escaped to England, then returned to Ethiopia when the British drove out the Italians. He is still alive, but a very old man now."

Purcell wondered if Father Armano could follow all this, but the priest said, "So, they are not all dead, then. Good. Someone lives from my time. This emperor was a brave man. His army was ill-equipped, but they fought like lions against our tanks and planes. But we won that war. That much I could see before my imprisonment."

"Yes," Mercado said, "you won that war. But you lost the big one afterwards. The one with the Americans and the English. Italy fought with Germany."

"With Germany? Insanity. Which war is this one, then?"

Mercado was pulled in two directions. On one hand,

he wanted to put the old priest's mind to rest about all that had transpired in forty years. He actually enjoyed telling it to him. But on the other hand, there was the priest's own story, which had to be finished.

He glanced at Purcell, who now seemed resigned to the priest's recounting of all he remembered of the past and all his questions about the present. Mercado said to Father Armano, "It is a civil war, Father. Ethiopia now owns the old Italian colony of Eritrea. Some Eritreans, mostly the Muslims, want independence. They are fighting the Ethiopians. Inside Ethiopia itself, there are Christians and Muslims who no longer want the emperor. Mostly it is the army that no longer wants Haile Selassie as emperor, and they have arrested him, but he is well. He lives in his palace under house arrest. There are some Royalist forces who still fight the army. There are others who want neither the army nor the emperor. It is a very confused war and there is much unhappiness in this land. Also, there is famine. Famine for two years now."

"Yes, I know of the famine." He asked, "And the Gallas? I heard you mention them. They are not to be trusted. In the last war, they took advantage of the fighting and killed many on both sides. They love fighting. They love it when there is strife in the land." There was actual anger in the old priest's gentle voice. He said, "It was the Gallas who attacked the place where I was imprisoned...they killed everyone..."

Henry Mercado remembered the Gallas very well—fierce tribesmen with no loyalty beyond their clans. He said to the priest, "Yes. I remember from the last war. I was here then. I am from your time, too, Father."

The old priest nodded and said, "You must not fall into their hands." He looked at Vivian.

Mercado did not respond, but the priest's warning awakened old and bad memories of that colonial war, and especially of the Gallas. Between 1936 and 1940, they fought the Ethiopian partisans who still carried on the fight against the Italians, and when the British took Ethiopia from the Italians in 1941, the Gallas harassed the retreating Italians as well as the advancing British and the reemerging Ethiopian partisan forces. Wherever there was a clash of arms, the Gallas heard it and rode to it on their horses. This was how they lived; on military plunder. And they didn't know a white flag or a press card when they saw one. In quiet times, they stayed in the Danakil Desert, near Eritrea, or the Ogaden Desert, near Somalia. But when the dogs of war were let loose, as now, thought Mercado, they were all over the countryside, as though someone had shaken a beehive, and the famine had made them more fierce and more predatory than usual.

Mercado had suspected and the priest had confirmed that the Gallas were in the area, that the battle in the hills between Prince Joshua's Royalist forces and the army forces of the Provisional government had drawn them like sharks to the smell of blood. They would sit in a place just like this spa and wait patiently for stragglers from one or the other army. Or if an army was badly beaten and retreating, they would attack the whole force. Yes, Mercado remembered them well. They butchered more than one beaten Ethiopian army and never spared the Western reporters who were with the army, and the Azebe Gallas, who populated this region, and who were neither Muslim nor Christian but pagan, were the worst of a bad lot. They hated the indigenous Amhara passionately, but they saved their most creative torture and death for Westerners.

The priest was sleeping again, and Mercado's mind went back to the first weeks of the Italian invasion, which he had covered for the *Times* of London. He'd had the misfortune to be with the Amharic Prince Mulugeta in February 1936, at a place called Mount Aradam, a place historically and topographically like Masada, where the Israelites made their last stand against the Romans, and where the prince was making his last stand against the new Roman legions of Mussolini. Prince Mulugeta's force of seventy thousand was being systematically destroyed by the Italians as the days dragged on. Mercado was with the prince at his headquarters, and with them was a British Army advisor with the evocative name of Burgoyne and a strange Cuban-American soldier of fortune named Captain Del Valle.

The prince, Mercado remembered, was weeping in his tent at the news that his son had been mutilated and killed by Azebe Gallas at the edge of the battle, and he decided to go down to the foot of Mount Aradam to find his son's corpse. Mercado, Burgoyne, and Del Valle, young and foolhardy and playing the part of Kiplingesque Europeans, volunteered to go with him and his staff. When they got to the area where the scouts— supposedly Gallas loyal to the prince—had said the body was located, they themselves were surrounded by Gallas. The Gallas would have butchered them all, except that a flight of Italian Air Force planes swooped down on them and began machine-gunning the whole area, killing not only the Ethiopians but also the Gallas. Prince Mulugeta was killed and so was most of his staff. Del Valle and Burgoyne were killed also. The surviving Gallas stripped and castrated all the bodies, and Mercado escaped only by stripping himself and smearing blood over his body so that he looked to any passing Galla as though he had already been killed and mutilated.

Mercado suspected, thinking back on it, that the whole thing had been an elaborate trap, perhaps with Italian connivance. But that was another time. The place was the same, however. They were not too far from Mount Aradam, where Mercado had lain naked, trying very much to look dead.

He took a deep breath, then looked at Father Armano, who was awake, and asked him, "Were you at Mount Aradam?"

"Yes. I was there. It was a few weeks before I was captured. It was the biggest slaughter yet. Thousands. I was made very busy in those weeks."

Mercado thought it was a stunning coincidence that he and this priest were at the same battle almost forty years ago. But maybe not. Priests, reporters, and vultures were attracted to death; they all had work to do.

Purcell lit another cigarette. A false dawn lit the eastern sky outside the gaping windows. He said to Mercado, "People die at dawn more frequently than other times. Ask him to finish."

"Yes. All right. I was just remembering Aradam."

"Remember it in your memoirs."

"Don't be insensitive, Frank," said Vivian.

Mercado looked at Father Armano. "Would you like to continue, Father?"

"Yes. Let me make an end of it. So, you asked about Aradam. Yes. The mountain was drenched in blood and the Gallas came afterwards and slaughtered the fleeing army of Ethiopia. And General Badoglio tried to make common cause with the Gallas because there were many Italian units, like my own battalion, that were weak and exposed to the Gallas, and the Gallas were bought with food and clothes by the Italian generals. But the Gallas were treacherous; they massacred small Italian units that were weakened by the fighting. My battalion—perhaps four hundred men remained out of a thousand—was told to march to Lake Tana at the source of the Blue Nile. The Gallas harassed us as we moved, and the remnants of the Ethiopian army harassed us, and the Gallas also attacked the Ethiopians. Was there ever so much bloodshed in such a confused, senseless manner? Everyone was like the shark and the vulture. They attacked the weak and the sick at every opportunity. I buried boys who had been baptized in my church. But we arrived at Lake Tana and made a camp, with the lake at our backs, so we could go no further."

Father Armano fell silent, and Mercado had no doubt the old man was not so much remembering as he was reliving that terrible battle and its aftermath.

After a full minute, Father Armano continued. "Now, the battalion commander was a young captain—all the senior officers were dead—and we had perhaps two hundred men left. And this young captain sent a patrol into the jungle to see what was there. Ten men he

sent and only five came back. These five said they were
ambushed in the jungle by Gallas. The Gallas captured
two or three of the five missing men. The returning
patrol said they could hear the screams of the men as
they were being tortured...and the men of the patrol
also told of seeing a high black wall in the jungle. Black
like coal. It was like a fort, they said, but they could see
a cross coming from a tower within the walls, so perhaps it was a monastery. I asked the captain if I could
go back and find the bodies of the lost soldiers. He said
no, but I said it was my duty as the priest of the battalion and he conceded to my wish. Also, I wished to see
this black wall and the tower in the jungle...but I said
nothing of this."

Vivian translated for Purcell, who commented,
"This guy had balls."

"Actually," said Mercado, "he had orders from the
pope, and he had his faith."

Vivian added, "And he knew he had found what he
was looking for."

Father Armano looked at his three benefactors as
though he knew what they were saying, and he nodded, then continued. "So with the five soldiers who had
survived the ambush, and who were not happy to go
back, and five others, we returned to the place of the
ambush. The soldiers we were looking for were dead, of
course. The ones who had been captured alive—three
of them—had been tied to trees by the Gallas and castrated. I gave the last rites and we buried them all."

Father Armano stayed silent awhile, then said, "So
now I had to make a decision...I had to know...so I
opened the envelope that was with me since Rome, and

I read the words...and I had to read the words in Latin again and again to be certain..."

Mercado asked, "What did the letter say?"

The priest shook his head, drew a long breath, and continued, "So now I imposed upon the leader of this patrol, a young sergeant, whose name I only remember as Giovanni, to show me the place of the black walls that he had seen. He asked my forgiveness and he refused. So then I told him and the men of the patrol of my mission to find the black monastery...I showed them the letter with the seal of the Holy Father and I told them that the Holy Father himself had asked me to do this...that within the monastery was a sacred object of the time of Jesus...I promised them that if we found this monastery and the sacred relic, I would petition the Holy Father to bring them home and they would receive great honors... Perhaps I promised too much, but they spoke among themselves and agreed, so we set off into the jungle."

Father Armano stared into the darkness awhile. "It was a long distance and took many days and we were lost, too, I think. The sergeant was not sure. I felt that the Ethiopians or the Gallas were following...Please, some water."

Vivian gave it to him as she translated for Purcell. The dark hour before the dawn had come and gone and now the sky began to lighten again.

"We can move in about a half hour," announced Purcell.

Mercado said, "We can leave now. We need to get him to Gondar."

Purcell replied, "He needs to finish his story, Henry. He's left us hanging."

Mercado was again torn, but there were no good choices.

Vivian said, "I agree with Henry."

"Well," said Purcell, "I don't. And it's my Jeep." He added, to soften his words, "It's not only about the monastery. Father Armano wants us to tell his people and the world what happened to him—if he dies."

Mercado said, "It's actually about the monastery and the relic. But you make a point, Frank."

The priest had sat himself up higher in the corner. In the dawning light, his features began to materialize, and he was no longer the shadow of a voice. They stared at him as their eyes became accustomed to the gray light. The priest looked like death, but his eyes were much brighter than they should have been, and his face—what they could see through the dirt and the beard—was rosy. But the rosiness, Purcell knew, was the fever, and the brightness of the eyes was also the fever, and perhaps a little madness too.

Mercado wiped the priest's forehead. "Father. We will be moving shortly."

The priest nodded, then said, "But I must first finish."

Purcell looked at him. He had become real all of a sudden. The voice had a body. Purcell became melancholy and felt a great sadness, not only for the priest but also for himself. He saw himself as he was in the prison camp. The priest's bearded face brought it back, and he felt uncomfortable with that face. It was the face of all suffering. Indochina had settled into his brain again and he could not cope with it so early in the morning.

The priest breathed softly and continued. "So, we

came upon it. In a deep jungle valley. In a million years you would not find it, but this sergeant was a good soldier, and having found it once by accident, he remembered how to find it again. A rock. A tree. A stream. You see? So we approached the black place. The jungle came up to the walls of the place, and hid it from view, but a tree had fallen and exposed some of the wall. We walked in a circle through the jungle and around the wall, which was of black stone, with a shine like glass, and it was constructed in the old style of the monasteries and had no gate or door."

Father Armano asked for more water on his face, and Vivian washed him with a wet handkerchief. Purcell was briefly touched by her compassion; he could see why old Henry had taken a liking to her.

Father Armano said, "We came around to the place from which we started. There was now a basket there on a rope, as in the old style of the monasteries of the Dark Ages. The basket was not there before, so we took this as a sign of hospitality. We called up to the walls, but no one answered. The basket was large and so we climbed into it . . . all of us. It was made of reeds, but it was strong. And we all fit—eleven—and the basket began to rise."

He stopped, took a long, deep breath, then went on. "The men were somewhat uneasy, but we could see crosses cut into the black stone so we knew it was a Christian place and we were not so much afraid, though I remembered the words of the cardinal about the monks. The basket came to rest at the top of the wall. There was no one there. The basket had been raised with a device of stones and gears and it was not necessary to stand by it once it was started. You understand? So we were alone on top of the wall… We climbed out of the basket, over the parapet, and stepped onto a walk."

The priest's face contorted and he grabbed his stomach with both hands.

Vivian knelt beside him and said in Italian, "You must lie down and rest."

Mercado said, "He's actually better off sitting up. That's why he sat up in the first place."

Vivian said, "We need to get him to the hospital. Now."

Purcell suggested, "Ask *him* what he wants to do."

Mercado asked Father Armano, and the priest replied, "I need to finish this…I am…near the end…"

Mercado nodded.

Father Armano took a deep breath and spit blood into his beard. He stayed silent for a time, then began. "Within the walls of the monastery lay beautiful buildings of the black stone and green gardens and blue ponds and fountains. The men were very happy at the sight and asked me many questions, which I could not answer. But I told the sergeant, Giovanni, about the monks and he ordered his men to keep their rifles at the ready. We called down into the monastery, but only the echoes of our own voices answered us. Now everyone was troubled again. But we found wooden steps to the ground. We walked with caution like a patrol because we were uneasy. We called out again, but only our own voices answered, and the echoes made us more uneasy, so we did not call out again, but walked quietly. We walked to the main building…a church. The doors of the church were covered with polished silver and they blinded us in the sunlight. On the doors were the signs of the early Christians...fish, lambs, palms. We entered the church. Inside, we observed that the roof was made of a substance like glass, but not glass. A stone, perhaps alabaster, and it let in the sunlight and the church was bathed in a glow that made my head swim and hurt my eyes. I had never seen such a thing and I am sure there is not such a thing, even in Rome." He laid his head back in the corner and closed his eyes.

Purcell, Mercado, and Vivian watched him closely in the dim light. Mercado asked, "Are we doing the right thing? Or are we killing him?"

Purcell said, "I think he's accepted death, so we need to accept it."

Vivian concurred and added, "He wants the world to know his story...and his fate."

Purcell agreed, "That's what we do best. So I think we need to wake him."

Mercado hesitated, then crouched and shook the priest gently.

The priest opened his eyes slowly. He said, "I can see you all now. This woman is very beautiful. She should not be traveling like this."

Purcell informed him, "Women do whatever men do these days, Father." But no one translated.

The priest took a deep breath. "So, now we make an end of it. And listen closely." He pressed his eyes with his shaky hands. "So we walked through the strange light of the church and into an adjoining building. A bigger place it seemed, but perhaps it was the darkness that made it look so. It was a building of many columns. We walked in the darkness, and the soldiers had removed their helmets because they were in a church, but they did not sling their rifles on their shoulders, but held them ready. Though it made no difference. In a second, every column produced a robed monk. It was over in a second or two. Everyone was clubbed to the ground and not a shot was fired. There was very little noise..."

Father Armano seemed to be failing, but he was determined to go on and spoke quickly. "I wore on my helmet a large cross which was the army regulation. So perhaps this is what saved me. The others were clubbed again and taken away. I remember seeing this, although I was stunned by the blow. But you see, I had left my helmet on, as it was not required of me to remove a head covering in church. You understand? So the steel absorbed the blow and God saved me. The monks dragged me away and put me in a cell."

The priest suddenly became rigid, and his face turned pale. His gums bit into his bearded lip, then the pain passed and he exhaled, drew a long breath, and said something in Latin that Mercado recognized as the Lord's Prayer. He finished the prayer, then he picked up his story in Italian. "A monk's cell...not a prison...they cared for me...two or three of the Coptic monks spoke some Italian...so I said to them...I said, 'I have come to see the sacred relic...' and one who spoke Italian answered, 'If you have come to see it, you will see it.' But he also said, 'Those who see it may never speak of it.' I agreed to this, though I did not understand that I had sealed my fate..."

Purcell waited for Vivian's translation, then commented, "I think he understood that."

And in fact, Father Armano added, "But perhaps I did understand...though when I saw the sacred relic, it did not matter..."

Mercado asked Father Armano, almost casually, "What was it, Father? What did they show you?"

The priest stayed silent for some time, then said, "So...so they brought me to it, and I saw it...and it was the thing that was written in the letter...and I fell to my knees and prayed, and the monks prayed with me...and the pain of the blow to my head vanished...and my soul was at peace."

Father Armano smiled and closed his eyes, as though reliving the peace that had filled him then. His body shook, then he lay motionless.

Mercado felt for a heartbeat and Purcell felt for a pulse. They looked at each other, and Mercado said, "Dead."

They waited for more light so they could bury him.

Vivian remained at the priest's side, holding his hand, which was still warm. She felt something—his fingers tightening the grip on her hand. "Henry."

"Yes?"

"He's...squeezing my hand."

"Rigor mortis. Let go, Vivian."

She tried to pull her hand out of the priest's grip, but he held tightly. She pressed her cheek on his forehead which was still burning with fever. "Henry...he's alive."

"No—"

The priest suddenly opened his eyes and stared up at the sunlight coming through the open ceiling.

Purcell quickly gave him water and they knelt beside him. Mercado said, "Father—can you speak?"

He nodded, then said in a weak voice, "I have seen it…it was very bright. It was the sun in Berini. I went home…it was so beautiful…"

No one responded.

"My sister, Anna…you must go to her and tell her. She wishes to hear from you."

Mercado said, "We will go to her."

He nodded, then seemed to remember what he needed them to know. He licked his cracked lips and spoke. "So then…I was taken into the jungle and given over to some soldiers of the emperor's army. I thought I was being released…being exchanged, perhaps, for Ethiopian prisoners who were held by our army…but I was taken to a local ras, a prince named Theodore who kept a small garrison in the jungle…" He paused in thought, then continued, "That was almost forty years ago. And last night I walked out of that fortress." Father Armano looked at Mercado, Purcell, and Vivian and said, "So now you know it, and I can rest in peace. You must go to Berini and tell them what happened to Giuseppe Armano. And go also to the Vatican. Tell them I found the black monastery…and saw the relic."

Purcell felt that he had missed something in the story or the translation. He looked at Vivian, but she only shrugged.

Mercado asked, "Father, what was in the monastery?"

Father Armano looked up. "You will never find it. And you should not look for it."

"What was it that you saw?"

Father Armano did not reply directly, but said, "My

head was bleeding from the blow of the club. The iron helmet took the blow, but still I cut my head somehow. They touched some of it to my head and the pain was gone and the wound healed immediately... and the monks said I was one of the blessed. One who believed..."

Purcell listened to the translation and said, "Maybe he didn't understand the question, Henry."

Mercado let out a breath of exasperation. "Frank—" He turned to the priest. "Please tell us what it was, Father."

The priest smiled. "Of course you want to know what it was. But it has caused so much suffering already. It is blessed and cursed at the same time. Cursed, not of itself, but cursed because of the greed and treachery of men. It should stay where it is. It is meant to stay hidden until men become less evil... The monks said this to me."

"What *was* it?" asked Mercado firmly.

He asked for water. Vivian gave him all he wanted, and he drank too much of it, but no one stopped him. The priest closed his eyes, then said in a soft voice, "The Holy Grail... the sacred vessel which Christ himself used at the Last Supper... It is filled with his most precious blood. It can heal mortal wounds and calm troubled souls. If you believe. And the lance that the Roman soldier, Longinus, used to pierce the side of our Lord... it hangs above the Grail, and the lance drips a never-ending flow of blood into the Grail. I have seen this, and I have experienced this miracle." He looked at Mercado. "Do you believe this, Henry?"

Mercado did not reply.

The priest said, in a surprisingly clear voice, "If you find it, you will believe in it. But I would advise you to leave here. Go to Rome, to the Vatican, and tell them I found it, and that it is safe where it was. And then forget all that I have said." He asked, "Will you do this?"

No one replied.

"And go to Berini." Father Armano blessed them, then recited the Lord's Prayer in Latin and closed his eyes.

The sun was yellow now and small birds, nesting in the cavernous lobby ceiling, flew around the ruined vaults overhead and made morning noises at the new sun.

They knelt around the old priest and spoke to him, but he did not answer, and within the next quarter hour he died peacefully.

Vivian bent over and kissed the old priest's cold forehead.

Chapter 5

Henry Mercado retrieved a short spade from the Jeep, and Frank Purcell carried the body of the dead priest, wrapped in the blanket, into the courtyard of the spa.

Vivian chose a spot in the overgrown garden near the dry fountain, and Purcell dug a grave deep enough to keep the jackals from the body.

Purcell, Mercado, and Vivian lowered the body into the grave and took turns filling it with the red African earth. When they were done, Mercado said a short prayer over the grave.

Vivian wiped her sweating face, then picked up her camera and took photographs of the unmarked grave and the surrounding ruins. They had agreed not to make notes of this encounter, in case they or their notebooks fell into the wrong hands, and Purcell wasn't sure Vivian should be taking pictures, but he said nothing. She said, "We can show these to his family." She added, "They may want to bring the body home."

Purcell didn't think that after forty years there was anyone in Berini who would want to do that. But it was possible, and nice of Vivian to think of it.

Mercado looked at the grave, then said to his companions, "I somehow feel that we killed him with our prodding...and all that water..."

Purcell replied, "He was a dead man when we found him, Henry." He added, "We did what he wanted us to do. We listened to him." He reminded Mercado, "He wanted us to let his people know what happened to him. And we'll do that."

Vivian sat on a stone garden bench and stared at the grave. She said, "He also wanted us to know about the black monastery...and the Grail. He wanted us to go to Rome...the Vatican, and tell them that Father Giuseppe Armano had found what they sent him to find."

Purcell glanced at Mercado and he was sure they were both thinking the same thing: They weren't going to break this story to the Vatican. At least not now. In fact, Father Armano himself had suggested that the Grail was safe where it was, meaning leave it there.

Mercado sat beside Vivian, looked around at the crumbling faux-Roman spa, and said, "This is a fitting place to bury him." He asked, "Well, what do we think about what Father Armano said?"

No one replied, and Mercado prompted, "About the black monastery...and the Holy Grail?"

Purcell lit a cigarette. "Well...I think his story was basically true...I mean about the cardinal, the pope, his war experiences, and the monastery. But he sort of lost me with the Lance of Longinus dripping blood into the Holy Grail."

Mercado thought a moment, then nodded and said, "I'm supposed to be the believer, but...you know, in the Gulag, there was a prisoner who said he'd been sent there for trying to kill Stalin. But he was actually there for pilfering state property—twenty years. But you see, he needed a crime big enough to fit the sentence, instead of the other way around."

No one responded, so Mercado continued. "We don't know what Father Armano did to spend forty years in a cell. But I think he convinced himself that he was there because he'd seen what he wasn't supposed to see."

Vivian said, "But his story was so full of *detail*."

Mercado said to her, "Vivian, if you had forty years to work on a story, you would get the details down quite well." He added, "He wasn't actually lying to us. He had just deluded himself to the point where it became truth in his own mind."

Purcell wiped his face with his sleeve. The sun was a brutal yellow now. He asked Mercado, "Where do you think the story became delusional?"

Mercado shrugged, then replied, "Maybe after the Lake Tana part. Maybe he had been captured by the Ethiopian army and they put him in jail as a prisoner of war."

Purcell asked, "But why lock him up for forty years? The war with the Italians ended within a year."

Again Mercado shrugged and replied, "I don't know...the local ras, Prince Theodore, had captured an Italian enemy...a priest who they didn't want to kill...so they threw him in jail and forgot about him."

Purcell pointed out, "But when the Italians won the war, the prince would have given Father Armano to them to curry favor, or for a price. Instead, they kept him locked in solitary confinement for four decades. Why?"

Mercado conceded, "I suppose it is possible that

Father Armano did find and enter this black monastery, and maybe the monks did kill the Italian soldiers who were with Father Armano, and that's why the monks handed him over to the Ethiopian prince and had him put away for life—so he couldn't reveal what they'd done, or reveal the location of the monastery." He added, "They silenced a witness without killing him. Yes, I can see that happening if the witness was a priest."

Purcell suggested, "So maybe what the priest said is all true—except for the part about the Holy Grail and the lance dripping blood."

Mercado replied, "That's very possible."

Purcell asked, "So should we look for this black monastery?"

"It would be a dangerous undertaking," said Mercado.

"But," said Purcell, "worth the risk if we're actually looking for the Holy Grail."

"Yes," agreed Mercado, "but the Holy Grail does not actually exist, Frank. It is a legend. A myth."

"I thought you were a true believer, Henry."

"I am, old boy. But I don't believe in medieval myths. I believe in God."

Vivian was looking at Mercado thoughtfully and said to him, "I think, Henry, that you're not so sure of what you're saying."

"I am sure."

Purcell speculated, "Maybe you're trying to cut us out of the deal, Henry. Or cut *me* out, and take your photographer along to look for the black monastery."

Mercado looked offended and said, "You've been in the sun too long."

"Look, Henry," said Purcell, "you and I and Vivian all believe every word of Father Armano's story, including him finding the Holy Grail in the monastery. But the problem is the Grail itself. The priest saw it, but is it actually *the* Grail? The cup used by Christ at the Last Supper? Or is it something that the monks *think* is the Holy Grail?"

Mercado nodded. "That's the most logical conclusion." He asked rhetorically, "How many false relics are there in the Catholic Church?" He answered his own question: "Probably hundreds. Such as a piece of the true cross. The nails used to crucify Christ. A piece of his robe. That is what the priest saw—a false relic."

"Correct," agreed Purcell. "But what we need to decide is whether or not we want to look for this black monastery, and the so-called Holy Grail. Is that enough of a story to risk our lives for?" He added, "Don't forget what happened to . . ." He nodded toward the grave.

Mercado glanced at the fresh earth, but didn't reply.

Vivian reminded them, "Father Armano said that the sacred blood healed his wound."

Purcell explained, "If you believe strongly enough, you can experience a psychosomatic healing of the body, and certainly of the mind. We all know this."

"Well . . . yes . . ." replied Vivian. "But he also described the Lance of Longinus dripping a never-ending supply of blood into the Grail."

"Well, you got me there, Vivian."

She continued, "And apparently the Vatican believes in this—if you believe that part of Father Armano's story. And I do."

Purcell pointed out, "The Vatican does not necessarily

believe that the Holy Grail even exists, or that it somehow wound up in Ethiopia. But they decided to take advantage of the Italian invasion of Ethiopia and send a bunch of priests here with the army to check out something they heard or read—and while they were at it, grab anything they could find."

Mercado agreed and said, "The Italian army looted a great number of religious artifacts from Ethiopia." He further informed them, "The steles sitting in front of the Italian Foreign Ministry in Rome were taken from the ancient Ethiopian capital of Axum." He added, "The Ethiopians want them back."

"The spoils of war," Purcell said, "go to the victors."

Mercado agreed. "Europe, the Vatican, the British Museum are filled with objects looted from the rest of the world. But those days are over, so even if we decide to look for this relic, and we find it, we have no right to try to...take it."

Purcell said, "You're getting ahead of yourself, Henry. We're not sure we're going to look for it. And if we do look for it and we find it, what we're going to do is take a few photos and write about it—not steal it."

Mercado clarified, "We don't believe it is the actual cup used by Christ at the Last Supper, and we could not prove that in any case. And we most definitely do not believe it has any mystical powers, contrary to legend. But the priest's story—the Vatican, the cardinal, the pope, the monastery, the monks, the Grail, and the lance—are the stuff of a great news story." He added, "A human interest story. The dying priest who has been imprisoned since the Italian invasion—"

"Correct, but we couldn't write only about what the

dying priest told us and then not report that we followed up by looking for the black monastery." Purcell added, "We'd look like all those journalists sitting in the Hilton bar in Addis, rewriting government press releases."

Mercado replied, "We are certainly not that." He added, "We're *here*."

Purcell asked rhetorically, "So have we talked ourselves into this? Are we willing to risk our lives to look for the Holy Grail that probably says 'Made in Japan' when you turn it over?"

Mercado forced a smile, then said, "I think the story is good enough to pursue to the end."

Purcell reminded him, "So did Father Armano."

No one spoke for a while, each lost in thought. Finally, Vivian said, "If we don't do this, we'll regret it all our lives."

"Which might be very short if we do," Purcell pointed out.

Mercado said, "Or even shorter if we can't get out of here." He reminded his companions, "Our immediate problem is that we are in dangerous territory. I don't suggest we try to drive back to Addis. I have a safe-conduct pass from the Provisional government, so we need to join up with the Ethiopian army, which is less than an hour from here. Or if that's not possible, we'll join up with the Royalist forces. What we don't want to do is run into the Gallas."

"That's not a good story," Purcell agreed. He suggested, "We'll spend a few days with the army, reporting on their victory, then we will offer them our Jeep in return for a helicopter ride back to Addis. Then when we come to our senses, we can decide over a drink if we want to come back here and look for the black monastery."

Vivian said, "I've already decided."

"Don't be impulsive," Purcell advised.

Mercado said, "We can't be sure this monastery still exists after forty years—or if it ever existed. We'll need to do some research at the Italian Library in Addis, and we'll need terrain maps and all that, and some better equipment—"

"Right," Purcell interrupted, "but let's first get away from this spa before the Gallas arrive for a bath."

Mercado and Vivian stood, and they made their way across the courtyard, then walked through the colonnade, back toward their Jeep.

Vivian asked, "How do we find the army headquarters?"

Mercado replied, "Probably by accident. We just need to drive into the hills and with luck we'll come across an army unit or an outpost." He suggested, "Practice waving your press credentials."

They got back to the lobby of the spa hotel and jumped into the Jeep. Purcell started it up and they drove across the lobby, out to the portico, then down the steps they'd ascended the night before. Purcell continued across the grass field and onto the narrow jungle road, then turned toward the hills and accelerated.

They were aware that they were in a battle zone and that anything was possible, especially bad things. The Provisional Army forces were supposed to honor their safe-conduct pass, issued by the Provisional government. The Royalist forces, who'd probably been beaten last night, might not be in a good mood. But their imprisoned emperor, Haile Selassie, had an affinity for the West, and Purcell thought that the Royalists, all Christians, would treat them well if they ran into them first. But as with all armies, you never knew for sure. What Purcell did know for sure was that the Gallas would butcher them without a thought about their status as accredited journalists.

Purcell tried to focus on the bad road and on the problem of avoiding the Gallas. But his thoughts kept returning to the priest and his story. Father Armano had found the black monastery that the Vatican knew existed. Purcell was sure of that part of the story. After that...well, as Henry Mercado said, it was all medieval myth. The search for the Holy Grail had been going on for about a thousand years, and the reason it was never found was because it never existed. Or it did exist for a brief hour or two at the Last Supper—but it had been cleared with the dishes and it was lost forever. More importantly, it had no special powers; that was a tale spun by storytellers, not historians or theologians. That fact, however, had never stopped anyone from looking for it.

Purcell wondered how many people had spent their lives or lost their lives in a quest to find this thing that didn't exist. He didn't know, but he did know that there might soon be three more idiots to add to that list.

Chapter 6

Purcell saw that the narrow mountain road hadn't been repaired since the rainy season ended. As they climbed, the jungle thinned, and behind them, through the dust, they could see the ruins of the white spa in the valley. Ahead, red rock formations jutted out from the red earth. There were no signs of the night's battle, noted Purcell, but he caught the faint odor of cordite and ripe flesh drifting down the hills with the mountain winds.

Vivian asked, "Why are we not seeing anyone?"

Purcell glanced at her in the rearview mirror. They had taken the canvas top off the Jeep so they could be identified more easily as Westerners. The wind had sifted dust through Vivian's raven black hair and deposited a fine red powder on her high cheeks. She wore a floppy bush hat to keep the sun off her stark white skin. He said to her, "They will see our dust before we see them."

Mercado stared absently at the winding road. His mind was elsewhere. Since his release from the Russian Gulag, he had made a career of seeking out religious experiences. In his travels as a journalist, he had spoken with Pope John XXIII, the Dalai Lama, Hindu mystics, Buddhist monks, and people who claimed they were God, or good friends of God. His life and his writing, up to the time of his arrest, had been anti-

Fascist and pro-Socialist. But with the collapse of the former system and his imprisonment by a government of the latter, his life and his writings had also collapsed. Both became stale. Empty.

People had urged him to write about his years in the Soviet Gulag, but he had no words to describe his experience. Or, he admitted, he could not find the courage to find the words.

It was his search for God that had revived his flair for the written word and his ability to tell a good story.

He had written a *New York Times* piece on the Dalai Lama fleeing the Red Chinese and living in exile in India, which gained him new postwar fame as a journalist. In 1962, he had gone boldly back to Russia and done articles on religious persecution. He narrowly escaped re-imprisonment and was expelled. There had been some good pieces since, but lately the writing had become stale again.

Mercado was as worried about his career as he was about his flagging religious fervor. The two were related. He needed something burning in his gut—like the priest's mortal wound—to make him write well. His current assignment for UPI was to do a series of articles on how the ancient Coptic Church was faring in the civil war. He also had contacts with the Vatican newspaper, *L'Osservatore Romano*, and they bought much of his output. But there was no fire in his words anymore and his editors knew it. He had almost given up. Until now. Now his brain burned secretly with the experience of the previous night. He felt that he had been chosen by God to tell the priest's story. There was no other explanation for the string of coincidences that had made him privy to this secret. He remained calm on the outside, but his soul was on fire with the anticipation of the quest for the Grail. But that was *his* secret.

Purcell glanced at him in the passenger seat. "Are you all right?"

Mercado came out of his reverie. "I'm fine."

Purcell thought of Henry Mercado as his danger barometer. Henry had seen it all, and if Henry was apprehensive, then a shitstorm was coming.

Purcell, too, was no stranger to war, and both of them had probably seen more combat and death than the average infantry soldier. But Mercado was a seasoned pro, and Purcell had been impressed with the older man's instinct for survival during the three-day ride through the chaos and violence of this war-torn country. Henry Mercado knew when to bluff and bluster, when to bribe, when to be polite and respectful, and when to run like hell.

Purcell thought that despite their imprisonments, both he and Mercado had been mostly lucky as war correspondents, or at least smart enough to stay alive. But Mercado had stayed alive far longer than Frank Purcell. So when Henry Mercado and Vivian had approached him in the Hilton bar, armed with a safe-conduct pass from the Provisional government, and asked him if he'd like to accompany them to the current hot spot, he'd agreed without too much hesitation.

But now...well, what sounded good in Addis did not look good three days out. Purcell had been in worse places and much tighter situations, but after a year in a Khmer Rouge prison, facing death every day from starvation and disease, and seeing men and women executed for no apparent reason, he felt that he'd used up his quota of luck. Unfortunately, he hadn't come to that realization until he was a day out of Addis Ababa. And now they had reached that point of no return. *Avanti.*

Purcell lit a cigarette as he kept the wheel steady with one hand. He said, "I'm hoping we hook up with the army. I'm sure they beat the hell out of Prince Joshua last night, and I'd rather travel with the winner. The Gallas travel with the losers."

Mercado scanned the high terrain with his field glasses as he replied, "Yes, but I think the better story is with Prince Joshua." He added, "Lost causes and crumbling empires are always a good story."

Vivian said, "Can we stop speaking about the Gallas?"

Mercado lowered his field glasses and told her, "Better to speak *of* them than *to* them."

They continued on, and Mercado sat back in his seat. He said, "The dangerous thing about a civil war is that the battle lines change like spaghetti bouncing in a colander."

Purcell inquired, "Can I quote you on that?"

Mercado ignored him and continued. "I covered the Spanish Civil War. As long as you travel with one side or the other, you are part of their baggage train. But if you get caught in between or out on the fringes and try to get back in, you become arrestable. You know, Frank, if you had been traveling with the Khmer Rouge, you probably wouldn't have been arrested. I suppose it all has something to do with spy-phobia. They don't like people who run between armies. The trick is to get inside the battle lines without getting shot. If you're challenged by a sentry, you must be bold and wave around your press cards and cameras, as if you had been specially invited to the war. Once you get inside, you'll usually find the top dogs are courteous. But you must never appear to be arrestable. The business of armies, besides fighting, is arrest and execution. They can't help it. They are programmed for it. You must not look arrestable or executable." He asked Purcell, "Do you understand?"

"Why don't *you* drive, Henry, and I'll pontificate?"

Mercado laughed. "Did I hit a sore spot, Frank? Don't fret. I'm speaking from personal experience."

Purcell thought he was speaking to impress Vivian.

Mercado continued, "There was one moment there in East Berlin when I could have blustered my way out of arrest. But I started to act frightened. And then they became more sure of themselves. From there on, it was all just mechanics. From a street corner in East Berlin, less than a thousand yards from the American sector, to a work camp in the Urals, a thousand frozen miles away. But there was that one moment when I could have brazened my way out of the situation. That's what happens when you deal with societies where the rule is by men and not by law. I had a friend shot by the Franco forces in Spain because he was wearing the red-and-black bandanna of the Anarchists. Only he didn't know it was an Anarchist bandanna. He was just wearing something for the sweat. A handkerchief he had brought from England, actually. They stood him against a wall and shot him by the lights of a truck. Poor beggar didn't even speak Spanish. Never knew why he was being executed. Had he made the appropriate gestures when he realized that it was the bandanna that was offending them, had he whipped it off and spat on it or something, he'd be alive today."

"He'd have screwed up someplace else and gotten shot."

"Perhaps. But never look arrestable, Frank."

Purcell grunted. There had been one moment there, back in Cambodia...a French-speaking Khmer Rouge officer. There were things he could have said to the officer. Being an American was not necessarily grounds for arrest. There were Americans with Communist forces all over Indochina. There were American newsmen with the Khmer Rouge. Yet he had blown it. Yes, Mercado had hit a sore spot.

Purcell came around a curve in the road and said, "Well, you have a chance to prove your point, Henry. There's a man up ahead pointing a rifle at us."

Vivian sat up quickly and looked. "Where?"

Mercado shouted, "Stop!"

Purcell kept driving and pointed. "You see him?"

Before Mercado or Vivian could reply, the man fired his automatic weapon and red tracers streaked high over their heads.

Purcell knew the man's aim couldn't be that bad, so it was a warning shot. But Mercado dove out of the Jeep and rolled into the ditch on the side of the road.

Purcell stopped the Jeep and shouted to him, "You look arrestable, Henry!" He stood on his seat and waved with both arms. He shouted, "Haile Selassie! Haile Selassie!" He added, "Ras Joshua!"

The soldier in the dirty gray *shamma* lowered his rifle and motioned them to approach.

Vivian peeked between the seats. "Frank, how did you know he was a Royalist?"

Purcell slid back in the seat and put the Jeep in gear. "I didn't."

Mercado climbed out of the ditch and crawled into the passenger seat. "That was a bloody stupid chance you took."

"But you weren't taking any chances at all." Purcell moved the Jeep slowly up the road.

Mercado, trying to explain his dive into the ditch, said, "I thought he was a Galla."

"I could see that he wasn't."

"Do you even know what a Galla looks like?"

"Actually, no."

They drove closer to the man, who they could now see was wearing a sash of green, yellow, and red—the colors of Ethiopia and of the emperor.

Purcell said, "Well, we're now in the Royal Army."

Mercado replied, "Good. This is where the story is."

Purcell reminded him, "The Provisional government forces could have gotten us back to Addis. Prince Joshua probably can't even get himself out of here."

"We don't know what the situation is."

"Right. But I know that your safe-conduct pass from the Provisional government won't do us much good with the prince."

Mercado didn't reply for a moment, then said, "I've actually met Haile Selassie here in '36, then again when he was in exile in London." He assured Purcell and Vivian, "I will tell that to Prince Joshua."

Vivian, who knew Henry Mercado better than Purcell did, asked, "Is that true, Henry?"

"No. But it will get us royal treatment."

Vivian said, "That's why I love you, Henry."

Purcell advised, "Don't look arrestable."

They were within twenty meters of the soldier and they waved to him. He didn't return the greeting, but he pointed to the right.

Mercado said, "He wants us to take that small path."

"I see it." Purcell swung the Jeep to the right and gave a parting wave to the tattered soldier on the rock. The smell of the dead began to permeate the air, although they saw no bodies yet. Purcell navigated the Jeep up the narrow path that looked like a goat track.

Mercado pointed to a flat area ahead. About a dozen bodies lay ripening under the sun. A soldier with an old bolt-action rifle walked toward them. Purcell wove around the dead bodies and drove the Jeep toward the man, who was looking at them curiously.

Mercado stood up and yelled a few Amharic words of greeting. "*Tena yastalann!*"

"That's the stuff, Henry," said Vivian. "Ask him how his kids are doing at Yale."

"I did."

The man approached the Jeep and Purcell stopped. Mercado waved his press card and said, "Gazetanna," as Purcell held out a packet of Egyptian cigarettes.

The soldier wore a shredded *shamma* and bits and pieces of web gear. He smiled and took the cigarettes. Purcell lit one for him. "Ras Joshua."

The man nodded and pointed.

Purcell moved the Jeep farther up the hill through grass that came up to the windshield. There was little evidence of military activity and few physical signs of the night's artillery barrage. As in most third world armies, Purcell knew, the weapons of modern war were more for the sound and the fury than anything else. The artillery barrages were small compared to modern armies, and most of the ordnance went wide of the mark. The real killing was done in a manner that hadn't changed much in two thousand years—the knife, the spear, the scimitar, and sometimes the bayonet of the rifles without ammunition.

They continued on and Purcell realized he was in the middle of the prince's headquarters. Low tents, much too colorful for tactical use, sprang up out of the high grass and bush. Ahead, down a small path, Purcell could make out the green, yellow, and red flag of Ethiopia emblazoned with the Lion of Judah. As he drove toward it, the bush around him came alive with soldiers. No one spoke.

"Wave, Henry," said Vivian. "Invite them all to your country place in Surrey. That's a good chap."

"Vivian, keep still and sit down."

Purcell stopped the Jeep a respectable distance from the tent with the imperial flag. They all climbed out, waved friendly greetings, and smiled. Some of the soldiers smiled back. A few, however, looked gruff and mean, Purcell noticed, like infantry soldiers all over the world fresh out of battle. They didn't like relatively clean and crisp-looking outsiders walking around. Especially if the army had been beaten. A beaten army was a dangerous thing, Purcell understood, much more dangerous than a victorious one. Morale is bad, respect for superiors is bad, and tempers are rotten. Purcell had seen this with the South Vietnamese Army as the war was being lost. Mercado had seen it all over the world. The embarrassment of defeat. It leads to rape, pillage, and random murder. It's a sort of catharsis for the soldiers who can't beat the other soldiers.

They walked quickly toward the prince's tent, as though they were late for a meeting. Purcell worried about the equipment, but any attempt to carry it with them or to make prohibitory gestures toward the Jeep would have invited trouble. The best thing was to walk away from your expensive possessions as though you expected that they would all be there when you returned. Vivian, however, took one of her cameras.

The prince came toward them. There was no mistaking him. He was young, about forty, and very tall. He wore a European-style crown of gold and precious stones, but he was clad in a lionskin *shamma* with a cummerbund of leopard. He also carried a spear. His aides, who walked behind him, were dressed in modern battle fatigues, but wore lions' manes around their necks. They had obviously put on all the trappings for the Europeans. Mercado knew this was a good sign.

The prince and his entourage stopped. The beaten-down track through the high grass was lined with curious soldiers.

Mercado stepped up his pace and walked directly to the prince and bowed. "Ras Joshua." He spoke in halting Amharic. "Forgive us not announcing our coming. We have traveled a long distance to be with your army—"

"I speak English," the prince responded in a British accent.

"Good. My name is Henry Mercado. This is Frank

Purcell, an American journalist. And our photographer, Vivian Smith." He bent at the waist again as he took a step to the side.

Vivian came up beside Mercado, who whispered, "Curtsy." She curtsied and said, "I am pleased to meet you." Purcell nodded his head in greeting and said, "Thank you for receiving us."

"Come," said Prince Joshua.

They followed him to his tent and entered. The red-and-white-striped pavilion was sweltering and the air smelled sour. The prince motioned them to sit on cushions around a low wood-inlaid table that looked like a European antique with the legs cut down. This, thought Purcell, was as incongruous as everything else in the country.

Ethiopia, he had discovered, was a blend of dignity, pageantry, and absurdity. The antique table with the shortened legs said it all. The battle fatigues with lions' manes maybe said it better. The country was not a mixture of Stone Age, Bronze Age, and modern, like most of Africa below the Sahara; it was an ancient, isolated civilization that had reached towering heights on its own, long before the Italians arrived. But now, as Purcell could see, the unique flavor of the old civilization was dying along with the old emperor.

Mercado asked, "Would you like to see our press credentials?"

"For what purpose?"

"To establish—"

"Who else could you be?"

Mercado nodded.

Prince Joshua inquired, "How did you get here?"

Purcell answered, "By Jeep, from Addis Ababa."

"Yes? I'm surprised you got this far."

"So are we," admitted Purcell.

The prince's servants brought bronze goblets to the table and poured from a bottle of Johnnie Walker Black Label. Mercado and Purcell pretended not to be surprised by the good choice of refreshment, but Vivian made a thing of it, as though she had expected fermented sheep dip. "Well, what have we here?" She leaned across the table and raised her camera, saying to the prince, "Do you mind?" and shot a picture of the bottle with Prince Joshua in the background. "Great shot."

Mercado was mortified. Bad manners were one thing he could not accept from the very young. It was cute in New York and London, but it was dangerous in countries like this. The prince seemed a charming enough fellow, but you never knew what would set these people off. He smiled at Prince Joshua and said, "Wattatacc," the Amharic word for "youth."

The prince smiled in return and nodded. "No soda, I'm afraid. And no ice for the American." He smiled at Purcell. But Mercado knew it was a strain to be polite when a three-thousand-year-old dynasty was coming to an ignominious end, your emperor was under arrest, and about a hundred members of the royal family had already been executed.

Prince Joshua looked at his guests and asked, "So, you have come into the lions' den? Why?"

Mercado was keenly aware that this was an Old Testament country, and important things were always said with biblical allusions. He replied, "So the Lord was with Joshua; and his fame was noised throughout all the country."

The prince smiled again.

Vivian said, "Can the Ethiopian change his skin, or the leopard his spots?" She, too, smiled.

Mercado looked at the prince, then at Vivian. "Vivian."

"Book of Jeremiah, Henry." She looked around. "Bad choice?"

The prince stared at her, then said, "I am black but comely; thy two breasts are like two young roes that are twins, which feed among the lilies. Song of Solomon." He eyed her for a long second.

Vivian smiled. "I like that."

The prince raised his goblet and said, "Welcome."

They all raised their goblets and Mercado said, "To the emperor."

Everyone drank, but the prince said nothing further.

Mercado took the lead and began conversationally, "I was here in 1935 when the Italians invaded your country. I had the honor, then, of meeting his royal highness. And then again in England, when the emperor was in exile, I had the honor of writing a news story on him."

Prince Joshua looked at Henry Mercado with some interest, then said, "You don't look old enough for that, Mr. Mercado."

"Well...thank you. But I assure you I'm that old."

The prince asked, "So what can I do for you?"

"Well," Mercado replied, "we have come from Addis Ababa to find you and your army. But we have had many mishaps along the way. The Gallas roam the countryside and the fighting is confused. So we ask you to give us safe-conduct passes—perhaps provide us with soldiers so we may return safely to the capital and report—"

"Mr. Mercado. Please. I am no fool. You are here because you couldn't find the Provisional government army forces. I cannot give a safe-conduct pass anywhere. I am in control of nothing more than this hill. My forces are badly beaten and at any moment the army will ask for my surrender or they will attack again. Unless, of course, the Gallas attack first. My men are deserting by the hundreds. We are living on borrowed time here."

Mercado glanced at his companions, then said to the prince, "I see...but...that puts us in a rather tight situation..."

"Well, I am sorry for that, Mr. Mercado."

Purcell said, "We certainly understand that your situation is worse than ours. But we would like to be able to tell your story and tell of the bravery of the Royal forces. So if you could spare a few armed men—"

The prince interrupted, "I will see what I can do to get you into the army forces. From there, perhaps, you can get a helicopter or a resupply convoy to the capital. I have no wish to see you die here with me." He spoke the words simply, but they were strained. He asked, "Any news of the emperor?"

Mercado replied, "He is still well. The army moves him from one palace to another in and near the capital, but he is reported in good health. A fellow journalist saw him last week."

"Good." He sipped his scotch. "I have here another

Englishman. A Colonel Sir Edmund Gann. Do you know him?"

Mercado nodded. "Heard of him, yes."

"He is my military advisor. He is out inspecting the positions. I told him there were no positions left to inspect, but he insisted." The prince shook his head at the lunacy. "The English are sometimes strange."

Purcell lifted his glass. "I'll drink to that."

"He is overdue now. But when he comes, I will try to make plans to get you all to safety if I can."

"Thank you, Ras." Mercado felt the old sadness return. It was the Spanish Civil War again; Mount Aradam, 1936; the trapped men at Dunkirk; fleeing Tibet with the Dalai Lama. All the losing causes met here on this hilltop. And always, he, Henry Mercado, had slipped away at the last moment while brave and doomed men waved at him and wished him bon voyage. But he had gotten his. Berlin, 1946. With a lousy U.S. Army surplus Kodak camera. He no longer felt any guilt at slipping away. He felt relief. "Yes. That would be fine."

"And if you should get away from here, write a good story about the emperor and his army—as you did when the Italians invaded."

"I will do that."

"Good." The prince rose. "I must see to my duty."

Purcell, Mercado, and Vivian stood and bowed. As the prince was turning to leave, Vivian called to him, "Prince Joshua?"

"Yes?"

"You must know of a Prince Theodore. He fought the Italians when they invaded and he had a fortress in the jungle a few days' march from here."

The prince nodded. "Theodore was my uncle. He was killed fighting the Italians with a band of partisans in 1937. My cousin, also Theodore, still keeps the garrison in the jungle. It is a fine fortress. Cement and stone. Why do you ask?"

"I heard there was fighting there. I just wondered if you knew of it."

"No. I have heard nothing. I would not even know which side controlled the fortress or who attacked it. Why are you asking?"

"Oh, I just thought that if perhaps the fighting were over, we could find sanctuary there."

"I think not. Excuse me."

"Prince Joshua?"

The prince turned and breathed a sigh of impatience. "Yes, madam?"

"There is also a monastery in the area. We thought, perhaps, we could reach that. A monastery of black stone, I think."

"There is no such place. You will be joined by Sir Edmund shortly and you can ask him your questions. Excuse me." He turned and left.

Purcell wiped the sweat from his neck. "You are a pushy bitch, Vivian. But good questions."

Mercado sat down on a cushion and said to Vivian, "The man is contemplating a Galla massacre or an army firing squad and you have to annoy him. Really, you are insensitive."

Vivian sat also and poured another scotch. "We aren't exactly at the Hilton in Addis, you know, Henry. His fate could very well be ours."

"Yes. You're right, of course. But *we* have a chance."

Purcell sat on the low table and helped himself to the scotch. He said, "Well, at least we know that the garrison in the jungle is real."

They could hear excited noises outside the tent and the unmistakable sounds of military deterioration. Arguments broke out, and at least one disagreement was settled with a gun. Tents around them were being plundered by the fleeing soldiers, but the flag of the Lion of Judah kept their tent inviolate for the time being, though they felt their perimeter of safety shrinking as they sat sipping scotch in the hot, fetid enclosure.

Purcell said to Mercado, "You were right, Henry. This is where the story is. And I think we're about to be part of it."

Mercado did not reply.

Vivian said, "I'd like to get some photographs."

Purcell motioned toward a row of ceremonial shields and spears leaning against the tent wall. "Henry, dress up a bit."

Again, Mercado did not reply, but he said to Vivian, "You will not leave this tent."

Purcell suggested they look around to see if there were any other weapons in the tent aside from the spears.

Mercado said firmly, "We cannot be found carrying a firearm. We are journalists."

"Everyone else has one."

"That's the point, Frank. We can't shoot our way out of here." He added, "This is not an American cowboys and Indians movie."

Purcell stayed silent for a moment, then said, "I was thinking more along the lines of avoiding a fate worse than death."

No one replied, then Mercado said, "You're being a bit fatalistic, Frank." He asked, "What would you like to do?"

Purcell thought a moment, then replied, "There's only one option left."

"What is that?"

"Another round." He emptied the remaining scotch into the three bronze goblets and said, "I hope those lances can drip more scotch into our cups."

"Don't be blasphemous."

Purcell took one of the spears and stuck it in the ground next to the table. They all sat on the tabletop, facing the closed tent flap.

Purcell had no idea who would come through that flap—mutinous soldiers, Colonel Gann, the prince, or Gallas. With luck, the cavalry in the form of the government soldiers would arrive and Henry would wave his press credentials and safe-conduct pass and remember how to say in Amharic, "Thank you for rescuing us from the prince."

Meanwhile, the sounds of desertion and disintegration outside the tent were growing quieter. In fact, ominously quiet.

Vivian said, "I think we're alone."

The tent flap opened and Purcell said, "Not anymore." He reached for the spear.

Chapter 7

A tall, thin man wearing a sweat-stained khaki uniform stooped and entered. He glanced at the spear in Purcell's hands, then said in a British accent, "Hello. I think we've lost the war."

Purcell noted that Colonel Sir Edmund Gann wore a reddish mustache and carried a riding crop. He was hatless, but there was a tan line on his forehead, so he'd lost his hat somewhere, though not his service revolver, which he wore on his hip. He also had a pair of field glasses hanging around his neck. Purcell stuck the spear back in the ground and stood.

Mercado introduced himself, and Colonel Gann said, "Yes, I've read your stuff."

"Thank you." Mercado introduced his companions, and Vivian said to Colonel Gann, "If you've read Henry's stuff, I like you already."

Colonel Gann forced a smile and told them, "We have to move quickly." He informed everyone, "There are several hundred nasty-looking Gallas less than a thousand yards from here."

No one replied, but Purcell saw that Mercado had gone pale.

Colonel Gann added, "But they are dismounted and moving slowly." He explained, "Stripping corpses, finishing off the wounded, and looking for booty."

And, Purcell knew, mutilating the dead and wounded, and that takes a while.

Purcell exited the tent and looked around. The entire camp was deserted, and he noticed that the prince's flag was gone. More importantly, their Jeep was also gone.

Mercado, Gann, and Vivian came out into the bright sunlight, and Purcell asked Gann, "Do you have horses to go with that riding crop?"

"I'm afraid not."

Vivian asked, "Where's our Jeep?"

Gann replied, "Last I saw it, there were a dozen Royalist soldiers in it, headed south toward the jungle valley."

Vivian said, "Everything we own was in that Jeep."

Mercado added, "Including our chance to get out of here." He asked Gann, "Where is Prince Joshua?"

"Last I saw of him, he and six of his staff were on horseback, also heading south."

Purcell remarked, "I hope he remembered to take his crown."

Vivian said, "This is not funny, Frank."

"Look at the bright side, Vivian."

"And what is that?"

"The Gallas can't castrate you."

Colonel Gann interjected, "The Provisional government forces are to the north. I would advise you to try to reach their lines and show your press credentials. However, they apparently have allowed the Gallas to have some fun before the army advances. So that puts the Gallas between you and the government army."

No one replied, and Colonel Gann continued, "But you can give it a go if you'd like."

Vivian asked, "And will you come with us?"

"No. I'm a known advisor to the Royal Army. The government forces would probably shoot me."

Purcell said, "So let's all head south and catch up with the retreating Royalists."

Colonel Gann informed them, "I'm afraid they don't fancy me much." He explained, "I was a strict disciplinarian. You understand?"

Purcell observed, "It seems no one likes you, Colonel."

"I'm not here to be liked."

Vivian said, "Well, I like you. So come with us."

Mercado inquired, "Where are we going?"

Colonel Gann suggested, "We can follow the rear guard of the Royal Army, keeping our distance from them, and staying a few steps ahead of the advancing Gallas."

"Between a rock and a hard place," said Purcell.

Colonel Gann also suggested, "You three can probably join up with the Royalist rear guard...though I'm not sure they'd treat you well." He explained, "The prince is on the run and discipline has broken down."

"And," Purcell reminded him, "you're no longer in a position to enforce good order and discipline."

"Correct."

"Well..."

In the distance, to the north, they could hear a man scream.

Colonel Gann said, "The Gallas have arrived."

Mercado, without a word, began moving quickly downhill toward the goat trail.

Vivian snapped a few quick pictures of the prince's tent and the deserted camp, then she and Gann started to follow, but Purcell said, "I'll look for water in the tent and catch up."

Gann informed him, "We looked. There is no water." He added, "Whiskey's gone, too, I'm afraid."

They caught up to Mercado and headed south, retracing the route they'd taken from the spa to Prince Joshua's headquarters. They passed the open area where the bloated bodies lay and found the small, ravine-like goat path, then took it downhill, continuing south toward the jungle valley. Purcell noted that their tire marks had been completely obliterated by the sandal prints and bare feet of Royalist soldiers fleeing toward the jungle.

The sun was hot and bright, and the rocks radiated an intense heat. Behind them, they could hear the war cries of the Gallas, and Purcell guessed that they had reached the prince's deserted camp.

Mercado was having difficulty breathing so they stopped to rest. Colonel Gann pulled an old Italian survey map from his pocket and studied it. Purcell lit a cigarette and studied Henry Mercado. Mercado had seemed to be in good physical shape, but his age was showing now.

Vivian was patting Mercado's face with a handkerchief, and she said, "We need some water."

Gann looked up from his map and replied, "There are a few mountain streams close by, but probably dry now."

Purcell noticed that Vivian had left her bush hat in the Jeep and her cheeks were bright red.

Colonel Gann climbed out of the ravine and surveyed the terrain through his field glasses. He called softly down to his companions, "Some of the Gallas on horseback have actually gotten in front of us—between us and the rear guard of the Royal Army. In fact, they are all around us."

Purcell climbed out of the ravine and took a look through Gann's field glasses. Down the hill, on both sides of the ravine, he saw the mounted men picking their way carefully but skillfully down the rock-strewn slopes.

Farther up the slope, coming toward them, were more horsemen, dressed in black robes, their heads and faces swathed in black scarves. They carried scimitars, and they looked to Purcell like Death.

At the top of the hill where they'd come from, Purcell could see dust clouds that meant more horsemen.

He looked across the ravine to the west. A high, razorback ridge of rock ran up to a neighboring peak.

Purcell lowered the field glasses and pointed to the ridgeline.

Gann nodded and said, "Yes, almost impassable for horses..." He consulted his map and said, "If we can get onto that ridge, it will take us up to that peak." He showed Purcell the map and pointed. "A descending ridge will take us to this plateau below the highlands where the government forces are dug in." He asked Purcell, "Can you read a terrain map?"

"A little. And I can climb mountains."

"Good. If we should become separated, just follow the ridgelines—west, then north."

Purcell and Gann scrambled back into the ravine, and Purcell said, "Okay, there seems to be a route out of here, but it's a lot of uphill." He looked at Mercado and asked, "Can you make it, Henry?"

Mercado nodded, but Purcell noticed he wasn't springing to his feet. Purcell gave him a hand and pulled him up.

Vivian asked Mercado, "Are you all right?"

"Yes...can't wait here for the Gallas."

Gann took the field glasses from Purcell and climbed up the west side of the ravine. He scanned the area, then waved everyone up.

Purcell and Vivian helped Mercado out of the ravine, and they all crouched around the jagged boulders, looking for signs of Gallas between them and the base of the ridgeline about three hundred yards across a rock-strewn slope that was covered with chest-high brown brush.

There were dust clouds upslope and downslope, but no visible horsemen.

Gann led the way, followed by Vivian and Mercado, and Purcell brought up the rear, urging Mercado on. They dashed in a crouch, keeping below the brush, from boulder to boulder.

Now and then, Purcell caught a glimpse of the Gallas and saw that some were dismounted, leading their horses, while others remained mounted. They were proceeding at a leisurely pace, like the scavengers they were, he thought, more interested in fallen men and abandoned equipment than engaging the rear guard of the prince's army.

Gann called for a rest among high, jagged rocks, and commented, "When the Gallas have picked the field clean, they will regroup, then decide if they are strong enough to attack the Royal Army." He added, "They would very much like to get the prince's crown and his head with it."

"Not to mention the prince's family jewels," said Purcell.

On that note, Mercado rallied a bit and said, "Let's get moving." They covered the remainder of the three hundred yards in a few minutes and stopped at the base of the ridgeline.

Purcell looked up the narrow ridge. It was a steep rise, comprised of large jagged red rocks, and between the rocks was more brown scrub brush.

Gann said, "Good cover and concealment, not passable on horseback." He asked, "Are we ready?"

Purcell looked at Mercado, who nodded without enthusiasm.

They began the climb, picking their way up the ridge between the large rocks. Now and then they had to squeeze sideways between close rock formations, which assured them that Gallas on horseback could not follow—though Gallas on foot could.

About halfway up the ridge, they stopped for a rest and sat in the shade of a large rock formation.

Gann, noticed Purcell, seemed okay, though he wasn't a young man. But he had been hardened by a few wars and he'd probably pushed himself harder than this the night before, trying to rally the prince's army.

Purcell looked at Mercado. He, too, had experienced hardships, but those hardships had taken their toll.

Vivian was wiping Mercado's face again, but Purcell noticed that Mercado was barely sweating, which was not a good sign.

Vivian herself seemed in decent shape, but her arms and face were burning red from the sun. Purcell took off his bush jacket, leaving him in a sweat-soaked T-shirt. He pitched the bush jacket toward her and said, "Drape that over your head."

She hesitated, then picked up the khaki jacket and threw it back to him.

Colonel Gann had climbed onto a tall rock and was scouting the terrain through his field glasses. He said, "The Gallas are coming together...perhaps two or three hundred of them...heading down into the valley. They'll harass the remnants of the Royal Army...and if they think the army is very weakened, they'll go in for the kill."

No one had anything to say about that, but everyone felt relieved that the Gallas had shifted their attention to the retreating army.

Purcell was hoping he'd see some signs of the Provisional Revolutionary government army in pursuit of the Royalists. That would save them a long hike. He asked Gann, "Do you see any signs of the army?"

Gann kept scanning as he replied, "No. They're letting the Gallas do the work. Lazy beggars." He added, "Bunch of damned Marxists."

Vivian said to Gann, "If we reach the Provisional Army, we can pass you off as a journalist."

Purcell added, "But you need to take off your royal insignia, and get rid of that gun and lose the riding crop."

Gann replied, "I appreciate the offer. But my presence will endanger you." He added, "They'll know who I am, even without the royal insignia on my uniform, and then they can shoot me as a spy instead of as a Royalist." He informed them, "I'd rather be shot as a soldier."

Purcell didn't see what difference it made, but Colonel Gann did, and he made a good point—about him endangering them all. Also, their safe-conduct pass from the Provisional government in Addis had only three names on it, and one of those names wasn't Colonel Sir Edmund Gann.

Purcell looked at Mercado, who hadn't said anything on the subject. "What do you think, Henry?"

Mercado replied, "We should cross that bridge when we come to it. We're still in a bad situation."

Gann agreed, and said, "I'll try to get you as close as I can to the army lines, then I'll scoot off."

Vivian asked him, "To where?"

He informed them, "Most of the Amharic peasants around here are loyal to the emperor, and I'll look for a friendly village."

No one replied, but Purcell didn't think much of Colonel Gann's plan. In fact, Purcell thought, Colonel Gann probably didn't think much of it either. Most likely he would die of thirst, hunger, or disease in the hills or in the jungle. But the Gallas would not get him. Not as long as Colonel Gann had his service revolver and one bullet left. Purcell said to Gann and to Mercado and Vivian, "I think we should stay together. Maybe we can find this Prince Theodore, or some other ras."

Gann said, "Nonsense. You have press credentials and a safe-conduct pass. Your best bet is the Provisional government forces, and they are close by."

Again, no one replied, but then Purcell said, "Let's play it by ear. Ready?"

Everyone stood and they continued up the ridge. Within half an hour, they reached the summit, which gave them a clear view of the surrounding terrain.

The sun was almost overhead now, and there wasn't much shade, but Mercado lay down in a sliver of shadow at the base of a tall rock. Vivian knelt beside him and put her damp, sweaty handkerchief over his face.

Gann was scanning the terrain with his field glasses,

and he said, "I can see soldiers dug in on the ridge-lines." He passed the glasses to Purcell.

Below was a grassy plateau, like an alpine meadow, between them and the hills to the north, and rocky ridges ran from the hills to the plateau.

Purcell focused on the closest ridge, less than a kilometer away, and saw a group of uniformed men. They'd piled up some rocks to construct a safe firing position, and he thought he saw the long firing tube of a mortar protruding above the rock. He looked farther up the ridge at the next summit and saw more gun positions.

Gann said, "The bulk of the Provisional Army are in those hills." He told them, "They attacked us in force last night, right there on that plateau, and we inflicted a good number of casualties on them. Unfortunately, they had heavy mortars and they pounded us through the night."

Purcell nodded. That's what they'd seen from the spa.

Gann went on, "At daybreak we expected another attack, and I was preparing for it, but panic had set in, and the troops started deserting. And once that starts, it's impossible to stop."

Purcell asked Gann, "Was the prince paying you enough for this?"

Gann thought about that, then replied, "A soldier's pay is never enough. You must also believe in the cause."

Purcell reminded him, "You're a mercenary." He added, "An honorable profession, I'm sure. But not one that believes in causes."

Gann informed everyone, "I was here in 1941 with the British Expeditionary Force that drove out the

Italians." He added, "I developed a fondness for Ethiopia and the people. And the monarchy. The emperor. He's a remarkable man . . . the last in a three-thousand-year-old line of succession."

"Right," said Purcell. "The last."

Gann turned the question around and asked, "Why are *you* here?"

Purcell replied, "To cover the war."

"Are they paying you enough for this?"

"No." He suggested, "Let's get moving." He looked at Vivian, who was kneeling beside Mercado and blocking the sun from him. "Is he all right?"

"No."

Purcell said, "Try to wake him, Vivian."

"No. He needs sleep."

"It's all downhill to the plateau."

Gann suggested, "Look, I'm not going with you into the army lines, so I'll stay here with him and you two make contact with the government forces, then come back for him with an army medic and a few men to carry him." He added, "I'll scoot off before you get up here."

Purcell thought that was a good idea, but Vivian said, "I'm not leaving him."

Gann explained, "You're not leaving him. You're going for help."

Purcell said to her, "You can stay here, too. I don't need company."

Mercado was awake now and he sat up with his back against the rock. He'd heard the discussion and said to Vivian in a weak voice, "Go with Frank."

"No. I'm staying with you." She knelt beside him and put her hand on his forehead. "You're burning . . ."

Purcell looked at Gann and they both knew that Mercado was close to heatstroke.

Gann said to Purcell, "You'd better start off now."

Mercado pulled a plastic-wrapped paper from his pocket and gave it to Vivian, saying, "The safe-conduct pass...go with Frank."

She took the pass and handed it to Purcell, but remained kneeling beside Mercado. Purcell put the pass in his pocket and said to Gann, "I won't be seeing you later. Thanks for your help."

They shook and Gann said, "Well, good luck." He added, "The commander of the Provisional government forces is a chap named Getachu. Nasty fellow. Red through and through. Likes to shoot Royalists. Doesn't think much of Westerners either. Your pass from the Provisional government should be all right, but be careful with him."

Purcell replied, "I know who he is." He said to Vivian and Mercado, "See you later."

Purcell moved toward the descending ridge, then turned and asked Gann, "Have you ever heard of a black monastery in this area?"

Colonel Gann didn't reply immediately, then said, "Yes. But not worth the side trip." He added, "Maybe after the war is over."

Purcell nodded, then started to pick his way down the rocky ridge.

Chapter 8

Below, the grassy plateau looked inviting, and Purcell thought there could be water there. Or Gallas.

Across the plateau was the base of the rocky hills, and in those hills was the victorious army of the Provisional government. But even if he made it to an army outpost, he wasn't sure what kind of reception he'd get. Theoretically, his American passport and press credentials and the safe-conduct pass from the Provisional Revolutionary government would ensure a good reception—which was why he and his traveling companions were trying to reach the army forces to begin with. But theory, when it butts up against reality, sometimes produces unexpected results. Especially if he had to deal with General Getachu, who was notoriously cruel, and probably insane; the perfect subject for a press interview—if he didn't kill the reporter.

Purcell heard something behind him, and he froze, then squeezed himself into a rock cleft. He listened and heard it again. Someone was coming down the ridge.

He waited, then saw her sliding on her butt down a long flat rock, holding on to her camera that was hanging from her neck. She jumped off the rock and he let her get a little ahead of him, then fell in behind her as she was scrambling over another large rock.

"Change your mind?"

She made a startled sound, then turned toward him. "God...Frank...you scared the hell—"

"Me too. Where you going?"

"To find you..." She took a deep breath, then said, "Henry gave you...he didn't give you the pass."

"Really?" Purcell took the plastic-wrapped sheet from his pocket and opened it. He smiled and said, "Looks like his bar bill from the Hilton."

She didn't reply to that but said, "I have the pass."

"Good. I'll take it."

She gave it to him.

He looked at it, put it in his pocket, and said, "Thanks. See you later."

She glanced up at the ridge.

He said, "Right. The climb up will kill you. Stay here."

"I'm coming with you."

He didn't respond to that and asked, "How's Henry?"

"A little better."

"Good. And how are you?"

"Dizzy."

He put his hand on her blistered forehead and asked her, "Tongue swollen?"

"A little..."

He took off his bush jacket and draped it over her head. "Okay. Let's go."

She followed him as he moved down the ridge.

She said to him, "Colonel Gann saw three Gallas on horseback riding through the tall grass ahead."

"News I can use."

They continued on and she said, "I wouldn't have left him...but he tricked me. Tricked you."

Purcell didn't reply.

She said, "He and Colonel Gann thought you'd have a better chance if I were along."

"You have not increased my chances."

"In case you got hurt. Or...whatever. Better to send two people on a rescue mission."

"True." Unless one of them was an attractive woman.

The ridge flattened and they stopped a hundred feet from the high grass of the plateau. Purcell said to her, "You stay here. If all goes well, I'll be back with a medic and some soldiers to collect you and get Henry. If I'm not back in, say, two hours—"

"I am not staying here."

"You will do what I tell you—"

"Frank, if something happens to you, I'm as good as dead here. And so is Henry."

"Vivian—"

"I can't get back up that hill, and I will not sit here waiting for the Gallas—or dying of fucking thirst." She moved toward him and gave him a push on the chest. "Let's go."

They continued on and entered the tall grass. Purcell said, "Keep a separation of twenty feet, and if you hear hoofbeats, drop and freeze."

They walked silently through the elephant grass, which was taller than they were. Purcell could see evidence of the battle that had been fought here during the night—naked bloated bodies lay strewn in the high grass, covered with big green flies. There was no mutilation, and Purcell guessed that it was not the Gallas but the victorious government forces that had carried off the pitiful war spoils from the slain soldiers of Prince Joshua. Fresh graves marked the spots where the government forces had buried their own dead. If he'd hoped to find a canteen of water among the carnage, that hope quickly faded.

They continued on and the nauseating stench of death hung in the hot air. Vultures circled overhead, and one swooped down and landed near a naked body, then bent its long neck and plucked out an eyeball. Vivian, who had come up behind him, let out a stifled cry of disgust.

Purcell rushed toward the vulture and it flew off. They continued on.

The tall grass was beaten down where horses had passed through, and where men had fought and fallen. He saw craters made by impacting mortar rounds that had set the grass on fire, and in the ash he saw jagged shrapnel and burned body parts. Brass shell casings littered the ground.

Purcell tried to imagine what had gone on here during the night, but despite his years of war reporting he could not conjure up the images of men joined in close combat. But he could imagine how Colonel Gann had felt when he realized the battle was lost.

The plateau began to rise toward the base of the high hills and the ground became rocky and the grass began to thin as they continued up the slope.

Somewhere to the west he could hear hoofbeats, and he hoped Vivian also heard them. Ignoring his own advice to freeze and drop, he doubled back and saw her walking toward him. The hoofbeats got louder and she heard them at the same time as she saw him. They both dove to the ground in the thin grass and remained motionless, staring at each other across a patch of open space.

The hoofbeats were close now, and Purcell guessed

there were three or four horses, about twenty or thirty yards' distance. The hoofbeats stopped, and he could hear the rustle of grass as the riders moved slowly, looking for anything of value, and for anyone unfortunate enough to still be alive.

Purcell made eye contact with Vivian and he could see she was terrified, but she remained motionless and resisted the instinct to run.

The Gallas were so close now that he could hear them speaking. One of them laughed. A horse snorted.

After what seemed like an eternity, he heard them ride off.

He motioned for Vivian to remain still, tapped his watch, and flashed five fingers twice. She nodded.

They waited the full ten minutes, then Purcell stood and Vivian moved quickly toward him. He glanced at the rising ridge about three hundred yards away and said, "We're going to make a run for that. Ready?"

She nodded, but he could see she was close to collapse.

He took her arm and they began moving at a half run toward the rising ridge of red rock, which he could see was impassable for mounted riders.

They had to stop every few minutes and rest, and Vivian scanned the ground for water. At one rest stop she announced she saw a pool of water that turned out to be a flat rock. Purcell recognized the signs of severe dehydration, which were confusion and hallucination. Water, water everywhere. He thought of all those bloated bodies—ninety-eight percent water...but he wasn't that desperate yet.

They reached the base of the ridge and continued up the exposed slope of sun-baked rock. Vivian suddenly scrambled away from him and he caught her by the ankle, but she kicked free and continued off to her left.

Purcell followed and saw what she'd seen; a clump of what looked like spiky cactus, nestled between two flat rocks.

She grabbed at the vegetation and brought it directly to her mouth. Purcell did the same and guessed, by the soft viscous flesh of the plant, that it was some sort of aloe. He squeezed some pulp into his hand and rubbed it across his burning face, then did the same for Vivian as she continued to chew on the plant.

Within a minute or two, the aloe plants were eaten and Purcell dug out the shallow roots with his penknife and they ate those as well.

Neither of them spoke for a while, then Vivian said, "Thank God..."

Purcell retrieved his bush jacket, which she'd let fall off her head, and covered both their heads with it as they sat and looked down onto the plateau below. He treated himself to a cigarette.

A few hundred yards away, he could see four Gallas on horseback, riding slowly through the elephant grass, heads down, still looking for the living and the dead.

Vivian followed his gaze and said softly, "Ghouls."

Purcell looked across the plateau at the mountain they had descended, and where Henry and Colonel Gann were hopefully still alive. Possibly Gann was able to follow their progress through his field glasses, so Purcell waved his arms.

Vivian, too, was waving, and Purcell heard her murmur, "Hang on, Henry."

Purcell didn't want to attract the attention of the

Gallas, who, if they spotted them, would start taking potshots at them—or they'd dismount and start climbing up the ridge. Assuming the Gallas were in better shape than he or Vivian, they would catch up with them before he and Vivian reached the army lines.

He glanced at Vivian. Her lips were cracked and her face was a mess, but her eyes looked more alert now. Her torn khakis were crusted with sweat salt, but not damp with new sweat. He guessed she had been very near heatstroke, but she should be able to finish the climb. He, himself, felt better. He'd had worse days in the Khmer Rouge prison camp, sick with dysentery and fever…Another interned reporter, a Frenchman, had saved his life, then died a few weeks later.

He asked Vivian, "How are you doing?"

She stood and moved up the ridge and Purcell followed.

They continued the climb, rock by rock. It would have been an easy climb if they'd had something in their stomachs aside from a few aloe plants. Also, their goal—the government forces—might not be a touchdown if Getachu was playing by his own rules.

Purcell stood on a flat rock, shielded his eyes with his hand, and scanned the jagged slope ahead. Less than two hundred yards up the ridgeline he spotted what looked like a revetment of stones. Then he saw a figure moving among the rocks. He said to Vivian, "I think I see an army outpost."

They continued up the ridge. As they got closer to the piled stone, Purcell could see at least five men in camouflage uniforms sitting beneath a green tarp that had been strung between tent poles. The men seemed engaged in conversation and didn't notice that anyone was approaching.

This was the critical moment, Purcell knew, the two or three seconds when the guys with the guns had to decide if you were friend or foe, or something else.

He motioned for Vivian to lie flat behind a rock, then he took his white handkerchief from his pocket and shouted one of the few Amharic phrases he knew. "Tena yastalann!" Hello.

A shot rang out and Purcell threw himself on the ground. More shots rang out and Purcell realized the shooting was coming from behind him—the Gallas—then return fire started coming from the soldiers. He put his hand on Vivian's back and pressed hard to keep her from moving.

The exchange of gunfire lasted a few minutes, then abruptly stopped.

Purcell whispered to Vivian, "Don't move."

She nodded.

He raised his body slightly and craned his head around the rock to see if the Gallas were behind them. He didn't see any movement below and he turned his head toward the army outpost. An arm's length from his face were two dark feet in leather sandals. He looked up into the muzzle of an AK-47.

The soldier motioned with the barrel of his gun for him to stand.

Purcell got slowly to his feet. Keeping his hands up, he smiled and said to the man dressed in camouflage fatigues, "Amerikawi. Gazetanna."

Vivian was also standing now and she asked, "Capisce Italiano?"

The soldier understood the question, but shook his head. He kept his automatic rifle pointed at them, but glanced down the ridge to see if the Gallas were still coming.

Purcell motioned up the ridge and said in English, "Okay, buddy, we're here to see General Getachu."

Vivian added, "Giornalista. Gazetanna." She tapped her camera. "General Getachu."

The soldier stared at her.

Two more soldiers in cammies came down from the gun emplacement carrying their Soviet-made AK-47s. The three men began conversing in what sounded like Amharic. As they spoke, they kept glancing at Vivian, who Purcell thought looked awful, but maybe not to the soldiers.

Vivian tapped her pants pocket to indicate she had something for them, then slid out her passport and press credentials.

One of the soldiers snatched the items from her hand and stared at the press credentials, which were written in several languages, including Amharic. He then opened Vivian's passport, which Purcell knew was Swiss—a good passport to have—and flipped through it.

Purcell drew his American passport and press credentials from his pocket along with the safe-conduct pass wrapped in plastic. One of the soldiers took the documents from him and all of them gave a look, though it appeared that none of them could read even Amharic.

Purcell pointed to the safe-conduct pass and said, "Signed by General Andom." He added, "Brezhnev is numero uno. Power to the people. Avanti."

One of the soldiers looked at him, then motioned

for him and Vivian to walk up the ridge. The soldiers followed.

On the way up, Vivian asked, "Are we going to get a bullet in the back?"

Purcell remembered the executions he'd seen in Cambodia; the victims were almost always naked so that their clothes wouldn't be ruined. Also, the women were usually raped first. He suspected it was the same here. "No," he replied. "Reporters can be shot only by the general."

They reached the gun emplacement and Purcell could see an 81-millimeter mortar surrounded by piled stone. A fire pit held the charred wooden remains of ammunition crates and the blackened bones of small animals.

They stopped and Purcell said, in Amharic, "Weha."

One of the soldiers indicated a five-gallon jerry can, which Purcell lifted and poured over Vivian's head and clothes to bring down her body temperature. She took the can and did the same for him, saying, "Spa, Ethiopian style." A soldier handed them a canteen and they drank.

Vivian smiled at the soldiers and thanked them in Amharic: "Agzer yastallan."

Purcell gave the soldiers his last pack of Egyptian cigarettes and they all lit up. So far, so good, he thought, though Vivian's gender was a complication.

One of the soldiers was talking on a field radio, then he said something to his companions. The soldier who seemed to be in charge handed them their documents and motioned them up the ridge.

Before anyone changed their minds, Purcell took Vivian's arm and they continued unescorted up the mountain.

Vivian said, "I think we're all right."

"I think I could have done this on my own."

"Me too."

He didn't reply and they continued on in silence.

Finally, she said, apropos of something she was thinking, "Go to hell."

"Already here."

She asked him, "Are you married? Girlfriend?"

"No."

"I can't imagine why not."

"Can we save this for the Hilton bar?"

"I don't ever want to see you again after this."

"Sorry you feel that way."

"And we don't need you to look for the black monastery."

He didn't reply and they continued on toward the top of the mountain.

Purcell thought about Father Armano, the black monastery, and the so-called Holy Grail. There was no Holy Grail, but sometimes his editors or other war correspondents described a story as the Holy Grail of stories—the story that would win a Pulitzer, or a National Journalism Award, or at least the admiration of their colleagues and a few drinks in a good bar.

He glanced at Vivian, and thought of Henry Mercado. Could he let them go without him? What if they died? What if they didn't and they found something? He wished he had something better to do with his life.

Chapter 9

Purcell and Vivian sat side by side on a cot inside the medical aid tent. Vivian's face was covered with white ointment and she wore a reasonably clean gray *shamma*, as did Purcell.

The army doctor sat in a camp chair and smoked a cigarette. Purcell also smoked one of the doctor's cigarettes, while Vivian finished the bowl of cooked wheat that Dr. Mato had brought.

Vivian said in Italian, "Thank you, Doctor. You have been very kind."

The big Ethiopian smiled. "It was nothing. You are both fine. Continue to rehydrate." He added, "You may keep the ointment."

Vivian translated for Purcell, then she asked the doctor, "Any word on our colleague?"

Doctor Mato replied, "As I said, we have sent ten armed men and a mule. I'm sure your colleague will be joining you shortly."

Vivian nodded, and again translated for Purcell.

The doctor stood. "I have many sick and wounded. Excuse me." He left.

Purcell said, "I'm sure Henry is enjoying the mule ride."

She nodded absently, then said, "I hope they reach him in time."

He didn't reply.

She continued, "I worry about the Gallas."

"The Gallas," said Purcell, "attack the weak and the dying. Not ten armed soldiers."

She looked at him, forced a smile, and said, "You do know how to con a worried lady."

He smiled in return, though he found himself for some reason annoyed at her worry about Mercado, justified as it might be. He stood and looked around the aid tent. His and Vivian's personal possessions were in neat piles at the foot of their cots, but their clothes and boots were gone, and he didn't see any native sandals for either of them. He said, "I'm going to take a look around."

She stood. "I'll go with you."

"Be here when they bring Henry in."

She hesitated, then nodded, and said, "Find a toothbrush."

As he began walking, he could see soldiers lounging under jerry-rigged tarps, eating, talking, and smoking, which was what soldiers did when they weren't killing other soldiers. In any case, they didn't seem that interested in the white guy walking around barefoot in a gray *shamma*—though a few did point to him. If Vivian had been with him, the soldiers may have shown more interest.

He passed a long open-sided tent marked with a white medical cross, and inside the tent he could see men lying close together on the dirt floor, mostly naked and bandaged. An overpowering stench came from the tent, and he could hear the moaning and crying of men in pain. Human misery. War, pestilence, famine, and civil strife. Ethiopia had it all.

In the distance, on a low hill, he noticed a big pavilion-style tent that flew the revolutionary red-starred flag of the new Ethiopia. That must be the headquarters, and when—or if—Henry arrived, they'd all go over there and see if General Getachu was in a good enough mood to offer them a helicopter ride to Addis—after they interviewed the victorious general, of course. There wasn't much frontline reporting in this war, and based on the events of the last forty-eight hours, he could see why.

Near the hill, he saw a windsock, indicating a helipad, though there was no helicopter there. He pictured himself in Getachu's helicopter, with Mercado and Vivian, high above the heat and stench of this place. The helicopter was the magic carpet of modern war, and if they left here by noon tomorrow, they could be in the Hilton bar tomorrow night, answering questions from their colleagues about their excursion into the interior of this benighted country. The etiquette was to modestly downplay the big dangerous adventure, but make it interesting enough to keep everyone's attention, and keep the drinks flowing. He thought about how to mention finding the dying priest without giving away the whole story.

He thought, too, about Colonel Gann. He'd taken a liking to the man and had acquired a respect for him after seeing that battlefield. Purcell hoped the colonel could find a village of friendly natives and eventually make his way out of Ethiopia. But the chances for that were not good, and Purcell thought about writing a posthumous story, titled "Knight Errant." Also a trip to England to find Edmund Gann's family.

The sun was going down and deep purple shadows filled the gullies and gorges that ran through the camp, and which held the human excrement of thousands of soldiers. A few military vehicles were parked haphazardly, but the main form of transportation seemed to be the mules and horses that were tethered to tent poles.

Purcell had seen a hundred army field camps in the course of his career, and every one of them—whether they were filthy like this place or spotless like the American camps—had the same feeling of life on hold, and death on the way.

Purcell felt he had seen enough of Getachu's camp, and he decided that he would go see General Getachu himself, without informing his photographer, who would insist that they wait for the missing Mercado. In any case, he felt that he should at least register their presence, which was the protocol.

As he made his way toward the headquarters tent, Purcell recalled what he'd read about General Getachu in the English-language newspaper in Addis. According to this government-censored and self-censored puff piece, the general was quite a remarkable man—loyal to the revolution, a competent military commander, and a man of the people, born into a poor peasant family. His parents had put themselves on starvation rations to have enough money to send their young son to the British missionary school in Gondar. Mikael Getachu had proven himself a brilliant student, of course, and he had learned English before he was seven. Also, he'd rejected most of his bourgeois teaching and secretly embraced Marxism at an early age. He never attended university, but had returned to his village and organized the oppressed peasants in their struggle against the local *rasses*, whom Purcell thought must have included *Ras* Joshua.

The flattering article went on to say that Mikael Getachu joined the Royal Army to infiltrate its ranks, and was stationed in Addis Ababa. And when the military seized power and overthrew the emperor, young Captain Getachu was in the right place at the right time, and he was now a general, and the commander of the army in his former province. Local boy makes good and comes home to bring peace and justice to his people.

According to the word in the bars and embassies in Addis, however, Getachu was a psychopath, and was rumored to have strangled a dozen members of the royal family in their palaces, including women and children. Even the revolutionary council—the Derg—feared him, and they'd made him commander of the Northern Army to keep him out of the capital.

As Purcell walked up the hill toward the large headquarters pavilion, he noticed something on the far side that he hadn't seen before. He couldn't quite make it out in the fading light, but as he got closer he realized that what he was seeing was a pole suspended between two upright poles—and hanging from the horizontal pole were about a dozen men. As he got closer he saw they were dressed in the uniforms of the Royal Army.

He stopped about ten feet from the scene and could see that the men had been hanged by their necks with what looked like commo wire, to ensure a slow, painful strangulation. Their hands were not tied so that they could grip the wire around their necks and try to ease the stranglehold, but in the end they'd become exhausted and lost the battle with gravity and with death.

Purcell took a deep breath and stood there, staring at the contorted faces, the bloody fingers and bloody necks. He counted thirteen men hanging motionless in the still air. He wondered how many more Royalists had been shot where they were captured. Taking prisoners was not a well-understood concept in this country and in this war.

Purcell noticed that a few of the sentries posted near the headquarters tent were watching him, and he rethought his visit to General Getachu.

He turned and made his way back toward the medical tent. Vivian was not there, and the sole orderly in the tent was not helpful in answering his pantomimed questions.

The standard procedure in situations like this was to stay put in a known location and wait for the missing colleague. If he went looking for her, they'd probably miss and keep coming back to the tent to see if the other was there, sort of like a Marx Brothers routine. He looked to see if she'd left him a note. She hadn't, but he saw that her camera, passport, and press credentials were gone, which meant she'd taken them. But then he noticed that his passport was also gone, and so was his wallet, his press credentials, and the safe-conduct pass. "Shit."

He walked out of the tent, looking for any sign of her in the darkening dusk. Maybe she'd gone to find a latrine, which didn't exist here, so that could take some time. He decided to give it ten minutes, then he'd go straight to the headquarters tent and demand to see

Getachu. Or Getachu would send for him. In fact, he thought, that's what might have happened to Vivian.

He waited, but he wasn't the waiting type. After about five minutes, he headed toward Getachu's headquarters.

He saw a figure running toward him in the darkness. It was Vivian and she spotted him and called out, "Frank! They've got Henry!"

"Good."

She stopped a few feet from him, breathless, and said, "They've got Colonel Gann, too."

Not good.

She explained quickly, "Colonel Gann had passed out on the mountain. Henry, too. The soldiers found them both—"

"Hold on. Who told you this?"

"Doctor Mato. They're in the hospital tent. Under arrest. Doctor Mato says they'll be all right, but—"

"Okay, let's go see them."

"They won't lct me in the tent."

Which, he thought, was just as well. "Okay, let's see the general."

"I tried, but—"

"Let's go."

They moved quickly up the hill to where the headquarters tent sat. A few of the side flaps were open and they could see light inside.

He'd noticed she didn't have her camera, and there was no place in her *shamma* where she could have put their papers, but she may have hidden everything, so hc asked, "Do you know where our passports and papers are?"

"No...when Doctor Mato came to get me, I ran out—"

"Well, everything is gone, including your camera."

"Damn it..."

"That's all right. Getachu has it all."

"That bastard. That's *my* camera, with thirty pictures—"

"Vivian, that is the least of our problems."

He could see that she was distraught over Mercado's arrest, and now was becoming indignant over the confiscation of her property. This was all understandable and would have been appropriate in Addis, but not here at the front.

She needed a reality check before they saw Getachu, so Purcell steered her around to the far side of the headquarters tent and said, "That is what General Getachu does to Royalists. We don't know what he does to Western reporters who annoy him."

She stared at the hanging men. "Oh...my God..."

"Ready?"

She turned away and nodded.

They approached the guarded entrance of the headquarters tent. Two soldiers carrying AK-47s became alert and eyed them curiously. They'd already sent the woman away, and they wondered why she'd returned. One of the men made a threatening gesture with his rifle, and the other motioned for them to go away.

Purcell said to them in the Amharic word that all reporters in Ethiopia knew, "Gazetanna." He added, "General Getachu." He tapped his left wrist where his missing watch should be, hoping they thought he had an appointment.

The two soldiers conversed for a second, then one of them disappeared inside the tent. The remaining soldier eyed Vivian's ointment-splotched face, then her legs beneath the *shamma*.

Vivian said softly, "I'm frightened. Are you?"

"Check with me later."

The soldier returned and motioned for them to follow.

They entered the pavilion, which Purcell noticed was much larger than Prince Joshua's. He noticed, too, that there were no ceremonial spears or shields in this sparse tent—only field equipment, including two radios on a camp table. Coleman-type lamps barely lit the large space.

The tent was divided by a curtain, and the soldier motioned for them to pass through a slit. It was darker in this half of the tent, and it took them a few seconds to make out a man sitting behind a field desk. The man did not stand, but he motioned toward two canvas chairs in front of his desk and said in English, "Sit."

They sat.

General Getachu lit a cigarette and stared at them through his smoke. A propane lamp hung above the desk illuminating his hands, but not his face.

As Purcell's eyes adjusted to the dim light he could see that Getachu wore a scruffy beard, and his head was bald or shaven. A tan line ran across his forehead where his hat had sat, and his skin was naturally dark, but further darkened by the sun.

Purcell had seen a photograph of General Getachu in an Ethiopian newspaper, and he'd noted that Getachu had the broader features of the Hamitic people and not the Semitic features of the aristocracy or the Arabic population. In fact, that was partly what this war was about—ancestry and racial differences so subtle that the average Westerner couldn't see them, but which the Ethiopians equated with ruler and ruled. Indeed, he thought, the Getachus of this country were getting their revenge after three thousand years. He couldn't blame them, but he thought they could go about it in a less brutal way.

He had dealt with the newly empowered revolutionaries in many countries, and what they all had in common was xenophobic paranoia, extravagant anger, and dangerously irrational thinking. And now he was about to find out how psychotic this guy was.

Getachu seemed content to let them sit there in his office while he perused the papers on his desk. Also on Getachu's desk was Vivian's camera, his wallet and watch, their passports, and their press credentials, but he couldn't see what would have been their safe-conduct pass, issued by the Provisional Revolutionary government. It occurred to Purcell that Getachu had chosen to deal with that inconvenient document by destroying it.

Getachu lit another cigarette and took a drink from a canteen cup. He looked at them and asked with a slight British accent, "Why are you here?"

Purcell replied, "To report on the war."

"To spy for the Royalists."

"To report on the war."

"Spies are shot. If they are lucky."

"We are reporters, certified by the Provisional Revolutionary government, and we have a safe-conduct pass issued by the Derg and signed by General—"

"You have no such thing."

Vivian said, "We do." She asked, "Why have you arrested our colleague?"

He looked at her and said, "Shut up."

Again, Getachu let the silence go on, then he said, "You two and your colleague were in the Royalist camp."

Purcell replied, "We got lost. On our way here."

"You met your colleague Colonel Gann."

"He is not our colleague."

"You fled with him to escape the Revolutionary Army that you say you were trying to find."

"We fled to escape the Gallas." Purcell also pointed out, "We climbed this mountain to find you."

Getachu did not reply.

Purcell didn't think he should bother to explain the actual circumstances of what had happened. General Getachu had drawn his own conclusions, and though he probably knew they were not completely accurate conclusions, they suited his paranoia.

Purcell said, "We are here to report on the war. We take no sides—"

"You have a romantic notion of the emperor and his family, and of the rasses and the ruling class."

Purcell thought that might be true of Mercado and maybe Vivian, and certainly of Colonel Gann, but not of him. He said, "I'm an American. We don't like royalty."

"So do you like Marxists?"

"No."

Getachu stared at him, then nodded. He said, "Colonel Gann has caused the death of many of my men. He has been condemned to death."

Purcell already guessed that, but he said, "If you spare his life and expel him, I and my colleagues promise we will write—"

"You will write nothing. You are all guilty by association. And you are spies for the Royalists. And you will be court-martialed in the morning."

Purcell saw that coming, and apparently so did Vivian, because she said in a firm, even voice, "My colleague, Mr. Mercado, is an internationally known journalist who has met frequently with members of the Derg and who has interviewed General Andom who is your superior. It was General Andom who signed the safe-conduct pass—"

"General Andom did not give Mercado—or you— permission to spy for the counterrevolutionaries."

Purcell tried another tack. "Look, General, you won the battle, and you've probably won the war. The Provisional government has invited journalists to—"

"I have not invited you."

"Then we'll leave."

Getachu did not reply, and Purcell had the feeling that he might be wavering. Getachu had to weigh his desire and his instinct to kill anyone he wanted to kill against the possibility that the new government did not want him to kill the three Western reporters. In any case, Colonel Gann was as good as dead.

Purcell had found himself in similar situations, each with a happy ending, or he wouldn't be here in *this* situation. He recalled Mercado's advice not to look arrestable, but he was far beyond that tipping point. He wasn't quite sure what to say or do next, so he asked, "May I have a cigarette?"

Getachu seemed a bit taken aback, but then he slid his pack of Egyptian cigarettes toward Purcell along with a box of matches.

Purcell lit up, then said, "If you allow me access to a typewriter, I will write an article for the *International Herald Tribune* and the English-language newspaper in Addis, describing your victory over Prince Joshua and the Royalist forces. You may, of course, read the article, and have it delivered to my press office in Addis Ababa along with a personal note from me saying that I am traveling with General Getachu's army at the front."

Getachu looked at him for a long time, then looked at Vivian, then at her camera. He asked her, "And if I have this film developed in Addis, what will I see?"

Vivian replied, "Mostly our journey from the capital to an old Italian spa...then a few photos of Prince Joshua's camp."

"Those photographs will be good to show at your court-martial, Miss"—he glanced inside her Swiss passport—"Miss Smith."

Vivian replied, "I am a photojournalist. I photograph—"

"Shut up." He leaned forward and stared at her, then said, "On the far side of this camp is a tent. In this tent are ten, perhaps twelve women—those with Royalist sympathies, including a princess—and they are there for the entertainment of my soldiers." He pushed Vivian's camera across the desk. "Would you like to photograph what goes on inside that tent?"

Purcell stood. "General, your conduct—"

Getachu pulled his pistol and aimed it at Purcell. "Sit down."

Purcell sat.

Getachu holstered his pistol and said, as if nothing had happened, "And you, Miss Smith, can also photograph the Royalists that you saw hanging. And also photograph Colonel Gann's execution. And your friend Mr. Mercado's execution as well. Would you like that?"

Vivian did not reply.

Getachu stared at her, then turned his attention to Purcell and said, "Or perhaps, as Mr. Purcell suggested, he can write very good articles about the people's struggle against their historic oppressors. And then, perhaps, there will be no court-martial and no executions."

Neither Purcell nor Vivian replied.

Getachu continued, "The enemies of the people must either be liquidated or made to serve the revolution." He added, "You could be more useful alive."

Vivian asked, "And Mr. Mercado?"

"He was once a friend of the oppressed people, but he has strayed. He needs to be reeducated."

Purcell asked, "And Colonel Gann?"

"A difficult case. But I respect him as a soldier. And I have a certain fondness for the British." He explained, "I attended a British missionary school."

And apparently missed the class on good sportsmanship and fair play, Purcell thought.

Getachu added, "The headmaster was fond of the switch, but perhaps I deserved it."

No doubt.

Getachu said, "Perhaps Colonel Gann can be persuaded to share his military knowledge with my colonels."

Purcell said, "I will speak to him."

Getachu ignored this and said, "Shooting a man—or a woman—is easy. I would rather see men broken."

Purcell had no doubt that Getachu was sincere.

Getachu said, "You may go."

Vivian said, "We want to see Mr. Mercado. And Colonel Gann."

"You will find them in the hospital tent."

Purcell took Vivian's arm and turned to leave, but Getachu said, "Before you go, something that may interest you."

They looked at him and saw he was retrieving something from the shadow beside his chair. Getachu held up a gold crown, encrusted with jewels. Purcell and Vivian recognized it as the crown of Prince Joshua.

Getachu said, "I allowed the Gallas free rein to hunt down the Royalists. All I asked in return was that they bring me the prince, dead or alive, along with his crown. And here is his crown."

Again, Purcell and Vivian said nothing.

Getachu examined the crown under the hanging lantern as though he were considering buying it. He set it down on his desk, then said, "Let me show you something else." He moved to the far side of the tent, and a soldier in the shadows lit a Coleman lamp.

Lying facedown on the dirt floor of the tent were three men, each naked. Getachu motioned for Purcell and Vivian to come near and they took a few steps toward the circle of light. They could see that the men's backs and buttocks were streaked with blood as though they'd been whipped.

Getachu barked something in Amharic and the men rose to their knees.

Each man had a collar around his neck—like a dog collar—with a chain attached to it. In the lamplight, Purcell could make out three battered faces, one of which was that of Prince Joshua. His long aristocratic nose was broken, and his eyes were swollen almost shut, but the prince was looking at him and Vivian.

Getachu said, "You see, I did not shoot them or hang them as I thought I would. But if you look closely, you will see that the Gallas have castrated them."

Purcell kept looking at the prince's face, but Vivian turned away.

Getachu reached into the pocket of his fatigues and extracted a piece of bread, which he held to the prince's swollen lips, and said, in English, "Eat."

The prince bit into the bread. Getachu did the same with the other two men, who Purcell thought must be what was left of the prince's staff.

Getachu dropped the bread to the ground and said, "The Revolutionary government has executed nearly all of the royal family and many rasses, so they are becoming more rare. It is my idea to put them to some use." He further explained, "These men are now my servants, and they attend to my personal needs. When I am sick of looking at them—which will be soon—they will become the eunuchs assigned to the tent of the women who are their loyal subjects." He added, "These men will also give pleasure to my soldiers who enjoy something different."

Vivian had turned her back to the scene, but Purcell continued to look at Prince Joshua, whose head was now bowed.

Getachu said to the prince, "Is this not better than death?"

The prince nodded his head.

Getachu again barked something in Amharic and the three men dropped to their hands and knees. Getachu produced a riding crop from the deep cargo pocket of his pants and moved behind the men. He said, "Colonel Gann's riding crop." He swung the leather crop across the prince's buttocks and the man yelled out in pain. The soldier holding the lamp laughed.

Getachu delivered a blow to each of the other two men, who also cried out, causing the soldier to laugh louder.

Getachu put the crop away and said, "Much better than hanging or shooting. Better for me." He came around to the front of the men and made an exaggerated bow, saying to Prince Joshua, "Forgive me, Ras. I am just a simple peasant who does not know how to show proper respect to my master."

The soldier again laughed.

Getachu turned to Purcell and Vivian. "That will be all."

Purcell took Vivian's arm and they passed through the curtain and out of the tent. Vivian was shaking and Purcell put his arm around her.

As they walked toward the hospital tent, she said in a breaking voice, "Those poor men...Frank...promise me..."

"That will not happen to us."

"He's insane...sadistic..."

"Yes." And he was history, getting its revenge. Purcell said, "But he's not stupid. He knows what he can get away with and what he can't get away with."

Neither of them believed that, but it was all they

had at the moment. Purcell thought about their ill-advised decision to leave the relative safety of the capital to find General Getachu. Henry Mercado had miscalculated the situation, and ironically Mercado had half believed the good press that General Getachu was getting in the English- and Italian-language newspapers in Addis. Purcell was angry at Mercado, and angry at himself, but anger wasn't going to get them out of here. They needed to work on Getachu. A little flattery, a little bluster, and a lot of luck.

Vivian, however, had another thought and she said in a barely audible voice, "We will get out of here because we are supposed to find the black monastery and the Grail." She asked him, "Do you believe that?"

"No. But you do. And I'm sure Henry does."

"The signs are all there, Frank."

"Right." The signs all said Dead End. But he recalled that Henry had said that faith had kept him alive in the Gulag, so he said to Vivian, to keep her spirits up, "You may be right."

She took his arm and they moved quickly toward the hospital tent.

Chapter 10

Purcell and Vivian entered the long hospital tent, which was badly lit by candles and oil lamps. The air was filled with the stench of blood and excrement, and with the moans and cries of the sick and wounded. A bright Coleman lamp hung in the rear, and Purcell could see three men with surgical masks standing around a table, attending to a patient.

Purcell took Vivian's arm and they picked their way between the rows of bandaged men who lay naked on dark blankets. Huge flies landed on their faces and Vivian covered her mouth and nose with her hand as she walked, her head and eyes darting around the darkness, looking for Mercado and Gann.

Doctor Mato spotted them and pulled off his surgical mask, and he and Vivian exchanged a few sentences in Italian, then Dr. Mato returned to his patient.

Vivian said to Purcell, "Henry and Colonel Gann were taken away as soon as Doctor Mato pronounced them well enough to be moved. They are under arrest."

"We know that. Where were they taken?"

"He says there is a campo...parata militare—a parade ground where prisoners are kept. Due east about five hundred meters."

Purcell took her arm and led her quickly out of the tent.

A nearly full moon was rising over the eastern hills, and the quiet camp was bathed in an eerie silver glow. Red sparks rose from a hundred campfires, and the air was heavy with the smell of burning straw and dried dung.

They headed east, avoiding the clusters of men around the fires, and avoiding the scattered tents as they tried to maintain their heading across the sprawling camp. In the dark, in their *shammas*, they attracted no attention.

No military camp, thought Purcell, was complete without a stockade where an army's misfits and criminals were held to await trial and punishment, and he scanned the moonlit camp for a structure in a field that could serve as a stockade, but he didn't see anything more substantial than canvas tents.

They continued on, and Purcell spotted the other thing that was a necessity in many military camps; the thing that Getachu had mentioned to Vivian. A long line of soldiers stood smoking and joking in front of a large tent, waiting their turn.

Vivian asked, "What's going on there?"

Purcell did not reply, and Vivian said, "Oh..."

They moved on.

Vivian was becoming concerned, and she said, "I think we missed it. Let's ask—"

"Let's not."

They continued on and ahead was a large sunken field, which formed a natural amphitheater. At the end of the field, Purcell saw a raised wooden platform, and he realized that this was the parade ground and the muster area where General Getachu and his officers could address their troops.

In front of the platform Purcell also saw a line of poles driven into the ground, which he recognized from too many other third world military camps as whipping posts, or tethering posts where soldiers were chained for punishment and humiliation in front of their comrades. He saw a movement near one of the posts and said, "There."

They ran toward the posts, and as they got closer they could see three men with their arms over their heads, hanging by their wrists.

Purcell saw that Mercado and Gann were still wearing the clothes he'd last seen them in, but they were barefoot. The third man, a naked and unconscious Ethiopian, hung between Gann and Mercado.

Vivian ran up to Mercado and threw her arms around his chest. He, too, seemed unconscious—or dead—but then Purcell saw his chest heave. Vivian sobbed, "Henry...wake up..." She shouted, "Henry!"

He opened his eyes and looked at her. She stood on her toes and kissed his cheeks.

Purcell saw that the three men wore wrist shackles connected to chains that hung from iron rings embedded in the posts. Their feet touched the ground so they could stand until their knees buckled from fatigue or unconsciousness.

Purcell looked at the Ethiopian in the bright moonlight and saw that the man's face was puffy and blistered, and his dark skin showed the result of a whipping.

Mercado was fully awake now and standing straight up as Vivian put her face into his chest and sobbed as she squeezed him in her arms.

Purcell moved over to Gann, who was awake and

alert, and Gann said to him, "I'm very glad to see you and to see that you and Miss Smith are well and free."

Purcell found he was slightly embarrassed by their relative fortunes. But that could change quickly. He did not want to give false hope to a man hanging by chains who was condemned to death, but he said, "I've spoken to Getachu and there is a chance—"

"Getachu plays with his intended victims. Save your breath."

Purcell changed the subject and asked, "Is there anything I can get you?"

"We were fed by Doctor Mato and made well enough to hang here until dawn." He added, "I will be able to walk to my own execution."

Purcell didn't respond.

Colonel Gann continued, "Just see if you can convince Getachu to make it quick and clean with a firing squad."

"He said he respects you as a soldier."

"I can't say the same for him. But I'll take him at his word and expect a proper firing squad."

Purcell did not reply, but he nodded, then said, "We'll stay with you through the night."

"Good. Plenty of empty poles, old boy."

Purcell smiled at the gallows humor despite the circumstances. He looked up at the shackles and saw they were held by a padlock, as were the chains on the iron ring. If he could find something to cut the locks or the chains, he could free Gann and Mercado and they could all make a run for it.

Gann saw what Purcell was looking at and said, "There hasn't been a single guard by here, but if you look to your right, you'll see a watchtower a few hundred meters' distance."

"Okay…maybe after the moon sets." Purcell considered telling Colonel Gann that his old boss, Prince Joshua, had been captured and was no longer a prince or a man. But that wasn't news that Colonel Gann would find helpful or hopeful. He said to Gann, "I'll be right back."

"I'll be here."

Purcell walked past the Ethiopian, who was still unconscious, and came up beside Vivian, who was murmuring to Mercado and caressing his chest and hair.

He stared at Mercado and they made eye contact. Finally Mercado took a deep breath and said, "Sorry about all this."

"It's been interesting, Henry."

"Good story if you can file it."

"Right."

Mercado said to Vivian, "Go see Colonel Gann. He's feeling left out."

She hesitated, then moved past the Ethiopian, but then came back and looked at him. She put her hand on his face and his chest and said, "He's dying."

Purcell looked at the three men hanging from the posts. In the morning, Getachu would muster his troops so they could see what happens to people who annoy the general. If he was insane, which he was, he would harangue the troops and threaten them with the same punishment if they stepped out of line. But if he was an accomplished sadist, he would speak to them about their victory, or some other matter, without explaining the three men hanging there. The soldiers could draw their own conclusions.

It also occurred to Purcell that he and Vivian might be paraded out at first muster and also chained to the poles. Or...Vivian could be taken to the tent. Recalling the prince's fate, he also knew that he, Mercado, and Gann could be serving time in that tent.

It was not a good thing to be at the mercy of an omnipotent psychopath who was probably also a sexual sadist. He realized he had to do something while he could. But what? Escape was still possible. But could he leave Henry and Colonel Gann? And should he take Vivian?

Mercado said, "My fault, really. Shouldn't have left Addis."

"Seemed like a good idea at the time."

"Shouldn't have gone to sleep. Gann asked if I could stay awake while he caught a few winks...I said, 'Get some rest, old man,' and next thing I know, we're surrounded by soldiers and a donkey."

"Mule."

"Whatever. And now we're all guilty by association."

"Henry, we are guilty of nothing except being stupid enough to come here expecting to be treated as accredited journalists."

"Well...it may have gone better if we hadn't teamed up with Colonel Gann."

Purcell thought that Colonel Gann had probably saved them all from the Gallas, but Henry needed to share the blame.

Mercado sensed that Purcell was not sympathetic to his interpretation of their predicament, so he said, "Fate. Fate is what brought us here. There is a reason for this..."

"Let me know when you find out."

Mercado continued, "When Doctor Mato told me that you and Vivian were here and well, I knew that there was a higher power watching over us."

"That thought never once crossed my mind, Henry."

"You need to have faith, Frank. Faith will see us through this."

Purcell was tempted to point out that he of little faith was not hanging from the pole, but instead he said, "Vivian and I saw Getachu."

Mercado did not respond.

Purcell continued, "He's basically held a court-martial in his head and condemned Gann to death."

Again, Mercado didn't respond, and Purcell looked at him to see if he was conscious. He was, and he was staring at Purcell waiting for news of his own fate. Purcell said, "You, I, and Vivian are to be court-martialed in the morning." He added, to ease Mercado's anxiety, "But maybe not."

Mercado had no response, so Purcell related his and Vivian's meeting with Getachu, trying to sound optimistic, but also realistic, though he didn't mention Getachu's thinly veiled threat to put Vivian in the camp bordello. Henry had enough on his mind. Purcell concluded, "Getachu may be waiting to hear from his bosses. Or he may have something else in mind for us that he's not saying."

Mercado did not respond immediately, then said, "We're more useful to him alive than dead."

"Unfortunately, that may be true."

"Or the Provisional government will just order him to release us. In fact, I'm sure they will." He added, "General Andom and I have a good relationship."

"Good. I hope General Andom and General Geta-chu have as good a relationship."

Mercado did not reply.

Purcell asked, "Did Vivian tell you that the Gallas captured Prince Joshua and two of his staff and turned them over to Getachu?"

"No...God take pity on them."

"God is on holiday this week, Henry. In the mean-time, I'll do what I can for all of us as long as I'm not hanging on the next pole."

"I know you will, Frank. If you can keep talking to Getachu—"

"But I have to tell you, Henry, I may decide to bust out of here. Without Vivian. If I can get to Gondar, I may be able to get a flight to Addis and get to the American, Swiss, or British embassy, and get you all sprung." He looked at Mercado and asked, "Are you all right with that?"

Mercado seemed to be thinking, then replied, "You'll never make it, Frank."

"Worth a try."

"You have no money, no credentials, no...no shoes for God's sake."

"I'll try to do what Gann was going to do—find some friendly Royalists."

"They can't even help themselves. They're finished. Hunted down like dogs." He said, "You need to stay here. To help us all here."

"I'll leave you here in God's hands."

Vivian returned and embraced Mercado, saying to Purcell, "We need to get them some water, Frank."

"All right. Stay here."

He headed up the slope of the amphitheater, got his bearings, and walked west toward the hospital tent— the only oasis of humanity in this desert of death. Though to be less cynical, probably any man here would offer water, as the soldiers did at the outpost. These were not bad people, but war, as he'd seen too many times, in too many places, changes people.

Whenever he started to believe in humanity, he thought of the Khmer Rouge who murdered millions of their own people. And now he'd made the acquaintance of the Gallas, who were a barbaric throwback to the dark side of humanity. In fact, he admitted, his chances of making it to Gondar and Addis were nil.

Faith, said Henry Mercado. *A higher power is watching over us. There is a reason for all this.* Well, he thought, it better be a very good reason. And, he supposed, Henry, and also Vivian, thought the reason had to do with them coming upon Father Armano, which Purcell thought was pure chance, but which Henry and Vivian believed was divinely ordained. In any case, they'd see in the morning who was right.

He reached the hospital tent and helped himself to two canteens of water that he found among what was called the muddied and bloodied—the discarded uniforms and field gear of the dead and wounded.

He looked, too, for a knife or bayonet, or anything else that could be useful, but the pile had been picked over.

Purcell wrapped the canteens in a fatigue shirt and made his way back.

He wasn't quite sure why Getachu had allowed him and Vivian to wander around freely, but his experience with sadistic despots had always had an element of inconsistency—random acts of cruelty, tempered with expansive acts of kindness. The despot wants to be feared, but also loved for his mercy. The despot wants to be like God.

Purcell got back to the parade ground and handed a canteen to Vivian, who held it to Mercado's lips.

Purcell moved to the Ethiopian, but it appeared that the man was dead. Purcell put his hand on the man's chest, then put his ear to his still heart.

Gann, on the next pole, called out, "Saw him go through his death throes."

Purcell moved to Gann and held the canteen to his lips while he drank.

Gann said, "Save some of that."

Purcell assured him, "This will all be over in the morning."

"Indeed."

There wasn't much else to say, so Purcell moved toward Vivian, who was washing Mercado's face with the water.

Purcell stood there, watching this display of womanly compassion and grief. *Pietà*. Which he knew in Italian meant both pity and piety. The dying son or husband, the warrior or father, comforted in the hour of death by the mother or wife, the pious woman, filled with love and pity. We should all be so fortunate, Purcell thought, to die like that.

He said to Vivian and to Mercado, "I'm going to go up on that platform and get some sleep." He assured Mercado, "I'm here if you need anything." He gave Gann the same assurance, then climbed the three steps onto the crudely built platform. The moon was overhead now and illuminated the large, empty field.

He counted ten poles running in front of the platform. Gann was to his left, standing straight, and the Ethiopian was also to his left, hanging dead by his wrists. He wondered what the man had done to suffer a death like that. Probably not much. To his immediate front was Henry Mercado, barely ten feet away, and he could hear Vivian speaking softly to him as she stroked his face. Mercado said something now and then, but Purcell couldn't hear the words, and in any case he didn't want to eavesdrop on their private moment— if one could call this place of public punishment and death private. He did hope, however, that Mercado was man enough, like Gann, to suffer in dignity, and that his words to his lover were as comforting as hers to him.

Purcell spread the shirt from the hospital on the logs that made up the floor of the platform and lay down. He was fatigued beyond sleep and found he couldn't put his mind to rest.

At some point, maybe fifteen minutes later, Vivian joined him and without a word lay down beside him, though the platform was large.

He shifted to his left and said to her, "Lie on this shirt."

She moved onto the shirt and lay on her back, staring at the sky.

A wind came down from the surrounding mountains, and she said, "I'm cold. Move closer to me."

He moved closer to her, and she rolled on her side, facing him, and he did the same, and they wrapped their bare legs and arms around each other and drew closer for warmth.

He could feel her heart beating, and her breathing, and her breasts pressing against him. Their *shammas* had ridden up to their thighs, and she rubbed her legs and feet over his, then rolled on her back with him on top.

He hesitated, then kissed her, and she threw her arms around his neck and held her lips against his.

He pulled both their *shammas* up to their waists and entered her without resistance. She raised her legs, then crossed them over his buttocks and pulled him down farther as he thrust deeper into her.

Her body began to tremble, then stiffened, and suddenly went loose as she let out a long moan. He came inside her and they lay still, breathing heavily into the cool night air.

"My God..." Tears ran down her cheeks.

They lay on their backs, side by side, holding hands, staring up at the starry sky.

They hadn't spoken a word, and Purcell thought there was nothing to say, but finally he said, "Try to get some sleep."

"I need to check on Henry. And Colonel Gann."

He sat up. "I can do that."

She stood, took the canteen, and said, "Be right back."

Purcell stood as she descended the steps, and he watched her as she moved first toward Gann.

The moon was in the west now and it cast moonshadows down the line of poles. Purcell realized that

Mercado had walked himself around his pole and was now facing the platform.

Vivian checked on Gann, then moved slowly toward Mercado, who was not looking at her but looking up at him.

Was it possible, he wondered, that Mercado had seen—or heard—what happened?

Vivian approached Mercado and he seemed to notice her for the first time.

As she lifted the canteen to his lips and touched his face, he said in a surprisingly strong voice, "Get away from me."

She spoke to him softly, but he shook his head and wouldn't drink from the canteen. She tried again, but again he said, "Get *away* from me."

Finally, she turned and moved back to the platform, and Purcell noticed that she was walking slowly, with her head down.

He glanced at Mercado, who was looking at him again, and they made eye contact in the bright moonlight.

Purcell turned and watched Vivian come up the steps. She threw the canteen on the floor, then lay down on the shirt and stared up at the sky.

Purcell knelt a few feet from her and said, "Sorry."

She didn't reply.

He put ten feet between them and lay on his back.

He heard her say, "Not your fault."

No, he thought, it certainly was not. He said, "Get some sleep. We're going to have a long day."

"We'll all be dead tomorrow. Then none of this matters."

"We will be in Addis tomorrow."

"I think not." She asked him, "Will you make love to me again?"

"No...not here. In Addis."

"If we get out of here, this won't happen again."

He asked, "Will you be with Henry?"

"Maybe...he'll get over it."

"Good. We'll all get over it."

"We will." She said, "Good night."

"Night."

He looked up at the starry African sky. Beautiful, he thought. So very beautiful up there.

He closed his eyes, and as he was drifting into sleep he heard her sobbing silently. He wanted to comfort her, but he couldn't, and he fell into a deep sleep, and dreamt of Vivian naked in the water, and of Mercado shouting her name.

Chapter II

At dawn, Purcell watched as a squad of soldiers marched through the ground mist toward the three men hanging from the posts.

It was too early for a firing squad, he thought—the troops had not yet arrived to witness the execution.

Purcell let Vivian sleep and he came down from the platform.

The ten soldiers didn't seem bothered by his appearance—they had no orders regarding him, and they didn't know if he was the general's guest or his next victim, so they ignored him.

Purcell saw that Mercado was half awake, watching the soldiers approach. Purcell asked him, "How are you doing?"

He looked at Purcell but did not reply.

Purcell held the canteen to Mercado's lips, and he drank, but then spit the water at Purcell.

Purcell said to him, "You were delirious last night."

"Get out of my sight."

In fact, Purcell thought, Henry was having a recurring nightmare about Vivian that had come true.

The soldiers were now unshackling Gann, who was able to stand on his own, then they moved to Mercado, leaving the dead Ethiopian hanging for the troops to see at the morning muster.

Purcell went over to Gann, who was rubbing his raw wrists, and handed him the canteen. Gann finished the last few ounces, then asked, "How is Mercado?"

"Seems okay."

"He had a bad night."

Purcell reminded Gann, "Neither of you would be hanging here if he'd stayed awake on the mountain."

"Don't blame him. I should have stayed awake."

Purcell didn't reply, and Gann said, "He was shouting at God all night."

Again, Purcell did not reply, but he'd heard Henry shouting at God, and also cursing him and Vivian, and Gann had heard that too, and probably surmised what and who Henry was angry at. But that was the least of their problems.

Gann asked, "Where is Miss Smith?"

"Sleeping." He asked Gann, "What's happening?"

"Don't know, old boy. But it's either something very good, or very bad."

"I'll settle for anything in between."

"That doesn't happen here." He asked Purcell, "Why didn't you make a run for it last night?"

"I fell asleep."

Purcell noticed now in the dawn light that the post from which Gann had hung was splintered and pocked with holes that could only have been made by bullets.

Gann, too, noticed and said, "Well, the good news is that they do execute people by firing squad." He nodded toward the dead Ethiopian. "Not like that poor bugger."

Purcell didn't want to get into that conversation, so he returned to Gann's other subject and said, "If I did make a run for it, where would I go?"

Gann replied, "Well, first, I'd advise you to go alone. You don't need a photographer."

Purcell did not reply, but he didn't want to leave Vivian here.

He continued, "About ten kilometers south and east of the Italian spa is a Falasha village. Ethiopian Jews. They'll take you in and you'll be safe there."

"How do you know?"

"I know Ethiopia, old boy. That's where I was going to head. They're Royalists."

Recalling what Mercado had said, Purcell pointed out, "The Royalists are being hunted down."

"The Falashas are immune for the moment."

"Why?"

"It's rather complex. The Falashas trace their ancestry to the time of Solomon and Sheba, and they are revered by some as a link to the Solomonic past, as is the emperor."

"And we know what happened to him."

"Yes, but the Ethiopians are a superstitious lot, and they believe if you harm a Falasha you have angered God—the common God of Christians, Jews, and Muslims."

"Works for the Falashas."

"For now. The name of this village is Shoan." He suggested, "If you're not being shot or chained up today, you should give it a try tonight."

"I was hoping for a helicopter ride to Addis this morning."

"And I hope you are having a whiskey for me tonight in Addis. But you should have an alternate plan."

"Right."

"And if you should ever find yourself in Shoan, tonight or some other time, they will know a thing or two about the black monastery." He looked at Purcell. "If you are still interested in that."

Purcell had the feeling he'd stepped into Tolkien's Middle-Earth. The mysterious dying priest, the surreal Roman ruin, the fortress city of Gondar, the good Prince Joshua, the evil General Getachu, Sir Edmund Gann, and the black monastery. And the Holy Grail, of course. And now the village of the Falashas. None of this seemed possible or real—but it was. Except for the Grail.

Purcell looked at Gann. "Thanks." He felt he needed to tell Gann about his former employer, Prince Joshua, so he did, sparing no detail.

Gann listened without comment, and Purcell could see he was more angry than he was frightened that this could also be his fate. When Purcell had finished, Gann said, "Bloody bastard."

"He's insane."

"Yes, but I'm sure you can convince him that a British soldier rates a firing squad, or at least a quick bullet in the head."

"I'll try to do better than that." He reminded Gann, and himself, "I'm not sure what Getachu has planned for any of us."

"He's treading lightly with you and Miss Smith, or you'd be hanging on these posts."

"Good thought."

"Getachu may be insane, but he's not reckless enough to endanger his own position with the Derg." He explained, "They'd like nothing better than to find an excuse to summon him to Addis, and General Andom would be glad to arrest his rival and have him shot."

"That's good."

"Or strangled."

"Even better."

"The Revolution," said Colonel Gann, "eats its own."

"It always does."

"I predict that Getachu will put you and Miss Smith on a helicopter to Addis."

"And Mercado?"

"Getachu will send him off to Addis to be dealt with at a higher level. Probably get expelled." He added, "They're not shooting Western reporters yet."

"Good. Well, you seem to know these people." He informed Colonel Gann, "Getachu hinted that he may want you to train and advise his officers."

"That will not happen."

"Don't turn down that job."

Gann did not reply, and Purcell pointed out, "The war is almost over. You won't be helping him much."

"I won't be helping him at all."

"Don't be stupid."

"I've asked a favor of you. Please do it."

"Do it yourself." He made eye contact with Gann and said, "Look, Colonel, I'm trying to save your life, and you're not helping. Don't take the knight thing too seriously."

Gann didn't reply, but he looked past Purcell and said, "I think it's time to go."

Purcell turned around and saw that Mercado was on his feet without help from the soldiers, and Vivian had awoken and was trying to minister to her lover, who was having none of it—which seemed to confuse the soldiers who'd missed the reason for Mercado's bad behavior toward the lady.

Purcell looked up at the dead Ethiopian, who seemed almost Christlike hanging there with his flesh torn. It occurred to Purcell that the new Ethiopia didn't look much different than the old Ethiopia.

Purcell turned to the rising sun above the eastern mountains, then to the large open field shrouded in morning mist. God did a good job with the heaven and the earth. Not so good with the people.

The squad leader formed everyone up in a line of march and barked something in Amharic, then shouted, *"Avanti!"*

Forward.

Chapter 12

General Getachu sat at his camp desk in his head-quarters tent, speaking to an aide in Amharic and ignoring his four guests who were sitting facing him.

Mercado sat on the far right, and Vivian had taken the chair next to him, though Mercado was pointedly ignoring her. Gann had sat himself between Vivian and Purcell, and behind them was a soldier armed with an AK-47 automatic rifle.

Purcell was surprised that Getachu had included Gann in this meeting, but possibly this was a summary court-martial, with the general acting as judge and jury, and the soldier as instant executioner.

The tent was not as dark as it had been at night, and the morning sun shone through mosquito net windows, revealing a dirt floor strewn with cigarette butts. Getachu took a call on his field phone, and spoke as he signed papers for his aide. A busy executive, thought Purcell, but there's always time for fun and sport.

On that subject, Purcell saw that neither Prince Joshua nor his two officers were present, and Purcell wondered if Getachu had sent his royal highness to the women's tent.

The aide left and Getachu looked at Gann and asked, "Do you know that your prince is here?"

Gann did not reply, and Getachu seemed angry at the insolence.

Purcell volunteered, "I informed him."

"Do not speak unless spoken to." Getachu looked at Gann again, smiled, and said, "That is what I learned in the English missionary school." He also informed Colonel Gann, "The prince has confessed that you and he have engaged in war crimes."

Gann had no response.

Getachu saw that this was not productive, so he looked at Purcell and asked, "Who gave you permission to leave the medical tent and walk through my camp?"

"We had no indication that we were under confinement."

"This is a secure military facility."

"As you know, we were looking for our colleagues."

"Yes? And is Colonel Gann your colleague?"

"According to you he is."

"Then you are all guilty by association."

"According to you."

Getachu was sipping water from a canteen cup and Purcell said, "We need something to eat and drink."

"Why should I waste food and water on people who are to be executed? But I promise you a cigarette before you are shot." Getachu thought that was funny and he translated for the soldier, who laughed.

Getachu tapped Vivian's camera, then held up three notepads and said, "There is enough evidence here to condemn you, Mr. Purcell, and you, Miss Smith, and you, Mr. Mercado, to death by firing squad."

Purcell didn't think so, but he also knew that

Getachu didn't need any evidence, except maybe to justify an execution to his superiors in Addis.

Purcell said, "I must ask you, General, to return our personal property, including our credentials and passports, and to provide us transportation to the capital." He reminded Getachu, "We came here expecting to be treated as journalists, not as criminals."

Getachu pointed out, "I think we have had this conversation."

"I think we need to have it again."

General Getachu looked at Colonel Gann, then said to his other guests, "Before we discuss your status, do you agree that this man deserves what he is to suffer?"

Purcell replied, "No, we do not. Colonel Gann was captured in uniform and he is to be treated as a prisoner of war under the Geneva Convention, which Ethiopia has signed."

"That was the previous government."

Gann said to Purcell, "Save your breath."

"Excellent advice," agreed Getachu.

Mercado cleared his throat and said, "General...if you agree to release us, we will write and sign statements of any wrongdoing that we may have engaged in. We will also write a press story praising your victory and your qualities as a leader. We also agree to have our passports held by your foreign office and to stay in Addis writing articles for the duration of this war."

Getachu looked at Mercado. "Well, you are offering less than Mr. Purcell and Miss Smith have already offered." He informed Mercado, "They offered to stay here with me for the duration of the war. I was looking forward to their company."

Vivian took a deep breath, hesitated, then said, "General, if this is supposed to be an inquiry or a trial, it's actually a farce." She concluded, "You are keeping us here unlawfully and against our will, and our press offices and our embassies know where we are, and they will be making inquiries, if they haven't already. Please provide us with transportation to the capital and please return our belongings."

Getachu stared at her for a long time, then said, "But you look very good in the shamma."

Vivian did not reply, but she held Getachu's stare.

Finally, he said, "The Revolutionary Army came into possession of some interesting equipment which the Americans provided to the Royal Army. One such item was a device called a starlight scope. You know of this? A telescopic sight that allows one to see in the dark, which my sentries use in the watchtower to look for the enemy, outside and inside the camp."

No one responded, and Getachu continued, "So it appeared—to my sentry at least—that you, Miss Smith, and you, Mr. Purcell, engaged in a behavior that did not please Mr. Mercado." He asked, "Or did my sentry misunderstand what he saw?"

Again no one replied, and if anyone thought that Getachu had brought this up solely to amuse himself, Purcell knew otherwise.

Getachu said to Mercado, "So perhaps you will write in your confession that you discovered that Mr. Purcell and Miss Smith were spying for the Royalists." He assured Mercado, "You need not write that about yourself. That would condemn you to death."

Purcell glanced at Mercado, expecting that Mercado

understood that he needed to reply with a firm fuck you, but Mercado did not reply.

"Mr. Mercado?"

"I...don't know what you're talking about, General."

"You do. And you should consider my offer."

Again, Mercado made no reply.

Getachu glanced at his watch as though this was all taking more time than he'd allowed for it. He said, "To my mind, you are all guilty, but as I said to Mr. Purcell and Miss Smith last night, it is possible to make your punishment less severe." He looked at Gann. "Even you, Colonel, could be spared from death."

"As you spared Prince Joshua?"

"I'm glad to see that Mr. Purcell has told you everything, and I'm glad to see that you speak."

"Go to hell."

"There is no hell. And no heaven. There is no more than what you see here."

Gann did not reply, and Getachu continued, "They taught me otherwise in the missionary school, but I did not believe them then or now. But I do believe in the use of earthly pain to punish bad behavior, or to make a person confess to his sins." He pulled Gann's riding crop from his pocket and said, "Or simply to give me pleasure." He flexed the crop.

Gann stared at Getachu and they made eye contact.

Getachu stood and said to Gann, "So, the good headmaster beat me in that English school, and he taught me something. But not the lesson he thought. He taught me that some men can be broken with the whip, and some cannot. My spirit was not broken."

Purcell thought Getachu's mind was broken, and he

saw what was coming, so he said, "General, we will not sit here and witness—"

Getachu slapped the crop on his desk. "Shut up!" He said to Gann, "I will spare your life if you drop your pants, as I did many times, and allow me to deliver thirty blows to your bare buttocks." He added, "Here and now, leaning over this desk, in front of your friends."

"I think it's you, Mikael, who needs another good beating."

Getachu literally shook with rage, then pulled his pistol, aimed it at Gann, and shouted, "I give you five seconds to do what I say!"

"You can give me five years and I will tell you to go to hell."

"One—"

Purcell stood. "Stop this."

The soldier behind Purcell pushed him down into his chair.

"Two."

Vivian said, "Colonel, please. Just do what he wants...please..."

"Three."

Mercado closed his eyes and lowered his head.

"Four."

Gann stood and Getachu smiled. Gann turned, dropped his pants, and said, "Kiss my arse."

Purcell thought he'd hear the loud explosion of the gun, but there was complete silence in the room.

Finally, Getachu let out a forced laugh, then said, "Very good, Colonel, you may sit."

Gann pulled up his pants, but did not sit and kept his back to Getachu.

Getachu saw that Gann was not going to turn around, and he said, "You will not provoke me into giving you an easy death."

Gann remained standing with his back to the general, and Getachu said something to the soldier, who came around and drove the butt of his rifle into Gann's groin. Gann doubled over, and the soldier pushed him into his chair.

Getachu holstered his gun and put down the riding crop, but remained standing. "You all understand, I hope, that I can have each of you shot as spies."

Vivian surprised everyone, and herself, by saying, "If that were true, you would have done it."

Getachu looked at her and said, "It *is* true, Miss Smith, but as we discussed, there are some men—and women—who I would rather see broken than dead." He reminded everyone, "And those who agree to serve the people's revolution may also be spared."

Mercado spoke up. "I did serve the revolution for many years, and I would be willing to serve it again with my written words—"

"Your written words are like adding your shit to a fire."

Mercado seemed to shrink in his chair.

Getachu looked at Gann, who was obviously in extreme pain, and said, "Colonel, if you agree to become an advisor to my army—as you did for the former prince's army—I will spare your life."

Gann shook his head.

Getachu seemed frustrated with the man's stubbornness and said, "I will take you to see your former employer and also his aides, who I am sure you know, and then you can decide if you wish to help the revolution or if you wish to assist the prince in his new duties."

Gann did not reply, and Getachu said, "Or perhaps I will turn you over to the Gallas, and wash my hands of you."

Purcell leaned toward Gann and said softly, "Just *say* you'll do it."

Gann shook his head, and Purcell wondered if Getachu really wanted or needed Colonel Gann's military skills, or if he just wanted the satisfaction of seeing the Englishman—the knight—crawling to him before he killed him. Getachu had tried the carrot and the stick, and neither was working on Gann, who Purcell suspected knew Getachu's game better than anyone.

Getachu's field phone rang, he answered it, spoke briefly, then hung up and said, "My helicopter has arrived from Gondar." He asked, "Would you all enjoy a ride to the capital?"

Purcell assumed there was a small catch, but the carrot sounded good. He said, "We're ready to go."

"So you said. But first I need some information from all of you. If you give me this information, you will be put on my helicopter and flown to the capital. If you do not give me what I am looking for, then a fate worse than death awaits you here." He looked at Vivian and said, "Unless, of course, you enjoy the attention of thirty or forty men a day."

Purcell knew these were not empty threats, but everyone seemed to have become numb to Getachu's words, and Getachu sensed this as well, so he sat and lit a cigarette, then remembered to offer the pack to Purcell, who declined.

Getachu seemed deep in thought, then began, "A company of my soldiers occupied the Italian spa, where they found empty cans of food and tire tracks." He looked at Purcell. "You were there?"

Purcell replied, "We said we were."

"Correct." He continued, "My men also found fresh earth which they took to be a grave, and which they dug up." He asked his guests, "Did you dig that grave?"

The easy answer, Purcell thought, was, *Yes, so what?* But Getachu was not asking out of idle curiosity, and a better answer might be no. Vivian, however, had taken a photograph of the grave, and her camera was sitting on Getachu's desk. Still, they could deny digging the grave, and he would have done so if it was only he and Vivian answering this psychopath's questions; but Henry, he realized, was ready to say or do anything to save himself from death or torture. Some men, like Gann, could hang from a pole all night and say, "Kiss my arse." Others, like Henry, cracked easy and early. But Purcell couldn't judge Mercado unless he himself had been hanging from the next pole.

"Did you dig that grave?"

Purcell replied, "We did."

"Who did you bury?"

"We buried who you dug up."

"My men dug up the body of an old man, Mr. Purcell. I am asking you who it was."

"A man we found dying in the spa."

"Why was he dying?"

"He had a stomach wound."

"How did he get this wound?"

"I have no idea."

"Did you not speak to him?"

Purcell thought it was time to turn this over to Henry to see what, if anything, he had to say about this, so he replied, "The man spoke Italian and I do not."

Getachu looked at Mercado. "Doctor Mato informs me that you speak Italian."

Mercado nodded.

"Did you speak to this dying man?"

"I...I did...but, he died before I could...find out much about him."

Purcell was not completely surprised that Mercado was keeping a secret from Getachu, because to Mercado it was a secret worth keeping.

Getachu looked long at Mercado. "If you are lying to me, I will find out and then we have no agreement, Mr. Mercado. And then...well, you have sealed your fate."

Mercado kept eye contact with Getachu. "The man died without telling us who he was."

Getachu kept staring at him, then shifted his attention to Vivian. "And Doctor Mato informs me that you speak Italian."

"I do."

"And what did this dying man say to you?"

Purcell wondered if Vivian would take this opportunity to repay Mercado for not firmly defending her against Getachu's charges of spying. But women, Purcell had learned, are loyal to men who don't deserve loyalty. On the other hand, it was Vivian who'd been disloyal first, and probably she was feeling as guilty as Henry was feeling angry. Sex has consequences beyond the act.

"Miss Smith?"

Vivian replied, "The man said nothing more to me than he said to Mr. Mercado."

"How convenient. Well, let me tell you who I think this old man was. It could only have been Father Armano." He looked at his guests. "As I'm sure he told you."

No one replied, and Getachu continued, "Two nights ago, one of my artillery batteries bombarded the nearby fortress of Ras Theodore, who is of the family of my present guest, Joshua. Within this fortress was this Father Armano, who had been imprisoned there since the days of the Italian war." He asked his guests, "Do you know this story?"

Vivian and Mercado shook their heads.

Getachu went on, "The bombardment attracted the attention of the Gallas, as it always does, and they descended on the fortress and massacred the Royalist survivors, though some managed to flee into the jungle. But my infantry company captured some of these men and brought them here. In fact, you may have seen these soldiers of Ras Theodore hanging outside this tent alongside the soldiers of Ras Joshua."

Getachu lit another cigarette, sipped some water, then continued. "But before they were brought here, they were brought back to their fortress. Why? To assist my men in determining the fate of Father Armano—and as they discovered, the prison cell of this priest was empty, and the captured soldiers could not identify a body as that of the priest. But they did find a Bible, in Italian, on the floor of his cell, with a hole in it—perhaps a bullet hole. So it is my assumption that the wounded man you discovered was Father Armano." He looked at his guests closely, then asked Mercado directly, "Why do you think this priest who you came upon was so important?"

Mercado replied, "I don't know."

"Then I will tell you. Well, perhaps I won't. You seem to have no information about this man or this matter, so we have nothing to discuss, and you have nothing to trade for your freedom or your lives."

Purcell said, "I hope you had the decency to rebury the old man."

"I have no idea if he was reburied, and I don't care if the jackals eat his body. But it is interesting that you took the time and effort to give an unknown man a burial."

"Interesting to you. Common decency to us."

"I don't like your attitude of moral superiority, Mr. Purcell. I had enough of that in school."

"Apparently not."

"Don't provoke me."

"We have no information for you, General. May we leave?"

Getachu seemed not to hear him, and he sat back in his chair and said, "I will be open with you, and perhaps you will do the same for me." He looked at each of them, then said, "The black monastery. You know of this place. What is in it, I do not know, nor do I know its exact location. But Father Armano knew its location and he may have told you something of this."

He looked at Purcell, then Vivian, then Mercado, and said, "I hope for your sake that he did."

Mercado said, "He did not."

"I will ask you again later. But for now, I will explain to you my interest in the black monastery." He leaned forward and said, "The Provisional Revolutionary government is interested in selling precious objects to museums and churches outside the country. The government is selling most of the emperor's trinkets now. We need the money for food and medicine for the people. But when a very old regime ends, some people become upset. Nostalgic. Some people are fond of kings and emperors and aristocrats on horses—as long as it's not in their own country. You understand? The end of the empire is a historical necessity. And gold and jewels are worthless in a modern state. We need capital. And we are acquiring it in the only way we can. The traditional way of revolutionary governments. We rob the rich of their baubles. A few suffer. Many gain. The churches, especially, are better off without their gold. They can concentrate more on God and saving souls without the worry of keeping their property intact. Everyone benefits. So in exchange for any information you might have on the location of this monastery—and what is in it—I will allow you all to return to the capital, including Colonel Gann, who will be dealt with at a higher level, and therefore dealt with less severely than I would here at the front." He added, "You all have my word on that."

Purcell wondered if Getachu knew specifically about the so-called Holy Grail, or if he was just interested in looting another Coptic monastery. It made no difference to Purcell, but it did to Henry Mercado. Henry wanted to get out of here and go look for the monastery and the Grail; Henry wanted to have his cake and eat it too. But he couldn't.

Getachu suggested, "Perhaps you would like a private moment to discuss this."

Purcell knew, and he hoped Henry and Vivian also knew that even if they could take Getachu at his word, what little they knew was not enough to get them out of here. But it *was* enough to keep them as Getachu's guests for a long time—just as Father Armano had been a guest of Ethiopia for a very long time. Or Getachu would just do away with them if Henry decided to clarify his lie.

"Mr. Mercado?"

Mercado said, "We told you all we know about this man. He was dying, and in pain, and he said almost nothing except to ask for water."

"I know you are lying."

Purcell didn't think that Mercado was doing a good job of putting this to rest, so he pointed out, "Why would we lie about something that has no meaning to us?"

"I told you. Some people are fond of the old regime and the old church, which are one."

"I don't care about either." Purcell added, "And if this old man did speak to us, and if he was Father Armano, what do you think he would tell us? The location of the monastery? I don't understand how he would know that. You said he was in this fortress for almost forty years. I'm not understanding what you think we should know."

Getachu seemed to have a lucid moment, and he nodded. "You make a good point. In fact, you have nothing to give me." He added, "And I have nothing to give you."

"Except," Purcell suggested, "our belongings, and a ride to Addis." He added, "Our embassies and our offices are awaiting word from us."

"Then they will have a long wait." Getachu informed everyone, "This proceeding is finished. I will consider my judgment. You remain under arrest." He said something to the soldier, who escorted them out into the bright sunlight where a squad of soldiers waited with leg shackles.

Chapter 13

They were marched to a deep ravine, and Purcell saw that there was fresh earth at the bottom, and shovels, and it was obvious that this was a mass grave, and perhaps a place of execution. They were ordered to climb into the ravine, and it seemed to Purcell that Getachu's judgment had traveled faster than they had. But to be more optimistic, he didn't think that Getachu was through with them yet.

At the bottom of the ravine, they could smell the buried corpses. Purcell and Gann looked up at the soldiers, to see if these men were their executioners, but the soldiers were sitting at the edge of the ravine smoking and talking.

Gann said to Purcell, "Sloppy discipline."

"You should have taken the job."

"They're a hopeless lot."

"Right." But they won.

No one had anything else to say, and Purcell was sure that each of them was thinking about what had transpired in Getachu's office. It had been a very unpleasant experience, he thought, but it could have gone worse, though not better. In any case, everyone seemed relieved that it was over, even if it wasn't.

Finally, Gann said, "The man's a bloody lunatic."

No one argued with that, and Gann added,

"Ungrateful bastard. Got a decent education from the good Church of England missionaries, and he complains about a few strokes on his arse. Did him more good than harm, I'm sure."

Purcell smiled despite the fact that little Mikael had grown up fucked up and was looking for payback. And he didn't have to look too far.

Vivian admitted, "I was very frightened."

Purcell wanted to tell her she did fine, but that was Henry's job, though Henry wasn't speaking to her. Mercado, in fact, was glancing nervously up at the soldiers with the automatic rifles.

Gann noticed Mercado's anxiety and assured him, "We're not getting off that easily, Mr. Mercado."

Mercado did not reply.

Vivian looked at Purcell and said, "You gave me courage, Frank."

He didn't reply.

Vivian said to Gann, "You're very brave."

"Thank you, but you were seeing more anger than bravery." He added, "Men like that are taking over the world."

That might be true, Purcell thought. He'd seen the Getachus of Southeast Asia, and they seemed to be springing up everywhere. Or maybe they'd been around since the beginning of time. He'd written about these men and about their so-called ideologies without comment or judgment. He reported. Maybe, he thought, if he got out of here, he should start being more judgmental. But then he'd sound like Henry Mercado.

Purcell looked at Mercado, who was sitting on a pile of fresh earth, staring off into space, unaware that there was probably a rotting corpse under his ass. No one had told Henry how brave he'd been. Maybe because he hadn't been. But he *had* lied, boldly and recklessly, to Getachu about Father Armano. And Vivian had loyally backed him up on that lie. It was a good lie and the right lie, but Purcell knew that Mercado had lied for the wrong reason. So, this being the private moment that Getachu had offered them, he said to Mercado, "You put us in some jeopardy, Henry, by lying about the priest."

Clearly, Henry Mercado had nothing to say to Frank Purcell, but he replied for everyone's benefit, "Getachu has no way to discover the truth."

"Well, he does if he hangs us all from a post for a few days."

Mercado said impatiently, "It may have occurred to you that even if I told him what little we knew, he wouldn't have released us."

"Right. In fact we'd be here forever. But you're not answering my question, Henry. *Why* did you risk lying to him about Father Armano and the black monastery?"

Mercado replied sharply, "You know damned well why."

"I do, but if we do get out of here, none of us should be coming back to find the black monastery."

Mercado glanced at Gann and said to Purcell, "I don't know if we're getting out of here or if I'm ever coming back, but I don't want *them* to find it."

Henry Mercado, Purcell knew, was comforted by thinking he was protecting the Holy Grail from the Antichrist, or whatever, and he could go to his martyrdom happy in the knowledge that when he met Jesus he could say, "I saved your cup."

Colonel Gann could feel the tension between the two men, and he knew the cause of it, which was a very old story; one chap had cuckolded the other, and to make matters worse, the lady in question was not declaring herself for one or the other. Awkward, he thought, and though he was sure he had far greater issues to worry about, it made him uncomfortable nonetheless.

To clear the air on at least one thing, however, Gann said, "As I've acknowledged to Mr. Purcell, I know about the black monastery, and though it's well hidden in the jungle, Getachu will eventually find it. You can be sure of that."

No one responded, and Gann continued, "As you may also have heard, perhaps from this Father Armano, there is a legend that this monastery is the resting place of the Holy Grail."

Again, no one responded, and Gann went on, "Can't say I believe in all that, but I can assure you that whenever the revolutionary bastards here show up at a church or monastery, the priests and monks make off with their earthly treasures."

Purcell figured as much. There were two things the churches were good at: acquiring gold and keeping gold. Half the world's priceless religious objects had been on the lam at one time or another. And there was no reason to think that this would be any different when the Ethiopian revolutionaries got close to the black monastery. Same if Henry Mercado or Vivian got close. Poof! The Grail disappears again.

Purcell said to Mercado, "We *are* getting out of here, and I can guarantee you I'm never coming back.

My advice to you and to Vivian is to forget you ever met Father Armano or ever heard of the black monastery. This is not a good thing to know about."

Mercado did not reply.

Purcell added, "God is not telling you to find the Holy Grail, Henry. He is telling you to go home."

"And I'm telling you to mind your own business."

Purcell changed the subject to something more immediate and asked Gann, "Do you think Getachu is at all concerned about overstepping his authority?"

"That's the question, isn't it? Well, I can tell you that he can't overstep his power, which is absolute here, as you see. But he *can* overstep his authority and get on the wrong side of the Derg and his rival, General Andom. Not that those two care about us, or about international law, but Andom has to decide if it would be good for him or bad for him if Getachu kills us."

Vivian asked, "Do we think anyone outside of the Revolutionary government even knows we're here?"

Mercado reminded everyone, "Our press offices know we were heading this way, and we mentioned to some of our colleagues that we had a safe-conduct pass to make contact with General Getachu."

Which, Purcell thought, meant very little. Basically, they were all freelancers, which worked well except when they got in trouble or went missing. Possibly, if they didn't show up in the Hilton bar in a week or so, someone might think to contact their respective embassies if they could remember their drinking buddies' nationalities.

As for himself, Purcell was aware that the American embassy in Addis was barely open, and not on good terms with the new government. If he wasn't wearing leg shackles, he'd have kicked himself in the ass for making this trip.

And as for Mercado with his UK passport, and Vivian with her Swiss passport, any requests for information made by their respective embassies to the Ethiopian government would be met by indifference on a good day, and hostility and lies on most days.

Bottom line here, Purcell thought, there was no outside help on the way. Mercado should know that, but maybe Vivian should not.

The sun was higher and hotter now, and the temperature at the bottom of the ravine had to be over a hundred degrees. Purcell noticed that most of Vivian's white ointment was gone, and her face and arms were getting redder. He called up to the soldiers at the top of the ravine, "*Weha!*"

They looked down at him, then one of them unhooked a canteen from his belt and threw it to him.

He gave the canteen to Vivian, and she drank, but then seemed uncertain who to pass it to. Old lover? New lover? She gave it to Gann. He drank and passed it to Mercado, who drank and held it out for Purcell to take.

Purcell finished the last few ounces, then suggested to Mercado, "Give Vivian your shirt for her head."

Mercado seemed angry at being told by Purcell to be a gentleman, and he snapped, "Give her your own shirt."

Purcell would have, if he'd had a shirt, but he had a *shamma*, and no underwear, and he didn't want to bring that up. He stared at Mercado, who started to unbutton his khaki shirt.

But Gann had already taken off his uniform shirt and handed it to Vivian, who said, "Thank you," and draped it over her head.

Purcell understood Mercado's anger, but it amazed him that the man could hold on to it while he was contemplating a firing squad or worse. But on second thought, men are men. He thought, too, that if he had a chance to do last night over, he'd do the same thing, but twice. No regrets. He wondered if he could convince Mercado that what happened last night was God's will.

He looked at Vivian sitting at the side of the ravine, closer to Mercado than to him. They made eye contact, and she held it, then looked away.

He wondered what she was thinking or feeling. Probably he'd never know, and that was just as well.

Another group of soldiers appeared at the top of the ravine, and it was obvious that something was going to happen, and probably not anything good.

Vivian suddenly moved closer to Mercado and grabbed his arm. "Henry…"

Mercado appeared more aware of the soldiers, thought Purcell, than of Vivian's hold on him. Purcell could hear her say softly, "I love you…please forgive me."

Mercado seemed to notice her for the first time, and he hesitated, then asked, "Are you truly sorry?"

"I am."

"Then I will forgive you."

She put her arms around him and buried her face in his chest.

Purcell assumed that Mercado's absolution didn't include him, even if he asked for it, but he didn't think

he needed forgiveness, so he didn't ask. He did, however, want to say something to Vivian, in case this was
the last time they'd see each other. But what he wanted
to say, he couldn't say, so he turned away and looked at
the soldiers, who were speaking rapidly and glancing
down at the prisoners at the bottom of the ravine.

Mercado spoke some Amharic, but he seemed pre-
occupied, so Purcell asked Gann, "Can you understand
what they're saying?"

"A bit...I think you three are going to be taken
somewhere else."

"Why do you think that?"

"The leg shackles are for traveling, old boy. When
they tie your hands behind your back, you know you're
not going far."

Purcell knew this made sense, but he pointed out,
"Your legs are also shackled, Colonel."

"Yes, I noticed. Can't say why, though."

Henry and Vivian seemed oblivious to what was
going on, but then one of the soldiers shouted to them,
"Come! Come!" He motioned for all of them to climb
out of the ravine.

They all looked at one another, then stood and began
climbing up the slope, dragging their chains with them
as the soldier kept shouting, "Come! Come!"

They reached the top of the ravine and stood among
the soldiers, who seemed indifferent to them. Purcell
noticed that in the distance, where he'd spotted the
helipad, an American-made Huey sat with its rotor
spinning.

The soldier in charge pointed to the helicopter and
shouted, "Go! Go!"

Purcell looked at Gann, expecting that he'd be pulled aside, but one of the soldiers gave Gann a push and shouted, "Go!"

Vivian and Mercado joined hands and began running as fast as their chains allowed. Purcell and Gann followed. Four soldiers accompanied them, urging them to move faster. Vivian stumbled and Mercado helped her up, and they continued toward the helicopter.

Vivian and Mercado reached the open door of the aircraft and were pulled aboard. As Purcell got closer, he could see a large red star painted on the olive drab fuselage—the red star of the revolution, which he knew covered the old emblem of the Lion of Judah.

Gann scrambled aboard without help, and Purcell followed.

Vivian called out over the noise of the engine and rotors, "Pilot says we're going to Addis!" She flashed a big smile and shouted, "*Avanti!*"

The helicopter lifted, pivoted, and headed south toward Addis Ababa.

PART II

Rome, December 1974

Tutte le strade conducono a Roma.
All roads lead to Rome.

Chapter 14

Hello, Henry."

Henry Mercado didn't turn toward the voice behind him, but he did glance into the bar mirror.

Frank Purcell took the empty stool beside Mercado and ordered a Jack Daniel's on the rocks. He said, "You look well."

"Is this an accident?"

"I heard you were in Rome."

Mercado did not reply.

"Can I buy you a drink?"

"I was just leaving."

The bartender poured Purcell's drink and he raised his glass. "Centanni."

Mercado called for his tab.

Purcell stirred his drink and said, "I left you a note at the Addis Hilton."

"I was taken directly from the prison to the airport."

"Vivian left you a note, too."

He didn't reply.

Mercado's bill came and he put a twenty-thousand-lire note on the bar, which Purcell reckoned was about three drinks at Harry's Bar prices.

It was four in the afternoon, and the quiet, elegant bar was not yet in full swing. A few perfunctory but tasteful Christmas decorations were placed here and there.

Outside, the Via Veneto was crowded with cars and people as always, but maybe more so, thought Purcell, because of the Christmas season. The sky was low and gray, and the air was damp, so he wore a trench coat, but he noticed that Mercado was wearing only a tweed sports jacket, which seemed too big for him. In fact, Henry did not look well and there was a lot of space between his neck and his collar and tie. They'd both lost their Ethiopian tans, and Mercado's skin looked as gray as the winter sky.

Mercado slid off his stool and said, "I'm living at the Excelsior, and usually at the bar there."

"I know."

"Then you also know not to run into me there."

Purcell nodded and said, "Merry Christmas, Henry."

Mercado turned toward the door, then turned back and said, "All right, I will ask you. How is she?"

"*Where* is she might be a better question."

"All right, *where* is she?"

"Don't know. She left me in Cairo, end of October. Said she had business in Geneva, and she'd be back in two weeks. What's today?"

Mercado stood there awhile, then asked, "How long have you been here?"

"Two days. Let me buy you a drink. I came to Rome to see you."

"Why?"

Purcell slid off his stool and took Mercado by the arm. "I need ten minutes of your time. I have some good news about Colonel Gann."

Mercado hesitated, then let Purcell steer him to a table by the window. Purcell called out to the bartender, "Another round, please."

They sat across from each other, and Mercado glanced at his watch. "I'm meeting someone at five."

"Okay. Well, I just heard from a guy named Willis at the AP office in Addis. You know him? He says that Gann has been released from jail and will be flying to London in time for Christmas."

Mercado nodded. "I'm glad to hear that."

"Me, too. Only in a place like Ethiopia can you be condemned to death, then released on bail and allowed to leave the country."

"I'm sure the British government paid dearly for their knight errant."

"Right. Money talks, and the Revolutionary government needs money, so they sold Gann. Works for everyone." He also informed Mercado, "The bad news is that Gann has to return to Addis after the holidays for a hearing on his appeal or he forfeits his bail." He smiled. "I don't think he'll be making that trip."

Mercado smiled in return. "If he does, he *deserves* a firing squad."

"*Two* firing squads."

Mercado said, "It's important for these people to save face. Before they kicked me out, I got handed a five-year sentence for my association with counterrevolutionaries."

"Only five? When are you supposed to report back?"

"I'm not clear about that." He asked Purcell, "How about you?"

"I just did that week in the slammer."

"Then a week of house arrest in the Hilton."

"Correct."

"With Vivian."

"Correct."

"You both got off easy."

"Right." He reminded Mercado, "You're the one who got caught sleeping with Gann. Vivian and I didn't do anything wrong."

"Well, I'm sure you did in the Hilton."

Purcell changed the subject. "We should go see Gann in London."

Mercado kept to the subject, "I didn't do anything wrong and I spent a month in the foulest prison I've ever seen, while you and Vivian—"

"Was it that long? Well, we've both been in worse places."

"Where did you go after you left Addis?"

"I went to Cairo."

"Alone?"

"No." Purcell explained, "It wasn't our choice to go there . . . or to go together," which was partly a lie. He said, "Cairo seems to be the dumping ground for people expelled from Ethiopia." He asked, "Where did they send you?"

"Cairo."

"I wish I'd known you were there."

"I was there two hours and took the first flight to London." Mercado asked, "Why did you stay?"

"I needed a job. So I contacted the AP office, and the bureau chief, Gibson, was looking for a freelancer." He added, "He's expecting another war with Israel, and I am a very good war correspondent."

Mercado didn't respond to that, nor did he ask why

Vivian stayed in Cairo. In fact, she had told Purcell she was excited about photographing the pyramids and all that, plus she wanted to be his photographer if another war broke out. Also, they were in love.

The waiter brought their drinks and Purcell saw that Henry was still drinking gin and Schweppes. Purcell raised his glass and Mercado hesitated, then did the same. Purcell said, "To freedom."

"And life."

They touched glasses and sat back in their chairs and watched Rome go by.

Rome, Purcell had noticed, wasn't as garishly decorated for Christmas as, say, London or New York. He'd like to be in one city or another for the holiday, and he had thought he'd be with Vivian, but that didn't look likely. Christmas in Cairo would not be festive.

He thought back to Addis. The whole two weeks had a surreal feeling. They'd all been taken from the helicopter in separate vehicles, still in chains, to the grim central prison and kept in separate cells, unable to communicate. Some prosecutor with a loose grasp of English had interrogated him every day and told him that his friends had all confessed to their crimes, whatever they were, and had implicated him.

The prison had an enclosed courtyard, with a gallows, and one or two men were hanged each day. He asked Mercado, "Did you have a room with a view of the hangings?"

"I did. Hoped I'd see you."

They both smiled.

Purcell lit a cigarette and stirred his drink.

After a week in prison, with no bath or shower,

rancid food, and putrid water, a nice lady from the American embassy arrived and escorted him, still barefoot and wearing his *shamma*, to a waiting car and took him to the Hilton a few blocks away.

The lady, Anne, had instructed him to stay in his room, which the hotel had held for him and were billing him for. She didn't suggest a bath, but she did suggest he call a doctor to his room for a checkup. In answer to his questions about Vivian, Gann, and Henry Mercado, she replied, "Miss Smith is here. The others remain in custody."

She offered to walk him to the front desk, but he declined, and she handed him his passport and wished him luck.

He walked barefoot in his *shamma* to the front desk, where the clerk said, "Welcome back, Mr. Purcell," and gave him his key.

His room had been searched and most of his possessions had been taken, including his notebooks, but that was the least of his problems.

He had waited a full day before calling Vivian, and they met in her room for drinks because they were both confined to quarters, and in any case neither of them wanted to run into their colleagues in the bar, or the security police in the lobby.

Vivian, too, had had her room ransacked and all her film had been taken, which made her angry, but she, too, understood that their real problem was getting out of Ethiopia.

As he'd finished his drink, she'd reminded him, "As I said, nothing is going to happen between us here."

"I understand."

Later, in bed, she told him, "When they release Henry..."

"I understand."

"Sorry."

"Me too."

But they didn't release Henry, and a week later Purcell and Vivian were officially expelled from Ethiopia and found themselves on an EgyptAir flight to Cairo.

Purcell said to Mercado now, "Vivian and I made daily inquiries to the British embassy about you and Gann, and they assured us you were both well, and they were working on your release." He added, "We were worried about you."

"And you didn't want me showing up unexpectedly."

Which was true, but Purcell stuck to the subject and said, "I was sure they were going to shoot Gann. Or hang him."

"All's well that ends well."

"Right." Purcell looked out at the Roman wall that surrounded the city. He realized that the bricks of the ancient city wall looked exactly like the bricks of the Italian-built prison in Addis. He pointed this out to Mercado and said, "The Italians know how to build."

Mercado did not respond.

"Those mineral baths were impressive."

"Don't get nostalgic on me, Frank."

"Henry...have you thought about going back?"

Mercado stayed silent for a moment, then replied, "I have, actually. But it's obviously too risky."

"Well, if you decide to go back, let me know."

"You'll be the last to know."

The waiter came by and Purcell ordered two more. He asked Mercado, "Did you hear the news out of Ethiopia today?"

"I did not."

"Well, a guy named General Banti took over the military council and announced a new government. Same group of thugs in the Derg, but with different leaders, and I'm thinking it may be possible now to go back if these new guys are not as crazy as the last bunch."

"Speaking of crazy."

"Just a thought." He informed Mercado, "The big story is the Mideast. The canal is still closed and Sadat is saying things like, 'Mideast time bomb.' He's pissed off at all the Russian Jews immigrating to Israel. It really looks like there could be another war."

"If there is, cover this one from Cairo."

"Right. Those safe-conduct passes to the front don't work that well." He smiled, then said, "I hear you're working for *L'Osservatore Romano*."

"Yes. I'm doing some English-language stuff for them on the coming Holy Year. Mostly press releases."

"Bored?"

"I like Rome."

"Cairo sucks." He asked, "Are you working on anything else?"

"You mean like our Ethiopian adventure?"

"That's what I mean."

"No, I'm not. But I expected to see something from you about that."

"I'm holding off," Purcell replied. "I wanted to speak to you first."

"You don't need my permission or my collaboration."

"I thought we'd do something together."

"I'm not interested."

"Really?"

Mercado thought a moment, then said, "If you—we—wrote about this, then not only Getachu but a lot of other bastards and idiots would be smashing through the jungle looking for the black monastery."

Purcell nodded. He'd certainly thought about that. He said to Mercado, "Getachu may have already found it."

"Perhaps. But if he did, I think we'd have heard that an important religious object was for sale."

"A lot of that stuff is sold privately," Purcell reminded him.

"True. And this one goes to the Vatican." He added, "Or perhaps the monks have spirited it away."

"Well, we could go check."

"Not interested."

"All right." He asked Mercado, "Did you report Father Armano's death to the Vatican?"

"No."

"Why not?"

"I . . . there doesn't seem to be any urgency. I'll get around to it."

"Your offices are in Vatican City, Henry."

"I'll get around to it."

"Good. Maybe we should go to Berini and look up his family."

"Why?"

"He asked us to do that. He also asked us to tell his story to someone in the Vatican. Or you can tell your people at *L'Osservatore Romano*."

"All right. I'll do that."

"I'm not quite understanding, Henry, why you're sitting on this."

"Why have *you* sat on it?"

"I told you. I wanted to speak to you first." He reminded Mercado, "We made sort of a pact."

Mercado asked, "What does Vivian think?"

"She wants to go back and find the Holy Grail. That's what she thinks."

"Insane."

"I'm sorry you've lost your enthusiasm for this, Henry."

"I'm sorry you've found it."

"I've been thinking."

"Try not to do that."

"It's a great story, Henry."

"It seemed so at the time."

Purcell looked at him and asked, "Have you been snooping around the Vatican archives? Like, on your lunch hour?"

"Yes . . . to satisfy my curiosity about a few things."

"Find anything?"

"I'll get you a pass and you can do your own research."

"May be a language problem."

"You can hire translators there."

"I need to get back to Cairo in a few days."

"Forgive my curiosity, Frank, but I don't understand why you're not going to Geneva."

Purcell ordered another round, and Mercado did not object.

Neither man spoke for a while, then Purcell said, "I received one letter from Geneva telling me . . . well, telling me that she felt awful about leaving you in Addis, and that she was feeling guilty because of what happened and how it happened."

"And well she should."

"Right. Me too."

Mercado stared into his drink, then said, "I've gotten over this, Frank. Except for the anger. You both behaved badly."

"We know that."

"And I did too...that moment in Getachu's tent... when he asked me—"

"You are forgiven."

Mercado looked at him. "Thank you for that."

"Vivian never once mentioned it."

"I'm sure she thought about it."

"We all need to move on." He smiled and said, "Avanti."

"I need to go."

"Some news, too, about Prince Joshua. They executed him in Addis."

"That was a mercy."

"It was." He asked Mercado, "Did you read about the mass executions at the end of November?"

"I'm not really following Ethiopia."

"You should."

Mercado asked, "What happened?"

"Well, they shot another bunch of guys from the old regime. The former premier, Makonnen, a general named Aman who was former chief of staff or something, another former premier named Wolde, and Rear Admiral Alexander Desta, a grandson of the emperor."

Mercado nodded and observed, "The revolution lives on blood."

"Right. And they shot fifty-six other guys, including Prince Joshua."

"Let me know when they shoot Getachu and Andom."

"I'll keep an eye on the wire."

Mercado stood and walked unsteadily to the *bagno*.

Purcell lit another cigarette and watched the Romans. It was almost dark now, and the cafés along the Via Veneto would be getting full.

Inside Harry's, the bar and the tables were filling up with what looked like mostly American tourists who needed to have a drink with the ghost of Ernest Hemingway, or to experience a little of *la dolce vita*.

Purcell had not expected to find Henry Mercado in a place like Harry's, but the bartender at the Excelsior said he might be here, and here he was, drinking with the tourists. But, Purcell thought, Henry was a pre-war character and he'd probably started coming here when it was the thing to do, and when it was a hangout for journalists and expat writers. Henry didn't seem to notice that the world was changing, and Purcell pictured himself at Henry's age—if he lived that long—staying at the wrong hotels, eating in the wrong restaurants, and getting drunk in the wrong bars with the wrong people.

He half understood Vivian's attraction to Henry Mercado in Ethiopia, but he didn't understand why she remained emotionally attached to him in absentia. Or why she hadn't tried to find him. It occurred to him, though, that she wanted Frank Purcell to find Henry Mercado. In fact, her letter hinted at that. She wanted the three of them to go back to Ethiopia to find the black monastery and the Holy Grail. Well, that sounded like a trip to hell on several levels. And yet...it made him think about it. And maybe that's why he had asked around about Henry Mercado.

Mercado returned but did not sit, and said, "I have to go. Let's split the bill."

Purcell stood. "You buy tomorrow night."

"I think we've said what we had to say."

"I'm staying at the Forum. Rooftop bar. Six P.M." He put out his hand, and Mercado hesitated, then took it. Purcell said, "I'm sorry about what happened."

"If you're looking for forgiveness, there are nine hundred churches in Rome."

"Let's be happy we're alive. We survived the camps and we survived Ethiopia. We'll survive cocktails. See you tomorrow night."

Mercado turned and walked out into the cold night.

Purcell watched him disappear into the crowd, then sat and finished his drink. He understood, as did Vivian, that they were not all through with each other yet. And Henry understood that, too.

Chapter 15

Frank Purcell sat at the bar of the glass-enclosed Hotel Forum restaurant. The real Forum lay five stories below, its marble ruins bathed in floodlights. A crescent moon hung above the Colosseum, and three thousand years of history hung over the city.

He'd spent the morning writing in his room—a piece about Egyptian president Anwar Sadat, whom he'd characterized as a Jew-hater with a pro-Nazi past, and not the moderate peacemaker and reformer that the rest of the news media were making him out to be.

His editors in the States would cut that, of course, or kill the whole story, and the Cairo bureau chief would remind him that he wasn't hired to write an opinion column. But he'd written it because he—and thus his writing—had been transformed.

In the afternoon, he'd taken a long walk, first to the Piazza Venezia where Mussolini used to stand on the balcony of the Palazzo, making a fool of himself *Urbi et Orbi*—to the city and the world. But the city and the world should have taken him more seriously, as Father Armano had at the blessing of the guns.

Next, he walked through the baths of Caracalla, the mother of all Roman spas, then over to the Fascist-built Foreign Ministry where the looted stone steles from Axum sat out front, a monument to European imperialism and good taste in stolen art. Rome, in fact, was filled with looted treasures going back over two thousand years, and, he admitted, they all looked good in their extrinsic settings. And in return for what they'd taken, the Romans had built roads and bridges all over their empire, amphitheaters and baths, temples and forums. So what Mussolini had done in Ethiopia was just a continuation of a long and venerable tradition of imperial stealing and giving. The Vatican, however, had planned a snatch of the Holy Grail without so much as an IOU.

The point of his walk, aside from physical exercise, was to get his head into the right mindset regarding the story—which was turning into a book—that he was writing about Father Armano, the black monastery, and the Holy Grail.

That story, however, would never see the light of day unless or until he went back to Ethiopia to discover the ending. Or, he supposed, it could be published posthumously, with an editor's epilogue regarding the fate of the author.

Now, Jean, the attractive lady next to him at the bar, was looking through her guidebook and said, "It says here that the Piazza Navona is all decorated for Christmas."

"I actually walked through there last night. Worth seeing."

"All right. Campo de' Fiori?"

"Produce market by day, meat market by night."

"All right…" She went back to her Roman guidebook, and Purcell went back to his Ethiopian book. The questions raised in his story, and in his mind, were: Who owns a two-thousand-year-old relic? Obviously, whoever has it owns it. But how did the present owner get the object? And does the object, if it is priceless, actually belong to the world?

The other question, of course, had to do with the authenticity of the object. Purcell had no doubt that whatever it was that now sat in the black monastery had no mystical powers, despite Father Armano's claim that it healed his wound and his soul, whatever that was. But the cup could be authentic in the sense that it was the actual chalice used by Christ at the Last Supper. Or it could be an object of faith, like most religious relics he'd seen in Rome and elsewhere.

He recalled what he'd once seen in the small chapel of Quo Vadis on the Appian Way, outside the gate of the city wall: a piece of black basalt paving stone, in which was a footprint. Specifically, the footprint of Jesus Christ, who had appeared to Peter on the Appian road as the saint was fleeing for his life from Rome. Peter, stunned at seeing his risen Lord, blurted, "*Domine, quo vadis?*" Where are you going, Lord? And Christ had replied, "To Rome, Peter, to be crucified for a second time." And Peter, feeling guilt at fleeing, and understanding what Christ was saying to him, returned to Rome to meet his fate and was crucified.

The story, Purcell understood, was apocryphal, and the outline of a foot in the paving stone was not actually made by Jesus's size nine sandal. But an Italian friend once said to him about the stone of Quo Vadis, "What is real? What is true? What do you believe?" *Quo Vadis?*

Well, he thought, maybe he was going back to Ethiopia to be crucified a second time. And that depended on Henry Mercado, who was half an hour late for his date with destiny. Purcell knew he was coming; Mercado had no choice, just as Peter had no choice.

Purcell ordered another Jack Daniel's and another red wine for the lady. The bar was full—best view in Rome—but the dining tables were almost empty—not the best food in Rome.

Jean, aged about forty, was a blonde Brit, and looked nothing like Vivian, but she made him think of Vivian because she was a woman. She was interesting and interested, and they were both staying at the Forum, alone, and what the hell, it was Christmas in Rome. Coffee and *cornetti* in bed. A wonderful memory.

She observed, "Your friend is late."

"He's always late."

"He must be Italian."

"No. But when in Rome."

She laughed, then informed him, "Did you know that this hotel was once a convent?"

"I'm checking out tomorrow."

She laughed again and returned to her guidebook.

His mind went back to Addis Ababa. The week at the Hilton after their release from prison had been intense and tense as they waited for news of Henry and Gann, and also waited for a midnight knock on their door, or a call or visit from their respective embassies telling them they were free to leave Ethiopia. That was the tense part. The intense part was their lovemaking, knowing or believing that this was all coming to an end, one way or the other.

He thought that if they'd left it there—if they'd separated at the airport in Cairo, as they said they would—then that would have been the end of it. She'd be with

Mercado now, and they'd all be going to London to see Gann. But they had decided to spend a last night together in Cairo at the Grand Nile. Then they found a furnished sublet together.

Cairo, as he knew from previous experience, was not Paris, or London, or Rome; Cairo was a challenge, and whatever romance it had in its streets and its stones was overshadowed by its repressive atmosphere.

Despite that, and despite the rumors of war, and the unpleasant memories of Ethiopia, he and Vivian had had a very good month in Cairo before she announced her departure for Geneva, where she had, she said, business and family.

In retrospect, he should have asked her to be more specific about her plans to return to Cairo, but it never occurred to him that she wasn't coming back. He had no phone number for her, and the return address on her single letter was a post office box. His reply letter, as he recalled, had been short and not filled with love or longing, or understanding. In fact, he was angry, though that didn't come through either. This was not the kind of writing he was good at, and his note may have sounded terse and distant. And that was the end of the letters, and presumably the end of the affair. And that was what he'd implied to Mercado, and that was the truth—or the truth as it stood at this time.

Also, in retrospect, he realized that the good news they'd gotten from the British embassy in Cairo—that Henry Mercado was about to be released—had something to do with her departure. He'd had a brief thought that she had left to find Henry, but if that were the case, she'd have told him to his face in Cairo. Vivian was forthright and honest, and brave enough to say, "It's over. I'm going back to Henry."

But Vivian knew that despite Henry's forgiving her for her one-night indiscretion when they thought they were about to be shot, he would not forgive her for her week with Frank Purcell in Addis or for their month together in Cairo. Yet for some reason, she couldn't stay in Cairo with him after Henry was free. He sort of understood that, but he also understood that she wanted the three of them to be together again, in some fashion or another, and to go back to Ethiopia together.

Jean asked, "Is that your dinner date?"

He looked at the entrance, where Mercado was standing, scanning the bar. Purcell caught his attention, and Mercado headed toward him. Henry still didn't have a topcoat, and he was wearing what he'd worn last evening, except he'd added a scarf.

They didn't shake, and Purcell introduced him to Jean, whose last name Purcell didn't know, along with not knowing her room number. They made small talk for a minute, and Purcell noted that Henry seemed to be in a better mood, and also that Henry could be charming to an attractive lady. He pictured him in the Addis Hilton bar, chatting up Vivian for the first time.

Under normal circumstances Purcell might have asked Jean to join them for dinner, but tonight he needed Henry to himself, without Jean, and without the absent presence of Vivian. He said to Jean, "Try the Piazza Navona tonight."

Henry suggested, "Trastevere would be better." He gave her the name of a restaurant.

Jean thanked them and went back to her guidebook.

Purcell led Mercado to a reserved table near the window and they sat.

Mercado said, "I'm not actually staying for dinner. But let's have a bottle of good wine."

"Whatever is your pleasure."

Mercado scanned the wine list, summoned a waiter, and they discussed vino in Italian.

Purcell lit a cigarette and looked out at the city. He never quite understood why Peter, and then Paul, had traveled all the way from their world to Rome, the belly of the beast. Surely they knew that was suicidal.

Mercado said, "You got off easy with a 150,000-lire bottle of amarone."

"I thought you were buying tonight."

"Let's first see what you're selling."

"Right." Purcell pointed to the Forum. "What's that building?"

"That's where the Roman senate sat and debated the affairs of the empire."

"Amazing."

"Truly the Eternal City. I think this is where I will end my days."

"Could do worse. Which is what I want to talk to you about."

"I am not going to Ethiopia."

"Okay. But hypothetically...if we could get back in, legally, as accredited reporters, would you consider it?"

"No."

"Let's say you said yes. Would you feel comfortable with the three of us going?"

"I do not want to see her—or you—again."

"We're making progress."

"Frank, none of us will ever be allowed back. So even if I said yes, it's moot."

"Right. But if we could swing it—"

"I'm facing a five-year prison sentence the moment I set foot on Ethiopian soil."

"Okay. Maybe we should sneak in."

"Maybe you should just step out into Roman traffic and save yourself some time and effort."

The waiter brought the wine, Mercado tasted it and pronounced it *meraviglioso*, and the waiter poured.

Purcell held up his glass and said, "To Father Armano, and to God's plan, whatever it is."

"I'm sure you're going to tell me what it is."

"It's coming to me." Purcell informed him, "I actually have a private pilot's license. Single-engine. Did I ever mention that?"

Mercado swirled his wine.

"If we could rent a bush plane in Sudan—"

"You're not making God's plan sound attractive." He asked, "What do you think of the wine?"

"Great. So let's think about false IDs. I have several sources in Cairo."

Mercado pointed out, "You don't actually need me along. It would be easier for you to just apply for a visa and see what happens. The new regime may let you in."

"I want you with us."

"By *us*, I assume you mean Vivian as well."

"Right."

"But she's left you, old boy. Or at least that's what you seemed to have told me last night."

"Right. But I also told you she wants us to go back to look for the black monastery."

Mercado mulled that over, then said, with good insight, "There are easier ways for you to regain her affection."

Purcell did not reply.

"If you, Mr. Purcell, want to go back, you need to go for the right reason. Your reason is not the right reason."

Purcell thought a moment, then replied, "I'm not going to tell you that I believe in the Holy Grail. But I do believe there is a hell of a story there."

"But Vivian, dear boy, believes in the Grail. You need to believe in it as well if you're going to drag her back there—or if she's dragging you back."

Purcell asked, "What do you believe?"

"I believe what Father Armano told us."

"All of it?"

"All of it."

"Then how can you *not* go back?"

He reminded Purcell, "Father Armano seemed to think that the Grail should be left where it was in a Coptic monastery—and he's a Catholic priest who was under papal orders to find it and take it for the Vatican."

"I'm not suggesting we should steal it. Just...look at it. Touch it."

"That would probably end in life imprisonment. Or death."

"But if you really believe, Henry, that we're going back to find the actual Holy Grail, what difference does death make?"

Mercado looked closely at Purcell.

"Father Armano risked death by going on that patrol to find the black monastery. Because he believed in the Grail, and he believed in eternal life."

"I understand that. But..."

"The Knights of the Round Table risked their lives to look for the Grail—"

"Myth and legend."

"Right. But there's a moral to that myth."

"Which is that the Grail will never be found."

"Which is that we should never stop looking for what we believe in. Death is not the issue."

Mercado did not reply.

"Why did Peter come to Rome?"

Mercado smiled. "To annoy the Romans with his arguments, as you are annoying me with yours."

"And to bring them the word of God. And why did Peter return to Rome?"

"To die."

"I rest my case."

Mercado seemed lost in thought, then said, "Look, old man, get a good night's sleep"—he nodded toward Jean, who was still at the bar but settling her bill—"and if you're still suicidal in the morning, give me a call." He put his business card on the table and stood.

Purcell stood and said, "Henry, this is what we have to do. We think we have a choice, but we don't."

"I understand that. And I also understand that you're not as cynical as you think you are or pretend to be. You are not going to risk your life for a good story—or for a woman. You're not *that* much of a reporter or that romantic. But if you believe in love, then you believe in God. There may or may not be a Holy Grail at the end of your journey, but the journey and the quest is itself an act of faith and belief. And as we Romans say, 'Credo quia impossibile.' I believe it because it is impossible."

Purcell did not reply.

They shook hands and Mercado went to the bar, spoke to Jean, then left.

Jean walked toward his table, smiling tentatively. Purcell stood, and thought: Good old Henry, up to his old tricks again, sticking me with the bill, the lady, and the next move.

Chapter 16

Rome was always crowded at Christmas with visiting clergy, pilgrims, and tourists, and even more so this year in anticipation of the pope's Christmas Eve announcement of the coming Holy Year. The taxi driver was swearing at the holiday traffic and at the foreign *idioti* who didn't know how to cross a street.

Purcell had decided to stay in Rome for Christmas and he'd sent a short telex to Charlie Gibson in Cairo telling him that. The return telex, even shorter, had said, YOU'RE FIRED. HAVE A GOOD CHRISTMAS.

He'd hoped that would be Charlie's response, and he dreaded a second telex rescinding the first. But if war broke out, as it might after all the Christian tourists left Jerusalem, Bethlehem, and Nazareth, then the Cairo office would want him back. In the meantime, he was free to pursue other matters. Also, as it turned out, Jean needed to get back to England for Christmas, which further freed him to write, and to think about what he wanted to do about the rest of his life.

He hadn't called Henry the morning after as Henry had suggested, and Henry hadn't called him, nor would he ever. So now, three days later, Purcell had made the call to *L'Osservatore Romano* that morning and he had a 4 P.M. meeting with Signore Mercado. It was 3:45 and the traffic was slower than the pedestrians, so Purcell asked

the driver to drop him off at the foot of the Ponte Vittorio Emanuele, and he walked across the Tiber bridge.

It was windy, and the sky was dark and threatening
with black clouds scudding across the gray sky, and the
Tiber, too, looked black and angry.

Saint Peter's Square was packed with tourists and with
the faithful who were praying in large and small groups.
In the center of the square stood the three-thousand-
year-old Egyptian obelisk, and at the end of the square
rose the marble mountain of Saint Peter's Basilica,
beneath which, according to belief, lay the bones of the
martyred saint, and Purcell wondered if Peter, dying on
the cross, had regretted his decision on the Via Appia.

Purcell did not enter the square, but walked along
the Vatican City wall to the Porta Santa Rosa where
two Swiss Guards with halberds stood guarding the
gates of the sovereign city-state. He showed his passport and press credentials to a papal gendarme who was
better armed than the Swiss Guards, and said, "Buona
sera. *L'Osservatore Romano*, Signore Mercado."

The man scanned a sheet of paper on his clipboard,
said something in Italian, and waved him through.

He'd been there once before and easily found the
press office on a narrow street lined with bare trees.
The windows of the buildings cast squares of yellow
light on the cold ground.

He was fifteen minutes late, which in Italy meant he
was a bit early, but maybe not in Vatican City. The male
receptionist asked him to be seated.

The offices of *L'Osservatore Romano* were housed in
a building that may have preceded the printing press,
but the interior was modern, or had been when the

paper was founded a hundred years before. Electricity and telephones had been added, and the result was a modern newspaper that published in six languages and was a mixture of real news and propaganda. And not surprisingly, the pope made every issue.

A lot of articles focused on the persecution of Catholics in various countries, especially Communist Poland. Occasionally the paper covered the plight of non-Catholic Christians, and Purcell recalled that Henry Mercado had been in Ethiopia to write about the state of the Coptic Church in the newly Marxist country, as well as Ethiopia's small Catholic population. Now Henry was writing press releases about the Holy Year. Purcell was sure that Mercado would like to return to Ethiopia to continue his important coverage. And hadn't Henry promised General Getachu a few puff pieces about the general's military prowess?

Mercado came into the waiting room wearing a cardigan over his shirt and tie. They shook hands and Mercado showed Purcell into his windowless office, a small room piled high with books and papers, giving it the look of a storage closet. He could see why Henry was in Harry's Bar at 4 P.M.

Mercado shut off his IBM electric typewriter and said, "Throw your coat anywhere." He spun his desk chair around and faced his guest who sat in the only other chair. Purcell asked, "Mind if I smoke?"

Mercado waved his arm around the paper-strewn room and replied, "You'll set the whole Vatican on fire."

But he did have a bottle of Boodles in his desk drawer and he poured into two water glasses.

Mercado held up his glass and said, "Benvenuto."

"Cheers."

They drank and Mercado asked, "Are you here to tell me you've come to your senses?"

"No."

"All right." He informed Purcell, "Then I've decided to go to Ethiopia."

Purcell was not completely surprised that Mercado had changed his mind. In fact, he hadn't. Whatever it was that had taken hold of him that night at the mineral spa still had him, and Henry, like Vivian, had been transformed by Father Armano and by that admittedly strange experience that Henry and Vivian took as a sign.

Mercado continued, "But I can't promise you that I will go any farther than Addis. I am not keen on going back into Getachu territory."

"I thought you wanted to write a nice piece about him."

"I do. His obituary." He tapped a stack of papers on his desk and said, "I am calling in favors and pulling some strings to get you and Vivian accredited with *L'Osservatore Romano*."

"Good. I just lost my AP job."

"How did you do that?"

"Easy."

"All right, we will be covering the religious beat, of course, and your starting salary is zero, but all expenses are paid to and in Ethiopia."

"And back."

"Your optimism amazes me." He asked, "Should I finalize this?"

"Where do I sign?"

Mercado finished his gin and contemplated another,

then reminded Purcell, "This will all be moot if we can't get visas."

"It's a good first step."

"And *L'Osservatore Romano* will look good on our visa applications."

"Si."

Mercado smiled, then asked, "Are you sure Vivian wants to go?"

"She said so in her letter."

"Have you heard from her?"

"I have not."

"Can you contact her?"

"I'll try her last known address. A P.O. box in Geneva."

Mercado nodded and said, "Tell her to come to Rome."

Purcell replied, "Tutte le strade conducono a Roma."

"Did you practice that?"

"I did." Purcell asked, "Are you all right with this?"

"I told you, old man, I'm over it."

Purcell didn't think so, and he had issues of his own with Vivian.

Mercado, in fact, asked, "Are *you* all right with Vivian coming along?"

"No problem."

"I'm not sure I'm understanding your relationship."

"That makes two of us. Probably three."

"All right . . . By the way, how did you make out with that lady? Jean?"

"She had to go back to England." Purcell added, "She did nothing but talk about you."

Mercado smiled.

Purcell asked, "What do you think our chances are of actually getting a visa?"

"I think you were right about the regime change. They seem to want to smooth things over with the West."

"They're just playing the third world game—flirting with the West while they're in bed with the Russians."

"Of course. But that could work for us."

Purcell asked, "Would you be suspicious if those visas were granted?"

"'Will you walk into my parlor? said the spider to the fly.'"

"Precisely."

"Well, if you want my opinion, old man, this whole idea is insane. But I think we've decided, so save your paranoia for Ethiopia."

"Right."

"And have you thought about *why* you are going back into the jaws of death?"

"I already told you."

"Again, please."

"To find the Holy Grail, Henry, to heal my troubled soul. Same as you."

"Well, we should save this discussion for when Vivian joins us."

Purcell did not reply.

Mercado poured two more gins and said, "I'm going to ask Colonel Gann to join us in Rome."

"Why?"

"I think he'd be a good resource before we set out. Also, I'd like to see him and thank him."

"Me too."

"I want you to buy him a spectacular dinner at the Hassler."

"Don't you have an expense account, Henry?"

"Yes, a rather good one, which is why they're putting me up at the Excelsior until I find an appartamento."

It seemed to Purcell that Henry Mercado had more influence at *L'Osservatore Romano* than his office or his job would indicate. The thought occurred to him that Henry had spoken to someone here about their Ethiopian adventure, including—contrary to what Mercado had told him—the appearance and death of Father Giuseppe Armano. If that were true, then someone here had probably gotten excited about pursuing this story. And maybe Henry had been stringing his bosses along, like the old trickster he was, sucking silver out of the Vatican treasury. And he'd been at it for a few months, and the time had come to put up or get out.

Purcell asked, "Will you do a piece on Father Armano for your paper?"

"Of course. But not until we get back, obviously. And you?"

"I work here, Henry. Remember?"

"That's right." He drained his glass. "We'll do a series of stunning articles together—yours in English and mine in Italian—and they will be translated into every world language, and you will achieve the fame and respect that has always eluded you, and I will add to my global reputation."

Purcell smiled.

"We'll do the talk show circuit. Who carries the Grail?"

"Vivian."

"Yes, the pretty girl. And we'll do a slideshow with her photography."

Neither man spoke, and Purcell thought about what would actually happen if they *did* find the black monastery and somehow got possession of the Coptic monks' Holy Grail. He said to Mercado, "Be careful what you wish for."

Mercado changed the subject. "It would be very good if Colonel Gann could come along."

"The Ethiopian government would love to see him."

"I mean, if he could be pardoned or cleared of all charges."

"That's not going to happen."

"Perhaps he could offer his services as a military advisor."

"That's a long shot, Henry. And I'm sure he's not interested."

"We'll find out at our reunion. I'll get Gann's contact information in the UK, and call or write him. I'll suggest early January for our reunion."

"I'll be here."

"And Vivian, too, I hope."

"I'll let you know."

"And we'll go to Sicily where it's warmer, and visit Father Armano's village and find his people."

"That would be a good first step on our journey."

"It is the right thing to do," Mercado agreed. "Meanwhile, if you are not too busy, I will meet you day after tomorrow at eight A.M., at the Vatican archives, and show you what I've found."

"It doesn't really matter, Henry. We are going forward on faith."

"Indeed, we are. But you might find this interesting, and even informative and useful. Good background for your story."

"Our story."

"Our story." He asked Purcell, "Have you written anything not for immediate publication?"

"I have."

"Good. Saves us some work. Leave out the illicit sex for *L'Osservatore Romano*."

Purcell did not smile.

Mercado asked, "Will you be in Rome for Christmas?"

"I'm undecided."

"Where is home?"

"A little town in upstate New York."

"Friends? Family? Old girlfriends?"

"All of the above."

"Then go home."

"How about you?"

"Christmas in Rome."

"Could do worse."

"If you're around, I'll get us in the back door for Christmas Eve Mass at Saint Peter's. You need a papal blessing."

"I'll let you know."

Mercado stood. "I'll see you day after tomorrow. Your name will be at the library door."

Purcell stood and put on his trench coat. On their way out, he said, "It doesn't matter if we never even get into Ethiopia, or if we do, it doesn't matter what happens there. It matters that we try."

"I've lived my life that way, Frank." He reminded Purcell, "This will be my third trip to Ethiopia, and

I nearly got killed the first two times." He added, "As they say, boats are safe in the harbor, but that's not what boats are made for."

Purcell left the offices of *L'Osservatore Romano* and walked along the lane lined with bare trees. It was dark now, but the narrow streets were lit, and with no place to go, he walked farther into the papal enclave until he reached the open spaces of fields and gardens behind the basilica.

He found a bench by a fountain—the Fountain of the Eagle—and sat. He lit a cigarette and watched the tumbling water.

The troubling thought came to him that Henry Mercado might be right about Frank Purcell's motives. That somewhere, deep in his mind or his soul, he believed what Henry and Vivian believed. And what Father Armano believed. And he believed it because it was impossible.

Chapter 17

Frank Purcell and Henry Mercado sat at a long table in a private reading room within the large Vatican Library. The windowless room was nondescript except for a few obligatory religious portraits hanging on the yellowed plaster walls. Three ornate lamps hung from the high ceiling, and Jesus Christ hung from a wooden cross at the end of the room.

On the long mahogany table, neatly arranged documents were enfolded in green felt, and Mercado informed Purcell, "I assembled all of this over the last month or so. Some of these parchments and papyri are almost two thousand years old."

"Can I smoke?"

"The library monks will execute you."

Purcell took that as a no. Also, it was interesting that Henry had spent so much time here.

Mercado had a briefcase with him that he emptied onto the table, and Purcell could see pages of handwritten notes.

Mercado gave him a notebook to use, then motioned toward the documents and said, "I employed the services of the library translators—classical Greek and Latin, Church Latin, Hebrew—"

"I get it."

"We will begin at the Last Supper."

"Coffee?"

"After the Last Supper." He explained to Purcell, "I'm not only trying to prove the existence of the Grail, but also to plot its long journey from Jerusalem to Ethiopia."

"Why?"

"This will be useful information when we write our series of articles. And perhaps a book. Have you thought about a book?"

"I have."

He also informed Purcell, "When we're finished here, we will go to the Ethiopian College, which is here in Vatican City."

"Why is it here?"

"Good question. The answer is, the Italians and the Vatican have had a long interest in Ethiopia, going back to the arrival in Rome of Ethiopian pilgrims in the fifteenth century. Interest was renewed when the Italians colonized Eritrea in 1869, then tried to conquer neighboring Ethiopia in 1896, then invaded again in 1935."

"Did you also cover the 1896 war?"

Mercado ignored that and continued, "The Ethiopian College is also a seminary where the Vatican trains and ordains Catholic priests, and instructs lay people, mostly Ethiopian, to go to Ethiopia and spread the Catholic faith."

"And maybe to look for the Holy Grail."

Mercado did not respond to that but informed Purcell, "The Ethiopian College has a good library and a cartography room with some rare ancient maps of Ethiopia and some hard-to-find modern ones, made in the 1930s by the Italian Army. We can use those maps to narrow down the location of the black monastery, based on what we know from Father Armano."

"Good idea. Let's go."

"We need to start at the beginning." Mercado slid a large English-language Bible toward him and thumbed through the pages. "Here—Matthew, at the Last Supper." He read, "And he took the cup, and gave thanks, and gave it to them, saying, 'Drink ye all of it; For this is my blood of the new testament for the remission of sins.'"

Mercado looked at Purcell and said, "Mark and Luke make similar brief references to what has become the central sacrament of Christianity—the Holy Communion, the transubstantiation of the bread into the body of Christ, and the wine into his blood." He added, "But John does not mention this at all."

Purcell had had similar reporting lapses—missing or downplaying something that later turned out to be very important. "John may have been out of the room."

Mercado responded, "The fact that the gospels differ actually give them credibility. These are men recording from memory what they saw and experienced, and the differences show they were not colluding to make up a story."

"That's what I tell my editors."

Mercado continued, "Notice that the cup—the Grail—has no special significance in the telling of this story of the Last Supper. But later, in myth and legend, the cup grows large."

"It gets magical."

"Indeed it does. As does the lance of the Roman soldier Longinus, and the robe of Christ, and the thirty pieces of silver that Judas took to betray Christ, and everything else that has to do with the death of Jesus Christ."

Purcell observed, "You're making a good case for why Christ's cup at the Last Supper is just a cup."

"Perhaps ... but of all the artifacts associated with the New Testament, the cup—the Grail—has persisted for two thousand years as a thing of special significance." He continued, "And I think one of the reasons is that the chalice is used in the sacrament of Holy Communion. The priest literally—or figuratively—turns the wine into the blood of Christ, and that miracle—or mystery—has taken hold in every Christian who ever went to church on Sunday."

"I guess ... I never thought much about it."

"Then you should be taking notes, Mr. Purcell. You have a story to write."

"More importantly, we have a Grail that needs to be found."

"We are finding it—first in our heads, then in our hearts." He reminded Purcell, "This is a spiritual journey before it becomes a physical journey."

Purcell picked up his pen and said, "I will make a note of that."

Mercado continued, "The chalices used by priests and ministers are often very elaborate. Gold and precious stones. But the cup used by Christ was a simple kiddush cup—probably a bronze goblet used at the Passover. So the kiddush cup, like the story itself, has been embellished over the years, and now looks very different at the altar. It gleams. But that is not what we are looking for. We are looking for a two-thousand-year-old bronze cup—something that would have disappointed many of those who have searched for it, if they'd found it."

Purcell nodded, trying to recall what, if anything, Father Armano had said about the cup that he claimed he saw.

Mercado went on, "But there is an essential truth to this story—Jesus saying, in effect, 'I have turned this wine into my blood for the remission of your sins.'"

"But that has more to do with Jesus than it has to do with the wine or the cup."

"You make a good point."

"Also," Purcell pointed out, "there is a lot of allegory and symbolism in the Old and New Testaments."

"That is where some Christians, Jews, atheists, and agnostics disagree."

"Right."

"You either believe or you don't believe. Evidence is in short supply. Miracles happen, but not often, and not without other explanations."

"We should have mentioned that to Father Armano."

"I completely understand your skepticism, Frank. I have some of my own."

That wasn't what he'd said on previous occasions, but Purcell left it alone.

Mercado had his Bible open again, and he said, "We move on from the Last Supper, and through the crucifixion, and we come to Joseph of Arimathea, who plays a central role in subsequent Grail legends." He looked at the open Bible. "From Mark 15:42–47." Mercado read, "And now when the even was come, because it was the preparation, that is, the day before the Sabbath, Joseph of Arimathea, an honorable counselor, who also waited for the kingdom of God, came, and went in boldly unto Pilate, and craved the body of Jesus. And Pilate marveled if he were already dead: and calling unto him the centurion, he asked him whether he had been any while dead. And when he knew it of the centurion, he gave the body to Joseph. And he bought fine linen, and took him down, and wrapped him in the linen, and laid him in a sepulcher which was hewn out of a rock, and rolled a stone unto the door of the sepulcher."

Mercado looked up from the Bible and said, "This is the last we hear of Joseph of Arimathea in the New Testament, but not the last we hear of him from other sources."

"Are these sources credible, Henry?"

Mercado pulled a notebook toward him and said, "I've read several accounts of the journey of the Holy Grail. You can call them legends or myths, or quasi-historical accounts. I've had access here to some primary source material, written on parchment and papyrus"— he motioned toward the green felt folders—"and the earliest date I was able to determine is from a papyrus, written in classical Greek, about forty or fifty years after the death of Christ." He informed Purcell, "I've written a summation of all these stories, based on the parts that seem to agree."

Purcell agreed with Mercado that it would be useful to get some backstory, but he was here mostly to . . . well, to humor Henry. To bond with him. Or maybe he was here in the musty Vatican Library, on what turned out to be a gloriously sunny morning, because he felt guilty that he'd taken Vivian from Henry. That was it. This was atonement. Punishment, actually. And he deserved it.

Henry was looking at his notebook and said, "Here's what I've written, combining most of what I've read. It begins as a continuation of the New Testament account of the crucifixion." He began, "And Joseph of Arimathea, believing in Christ, wished to possess something belonging to him. He therefore carried off the chalice of the Last Supper—"

"Was he there to clean up?"

Mercado ignored the interruption and continued, "And having begged Pilate for the Lord's body, Joseph used the chalice to collect the blood flowing from Jesus's wounds. And it came to pass that Joseph of Arimathea was imprisoned for his good deed by Pilate, at the urging of the same angry crowd that had demanded Christ's death. And Joseph lay forty years in a hidden dungeon, but he was sustained by the Holy Grail, which was still in his possession."

Mercado stopped reading and looked at Purcell.

Purcell nodded. Indeed, this ancient tale had a little of Father Armano's story in it. And Father Armano probably knew the story.

Mercado continued, "And in the fortieth year of Joseph's imprisonment, the Roman emperor, Vespasian, was cured of his leprosy by the veil of Saint Veronica, and believing now in Christ, the emperor took himself to Jerusalem to avenge the death of Christ, but all who had been responsible for his death were now themselves dead. But through a vision, Vespasian learned that Joseph, who was believed dead, was still imprisoned in the hidden dungeon. Vespasian had himself lowered into the dungeon and freed Joseph. The emperor Vespasian and Joseph of Arimathea were then baptized together by Saint Clement."

Mercado put his notebook aside and said, "There are a number of historical inaccuracies—or stretches—in that story. But the story has persisted for two thousand years, and is believed by millions of Catholics and others."

"And what does the Church of Rome think?"

"The Church of Rome neither confirms nor denies. The Church of Rome likes these stories, but understands, intellectually, that they are a stretch. But stories like this are good press, and they circulate among the faithful and reinforce their beliefs."

"That's what good propaganda does."

"So we've heard that Joseph took Christ's cup after the Passover meal, and we've heard that Joseph had it with him in the dungeon, and that the Grail sustained him for forty years."

Purcell made a note to show he was listening.

Mercado flipped a page in his notebook and read, "Joseph journeyed with a flock of new Christians through the Holy Land and in time came into Sarras in Egypt. In Sarras, Joseph was instructed by the Lord to set out a table in memory of Christ's Last Supper, and the sacrament of Communion was performed with the Grail for the new converts. After a time, Joseph was instructed by the Lord to journey to Britain, and there the Grail was kept in the Grail Castle, which was located, some say, near Glastonbury. The Grail was kept there by a succession of Grail Keepers, who were all descendants of Joseph of Arimathea, and after four hundred years, the last in the line of the Grail Keepers of the castle lay sick and dying."

Mercado stopped reading and said, "So now we have the Grail in Britain, which also seems a stretch, but Britain was a Roman province, part of Joseph's Roman world, so this is possible."

"Henry, I don't mean to be cynical, but this whole thing is a stretch."

"If you had read all that I have read here—"

"You started with a belief, and you cherry-picked your facts and gave credence to unconfirmed sources. The worst kind of reporting." He added, "You know better than that." Or maybe, Purcell thought, Henry had been working at *L'Osservatore Romano* too long.

"I'm not the first one to do this scholarship and come up with the same conclusions."

"There's a guy now writing books based on his scholarship saying that extraterrestrials visited the earth and built the pyramids."

Mercado did not reply for a few seconds, then said, "We are all searching for answers to who we are, what our place is in this world and this universe. We hope there is more than we know and see. We hope there is a God."

"Me too, Henry, but... okay. The Holy Grail is in Glastonbury."

Mercado referred to his notes and continued, "This brings us to the time when the Roman legions withdrew from Britain. The Roman world is disintegrating and Britain has been invaded by various Germanic tribes. The legendary—or historical—Arthur is king of the Britons and we begin the well-known legend of Arthur and the Knights of the Round Table."

Purcell had seen the movie, but he let Henry continue.

Mercado read from his notebook, "The magician Merlin told King Arthur of the presence of the Holy Grail in Britain and bid him form the Round Table of virtuous knights to seek out the Holy Grail. The table was formed, with an empty place to represent Judas, in the tradition of the Last Supper and the table of Joseph of Arimathea. After many adventures and dangers during their quest for the Grail, one of Arthur's knights, Sir Perceval, who was unknowingly a descendant of Joseph of Arimathea, discovered the Grail Castle and there found the Holy Grail, and also the lance of the Roman soldier, Longinus, that had pierced the side of Christ on the Cross. The lance hung suspended in thin air and dripped blood into the Grail cup."

Purcell looked at Mercado, who had stopped reading. It must have occurred to Mercado that this was a story known by all, but believed by virtually no one in the modern world. Except maybe Henry Mercado, Father Armano, maybe Vivian, and a few select others. But Purcell understood that even if the legends were untrue, that didn't mean that the Grail did not exist. The paving stone with Christ's footprint existed in the physical world, as did the Shroud of Turin and a thousand other religious relics. The Grail, however, was always associated with the power to heal. So if they found the black monastery and the Grail, then they would know if it was real. Especially if there was a lance hanging above it in thin air, dripping blood. He'd believe *that* if he saw it.

Mercado continued, "Sir Perceval was told by the

old Grail Keeper of their kinship, and when the Grail Keeper died, Sir Perceval and Sir Gauvain, perceiving that the times had grown evil, knew that the Grail must again be hidden from sinful men. The Lord came to them and told them of a ship anchored nearby the castle, and bid them take the Grail and the Lance back to the Holy Land. The two knights set off in a fog and were never seen or heard from again."

Mercado closed his notebook.

After a few seconds, Purcell inquired, "Is that it?"

Mercado replied, "No. The Grail, and sometimes the Lance, appear again in other references throughout the Dark Ages, Middle Ages, and into modern times."

Right, Purcell thought. Like a few months ago.

Mercado asked, "Did you find any of that interesting or useful?"

"Interesting, but not useful."

"Do you believe any of it?"

"You lost me after Mark."

"Why even believe in the New Testament?"

"You're asking questions I can't answer, Henry."

"That's why we're here. To find answers."

"The answers are not here. Half of the archives in the great Vatican Library are myths and legends. The answer is in Ethiopia."

"The answer is in our hearts."

"Let's start with Ethiopia." Purcell reminded him, "And we have less than a fifty-fifty chance of being allowed back there."

"We are going to Ethiopia."

"You have our visas?"

"No. But I will." He looked at Purcell. "You don't

understand, Frank. We—you, me, Vivian, and also Colonel Gann—have been chosen to go back to Ethiopia to find the Holy Grail."

Purcell didn't bother to ask who had chosen them.

Mercado agreed it was time for a coffee break, and they walked out into the sunshine.

Purcell easily understood how early humans believed in the sun as God; it acted in mysterious ways, it rose and set in the heavens, and it gave life and light. The religion of the Jews, Christians, and Muslims, however, was more complex. They asked people to believe in things that could not be seen or felt like the sun on his face. They asked for faith. They asked that you believe it because it was impossible.

And on this basis, he was going back to Ethiopia.

Chapter 18

They walked the short distance to the commissary, where they got coffee and biscotti that they took outside to a bench. The barracks of the Swiss Guard was across the lane, and Purcell watched them forming up for some occasion. The Vatican post office, too, was run by the Swiss, and he said to Henry, "Swiss efficiency and Italian biscotti. Truly a blessed place."

Mercado responded, "The Italians are the only people on earth who have monumental egos *and* an inferiority complex." He added, "I find it charming."

"So you're staying here?"

"I will die here or in Ethiopia."

"Can I ask . . . do you have a lady here?"

He hesitated before replying, "I . . . have a lady of my own age whom I see whenever I'm in Rome."

Purcell didn't pursue that. He lit a cigarette and watched the people.

There were no tourists in this part of Vatican City, and everyone on the streets here was employed by the Vatican in one way or another or they were official visitors like himself. There were, he knew, about a thousand actual residents of this sovereign city-state, mostly clergy, including the pope's staff or retinue, or whatever they were called. The art and the architecture here were without parallel in the world, and he understood, sitting there, why the popes and the cardinals and the hierarchy believed that this was the one true church of Jesus Christ. This was where the bones of Peter, the first pope, were buried somewhere beneath the basilica that bore his name, and Peter had taken the cup from Jesus's hand and drunk his Lord's blood. And so, the argument would go, this was where that same Holy Grail, if it existed, belonged. Case closed.

But even Father Armano had second thoughts about that. And so did Frank Purcell.

Mercado asked, "Are you thinking about what you've just learned?"

"No. I'm thinking about Father Armano and the black monastery."

"We will get to the black monastery."

Purcell didn't know if Henry meant get to it in the next library seminar or get to it in Ethiopia. Hopefully the latter. He said, "Good coffee."

"Made from holy water."

Purcell smiled.

"And Ethiopian coffee beans."

"Really?"

"The Italians still own and run some coffee plantations in Ethiopia. Though they've probably been seized by the bloody stupid Marxists."

"Right."

"There's a chap lives in Addis. Signore Bocaccio. Owns coffee plantations around the country. Visits them with his airplane."

Purcell nodded.

"They may have kicked him out, of course, or put

him in jail, but if he's still in Addis, we may want to look him up when we get there."

"What's he fly?"

"I don't know. Never been up with him, but a few journalists have."

"Would he rent the plane without him in it?"

"Ask."

Purcell nodded. His piloting skills were not great, but he thought he could fly nearly any single-engine aircraft if someone gave him an hour or so of dual flying instructions.

Also, he realized that Henry had already thought some of this out. They couldn't just head off into the jungle and expect to run into the black monastery. Few people had been so lucky, and those who had, like Father Armano and his army patrol, had discovered that their luck had run out at the monastery—or before then, when they met the Gallas. And now General Getachu was also interested in the monastery.

So, yes, they should do aerial recon to see if they spotted anything that looked like a black monastery— or like something they didn't want to run into on the ground.

Mercado glanced at his watch and said, "We'll go back to the library, then over to the Ethiopian College."

"Are you taking the day off?"

"No. I'm working. And so are you."

"Right. I work here." Purcell asked, "When do I get my creds?"

"In a week or two. Or three." He smiled. "This is not Switzerland." He said, "After you left my office the other night, I sent a telex to the British Foreign Office, who have taken responsibility for the repatriation of Colonel Sir Edmund Gann. I asked them to have Gann call or telex me at my office."

"Good."

"Have you written to Vivian?"

In fact, he had after he'd left Mercado's office that night and returned to the Hotel Forum. The letter had said, simply, "I am in Rome, staying at the Forum. Henry is here, working for *L'Osservatore Romano*, and we have met and spoken. We would like you to join us in Rome, before Christmas if possible. We are discussing the possibility of returning to Ethiopia, and we would like to include you in those discussions if you are still interested. Please telex me at the Forum either way. Hope you are well. Frank."

He'd felt that the letter, like his last, was a bit distant, and he wanted her to respond, so he'd added a P.S.: "I have been very lonely without you."

"Frank?"

"Yes . . . I wrote to her. Posted it yesterday morning."

"Hopefully the Italian postal service is not on strike this week." He joked, "Half of Paul's letters to the Romans are still sitting in the Rome post office."

Purcell smiled. "I actually sent it from the Swiss post office here."

"Excellent thinking. It should be in Geneva today." He stood. "Ready?"

Purcell stood and they walked back to the library.

Mercado informed Purcell, "There are over half a million printed volumes in this library, and over fifty thousand rare manuscripts, including many in the hand of Cicero, Virgil, and Tacitus."

"So no coffee allowed."

Mercado continued, "It would take a lifetime to read just the handwritten manuscripts, let alone the printed volumes."

"At least."

"In any case, after a month of research, I have no documentary evidence of how the Grail, which was bound for the Holy Land, wound up in Ethiopia. But I have a theory." He said to Purcell, "If you know your history, you will know that the Council of Chalcedon was called in A.D. 451 to try to resolve some of the theological differences that existed in the early Christian Church."

"Right."

Mercado continued, "The pope, Leo I, and the Christian emperor of the Eastern Roman Empire, Marcian, had a disagreement with the Egyptian and Ethiopian emissaries to this meeting because these emissaries refused to accept the complex doctrine of the Trinity and insisted that Christ was one and that he was wholly divine. These emissaries were expelled, and the dissenting churches came to be called Egyptic, and later Coptic, and this was the beginning of Ethiopia's isolation from the larger Christian world, which persists to this day."

"I noticed."

"In any case, the missing piece of the journey of the Grail could be this—Perceval and Gauvain—"

"Who we last saw sailing off in a fog."

"Reached the Holy Land, which was part of the

Eastern Roman Empire, ruled by the emperor in Constantinople." He continued, "Perceval and Gauvain
would have given the Grail to the Christian bishop
in Jerusalem, who was at that time a powerful figure
in the church." He informed Purcell, "There is some
documentary evidence here in the archives that the
Grail was circulated among the important Christian
churches in Jerusalem over the next few centuries."

Mercado continued, "But in A.D. 636, Jerusalem
was conquered by the armies of Islam, and many important Christian religious objects were lost or were spirited
away to Rome, Constantinople, and Alexandria, Egypt,
which was still part of the Eastern Roman Empire."

"How'd it wind up in Ethiopia, Henry?"

"I'm speculating that the Grail wound up in Alexandria, or someplace else in Egypt, and six years later, in
642, Christian Egypt fell to Islam. I'm further speculating that the Grail, now in the possession of Coptic
priests or monks in Egypt, was taken by Nile riverboat to
Ethiopia for safekeeping in Axum." He explained, "That
would make sense, historically, geographically, and in
terms of theology—the Egyptians were Copts, and they
came into possession of the Grail from Christian refugees from Jerusalem who were fleeing Islam. Six years
later, they themselves were conquered by Islam, and they
needed to safeguard the Grail, so they took it by a safe
route on the Nile to their co-religionists in Ethiopia."

"That's an exciting story."

"And based on known historical events. Also, after
this time, there are historical references to the Holy
Grail in Ethiopia—and no references to it being anywhere else."

Purcell did not respond.

"I'm not asking you to suspend belief. I'm trying to fill in the blanks between when the Grail left Glastonbury and when it is mentioned in primary source documents as being in Ethiopia."

A far simpler explanation, Purcell thought, was that the cup used by Christ at the Last Supper had never left Jerusalem. But the Brits liked their story of King Arthur and the Knights of the Round Table and the Holy Grail, and people like Mercado worked it into the legend. In the end, it didn't matter how it got to Ethiopia, assuming it did, and assuming it existed.

Purcell said, "You understand, Henry, that we are not trying to locate the Holy Grail or even figure out how it got to Ethiopia. We have been told by a credible source—Father Armano—that it's sitting in the black monastery. Now all we have to do is go find this place."

"And I've explained to you that our journey—spiritual and intellectual—begins here."

"I'm not arguing with you, Henry. I just want this part of the journey to end before lunch."

"If we do find the Grail, it would be important if we could establish its provenance, as you would do with any ancient object—to establish its authenticity."

"If we find the Grail, Henry, we will know it is authentic. Especially if it has a lance dripping blood into it. And even if it doesn't, we will know it when we see it. We will *feel* it. That much I believe. And that's what *you* should believe. So it doesn't matter how it got there, and *we* don't have to prove anything to anyone." He said, "Res ipsa loquitur. The thing speaks for itself."

Mercado looked at him and said, "I didn't know you spoke Latin."

"Neither did I."

Both men stayed silent. Then Mercado asked, "But did I make my case?"

"You did an excellent job." He asked Mercado, "Did you do all this on company time? Or are you doing it *for* the company?"

Mercado did not reply.

Purcell closed his notebook and said, "Well, I have enough to write the story. Now let's find the black monastery so I can write the end."

Purcell stood, and Mercado said to him, "For a writer, a journey of a thousand miles begins in a library and ends at the typewriter."

"We should be so lucky as to end this journey at a typewriter."

They left the room and Mercado said something in Italian to a monk, who walked toward the reading room with a large key in his hand.

They walked out into the December sunshine, then headed into the Vatican gardens toward the Ethiopian College, where Purcell hoped they'd find a map with a notation saying, *Black monastery—home of the Holy Grail*.

They should be that lucky. Or not.

Chapter 19

Priests and nuns strolled the garden paths, and Purcell thought that wherever they had come from, they had arrived here at the center of their world and their faith. Their spiritual journey would never end, until they were called home, but their physical journey had ended and they seemed at peace with themselves.

He and Henry, on the other hand, had a ways to go to find whatever they were looking for. And Vivian, too, who had seemed happy just to be out of Ethiopia and to be with him, had not gotten Ethiopia, Henry, or Father Armano out of her head. But if everything went right, three troubled souls would come together in Rome and make their peace and begin their journey.

Mercado spoke as they walked. "The next significant mention of the Grail in Ethiopia is dated 1527."

"Are we back in the library?"

"Yes. I found a report, written in Latin by a Portuguese Jesuit named Alvarez, written for Pope Clement VII. Father Alvarez says to Pope Clement that he has just returned from Ethiopia and while there he met another Portuguese gentleman, an explorer named Juscelino Alancar, who had reached the Ethiopian emperor's court at Axum with his expedition forty years earlier. Father Alvarez further states that Alancar had been treated well, but he and his men had been put under house arrest by the Coptic pope for the remainder of their lives."

"That seems to be a recurring theme in Ethiopia."

"I also learned that as a result of Alancar's visit to Axum, a number of Ethiopians, most of them Coptic monks, made a pilgrimage to Rome to see the Holy City and were welcomed by Pope Sixtus IV, who granted them the use of the Church of Saint Stephen, near Saint Peter's Basilica, and this was the founding of the Ethiopian College that we are about to visit."

"Very generous of the pope. What did he want in return?"

"Perhaps some information." Mercado returned to the story of Father Alvarez. "Father Alvarez with some other Jesuit priests had been looking for Axum because its name appeared in many ancient writings that were being circulated during the Renaissance. Also, Father Alvarez believed that Axum was the legendary lost Christian kingdom of Prester John."

"Did he find that?"

"No, what Father Alvarez actually found was the capital of Ethiopia and the seat of the Ethiopian Coptic Church. He also found the last surviving member of the Alancar expedition, who was Alancar himself." Mercado added, "Father Alvarez says in this report to Pope Clement VII, that, quote, 'Juscelino Alancar told me that he found and saw the cup—the *gradale*—that his Holiness Sixtus had sent him to find.'"

"Which got Senhor Alancar life in Ethiopia."

"Apparently. And because Alancar told Father Alvarez what it was that he had found and seen, Father Alvarez was also kept in Axum under house arrest."

"But he got out and wrote to the pope."

"Yes, what happened was that Ethiopia was being attacked by the Turks, so the Ethiopian emperor, Claudius, let Father Alvarez go so he could tell King John III of Portugal about the lost Christian empire of Ethiopia, and to ask the Portuguese king for military aid. Alancar himself was dead by this time, so Father Alvarez and his fellow Jesuits left Axum and made their way back to Portugal. King John actually sent an expeditionary force to Ethiopia, and in 1527 a combined Ethiopian and Portuguese force defeated the Turks, and the Ethiopian emperor Claudius pledged everlasting thanks to King John III and to the Jesuits, who, Father Alvarez says in his report to the pope, are now welcomed back into Ethiopia by the emperor Claudius."

They continued through the acres of gardens, and Purcell could see a building ahead that Mercado identified as the Ethiopian College.

Mercado slowed his pace and continued his story. "There is another report from a Jesuit priest named Father Lopes to the next pope, Paul III, which tells of the Jesuit missionary influence in Ethiopia, and of all the good works that they had done in spreading the Catholic faith. But this report also says that the Jesuits are being expelled again because the Ethiopian emperor and the Coptic pope have accused them of excessive prying into the affairs of the Coptic Church and for making inquiries about the monastery of obsidian." He added, "This is the first reference to the black monastery and to the Grail possibly being there."

"Where it remains."

"Yes. Also, it would seem that a succession of Catholic popes had an interest in Ethiopia, and in the black monastery, and therefore the Grail." Mercado continued, "I guess you could make the case that this is a secret passed on from pope to pope, and that's why Father Armano got the sealed envelope from Pius XI. And it also appears, from other oblique references I've read, that the Jesuits, who are the shock troops of the papacy, have been tasked with the mission to find the Holy Grail."

"If that's true, they haven't done a good job of it."

"They are patient." He thought a moment, then said, "Or, more likely, they and the recent popes have lost interest in this because they no longer believe in the existence of the Holy Grail."

"It's a hard thing to believe in, Henry."

"It is. But—"

"You believe it because it is impossible."

"I do."

They reached the Ethiopian College, a Romanesque-style structure that Mercado said was built in the 1920s when the college was moved from the five-hundred-year-old monastery of Saint Stephen. Purcell saw a number of black-robed, dark-skinned monks going in and out of the main entrance, and he couldn't help but recall Father Armano's story of the monks in the black monastery who'd greeted him and the Italian soldiers with clubs. "Is this place safe, Henry?"

Mercado smiled. "They're good Catholics, old man. Not Copts with clubs."

"Good."

But he saw that Mercado crossed himself as he entered, so he did the same.

Mercado confessed, "I haven't been here before, but we have permission and we have an appointment and we are on time."

They stood in the large antechamber and waited.

A tall, black, and bald monk came toward them and Mercado greeted him in Italian. They exchanged a few words, and Purcell could tell that there seemed to be some problem, notwithstanding their appointment.

Purcell suggested, "Tell him all we want to do is see the map that shows the black monastery."

Two more monks appeared from somewhere and the discussion continued. Finally, Mercado turned and said to Purcell, "They are refusing entry. So I'll need to go through channels again."

"Try a different channel."

"All right, let's go. I'll work this out."

They exited the Ethiopian College and walked down the path through the gardens.

Purcell asked, "What was that all about?"

"Not sure."

"When you asked permission, to whom did you speak?"

"I spoke to a papal representative." He explained, "The pope is considered the special protector of the college."

"Doesn't look like that place needs any outside protection."

Mercado didn't respond.

"So what did you tell this papal representative?"

"The truth, of course." He added, "That I had just returned from Ethiopia and I wanted to do some research on a series of articles I was writing for our newspaper about the Coptic and Catholic churches in post-revolutionary Ethiopia."

"Which is the truth, but not the whole truth."

Mercado did not reply and they continued to walk back toward the Vatican Library, or, Purcell hoped, the offices of *L'Osservatore Romano*, or, better yet, lunch. He said, "I assume you didn't mention the black monastery."

"It didn't come up."

Purcell thought about this. If Henry were actually in league with someone or some group here in the Vatican who wanted him to look for the Holy Grail, then there must be another group here who didn't want him to do that. Or the only people here whom Henry Mercado was working for were his editors at *L'Osservatore Romano*, and he, Purcell, was seeing conspiracies where there were only bureaucratic screwups or miscommunication. He wasn't sure, but at some point, here or in Ethiopia, he'd know what, if anything, Henry was up to.

Mercado said, "Just as well. When Gann gets here, we'll have this all straightened out, and I'm sure Colonel Gann can read a map far better than you or I."

"Good point."

"Would you like to go back to the library? There's more."

"The monk locked the door."

"He'll open it."

"Let me buy you lunch."

"All right..."

"The Forum." Purcell explained his restaurant choice: "I'm waiting for a telex."

Mercado looked at him and nodded.

They exited the Vatican through Saint Peter's Square and hailed a taxi on the Borgo Santo Spirito, which took them to the Hotel Forum.

Purcell said, "Go on up and get us a table by the window, and a good bottle of wine."

Mercado hesitated, then walked to the elevators.

Purcell went to the front desk and asked for messages. The clerk riffled through a stack of phone messages and telexes and handed him a sealed envelope.

He opened it and read the telex: ARRIVING FIUMICINO TONIGHT. WILL TAXI TO CITY. HOTEL UNDECIDED. WILL MEET YOU AT FORUM BAR, 6 P.M. I MISS YOU, V.

He put the telex in his pocket and walked to the elevator.

Well...no mention of Henry. Hotel undecided. Don't meet me at the airport. See you at six. I miss you.

And, Purcell thought, I miss you too.

He rode up to the Forum restaurant and found Henry speaking on the maître d's phone. Henry motioned to a table by the window, and Purcell sat.

Mercado joined him and asked, "Any messages?"

"No."

Mercado looked at him and said, "It's all right."

He wasn't sure what that meant, but he nodded.

"I ordered the same amarone."

"I thought we drank it all."

"Do you feel that you are intellectually and spiritually prepared to go on this quest?"

"I do, actually."

"And do you think Vivian will come with us?"

Purcell reminded Mercado, "You seem to think that the Holy Spirit has told her to go. So ask him. Or her."

Mercado smiled.

Purcell suggested, "Let's talk about something else."

"All right. I just spoke to my office. Colonel Gann telexed. He can come to Rome right after the New Year and may be able to go to Berini with us."

"Good. Did he mention Ethiopia?"

"He said he would go if he could get in."

"Getting in is easy. Getting out, not so easy."

"I assume he meant getting in without being rearrested."

The wine came, and Henry poured it himself. He raised his glass and said, "Amicitia sine fraude—to friendship without deceit."

"Cheers."

Chapter 20

The Forum bar was crowded when Purcell arrived at 5:30, so he took a table by the window and sat facing the entrance, nursing a glass of red wine.

This wasn't the first time in his life that an ex-lover or estranged girlfriend had wanted to meet in a public place, and sometimes he'd suggested it himself. And maybe with Henry still in the picture, this was a good idea. In fact, he wasn't sure himself what he wanted to happen tonight, except that he wanted Vivian to go with him—and Henry—to Ethiopia. And that, apparently, was what she wanted, though it had to be worked out if she was with him, or with Henry, or with neither.

In any case, despite Henry's toast, Purcell had no guilt about deceiving Henry regarding Vivian's arrival. In fact, Henry probably knew he'd heard from Vivian, and Henry understood that a three-person reunion would not be a good first step toward a return trip to Ethiopia. Purcell had made his separate peace with Henry Mercado, and now he'd do the same with Vivian. Eventually they'd all have a drink together and be civilized—even if Vivian decided to be with Henry. Actually, he was sure Henry would not take her back, even if she wanted that. Henry, like his Italian friends, had a monumental ego—and if he didn't have an inferiority complex before, he'd acquired one in Ethiopia.

It was past 6 P.M., but Purcell knew she'd be late, though he had no idea what time her plane had arrived from Geneva. But the traffic from Fiumicino was always bad, and it was rush hour in Rome, and Christmas, and maybe she was looking for a hotel, which was difficult during the holy season.

He lit a cigarette and looked out at the Colosseum. Or maybe she'd changed her mind. And that was okay, too. Less complicated.

"Hello, Frank."

He stood and they looked at each other. She hesitated, then put her hand on his arm. He leaned forward and they kissed briefly, and he said, "You're looking very good."

"You too."

She was wearing a green silky dress that matched her eyes, and her long black hair framed her alabaster skin, and he remembered her as he'd seen her that night at the mineral spa when he realized he was taken with her.

"Frank?"

"Oh . . . would you like to sit?"

A hovering waiter pulled a chair out for her, she sat, and Purcell sat across from her. She said to the waiter, "Un bicchiere di vino rosso, per favore."

They looked at each other across the table, then finally she said, "I'm sorry."

"You don't need to apologize or explain."

"But I'd better do that."

He smiled.

"I just needed to sort things out."

"How did that work out?"

"Well, I'm here."

That didn't answer the question, but Purcell said, "Thank you for coming."

"Did you throw my stuff out?"

"Tempted."

The waiter brought her glass of wine and Purcell held up his glass. "Sono adirato."

"Why are you angry?"

"I thought that meant, 'I adore you.'"

She laughed and they touched glasses. She said, "Ti amo."

"Me too."

She put her hand on the table and he took it. They didn't speak for a while, then she asked, "Did you come to Rome to see Henry?"

"I did."

She nodded, then asked, "Does he know I'm here?"

"No."

She nodded again and asked, "How is he?"

"Adirato."

"Well...I don't blame him...but...at least you two are talking."

"I think he's ready to talk to you."

"That's good. So he's working for *L'Osservatore Romano*?"

"He is. Seems to enjoy it. Loves Rome."

"I'm happy for him."

"Any other feelings for him that I should know about?"

She shook her head.

"All right...but when you see him, you can work that out with him."

"I will." She added, "I'm sure he's over it."

"He said he was."

She changed the subject and asked, "How long are you staying in Rome?"

"That depends. How long are *you* staying in Rome?"

"As long as you are."

"All right." He informed her, "I've resigned from the AP office in Cairo."

"Why?"

"Because Charlie Gibson fired me."

"Good. You hated the job and you hated Cairo."

"I wasn't fond of either," he admitted, "but it was tolerable with you there."

She smiled. "I can make any place tolerable, Frank."

"Even Ethiopia."

"That may be overstating my powers." She asked him, "What about our apartment in Cairo?"

"That's the only home I have at the moment."

"Me too."

"We'll keep it awhile." He asked, "Where did you stay in Geneva?"

"My old boarding school." She explained, "We're always welcome back. Twenty francs a night in the guesthouse. Best deal in Geneva." She added, "No men allowed."

"Can you at least drink?"

"Yes. You *must* drink to stay sane there."

He smiled.

She told him, "I'm not a writer, but I did write a sort of diary about what happened in Ethiopia." She told him, "I also wrote about us in Cairo."

"Can I see it?"

"Someday." She added, "I'm still angry about losing all my photographs."

"You can ask Getachu for them when we go back."

She looked at him for a few seconds. "Are we actually doing that?"

"Well...that's the plan." He asked, "Are you still interested?"

"I am." She added, "I'm surprised that Henry wants to go back."

"I'm not, and neither are you." He reminded her, "He believes he has been chosen by God to find...it."

She nodded.

"And you?"

Again, she nodded, and asked, "And *you?*"

"My motives, according to Henry, are confused at best."

"But you *do* want to go?"

"I do." He informed her, "Henry is working on getting us press credentials with *L'Osservatore Romano*, then we need to get visas. If none of that works, we may consider jumping the border from Sudan."

"That could be dangerous."

"No more dangerous than trekking through Getachu territory to find the black monastery."

She nodded.

He told her, "Good news. Colonel Gann has been released from prison."

"Thank God. I thought...they'd kill him."

"They would have, but they sold him instead." He added, "I don't know where he is now, but Henry got a telex from him and Gann says he's willing to accompany us to Ethiopia."

"That is insane."

"He probably had the same thought about us."

"But he's...an enemy—"

"Maybe he'll rethink that trip. In the meantime, he's coming to Rome after the New Year, and if you're up for it, all four of us will go to sunny Sicily for holiday. Berini."

She smiled. "I would like that."

He informed her, "There was a piece in the news... they shot Prince Joshua."

"I saw that...that poor man...and all those other members of the royal family, and all the former government people..." She looked at him. "How can people do that to other people?"

"It's been going on awhile."

"I know...but...there's such evil in the world..." She asked him, "Doesn't it test your faith in God?"

"Father Armano—and Henry—would tell you it's all part of God's plan."

"It can't be."

"The devil, then."

She nodded, then looked at him and said, "I always meant to ask you...that night...when we were driving, why did you suddenly turn off the road?"

"I don't know."

"You went right through a wall of bushes. Right where the spa was."

He'd thought about that himself, and he couldn't recall what had made him suddenly crash the Jeep through those bushes. He smiled. "A voice said, 'Turn right.'"

"Be serious."

"I don't know, Vivian."

"But don't you think it was beyond strange that you turned off the road exactly where the spa was?"

"Let me think about it." He changed the subject. "Henry and I discussed the possibility that Getachu or someone else has already found the black monastery."

"They haven't."

"All right..." He wanted their first night to be more romantic, so he asked, "Would you like dinner?"

"No. I want to take a walk."

"Good idea." He signaled the waiter for the bill, then asked her, "Where are you staying?"

"There is not a room to be had in Rome."

"Sorry to hear that." He inquired, "Where is your luggage?"

"In your room."

He smiled. "How did you manage that?"

"Really, Frank. We're in Italy."

He asked, seriously, "How did you know this would go well?"

"It didn't matter how it went. We're sleeping together tonight."

He didn't argue with that, and he suggested, "Let's get you unpacked."

"I need a walk. It's a beautiful night."

"Okay." He paid the bill while she got her coat, and they went down to the lobby and outside into the cool night.

The Roman rush hour had ended, and the streets were becoming more quiet, and pedestrians were strolling on the broad Via dei Fori Imperiali. The Christmas decorations, such as they were, were mostly of the religious type, and there was no sign of Santa or his reindeer.

They held hands and didn't speak much as they took

in the city and its people. Vivian said, "This is what I pictured when I received your romantic letter."

"I didn't know what tone to use."

"So you wrote it as a news release. If it wasn't for your P.S., I'd still be in Geneva."

"I know."

"Well, I don't blame you for being angry."

"Why should you?"

"I know I shouldn't have left under false pretenses. And I'm sorry for that. But I couldn't face you . . . and say . . ."

"Drop it."

She squeezed his hand and said, "I kept thinking to myself, 'Get thee to a nunnery, Vivian. Go think this out.'"

"Good. Let's move on. Avanti."

"I feel cleansed now, and pure."

"We'll take care of that later."

She laughed and they continued on. She asked him, "What is the most romantic spot in the city?"

"My room."

"Second most."

"I'll show you."

They walked around the Vittorio Emanuele monument, then up the steps of the Campidoglio to the piazza at the top of the ancient Capitoline Hill where dozens of hand-holding couples strolled past the museums and around the equestrian statue of Marcus Aurelius.

Purcell led her to a spot at the edge of the hill that looked out over the floodlit Forum below and at the Palatine Hill rising above the Forum ruins, with the Colosseum in the distance.

Vivian said, "Breathtaking."

"We'll come back here after Ethiopia."

"We will come back."

They descended the long flight of steps down the hill and walked back to the hotel.

Chapter 21

Purcell picked up his room phone and called Henry at his office to inform him that Vivian was in Rome, though he didn't say when she'd arrived, or where she was staying, and Henry didn't ask. Had he asked, Purcell would have told him that Vivian was in the shower.

Henry suggested lunch at a restaurant called Etiopia, which he thought would be a fitting place for their reunion. Purcell didn't think so, but he took down the address, which Henry said was near the Termini. Henry further suggested that he, Henry, meet Vivian there at 12:30, and that Purcell join them at one—or even later.

Purcell wasn't sure he liked that arrangement, but he'd leave it up to Vivian.

Later, as he and Vivian began a morning walk, he told her about his call to Mercado, and about lunch.

He thought she might want to return to the hotel to change out of her jeans, sweatshirt, and hiking boots for lunch with her old boyfriend, but she said, "I'm all right with that. If you are."

"I'm okay." He informed her, "It's an Ethiopian restaurant."

"That's Henry."

It was a warm and sunny morning, and it was the Saturday before Christmas, so traffic was light and the city seemed to be in a holiday mood.

They walked through the Campo de' Fiori, which made Purcell think of his advice to Jean, which in turn made him think of Henry sending Jean to his table under false pretenses. Henry Mercado, Purcell understood, was a manipulator and a man who knew how to compromise other people. But Henry was also a gentleman of the old school, and Henry would not mention Jean to Vivian. Unless it suited his purpose.

They then walked to the Trevi Fountain, made their secret wishes, and tossed their coins over their shoulders into the water, which according to tradition guaranteed that they'd return to Rome someday.

At 11:30, Purcell suggested they head toward Etiopia—the restaurant, not the country.

Their route took them past the Termini, Rome's central rail station, around which was Rome's only sizable black neighborhood, whose residents were mostly from the former Italian colonies of Ethiopia, Eritrea, and Somalia. The area around the Termini was crowded with African street vendors whose native wares were spread out on blankets.

As they walked, Purcell asked Vivian, "Are you still all right with this meeting?"

She nodded, but he could see she was apprehensive. The last time Vivian had seen Henry was when they'd gotten off Getachu's helicopter in Addis Ababa. The flight from Getachu's camp to Addis had been made mostly in silence, except for Gann telling them that as foreigners and journalists, the worst they could expect was a show trial, a conviction, and expulsion from the country.

Purcell had realized at the time that Colonel Gann

was not speaking about himself—he fully expected to be hanged or shot—and yet he'd put his own fears aside to boost the morale of three people he hardly knew. A true officer and gentleman. And now, according to Mercado, Gann was willing to return to Ethiopia, where he was under a death sentence. Fearless was one thing, but foolhardy was something else. He wondered what was motivating Colonel Gann.

From the helicopter, they had been made to run barefoot across the tarmac, wearing leg shackles, to four waiting police cars. Before they were separated, Vivian had called out to Henry, "I love you!"

But Henry had not replied—or maybe he hadn't heard her.

Then Vivian had turned toward him, and they made eye contact. She gave him a sort of sad smile before the policeman pushed her into the car.

And that was the last he saw of her until the Hilton, and the last Henry would see of her until about fifteen minutes from now.

He said to her, "If you're having second thoughts, I'll go with you."

"No. I just need to put it to rest, Frank. Then get on with what we have to do."

"All right." There was no script for this sort of thing—the eternal triangle in the Eternal City—and he supposed that Henry's request for half an hour alone with his former lover was not unreasonable, and that Vivian's acquiescence was meant, as she said, to put it to rest and move on. Henry, on the other hand, had many agendas, and Purcell didn't know which one was on the schedule today.

Vivian was looking at the blankets spread over the open spaces around the Termini, and the street vendors were calling out to her in Italian as she passed. She said something to one of them in Amharic and the man seemed surprised, then delighted.

She stopped and looked at the crafts on his blanket, and the man was speaking rapidly to her in Amharic, then switched to Italian.

Purcell looked at the items. There were a few objects carved out of what looked like teak and ebony, some beadwork, and a few sculptures carved from jet black obsidian, polished to a high gloss, including a model of the distinctive octagon-shaped Saint George Cathedral in Addis Ababa. He smiled. "We've found the black monastery."

"Frank, that's Saint George in Addis."

"Looks smaller than I remember."

A lady was selling embroidered *shammas* and Purcell suggested, "Let's wear these to lunch."

Vivian surprised him by saying, "The last time Henry saw us in shammas, he didn't like what he saw."

Purcell had no comment on that. He walked over to another blanket covered with bronze ware, and he spotted a wine goblet that reminded him of the goblets in Prince Joshua's tent. The vendor wanted fifty thousand lire, Purcell offered ten, and they settled on twenty.

Purcell moved back to Vivian, who was negotiating the price of Saint George's, and held up the goblet. "I have found the Holy Grail."

She laughed.

"Here. Give it to Henry and tell him mission accomplished."

She examined the goblet of hammered bronze, which looked ancient, but was probably made last week, and asked, "How will we know?"

"The thing will speak for itself."

She nodded, then handed it back to him, saying, "You give it to him."

The *polizia* were doing a scheduled sweep through the Termini area, chasing off the street vendors, who rolled up their blankets and wares and moved a few meters behind the sweep, then set up again on the pavement. No one seemed to take things too seriously here, he noticed, and maybe Henry had found the right place to live and die, if he didn't die in Ethiopia. Same for him and Vivian.

Purcell asked a policeman for directions to Via Gaeta, and he walked Vivian part of the way. They stopped and he said, "See you in half an hour."

"Don't be late."

"I might be early."

She smiled, then said seriously, "If he's willing to forget the past, and get over his anger, and be with us under these...I guess, awkward circumstances, then you—"

"I get it."

"All right..." She gave him a quick kiss, turned, and walked off.

Purcell checked his watch, then wandered the streets around the Termini. He found a taverna and went inside. The clientele was mostly black, though the taverna itself seemed to be traditional Roman.

He sat at the small bar and ordered an espresso, then changed his mind and asked for a *vino rosso*.

Henry Mercado had a flair for drama and stage setting. He was, in fact, a performer. An illusionist. Purcell could see it in some of Henry's writing. There were never any hard facts—just suggestions of fact, mixed with his profound insights. Henry manipulated words the way he manipulated people. Purcell had no doubt that Henry's epiphany in the Gulag was real, but Henry's inner pagan had remained the same. If Henry Mercado wasn't a Catholic journalist, he'd probably be a magician or a wizard. Purcell didn't think that Vivian would again fall under his spell, but Henry would use her guilt to his advantage.

He had a second wine and looked at the patrons in the bar mirror. Ethiopia was disgorging large chunks of its population, especially the entrepreneurs and the professional class, and also the old aristocracy who had escaped hanging and shooting, as well as the Coptic and Catholic clergy who felt threatened by the godless revolutionaries. Ethiopia was, in fact, a replay of the French and Russian revolutions; an isolated ruling elite had lost touch with the people, and with reality, so the people had brought reality to the palaces and churches. The three-thousand-year-old established order was crumbling, and for this reason, the Holy Grail was up for grabs.

It was only a matter of time, he thought, before the revolutionaries located the black monastery; it was well hidden, but nothing can be hidden forever, though he knew that the lost cities of the Mayans had remained undiscovered for hundreds of years in jungles far smaller than those of Ethiopia.

But no matter who found the monastery, he was sure

that the Holy Grail, or whatever else was there, would be spirited away before the first intruders got over the walls. And yet...

He took the bronze goblet out of his trench coat and looked at it.

The proprietor, an Italian, looked at it also, then nodded toward his clientele and said in English, "Ethiopian junk."

Not wanting the man to think he was a gullible tourist, Purcell informed him, "This is the Holy Grail."

The proprietor laughed. "What you pay for that?"

"Twenty thousand."

"Too much. Ten."

"This can turn wine into the blood of Christ."

The proprietor laughed again, then said, "Okay, for twenty is good."

Purcell left a ten on the bar, walked out into the sunshine, and headed for Etiopia.

Chapter 22

Purcell spotted Vivian and Mercado sitting in the rear of the dark restaurant. They weren't tête-à-tête, but they did seem at ease, talking and smiling.

He brushed past the hostess, walked to the table, and said, "Sorry I'm late."

Mercado replied, "You're a bit early, actually."

Purcell did not shake hands with Mercado or kiss Vivian; he sat, still wearing his trench coat. Henry, he noticed, was looking a bit more trendy in a black leather jacket and black silk shirt.

Vivian said, "Henry has brought me up to date."

"Good."

There was a bottle of wine on the table, and Henry poured into an empty glass for Purcell, then raised his glass and said, "Ad astra per aspera. Through adversity to the stars."

Purcell wondered how many Latin toasts Mercado had in him.

They touched glasses, and Vivian proposed, "To peace and friendship."

Purcell lit a cigarette and scanned the room. The place looked as if it had been decorated with the stuff from the blankets, including the blankets themselves that hung on the walls. The tables were half empty, and the clientele seemed to be mostly African and well dressed, probably, Purcell thought, the cream of Ethiopian society who'd washed up on the banks of the Tiber.

Vivian, trying to keep the conversation going, said, "Henry told me about the research he's done in the Vatican archives."

Purcell didn't respond.

Mercado said to her, "Frank was unimpressed."

Vivian waited for Purcell to respond, then said, "Odd that they wouldn't let you into the Ethiopian College."

Mercado assured her, "I'll work that out." He added, "That is the type of practical research that would appeal to Frank's practical mind."

Mercado and Vivian continued their two-way conversation, the way they had before Purcell arrived, and Purcell knew he was not being civilized or sophisticated, and this probably pleased Mercado to no end. So to avoid a scene later with Vivian and to avoid giving Mercado the satisfaction of seeing him uncomfortable in this situation, Purcell said, "Henry and I have agreed to disagree about some things, but we agree that the three of us are going back to Ethiopia—if we can get in—and we are going to pick up where we left off when we buried Father Armano."

Vivian nodded, then reminded Purcell, "You have something for Henry."

"I do? Oh…" He reached into his coat pocket and set the bronze goblet on the table.

Mercado picked it up and looked at it.

Purcell announced, "We have found the Holy Grail."

Vivian added, "At a street stall near the Termini."

Mercado laughed, then turned the goblet upside down and said, "Indeed you have. Made in Jerusalem, 10 B.C., property of J. Arimathea."

Vivian laughed.

Mercado said, "Well done, you two. Now Frank and I can get working on this story, then go our separate ways."

Purcell thought that would be nice, but to keep the ice from refreezing, he said, "You need to research this grail, Henry."

They all laughed, then Mercado picked up the wine bottle and poured into the bronze goblet. He said solemnly, "We will drink of this and this will be our covenant." He passed the goblet to Vivian, who put it to her lips and drank, then passed it to Purcell. He drank and passed it to Mercado, who finished the wine and said, "May God bless our journey."

Vivian reached out and took both men's hands, though Purcell and Mercado did not join hands. Vivian lowered her head and said, "God rest Father Armano and all those who suffer and die in his name, in Ethiopia and around the world."

"Amen," said Mercado.

The waiter, a tall, thin black man wearing a colorful *shamma*, saw that they had completed their prayers and came by with menus, but Mercado stood and said, "I will leave you to enjoy this wonderful food and enjoy each other's company—after your long separation."

Purcell forced himself to say, "Please stay."

"Yes, please stay, Henry."

"I've let some work pile up at the office."

Purcell stood and they shook hands, then Mercado came around and gave Vivian a peck on the cheek and left.

Purcell sat and the waiter left two menus.

Vivian said to Purcell, "Thank you."

Purcell perused the menu.

Vivian informed him, "We've worked everything out."

"Good. I hope you like lamb. Here's a fish called Saint Peter's fish."

"He understands what happened and how it happened, and he understands that we are in love."

"Good."

"Did you tell him we were in love?"

Purcell put down the menu. "At the time I spoke to him, I didn't know if we were."

"Well, you know now."

"I do." He looked at her and said, "A piece of advice, Vivian. Henry Mercado is a charming rogue. He is also a manipulator and a con artist." He added, "Don't get me wrong—I like him. But we need to keep an eye on him."

She thought about that, then replied, "He's not trying to . . . reseduce me."

"He would if he could. But what I'm talking about is our partnership with him." He nodded toward the goblet. "Our new covenant."

She stayed quiet for a few seconds, then said, with some insight, "I was easy for him. But I think he knows he's met his match with you."

Purcell couldn't have said it better, and he smiled at Vivian. "I have met my match with you."

"You never stood a chance, Frank."

"No, I never did."

She filled the goblet with wine and passed it to him. He drank and passed it back to her. She said, "If you believe in love, you believe in God."

Where had he heard that before?

Chapter 23

They didn't see Henry again for several days, but he, or a messenger, dropped off an envelope in which were their visa applications partly filled out, awaiting only their passport information and their signatures. A note from Henry said, "Bring these in person to the Ethiopian embassy, ASAP. Cross your fingers."

Purcell and Vivian visited the Ethiopian embassy the next morning and spent a half hour waiting for a consulate officer who seemed to be a relative of General Getachu. The former regime's diplomatic staff had been dismissed, of course, and had undoubtedly chosen not to go back to Ethiopia and face a possible firing squad, so they'd probably stayed in Rome and were hanging out with the other expats at Etiopia. The colonial ties between Italy and Ethiopia had been brief and not strong, but they persisted, as Purcell saw around the Termini, and he imagined that Italy would see even more upscale refugees as the revolution got uglier. Meanwhile, he had to deal with the unpleasant consulate officer, who didn't speak English but spoke bad Italian to Vivian, who maintained her composure and smiled. The man didn't seem to believe that anyone wanted to travel to the People's Republic for legitimate purposes, and he was right. The officer took their passports, which he said would be returned to them in a week or so at their place of business, which was *L'Osservatore Romano*, with or without their visas. He also took 100,000 lire from each of them for expedited processing.

The consulate officer's parting advice, which Vivian translated, was, "If you are denied visas, do not apply again. If you are accepted as journalists, you must refrain from all other activities in Ethiopia."

Vivian assured him they understood and wished him, "Buongiorno."

They spent the next few days before Christmas exploring the city. Vivian said she'd been to Rome twice on school trips, but she didn't know the city as an adult, so Purcell showed her Rome by night, including Trastevere and the fading Via Veneto, where he pointed out the Excelsior where Henry was living and presumably drinking. They didn't go into the hotel bar, but he did take her to Harry's, and after they'd had a drink at the bar, he told her about finding Henry there.

She said to him, "Thank you for doing that."

"That's what you wanted."

"Was it...awkward?"

"It was, but we moved on to bigger issues."

"I knew you would both be mature."

"I didn't say that."

She smiled, then leaned over and kissed him at the bar, and the slick bartender said, "Bellissimo."

During the day they walked the city and he took her to out-of-the-way places, including the Chapel of Quo Vadis, where Vivian was intrigued by Christ's footprint in the paving stone, and she said, "This *could* be real."

"You never know."

A call to Henry had gotten them put on the visitor's list at Porta Santa Rosa, and they walked the hundred acres of Vatican City, and Purcell showed her Henry's office building, and also the Ethiopian College where black-robed monks and seminarians entered and exited. Vivian asked, "Will I be allowed in there?"

"Good question. I don't think it's coed. But we'll try."

"I'll wear your trench coat."

"They're celibate, Vivian, not blind."

Henry had gotten them passes to Saint Peter's for Midnight Mass on Christmas Eve, and they met Henry at Porta Santa Rosa at eleven and walked to the basilica without having to go through the throngs in Saint Peter's Square.

The Mass looked to Purcell as it had looked on television when he'd seen it sitting in a New York bar one Christmas Eve.

Vivian, as expected, was moved by the pageantry and the papal address, and the pope's announcement that 1975 would be a Holy Year. Purcell, though he spoke neither Italian nor Latin, was also impressed by the history and the grandeur of the Roman Mass. He wondered if they'd keep the Holy Grail at the altar of the basilica or in the Vatican Museums. He'd suggest the altar, and maybe he would make that part of the deal. He smiled at his own absurd thoughts and Vivian whispered to him, "It's good to see you happy."

Henry had secured late supper reservations in the Jewish ghetto, explaining, "There is nothing else open in Rome tonight."

And there were no taxis or public transportation

either, so they walked along the Tiber to the ghetto and entered Vecchia Roma on the Piazza di Campitelli.

The restaurant was standing room only, but the hostess seated them immediately, and Henry confessed, "I promised them a four-star review in *L'Osservatore Romano*."

Vivian asked, "Do you do restaurant reviews?"

"No, and neither does the paper."

Vivian and Purcell exchanged glances.

Henry asked, "Red or white?"

"Both," Purcell replied. He looked around at the fresco walls, seeing nothing that looked particularly Jewish. In fact, the restaurant was decorated for Christmas.

Mercado commented, "The Jews have been in this ghetto since before the time of Christ and I'd say they are more Roman than the Romans." He added, "I'm sure Peter and Paul found comfort here among their fellow Jews."

Vivian said, "Amazing."

The wine came and Henry toasted, "Merry Christmas to us."

Vivian added, "And a happy, healthy, and peaceful New Year."

Purcell didn't think their immediate plans for the New Year included any of that, so he also proposed, "To a safe and successful journey."

Vivian said to Henry, "And thank you for this night."

Purcell offered, "We'll split the bill."

"No, no," said Mercado. "This is my Christmas gift to you both."

"Thank you," said Vivian.

Purcell noticed that the table was set for four, and he wondered if Mercado's lady friend was joining him, but he didn't ask. Henry, however, brought it up. "I have an old friend in Rome—Jean—whom I mentioned to Frank, but she couldn't join us."

Purcell doubted if the lady was named Jean, and he looked at Henry, who smiled at him. *Bastard*.

Vivian said, "We'd like to meet her."

They looked at the menus and Vivian noted that the food didn't seem much different than traditional Italian, but Mercado assured her that there were subtle differences, and he offered to order for everyone, which he did. Mercado then held court for the rest of the evening, and if Purcell didn't know better, he'd think that Henry was trying to re-impress Vivian, who handled the balancing act well, giving equal time to her host and former lover and to her new beau.

They left the restaurant at 3 A.M. and Mercado walked with Vivian and Purcell part of the way to their nearby hotel, then wished them Merry Christmas and continued on to the Excelsior.

Purcell and Vivian strolled hand in hand through the quiet streets and Vivian said, "I didn't know Henry had a lady friend in Rome."

"I'm sure Henry has a lady in every city."

"And you?"

"Only four—Addis Ababa, Cairo, Geneva, and Rome."

She leaned over and gave him a kiss. They continued on and Vivian said, "Wasn't that a beautiful Mass?"

"It was."

"Could you live in Rome?"

"I would need a job."

She pointed out, "If we find the Holy Grail, you probably won't need a job."

"Right. Let's ask ten million. Dollars, not lire."

"We're not going to steal the Grail or sell it. But you and Henry will write a book, and I'll supply the photographs, and we'll all be famous."

"Don't forget your camera."

On the subject of money, Purcell had informed Vivian in Cairo that the AP, which he'd been working for when he went missing inside a Khmer Rouge prison camp, had generously given him a year's back pay on his release. As with Henry's back pay after four years in the Gulag, it wasn't the easiest money Purcell had ever made, but the lump sum came in handy when he'd collected it in New York. He still had most of it, and this was paying for his Roman Holiday, and *L'Osservatore Romano* would pay the expenses for his Ethiopian assignment, sans salary. He assumed Henry would work out something similar for his photographer.

As for Vivian's finances, she'd told him in Cairo that she had a small trust fund, though she never mentioned its source or anything about her family. All he knew about her past was that she'd gone to boarding school in Geneva. If there was anything more she wanted to tell him, she would. Meanwhile they were in Rome and in love. *La dolce vita.*

Most of the restaurants in Rome were closed on Christmas Day, but the concierge booked Christmas dinner for them at the Grand Hotel de la Minerva because he said Vivian was as beautiful as the goddess Minerva. That cost Purcell thirty thousand lire, but Vivian paid for dinner, which was her Christmas gift to him. His to her would be a trip to Tuscany.

Purcell rented a car and they drove to Tuscany and spent the week touring, staying at country inns, then they drove up to Florence for New Year's Eve, where they joined the crowd in the Piazza della Signoria and celebrated the arrival of the New Year on a cold clear winter night.

They drove back to Rome on New Year's Day and returned to the Hotel Forum in midafternoon.

There was a handwritten message at the desk from Henry that said, "Col. Gann will arrive at Fiumicino Jan. 4. Staying at Excelsior. Dinner at Hassler Roof 8 P.M. Call me when you've returned. Can you go to Berini next week? Good news about our visas." It was signed, "Love, Henry."

Purcell said, "Well, it seems that we are going to Ethiopia."

Vivian nodded.

They returned to their room and Purcell called Henry at the office. "Happy New Year," Purcell said.

"And to you. Are you in Rome?"

"We are. Got your message."

"Good, come join me for cocktails and we'll catch up. Excelsior, say five."

"Six. See you then." He hung up and said to Vivian, "I can go alone."

"I'll come. Lots to talk about."

"There always is with Henry."

"Now that it's becoming real...I'm getting a little apprehensive."

He looked at her. "I always feel that way before an assignment into a hostile area." He assured her, "It's normal."

"Ethiopia was my first time in a war zone." She smiled. "I was excited and clueless."

"Now you're an experienced veteran."

"God will watch over us. He did last time."

Purcell thought that God's patience with them might be wearing thin, and he didn't reply.

Chapter 24

The Excelsior bar and lounge, Purcell guessed, was probably Old World when it was brand-new, and Henry was at home here, and everyone seemed to know him. Someday they'd name a drink after him.

They were escorted to a good table by the window, and they gave their orders to a waiter, Giancarlo, who had greeted Signore Mercado by name, of course, and knew what he was drinking.

Purcell thought back to Harry's Bar when Signore Mercado had told him never to darken his doorstep at the Excelsior. They'd come a long way. Purcell noted that Henry was wearing a sharp blue suit with a white silk shirt, and what looked like an Italian silk tie. Apparently Henry had gone shopping. Vivian, too, had gone shopping, in Florence, and she looked good in a white winter silk dress, which Henry complimented.

Purcell was feeling a bit underdressed in the only sport jacket he'd brought from Cairo. He would have gone shopping, too, but they weren't going to be here long.

It was New Year's Day evening, a quiet night back in the States, Purcell recalled, but the Excelsior bar and lounge was full, and Mercado informed them, "The Italians will take the rest of the week off."

Purcell inquired, "And you?"

"The printing presses never stop, as you well know." He added, "I'll do half days."

Vivian asked, "Will Jean be joining us?"

Mercado replied, "She had to go to London."

Purcell lit a cigarette.

Vivian asked him, "So do we have our visas?"

Mercado pulled two passports from his inside pocket and handed the blue one to Purcell, then opened Vivian's red Swiss passport and said, "This photo never did you justice."

Vivian reached across the table and Mercado gave her her passport.

By this time, Purcell thought, he'd have clocked the guy, who was pissing him off, but he decided to see if Henry continued to be an asshole, then take it from there.

Henry said, all businesslike now, "Same as last time, the visas are stamped inside." He drew two sheets of paper from his pocket. "And these are copies of your visa applications, signed and stamped by the consul general." He handed a visa to each of them.

Purcell glanced inside his passport and saw that the new visa stamp, unlike his last one, had been altered by someone, who'd scratched out the Lion of Judah in red ink. His visa application had the same rubber stamp, similarly altered to show that things had changed in Ethiopia.

Their drinks came and Henry informed them, "Tonight is on *L'Osservatore Romano*."

They touched glasses and Purcell asked, "Do you have our press credentials?"

"I do." He handed each of them a press card, and also a larger document written in several languages, including Amharic, Arabic, and Tigrena, which he said was sort of a journalist's safe-conduct pass. He smiled.

Neither Purcell nor Vivian returned the smile.

The waiter brought over an assortment of nuts, olives, and cheese, which Purcell suspected was Henry's dinner on most nights.

Purcell asked, "Any good news about the Ethiopian College?"

"Not yet." Mercado explained, "The college is closed until the Epiphany."

"Good time to break in."

Mercado looked at him, but did not respond.

Vivian, too, had nothing to say about that, but she asked, "Will I be allowed in?"

"No."

Purcell inquired, "What do you make of this refusal to let us see their library?"

Mercado pondered that, then replied, "That depends on your level of paranoia." He informed them, "The Ethiopian College is a very cloistered place. I'm sure there is nothing strange or secretive going on there, but they like their privacy."

"We all do, Henry, but this place is not a monastery on a mountain—or in the jungle. It's on Vatican City property, under the authority of the papal state. Who makes the rules? Them or the Vatican?"

"They are semi-autonomous." He let them know, "I'm pushing our cover story that we want to do some research for our Ethiopian assignment—which is actually true. But I'm not pushing so hard that someone would think there is more to my interest."

"All right." He asked, "Is this library worth the trouble?"

"I think the maps will be invaluable. But I may be wrong."

Purcell nodded. Henry's time in the Vatican Library and his request for access to the Ethiopian College were well within his needs as a reporter for *L'Osservatore Romano.* On the other hand, if someone in the Vatican hierarchy was putting the pieces together—including Henry asking to go back to hell with the same reporter and photographer he'd been with in prison—then a picture was taking shape. Actually, two pictures: one that looked like a reporter doing his job, and one that looked like a reporter who was getting nosy about something he wasn't supposed to know. The thing that would put the picture in focus would be Henry's notifying the Vatican of Father Armano's death, saying in effect that he'd heard the dying words of Father Giuseppe Armano, who once had a papal letter in his pocket telling the good father to grab the Holy Grail from a Coptic monastery.

Mercado asked, "What's on your mind, Frank?"

"Our cover story."

"The beauty of our cover story is that it is real."

"Right." Up until the point where they went off into the jungle. And even then, they were on assignment, though not necessarily for *L'Osservatore Romano.*

Also, Purcell thought, Henry was driving this bus with a lot more enthusiasm than he'd shown at Harry's Bar. He'd been touched by the Holy Spirit, or he just smelled a good story—the Holy Grail of stories. Plus, of course, Henry wanted to make up for his past poor performance in Ethiopia. It was important to him that neither Vivian nor Frank Purcell thought he had lost his nerve. Henry should take his own advice about going to Ethiopia for the right reasons.

Henry seemed to be done with business, and he inquired about their trip to Tuscany, and Vivian provided most of the answers. Henry said it sounded like a wonderful trip, and added, "If you are still here in the spring, or the fall, Tuscany is at its best." He further advised, "But stay away in the summer. It's overrun with Brits." He smiled and said, "The Italians call it Tuscanshire."

Henry continued with his travel advice, and it occurred to Purcell that he might be lonely. He obviously knew people in Rome, including his colleagues at the newspaper as well as every bartender and waiter on the Via Veneto. And there was also the mysterious lady whose name was not Jean. But Purcell could detect the loneliness—he'd experienced it himself. In a rare moment of empathy, Purcell understood that Henry had lost more than a lover in Ethiopia—he'd lost a friend. Or, considering the age difference, he'd lost a young protégée—someone he could teach. Or was it manipulate?

He looked at Vivian as Henry was going on about Perugia or something, and it seemed to Purcell that Vivian had lost the stars in her eyes for Henry. In fact, Vivian, like himself, had been transformed by her experience in Ethiopia. She had seemed then, to him, a bit...immature, almost childish in Addis and on the road to the front lines, not to mention the mineral baths or Prince Joshua's tent. But she'd grown up fast, as people do who've been traumatized by war. He knew, too, that the encounter with Father Armano had affected her deeply, as had her recent romantic complications. It was a mature decision to get herself to a nunnery, and though he loved the woman who'd left him in Cairo, he liked the woman who'd met him in Rome.

Henry, on the other hand, seemed to be regressing. But Purcell was not going to underestimate the old fox.

Henry had moved on to Milan, and Vivian was nodding attentively, though her eyes were glazing over.

It occurred to Purcell, too, that Henry must hear time's wingèd chariot gaining on him. So for Henry, a return to Ethiopia was a no-lose situation; if he died there, he wasn't missing much more of life. But if he returned—with or without the Holy Grail—he would have stories to tell for the rest of his life. Hopefully to a nice woman, but anyone would do.

For Vivian and Purcell, however, the timeline was different. Especially for Vivian. Henry Mercado was at the end of that timeline, while he, Purcell, was somewhere in the middle, and Vivian was just beginning her life and her career as a photojournalist. By now, she'd figured out that it wasn't easy or glamorous, but it *was* exciting and interesting. Unfortunately, the exciting parts were dangerous and the interesting parts had nothing to do with the job. And it was often lonely.

He didn't know if Henry had ever had this conversation with Vivian, and he would advise against it in any case. Frank Purcell was not going to give her The Lecture. She'd figure it out on her own. Meanwhile, Vivian thought they had something together, and they did, but the future was something else. He'd had a few Vivians in his life, and the odds were that Vivian would have a few more Frank Purcells in her life, and maybe one or two more Henry Mercados.

Or Ethiopia would join them together forever, one way or the other.

"Frank?"

He looked at Henry.

"Are you mentally attending?"

"No."

Mercado laughed. "Learn to lie a bit, old man. You're offensive when you don't."

"I'm learning from a master, Henry."

"That you are." He said to Purcell, "I was just telling Vivian the terms of her employment. All expenses paid, but no pay."

"Right. Money is tight at the Vatican."

Henry laughed, then informed him, "We try to keep the newspaper self-sufficient."

"Sell tobacco ads."

"The assignment is for one month." He looked at both of them and said, "That should be enough time... one way or the other."

Neither Purcell nor Vivian replied.

Mercado said, "I have a contract for each of you to sign."

Purcell informed him, "I stopped signing contracts in bars years ago."

Mercado laughed. "They're in my office, old man. Not here." He let them know, "Anything you write— or photograph—becomes the exclusive property of *L'Osservatore Romano*."

"Who gets to keep the Holy Grail?"

"We will see."

The waiter brought another round along with a plate of canapés. Main course.

Mercado announced, "By the way, I've informed the Vatican, by letter, of the death of Father Giuseppe Armano of Berini, Sicily, with copies of my letter to several Vatican offices, which is what one does in a bureaucracy, and a copy to the Ministry of War because the deceased was in the army serving the fatherland in Ethiopia."

Purcell asked, "Have you had a response?"

"No."

Vivian asked, "Did you relate the circumstances of his death?"

"Yes, of course, but I neglected to mention the black monastery or the Holy Grail."

Purcell asked, "Did you use our names in the letter?"

"I did." He explained, "I didn't want them thinking I was hallucinating at the sulphur baths."

Purcell said, "We'd like to see a copy of the letter."

Mercado took a photostated page out of his pocket and handed it to Purcell. Purcell read it and saw it was a fairly straightforward account of what had happened that evening, though Father Armano's tale had been condensed to a few lines about his capture by Ethiopian forces—though he'd actually been captured by Coptic monks—and his forty-year imprisonment in a Royal Army fortress. Purcell noticed, too, that Henry had not mentioned the nude bathing.

He passed the letter to Vivian and said to Mercado, "I would think someone would have replied to this."

"Communication with the Vatican is usually one-way. Same with government ministries."

"Yes, but they'd want more information."

"Not necessarily."

"How about a thank-you?"

"A good deed is its own reward." He popped a canapé in his mouth, then said, "I wasn't actually sure whom to notify, so I copied six Vatican offices, and I admit I am a bit surprised myself that no one from the Vatican has gotten back to me—though someone else did."

"Who?"

"The order of Saint Francis. And they have no one in their files or records by the name of Giuseppe Armano of Berini, Sicily."

Vivian looked up from Mercado's letter.

Purcell asked him, "What do you make of that?"

"I'm not sure. Certainly Father Armano existed. We saw him. Or we saw someone."

Vivian said, "A man lying on his deathbed does not make up a lie about who he is."

Mercado agreed and said, "It gets curiouser." He continued, "I called the Franciscans in Assisi to follow up and someone there said they'd get back to me, though they haven't. Then I tried the Ministry of War, and some maggiore informed me that the 1935 war in Ethiopia was not his most pressing problem. He did say, however, that he'd make internal inquiries."

Purcell thought about all this, then said to Mercado, "Things, I'm sure, move slowly in the Vatican bureaucracy, but you may hear back soon."

"What is the date of my letter?"

Vivian looked at it and said, "Ten November."

"Which," Mercado said, "is less than a week after I arrived in Rome from London, and which is why, as you'll see in the letter, I didn't apologize for any delay in reporting this death to whomever I thought were the proper authorities."

Purcell reminded him, "You told me you didn't notify the Vatican."

"I lied." He smiled. "I didn't like you then." He added, "Now we are friends and partners in this great adventure and we have sealed our covenant with blood. Well...cheap wine. And we are, as they say, putting all our cards on the table."

Purcell thought Henry was still holding a card or two. He asked, "What do you think is actually going on?"

Mercado drained his gin and tonic and replied, "Well, obviously, something is going on. Someone, perhaps in the Vatican, instructed the Franciscans to post a reply, and further instructed them to say there is no Father Armano."

"Why?"

"Your guess is as good as mine, old man."

Vivian said, "The Vatican knows who Father Armano is, and they know what Father Armano was doing in Ethiopia. And now they're wondering how much we know."

"That's very astute, Vivian. And they will continue to wonder how much we know—what Father Armano's last words were to us."

Again Purcell thought about this. He wasn't a believer in grand conspiracies or a fan of those who did believe in them. But Father Armano had, in effect, spelled out a Vatican conspiracy to steal the Holy Grail. It would follow, then, that there still existed a conspiracy of silence regarding what seemed to be an ongoing Vatican mission to relieve the Coptic Church of their Holy Grail.

Vivian asked Mercado, "Will you do any further follow-up?"

"That would not be a wise thing to do."

She nodded.

Purcell commented, "It would have been wiser for someone in the Vatican to just say, 'Thank you, we will notify next of kin, and God bless you.'"

Mercado nodded. "That would have been the wise thing for them to do. But I suspect my letter caused some worry and they decided to...what is the expression? Stonewall it."

Purcell also pointed out, "Maybe you shouldn't have sent the letter at all."

"I thought about that. About not tipping my hand. But then the job in Rome came up with *L'Osservatore Romano*, and I thought ahead to writing about this, so I couldn't very well reveal this story in an article months or years later without having to explain why I'd kept this information to myself."

Purcell suggested, "Your letter to the Vatican may actually be the reason you're working in and for the Vatican."

Mercado looked at Purcell. "Interesting."

"And," Purcell pointed out, "why Vivian and I are now working for the Vatican."

"Actually, you're working for the Vatican newspaper, Frank, but I won't split hairs with you."

Vivian was taking this all in, then said to Mercado, "You did the right thing, Henry, by reporting Father Armano's death."

"Yes, you can never do wrong by doing right." He suggested, "Let's put conspiracy aside and think this could be typical bureaucratic indifference, coupled with bad record-keeping in all departments." He added, "The Italians, like the Germans, would just as soon not be reminded of the 1930s and '40s."

Purcell replied, "That could explain the indifference of the Ministry of War. But not the Vatican."

Mercado did not reply.

Vivian said, "Father Armano was real, and we are going to make sure that his suffering and death are acknowledged by the people who sent him to war."

Mercado looked at her, and it seemed to Purcell that Henry was just noticing the change in his former playmate.

Vivian continued, "We will go to Berini and find his family."

"That is the plan," Mercado agreed, and ordered another round.

Vivian had two full glasses of red wine in front of her, and Purcell was still working on his last Jack Daniel's, and he wondered where Henry put all that gin.

They spoke awhile about the timing of their trip to Berini, then Ethiopia, and how they'd approach the problem of covering their assignments while actually trying to find the black monastery, which was in Getachu territory.

Vivian surprised everyone and herself by saying, "I hope Getachu gets arrested and shot before we get there."

Mercado informed her, "Men like that do not get eaten by the revolution. They do the eating."

Vivian nodded, then said, "Maybe we should not be asking Colonel Gann to come with us."

Mercado suggested, "Let's discuss that further when we see him."

Vivian got up to use the ladies' room and Purcell said to Mercado, "As I mentioned to you in your office, these entry visas are not necessarily exit visas."

"And as I said to you, save your paranoia for Ethiopia."

"I'm practicing."

Mercado changed the subject and said, "She looks very happy."

Purcell did not respond.

"I told you, old man, I'm over it, and I'm over the anger as well." He asked, "Can't you tell?"

"We don't need to have this conversation."

"It's not about us, Frank. And it's not even about her. It's about our . . . assignment."

"We all understand that. That's why we're here."

"I'd like us to be truly friends."

"How about close colleagues?"

"I didn't steal her from you, old boy. You stole her from me."

"You sound angry."

"Put yourself in my shoes. I'm hanging there from a fucking pole, and what do I see? *Fucking*."

"You're drunk, Henry."

"I am . . . I apologize."

"Accepted." Purcell stood. "And if you mention the name Jean one more time, I am going to clock you."

"What does that mean?"

"You don't want to find out."

Mercado stood unsteadily and offered his hand to Purcell. Purcell saw Vivian coming back, so he took Mercado's hand.

Vivian asked, "Are we leaving?"

"We are."

She said to Henry, "We had a long drive from Florence. Thank you for drinks."

"Thank our newspaper."

She looked at him and suggested, "You should turn in."

He leaned toward her, she hesitated, then they did an air kiss on both cheeks. "Buona notte, signorina."

"Buona notte."

Purcell took Vivian's arm and they left.

As the doorman signaled for a taxi, Vivian said, "I've never seen him so drunk."

Purcell did not respond.

She glanced at Purcell. "Well...I only knew him a few months."

The taxi came and they got in. Purcell said, "Hotel Forum."

They stayed quiet on the ride to the hotel, then Vivian said, "If I hadn't met him, I wouldn't have met you."

Purcell lit a cigarette.

She took his hand. "Did something happen when I was gone?"

"No."

"I love you."

He took his hand out of hers and put his arm around

her shoulders. He said to her, "You once told me to go
to hell."

"I was so angry at you." She mimicked him: "I think
I could have done this on my own. Can we save this for
the Hilton bar?" She said, "Bastard."

He drew her closer and she put her head on his
shoulder. She said, "It was my idea to invite you along."

"I thought it was God's plan."

"It was. I just went along with it."

"What's the rest of the plan?"

The taxi stopped. "Forum."

She said, "To get upstairs and get our clothes off."

"Good plan."

Chapter 25

The golden domes and crosses of the churches caught the first rays of the rising sun, and Purcell watched the dawn spreading over the city.

He looked back at Vivian lying naked in the bed, her skin as white as the sheets, making her appear wraithlike.

"Come to bed, Frank."

He sat at the edge of the bed and she ran her hand over his back. She said, "You were talking in your sleep."

"Sorry."

She sat up and said, "I dreamt that we were at the mineral baths, and we were swimming, and we made love in the water."

Purcell wondered where Henry was, but he didn't ask.

"And then we went back to the Jeep, and Father Armano was there...and we were still naked..."

"Sounds like a Catholic schoolgirl's nightmare."

She laughed, then stayed silent awhile. "Why did he have that skull?"

"I don't know."

"Was it a warning?"

"I'm not good at symbolism, Vivian."

"What did *you* dream about?"

"Henry, in the Vatican archives. A nightmare."

"Tell me."

"Henry has solved the mystery of how the Holy Grail wound up in Ethiopia."

"What difference does it make?"

"That was my point." He lay down beside her and asked, "Do you believe that the actual Holy Grail is sitting in a black monastery in Ethiopia?"

"I told you I believe what Father Armano said to us. I believe that God led us to him, and him to us." She also told him, "I believe that if we find the Grail, and if we believe in it, it will reveal itself to us. If we do not believe in it, it will not be real to us." She made him understand, "It's not the Grail by itself—it is our faith that heals us."

This sounded to Purcell almost as complex as the doctrine of the Trinity, but he understood what she was saying. "All right...but do you believe that we should risk our lives to find it?"

She stayed silent a moment, then replied, "If this is God's will...then it doesn't matter what happens to us—it only matters that we try."

Purcell glanced at her. He wondered if Mercado had told her what he'd said to him.

She asked, "Do you believe in this, Frank?"

"Henry says I do."

"And you say...?"

"Depends on the day."

"Then you shouldn't be going to Ethiopia."

"I am going."

"Go for the right reasons."

"Right."

She moved closer to him and said, "There is another miracle. Us."

"That's one I believe in." He asked her, "Would you like breakfast in bed?"

"It's early for breakfast."

"It's two hours to get room service. You're not in Switzerland anymore."

She laughed and said, "I want you to fill the tub and make love to me in the water. That's what I wanted you to do at the spa."

"I didn't know that."

"You did."

"Never crossed my mind."

"Do you think I take my clothes off in front of any man I just met?"

In fact, he'd thought that she and Henry were just being worldly and sophisticated, and maybe trying to shock his American sensibilities.

"Frank?"

"I thought that was a rhetorical question." He got out of bed. "I'll run the water. You call for coffee."

He filled the tub and she came into the bathroom and they got into the steamy water together, facing each other. They moved closer, embraced, and kissed. She pressed her breasts against his chest, then rose up and came down on his erect penis. She gyrated her pelvis as she clung to him in the warm water, and they climaxed together.

They sat at opposite ends of the tub, and Vivian lay back with her eyes closed, breathing in the misty air.

He thought she'd fallen asleep, but she said softly,

"It doesn't matter what happens, as long as it happens to us together."

"I believe that...but I want to make sure we're not choosing death over life."

"We are choosing eternal life." She added, "As Saint Peter did."

"Right...but I'm not a martyr, and neither are you. We're journalists."

She laughed. "Journalists go to hell."

"Probably...and we're not saints either, Vivian."

"Speak for yourself."

They sat back in the water with their eyes closed, and Purcell drifted off into a pleasant sleep. He thought he heard Vivian saying, "Take this cup and drink of it, for this is my blood."

"Frank?"

He opened his eyes.

Vivian stood over him in a robe, holding a cup. "Have some coffee."

He took the cup and drank it.

Chapter 26

The Hassler Hotel sat high above the Spanish Steps, offering a panoramic view of Rome and the Vatican. It was Saturday, and the elegant rooftop restaurant was filled with well-heeled tourists, businesspeople, and celeb types, but Mercado had gotten them a choice table by the window.

Purcell had no doubt that Signore Mercado used his connection to *L'Osservatore Romano* all over town. No one actually *read* the paper, of course, but it was widely quoted over the wire, and its name had cachet, especially in Rome.

Henry Mercado and Colonel Sir Edmund Gann had arrived together from the Excelsior, and Gann, thin to begin with, looked like a man who'd been on starvation rations for a few months, which he had, and he hadn't put on any weight in London. His tweed suit hung loosely and his skin had a prison pallor. As Purcell knew from firsthand experience, it took a while before the body got used to food again.

Gann's eyes, however, were bright and alert, and his demeanor hadn't changed much. His mind had stayed healthy in prison, and his body just needed a few Italian meals. Then back to Ethiopia for another round with fate. Purcell wondered again what was driving Colonel Gann.

Purcell noticed that Henry had slipped into his British accent to make the colonel feel at home away from home, and Colonel Gann had now become Sir Edmund.

Mercado informed them that he'd briefed Sir Edmund over a few drinks at the Excelsior, but Purcell wasn't sure how detailed that briefing had been. Sir Edmund, however, did seem to know that Miss Smith was now with Mr. Purcell, and that Mr. Mercado was okay with that—so there'd be no unpleasantness at dinner.

Cocktails arrived at the table, and Henry toasted, "To being alive and being together again."

Vivian added, "And thanks to Sir Edmund for keeping us alive."

They touched glasses and Sir Edmund said modestly, "Trying to save my own skin, actually, and I was glad for the company—and your assistance."

Purcell was sure that Gann didn't want to talk about his three months in an Ethiopian prison, so Purcell picked another unhappy subject. "I assume you heard about Prince Joshua."

"I did."

Gann didn't seem to want to talk about that either, so they perused the menu. Purcell remembered that he was buying, and the prices, in lire, looked like telephone numbers. But he supposed he owed this to Colonel Gann for saving their lives, and he owed it to Henry for stealing his girlfriend.

The waiter came and they ordered. Henry found the same amarone at double the price of the Forum.

Mercado said to Vivian and Purcell, "I've told Sir

Edmund that we have our visas, and I took the liberty
of telling him that this black monastery may be of interest to us when we return."

Gann reminded Purcell, "Last time we discussed
this—in that ravine—I believe you said you were never
going back."

"I've changed my mind." He added, "Actually,
we've all *lost* our minds."

Colonel Gann flashed his toothy smile. He thought
a moment, then replied, "I grew up with King Arthur
and his Knights of the Round Table, Mr. Purcell. And
when I was a boy, my greatest dream was to join in a
quest to find the Holy Grail."

"So you're crazy, too."

Everyone laughed, and Gann continued, "Now, of
course, I, like most rational men, do not believe any
of this...but it is a wonderful story—it is the story of
our unending search for something good and beautiful...which is why it appeals to us...to our hearts
and our souls. And I loved those stories of Arthur and
his knights, and they affected me deeply. And then I
grew up."

Everyone stayed silent, so Gann continued, "But
those stories have stayed with me...and they are still
part of me."

Again no one spoke, then Mercado confessed,
"I believe there *was* a King Arthur, and a Camelot. I also
believe there was a round table of virtuous knights, and
I believe they sought the Holy Grail." He hesitated, then
continued, "I also believe that Perceval and Gauvain
found the Grail Castle in Glastonbury and sailed off into
a fog with the Grail and returned it to Jerusalem."

Again, no one spoke, then Gann said, "I don't seem to remember the Jerusalem bit."

Mercado said, "That's my theory."

"Yes . . . well, I suppose that's possible."

Mercado took the opportunity to explain to Gann, and also to Vivian, how the Holy Grail was then taken from Jerusalem to Egypt, then to Ethiopia, a half step ahead of the armies of Islam.

Both Gann and Vivian seemed to agree that Henry's scholarship was impressive and logical.

Purcell said to Gann, "More importantly, we have been told by this Father Armano, who Getachu was asking us about, that the Grail—or something called the Holy Grail—is sitting in this black monastery."

"I see."

"So we're going back to Ethiopia to see who's crazier—us or Father Armano."

Gann said, "There is a thin line, Mr. Purcell, between bravery and insanity."

"No argument there."

"Some people are content to accept things on faith. Others are driven to extraordinary efforts to find and see the thing they want to believe in. Vide et crede. See and believe. And that is where bravery and insanity become one."

"And that's when you buy a ticket to Ethiopia."

Gann smiled and suggested to his dining companions, "And while you are there looking about for the Holy Grail, you might as well try to get a look at the Ark of the Covenant."

"Is that there too?"

"Apparently, but not in the black monastery. It's in the ancient ruins of Axum."

Purcell asked Mercado, "Have you heard of that?"

"I have."

It seemed to Purcell that Ethiopia had at least two amazing biblical relics, making him start to wonder about the first one. He asked Gann, "Has Noah's Ark also shown up there?"

Again Gann smiled, then said, "Not that I'm aware of. But I have seen the resting place of the Ark of the Covenant."

Vivian encouraged him to tell them about it, and Purcell wished she hadn't.

Gann explained, "The Ark of the Covenant is hidden in a small Coptic chapel in Axum, and it is guarded by one monk, a man named Abba who is called the Atang—the Keeper of the Ark." He further explained, "This is the most solemn position in the Ethiopian Orthodox Church—the Coptic Church. Abba can never leave the grounds of the chapel and he will hold this position of Atang until he dies."

Vivian asked, "And you've seen this man?"

"And I've spoken to him." He added, "He is the only living person who has ever actually seen the Ark, but he has never opened this chest to see the stone tablets on which God gave Moses the Ten Commandments." Gann explained, "Abba told me that whoever opens the Ark will be struck dead."

Purcell inquired, "Did the Ark of the Covenant arrive in Ethiopia along with the Holy Grail?"

Gann smiled again and replied, "No, the time and the circumstances were quite different." He explained,

"As you know, the Queen of Sheba, who ruled in Axum three thousand years ago, went to Jerusalem and was impregnated by King Solomon. She returned to Axum and bore a child whom she named Menelik, and this was the beginning of the Solomonic dynasty that has ruled Ethiopia until...well, a few months ago." He continued, "When Menelik was a young man, he traveled to Jerusalem to meet his father. Menelik stayed for three years, and when he left, Solomon ordered that the Ark of the Covenant accompany his son to protect him. Menelik brought the Ark to a monastery called Tana Kirkos on the eastern shore of Lake Tana, which feeds its waters into the Blue Nile. The monastery is still there, guarded by monks, and I have actually been a guest at this monastery."

Purcell inquired, "Did the monks insist that you stay forever?"

"Sorry?"

"Please go on."

Gann went on, "After Menelik died, the new emperor, Ezana, sent for the Ark, and it was brought to Axum, where it remains to this day."

Purcell asked, "Why hasn't the Marxist government grabbed it?"

"Interesting question." Gann explained, "They've appropriated some church property, but there is a backlash growing among the Coptic faithful, so the government has backed off a bit." He added, "The stupid Marxists have actually stirred a religious revival amongst the peasants."

Purcell nodded. That wasn't what happened in Russia when the Communists crushed the churches, but it was interesting that it was happening in Ethiopia. More importantly, if the Ark of the Covenant was safe for the time being, then maybe the black monastery and the Holy Grail were also safe for now—at least until the team from *L'Osservatore Romano* arrived.

Mercado had come to a similar conclusion and said, "The black monastery is also on borrowed time."

Gann said, "The new government is trying to consolidate its power, and it doesn't wish to anger the masses whom it purports to represent. But as you say, it's only a matter of time before they resume their confiscation of church property. For now, they are satisfied with executing the royal family and the rasses, and appropriating their palaces and wealth."

Purcell asked Gann, "Are you still working for the Royalists?"

Gann hesitated, then replied, "I am in contact with counterrevolutionary elements here in Rome, in London, and in Cairo and Ethiopia."

"How's that counterrevolution looking?"

Gann replied, "Not very good at the moment. But we are hopeful."

Their antipasto arrived and Mercado picked at his food, then said, "I am convinced that the Holy Grail could eventually wind up in the hands of the Marxist government. And if that happens, the Grail may not be sold to the highest bidder—it may be destroyed."

Purcell looked at Mercado. It was inevitable, he thought, that Henry, or one of them, would find a justification for stealing the Grail from the monastery—for its own protection, of course. And, in truth, Henry had a point.

Mercado went on, "After three thousand years of relative stability under the Solomonic dynasty, the whole country is in chaos." He pressed his point. "And if the black monastery is looted by revolutionary troops— soldiers of Getachu, for instance—the Grail is in jeopardy. Even if it is sold to the highest bidder, that bidder could very well be someone like the Saudi royal family, who have billions to spend on whatever they fancy." He concluded, "I don't want the Holy Grail to wind up in Mecca."

Purcell pointed out, "You've done a quantum leap, Henry."

"Perhaps, but you see what I'm getting at."

"You're making a case for why we should relieve the Coptic monks of their property."

"I am trying to protect the Grail."

Purcell inquired, "And where do you think it would be safe?"

"The Vatican, of course."

"I thought you might say that."

Everyone got a small laugh from that.

Vivian said, "I agree with Henry."

Gann, too, said, "I agree that you—we—need to get this relic out of Ethiopia."

Purcell, too, agreed, but he advised, "Not permanently. Just until the times in Ethiopia grow less evil."

Mercado pointed out, "The Grail has been taken on long journeys over the last two thousand years to safeguard it from evil, and I believe it has fallen to us to do that again."

Purcell said, "So we are all agreed that if we find the black monastery and the Holy Grail, we are morally justified in stealing the Grail for its own protection."

Everyone nodded.

Colonel Gann looked at Mercado, Purcell, and Vivian and said, "I should tell you that I am not a believer in this relic as the true cup that Christ used at the Last Supper, and neither do I believe that the Ark of the Covenant and the Ten Commandments are in a hidden chapel in Axum. But these artifacts are central to the Coptic Church in Ethiopia, as well as in Egypt." He continued, "Egypt may never be Christian again, but Ethiopia will be. And it is important that all the religious objects that are in jeopardy be safeguarded for the time when the Marxists are overthrown and the emperor is restored to the throne."

Purcell thought that if by some miracle they actually got hold of the Holy Grail and got it to the Vatican— for safekeeping—it wouldn't get out of there until the second coming of Christ. But that wasn't his problem.

Gann asked, "Can you tell me a bit more about this Father Armano?"

Mercado looked at Purcell and Vivian, who both nodded. Mercado said to Gann, "I'm sure you know of the Italian spa that Getachu was talking about."

"I do indeed." He told them, "You shouldn't have spent the night there." Gann explained, "The Gallas fancy the place. I don't think they bathe there—or bathe at all—but there is fresh water for their horses and for themselves." He advised, "It is a place to avoid."

Purcell commented, "We had an old guidebook."

Mercado continued, "Well, we put up for the night— had a quick wash—and when we returned to our Jeep, we came upon Father Armano, who was wounded and dying."

"And I'm sure he said more to you before he died than you told Getachu."

"Correct." Mercado suggested that Vivian relate the story, which she did.

Gann listened attentively, nodding now and then, and when Vivian had finished, he said, "Remarkable. And do you believe this man's story about the Lance of Longinus hanging in thin air, dripping blood? Or that this blood healed the priest?"

Vivian said she did, as did Mercado.

She also said, "We think it was more than chance that we and Father Armano arrived at the same place at the same time. And now you tell us that the Gallas are usually there, but they weren't that night." She concluded, "We think it was a miracle."

Colonel Gann nodded politely.

Vivian added, "And it was an eerie coincidence, I think, that Father Armano and Henry were at the same battle of Mount Aradam in 1935."

"Yes...striking coincidence." He looked at Purcell.

Purcell said, "I believe the substance of Father Armano's story, but I'm a bit skeptical about the Lance of Longinus hanging in thin air, or about the Holy Grail healing Father Armano."

Gann replied, "Yes...that seems a bit unnatural, doesn't it? But we agree that this relic is probably in the black monastery."

Everyone agreed.

Gann asked, "Do you have any specific operational plans to find this monastery?"

Mercado replied, "We hoped you could help us with that."

"I believe I can." He informed them, "I have a general idea where it is."

"So do we," said Purcell, "based on what Father Armano said about his army patrol from Lake Tana to the black monastery, then being taken by foot to the Royalist fortress, then his escape forty years later and his walk that night to the Italian spa." He suggested, "Maybe we could triangulate all of that if we had a good map."

Gann nodded again. "It's a starting point." He advised, "You ought to begin with aerial reconnaissance if you can."

Purcell informed him, "We might have access to a light plane in Addis."

"Good. That will save you time and effort, and help keep you out of the hands of the Gallas—or Getachu."

Mercado told Gann, "There are possibly some good Italian Army maps in the Ethiopian College in Vatican City."

"Excellent. I'd like to take a look at them."

"I'm working on that."

Gann also informed them, "There is a Falasha village in the vicinity, as I mentioned to Mr. Purcell at Getachu's parade ground. These Jews may be a key to locating the black monastery." He explained, "There seems to be some . . . ancient relationship there."

Vivian asked, "What is that relationship?"

Gann further explained, "The royal family, of course, has Jewish blood from Solomon, and they are proud of that. Proud, too, that they, through the

Coptic Church, are the keepers of the Ark of the Covenant, which presumably they are keeping safe for the Jews. The Jews there, the Falashas, see Jesus as a great Jewish prophet and they revere him, and presumably they also believe in the Holy Grail—the kiddush cup of Jesus's last Passover meal." He asked his companions, "Do you see the connection?"

Everyone nodded.

Gann continued, "Also, it would appear that the only connection the black monastery has with the outside world is through this Falasha village. Shoan."

Purcell inquired, "What sort of connection?"

Gann replied, "A spiritual connection. But also a practical connection. Food, medical supplies—"

"They have the Holy Grail," Purcell reminded him. "Cures what ails you."

"Yes...well...good point." He continued, "The monastery, like most monasteries, is self-sufficient, but even a monk needs new underwear now and then. Sandals and candles. And a bit of wine."

Purcell asked, "How do you know all this?"

"We can discuss that in Ethiopia."

"All right." Purcell said, "It would seem, then, that the Falashas know how to find the black monastery."

Gann replied, "My understanding is that there is a meeting place somewhere between the monastery and the village."

Purcell nodded. He had this feeling, as he'd had in Ethiopia, that he'd fallen through the rabbit hole. He said to Mercado, "This is a whole chapter in our book, Henry. Jews for Jesus."

Gann changed the subject. "Have you thought

about how you will actually get into this walled monastery if you find it?"

Purcell admitted, "We haven't thought that far ahead—about pulling off a heist in a monastery filled with club-wielding monks."

Gann nodded. "Well...we can discuss that if or when the time comes."

"Right." But the more Purcell thought about all this, the more he believed that time might never come. More likely, they'd wind up in Getachu's camp again, or if they were really unlucky, they'd meet up with the Gallas. Henry and Vivian, however, believed they were chosen to find the Holy Grail, and that God would watch over them. As for himself, he half believed half of that.

Purcell asked Gann, "If you can get back into Ethiopia, will you actually come with us to the monastery?"

"Am I invited?"

Vivian cautioned, "This would be more dangerous for you than for us." She asked, "And how would you get into the country?"

Gann reminded them, "I am officially a fugitive from Ethiopian justice, so I will not be applying for a return visa. I will acquire another identity and fly in from Cairo on a commercial flight." He informed them, "I have access to everything I need in regard to a passport and a forged visa."

Vivian said, "Sounds risky."

"Not too." He explained, "The security people at Addis airport are totally inept—except the ones who are corrupt." He informed them, "That was how I flew in last time. I was Charles Lawson then, a

Canadian citizen, and within a few days I was Colonel Sir Edmund Gann again, up north with Prince Joshua."

Vivian pointed out, "They know what you look like now."

"You, Miss Smith, will not know what I look like when I see you in Ethiopia."

Purcell inquired, "What is your motivation, Colonel, in risking your life?"

"I believe we had this discussion on a hilltop." He informed everyone, "I *am* being well paid by the Ethie expat community, but even if I weren't, I'd do this because I believe in it."

"And what is it that you believe in?"

"The restoration of the monarchy and the liberation of the Ethiopian people from Communism, tyranny, and terror."

"Do you get paid for trying? Or only for success?"

"Both." He admitted, "The princely payment comes when the emperor or his successor is back on the throne."

"Do you get a palace?"

"I get the satisfaction of a job well done—and the honor of having changed history."

Vivian asked Gann, "Will you be coming to Sicily with us?"

"I'm afraid not. As I explained to Mr. Mercado earlier, I have related business here in Rome."

Mercado informed Gann, "Neither the Vatican nor the Ministry of War nor the Franciscans seem to have any record of Father Giuseppe Armano, which is why we need to go to Berini—to establish his existence. And also to notify next of kin of his fate."

Gann thought about that, then replied, "Well, I suppose his name could have been lost." He added, "But if the Vatican *wants* his name lost, then they've been to Berini before you."

That thought had briefly crossed Purcell's mind, but it seemed outlandish to believe that Father Giuseppe Armano was disappearing into an Orwellian black hole. But maybe not so outlandish. They'd find out in Berini.

Chapter 27

Mercado said, "In 1868, the Ethiopian emperor Theodore wrote a letter to Queen Victoria. She did not respond, and Theodore, to avenge the insult, imprisoned a number of British nationals, including the consul. The British then landed an expeditionary force on the African coast and marched on Ethiopia to rescue these people."

Colonel Gann said, half jokingly, "Now we've got to pay the bloody beggars to get her majesty's subjects released."

Purcell didn't know if he was actually back in the reading room of the Vatican Library, or if this was a recurring nightmare. Vivian, however, seemed fascinated by the library and impressed with all the documents that Henry had assembled.

Mercado had assured Purcell that this would be a quick visit, to wrap up his background briefing. Next stop was the Ethiopian College, and if they weren't kicked out again, he, Mercado, and Gann had been allowed one hour in the college library. Vivian, because of her gender, was not welcome.

Mercado continued, "The British Expeditionary Force was led by Sir Robert Napier, and they advanced on the new Ethiopian capital of Magdala. Theodore was beaten in battle and committed suicide on Easter Day 1868."

Purcell glanced at his watch. Vivian had volunteered to stay in this room and read through Henry's notes. She'd also brought her camera with her, a brand-new Canon F-1, to begin her photographic documentation of their story, starting with this reading room, and ending, Purcell hoped, with cocktails in the papal reception hall, with everyone holding up the Holy Grail like it was the Stanley Cup.

Vivian saw Purcell smiling and took his picture.

Mercado continued, "Napier, in good imperial tradition, sacked the emperor's palace and the imperial library at Magdala, carrying off a trove of ancient documents. He took four hundred or so of the most promising of them back to England. He also took the ancient imperial crown that wound up in the British Museum."

Gann said, "I believe we gave it back."

"You did," said Mercado. "And now it's probably in the hands of the Marxists—or it's been sold or melted down for the gold and gems."

Purcell said, "We get the point, Henry."

Mercado continued, "Inside the rim of the crown is engraved, in Geez, the ancient language of Ethiopia, which remains the language of the Coptic Church, these words"—he glanced at his notes—"King of Kings, Conquering Lion of Judah, Descendant of the House of David, Keeper of the Ark of the Covenant, and Keeper of the Holy Vessel." Mercado looked at his audience and said, "We can assume that is the Holy Grail."

No one argued with that translation, but everyone knew that kings and emperors liked to give themselves titles. Theodore may have descended from the House of David, Purcell thought, but he wasn't the conquering

Lion of Judah on Easter Day 1868. Nor was he King of Kings. He was dead. As for keeper of the Ark of the Covenant and the Holy Grail, Purcell was sure that Theodore believed it, but that didn't make the relics real.

Mercado continued, "Napier, now Lord Napier of Magdala, sold some of the looted documents at auction, and a few of them found their way into the Vatican archives, and this"—he took a curled, yellowed parchment out of a velvet folio—"is one of them."

Mercado held up the parchment by a corner and said, "It is written in Geez, and I had one of the Ethiopian seminarians who can read Geez translate it for me."

Gann was looking closely at the parchment as though he could read it, but he said, "It's Geez to me."

Mercado smiled politely and replaced the parchment in its velvet folio. "The seminarian thought that based on the style of Geez used, and on the historical event described, this is from about the seventh century— about the time that Islam conquered Egypt."

Mercado referred to his notes and continued, "This parchment is unsigned, and the author is unknown, but it was probably written by a church scribe or monk and it is an account of a miraculous healing of a Prince Jacob who was near death from wounds sustained in battle with the Mohammadans, as they are called here, who had invaded from Egyptian Sudan. According to this account, Prince Jacob was carried to Axum to die, and was taken to the place—it doesn't say which place—where the Holy Vessel was kept. The abuna of Axum, the archbishop, gave this prince the last rites, then anointed him with the blood from the Holy Vessel, and Prince Jacob, because he was faithful to God, and because he loved Jesus, and also because he fought bravely against the Mohammadans, was healed of his wounds by the sacred blood of Christ, and he rose up and returned to battle." Mercado said, "Unfortunately, there is no actual mention of the Lance of Longinus."

Purcell thought there were other problems with that story. In fact, it sounded like propaganda to rally the troops and the citizens in time of war. But everyone understood that, so he didn't mention it.

Mercado, too, saw the story as a morale builder and possibly a bit of a stretch. He said, "This proves little, of course, but it does mention the Holy Grail being in Axum at this time, and it is one of the few early references to the Grail having the power to heal."

Vivian said, "The power to heal those who believe."

Mercado nodded at his former protégée, then said to everyone, "At some point after this time, with Axum being threatened by Islam, the Grail was taken to a safe place—or many safe places—and now we think we know where it is."

Mercado stayed silent a moment, then said, "Edward Gibbon, in his Decline and Fall of the Roman Empire, wrote, 'Encompassed on all sides by the enemies of their religion, the Ethiopians slept near a thousand years, forgetful of the world, by whom they were forgotten.'"

Mercado looked at his watch and said, "We will now go to the Ethiopian College."

Chapter 28

A short, squat Ethiopian monk met them in the antechamber and escorted them, without a word, to a second-floor library. The college appeared to still be closed for the long Christmas holiday, and they seemed to be the only people there.

A very large monk stood inside the entrance to the library, and the two monks exchanged a few words in what sounded like Amharic.

Purcell looked around the library, which was windowless and badly lit. Book-laden shelves extended up to the high ceiling, and long reading tables ran down the center of the room.

The short monk left, and the big one remained in the room. Apparently he wasn't leaving, so Mercado said something to him in Italian, and the monk replied in halting Italian.

Mercado informed Purcell and Gann, "He's staying."

Purcell asked, "Does it matter?"

"I suppose not." He said, "There's a map room here somewhere, and that's what we want to see."

Gann suggested, "Don't go right for it, old boy. We'll look around here a bit, then find the map room."

Mercado nodded and moved over to the shelved books and scanned the titles. Gann did the same, so Purcell took a look at the books. Most seemed to be in

Latin, some in Italian, and many in what looked like Amharic script.

Mercado said, "Here's a Bible in Geez."

Purcell's three minutes of pretending were up and he moved toward the far end of the long room, where there was a closed door, which he opened, expecting to be shouted at by the monk. But the monk didn't say anything, so Purcell entered the room, which was indeed the cartography room.

A long, marble-topped table sat in the center of the room, and hundreds of rolled maps sat stacked on deep shelves, each with a stringed tag attached. He looked at a tag that was handwritten in Italian, Latin, and Amharic.

He heard something behind him and turned to see the monk standing a few feet from him. Purcell asked, "Mind if I smoke?"

The monk did not reply.

Purcell moved along the shelves, looking at the hanging tags, though he couldn't read any of them.

Mercado and Gann joined him, and they seemed pleased to see all the maps. Mercado began immediately reading tags, and Gann said, "Here are the Italian Army maps." As he picked a few dust-covered maps off the shelf, Purcell unrolled them and laid them on the map table, weighting their corners with brass bars that had been stacked there for that purpose.

There didn't seem to be a card catalog, but Mercado soon figured out how the maps were grouped, and he took a few ancient maps, hand drawn on parchment and papyrus, and set them gently on the table.

The monk watched, but said nothing.

Gann was now sitting at the table, studying the unfurled army maps, and Purcell sat to his right and Mercado to his left. Sir Edmund was once again Colonel Gann.

Purcell saw that the army maps were color printed, with shades of green for vegetation, shades of brown for arid areas, and pale blue for water. The elevation lines were in dark brown, and the few roads were represented by black dotted lines. The symbols for other man-made objects were also in black, as were the grid lines and the latitudes and longitudes. The map legend and all the other writing was in Italian. Gann said, "We used these captured maps in '41, and map words are the extent of my Italian."

Gann pointed to a map and said, "This one is a 1:50,000 map of the east bank of Lake Tana. It was partially field checked by the Italian Army's map ordnance section that made it, but most of this map was compiled from aerial photographs. This map here is of the fortress city of Gondar and environs. It is a more accurate 1:25,000, and completely field checked. Everything else seems to be crude 1:100,000- and 1:250,000-scale maps, not field checked."

Purcell knew how to read aviation charts, but these were terrain maps, and unless you understood what everything meant, it was like looking at paint spills on graph paper.

Gann continued, "Most of Africa was accurately mapped by the colonial powers. Ethiopia, however, was not a European colony until the Italians invaded, and the Ethies themselves hadn't any idea how to make a map, or what use they were. Therefore, most of what exists is a result of the Italian Army's brief control of the country."

Mercado asked, "And nothing since then?"

Gann informed them, "The former Ethiopian government had a small cartography office, but they mostly reproduced Italian maps, and now and again they'd produce a city map or a road map, though never a proper field-checked terrain map." He added, "Both armies in the current civil war are using what we see here from 1935 until 1941."

Purcell pointed out, "I assume the black monastery hasn't been moved, so maybe these are better than nothing."

"Quite so."

Gann studied the maps closely, then unrolled a few more.

"Here. This is the area where we were, and this is the map I was using then." He ran his finger in a circle around a green-and-brown-shaded area. "This is the jungle valley where the spa is located, and this is the unimproved road by which you presumably arrived."

Purcell asked, "Where is the spa?"

"Not here, actually. Probably built after the map was done. But right here"—he pointed—"is where it is."

Gann bent over the map and said, "These are the hills where Prince Joshua set up his camp... These are the hills where Getachu's camp was located. And this is the high plains or plateau between the camps where... where the armies met."

Purcell stared at the map—the same one Gann had shown him—and that unpleasant day came back to him as it had just come back to Colonel Gann.

Purcell said to Mercado, "Puts me right there again, Henry. How about you?"

"Makes me wonder why we ever left."

They all got a laugh at that, and Gann continued his map recon. He glanced at the monk across the room, then joked, "Don't see the symbol for hidden black monastery."

Purcell asked, "Do you see anything that could be a fortress?" He reminded Gann, "Father Armano's prison for almost forty years."

"No . . . don't see any man-made structures . . ."

Mercado reminded everyone, "Father Armano walked through the night *from* this fortress *to* the spa."

"Yes . . . but what direction?"

Purcell said, "He mentioned something about Gondar to the north. And I'm assuming the fortress was in the jungle—the dark green stuff."

"Yes, possibly . . . here is something that would be a night's march to the spa . . ." He pointed to a small black square identified as "*incognita*"—unknown.

Gann surmised, "Probably seen from the air and put on the map, but never field checked to identify it."

Mercado said, "Could be the fortress. I don't see any other man-made structures in this jungle valley."

Gann agreed that *incognita* could be the fortress, but he advised, "The scale of this map is so large that even these hills, which we know are large from being there, look quite small."

In fact, Purcell thought, those hills had almost killed Henry.

The monk had moved and was now standing across the table, looking at them.

Gann said, "Don't assume he doesn't speak English."

Purcell said to Mercado, "Maybe this guy wants to back off."

Mercado said something to the monk, who moved a few feet away.

Purcell said softly, "The priest said he was taken *from* the black...place by the monks and handed over to soldiers of this Prince Theodore, who marched him to the fortress." He thought back to the spa and to Father Armano's dying words. "The priest didn't remark about the march, so maybe it was a day's march at most."

Mercado, too, was thinking about what Father Armano had said. "I don't know if we can make that assumption...I wish we'd known we were going to be looking for this place. I'd have asked him to be more specific."

Purcell replied, "We knew at some point, but there was a lot going on. He was dying."

Gann suggested, "Try to recall all that this man said. He may have given you a clue."

Purcell and Mercado thought about that, then Purcell suggested, "Let's back it up. The priest said his battalion had made camp on the eastern shore of Lake Tana." He pointed to the lake. "His patrol went out to find the place where the Gallas had ambushed the previous patrol. They found the ambush site...maybe the same day...then continued on to find the black walls and tower that the sergeant, Giovanni, said he'd seen on the previous patrol."

Mercado added, "The priest said this took several more days...Three? Four? And they were lost, so they could have wandered in circles."

Gann said, "I can tell you that you'd be good to make a kilometer an hour in this terrain. So if we assume a ten-hour-a-day march, from somewhere along this eastern bank of Lake Tana, we can reckon thirty kilometers in three days, perhaps, less if this patrol was moving cautiously, which I'm certain they did."

Gann took a notebook from his pocket and a pen, which caused the monk to say, "No!"

Gann said to Mercado, "Tell him I'm not going to mark his map."

Mercado spoke to the monk, and Gann measured the kilometers from the map legend on a piece of note-paper that he marked with his pen, then held the paper against the map and said, "This is ten K. But to find the ambush site, we would need to know where this man's battalion made camp along the lakeshore—which as you can see is about eighty kilometers long—then draw a ten-K radius from there, and somewhere along that radius would be the ambush site. But we don't know where on the lakeshore to start."

Mercado said, "And then they wandered around for several more days to find the black wall and tower—the monastery." Mercado said, "We've narrowed it down a bit, but that is still a lot of square kilometers of jungle to be walking through."

Gann said, "That is why aerial recon would be helpful."

They studied the terrain map and recomputed their numbers, based on different points along the shore of Lake Tana and different traveling times through the terrain, as well as trying to guess what Father Armano meant by "several days" from the ambush site to the black monastery. They then approached the problem the other way—from the fixed location of the fortress to the monastery, though Father Armano never said how long his march was from the monastery to the fortress. And what they thought was the fortress could be something else, though "*incognita*" was about five kilometers east of the spa—a night's march.

Mercado and Purcell tried to recall if Father Armano had said anything else that could be a clue, and Purcell pointed out to Mercado that the priest had spoken Italian and that Mercado and Vivian had translated, so Purcell may not have gotten the entire story, or gotten an accurate translation.

Mercado said, "Perhaps Vivian will recall some further details."

Purcell said to Gann, "This man did say something about a rock, a stream, and a tree."

"No rocks on this map, I'm afraid, and I'm not sure which of the million trees he was referring to, but here is a small, intermittent stream...and another here, and a larger one here, all flowing downhill to Lake Tana." He suggested, "Remember this when you are on the ground. But it's of no help here."

Purcell asked, "Where is this Falasha village?"

Gann replied, "Not on this map..." He pulled another map toward him and said, "Here, on the south adjoining map...the village of Shoan." He put the maps together and said, "About forty K west and south of the suspected fortress."

Purcell reminded Gann, "They might know the location of the monastery."

Gann replied, "They know where they meet the

monks. But they're not going to take us along for company."

They again looked at the maps, trying to transfer what little they knew to what was spread out in front of them.

Gann pointed out, "The Italian aerial cartographers saw this unknown structure, and noted it, but they apparently didn't see what we are looking for or they'd have noted that as well."

Mercado informed him, "Our friend said it was in a deep jungle valley, with trees that went right up to the walls."

"I see... Well, it could have been missed from the air."

Purcell added, "He said the area within the walls had trees, gardens, and I think a pond."

Gann nodded. "This whole area was photographed and transferred to a map, and the thing we are looking for was on one of those photographs, but the cartographers missed it when they made these maps." He further informed them, "Most aerial photography was done in black and white, so things—man-made and natural—are missed in black, white, and shades of gray that would be more apparent in color." He added, "What we're seeing here is what the cartographer thought he saw in black-and-white photographs, and there was little field checking. We can also assume the cartographers were a bit sloppy and perhaps overworked and under pressure to get these military maps to Il Duce's army."

Purcell said, "Maybe we'll have better luck when we fly over this area ourselves."

Gann agreed, but advised, "Don't do too much flying, old boy, or you'll attract attention." He asked, "Do
I understand that you have an aircraft and pilot?"

Purcell replied, "We're working on that." He confessed, "I'm the pilot."

"I see. Well, good luck."

"I thought you were coming with us."

"I will try my best."

Purcell said to Gann, "We are going to do this, Colonel. And we will find what we are looking for."

"I believe you will." He added, "That may be the
easy part."

Henry stood and moved to the antique maps, and
Purcell said, "Henry, you will not find what we're looking for there."

Gann agreed. "Those maps are more fantasy than
accurate representations of reality, old boy. Dragons
and all that."

Mercado ignored them and unrolled a few parchments on which were hand-colored maps of sorts,
showing lakes, mountains, and hand-drawn churches.
Mercado said, "This is written in Geez."

No one replied.

He said, "I think this one is showing Axum. I see
a crown, and here is a drawing of what looks like the
stone tablets of the Ten Commandments."

Purcell said, "Well, that proves it."

"And here, to the southeast of this lake that looks
like Tana...with the Blue Nile...is a drawing..." He
slid the map toward them and they saw a nice drawing of a golden cup, next to which was a black cross,
surrounded by well-drawn palm trees that Gann said

would be about a half kilometer tall if they were drawn to scale.

Purcell said, "We should have started with this map, Henry."

Gann suggested, "Offer this monk fellow ten pounds for it."

Mercado was not enjoying the jokes, and he said, "Well, this may not be very detailed or accurate, but it is significant that it shows . . . or possibly shows what we are looking for." He added, "Cross and cup. Monastery and Grail."

"We get it."

Gann said, "But it does show it southeast of Lake Tana . . . so that may actually be a clue on a real map, and on the ground."

The monk said something in Italian, and Mercado said, "Our hour is fini."

Chapter 29

They found Vivian sitting on a bench outside the Ethiopian College, and she informed them, "I was asked to leave the reading room."

Mercado seemed surprised. "Why?"

"No explanation except that the archive materials had been out too long, and the reading room was needed by others."

Purcell said to Mercado, "You have been abusing your library privileges, Henry."

"This is not funny."

Purcell pointed out, "You said we were done."

"We were, but..." He looked at Vivian. "Where is my notebook?"

"In my bag." She gave it to him.

Purcell said to Mercado, "If I were paranoid, I'd say you should not leave that notebook in your office."

Mercado nodded.

It was late afternoon, the sky was overcast, and Henry said he had a bottle of Strega in his office to lift their spirits.

On the way, Vivian asked, "How did you make out?"

Mercado replied, "We've narrowed it down."

Gann asked Mercado, "Is it possible to get back in there?"

"Another request is one too many."

Gann suggested, "If you contact the Ministry of War, they will have a complete set of army survey maps of Ethiopia." He also informed them, "If you know Father Armano's military unit, you should ask to see his unit logs to see where his battalion made camp on the shore of Lake Tana."

Mercado thought about that, then replied, "I will inquire about the maps. But we don't know Father Armano's army unit, and the War Ministry doesn't know Father Armano."

Vivian said, "Someone in Berini may have letters from him with a return military address."

"Good thinking," said Mercado.

Gann said, "There is a possibility, however, that these unit logs never made it back to Italy."

Purcell pointed out, "Even if they did, the Ministry of War's archives may not be open to us—or what we're looking for may no longer be there."

No one responded to that.

They continued their walk across the parkland of Vatican City. Purcell looked at Saint Peter's, rarely seen from the rear, and he realized it was much bigger than it appeared from its well-known façade. The basilica and the square with its encompassing colonnades was the public face of the Vatican. But there was more to this place. There were offices and archives, and there were people whose job it was to manage the money, to support charities, to stamp out heresy, to propagate the faith, and to put out the word of God and the word of the pope and the Sacred College of Cardinals—as Henry did at *L'Osservatore Romano*.

Purcell didn't think there were any great conspiracies being hatched behind the closed doors of all those offices—but he did think there was two thousand years of institutional memory that defined the Vatican and the papacy; there was an unspoken and unwritten understanding regarding what needed to be done.

Most times, he suspected, everyone was on the same page—the clergy, the hierarchy, and the bureaucracy who toiled here. But now and then there were quiet differences of opinion. And maybe that was what he was seeing now—assuming, of course, that the people here were on the same quest that he and his three companions were on.

Gann was saying, "If we can't get access to the military maps here, I know that the Italian Library in Addis has a collection of wartime maps." He added, "Problem is, the Provisional Revolutionary government may have confiscated all the maps as a security measure, or to issue to their fighting units in the field."

Purcell interjected, "One of the first places we need to find is the village of Shoan." He asked Gann, "Do you know how to get there?"

"I have been there." He continued before anyone could ask him about that. "As I said, finding the monastery may not be as difficult as we think, given what we know. The problem, as with any military objective, is to get inside the place, get what we want, then get out."

Purcell liked the way Gann thought. Military minds were generally clear, and geared to practical matters and problem solving. Lives depended on it. Vivian and Henry, on the other hand, were focused on the righteousness of their mission, with only passing thoughts about the logistics and the battle plan—like medieval Crusaders off to free the Holy Land. But, he supposed, the world needed those people too.

As for himself, he'd had enough of maps, archives, and religious experiences. He was ready to move.

They reached Mercado's office, and Henry produced the bottle of Strega, which he shared with his guests to warm them up. Regarding their trip to Sicily, he consulted his calendar and said, "The Italians have the most vacation days in Europe. Forty-two, I believe. The fourteenth looks good for me." He asked, "Is that good for everyone?"

Purcell and Vivian said it was, and Mercado asked Gann, "Are you sure you don't want to go to sunny Sicily?"

"I'm afraid I can't."

Mercado said, "I won't use the Vatican travel office, and I suggest we all use different travel agencies to book a flight to Palermo. We'll hire a car there and drive to Berini."

Purcell and Vivian agreed, and Henry poured more of the yellow liqueur into their water glasses.

Purcell said, "While we're making travel plans, I suggest we pick a date now to fly to Addis Ababa."

No one responded, and Purcell said, "As Colonel Gann would agree, we need to stop planning the invasion and we need to have a jump-off date."

Gann said, "I'm actually fixed to go on January twenty-fourth—or thereabouts."

"Good." Purcell suggested, "The *L'Osservatore Romano* team needs to go separately, in case there is a problem at the other end. I will go first—let's say

January eighteenth. If I telex all is well, Vivian will follow on January twentieth—"

"We're going together, Frank."

He ignored her and continued, "If you don't hear from me, take that as a sign that I may be indisposed." He said to Mercado, "You may have the most risk considering your prior conviction for consorting with an enemy of the Ethiopian people. But if I and Vivian are okay, you bring up the rear."

Gann agreed, "That is a safe insertion plan."

Purcell said, "Unless they're waiting for all of us to get there."

Mercado said, "If your paranoia has substance, Frank, then I should go first to see if there is a problem."

"Your offer is noted for the record." He added, "I leave on the eighteenth."

Gann informed them, "I have a number of safe houses in Addis. Where will you be staying?"

Purcell replied, "With all the other reporters at the Addis Hilton."

"Safety in numbers," said Gann.

"With the journalistic community, Colonel, it's more like dog eat dog."

Mercado reminded Purcell and Vivian, "Alitalia still has daily flights to Addis, and seats are not hard to come by. Same with rooms at the Addis Ababa Hilton. I will notify the newspaper and the travel office of our plans next week." He added, "Gives us time to think about this."

Purcell said, "There is nothing to think about."

Mercado nodded.

They discussed a few other operational details,

and in regard to their Berini trip on the fourteenth, Mercado consulted an Alitalia flight schedule and said to Purcell and Vivian, "Book the nine-sixteen A.M. Alitalia to Palermo. I'll meet you at the airport."

Mercado said he had work to do, and his three visitors left.

Gann said he wanted to wander around the seat of the papacy, and he wished them good day.

Purcell and Vivian exited Vatican City and walked along the Tiber.

Vivian said, "This has just become real."

"It gets even more real in Ethiopia."

Chapter 30

They landed in Palermo, rented a Fiat, and bought a road map of Sicily.

There were a few routes to Berini, which was in the mountains near the town of Corleone, and they decided to reverse the route that Father Armano had taken in 1935 from Alcamo to Palermo, though instead of a train, they drove the new highway to Alcamo. There, they took an increasingly bad road into the hills—the same road that the priest had undoubtedly walked forty years before with the other army conscripts who, like himself, were bound for Palermo, then Ethiopia. Father Armano, however, had taken a detour to Rome, and to the Vatican, before his fateful and fatal journey to Africa.

It was a sunny day and much warmer than Rome. The sky was deep blue and white clouds hung over the distant mountains. Lemon and orange groves covered the narrow valleys, and olive trees and vineyards rose up the terraced slopes. Clusters of umbrella pines shaded white stucco houses, and tall cedars stood sentry at the bases of the hills.

This, Purcell thought, was the last that Father Armano had seen of his native land, and he must have realized as he was walking to Alcamo with the other young men that he might never see it again.

Vivian said, "This is beautiful. Completely unspoiled."

Purcell noticed there was very little vehicular traffic, but there were a good number of donkeys and carts on the road, and a lot of people walking and biking. The villages, as expected, were picturesque—white stuccoed houses with red tile roofs, and church bell towers in even the smallest town. "They must pray a lot."

Mercado said, "I'm sure they're all in church every Sunday and holy day. And, of course, for weddings, funerals, baptisms, and such, not to mention Saturday confessions." He added, "They are a very simple, religious people and there are not many like them in Europe anymore."

Purcell suggested, "You should move here, Henry."

"After you, Frank."

Vivian said, "I can see having a summer place in Sicily."

Mercado reminded her, "You don't speak the dialect."

Purcell pointed out, "You both spoke to Father Armano."

Mercado explained, "He spoke standard Italian, a result I'm sure of his seminary training and his time in the army."

"Are we going to have trouble speaking to the citizens of Berini?"

"Sicilians understand standard Italian when they want to." He added, "The priest will understand my Italian. And the younger people as well, because of television and cinema."

"Then maybe we'll get some answers."

Mercado informed them, "Sicilians don't like to answer questions, especially from strangers."

"We're doing a nice story for *L'Osservatore Romano* on their native son."

"Doesn't matter. They are suspicious of the outside world."

"And with good reason."

Vivian suggested, "Use your charm, Henry."

Purcell said, "We may as well turn around now."

Mercado ignored that and said, "The key is the village priest."

They reached Corleone, consulted the road map and the signs, and headed southwest into the higher hills.

It would not have been too difficult, Purcell thought, to walk downhill to Alcamo. But it would not have been an easy journey home to Berini, on foot, though a soldier returning home would not think about that.

They had spotted a few classical Roman and Greek ruins along the way, and Mercado informed them, "The Carthaginians were also here, as well as the Normans, the armies of Islam, and a dozen other invaders." He further informed his audience, "Sicily was a prize in the ancient world, and now it is the land that time forgot—like Ethiopia."

"The world changes," Purcell agreed. "Wars have consequences."

"I have an English cousin who served with Montgomery, and he may have passed through here in '43."

"We'll keep an eye out for anyone with a family resemblance."

The village of Berini was strategically located at the top of a hill that rose above the valley, and the one-lane road hugged the side of the slope and wrapped around it like a corkscrew until it abruptly ended at a stone arch, which marked the entrance to the village.

Purcell drove through the arch and followed a narrow lane between whitewashed houses. The few pedestrians stood aside and eyed them curiously as they passed by.

A minute later they entered a small, sunlit piazza, and at its far end was a good-sized stone church, which according to the Vatican directory was San Anselmo. The parish priest, if the information was up to date, was Father Giorgio Rulli. There were no other priests listed.

On the right side of the square was a row of two-story stucco buildings, one of which had an orange awning and a sign that said, simply, "Taverna." On the other side of the piazza was a place called "Caffe," and next to that was a tabaccheria, a sort of corner candy store. That seemed to be the extent of the commercial establishments, and the other structures appeared to be residences and a village hall. A few miniature Fiats were parked around the perimeter of the piazza, but the main form of transportation seemed to be bicycles. Purcell noticed there were no donkeys.

The outdoor seating under the awning and umbrellas of the taverna and caffe was filled with people, and Purcell noted they were all male. He could also see that their full-sized Fiat had attracted some attention. It was a little past three o'clock and Mercado said, "This is the riposo—the traditional four-hour afternoon break."

Purcell inquired, "Break from what?"

Vivian suggested, "Park someplace."

"I'm looking for a parking meter."

"Wherever you stop the car is a parking place, Frank."

"Right."

He moved the Fiat slowly over the cobblestoned piazza and stopped a respectable distance from the church. They all got out and stretched. It was cooler here at the higher elevation, and the air smelled of woodsmoke.

They had been advised by one of Mercado's colleagues to dress modestly and in muted colors. The rural Sicilians, the colleague said, literally laugh at brightly colored clothing, the way most people would laugh at someone coming down the street in a clown outfit. Purcell and Mercado wore black trousers, white shirts, and dark sports jackets, and Vivian wore a black dress, a loose-fitting black sweater, and sensible shoes. She also had a black scarf to cover her head if they entered the church.

A few elderly men and women made their way up and down the steps of the church, and Mercado said to an old woman in a black dress, "Mi scusi, Signora," then slowly and distinctly asked her something.

She replied, pointed, and moved on, giving the strangers a backward glance and looking Vivian up and down. Mercado informed them that the rectory was behind the church and he led the way.

The rectory was a small stucco house set in a garden, and they went up the path to the door. They had discussed what they were going to say, and they'd agreed that Mercado would take the lead. There was a doorbell and Mercado rang it. They waited.

The door opened and a very young priest stood there and looked at them. "Si?"

Mercado inquired, "Padre Rulli?"

"Si."

Mercado introduced himself and his companions, and said they were from *L'Osservatore Romano*, then Purcell heard him say, "Padre Armano."

The priest didn't slam the door in their faces, but he seemed to hesitate, then invited them inside. He ushered them into a small, plain sitting room and indicated a narrow upholstered couch. They sat, and the priest sat opposite them on a high-backed chair.

The priest, as Purcell noted, was young, and also short of stature, though he had a presence about him. His nose looked like it could have its own mailing address, and his eyes were dark and intelligent. He had thin lips and an olive complexion, and the sum total of his appearance was handsome in an interesting way.

Purcell glanced around the room. A woodstove radiated heat, one floor lamp cast a dim light in the corner behind the priest's chair, and the crude plaster walls were adorned with colored prints of men with beards and women with veils. A white marble Jesus hung from an olivewood cross above the priest's chair.

This was obviously a small and poor country church in a poor parish, Purcell thought; a place where the priest answered his own door. This was not the Vatican.

Mercado said something to the priest, enunciating each word so the Sicilian priest would have no difficulty understanding.

The priest replied, "You may speak English if it is better than your Italian."

Mercado seemed surprised, then recovered and said, "Forgive us, Father, for not making an appointment—"

"My doorbell rings all day. It is the only doorbell in Berini. I am here."

"Yes...well, as I said, we are from *L'Osservatore Romano*. Signorina Smith is my photographer and Signore Purcell is my...assistant."

"I understand." He informed them, "I have taught myself English. From books and tapes. Why? It is the language of the world, as Latin once was. Someday..." He didn't complete his thought, but said, "So forgive me in advance if I do not understand, or if I mispronounce."

Mercado assured him, "Your English is perfect."

Father Rulli asked, "How may I be of assistance?"

Mercado replied, "My colleagues and I were in Ethiopia, in September, and while there we came across a priest who was dying—"

"Father Armano."

"Yes." He asked, "Have you been notified of his death?"

"I have."

"I see...When were you notified?"

"In November. Why do you ask?"

Purcell answered without answering, "We're writing a newspaper article on Father Armano, so we are collecting information."

"Yes, of course. But it is my understanding that you have all this information from the Vatican press office."

Purcell knew that the Vatican press office and *L'Osservatore Romano* were not one and the same, though sometimes they seemed to be. He glanced at Mercado.

Mercado said to Father Rulli, "I haven't had contact with the Vatican press office."

"They said they were in contact with *L'Osservatore Romano*."

"They may be ... but not me."

Father Rulli admitted, "I have no idea how these things work in Rome."

Purcell assured him, "Neither do we."

Father Rulli smiled. He then informed them, "But you do know about the steps toward Father Armano's beatification."

At first Purcell thought that the priest had mispronounced "beautification," and he was confused. Then he understood.

Mercado seemed dumbstruck.

Vivian asked, "What am I missing?"

Mercado told her, "Father Armano has been proposed for canonization—sainthood."

"Oh ..."

"Did you not know this?" asked the priest.

"We ... had heard ..."

"That is the purpose of your visit, is it not?"

"Yes ... well, we wanted to gather some background on his early life. His time in the army ... perhaps letters that he wrote to his family and friends."

Father Rulli informed them, "You could have saved yourselves the journey." He explained, "A delegation from the Vatican was here in November to let me know of Father Armano's death and his proposed canonization. As you know, if he is entered into the sainthood, and if a church is ever built in his name, a relic is needed to consecrate the church. And also a complete biography of the prospective saint is compiled. So a call was put out in Berini and we also searched the storage cellar of this rectory." He let them know, "We found some of his old vestments in trunks, and his family had photographs and letters they had saved. Some from Ethiopia." He told them, "The man from the Vatican press office interviewed the family and some childhood friends of Giuseppe Armano. So this has all been done."

Mercado replied, "*L'Osservatore Romano* likes to do this work themselves."

"As you wish." Father Rulli said, "We had a special Mass when the delegation from the Vatican announced this. The town was very excited, and the bells of San Anselmo rang all day. His family was filled with joy at the news of his beatification. And of the news that he had performed miracles in Ethiopia."

Mercado nodded, then said, "We are sorry we missed that day."

Well, Purcell thought, Colonel Gann had guessed correctly. The Vatican was here first, and it was Henry's unanswered letter that led them here. It was possible, of course, that there was nothing sinister about this; it was just the Vatican doing its job of making a death notification of a priest. And while they were at it, they sent a whole delegation to announce that Father Giuseppe Armano was being considered for sainthood. And they took what they needed. Purcell was impressed.

Father Rulli looked at his guests. "Did you say you were with Father Armano when he died?"

"Yes."

The priest nodded, then said, "I am not clear about the circumstances of his death." No one replied, so

Father Rulli went on. "Monsignor Mazza from the office of beatification told me that Father Armano had been imprisoned since 1936, and that he escaped and was found dying by three war correspondents from England who did not speak much Italian." He asked, "So that was you?"

Mercado nodded.

Father Rulli said, "Well, that is itself a miracle. After forty years, to be found by...English people who work for *L'Osservatore Romano*." He asked Mercado, "Can you tell me the circumstances of this encounter?"

Mercado related an edited version of what happened that night, and Father Rulli kept nodding with interest. Mercado concluded, "We buried him in a garden of this Italian spa...and said prayers over his grave."

"That is a wonderful story. And wonderful that this man did not die alone."

Mercado said, "He was at peace."

"Yes. Good." He thought a moment, then asked Mercado, "Is your Italian good?"

"It is passable."

The priest thought a moment, then said, "But Monsignor Mazza said to me he received a letter from one of the people who found Father Armano dying and that this man had little to report about Father Armano's last words—because of the language difficulties and because he died soon after he was found."

"He...was unconscious most of the time."

"I see." Father Rulli stayed silent awhile, then said, "As you know, there must be three miracles for a person to enter into the sainthood, and I am wondering how they in Rome would know of a miracle."

Mercado replied, "I'm not sure."

"Perhaps these miracles took place when he was serving in the army during that terrible war."

"Probably."

"And they were reported by the survivors of his military group."

"That's possible." Mercado added, "That's what we are investigating. For our story."

Purcell inquired, "Do you have any information as to Father Armano's military unit?"

"Well, his return address would have been on his letters, but that is all in Rome now." He looked again at his guest and said, "It seems to me that all this information is available to you in Rome."

"Of course."

Father Rulli informed them, "I was told not to speak of this to outsiders. Why is that?"

Mercado replied, "I have no idea." He added, "Rome is Rome."

Father Rulli nodded, then changed the subject. "The most important relic of a saint is part of his body. Monsignor Mazza said that he was going to send a mission to Ethiopia to locate this spa and recover the remains."

Mercado, wanting to appear more knowledgeable than he had been, replied, "Yes, we know that. In fact, we may return to Ethiopia ourselves."

The priest advised them, "It has become dangerous there."

Purcell reminded him, "We've been there."

"Yes, of course." Father Rulli looked at his watch and said, "I am to perform a burial Mass in half an hour."

Purcell asked him, "Can you put us into contact with any of Father Armano's family? Or anyone else who is still alive from his time? He mentioned a brother and two sisters."

"Yes, Anna is still alive. A widow. And I can have her and other family members, and perhaps some friends, meet you here if you wish."

"That would be very good of you."

"Anna would find some comfort in speaking to you who last saw her brother alive." He added, "She grieved for his loss, but now she has been delivered a miracle."

The priest rose and his guests also stood. Father Rulli showed them to the door and said, "Five o'clock. I will have coffee."

They thanked him, left the rectory, and walked along the side of the church and entered the piazza. The afternoon break seemed to be over and the taverna looked quiet, so they crossed the piazza and found a table under the awning.

Mercado said, "We were scooped by the Vatican press office."

Purcell added, "And they made off with all traces of Father Armano."

Vivian said, "This is hard to believe... I mean, is this canonization...legitimate?"

Mercado replied, "It could be."

Purcell lit a cigarette and looked at him.

Mercado met his stare and said, "It *could* be, Frank." He explained, "They'd want his army letters to see if he mentioned anything that could be construed as a miracle."

"They wanted his army letters to see if he mentioned

anything about the letter he was carrying from the pope."

"We don't know that."

Purcell asked, "Aren't there supposed to be eyewitnesses to these miracles?"

Mercado replied, "I'm impressed with your knowledge of the steps to sainthood." He added, "The Vatican office of beatification will be trying to find and interview men who served with Father Armano in Ethiopia."

Vivian said, "Even if he didn't *perform* a miracle, he experienced the greater miracle of...being healed."

Purcell inquired, "Does that count?"

Mercado surprised him by saying, "Even doubting Thomas had a place among the apostles." He assured Purcell, "We need a skeptic."

Vivian smiled. "I look forward to being there, Frank, when you are in the black monastery in the presence of the Holy Spirit."

"I will eat my words. Or drink them."

Vivian thought a moment, then said, "Father Armano asked us to tell his sister Anna of his death."

No one responded.

"Why did he say Anna? Why didn't he mention his other sister or brother?"

The obvious answer, as they all knew, was that Giuseppe Armano had indeed gone home to Berini, then returned to Ethiopia with the happy knowledge that Anna was still alive, and that she would be waiting to hear from them about his last hours on earth.

Purcell said, "The rational side of me says that Anna was closest to him."

No one responded.

Purcell continued, "But I like the other possibility better. He went home."

The proprietor saw they were still sitting in his chairs and he came out to see why. Mercado greeted him and asked politely for three glasses of *vino rosso* and *acqua minerale*. The man seemed all right with that and disappeared inside.

Mercado said, "The last strangers he saw were wearing British Army uniforms."

"He looks the right age to be your cousin."

Vivian returned to the subject. "Father Rulli seemed a bit confused, or even suspicious, that we didn't know about the Vatican delegation or much else."

Mercado assured her, "Catholic priests know better than anyone that the Vatican moves in mysterious ways." He added, "Rome is Rome."

Purcell said, "The Roman Church, in my opinion, is a continuation of the Roman Empire, also not known for openness or enlightenment."

Mercado replied, "The Church of Rome preaches and practices the word of God."

Purcell thought that every time Henry Mercado heard the word "God," he also heard a choir of heavenly angels. He said to Mercado, "You lied to the priest."

Mercado replied, "I was as confused as he was and I may have misspoken."

"You need to go to confession."

Mercado changed the subject. "We may be able to get some information on Father Armano's military unit from his family. But to be honest with you, the Ministry of War is not going to be cooperative in regard to providing us with maps or logbooks." He added, "We have been shut down."

Purcell agreed. "This is not a productive trip. But it could be good background for our story—though not the one we write for *L'Osservatore Romano*."

Vivian reminded them, "We also came here to inform his family—to tell Anna—of his death and to tell them we were with him at the end."

Purcell pointed out, "The Vatican beat us to the death notification." He added, "And whatever else we tell them might contradict what the Vatican delegation has already told Father Rulli and the family." He advised, "Keep it short, general, and upbeat."

Mercado reminded Vivian, "He was unconscious most of the time."

Vivian replied, "Lies just breed more lies."

Purcell said, "When in Rome."

Their wine and water came with a bill written on a slate board, and Mercado gave the proprietor a fifty-thousand-lire note. He said to his companions, "It's pay as you go."

"We look shady," Purcell agreed.

The proprietor made change from his apron and Mercado took it, explaining, "Overtipping is in poor taste." He left some coins on the table.

Mercado raised his glass. "God rest the soul of Father Giuseppe Armano."

"San Giuseppe," said Purcell.

Mercado pronounced the wine drinkable, then informed them, "Sainthood moves very slowly. We will not see his canonization in our lifetime."

"Well, not your lifetime, Henry."

Mercado pointed out, "None of us knows how much time we have left here, Frank." He nodded toward San Anselmo, where men, women, and children, dressed in black, were climbing the steps as the church bells tolled slowly and echoed through the piazza.

Vivian said, "Let's go to this burial Mass."

Purcell inquired, "Did you know the deceased?"

"I want to see Father Armano's church."

Purcell and Mercado exchanged glances, then Mercado said, "All right." He went inside to say *arrivederci* to the proprietor, then came out and informed his companions, "You never leave without saying good-bye."

Purcell said, "I'm impressed with your rustic etiquette."

Vivian said, "I think I could live in Sicily."

Purcell informed her, "Half the Italians in America are Sicilian. They couldn't live here."

"Maybe summers."

They walked across the piazza to the church and Vivian draped her scarf over her head as they climbed the steps.

The church of San Anselmo was big, built, Purcell thought, when more people lived here. The peaked roof showed exposed beams and rafters, and the thick stone walls were plastered and whitewashed. The altar, though, was of polished stone and gilded wood, and looked out of place in the simple setting, as did the intricate stained glass windows.

A white-draped coffin sat at the Communion rail and Father Rulli stood beside it, blessed it, then went up to the altar.

There were no pews, but a collection of wooden chairs were lined up in rows, and most of them were filled with the people of Berini and the surrounding farms. The three visitors took empty seats in the rear.

Father Rulli stood in the center of the altar, raised his arms, and greeted his flock in Italian. Everyone stood and the Mass of Christian burial began.

Purcell looked at Father Rulli, and he saw Father Armano, forty years ago; a young priest from this village who'd gone to the seminary and returned to his village, his family, his friends, and his church where he'd been baptized. In a perfect world, where there was no war, Father Giuseppe Armano might have stayed here until the burial Mass was for him. But the new Caesar in Rome had much grander plans for the Italian people, and the winds of war swept into Berini and carried off its sons.

Father Rulli was now at the lectern, speaking, Purcell imagined, of the mystery of death and of the promise of eternal life. Or maybe he was speaking well of the departed, because people were crying. Even Vivian, who had no clue who was in the coffin, was dabbing her eyes with a handkerchief.

Purcell returned to Father Armano, and wondered if the priest saw his life as wasted or as blessed for having seen and experienced a miracle. Probably, Purcell thought, the priest had had moments of doubt in his prison cell, but his faith and his experience in the black monastery had sustained him. And in the end, as he was dying, he had probably thought he was again blessed to be ending his life a free man, in the company of at least one, maybe two believers who would tell his family and the world of his fate and of what he had seen and experienced. He seemed at peace, Purcell recalled, ready for his journey home.

It occurred to Purcell that they didn't have to come to Berini, but it was the right thing to do; it was the right place to begin their own journey back to where this all began.

PART III

Ethiopia

The longest journey
Is the journey inwards
Of him who has chosen his destiny,
Who has started upon his quest
For the source of his being...

—Dag Hammarskjöld, *Markings*

Chapter 31

Frank Purcell stood with his back to the bar, a drink in one hand and a cigarette in the other.

The Addis Ababa Hilton cocktail lounge was filled with the usual clientele that one finds in times of war, pestilence, and famine, though it seemed to Purcell that there were far fewer news people here than in September—though more UN relief people and embassy reinforcements. And, as always, there were some shady-looking characters whose purpose here was unknown, but it had to do with either money or spying.

Another difference from the last time was that the rich Ethiopians seemed to have disappeared. The ones that weren't dead or in prison were at Etiopia in Rome. The Italian expats and businesspeople had also disappeared.

Purcell was happy to see that the newly arrived Soviet and Cuban advisors were not drinking in the Addis Hilton. The hotel demanded hard currency, which kept out the riffraff and the Reds.

He'd sent his telex to Vivian at the Forum Hotel, and to Mercado at the newspaper two days before, informing them he was alive and well at the Hilton. Now he was waiting for Vivian to arrive.

A few of his former colleagues had approached him in the two days since he'd been here, but they'd observed the unspoken rule of not asking any questions of a fellow reporter. He had, however, volunteered a few details about his trip to the front in September, his arrest and imprisonment, and his expulsion from the country. He was back, he said, on assignment for *L'Osservatore Romano.* This was old news and didn't rate getting bought a drink, but they wished him good luck.

One reporter, a nice lady named Fran from AP, had informed him, "The crazy fun phase of the revolution is over. Almost everyone they wanted dead is dead or in jail, or on the run. Now they have to govern and they can't deal with the famine or the Eritrean separatists."

Purcell had asked her about the Gallas, but she didn't know or care much. The Gallas were not on the radar screens of anyone in the capital; they were like marauding lions, somewhere out there, with no political agenda. Plus, they were not available for comment.

He also asked, "How about the Royalist partisans?"

"They're finished."

He thought about Colonel Gann, who was returning to fight a lost cause. Colonel Gann would wind up dead this time.

Fran also informed him that the Falasha Jews were beginning an exodus, to Israel, and that was a good story.

Purcell looked up at the huge stained glass window that diffused the dying afternoon sunlight throughout the modern bar, and which would do credit to a European cathedral. The window was the work of a contemporary Ethiopian artist, done in a neoprimitive style, and told the story of the founding of the Ethiopian royal line. The first panel showed the black queen,

Sheba, visiting Jerusalem with her attendants. The next panel showed them being received by King Solomon. The queen then returns to her homeland, and there she gives birth to a son, Menelik, the ancestor of the present emperor, who would also be the last emperor of Ethiopia, unless Colonel Gann could perform a miracle. Purcell wondered if the new government would allow that window to stay there. The hotel guests liked it.

He looked at his watch: 4:36. Vivian's plane had landed. Lovers meet at the airport. Reporters and their photographers do not if they are also lovers and don't want to advertise that relationship to the security apparatus, who might make use of the information. So for that reason, and also because *L'Osservatore Romano* was a Catholic enterprise, Vivian had her own room.

Purcell had, however, sent a hotel car and driver to meet her, and to report by telephone that the hotel guest had arrived and was safely through passport control.

Purcell informed the bartender that he was waiting for this call.

He ordered another Jack Daniel's and perused an English-language newspaper on the bar. A small item tucked away inside the paper reported that the former monarch, Mr. Haile Selassie, remained under the protective custody of the Provisional Revolutionary government.

If Mr. Selassie was a younger man, Purcell knew, they'd have already executed him. But one of the advantages of advanced age—if there were any—was that people who wanted you dead only had to wait patiently. Also, the now Mr. Selassie was still popular in the West and killing him would further strain relations with Europe and America. Even the Soviet and Cuban advisors would argue against regicide in this case. The murdered Romanovs had become martyrs, and the modern Marxists wanted to avoid that this time.

Purcell thought back to Berini. Coffee and cannoli at the rectory of San Anselmo had not been as awful as he'd expected. The sister of Father Armano, Anna, was a sweet woman and she had taken to Vivian, despite Vivian's exotic appearance.

Vivian had told Anna that her brother had mentioned her by name, which made Anna weep. Anna told them that she had seen her brother in a dream, last year when there was much news of Ethiopia, and her brother was smiling, which according to Sicilian belief meant he was in heaven. Unfortunately, Anna couldn't recall the exact date of the dream, though with Vivian's prompting she agreed it could have been in September.

Coincidence? Not according to Vivian or Mercado, who took this as a further sign of divine design. Even he, Frank Purcell, found himself wanting to believe that Father Armano had traveled home for a last visit.

Father Rulli's small rectory had become filled with the near and distant relatives of the late Giuseppe Armano, and as Father Rulli explained, unnecessarily, "Sicilian families are large."

There were some language difficulties, but mostly everyone understood each other, and Mercado and Vivian repeated the story of how they and Signore Purcell, who spoke no Italian, had found Father Armano, mortally wounded, and how the priest had asked them to tell his family that he was thinking of them in his last moments. Everyone was very moved by the story, and no one asked why it had taken so long for the three *giornalisti* to come to Berini, though Mercado mentioned he'd been in an Ethiopian prison. An older man, who'd fought in Ethiopia, and was a cousin of Father Armano, said, "Ethiopia is a place of death. You should not return."

Vivian informed him and everyone that they were going to find the grave of Father Armano and bring back a mortal relic of the saint-to-be. Purcell thought this custom was ghoulish, but no one else there did.

The women disappeared at about 6 P.M., and cordials were served. At seven, the men excused themselves and Father Rulli invited his three guests to stay for dinner. Vivian wanted to stay, but it was obvious that Father Rulli wanted his guests to clear up some inconsistencies between their story and that of the Vatican beatification delegation, so Mercado reminded Vivian of their flight to Rome—which was actually the next day.

They thanked Father Rulli for his hospitality and assistance and promised to return to Berini after their assignment in Ethiopia. The priest blessed them and their work and wished them a safe journey.

Outside, on the way to the car, Vivian said, "That was a very moving and wonderful experience."

Mercado agreed, and so did Purcell, though he'd had to rely on translations for the experience.

In the car, Vivian announced, "I got Father Armano's military address from Anna. She knew it by heart."

They drove to Corleone and spent the night in a small hotel, then caught a noon flight from Palermo back to Rome.

Mercado wrote to the Ministry of War on *L'Osservatore Romano* letterhead, saying he was doing an article on the Ethiopian war and requesting information such as unit logs on the battalion or regiment whose military designation he specified in his letter.

The response, unusually fast, informed him that all records of this regiment had been lost in Ethiopia.

And that was that.

As for Italian Army maps, which would be critical for their mission, Colonel Gann had informed them that he had a source in London for captured Italian maps. He also advised them not to visit the Italian Library in Addis Ababa, which he'd discovered was under some sort of state surveillance. So now they needed Colonel Gann and his maps before they could begin their journey, and Gann was scheduled to arrive on the twenty-fourth. He said he'd contact them at the Hilton, but if they didn't hear from him by the twenty-eighth, they were on their own.

Purcell looked at the telephone on the bar. He'd checked for telexes twice already, to see if Vivian—or Mercado—had tried to contact him. He picked up the phone, called the front desk, and asked again. The clerk informed him, "We will deliver any telex to you in the lounge, Mr. Purcell."

"And forward my phone calls here."

"Yes, sir."

He knew he should have gone to the airport to meet her, but they'd all agreed in Rome not to do that. Sounded good in Rome.

He ordered another drink and lit another cigarette. It was now 5:24, long past the time when she'd be through airport security. But probably the Alitalia flight from Rome was late.

He turned and looked at the patrons at the cocktail tables. People gravitated toward the hotel bars in times of stress. They came to get news, or hear rumors, or because there actually is safety in numbers. Some of the patrons were quiet and withdrawn, and some were hyper. A feeling of unreality always permeated these softly lit islands of comfort, and sometimes a feeling of guilt; there was death and famine out there.

He looked up at the stained glass window again. The mid-January sun was almost gone, and when the light struck the huge window at this angle, Purcell could make out in the modern scene of the panorama, as well as in the ancient scene, a church or monastery. The artist chose to use black glass for the depiction of the church, and around it were dark green palms. Purcell wondered if the church was black by design or by the random choice of the artist. The dark green glass of the palms made the black church almost impossible to see except in a certain light, yet the remainder of the panorama was a contrast in light and dark. He stared at the glass as the sun sank lower and both the modern and ancient depictions of the same church— or monastery—disappeared, and the soft glow of the lounge lighting gave the stained glass an altogether different appearance.

The phone rang and the bartender answered it, then gave it to him.

"Purcell."

A woman with an Italian accent said, "This an Alitalia customer servizio."

"Yes?"

"I hava deliver to your room a young a lady."

He smiled and asked, "Is she naked?"

"Due minuto."

"I'll be right there."

Chapter 32

Purcell and Vivian spent the next two days re-familiarizing themselves with the city, and rees-tablishing some press contacts and local contacts. *L'Osservatore Romano* had no office in Addis, but the paper shared space in the old Imperial Hotel with other transient reporters and freelancers who paid a small fee for a place to hang their hats and use the type-writers and telexes.

They also visited the American embassy to register their presence, and to see Anne, the consulate officer who'd come for Purcell in prison, and also for Vivian. Vivian gave Anne a pot of black African violets she'd picked up from a street vendor, and Anne gave them some advice: "You should not have returned."

Purcell assured her, "We'll try not to get arrested this time."

Purcell also wrote and filed a story about Ethiopian Catholic refugees from the fighting on the Eritrean bor-der. He knew nothing about this, so in Mercado style, he made up most of it. But to give it a little twist, he mentioned his visit to the Ethiopian College in the Vati-can, and praised the Catholic brothers there for their hospitality and their blessing of his journey to Ethiopia.

Vivian read his piece and asked, "How much of this is true?"

He reminded her, "The first casualty of war is the truth." He added, "We need to earn our keep. Take a picture of a beggar and caption it 'Catholic Refugee.'"

They checked for telexes twice a day to see if Henry Mercado had decided that Rome was a better place to be. But Mercado's only telex, that morning, said: ARRIVING ALITALIA, 4:23. CONFIRM.

Purcell sent him a telex confirming they were still alive and well, and looking forward to his arrival.

Purcell left a note for Mercado at the front desk saying he'd be in the bar at six, and now he and Vivian sat at a cocktail table waiting to see if Henry had made it past the security people at the airport. It was 6:35.

Vivian looked up at the stained glass window and asked him, "Where are they keeping the emperor these days?"

"They're not saying."

"Do you think he's still alive?"

"If he was dead, they'd announce he died of natural causes." He reminded her, "He's the reason the rasses are still fighting."

"Who is the successor to the throne?"

"Crown Prince Afsa Wossen. He escaped to London. Probably a pal of Gann."

She nodded.

Purcell glanced at his watch: 6:46. Henry was very late.

He said to Vivian, "Do you know that the Rastafarians in Jamaica consider Haile Selassie to be divine?"

"No, I didn't."

"We need to fly to Jamaica next and do a story on that."

She forced a smile.

Clearly she was worried about Henry, but she was reluctant to say that in case he misinterpreted her concern.

He pointed to the long bar and said, "Right over there. That's where I was sitting, minding my own business, when you and Henry came up to me."

She again forced a smile.

He mimicked Henry's slight British accent. "Hello, old man. Have you met my photographer?"

Her smile got wider. "I was immediately taken with you."

"You wanted my Jeep."

"I didn't even know you had a Jeep."

"Well, I don't anymore. The Gallas probably have it now. Pulling it around with their horses." He added, "I have to find the guy I rented it from and get my three-thousand-dollar security deposit back."

"Why should he give it back? You lost his Jeep."

"Wasn't my fault."

"It wasn't his fault either. Where did you get the Jeep? We need another one."

"An Italian resident of Addis. Probably gone by now."

"You need to find him."

"I think he's out of Jeeps." He informed her, "There's another guy here, Signore Bocaccio, who owns or owned a small plane. I've asked around, but no one seems to know if he's still here."

She nodded, then glanced at her watch. She said, "I'll go to the front desk to see if he's checked in. Or see if the flight is late."

"All right."

She got up and left the lounge.

Purcell sipped his drink. He had an after-hours emergency number for the British, American, and Swiss embassies.

It occurred to him that without Mercado and without Gann, the quest for the Holy Grail was going nowhere. He and Vivian could, of course, press on, but that would be crossing the line from brave to crazy. And yet... now that he was here, something was telling him that it was going to be all right—that what they'd felt and believed was correct; they had been chosen to do this.

He understood, too, that they had not necessarily been chosen to succeed, or even to live. But they'd been chosen to find the Holy Grail that was within themselves. And that was what this was always about; the Grail was a phantom and the journey was inward, into their hearts and souls.

Vivian and Henry walked into the lounge, smiling, arm in arm, and Purcell stood, smiled, and said, "Henry, have you met my photographer?"

"I have, old man. She's going to buy me a drink. And buy one for yourself."

Chapter 33

Purcell walked across the windy airstrip. The rising sun began to burn off the highland mist that still shrouded the valley floor. In the distance, along the same mountain chain, Addis Ababa was becoming visible as the ground fog dropped back into the valley.

Purcell noticed the condition of the concrete as he walked. Like much of the civil and military engineering in this country, this old airfield was an Italian legacy. The Italians were good builders, but forty years was a long time. The concrete runways were patched with low-grade blacktop and the hangar roofs were mended with woven thatch. A platoon of soldiers was forming up near the hangar. The Royalists may have been beaten, but the Eritreans, who were now trying to win independence from the new Ethiopian government, were winning, and the whole country was on a war footing.

The Ethiopian Air Force kept a wing of American-made C-47 transports here, and Signore Bocaccio, the Italian coffee dealer, whom Henry had found, also kept his American-made Navion here. He told Mr. Purcell, however, that he used to hangar it at the Addis Ababa International Airport, but the Ethiopian Air Force made him keep the ancient Navion within their grabbing distance in the event they should need it. It had in fact already been used as a spotter for jet fighters in the Eritrean conflict, and as a consequence of that, the Navion sported a rocket pod under its fuselage that Signore Bocaccio pointed out to Mr. Purcell. The rocket pod was used to fire smoke markers at the Eritrean rebels, the Royalist forces, or anyone else they didn't care for. The few French Mirage jets that the Ethiopians possessed would then try to place their bombs and rockets on the smoke markers, with varying degrees of success.

Purcell walked up to the stoutly built, low-wing craft and did a quick walk-around. Its black paint was not holding up well, and bare spots of aluminum were everywhere, except for the red-painted name of the plane—*Mia*. The nose wheel of the tricycle gear needed air and the plane pitched forward. Purcell noticed that the sliding canopy was pushed halfway back on its tracks, and a bullet hole was visible in one of the rear panes. He asked Signore Bocaccio, "Am I paying extra for the rocket pod?"

Signore Bocaccio made a classic Italian shrug. "What am I to do about it? You think this is America? Italy? Here, they do what they want. There is no war today, so you can have the plane. If you fly her well, perhaps they will make you a colonel in the air force. This is Ethiopia."

"Yes, I know."

"If you were not a journalist, they would not let me rent her to you at all. There was trouble as it was. I had to pay them to allow this."

"That's why they make trouble." He walked around the craft again. There were at least six bullet holes in it. "Do you file a flight plan?"

"Yes. You must. Before the trouble they did not care. But now they insist. They think everyone is a spy for the emperor. So they want a flight plan. There are ten airstrips in the whole country. They want a flight plan. Hah!" He assured Purcell, however, "Today we are doing only the check out. So we need no flight plan, but when you go to Gondar, you must file for Gondar."

The flight plan was an unforeseen problem. This morning he was just logging in some flight time with Signore Bocaccio, to see if the Navion was airworthy. But when he was with Vivian, Mercado, and Gann—if he showed up—they'd be doing aerial recon, and he did not want to land in Gondar, which was Getachu's Northern Army headquarters. He could, however, file a flight plan for Khartoum, where they could conceivably have business. He asked Signore Bocaccio, "Can I fly to Khartoum?"

"You can if you want to get arrested."

"They're not getting along with the Sudanese, I take it."

"They are not. Anyway, I would not want you to take Mia that far." He tapped the fuselage where the name appeared. "Khartoum is the limit of her cruising range. But if you come upon headwinds or bad weather, you will run out of fuel." He smiled as his hand did a nosedive.

"All right..." Purcell informed Signore Bocaccio, "Tomorrow, or the next day, I'll have one passenger. Perhaps two or three." He asked, "Are the rear seats in place?"

"Unfortunately, no." Bocaccio explained, "I took them out for the beans."

"Right, but—"

"I sometimes take samples from the plantations. I

carry items to trade. And things to eat. You cannot find Italian food outside of Addis." He added, "In fact, with the famine, sometimes you cannot find any food at all."

"Sorry about that. Can you replace the seat?"

"It was stolen."

"Of course. Well, my passengers can sit on your bean bags." He asked, "How does Mia handle with four?"

"How would you handle with four people on your back?" He inquired, "Who are the others?"

"Giornalisti."

"They are friendly with the government, I hope."

"Of course." Purcell could see that Signore Bocaccio was having second thoughts, so he distracted him with technical questions. "When was she built?"

"Twenty years ago. She is a young girl, but an old aircraft." He smiled. "She is American made, as you know, and all measurements are in feet, miles, and gallons."

"What is her stall speed?"

"She stalls at any speed. So go as slow as you please. She will stall when she wants. Just give yourself enough altitude to recover."

"What speed, Signore Bocaccio?"

He shrugged. "The airspeed indicator is inaccurate. And the needle jumps. The airplane is, how you say in English, out of trim. The leading edge is banged up."

"I noticed."

"Well, so, the stall speed is perhaps sixty. But when she was young, she could go forty-five. But what difference does that make? You must just give yourself the altitude to recover—and why would you want to approach stall speed?"

"I want to go low and slow. I want to make steep banks and turns. Will she do that?"

Signore Bocaccio looked at him closely. "That is not the way to Gondar, my friend. Gondar is three hundred miles due north. There are no steep banks or turns to be made."

"We are looking for the war, Signore."

"This is not a plane for that. She knows the way to Gondar as a straight line. She does not like to be fired at." He put his finger into a bullet hole, then patted his plane and dusted off his hands. He also informed Purcell, "The government does not want you looking for the war from the air. That is their job. If you do that, they will think you are spying for the Royalists. Or the Eritreans. Or the British or the Americans—"

"Cruising speed? Altitude?"

"This airfield is already at eight thousand feet. You will get the best cruising speed if you climb to perhaps twelve thousand. To go much higher would take too long. Especially with four people. As you go over the valleys you can drop down if you wish, but you must remember that at eight thousand feet, you may meet a nine-thousand-foot mountain. You understand?"

"Si. And what will she make?"

"Perhaps you can get a hundred fifty out of her. I make Gondar in two and a half hours, normally."

"How's the prop?"

"She wanders. Sometimes a hundred—two hundred rpm. Give it no thought."

"It can wander all it wants as long as it doesn't wander off the airplane."

"The hub is solid. It has no cracks."

"Let's hope so."

"Do you think I am"—Bocaccio tapped his head—"pazzo?"

"Well, Signore Bocaccio, if you are, so am I."

He laughed, then looked at Purcell and said seriously, "Do not try tricks with Mia, my friend. She will kill you."

"Capisco." He said to Signore Bocaccio, "Are you ready to teach me how to fly Mia?"

He smiled. "After all I have said, you still want to fly her?"

"If the Ethiopian Air Force can fly her, I can fly her."

Again Bocaccio looked at Purcell. "Whatever is your purpose, it must be important to you."

"As important as your coffee beans."

Apropos of nothing, Signore Bocaccio said, "This has become a sad land."

"You should leave."

"I will..." He smiled and said to Purcell, "Perhaps *L'Osservatore Romano* would like to buy Mia."

"I will ask." He looked up at the cockpit. "Ready?"

"I fly, you watch, then you fly and I watch you. Next time, you fly and I watch you from the ground."

"Let's hope for a next time."

Signore Bocaccio laughed, and they climbed into the aircraft.

Chapter 34

Henry Mercado, wearing a bathrobe and under-shorts, sat on the balcony of his top-floor room sipping coffee. The fog was lifting, and in the distance he could see a single-engine black aircraft rising off a hilltop airstrip. He said, "That must be Frank."

Vivian, sitting next to him, replied, "He said to look for him about seven."

Mercado glanced at her. She was wearing a short white *shamma* that she'd picked up somewhere, and she had obviously worn it to bed. The *shamma* reminded him of Getachu's camp. The parade ground. The pole. He wondered if she'd thought about that.

Vivian told him, "Frank said he'd do a flyby and tip his wings."

He supposed that meant she had to leave and get to her own room—or Purcell's room—so that Purcell would not see both of them having coffee on Henry Mercado's balcony at 7 A.M. But she didn't move.

To make conversation, he said, "This is a squalid city."

"It is not Rome."

"No. This is the Infernal City."

She laughed.

He had developed a strong dislike for Addis Ababa in 1935, and forty years later nothing he'd seen had changed his opinion. Even the Ethiopians disliked it. It was like every semi-Westernized town he'd seen in Africa or Asia, combining the worst aspects of each culture. Its only good feature was its eight-thousand-foot elevation, which made the climate pleasant—except during the June-to-September rainy season when mud slid down the hills into the streets.

He poured more coffee for both of them. Vivian put her bare feet on the balcony rail and her *shamma* slipped back to her thighs.

He was surprised that she had accepted his invitation for coffee on the balcony, and more surprised when she came to his door wearing only the *shamma* and little else. Or nothing else.

On the other hand, Vivian was of another generation. And sometimes he thought of her as a child of God: naturally innocent while unknowingly sensuous.

He looked out at the black aircraft in the distance. It was circling over the hills and making steep, dangerous-looking turns. He said, "I hope he's a good pilot."

She was staring at the aircraft and didn't reply.

He looked out again into the city. Like all the cities of his youth, he hated this place because it reminded him of a time when he was hopeful and optimistic— when he believed in Moscow and not Rome. Now he was burdened with years and disappointments, and with God.

If he looked hard enough into the swirling fog below, he could see Henry Mercado dashing across Saint George Square to the telegraph office. He could hear the roar of Italian warplanes overhead. He could and did remember and feel the pleasure of making love

to the nineteen-year-old daughter of an American dip-
lomat in the blacked-out lobby of the Imperial. Why
the lobby? He had a room upstairs. What if they'd
snapped on the lights? He smiled.

"What is making you smile, Henry?"

"What always makes me smile?"

"Tell me."

So he told her about having sex in the lobby of the
Imperial Hotel during an air raid blackout.

She listened without comment, then stayed silent
awhile before saying, "So you understand."

He didn't reply.

"We do things when we're frightened."

"We were not frightened of the air raid."

"We want to hold on to another person."

"I didn't follow this person to Cairo."

She didn't reply.

He looked out at the Imperial Hotel. Its surrounding verandas seemed to sag. He had the nostalgic idea
of checking in there instead of here, but maybe it was
enough to visit once a day when he went to the press
office. In fact, the places that once held good memories
were best left as memories.

The aircraft was climbing to the north, and Mercado
saw that it cleared a distant peak by a narrow margin.
Vivian didn't seem to notice, but he said to her, "I hope
you're prepared to do some aerial photography in a
small plane with a novice pilot."

"You should stay here, Henry."

"I don't care if I die, Vivian. I care if you die."

"No one is going to die. But that's very...loving of
you to say that."

"Well, I love you."

"I know."

He didn't ask the follow-up question and stared out at Addis Ababa. It was dirty and it smelled bad. Old men with missing pieces of their bodies were a walking reminder of old-style Ethiopian justice. Adding to the judicial mutilations were the wounded of recent and past wars. And then there were the deformed beggars, the diseased prostitutes, and the starving barefoot children running through donkey dung. A quarter million already dead from the famine. How was he supposed to believe in God? "How can this be?"

"How can what be?"

"*This.*" He swept his arm over the city.

She thought a moment, then replied, "It's good that you still care."

"I don't care anymore."

"You do."

He said to her, "Sometimes I think I've been around too long."

"I think you told me that once before."

"Did I? What did you say?"

"I don't remember."

But *he* did. She'd said to him, "How can you say that when you have me?"

He looked at her and his heart literally skipped a beat.

The aircraft was now directly over the city, making tight banking turns as they'd have to do when they were shooting photographs of the ground. He thought she should leave before Purcell decided to do a flyby. But she just sat there, her feet on the rail, with her legs parted too wide, sipping coffee, watching her lover fly. Finally he said to her, "You should go to your own balcony. Or his."

Again, she didn't reply.

Mercado stood, but did not go inside.

The sun was coming over the eastern hills, burning off the last of the ground mist. The capital of the former empire was a straggly city of empty lots with gullies and ridges everywhere. The few high-rise buildings were separated by miles of squalid huts that sat in clusters like primitive villages. Banana trees and palms shaded the corrugated metal roofs of the huts from the blazing sun. Vermin and insects swarmed through the city, and at night hyenas howled in the surrounding hills. Whatever hope there had been for this city and this country under the emperor's halfhearted reforms was now drowned in a sea of blood. A long night was descending on this ancient land, and if a new dawn ever arrived, he would not see it in his lifetime.

"Are you all right?" she asked.

"I see things more clearly now. And I am feeling sorry for myself, and for these people."

"You're a good man, Henry."

"I was."

"We will find that good, happy, and optimistic man. That's why we're here."

He nodded. This was the last quest. He hoped for salvation, but was prepared for the final disillusionment.

He looked down into the square dominated by the city's only beautiful building, the octagonal Cathedral of Saint George. The square was filled with beggars by day and prostitutes by night. To further desecrate the great Coptic cathedral, it had been built by Italian prisoners of war captured at Adowa during the first Italian invasion of 1896. He found that an irony of sorts, or maybe a great cosmic joke.

Vivian said, "Here he comes." She pointed.

The black aircraft was coming in from the east so that the pilot's side would be facing the hotel as it passed by. Mercado noticed the aircraft was flying dangerously low and slow as it approached the hotel. If he stalled, he had no altitude to recover.

Vivian seemed not to understand the danger, and she was smiling and waving.

Mercado could not take his eyes off the aircraft, expecting it to nosedive any second. What was Purcell thinking? That's what happens when you show off for a woman, Mercado thought. You die. And if Frank Purcell died . . . He looked at Vivian.

She was standing on her toes now, waving wildly. "Frank! Over here!" She jumped up and down.

The aircraft dipped its wings about a hundred yards from the balcony, indicating he'd seen them. Mercado gave a half wave, and as the plane passed by he could see Purcell's face, looking at them.

Vivian shouted, "He saw us! Did you see him, Henry?"

He didn't reply. Mercado watched the aircraft as it gained speed and continued west. He expected that Purcell would come around for another flyby, but he continued on and disappeared against the background of the tall western mountains.

Vivian remained standing at the rail, looking at the fog-shrouded hills.

Mercado was going to ask her to leave now, but he didn't. Finally he said, "I trust this will not cause a problem."

She turned her head toward him. "We had coffee. Waiting for Frank."

He nodded.

She turned and put her back against the rail. "You were not the jealous type."

"No."

"We all bathed together."

"Yes... well, bathing together and sleeping together are different things."

"One is a prelude to the other. And you knew that."

"Don't try that argument on me, Vivian."

She walked past him into his bedroom.

He stood on the balcony for a few seconds, then went through the sliding door.

She was lying on his unmade bed, her *shamma* still on, but pulled back, revealing her jet-black pubic hair.

He looked at her, but said nothing.

She said to him, "This will make everything right between us."

He understood what she meant. This was her way of saying, I'm sorry. I'm giving you back your pride. I'm taking away your anger.

He dropped his robe to the floor, then slipped off his shorts and got into the bed. He knelt between her wide-spread legs, bent forward, and started to pull off her *shamma*, but she said, "No. Like this."

He looked at her.

"Like this, Henry. You understand."

He nodded.

She reached out and took his hard penis in her hand and pulled him toward her. He lay down on top of her and she guided him in, then wrapped her legs around his buttocks and pulled him in tighter.

He began thrusting against her tight grip, and within a minute she climaxed and let out a long moan—the same moan he'd heard that night hanging from the pole. He kept thrusting inside her and she climaxed again, then he felt himself coming into her.

They lay side by side, holding hands, gazing at the paddle fan spinning slowly on the ceiling.

She asked him, "Do you understand this?"

"I do."

"And you understand that this is between two friends."

He didn't reply.

"I hurt you, and now I feel better, and I want you to feel better. About me. And about...all of us."

"I understand."

"I hope you do. If not right now, then later."

He knew that she meant when he next saw Purcell. When the three of them sat together having a drink, the score was even, even if Purcell did not know that. But Henry Mercado did.

And actually he did feel better already. The anger wasn't there any longer, or if it was, it was not helpless anger. But what remained was a sense of loss. He wanted to be with her.

He said to her, "At least tell me you enjoyed it."

"I always did."

"Encore?"

She glanced at the clock. "I'd better get moving."

"Rain check?"

"No. This will not happen again." She sat up and started to swing her legs out of the bed, but he put his hand on the back of her head and gently pulled her toward him.

She hesitated, then let him bring her head and face down on his wet penis, which she took into her mouth.

She knelt between his legs and her long, raven black hair fell across his thighs as her head bobbed up and down.

He came and his body arched up, and she stayed with him until there was nothing left inside him.

Vivian sat back on her haunches, and he looked at her, his semen running down her chin. Their eyes met and she smiled, then pulled off her *shamma* and stood on the bed. She turned completely around for him, and he watched her but said nothing.

Vivian jumped off the bed, wiped her face with a tissue, slipped on her *shamma*, and moved toward the door. "Thank you for coffee."

"Anytime."

She left, and he stared up at the rotating fan. "I love you."

Chapter 35

Purcell took a taxi from the airstrip to the hotel and called Mercado in his room to meet him for coffee. The two men sat in the Hilton cocktail lounge, which doubled as the breakfast room.

Mercado had hoped Vivian would be there so he could have that post-coital moment that she suggested would make him feel better. It wasn't the same, somehow, with only the two cuckolded men having coffee. He asked, "Where is Vivian?"

"I called both rooms, but she's not answering."

Mercado wanted to say, "Well, she's not still in my room." Instead he said, "Probably napping. She was up early." He suggested, "Try her again."

"She'll be down."

A waiter came by with breakfast menus and Mercado said, "Every time I eat, I think about the famine."

"Order light."

"That's very insensitive, Frank." He added, "You wouldn't say that if Vivian was here."

Purcell looked up from his menu, but didn't respond.

Purcell ordered a full breakfast, saying, "Flying makes me hungry."

Mercado ordered orange juice and a *cornetto* with his coffee. He asked Purcell, "How did it fly?"

"Not very agile. But it seems safe enough." He asked, "How did it look to you?"

"Well, I can't tell, of course, but you seem to know what you're doing."

"What did Vivian think?"

"She was excited when you did your flyby." He added, "You saw her."

"I did."

"Yes. And we could see you in the cockpit."

"And how did I look, Henry?"

"Sorry?"

"Did I look happily surprised to see Vivian on your bedroom balcony?"

Mercado did not answer the question, but said, "Hold on, old man. We had coffee, waiting to see you. I hope you don't take that as anything other than what it was."

Purcell stared at him, but didn't reply.

Mercado was not enjoying this moment as much as he'd thought he would. It would have been much better if Vivian and Purcell had already had a tiff about this, followed by Purcell being sulky at cocktails or dinner.

Mercado didn't want to protest too much, but he said, "We're all civilized, old man." He reminded Purcell, "We're going to be in close quarters when we get into the bush." He immediately regretted his choice of words. *Get into the bush.* Freudian slip? He suppressed a smile.

"All right." Purcell let him know, "It's nothing."

Nothing? Mercado wanted to tell him, "I fucked her, actually," but that would wreck the whole deal. So instead, he said, "She's very attached to you, Frank."

"End of discussion."

"In fact, you should have this discussion with her."

Purcell didn't respond, but he was getting annoyed with Mercado. The subject of Vivian was not a happy one between them, and Mercado's familiarity would have earned him at least a punch in the gut, as he'd told him in Rome. But Purcell didn't want to upset the mission. Also, he liked Henry.

Mercado said to him, "I'm not sure, but I think you were flying too slow as you passed by."

"Let me pilot the aircraft, Henry."

"I'm thinking about *me*, old man. Your passenger. And Vivian."

"Don't worry about it." Purcell informed him, "If it makes you feel better, Signore Bocaccio was impressed with my flying skills."

"Good. But will he let you fly it again?"

"He's thinking about it."

"We need that plane." Mercado asked, "And how is Signore Bocaccio? Is he trying to pretend that the Marxists haven't taken charge and that his privileged life will continue as usual?"

"No, I think he gets that it's over."

"He sounds more realistic than many of my colonial compatriots around the world."

"Right."

"The old world order is finished."

"Indeed it is." Purcell informed Mercado, "Signore Bocaccio wants to know if our newspaper wants to buy Mia."

"Who?"

"The airplane. Mia."

"Oh...I don't think so."

"Please ask." He explained, "Signore Bocaccio wants to get out."

"He should. And you should tell him we're considering buying his aircraft so he will let us continue renting it."

"I may have led him to believe that."

"You are devious, Frank."

"*Me?* You just told me to con him."

Their breakfast came and Purcell said, "On the taxi ride to the airstrip, I saw children with distended stomachs."

Mercado stayed quiet a moment, then said, "Sometimes I weep for this land."

"If you'd seen what I saw in Cambo, you'd weep for that land, too." He looked at Mercado. "We could weep for the whole world, Henry, but that won't change the world."

Mercado nodded. "When you get to be my age, Frank, you start to wonder...what the hell has gone wrong?"

"It's all gone wrong."

"It has. But then you see...well, Father Armano. And these UN relief people. And all the aid volunteers and missionaries who come to places like this to do good. To help their fellow human beings."

"That is a hopeful thing."

"For every Getachu, there is a decent human being trying to soften the world's suffering."

"I hope so." Purcell asked, "When will the good guys win?"

"When the last battle is fought between the forces of

good and evil. When Christ and the Antichrist meet at Armageddon."

"Sounds like a hell of a story. I hope I get to cover it."

"We cover it every day, Frank."

Purcell nodded.

Purcell wasn't as hungry as he'd thought, and he drank his coffee and lit a cigarette.

Mercado was looking up at the stained glass and said, "It doesn't actually show Solomon and Sheba in the act."

"You have to use your imagination."

"I think that scene would bring in the customers."

"Or the police." Purcell asked, "Have you heard anything about Mr. Selassie, as he is now called?"

"I have heard a rumor that they are gently grilling him about his assets here and abroad, and that he's giving them a little at a time in exchange for the lives of some of his family."

"And what happens when he's given them everything?"

He informed Purcell, "They've smothered a few old royals with pillows and announced a natural death. That will be his fate. Or something similar."

Purcell nodded. He asked, "Do you think the emperor knows the location of the black monastery?"

"That is a good question. The royal court used to travel throughout the kingdom to dispense justice, give pardons, give money to churches, and so forth. They would always visit the Ark of the Covenant at Axum. So it is possible that the emperor has visited the black monastery, but my instincts say he has not. And even if he had, he could not give his captors the grid coordinates."

"Right. I'm sure he wasn't driving the tour bus."

"More likely the Grail was brought to him at some location away from the monastery."

"Like the village of Shoan."

"Possible." Mercado informed him, "The royal court has been shrouded in secrecy for three thousand years. They make the emperor of Japan's court seem like an open house party."

"And the Vatican makes every other closed institution look like a public information office."

"Your anti-papist views are annoying, Frank." He reminded him, "You work for the Vatican newspaper."

"God help me."

"In any case, the imperial court of Ethiopia is no more."

"Unless Gann gets his way."

"That will not happen. There is no going back."

"I think you're right, Henry. And on that subject, where is Sir Edmund?"

"I'm beginning to wonder myself."

"He said he'd arrive on the twenty-fourth, which was yesterday. But we were to wait four days before we gave up on him."

"Then we will wait. But if he doesn't show, we will press on. Without him."

"We need those maps."

"We have an aircraft."

"Aerial recon is not a substitute for terrain maps. One complements the other. Also, Colonel Gann has skills we don't have."

"I believe we can do this without him. But I can't do this without you and Vivian."

Purcell looked at Mercado and asked, "Why are we actually doing this? Tell me again."

"My reasons, like yours, Frank, change every day. There are days I think of my immortal soul, and other days I think how nice it would be to become rich and famous on a world Grail tour. The only thing I'm sure of is that we—all three of us—were chosen to do this, and I believe we will not know why until we are in the presence of the Holy Grail and the Holy Spirit."

Purcell nodded. "All right. If Gann doesn't show up, I'm still in. I'll ask Vivian."

"You don't have to ask." Mercado looked toward the lobby. "But if you'd like to, here she is."

Vivian came into the room carrying a tote bag and wearing khaki trousers, a shapeless pullover, and walking shoes. She spotted them and came toward the table, smiling.

Mercado rose, smiled at her, and pulled out a chair.

Vivian gave them both a peck on the cheek, then sat and said, "I thought I might find you both in the bar as usual."

Mercado replied, "It is now the breakfast room. But I can get you a Bloody Mary."

"No thank you." She asked, "What have you two been talking about?"

Purcell replied, "Aerial recon."

She took his hand. "Frank, you were absolutely magnificent. What other skills do you have that you haven't told us about?"

"I can tie a bow tie."

She laughed, then took Purcell's toast. "I'm famished."

Mercado said to her, "I was telling Frank that we were impressed with his flyby."

Vivian glanced at Purcell, who was trying to get a waiter's attention, then she looked at Mercado and their eyes met. He smiled. She gave him a look of mock annoyance.

The waiter came and Vivian ordered tea and fruit, then ate one of Purcell's sausages. Mercado told her, "We were feeling guilty about the famine."

"Did you cause it, Henry?"

"I'm having only a cornetto."

"Well, you should keep up your strength. You're going to need it."

"Excellent point." Mercado was not getting the full satisfaction from this moment, so he suggested, "Perhaps we should clear the air about this morning."

Vivian responded a second too late. "What do you mean?"

"Frank was wondering why we were having coffee together on my balcony."

She looked at Purcell. "What were you wondering about?"

"I think Henry misconstrued my question."

She looked back at Mercado, who said to Purcell, "Sorry, old man. I thought you were showing a bit of jealousy."

Purcell looked at him and said, "I was actually wondering how you got your old ass out of bed so early."

"I set my alarm to see you, Frank. And then I thought, What if Vivian oversleeps? So I rang her up and asked her to join me for coffee while you buzzed by." He joked, "If you hadn't seen either of us, then perhaps you should have wondered where we were."

Purcell was not amused, and Vivian kicked Mercado under the table and said, "Can we change the subject?" She asked, "Have we heard from Sir Edmund?"

Mercado replied, "We have not."

"Should we be worried?"

"Frank thinks not."

"Can we do this without him?"

"Again, Frank thinks not." Mercado added, "The maps."

Vivian reached into her bag, withdrew a thick manila envelope, and put it on the table. "This was at the front desk."

Purcell saw that it had been hand-delivered, addressed to "Mercado, Purcell, Smith, *L'Osservatore Romano*, Hilton Hotel." There was no sender information.

Vivian asked, "Shall I open it?"

Purcell glanced around the room. "Okay."

Vivian used a knife to cut through the heavily taped flap, then peeked inside. "M-A-P-S."

Purcell said, "See if there's a note."

She slid her hand in the envelope and pulled out a piece of paper. She read, "I am in Addis. Will contact you. Good flying, Mr. Purcell." Vivian told them, "It is unsigned."

Mercado said, "Thank God he's here and safe."

Purcell pointed out, "Being here is not being safe."

"Well, in any case, we have the maps, and if he does not contact us, we three can continue on."

Vivian asked Purcell, "How did he know you were flying?"

"I suppose we're being watched by the Royalist underground."

Vivian said, "This is exciting."

Purcell assured her, "It gets more exciting when the security police knock on your door."

They finished their breakfast and Purcell said he'd call Signore Bocaccio to see if they could get the airplane for seven the next morning. He advised Mercado, "We don't need you on board, but another set of eyes would be good."

Mercado hesitated, then replied, "I wouldn't miss the experience, Frank."

"Good."

Mercado said he was going to the Imperial to check telexes and catch up on rumors and gossip. He added, "I will also write a story on the famine." He told Purcell, "I saw that story you filed about the Catholic refugees, saying that the Provisional government was not helping them."

"Hope you enjoyed it."

"Was *any* of it based on fact?"

"I'm taking a page from your notebook, Henry, and being creative."

Mercado did not reply to that, but said, "It is true that newspapers are a rough draft of history. But not a rough draft of historical fiction."

Purcell was getting annoyed. "Looking forward to your factual coverage of the famine."

"My story will stress the government's selling of national treasures to buy food for the people."

"That is not what is happening. They are buying guns."

"My point, Frank, has nothing to do with truth or fiction—it has to do with not writing anything that will get us expelled from the country. Or arrested."

"I think I know that, Henry."

"Good. We can tell the truth when we get out of here."

"When you're in Ethiopia, it's *if*, not *when*."

"Meanwhile, I've told the paper to hold your story."

Vivian, who had stayed quiet during this exchange, said, "*When* we get out of here, we will have a much bigger story to tell." She said to Mercado, "We have agreed to work together, Henry, and to be friends and colleagues, and to forget the past." She looked at him. "Didn't we?"

He smiled. "We did." He wished them a good day and left.

Vivian stayed quiet a moment, then said to Purcell, "I'm sorry."

"About what?"

"You know."

"Look, Vivian, I know you're still fond of him, and that's all right." He recalled what Mercado said and reminded her, "We're going to be in close quarters when we get out of Addis, so we all need to put aside the . . . jealousies."

She smiled and asked, "So can we all bathe together in the nude?"

"No."

"See? You *are* jealous."

"What do you want to do today?"

"I want to take pictures of everything I lost when I was in jail and those bastards ransacked my room."

"Sounds good."

"I need to get my camera." She stood and said, "Will you come upstairs with me, Mr. Purcell? I want to show you my new F-1."

He smiled and stood. "Remember that we work for the Vatican, Miss Smith."

"I will shout, 'Oh, God!' at the appropriate moment."

He picked up the envelope and they went to her room.

As he was getting undressed, he noticed the white *shamma* she had been wearing, draped over a chair. He also noticed the hotel bathrobe lying on her bed. It was a very cool morning and he thought she should have worn that on Henry's balcony.

Chapter 36

The small Fiat taxi climbed the fog-shrouded hills with Purcell and Vivian in the rear and Mercado in front with the driver.

They reached the airstrip, where a swirling ground mist obscured the runway and the hangars. Purcell said to Mercado, "It's okay if you want to go back." He added, "It's not a bad idea to have a potential survivor."

Mercado did not reply.

"Someone to carry on with the mission. Or tell our story."

Mercado opened the door and got out of the taxi.

Purcell told the driver to wait, and to Vivian he said, "In case there's a problem with the authorities. Or with Henry."

"He's not good in the mornings."

"I wouldn't know." He got out of the taxi and walked to the hangar to file his flight plan. He found, to his surprise, that he was still annoyed with Henry—and with Vivian—about their coffee date. There was no reason for her to be alone with him. But as they all knew, there would be more such moments in the weeks ahead.

A young air force lieutenant sat behind a desk in the hangar office, smoking a cigarette. Signore Bocaccio had given Purcell a few flight plan forms and advised him how to fill them out, which Purcell had done in

English, the international language of flight—except here, apparently.

The lieutenant looked at the flight plan, and it was obvious he couldn't read it.

"Where go you?"

"Gondar." Purcell pointed to the destination line of the form.

"Why?"

Purcell showed him his press credentials and his passport. "Gazetanna."

The man pointed outside. "Who go you?"

"Gazetanna." He held up two fingers.

The lieutenant shook his head. "No." He waved his hand in dismissal.

Purcell took the carbon copy of the flight plan out of his pocket and put it on the desk. The Ethiopian birr had collapsed, but there was a fifty-thousand-lire note—about forty dollars—paper-clipped to the form.

The lieutenant eyed the money—about a month's pay—then picked up his rubber stamp and slammed it on Purcell's copy of the flight plan, then wrote the time on it. "Go!"

Purcell took his copy and exited the hangar.

Henry hadn't taken the taxi back to the hotel, and he was talking to Vivian near the Navion. Purcell paid the cabbie, then walked to the aircraft.

Mercado asked, "Any problems?"

"Are we reimbursed for bribes?"

"There are no bribes in the People's Republic. Only user fees."

Vivian had her camera bag and said, "I was telling Henry that I dug up a wide-angle lens at the Reuters office, and they have a good lab for blow-ups." She added, "And they don't ask questions."

"Good. Are we ready? Pit stop? Henry? How's your bladder?"

"Everything down there works well."

Purcell tapped his canvas bag and said, "I have an empty water carafe from the hotel if anyone needs to use it." He asked Mercado, "Did you remember to buy binoculars?"

"I borrowed a pair from the press office."

As Purcell walked to the wing, Mercado asked him, "What is this?" He pointed to the rocket pod.

"What does it look like, Henry?"

"A rocket pod. Are we attacking?"

As Purcell was explaining about the rocket pod, Mercado noticed bullet holes in the fuselage and pointed them out to everyone.

Purcell assured Vivian and Mercado, "Lucky hits." He climbed onto the left wing from the trailing edge, unlatched the canopy, and slid it back. The odor of musty leather and hydraulic fluid drifted out of the cockpit. He reached down for Mercado, who took his hand and vaulted up onto the wing. Purcell said, "Pick any seat in the rear."

"There are no seats."

"Sit on the bean bags."

Mercado climbed unhappily into the rear as Purcell reached down for Vivian and pulled her up. She squeezed into the cockpit and crossed over to the right-hand seat.

Purcell got in and slid the canopy closed. "All right, Henry, there is a seat belt back there."

"I'm working on it."

Purcell fastened his belt and Vivian did the same. He said, "The time written on our flight plan is six thirty-eight. We are supposed to be in Gondar in under three hours. Anything longer will raise questions from the guy who takes our flight plan at the other end. But we need to make some unauthorized detours, so it might be after ten when we land. I will blame headwinds."

Mercado asked, "What if they know there are no headwinds?"

"They only know what is reported to them by other pilots who have landed. And I don't think there is much traffic from Addis to Gondar."

Purcell opened Signore Bocaccio's chart and glanced at it. He said, "What I will do is run her up to twelve thousand feet, and try to get a hundred and fifty out of her. When we see Lake Tana, I will go as low and slow as I can around the areas where we think the black monastery could be located." He added, "We'll also take a look at the spa and the thing marked incognita. Vivian will take wide-angle photos, then at some point we need to climb to six thousand feet, which is Gondar's elevation. With luck we will land in Gondar no later than ten A.M."

Vivian said, "If anyone asks, what are we supposed to be doing in Gondar?"

"We're doing an article on the ancient fortress city."

Mercado said, "That's a stretch, Frank."

"Okay. We're looking for an interview with General Getachu."

Vivian said, "I like your first idea better."

Purcell reminded them, "We're reporters. We have

no idea what we're doing." He looked at his watch: 6:52. "Ready?"

Vivian said, "If you are, I am."

He turned on the master switch, then pulled the wheel, and Vivian was startled when the wheel in front of her moved in concert with his. He pushed on the rudder pedals, and hers moved under her feet. He said to her, "This is dual control, but that does not mean that two of us are going to fly this. Keep your hands off the wheel and your feet off the pedals."

"Yes, sir."

He pumped the throttle a few times, then hit the starter. The engine coughed, and a black puff of smoke billowed out from under the cowl. The propeller went by once, twice, and the engine caught.

Vivian noticed a Saint Christopher medal that Signore Bocaccio had pinned to the headliner above the windshield. She touched it, and said, "Patron saint of travelers. He will watch over us."

"Good."

Purcell looked at the disarrayed and mostly inoperative gauges. Under the control panel was a new switch, marked in English, "Safety," and "Fire." A separate red button was the actual trigger for the smoke rockets. A round, clear plastic sighting device was mounted in front of him on a swivel near the windshield. He had noticed that there were still four smoke rockets left in the pod. According to Signore Bocaccio, this was not unusual; the Ethiopian ground crews minimized their workload. Signore Bocaccio had advised Purcell not to demand that the rockets be taken out. He also advised him not to fire them for sport.

Purcell glanced at the distant windsock, then released the handbrake and rolled toward the runways. He saw that a C-47 was sitting on the edge of the long runway that he had used with Signore Bocaccio the previous day. He had no time to wait for the C-47 to move, so he taxied to the shorter runway, which Signore Bocaccio had said was all right to use, depending on winds, fuel load, and cargo load. The fuel gauge said full, but Vivian was light and Mercado had skipped breakfast.

Purcell taxied to the end of the shorter runway. The noise level in the cockpit was tolerable and speech was possible if they raised their voices. He asked, "Everyone okay?"

Vivian nodded. Mercado did not reply.

Purcell checked the flight controls and the elevator trim position. He did a quick engine run-up and noticed that the magneto drop was neither good nor bad. He'd go with it.

He cycled the propeller through its range, then wheeled onto the runway, where the ground fog had mostly blown off. He lined up the nose on what was once a white line. The expanse of broken concrete was a little disturbing. He hesitated, then pushed the throttle in and the Navion began its run.

The aircraft bounced badly over the broken concrete. The control panel vibrated, the Plexiglas canopy rattled, and the controls shook in his hands. The thumping sound of the nose gear strut filled the cabin as it bottomed out. He glanced at Vivian and saw that she was playing with her camera.

The Navion ate up the runway at the rate of fifty

miles per hour, then sixty. The end of the runway was shrouded in fog, but he knew it was also the end of the flat-topped hill that he'd noticed when he'd flown over it with Bocaccio. Purcell saw that the land dropped away to his sides into fog banks. He was on a ridge and there was no aborting this takeoff anymore.

"Frank!"

It was Mercado, but there was nothing to discuss.

Vivian looked up from her camera, but said nothing.

Purcell glanced at his airspeed indicator and noticed that the balky instrument read zero. The throttle was fully open, but Mia showed no signs of lifting.

The runway suddenly ended and Vivian let out a startled sound, then reached out and put her fingers on Saint Christopher.

The control wheel felt light in Purcell's hands and the Navion hung for a moment, as though trying to decide whether to fly or drop into the valley.

The nose dipped down, and Purcell pulled back slowly on the wheel and pulled the hydraulic landing gear lever. Mia lifted slightly. The adjoining hill went by off his left wing, and he noticed that it had more elevation than the Navion. The sound of the landing gear banging into its wells gave Vivian a start, and Mercado said, "Oh!"

The aircraft began to climb. Purcell glanced at the altimeter. He was at seventy-eight hundred feet, which was not good considering he had started at seventy-nine hundred. Around him, the mountains rose ten and twelve thousand feet and seemed to hem him in. A peak rose up to his front.

The aircraft continued to climb, and at twelve thousand feet he relaxed a bit. He turned to a northwesterly heading and asked, "Mind if I smoke?"

No one seemed to mind, so he lit up. He asked, "Anyone need that carafe?"

Vivian replied, "Too late for that."

Purcell asked, "How you doing, Henry?"

No response.

Vivian turned her head. "Are you all right?"

"I'm fine."

"Would you like some water?"

"I'm fine."

Vivian asked Purcell, "Did you do that yesterday?"

"Yesterday we used the longer airstrip."

"Can we do that next time?"

"We can."

"How did the landing go?"

"Don't worry about it."

"Can I have a puff?"

He handed her the cigarette.

They continued on a northwesterly heading and Purcell said to Mercado, "You should familiarize yourself with those terrain maps."

"I thought you had them."

"Are you joking, Henry?"

"Oh . . . here they are."

Vivian laughed.

Purcell settled back and scanned the instrument panel. He was happy to see that the airspeed indicator was now working.

Mercado said, "The next time, I will volunteer to be the potential survivor."

"Happy to shed the takeoff weight."

They continued on and Purcell looked out his left side. It was a beautiful country from the air. This is what God had given the human race. In fact, the earliest remains of a human ancestor, over three million years old, had been found in the Awash Valley. And since then, it had been a long, hard climb toward...something.

Vivian snapped a picture of him, then of Henry sitting on the coffee bean bags in the rear. Henry took her camera and said, "Turn around."

She turned, smiled, and Mercado took a picture of her.

Vivian said to her companions, "We have begun our journey."

Mercado replied, "We almost ended it on takeoff."

Vivian assured him, "I felt Saint Christopher and the angels lifting our wings."

Purcell was about to say something clever, but when he thought about that takeoff, there was no aeronautical reason why it should have happened.

Vivian again touched the Saint Christopher medal over the windshield. "Thank you."

"How about me?"

"Next time, use the longer runway."

They continued on in silence as Ethiopia slid by beneath their wings. Somewhere down there, Purcell thought, was the thing they were looking for. And maybe that thing was waiting for them.

Chapter 37

An hour out of Addis, Purcell spotted the great bend in the Blue Nile. He banked right and followed it north. Their airspeed was one hundred fifty, and the flight so far had been smooth except for some mountain updrafts. The smell of the coffee beans in the burlap bags was pleasant.

Purcell had been thinking about the logistics of their quest, the devils that were in the details. He said to Vivian, "If there is any problem when we land in Gondar, they may confiscate your film. And if they see we've been shooting wide-angle photos of the terrain, we will have some explaining to do."

"I will hide the exposed rolls on my person."

"They may look at your person."

Mercado confided to them, "I once hid a roll of film in a place where the sun does not shine."

"Don't tempt me, Henry." He added, "We don't want the film found on us." He suggested, "Maybe the coffee bags."

Mercado replied, "The ground crew at Gondar will help themselves to a bag or two."

Purcell noticed a taped rip in the headliner above the windshield where the Saint Christopher medal was pinned. He pulled back the tape and said, "We can also put the maps in there."

Mercado pointed out, "Even if there is no trouble in Gondar, the authorities will do a thorough search of the cockpit when we leave the aircraft, and they will probably find that."

Purcell did not reply.

Mercado continued, "If we deny any knowledge of the maps or the film, which together may look suspicious, then Signore Bocaccio will be down at police headquarters in Addis answering questions, while we are answering questions at Getachu's headquarters in Gondar."

Purcell thought about that. Henry made some good points. "What do you suggest?"

"I say we take a chance that there will be no problems at the Gondar airfield, and we should carry the exposed film and maps with us." He added, "If there *is* a problem in Gondar, it is already waiting for us, and the film and the maps will be the least of our problems."

Purcell's instincts still told him not to carry around incriminating evidence in a police state. Especially with prior arrests hanging over their heads. But Henry Mercado had been at this game far longer than Frank Purcell. And there seemed to be no good choices.

Vivian said, "I will carry my exposed film in my bag." She added, "Naked is the best disguise. As soon as you try to hide something, you get in trouble."

Mercado commented, "You should know."

Vivian ignored him and continued, "Frank will carry the maps." She pointed out, "It's not as though we're carrying guns or a picture of the emperor."

Purcell nodded. "Okay. We land in Gondar and take

our things with us. I need to give our flight plan to the officer on the ground, then we take a taxi to town."

Mercado, too, had some thoughts about their destination. "If Getachu somehow knows we have returned to his lair, I believe he will not reveal himself to us. He will watch to see what we are doing back in Ethiopia."

Purcell replied, "I don't think he's that bright. I think he acts on his primitive impulses."

"We will find out in Gondar."

Vivian asked, "Can we change the subject?"

Purcell said, "Here's another subject. When we begin our search for the black monastery, we should not drive from Addis to the north again. Agreed?"

Vivian agreed. "I would not do that again."

"So," Purcell said, "at some point, after we've finished our aerial recon, and when we think we have a few possible locations for the black monastery, we need to fly to Gondar, ditch the aircraft, and buy or rent a cross-country vehicle to go exploring." He pointed out, "From Gondar to the area we need to explore is about four to six hours—rather than three or four days cross-country from Addis."

Mercado agreed. "Gondar should be our jump-off point."

They continued on in silence. Purcell followed the Blue Nile north and maintained his airspeed and altitude.

Vivian announced, "I need to go."

Mercado passed her the empty water carafe. She said, "Close your eyes. You too, Frank." She pulled down her pants and panties and relieved herself.

Purcell said, "My turn. Close your eyes, Henry." He unzipped his fly.

Vivian offered, "I'll hold it for you so you can fly." She laughed. "I mean the *carafe*."

Purcell suspected that Henry was not amused. He held the wheel with his left hand and himself with the other, and Vivian held the carafe for him.

"Finished."

She snapped the hinged lid of the carafe in place and passed it to Henry, who also used it. Indeed, Purcell thought, they would be in close quarters in the days and weeks ahead with many more close bonding moments. It was good that they were all friends.

At 8:32, Purcell spotted Lake Tana, nestled among the hills. The altimeter read eleven thousand eight hundred feet, and the lake looked like it was about six thousand feet below, which put the lake's altitude at about a mile high. In the hazy distance, about twenty miles north of the lake, would be Gondar.

He pointed out the big lake to his passengers and said, "We've made good time, so we may be able to snoop around for an hour."

Purcell began his descent. Within half an hour they were about a thousand feet over the terrain, and the altimeter read sixty-three hundred feet above sea level.

He made a slow banking turn over the lake's eastern shore, and Henry, who had a map spread out in the rear, said, "I can see the monastery of Tana Kirkos that Colonel Gann mentioned. See it on that rocky peninsula jutting into the lake?"

Vivian saw it and took a photo through the Plexiglas.

Mercado said, "Somewhere along that lakeshore is where Father Armano's battalion made camp, almost forty years ago."

The lake was ringed with rocky hills, which Purcell knew was very defensible terrain for Father Armano's decimated battalion. The monastery of Tana Kirkos, he thought, was also defendable because of its position on a rocky peninsula. The black monastery, however, was safe because it was hidden. Even from up here.

He made another slow banking turn and said, "We will see if we can find the spa."

Mercado peered through the canopy with his binoculars and Vivian had her nose pressed against the Plexiglas. "There! See it?"

Purcell lowered his right wing and reduced his airspeed. Below, off his wingtip, he could clearly see the white stucco spa complex and the grassy fields around it. He saw the main building where they'd parked the Jeep and found Father Armano, and he spotted the narrow road that they'd driven on to get there. He wondered again why he'd turned off that bush-choked road at exactly that spot.

Vivian said excitedly, "There's the sulphur pool!"

Purcell stared at the pool, then glanced at Vivian. A whole confluence of events had come together down there on that night, and from up here, in the full sunshine, it was no more understandable than it was in the dark.

Vivian said, "It looks so beautiful from here." She took several pictures and said, "We will go back there to find Father Armano's remains." She reminded them, "The Vatican needs a relic."

Purcell had no comment on that and said, "We will continue our walk down memory lane."

He turned the aircraft north and said, "The scene of the last battle."

Below were the hills where the last cohesive Royalist forces, led by Prince Joshua, had camped and fought, and died. Purcell dropped to two hundred feet. All the bright tents of the prince's army were long gone, and all that remained were scattered bones and skulls in the rocky soil.

Mercado said, "A civilization died there."

Purcell nodded.

The hills still showed the cratered shell holes on the bare slopes, and those scars and the bones were all the evidence left of what had happened here while he, Vivian, and Henry were bathing at the Italian spa. If they had arrived a day earlier—or a day later—who knows?

They flew farther north to Getachu's hills. The army had decamped long ago, and only the scarred earth of trenches and firing positions remained to suggest that thousands of men had been there.

Purcell could not determine where Getachu's headquarters tent had been, but then he saw where Getachu had hanged the soldiers with commo wire, and he spotted the ravine where they had all been shackled, and the helipad where they had been lifted out of this hell.

Purcell got lower and slower and they could see the natural amphitheater—the parade ground—and Purcell was certain that Vivian and Henry saw the ten poles that were still sticking out of the ground. But no one pointed this out. And neither did anyone point out the wooden platform where he and Vivian had clung to each other in what they both believed was their last night on earth.

Unlike the spa, this scene, from this perspective, made the events of that night more understandable.

Vivian did not take photographs and she turned away from the Plexiglas.

Henry, of course, had nothing to say, but Purcell would have liked to know what he was thinking.

Purcell circled around toward the plateau between the two camps. To their left he spotted the ridgeline that they'd all climbed to get away from the Gallas, and the peak where Henry and Colonel Gann had picked the wrong time to take a nap. He banked to the right, and the wide grassy plateau spread out before them between the hills.

Vivian asked him, "Is that where we were?"

"That's it."

"It looks very nice from up here."

"Everything does." He pointed. "That's the ridge we climbed to go get help from General Getachu."

It sounded funny in retrospect and Vivian laughed. "What were we thinking?"

"Not much."

He turned east and flew the length of the plateau between the hills where the armed camps had once been dug in.

Something caught his eye in the high grass ahead: a dozen Gallas on horseback riding west toward them.

Mercado saw them, too, and said, "Those bastards are still here." He suggested to Purcell, "Fire your rockets at them."

"They're not my rockets. And they're only smoke markers."

"Bastards!"

Henry, Purcell thought, was recalling Mount Aradam, where the Gallas had almost gotten his balls.

The Gallas saw the aircraft coming toward them, and Purcell was about to bank right to get out of rifle range, but he had a second thought and put the Navion into a dive.

Vivian asked, "What are you doing? Frank?"

Mercado called out, "For God's sake, man—"

Purcell got as low and slow as he dared, and the Gallas sat placidly on their horses, staring at the rapidly closing airplane. They must have seen the rocket pod, Purcell thought, because they suddenly began to scatter. A few horses reared up at the sound of the howling engine, and a few riders were thrown off their mounts.

Purcell got lower and gunned the engine as he buzzed over them. He banked sharply to the right to avoid giving them a retreating target, then flew over the Royalist camp and dropped lower toward the valley to put the hills between himself and the line of fire of the very angry Gallas.

Mercado shouted above the noise of the engine, "What the hell are you doing?"

"Looking for my Jeep."

"Are you insane?"

"Sorry. I lost it."

Vivian took a deep breath. "Don't do that again."

Purcell headed southeast along the jungle valley and said, "We will look for Prince Theodore's fortress."

He reduced his airspeed and his altitude as he followed the valley, which widened into a vast expanse of green between the neighboring hills.

Mercado leaned between the two seats with the map of the area and said, "Here is incognita." Purcell glanced at the map, then looked through the surrounding Plexiglas to orient himself. He made a slight right turn and said, "Should be coming up in a few minutes at about one o'clock."

He pulled back on the throttle and the airspeed bled off, and the Navion sank lower above the triple-canopy jungle. He was starting to recognize the warning signs of a stall in this aircraft, but its flight characteristics were still unpredictable.

He got down to two hundred feet and Vivian said, "It's all going by too fast."

He explained, "If we go low, we can see things in better detail, but everything shoots by fast no matter how slow I go. If we go high, the ground looks like it's going by slower, but we can't see smaller objects."

"Thank you, Frank. I never realized that."

"I'm telling you this because you are in charge of photography. What do you want?"

"I need altitude for the wide-angle lens. I'll get the photos enlarged and we can go over them with a magnifier."

"Okay. Meanwhile, if you'll look to your one o'clock position, I see something."

Henry learned forward and they all looked to where Purcell was pointing. He picked up the nose to slow the aircraft, and up ahead, to their slight right, they could see a break in the jungle canopy, and inside the clear area were broken walls and burned-out buildings. If they hadn't known it was intact five months before, they'd have thought it was an old ruin—except that the jungle had not yet reclaimed the clearing.

Purcell thought of the priest. He'd escaped death here, then walked out of his prison into the jungle.

And something—God, memory, or a jungle path—led him west, to the Italian spa. But he wasn't heading for the spa. It hadn't been built when he'd been captured, according to Gann and to the map, which did not show the spa. So what was it that took him west to that spa and to his rendezvous with three people who themselves did not know about the spa? Probably, Purcell thought, a jungle path, or a game trail. If he asked Vivian or Henry, the answer was simple: God led Father Armano to them. Purcell thought he'd go with the game trail theory.

Vivian shot a few photos as they approached, then the ruined fortress shot by and she said, "Can we come around higher?"

"We can." He climbed as he began a wide, clockwise turn.

In a few minutes, the fortress came into view again off their right side at about a thousand feet.

As Vivian took photos, she asked, as if to herself, "Can you imagine being locked in a cell in the middle of the jungle for forty years?"

Purcell wanted to tell her that if they found the black monastery, she might find out what that's like.

More importantly, he had confirmed another detail of Father Armano's story. Also, they'd fixed a few points of this tale—the east shore of Lake Tana, the spa, and the fortress. Now all they had to do was find the black monastery which they believed was in this area.

He looked at the thick, unbroken carpet of jungle and rain forest below. He'd once ridden in an army spotter plane in Vietnam, and the pilot had told him, "There are enemy base camps under that triple canopy. And thousands of men. And we can't see anything."

Right. Which was why the Americans defoliated and napalmed the jungle. But here, there were hundreds of thousands of acres of thick, pristine jungle and rain forest, and there could have been a city under that canopy and no one would ever see it. Also, they had only a vague idea where to look.

Mercado was having similar thoughts and said, "This is a rather large area of jungle."

"You noticed?"

"A clue might be that old map we saw in the Ethiopian College."

"Henry, please."

"And the stained glass window at the Hilton."

"You're sounding oxygen-deprived."

"What they have in common is that they show palm trees. And if you look, you won't see many clusters of palms down there."

Purcell glanced out the canopy. True, there weren't many palm trees, but...that wasn't a very solid clue. He said, "Okay, we'll keep an eye out for palms. Meanwhile, we have about a half hour before we need to head for Gondar, so I'll make ascending corkscrew turns and Vivian will begin shooting everything below as we climb." He suggested to her, "Try to overlap a bit—"

"I know."

"Good. Up we go." He pushed in the throttle and the Navion began to climb. Purcell said to Mercado, "Use the field glasses, and if you see any abnormalities below, bring it to my and Vivian's attention." He told them, "I'm going to slide open the canopy so Vivian can get clear shots." He unlatched the canopy and slid it open a few feet, and the roar of the engine filled the cabin.

Vivian unfastened her seat belt, leaned forward, and pointed her camera through the opening.

They circled the area east of Lake Tana—the forested land that matched up with Father Armano's story, which began on the east shore of the lake and ended at his fortress prison. The lakeshore was known, though not the exact location of the priest's starting point along the eighty-mile shoreline. And the fortress was no longer incognita. What *was* incognita, however, was everything under that jungle canopy, including the black monastery.

Purcell looked down at the land below. There seemed to be no man-made break in the green carpet of jungle. But they knew that.

Vivian, believing in Henry's inspiration about the palm trees, took lots of photos of palm clusters. There were a few small ponds below, and she also focused on them because the priest had mentioned a pond within the walls of the monastery.

As for the tree, the stream, and the rock, as Gann had pointed out, there were lots of trees, and a rock would not be visible unless it was huge, or sat in a clearing. Purcell and Mercado saw streams on the map, but they were not visible through the thick jungle.

Purcell thought about the Italian Army cartographers who'd created dozens of terrain maps based on their aerial photography. They'd spotted the fortress, and a few other man-made objects on their photographs that they'd transferred to their maps. But they had not spotted the black monastery, or anything else they might have labeled "incognita."

Needle in a haystack. Monastery in a jungle.

The key, he thought, might be the village of Shoan. He looked at his watch. It was almost 10 A.M. and they needed to head for Gondar, or they'd be unexplainably late on a flight from Addis.

He let Vivian take a few more photos, then shouted, "That's it!" He slid the canopy closed and latched it. The cockpit became quieter, but no one spoke. If they were disappointed in their aerial recon, they didn't say so.

Purcell picked up a northwesterly heading and began climbing to Gondar's elevation.

He had no idea what awaited them in Gondar, away from the relative safety of the capital. But if their last trip to Getachu territory was predictive, their search for the Holy Grail could be over in half an hour.

He had enough fuel to turn around and go back to Addis, but then he'd have no explanation for this flight.

He said, "We land in about twenty minutes."

No one replied, and he continued on.

Chapter 38

Lake Tana was coming up on their left, and beyond the lake were the mountains of Gondar.

Purcell said, "We'll catch Shoan on the way back."

Mercado informed him, "You may not see anyone down there." He explained, "There is a mass exodus of Falasha Jews under way."

"I heard that. But why?"

"They feel threatened."

"I know the feeling." He reminded Mercado, "Gann said the Falashas have a special place in Ethiopian society."

"Not anymore."

Vivian asked, "Where are they going?"

"To Israel, of course. The Israelis have organized an airlift." Mercado informed them, "Every Jew in the world has the right to emigrate to Israel under the Law of Return."

It seemed to Purcell that everyone who could leave was leaving. Soon the only people left would be the Marxist government, the Russian and Cuban advisors, the peasants, and idiot reporters. And for all he knew, the monks of the black monastery were gone, too, along with the Holy Grail.

Mercado continued, "The Falashas are the only

non-convert Jews in the world who were not part of the Diaspora. They are Ethiopians who have been Jewish since before the time of Sheba. Their ethnic origins are here, not Israel or Judea, so the Law of Return does not technically apply to them. But the Israeli government is welcoming them."

"That's good. But I hope they're still in Shoan, because we're going to put that on our itinerary."

"I think you're placing too much hope on Shoan for our mission."

"We'll see when we get there."

At 10:20, Purcell spotted the fortress city of Gondar rising from the hills. It looked like some movie set from a fantasy flick that featured dragons and warlocks. The reality, however, was worse; it was General Getachu's army headquarters.

The civilian-military airfield was perched on a nearby plateau, and without radio contact, Purcell had to swoop down to see the windsock, and for the tower to see him, making him feel like an intruder into enemy airspace.

The control tower turned on a steady green light for him, the international signal for "Cleared to land."

He lined up on the north-south runway and began his descent.

Mercado said, "I don't see a firing squad waiting for us."

"They're behind the hangar, Henry."

Vivian suggested, "Can we stop with the gallows humor?"

As the Navion crossed the threshold of the long runway, Purcell snapped the throttle back to idle, and the aircraft touched down. "Welcome to Gondar."

He let the Navion run out to the end of the runway as he looked around for any signs that they should turn around, take off, and fly to Sudan, or to French Somaliland, about two hundred fifty miles to the east.

Henry, too, was looking toward the hangars, and at the military vehicles nearby.

The Navion came to a halt, and Purcell taxied toward the hangars.

Vivian lifted her camera, but Mercado said, "You cannot take photos here."

She put the camera in her bag.

Purcell noticed a C-47 military transport parked near one of the hangars, and he wondered if it was the same one that had blocked him from using the longer runway at the Addis airstrip. The tail number seemed to be the same, but he couldn't be sure.

He taxied up to the hangar and killed the engine. The cockpit became quiet after four hours in the air, and it was easy now to speak, but no one had anything to say.

Purcell unlatched the canopy and slid it back, letting the cool mountain air into the stuffy cockpit. He said, "Take everything. Leave the carafe."

He climbed onto the wing, then helped Vivian and Mercado out.

Four men in olive drab uniforms, wearing holsters, were watching them.

They knew the Navion, of course, and Purcell could see they had expected Signore Bocaccio to come out of the cockpit, or maybe Ethiopian pilots who had commandeered the Navion to shoot smoke rockets at the enemies of the state.

Purcell said to his companions, "The good news is that they seem surprised to see us."

They all jumped down to the concrete apron and walked toward the four military men. One of the men, a captain, motioned them inside the hangar office. He took his seat behind a desk and looked at them.

Purcell noted that the captain was wearing the red star insignia of the new Marxist state, but he had probably worn the Lion of Judah six months ago. Hopefully, this guy was not Getachu's nephew, and hopefully he spoke the international language of flight, and also believed in the international brotherhood of men who took to the skies. Or he was an asshole.

The captain asked, in good English, "Who are you?"

Purcell replied, "We are journalists from Addis and friends of Signore Bocaccio."

"What is your business here?"

"We are here to see the ancient city of Gondar."

"Why?"

"Because it is famous."

The captain thought about that, then said, "Your flight plan, passports, and credentials."

Purcell gave him the flight plan, and everyone gave him their passports and press cards. He studied each passport, then checked their names against a typed list. Purcell, Vivian, and Mercado glanced at each other.

The captain looked at their press cards, then handed everything back to Purcell and informed him, "There is a landing fee."

"What is it today?"

The captain stared at him, then asked, "What do you have?"

"Lire."

"Fifty thousand."

Purcell said to Mercado, "Pay the gentleman, Henry."

Mercado looked both relieved and annoyed. He took a fifty-thousand-lire note out of his wallet and gave it to the captain.

The captain asked, "How long are you here?"

"A few hours."

"A long flight for a few hours in Gondar."

Vivian replied, "I am a photographer." She tapped her camera bag. "We are taking preliminary photographs today, and if our newspaper likes them, we will be back to do a photographic essay of the ancient city."

The captain stared at her, and he seemed to be processing that information. He asked Purcell, "What other business do you have here?"

"None."

"Do you know anyone here?"

"No one." Except General Getachu, of course, but that wasn't worth mentioning.

The captain looked at them for a long time, then said, "If a military situation develops, the Provisional Revolutionary Air Force has the right to make use of your aircraft, as I am sure Signore Bocaccio told you."

"We understand."

"Are you here to report on the war?"

"Not today."

"What is your next destination?"

"Addis."

The captain informed them, "Your fuel tanks will

be filled in your absence and you will pay for the fuel in Western currency." He reminded them, "You will file a flight plan for Addis, and there will be a takeoff fee."

"I understand."

"You will see me—Captain Sharew—before you take off."

"All right."

"You may leave."

They walked toward the door.

"Wait!"

They turned and Purcell saw that Captain Sharew was looking at their flight plan. He said to Purcell, "It has been over four hours since you left Addis."

"We had headwinds."

Captain Sharew pointed to the C-47 outside his window and informed them, "That aircraft left from the same airstrip after you. He arrived two hours ago and reported no headwinds." He asked, "Did you deviate from your flight plan?"

"Actually, I misread the chart, and I'm unfamiliar with the terrain, so I was lost for about an hour."

"So, headwinds *and* lost. You are an unlucky pilot."

"Apparently."

"I will be taking note of your total fuel consumption from Addis."

"Note that we started with only three-quarters fuel."

"Perhaps someone at Addis will remember that."

"I'm sure they will."

The captain kept staring at them, then said, "You may leave."

They turned and exited the hangar.

Mercado said, "He is not buying headwinds and lost, Frank."

Purcell had spotted the small commercial aviation terminal from the air, and as they walked toward it to get a taxi, he assured everyone, "My explanation, as a pilot, was logical and believable."

Vivian replied, "I think my explanation as a photographer for what we're doing here for two hours was more believable than your explanation about what took us over four hours to get here."

"You're a better liar than I am."

Mercado also reminded them, "They may borrow our aircraft while we're gone."

"They'll return it if it doesn't get shot down."

Vivian asked, "Is there a hotel in this town?"

Mercado replied, "There were a few good ones last time I was here."

"When was that?"

"Nineteen-forty-one."

They reached the passenger terminal and entered through the rear. The small, shoddy terminal building looked deserted, and Vivian asked, "Are there any commercial flights to Addis?"

Mercado replied, "There used to be one a day. Now, from what I've heard, perhaps one a week."

Purcell observed, "Obviously we missed that one."

Vivian said, "We could get stuck here."

Purcell replied, "That would be the least bad thing that could happen here." He noted that the only car rental counter was closed and he suggested, "While we're in town, let's see if we can find a cross-country vehicle to rent."

They exited the front of the terminal, where a single black Fiat sat at the taxi stand. Mercado woke the driver and they climbed in, with Mercado in the front. "Gondar," he said.

The driver seemed confused, as though he hadn't had a customer since the revolution.

Purcell said to Mercado, "Give him twenty thousand."

"That's about fifteen dollars, Frank. He makes about a dollar a day."

"That's more than *L'Osservatore Romano* is paying me. Let's go."

Mercado reluctantly gave the driver a twenty-thousand-lire note, and the man stared at it, then started his car and drove off.

On the way down the plateau, Mercado attempted a few words of conversation with the driver in Amharic, Italian, and English.

Vivian said to Purcell, "I don't think we should fly the Navion back here. That would be one trip too many." She suggested, "We'll take the commercial flight here when we're ready to begin our journey."

"We need one more recon flight to check out anything that looks interesting on your photographs."

"I'm not even sure we're getting out of here."

"We have been chosen to get out of here."

She didn't reply.

As they climbed the steep, narrow road toward the walls of the city, Mercado turned and said, "This driver was actually waiting for a Soviet Air Force general."

Vivian laughed. "Then why did he take us?"

Purcell replied, "Because Henry gave him a month's pay."

Mercado said, "Nothing has gone right today."

Purcell disagreed. "I didn't crash, and we didn't get arrested."

"The day is not over."

Chapter 39

Mercado directed the driver to the Italian-built piazza in the center of Gondar. They stood in the cool sunshine and looked around at the shops, cinema, and public buildings designed by Italian architects in 1930s modern Fascist style.

Mercado said, "This looked better in 1941."

"So did you," Purcell pointed out.

Mercado ignored that and said, "Gondar is where the Italian Army made its last stand against the British in '41." He stayed quiet awhile, then continued, "I was traveling as a war correspondent with the British Expeditionary Force by then...we'd taken Addis from the Italians six months before, and Haile Selassie was back on the throne."

Purcell looked at Henry Mercado standing in the piazza. The man had seen a great deal of life, and death, and war, and hopefully some peace. He had, in fact, seen the twentieth century in all its triumphs and disappointments, its progress and failures.

It was a wonder, Purcell thought, that Mercado had anything left in him. Or that he could still believe in something like the Holy Grail. Or believe in love.

Purcell glanced at Vivian, who was looking at Henry. Purcell hadn't meant to take Henry's lady.

Mercado nodded toward the cinema. "The British

soldiers watched captured Italian movies, and I stood on the stage and shouted the translations." He laughed. "I made up some very funny sexual dialogue."

Vivian laughed, and Purcell, too, smiled.

Mercado pointed to a large public building. "That was where the British Army put its headquarters. The Union Jack used to fly right there." He informed them, "Gann told me he was here as well, but we never met. Or if we did, it was in a state of intoxication and we don't remember."

Purcell wondered if thirty-five years from now he'd be here, or in some other place from his past, telling a younger companion about how it was way back then. Probably not. Henry had been exceedingly lucky at cheating death; Purcell felt lucky, too, but not *that* lucky.

Mercado continued, "The Italians carried on a surprisingly strong guerrilla war in the countryside against the Brits for two more years before they finally surrendered this last piece of their African empire. By then I was traveling with the British Army in North Africa." He stayed quiet a moment, then said, "I always meant to come back to Ethiopia, and especially to Gondar. And here I am."

Vivian said to him, "Show us around, Henry."

They left the piazza and walked into the old city, which was as otherworldly as it appeared from the air: a collection of brick and stone palaces, churches, fortifications, an old synagogue, and ruins. It looked almost medieval, Purcell thought, though the architecture was unlike anything he'd seen in Europe or elsewhere.

Vivian took photographs as Mercado pointed out

a few buildings that he remembered. He observed, "There seem to be fewer people here than I remember." He informed them, "Gondar and the surrounding area is where most of the Jewish population in Ethiopia lives. I think, however, the Jews have left, along with the nobility, the merchant class, and the last of the Italian expats."

Vivian pointed out, "If you lived where General Getachu lived, you'd get out, too."

Mercado also told them, "The Falashas, along with the last of the Royalists, and other traditional elements in the surrounding provinces, have formed a resistance against the Marxists. So Getachu is not completely paranoid when he sees spies and enemies all around him." He added, "The countryside is unsettled and dangerous."

Vivian asked, "Does that include the area where we will be traveling?"

"We will find out."

Most shops and restaurants were closed, including an Italian restaurant that Mercado remembered. Soldiers with AK-47s patrolled the nearly deserted streets and looked them over as they passed by.

Vivian said, "This is creepy."

Purcell suggested, "Tell them you know General Getachu."

They found a food shop that sold bottled water and packaged food and they noted its location for when they needed to buy provisions.

There was an open outdoor café in a small square near a church, and they would have stopped for a beer, but six soldiers, who were undoubtedly Cuban, were sitting at a table watching them approach. One of them called out to the señorita, and Vivian blew them a kiss. They all laughed.

Purcell wanted to find the English missionary school where young Mikael Getachu got his ass whipped, but an old man who spoke Italian told Mercado, "It is now the army headquarters."

Mercado suggested they skip that photo, and Purcell said, "Mikael is trying to work through some childhood issues."

Inquiries about the best hotel in town led them to the Goha, near the Italian piazza. They asked for an English- or Italian-speaking person, and were escorted into the office of the hotel manager, Mr. Kidane, who spoke both languages.

They inquired about rooms for the near future, though the hotel seemed deserted, and also asked about renting a cross-country vehicle. Mr. Kidane informed them he could get his future guests a British Land Rover, but unfortunately, due to the unsettled situation, the price would be two hundred dollars American, each day. A driver and security man would be extra, and he recommended both. Mr. Kidane also required a two-thousand-dollar security deposit in cash—just in case the vehicle and his guests never returned, though he didn't actually say that.

They took Mr. Kidane's card with the Goha's telex number. Purcell gave him a twenty-dollar bill for his trouble, and Mr. Kidane called them a taxi.

Purcell, Vivian, and Mercado headed back to the airport.

Vivian said, "That was fascinating."

Mercado replied, "Someday, Gondar will be a tourist attraction. Now it is Getachu's prize, if he can hold on to it."

Purcell said, "It looks like we have our vehicle, and we can also get provisions in Gondar. But we have to act fast in case the fighting starts again."

Mercado agreed. "These mountains have always been a place of desperate last stands."

Purcell suggested, "We'll make one more recon flight tomorrow or the next day, and if we still haven't heard from Gann, we need to decide our next move."

Everyone agreed, and they continued on to the airport, where Captain Sharew awaited them.

The Navion was still there, but Captain Sharew was happily not, so another kleptocrat took their fifty-thousand-lire takeoff fee, which Mercado paid while Purcell quickly filled out the flight plan.

Purcell didn't mind the bribes; it was when the authorities stopped taking bribes that you had to worry.

The new officer wrote their takeoff time as 1:30 P.M., and advised them, "Do not deviate." He then presented them with an outrageous bill for fuel, which needed to be paid in Western currency. Purcell said, "Your turn, Vivian."

They got quickly into the Navion and noticed that two bags of coffee beans were missing, as well as the urine-filled carafe. Purcell hit the ignition switch and said, "I hope they left the spark plugs."

The engine fired up and he taxied at top speed to the north end of the runway. He got a green light from the tower and pushed the throttle forward.

The Navion lifted off and he continued south, toward Addis Ababa.

A half hour out of Gondar, he took an easterly heading and said to Mercado, "Pass me the map that shows Shoan."

"I do not want to be late into Addis."

"We have tailwinds."

Mercado passed him the map and Purcell studied it. He asked Mercado, "Do you have any interest in flying over Mount Aradam?"

Mercado did not reply, and Purcell did not ask him again.

Purcell found Shoan on the map, and looked at the terrain below, then turned farther east. He picked out the single-lane north-south road that they'd used when they were looking for the war and found the spa. He noticed on the map that Shoan was only about thirty kilometers east of the road, located on high ground that showed on the map as agricultural, surrounded by dense vegetation. If Gann was correct about the village supplying the black monastery with candles and sandals, then Shoan should be a day or two's walk to the meeting place. The monastery, too, could be a day or two's walk to this meeting place. Therefore, Shoan could be a four-day walk to the monastery. But in what direction?

He looked again at the terrain map. They had narrowed it down a bit, but the area was still thousands of square kilometers, and most of it, according to the maps, was covered with jungle and forest.

Vivian asked, "What are you looking at?"

"I'm looking for a black dot in a sea of green ink."

"It's down there, Frank. And we will find it."

"We could walk for a year and not find it. We could pass within a hundred yards of it and miss it."

"I'll have the photographs developed and enlarged before noon tomorrow."

"Good. And if we don't see anything...then we need to start at a place we can easily find. Shoan." He looked out the windshield. "In fact, there it is."

He made a shallow left bank and began to descend.

As they got closer, they could see white farmhouses with corrugated metal roofs sitting in fields of crops. There were also what looked like fruit orchards, and pastures where goats roamed and donkeys grazed. There was also a horse paddock built around a pond. It looked peaceful, Purcell thought, an island of tranquility in a sea of chaos.

The village itself was nestled between two hills, and they could see a cluster of houses around a square. There were a few larger buildings, one of which Purcell thought could be the synagogue. Another large building at the edge of the village was built around a courtyard in which was a round pool and palm trees.

Mercado was looking through his binoculars and said, "Amazing."

Purcell asked, "Do you see any people?"

"Yes...and I see...a vehicle...looks like a cross-country vehicle...maybe a Jeep or Land Rover."

"Could it be military?"

"I really can't say, Frank. Get closer."

He glanced at his watch, then his airspeed. The phantom headwinds he'd reported on the northbound flight were real now, and they needed to get back to the flight plan and head directly toward Addis. "We're heading back."

He looked at his chart and compass and took a direct heading toward Addis Ababa with the throttle fully opened. He said, "If there's a vehicle in the village, then there is a passable road into the village. Probably from the one-lane road we took."

Mercado replied, "I don't remember seeing any road coming off that road."

Purcell said, "There wouldn't be a road sign saying, 'Shoan, population a few hundred Jews.'" He speculated, "The road might be purposely hidden."

Mercado agreed. "They don't want visitors."

"Well, they are about to get three." He said, "From what I see below, and from what we've experienced ourselves, most of this terrain is impassable, even for an all-terrain vehicle. What I suggest is that we have a driver in Gondar take us as far as the spa, and from there we'll walk to Shoan. Should be a few hours."

No one replied.

"I suggest we use Shoan as our base of operation and explore out from there."

Mercado said, "I'm not sure the Falashas would welcome our intrusion, old man. Nor would they be keen on us looking for the black monastery."

"Gann was telling us something. And I think what he was saying was, 'Go to Shoan.'"

Mercado informed him, "The English are not that subtle, Frank. If he wanted us to go to Shoan, he would have said, 'Go to Shoan.'" He further informed Purcell, "That's the way we speak."

"I think he was clear."

"What is clear to me is that we should avoid all human contact as we're beating about the bush. Nothing good can come of us trying to get help from friendly natives."

"I hear you, Henry. But as we both know, you can usually trust the outcasts of any society."

"The Falasha Jews are not outcasts—they are people who just want to be left in peace as they have been for three thousand years."

"Those days are over."

"Apparently, but if Sir Edmund is correct about the Falashas and the monks, and if we engage the Falashas, we may find ourselves as permanent residents of the black monastery."

"There are worse places to spend the rest of your life, Henry."

Vivian had stayed silent, but now said, "I think you are both right to some extent."

"Meaning," Purcell replied, "that we are both wrong to some extent."

She pointed out, "We could clear this up if Colonel Gann shows up."

No one responded to that.

They continued south, toward Addis.

Vivian said, "I think we are missing something."

"The carafe?"

"There was something that Father Armano said . . . He gave us a clue, without knowing it."

Purcell, too, had had the same thought, and he'd tried to drag it out of his memory, but couldn't.

Vivian said, "It's something we should have understood."

Mercado reminded them, "He didn't want us looking for the black monastery or the Holy Grail, so he wasn't giving us an obvious clue to where the monastery was located. But Vivian is correct and I've felt that as well. He told us something, and we need to understand what it was."

No one responded to that and they fell into a thoughtful silence. The engine droned, and the Navion bounced and yawed in the highland updrafts. Purcell scanned his instruments. This aircraft burned or leaked oil. The engine probably had a couple thousand hours on it, and the maintenance was probably performed by bicycle mechanics.

He glanced up at the Saint Christopher medal, which may have been the only thing that worked right in Signore Bocaccio's aircraft.

He tried to figure out if he'd taken leave of his senses, or if this search for the black monastery and the so-called Holy Grail was within the normal range of mental health. A lot of this, he admitted, had to do with Vivian. *Cherchez la femme.* His libido had gotten him into trouble before, but never to this extent.

And then there was Henry. He not only liked Henry, but he respected the old warhorse. Henry Mercado was a legend, and Frank Purcell was happy that circumstances—or fate—had brought them together.

And, he realized, the sum was more than the parts. He wouldn't be here risking his life for something he didn't believe in with any other two people. Also, they all had the same taste in members of the opposite sex. That ménage, however, was more of a problem than a strength.

Vivian was sleeping, and so was Henry, curled up on the remaining two coffee bean bags.

Within three hours of leaving Gondar, he spotted the hills around Addis Ababa, then saw the airstrip. The southern African sky was a pastel blue, and streaks of pink sat on the distant horizon.

Vivian was awake now, and she glanced in the rear to see Mercado still asleep. She said to Purcell, "I had a dream..."

He didn't respond.

"You and I were in Rome, and I was the happiest I've ever been."

"Did we have the Grail with us?"

"We had each other."

"That's good enough."

He throttled back and began his descent.

Chapter 40

Vivian came out of the Reuters news office carrying three thick manila envelopes in her canvas tote, which contained a total of ninety-two eight-by-ten photographs.

Purcell and Mercado met her outside and they walked toward Ristorante Vesuvio, which claimed to be the best Italian restaurant in Africa, and probably the only one named after an Italian volcano.

To add to the surreal and almost comic quality of Addis Ababa, the street was lined with Swiss Alpine structures, which seemed to fit the mountainous terrain, but which Mercado thought were grotesque parodies of the real thing. He explained, "The Emperor Menelik II, who founded Addis, commissioned a Swiss architect to design the city, and I think the Swiss chap had a bit of fun with the emperor."

"You get what you pay for," Purcell said.

They went into Vesuvio and took a table in the back. Mercado said, "This place has been here since the Italian Army conquered the city."

Purcell observed, "The décor has not changed."

"They took down the portrait of Mussolini. It used to be right above your head."

"Where was the portrait of the emperor?"

"Also above your head."

"What's above my head now?"

"Nothing. The proprietor is waiting to see who survives the Derg purges."

"The Italians are very practical."

Vivian gave an envelope to Purcell and one to Mercado, and they slid out the enlarged photographs. They all sat silently, flipping through the matte-finish color prints.

A few of the photos showed part of the wing, and some were almost straight-down shots, showing only a green carpet of jungle without wing or horizon, and these were not easy to orient, but they did penetrate into the jungle. All in all, Vivian had done a good job, and Purcell said, "You could work for the Italian cartography office."

"And you could work for the Italian Air Force."

Purcell looked closely at a few photos, studying the sizes, shapes, tones, and shadows of the terrain features. He said, "We'll look at these with a magnifier and good light in one of our rooms."

Mercado looked up from his photos and said, "We did not see anything that could be a man-made structure when we were in the air, and I don't think we will see anything more in these photographs than the Italian cartographers did forty years ago." He pointed out, "The monastery is *hidden*. By overhanging trees."

Purcell reminded him, "Father Armano said that sunlight came through the opaque substance used in the roof of the church. If sunlight came through, then the roof can be seen from the air."

Mercado nodded reluctantly, but then said, "That was forty years ago. Those trees have grown."

"Or died."

Vivian was looking closely at the photos in her

hands. "Father Armano also mentioned green gardens, and gardens do not grow well under a triple-canopy jungle. So what I think is that the monastery is hidden by palms—palm fronds move in the breeze and block the sun, but they also let in some sunlight."

Purcell observed, "We're back to palms."

"Makes sense."

"All right. But I don't remember Father Armano saying anything about palms."

Vivian reminded him, "He did say that on the doors of the church were the symbols of the early Christians—fish, lambs, palms."

"That's not actually the same as palm trees overhead."

"I know that, Frank, but..." She studied a photo in her hand.

Purcell thought, then said, "All right...in Southeast Asia, from the air, or in aerial photographs, palm fronds were a good camouflage. They create a sort of illusion because of their shape, movement, and the shadows they cast. They break up the image on the ground and fool the eye. Photographs, though, capture and freeze the image, and if you're a good aerial photo analyst, you might be able to separate the reality from the optical illusion."

Vivian looked at him. "Did you make that up?"

"Some of it." He said. "Okay, let's concentrate on clusters of palms. Also, there is something called glint."

Vivian asked, "What is glint?"

"If you buy me lunch, I'll tell you."

"I'll buy you two lunches."

The waiter came by, an authentic Italian who, like Signore Bocaccio, hadn't bought his ticket to Italy yet. Most of what his customers wanted on the menu was no longer available, but pasta was still plentiful, he assured them, though the only sauce today was olive oil. There was also a small and diminishing selection of wine, and Mercado chose a Chianti that had tripled in price. He said to his luncheon companions, "I miss Rome."

Purcell asked, "What makes you say that?"

Vivian reminded them, "There is a famine out there. Get some perspective, please."

Purcell admitted, "I hate eating in restaurants when there's a famine."

Mercado admonished, "That is insensitive."

"Sorry." He reminded Mercado, "I almost starved to death in that Khmer Rouge prison camp. So I can make famine jokes." He asked, "What do you call an Ethiopian having a bowel movement? A show-off."

"Frank. Really," said Vivian. "That is not funny."

"Sorry." He said to Mercado, "You can use that as a Gulag joke."

Purcell lit a cigarette and said, "This famine is mostly man-made by a stupid, corrupt government that has instituted stupid policies." He continued, "Half the famine relief food coming in is stolen by the government and sold on the black market. The birr is worthless and you can't buy food at any price unless you have hard currency. The UN relief workers are being harassed, and the military uses all the available transportation to move soldiers around instead of food." He told Mercado, "That's my next article for *L'Osservatore Romano.*"

"You can write it, Frank, but it will not run. And if it does, you will be lucky if you only get expelled."

"The truth will set us free, Henry."

"Not in Ethiopia. Save it for when we are out of here."

"What is worse—me not demonstrating the proper guilt about eating during the famine, or you not letting me write the truth about it?"

Mercado stayed silent awhile, then replied, "Your point is made, and well taken." He smiled, "Someday you will make a good journalist."

Vivian asked, "Is the pissing match over?"

Purcell said, "Pass the bread."

The wine came and they drank as they flipped through the photographs.

Purcell looked around the restaurant, which, if it could talk, would have some stories to tell. The clientele was mostly Western European embassy staff, though he spotted four Russians in bad suits at a table. Vesuvio, unlike the Hilton and other hotels, was not in a position to demand only hard currency, but the proprietor and staff did not go out of their way to welcome the Russians or Cubans who paid in birr.

This country was in bad shape, Purcell thought, and the worst was yet to come. The old Ethiopia was dead, and the new Ethiopia should never have been born.

Vivian said, "I assume there was no message from Colonel Gann at the hotel."

Mercado replied, "None."

"Do you think something has happened to him?"

Mercado replied, "If he's been arrested, and being held in Addis, someone in the press community would have heard through sources." He added, "But if he's been killed in the hinterlands, we may never know."

Purcell said, "We will hear from him."

Vivian reminded Purcell, "You were going to tell us what a glint is."

"It is what you see in my eyes when you walk into a room."

Purcell thought that was funny, but Vivian did not, though she might have if Henry was not at the table. Clearly she was still uncomfortable with the situation, but no more so than he was. Henry, too, was not amused, though he smiled for the record.

Purcell said, "A glint is what it sounds like—a quick reflection of light off a shiny surface. Pilots in combat look for the glint of an enemy aircraft, or the glint of a metal target on the ground." He picked up his wineglass. "Glass, too, can give off a type of glint. Glass roofs, even if opaque, may give off a glint." He drank his wine.

Mercado was nodding, and Vivian was flipping through the photographs again, looking for a glint.

Purcell continued, "Obviously, the sun has to strike the object, and the object has to be reflective enough to produce a glint."

Mercado nodded again, and Purcell continued, "Father Armano said he thought the roof could have been alabaster, and he said it let in the sunlight and bathed the church in a glow that made his head swim and hurt his eyes." He speculated, "It could also have been quartz, or, despite what the priest thought, it could have been a type of stained glass that was rippled and mostly clear, and that might account for the strange light." He concluded, "In any case, this substance did not let all the sunlight in, and that means it had to reflect some sunlight back."

Mercado asked, "So do we now believe in palm trees and glints?"

Purcell replied, "I can make a stronger case for that than I can for the existence of the Holy Grail."

Mercado did not respond to that, but said, "If we see a glint coming through palm trees, then I think we've found the black monastery."

Vivian said, "I see palm trees, but I'm not seeing any glints."

Purcell said, "We'll have the photographs done again in a high-gloss finish, and we'll go over them inch by inch in our rooms."

Vivian informed them, "The Reuters photo lab guy is very taken with me, but if I ask him to reprint ninety-two photographs in a different finish, I'll have to have a drink with him."

"Have several," Purcell suggested.

She smiled, then said, "He also asked me why I was taking aerial photos of jungle."

Mercado said, "He is not supposed to ask questions. What did you tell him?"

"I told him I was trying to find the right green for my drapes."

Mercado asked, "Is Father Armano's mention of this roof the unintended clue he gave us as to the location of the monastery?"

Purcell replied, "It *is* an unintended clue, but there is something else. Something keeps nagging at my mind, and it will come to me."

Vivian poured him more wine. "This might help."

"Can't hurt."

Their lunch came and Purcell said, "Buon appetito."

Chapter 41

They laid the photos out on the bed in Mercado's room. Each photograph was now in matte and gloss finish, and Vivian had also borrowed two lighted magnifiers from the smitten lab tech.

The drapes were open and they knelt around the bed, studying the photographs. Purcell was at the foot of the bed, and Vivian and Mercado on opposite sides. Vivian looked up to say something to Mercado and saw him looking at her across the bed that they'd shared a few days before. She met his gaze for a second, then looked down at the photograph in front of her.

They each had a grease marker that they used to circle palm clusters. Next, they looked closely for a glint, or a reflection of light, or anything that could be an anomalous source of light.

Purcell advised them, "Consider the position of the sun when looking for a glint or sparkle, and consider the direction we are looking at."

They also had the terrain maps spread out so they could match the photos with the maps, but this turned out to be difficult unless there was an identifying feature in the photo that was represented on the map. Real aerial photographers, Purcell knew, had methods of printing grid coordinates on their photos, but he, Vivian, and Mercado were trying to match the photo to the maps, then mark the maps, which they would use on the ground.

Mercado said, "This is more difficult than I thought it would be."

"It was never going to be easy or fun."

Vivian found what she thought was a glint close to the destroyed fortress, and they all took a look at it.

Mercado said, "It is definitely a reflection of some sort, but there are no palms around it."

Purcell added, "It's also too close to the fortress— maybe five hundred meters."

Vivian agreed that the monastery would not be that close to the fortress.

Mercado said, "It could be a pond, or one of the streams that run through the area. We will check it out when we get there."

Vivian pointed out the sulphur pool of the spa and said, "That is what a body of water looks like in these photographs. It is more reflective than...glinting."

Purcell agreed. "We are looking for something that...if we saw it from the air, we'd say something sparkled down there. Or maybe flashed. The problem with still photography is that you need to capture the glint at the moment it happens. And even then, it might not register on the film."

Vivian said, "I used both high- and low-speed film, but I'm not sure which would be better for capturing a quick glint of light." She added, "The matte finish actually seems better for showing a light anomaly."

Purcell also pointed out, "It was a mostly sunny day, but there are a few cloud shadows on these photographs, and when the sun is blocked, you won't get reflected or refracted sunlight."

Mercado said, "We will pray for clear skies on our next flight."

Purcell replied, "Remind God that we are chosen."

"We are being tested."

"Right. But tell him clouds are not fair."

They continued to study the photographs.

After half an hour, Purcell said, "I'm going blind and nuts." He stood and retrieved the photographs that Vivian had taken in Gondar for her bogus photographic essay.

He sat in a chair and flipped through the photos. One was an artistic shot of a palace garden with a reflecting pool, and the plants around the pool were reflected in the water of the pool, which was the idea. He thought a moment, then said, "Depending on what that church roof was made of, it might reflect what is above and around it." He suggested, "Look for a palm frond or maybe a tree branch that has an exact mirror image."

Vivian looked up at him, "All right...would you like to join us?"

"I'm just the pilot. Also, you have the only two magnifiers."

Vivian smiled. "I can get another one from the lab guy, but it will cost me."

"Go for it."

Vivian and Mercado continued to study the photos, then Mercado stood and said, "I need a break."

"I'm surprised your old eyes lasted this long." Purcell stood and took Mercado's place at the side of the bed, and Mercado sat and looked at Vivian's pictures of Gondar.

Vivian said, "I have three possible...glints. But I could be looking at ground water, or even moisture on leaves or palm fronds."

"That is another problem with photographs. They are two-dimensional, and depth of field can only be interpreted from what we know of the image." He added, "This is not an exact science."

"Thank you, Frank."

"Anytime."

He moved a photograph to the side and noticed something on the bedspread. He looked closer and saw that it was a long, straight jet-black hair, and he didn't need the magnifier to tell whose it was.

He looked up at Vivian, who was bent closely over the magnifier. He glanced at Mercado, who was looking at the Gondar photos. He tried to remember if Vivian had knelt at this side of the bed, but he knew she hadn't. Not today, anyway.

He had two choices: pick up the hair and bring it to everyone's attention—or forget it.

He looked again at Vivian. If he asked her what happened here, she would tell him the truth. But he already knew the truth. Or did he? It would not be unlike her to make herself comfortable on a male friend's bed and chat away while the poor guy was trying to talk his dick down.

On the other hand...but why would she have sex with Henry Mercado? He thought he knew, and thinking back to Henry's changed demeanor since that morning, he could imagine what Vivian's purpose was.

Or was he misinterpreting all those images the way he might misinterpret a photograph?

Vivian said excitedly, "I think I see a double image. Two palm fronds that are the mirror image of each other." She put a circle on the photograph and flipped it to him.

He looked at the circled image under the magnifier and said, "These are not exact doubles. These are two very similar palm fronds."

"Are you sure?"

"I am sure."

"Damn it."

He said to her, "Things are not always what they seem."

She looked at him, then some instinct, or prior experience, made her look at where his hand was resting on the light yellow bedsheet. She looked up at him again and said, "Sometimes things *are* what they seem."

He nodded and went back to his magnifier and the photograph in front of him.

At 5 P.M., Mercado determined that there was nothing else to look at, and he suggested a cocktail in the lounge.

They stopped at the front desk for messages, and the desk clerk gave them a hand-delivered letter-sized envelope addressed to "Mercado, Purcell, Smith, *L'Osservatore Romano*, Hilton Hotel." The handwriting was different from the writing on the manila envelope that had contained the maps, but they had no doubt who this was from.

Purcell carried the envelope into the lounge and they sat at a table.

Vivian said, "He's alive and well."

Purcell pointed out, "He was when he sent this."

"Don't be a pessimist. Open it."

"We need a drink first."

Mercado signaled a waiter and ordered a bottle of Moët, saying to his companions, "We're either celebrating something, or we need to drown our troubles in champagne."

"I like the way you think, Henry."

Vivian said, "Out of ninety-two photographs, there are only six circled locations that fit our criteria." She listed the criteria: "Palm trees, and/or a glint, in a location that is not too close to the fortress or to the spa, or the road, or to any place that would not be a likely location of a hidden monastery." She continued, "Only one photo has all three—palms, a glint, and a likely location."

Mercado suggested, "But we may have our criteria wrong."

"In fact," said Purcell, "we may have talked ourselves into palms and glints, so we need to look at the photos with a fresh eye in the morning."

Mercado informed them, "I need to go to work tomorrow to justify our existence here."

Purcell reminded him, "You're on the payroll. The rest of us are working for room and board."

They discussed photo analysis for a while, and their next recon flight over the area.

Purcell looked at Vivian, then at Mercado. There had definitely been a new spring in Henry's step since that morning. But interestingly, Vivian seemed the same. In fact, at breakfast on the morning of his flight with Signore Bocaccio, which would have been soon after

Vivian had sex with Henry, she had seemed herself—as though she'd put the encounter in a file drawer and forgot about it.

And then she'd invited Purcell to have sex with her.

It was possible, however, that nothing of a penetrating nature had happened. He was certain he would not have been happy to see what did happen in Henry's bedroom, but it might have fallen short of a legal definition of cheating on your boyfriend.

Henry, however, seemed to be happy with whatever had happened, even if the object of his affection didn't seem so moved by the experience.

He looked again at Vivian, who was chatting happily with her old friend.

In Vivian's mind, all was now right with her world, and they could *all* be friends, and continue with their mission here, which to Vivian was far more important than two horny men. No doubt she loved Frank Purcell, and he loved her, so now he had to decide what to do about what she had done.

Two waiters appeared with a wine bucket, fluted glasses, and a bottle of Moët & Chandon, which one of them displayed to Mercado. He pronounced the year *magnifique*, and told his companions, "This is on the newspaper."

Purcell suggested, "Tell them you entertained a member of the Derg."

"I always do."

The headwaiter popped the cork, which caused some heads to turn, then filled the flutes.

Henry held up his glass and proposed, "To us, and to Sir Edmund, and to our journey."

They drank and Vivian said, "Ooh. I love it."

Mercado suggested, "We will take a bottle with us on the road, and pop it when we see the black monastery in the jungle."

Purcell warned him, "That might be the last alcohol you ever see."

"Nonsense. The monks drink wine."

They finished their glasses and Mercado refilled them.

Purcell said, "Okay, one more flight to Gondar, and on the way we will check out whatever we've circled on the photographs. With any luck, we will be able to narrow the circles down to a few, or we will see something else that may be of interest. In any case, we will land in Gondar and go to the Goha Hotel. We'll shop for provisions without attracting too much attention, then we will spend the night, then get in the Land Rover with the driver and security man, and tell them we are hiking. We'll get dropped off near the spa, tell the driver to meet us there in six hours, and we are off on our quest. First stop is Shoan."

Mercado and Vivian processed all that, and Mercado said, "I think we should go first to the places in the photographs that are possibly what we're looking for."

"I don't want to traipse around the jungle for a week or two." He reminded Mercado, "That is rough country, old man, and I don't just mean the terrain. We want to minimize the walking, and not use up our provisions."

Mercado replied, "I've done this sort of thing before, Frank."

"Good. Then you agree." He continued, "The Falashas may be more helpful than those photographs."

"They may be the opposite of helpful—or they may all be gone."

Vivian said, "Our first objective should be the spa." She reminded them, "We said we'd bring back a relic... a bone of Father Armano."

"You carry the bone." He also said, "I will call Signore Bocaccio tonight about the availability of the plane. I'd like to go tomorrow."

Mercado thought about that, then asked, "Are you saying that we're leaving the aircraft in Gondar?"

"Well, it's not going to fly itself back." He assured Mercado, "I'll telex Signore Bocaccio from the Goha and let him know he can pick up his plane in Gondar, and keep our security deposit."

Neither Mercado nor Vivian replied.

"I don't think we'll be needing Mia one way or the other after we leave Gondar on our journey."

Again, no one responded.

Purcell further explained, "There is no reason for us to return here. We don't need any more photographs developed, and it is time we moved forward—before we get shut down by the authorities or by something outside our control." He looked at Mercado and Vivian. "Caesar crossed the Rubicon and burned his bridges behind him. And that is what we will do tomorrow."

Mercado said, "We should see what Sir Edmund has written to us. That may influence what we do next."

"Let's first have our own plan."

"All right, Frank. We have a plan. Now please open the envelope."

Purcell glanced around to see if anyone was paying too much attention to them, then tore open the envelope. He extracted a single piece of paper and looked at it.

Vivian asked, "What does it say?"

"It is…a poem." He smiled, then said, "Titled, 'The Explorer.'"

Mercado said, "That's Kipling, if you don't know."

"Thank you." He read, "Something hidden. Go and find it. Go and look behind the Ranges—Something lost behind the Ranges. Lost and waiting for you. Go!"

He looked up at Mercado and Vivian.

They stayed silent, then Vivian asked, "Is that it?"

"That is it—except for the signature."

Mercado asked, "Did Sir Edmund sign it?"

"Actually, no, and neither did Rudyard Kipling." He glanced at the signature and said, "It is signed, I. M. N. Shoan."

"Who?"

"You gotta say it fast, Henry."

Vivian said, "I am in Shoan."

Purcell passed the note to her. "You win."

She looked at it, then gave it to Mercado.

Purcell said, "We will join Sir Edmund in Shoan."

Mercado had a dinner date and left them in the lounge. They sat without speaking for a while, then Vivian said, "I don't want dinner. Let's have a bottle of wine sent to our room."

Purcell replied, "You can have one sent to your room."

She didn't reply.

He stood and said, "Good night."

"Frank…"

He looked at her in the dim light and he could see tears running down her face.

She looked at him. "Do you understand?"

"I do."

"I'm sorry."

"We will all stay friends, until we leave Ethiopia."

She nodded.

He turned and left.

Chapter 42

The Navion was available the next day for an overnight stay in Gondar and a return to Addis on the following day. Signore Bocaccio met them at the airport at noon to collect his rental fee and deliver the news. "This is unfortunately your last flight." He explained, "This is causing me worry."

"I'm the one flying this thing."

Signore Bocaccio smiled, then said seriously, "I want no trouble with the government."

"I understand."

He advised, "You, too, should be careful with the government. They will be curious about your flights to Gondar."

"We are journalists."

"There is a commercial flight once a week. So perhaps they will want to know why you need my aircraft."

"We don't want to spend a week in Gondar." Purcell asked, "How does that sound?"

"To me, it sounds good. To them...who knows?" He motioned toward Vivian and Mercado, who were standing near his aircraft. "You are nice people. Please be careful."

"We're not actually that nice." Purcell paid him in dollars for the two-day rental and informed him, "Some of your coffee was stolen in Gondar."

"It is there to be stolen."

"Right." He suggested to Signore Bocaccio that he meet them at the Hilton for dinner on their return from Gondar so that the Signore Bocaccio could release their security deposit.

"But you must let me buy you dinner, and I will keep the security deposit for the down payment on Mia." He smiled.

Purcell returned the smile and suggested, "Seven P.M., but check at the desk for a telex from us in case we are delayed getting out of Gondar."

The Italian looked at him. "Be careful."

"See you then."

Signore Bocaccio would actually be dining alone, but he had their two-thousand-dollar security deposit to keep him company—and also to pay for his commercial flight to Gondar to retrieve his aircraft.

Purcell was about to say *arrivederci*, but then said to Signore Bocaccio, "I have seen expats and colonials all over the world waiting for the right time to leave a place that has become unfriendly." He advised him, "That time has arrived."

Signore Bocaccio, the owner of coffee plantations and other things in Ethiopia, nodded. "But it is difficult. This is my home." He told the American, "I love Africa."

"It doesn't love you anymore."

He smiled. "It is like with a woman. Do you leave the woman you love because she is having difficulties with life?"

Purcell did not respond.

Signore Bocaccio informed Purcell, "My wife is

Ethiopian. And my children. Would they be happy in Italy?"

"I saw many Ethiopians in Rome."

"Yes, I know."

"At least take a long vacation."

"As soon as I leave, the government will take all I have."

"They'll take it anyway."

"This is true...so perhaps a long vacation." He smiled. "I will fly to Rome with my family in Mia."

"Bad idea." He suggested, "Bring your wife to dinner."

"That is very kind of you."

They shook hands and Signore Bocaccio wished them, "Buona fortuna."

"Ciao."

Purcell had already filed his flight plan for Gondar, and as a repeat customer with fifty thousand lire clipped to the form, he got his red stamp without attitude. The duty officer had written 12:15 as the departure time on the form, and that was fifteen minutes ago, so Purcell said to his flight mates, "Let's hit it."

Mercado and Vivian had loaded the luggage, which contained more than they needed for an overnight in Gondar, and most of what they needed for a few weeks in the bush, including a bottle of Moët for when they found the black monastery. Henry had also sent a hotel employee out early in the morning with three hundred dollars and a shopping list that included three back-packs, flashlights, and other camping equipment, all of which could be found in Addis's many secondhand s that were bursting with items sold by people who were getting out or who needed hard cash to buy food. The young hotel employee had found nearly everything on the list, including a compass. The only thing they needed now was food, which they could buy in Gondar, and luck, which could not be bought anywhere.

Purcell jumped on the wing and helped Mercado up, then took Vivian's hand and pulled her onto the wing. They looked at each other a second, then she released his hand and climbed into the cockpit and over to the right-hand seat.

Purcell got in, hit the master switch, and checked his flight controls, then pumped the throttle and hit the starter. The engine fired up quickly, and he checked his instrument panel. Oil pressure still low.

Mercado said, "It's a bit tight back here with the luggage."

Vivian said to him, "Do not disturb the pilot when he is doing his pilot stuff."

Purcell said, "Seat belts."

He released the handbrake and brought the Navion around. He saw Signore Bocaccio standing beside his old Fiat, waving to them. He returned the wave, then slid the canopy closed and taxied toward the end of the longer runway, which was clear of traffic this afternoon.

Vivian asked him, "Do I need to pray to Saint Christopher?"

He didn't reply.

Vivian had been trying to engage him in light banter all morning, but he wasn't in the mood. She'd been good enough not to call him in his room last night, or knock on his door, and he was fairly certain she hadn't spoken to Mercado about the new sleeping arrangement because Henry seemed himself.

Purcell ran the engine up, checked his controls and instruments again, then wheeled onto the runway. "Ready for takeoff." He pushed the throttle forward and the Navion began its run.

The aircraft lifted off and Purcell began banking right, north toward Gondar. To his right lay Addis Ababa, a city he would probably never see again, or if he did, it would be from a prison cell—unless they gave him the same view of the courtyard and gallows.

Purcell steered the Navion between two towering peaks, then glanced back at what he hoped was his last look at Addis Ababa.

Henry, as it turned out, had not gone to the press office that morning, but he'd sent a telex from the hotel to *L'Osservatore Romano* telling his editors that the team was going to Gondar for a few days to report on the Falasha exodus.

Purcell, Vivian, and Mercado had spent the morning in Henry's room, giving the photos a last look and marking the terrain maps with a few more suspected hiding places for the black monastery. The other suspicious thing in Mercado's room, the strand of black hair, was still there. Henry should speak to the maid. But they would not be returning to their hotel rooms ever. It was time, as Colonel Gann suggested, to go and find it.

Regarding where to go next if they did find it, Colonel Gann, in the maps he'd sent them, had included contiguous terrain maps from Gondar and Lake Tana to French Somaliland on the coast. Clearly Gann was suggesting an exit plan for them.

So, with or without the Holy Grail, they would make their way to French Somaliland, the closest safe haven, where many Westerners and Ethiopians on the run had gone. The French officials were good about providing assistance to anyone who reached the border. All they had to do was get there.

Vivian said to him, in a soft voice, "You told me we would be friends."

"We are."

"You've barely spoken to me all morning."

"I'm not good in the morning."

She glanced back at Henry, who was concentrating on a photograph with the magnifier. She said to Purcell, "It will never happen again. I promise you."

"Let's talk about this in Gondar." He added, "I'm flying."

She looked at him, then turned her head and stared out the side of the canopy.

They continued on, and Mercado said, "We have reached the point of no return on our journey."

Purcell replied, "Not yet. We have burned no bridges, and I can still fly back to Addis and say we had engine problems."

Mercado did not reply, but Vivian said, "Avanti."

Chapter 43

P urcell spotted the single-lane road and followed it north. Off to his right front, he could see Shoan about ten kilometers away. He banked right and began descending, saying to his passengers, "I want Colonel Gann to know we are on the way."

As they got lower and closer, Mercado leaned forward with his binoculars. "I don't see the vehicle."

Purcell replied, "We don't know if that vehicle had anything to do with Gann."

Purcell flew over the village at four hundred feet and tipped his wings.

Mercado said, "I saw someone waving."

"Did he have a mustache and a riding crop?"

"He was wearing a white shamma...but it could have been him."

"Going native."

They flew over the spa, then Purcell banked right, to the area east of the single-lane road where most of their photographs had been taken of the jungle and rain forests that lay between Lake Tana and the area around the destroyed fortress—an area that Purcell estimated at more than a thousand square miles.

Vivian had the large-scale maps on her lap, and Purcell asked her to hold up the one of the area below.

She held the map for him, and he glanced at the

circled sites, then banked east toward the first circle on the map. He dropped down to three hundred feet and slowed his airspeed as much as he could.

Mercado was leaning between the seats, dividing his attention between the map and the view from the Plexiglas canopy.

Purcell dropped lower as he approached the first site, marked Number One on the map, which had shown a light reflection in the corresponding photograph. He made a tight clockwise turn, then dipped his right wing so that it was not obstructing their view. Mia shuddered to warn him she was about to stall, and Purcell pushed in the throttle as he leveled his wings.

Mercado lowered his binoculars. "I think I saw a pond...or maybe swampland."

Vivian agreed, "It was water. Not a glass roof."

Purcell said, "At least what we saw in the photograph was not an illusion, and we've also marked the map position correctly. That's the good news."

Vivian agreed. "One of these circles will be the black monastery."

"If not, we have at least eliminated some locations."

They continued on to the next closest circle that showed a large cluster of palm trees in the photographs, and Purcell repeated his maneuvers. No one saw anything, so he made another pass, and this time Vivian said, "I definitely saw a body of water through the palms."

"Any shiny roofs?"

"No."

Purcell moved on to the next circle on the map, Number Three, which Vivian pointed to on the corresponding photograph. He glanced at the photo and saw a very large cluster of palms, surrounded by much taller growth. This looked more promising and he pulled off some power and lowered his flaps as if he intended to land. The airspeed indicator bounced between sixty and sixty-five miles per hour.

The cluster of palms was coming up fast at his one o'clock position and he dropped his right wing, causing the Navion to shudder, but giving Vivian and Mercado an unobstructed view as they passed by.

Vivian shouted, "I saw something! A glint of light... not water."

Mercado agreed, and Purcell, too, had seen something, and it was definitely not water.

He climbed as fast as he could, got to six hundred feet, and came around again, this time from the west so that the afternoon sun was at their back. He was higher than last time, so he could keep his nose down as he flew straight toward the cluster of palms.

Vivian had taken the binoculars from Mercado and she was unbuckled and leaning over the instrument panel, staring through the front windshield.

Purcell continued his dive until the last possible second, then pushed the throttle forward, pulled back on the wheel, and raised his flaps. The Navion continued downward for a few more seconds, then the nose slowly lifted and they leveled out over the jungle canopy at about two hundred feet, then began gaining altitude.

Mercado said, "That was a bit close, old man."

"Right." Purcell glanced at Vivian, who was sitting back in her seat with the binoculars in her lap. He asked, "See anything?"

She nodded. "It was... black rock. Just rock."

Purcell nodded. That was what he thought he'd seen, too. A shiny outcropping of black rock—probably obsidian. "Well, there is black rock in this area."

Vivian said, "Father Armano mentioned a rock, a tree, a stream..."

"Right. Lots of that down there." He added, "We'll check this out on the ground tomorrow."

He glanced at his watch. It had been three hours since they left Addis. They could keep flying over the area for maybe another half hour, and they should be able to recon all the sites marked on the maps, with maybe some time left over to look at anything else that seemed promising. They'd be late into Gondar again, but not two hours late as they'd been last time. He'd worry about that when they landed. The goal now was to complete the aerial recon, which, if they were very lucky, would reveal the location of the black monastery.

He said to Vivian, "Map."

She held the map toward him, and he looked at it, trying to determine what heading to take to get to the next circle on the map.

Vivian was glancing out the windshield, then suddenly shouted, "Look!" She dropped the map.

Purcell looked quickly through the windshield. Passing across their front was a helicopter, about a half mile away. "Shit!"

Mercado said, "I think he may have seen our maneuvers."

"You think?" Purcell had no way of knowing if the helicopter just happened to be in the area, or if it was sent to track them. He said, "If he has a radio, and I'm sure he does, he has radioed ahead to Gondar Airport."

Vivian said, "Maybe he didn't see us."

"We saw him, he saw us."

Purcell watched as the helicopter turned northwest, toward Gondar, which was where they were supposed to be heading. So Purcell took the same heading, but stayed to the left of the helicopter, and kept his distance at about half a mile.

Vivian asked, "How will he know it was us?"

Purcell informed her, "There are not too many black-painted vintage Navions in East Africa, Vivian. Probably one."

She nodded.

Mercado said, "We actually have done nothing illegal."

Purcell reminded him, "We didn't do anything illegal last time we wound up in jail here, and this time we are suspiciously diverting from the flight plan."

"Quite right." Mercado asked, "What do we do?"

Purcell watched the helicopter. He was flying at the same altitude, and he had definitely slowed his speed relative to the Navion, and the distance was closing. Purcell throttled back and the Navion slowed.

"Frank?"

"Well... what we don't do is continue on to Gondar Airport where a reception committee will be waiting for us."

No one replied to that, then Mercado announced, "We need to fly to French Somaliland." He asked, "Can we do that?"

Purcell glanced at his fuel gauge. "The fuel should not be a problem." But they could have other problems with that idea.

Purcell saw that the helicopter had also reduced its speed to maintain the distance between the aircraft. He understood that the helicopter pilot wanted the Navion to follow him into Gondar.

Mercado suggested, "You may want to turn east now." He reminded Purcell, "French Somaliland is that way."

"Right."

Vivian was slumped in her seat. She said softly, "It's over. We never got a chance..."

Mercado said comfortingly, "We will come back."

Purcell noticed that the helicopter had slipped to the right and was higher now, so that Purcell had a side view of it, and the pilot had a better view of the Navion.

Mercado said, "We have to turn east, old man." He asked, "Can we outrun this helicopter?"

"Depends on too many unknowns..." Purcell said to Vivian, "Give me the binoculars."

She gave them to him and Purcell focused with his left hand while he flew with his right. The helicopter was olive drab, definitely military, and on the side of the fuselage was a red star. He said, "It's a Huey... UH-1D...saw a million of them in 'Nam..." In fact, this was the same type of helicopter that Getachu had used, and maybe it was the same one that had taken them to prison in Addis. He added, "His top speed would be about the same as ours." He lowered the binoculars and said, "Also, I can see a door gunner."

"A what?"

"A fellow sitting in the door opening with a mounted machine gun. Probably an M-60, and there is probably another one on the other side." He added,

"I don't see anyone in the cabin, so General Getachu is not on board."

No one replied.

Purcell noticed that the distance between him and the helicopter was again closing. He was barely doing seventy miles per hour, and the helicopter pilot, of course, could do zero if he wanted to, so Purcell was going to pass alongside that machine gun unless he turned.

Mercado said again, "You really need to turn, Frank."

"Right...but I'm thinking this guy will follow us toward French Somaliland, and even if I can outrun him, I can't outrun a stream of 7.62-millimeter machine-gun rounds."

Vivian drew a deep breath. "Oh, God..."

Purcell continued, "Also, even if I could stay out of his machine-gun range, he will radio for support, and the Ethie Air Force might scramble some kind of fighter aircraft."

Mercado processed all that and said, "We have no choice then...we must continue on to Gondar."

Purcell told them, "I don't think we're going to be as lucky in General Getachu's headquarters as we were last time."

No one replied, but then Mercado said again, "We've done nothing illegal." He had an idea and said firmly, "We will jettison everything that is incriminating—the camera, the maps, the photographs, the film...our camping gear—everything."

Purcell replied, "That goes without saying, Henry. But I have to tell you both—Getachu knows, or will know, what we are doing here, and he will not hesitate to use any means that comes into his sick mind to get us to tell him everything he wants to know."

Vivian put her hands over her face. "Oh my God..."

Purcell continued, "And if he also asks us about Colonel Gann, one of us will eventually say Shoan."

Vivian was visibly shaken, but she sat up in her seat, took a deep breath, and said, "I would rather die trying to get away."

Purcell agreed. "That would be preferable to what awaits us in Gondar." He asked, "Henry?"

Mercado did not respond.

Purcell looked out the windshield and saw that he was only about five hundred yards behind and to the left of the helicopter. He could now see the left door gunner leaning out, attached to his harness, looking back at them, with the machine gun pointed at the Navion.

He slid the Navion to the right to get directly behind the helicopter, but the pilot also slid to the right, so his door gunner could keep them in sight. Purcell knew he couldn't play this game with a highly maneuverable helicopter, so he maintained his position, but reduced his airspeed as low as he could without going into a stall. He needed time to think.

Vivian said to him, "Frank...we have to get away from him. Can you do that?"

He was already considering his options. If he made a sudden dive left or right, one or the other door gunners could easily blow them out of the sky. If he climbed, he could possibly pass over the helicopter, and if he kept directly in front of him and got some distance, the door gunners might not be able to swivel their guns that far to the front—but the helicopter pilot only had to swivel his aircraft to give one or the other of his gunners an easy shot at the retreating Navion.

His only chance was to go into a dive—to get into the blind spot below the pilot and the door gunners. He'd have the dive speed he needed to possibly get beyond the accurate range of the machine guns before the helicopter pilot could position his aircraft to give one of his gunners a shot.

Vivian put her hand on his shoulder. "Frank?"

He asked Mercado, "Have you come to a decision, Henry? Run or follow this asshole to Gondar?"

Again, Mercado did not reply.

Purcell looked at the distant horizon. Lake Tana was coming up, and so was Gondar. It was possible, he thought, that the Ethiopian Air Force had already scrambled fighters or more helicopters to make sure they didn't lose them. He was a few minutes away from having no options left.

Mercado said, "Run."

"Okay..." He looked at his airspeed and altimeter and considered what to do, and how best to do it. His rate of descent in a dive would be greater than the Huey's, and his airspeed, too, would be greater. But, as he said, he couldn't outrun a bullet.

The helicopter was nearly hovering now, about three hundred yards away, and he saw the left door gunner making a sweeping motion with his arm, indicating that the Navion should pass and get in front of the helicopter on the approach into Gondar.

That was not what Purcell wanted to do, and it suddenly became clear to him what he needed to do. And he'd known this almost from the beginning.

He reached up and moved the plastic aiming disc on its flexible arm so that it was in front of his face.

Mercado asked in a forcibly controlled voice, "What are you *doing*?"

"What does it look like I'm doing?"

"Are you insane?"

Purcell moved the switch under the instrument panel to the "Fire" position.

Vivian watched him, but said nothing.

The helicopter was less than two hundred yards away, and the door gunner kept waving his arm for the Navion to pass.

Purcell dipped his right wing as though he were going to bank right, and the helicopter pilot, who'd either seen this or heard from his left door gunner, slid his helicopter to the right to keep the Navion on his left.

Purcell pushed forward on the throttle and shoved his rudder hard right, causing the Navion to yaw right, with its nose now pointed at the helicopter. He lined up the helicopter in the red concentric circles of the plastic disc and pushed the firing button, praying that the electrical connection to the rocket pod was working.

The rocket shot out of the pod with a rushing sound and trailed a white smoke stream toward the Huey, less than two hundred yards away now.

Vivian let out a startled sound and Mercado shouted, "Oh God!"

The rocket went high over the helicopter, just missing the rotor shaft.

The door gunner seemed frozen behind his machine gun.

Purcell fired the second rocket, which went low, passing between the landing skids and the cabin, right under the door gunner's feet.

The door gunner fired a long burst of rounds at the Navion and the tracers streaked over the Plexiglas canopy. Vivian screamed and dove onto the floor.

The helicopter pilot made the instinctive mistake of taking evasive action, which threw off the aim of his gunner and gave Purcell a better shot at the Huey as it tilted away from him and slipped sideways and downward. Purcell again kicked the rudder to yaw farther right, and pushed hard on the control wheel to lower the Navion's nose. He kept looking through the plastic disc as the Huey again passed into the concentric circles. The door gunner fired again, and Purcell heard the unmistakable sound of a round impacting the aircraft. He pushed the red button once, then again, firing his last two rockets.

The first smoke rocket sailed through the open cabin, past the head of the door gunner, and the second rocket hit the Plexiglas bubble and burst inside the cockpit. Billows of white smoke poured out the hole in the bubble and through the open doors of the Huey.

The pilots were either injured or blinded by smoke, or something critical was damaged in the cockpit, and the Huey's tail boom began swinging left and right.

Purcell did not change course and continued to fly straight at the unstable helicopter. He could see the door gunner through the billowing smoke, but the man, undoubtedly terrified, had let go of his machine gun and the barrel was hanging loose.

The Huey began a slow roll to the right, then suddenly inverted and dropped like a stone into the jungle canopy below, just as the Navion passed through the airspace that the helicopter had occupied a second before. There was a barely audible explosion behind them as Purcell gave it full throttle and began to climb hard.

Purcell turned off the firing switch, slapped away the plastic aiming disc, then said to Vivian, "It's over."

She rose slowly back into her seat.

He asked, "Mind if I smoke?"

No one replied, and he lit a cigarette, noticing that his hand was shaking.

He glanced at Vivian. Her skin, already pale, was now stark white. "Are you okay?"

She nodded.

"Henry?"

No reply.

Vivian turned in her seat. "Henry? Henry?" She leaned farther into the rear compartment. "Are you all right? Did you get hit?"

"By what?"

Vivian watched him awhile, then turned around.

Purcell kept the throttle open and the Navion continued to climb.

Mercado asked, "What happened?"

Vivian replied, "The helicopter...crashed."

He didn't reply.

Vivian looked at Purcell. "Now what?"

"Well...the French Somaliland option is again open. But that's over two hours from here...and the Ethiopian Air Force may be looking for us shortly."

Mercado seemed to be fully aware now, and he

cleared his voice and asked, "Do you think the helicopter pilot had time to radio anyone?"

Purcell didn't think the pilot even had time to piss his pants after the first smoke rocket went over his head. He replied, "I don't think so. But the helicopter is now obviously out of radio contact, so Gondar will be looking for him, and for us."

Mercado stayed silent, then said, "I don't see that we have any option other than French Somaliland . . . or perhaps Sudan. How far is that?"

Purcell glanced at his flight chart. "The Sudan border is less than two hundred miles—maybe an hour-and-a-half flight. But the Ethie Air Force won't hesitate to pursue over the Sudan border, though they probably won't pursue over the French territory's border."

Mercado seemed to be thinking, then said, "I will vote for the French border." He reminded everyone, "We will receive a better reception there than in Sudan."

Purcell nodded, then glanced at Vivian. "Your vote?"

She had already thought about it and said, "Shoan. Can you land there?"

Purcell thought about that. The single-lane road was too narrow, with towering trees on both sides. The open pastures, however, were a possibility.

Mercado said, "I'm not sure I'm following you, Vivian."

"You are, Henry." She let them both know, "We are not leaving Ethiopia. We came here to find the Holy Grail."

Mercado pointed out, "We are now hunted fugitives. We have just committed murder."

Purcell corrected him. "I engaged a hostile aircraft."

"Call it what you will, old man, if it makes you feel better as they put the noose around your neck." He said to Vivian, "We need to get out of here."

"We will, when we finish what we came here to do."

Purcell was still heading east, toward French Somaliland, and if they decided to change course to Sudan, they had to do it soon, before Sudan became a longer flight than the French territory. He said to Vivian, "You have two choices, and landing in Shoan is not one of them."

"How do you know you can make it to a border before the Ethiopian Air Force shoots us down?"

"I don't know."

"Then *land*. In Shoan. How far is it?"

"Maybe...twenty or thirty minutes."

She pointed out, "Colonel Gann is there. Waiting for us. The black monastery is down there, also waiting for us."

Purcell thought about that. Vivian was crossing the thin line between bravery and insanity—or obsession at best. But she made good arguments.

He was about three thousand feet above the ground and climbing. Airspeed was a hundred miles per hour in the climb, but he could get a hundred fifty in a descent. He banked right and the Navion began turning south.

Mercado asked, "What are you doing?"

"We are landing in Shoan, Henry." To be completely honest, he added, "Or we will die trying."

"No!"

Vivian turned in her seat. "Yes!"

Vivian and Henry looked at each other for several

seconds, and Purcell could imagine Vivian's green eyes staring into Henry's soul.

He heard Henry say, "Yes...all right." He added, "We have come a long way to find the Grail, and we are too close to turn back."

Vivian reached out and touched Henry's face, then turned in her seat and stared out the windshield as the Navion picked up a southwesterly heading toward Shoan and began descending.

She turned her head toward Purcell and looked at him until he looked at her. She said softly, "I love you."

"You love anyone who gives you your way."

She smiled. "What is best for me, is best for us."

He didn't reply.

They continued their rapid descent and Purcell said, "Shoan, about ten minutes." He added, "I will *attempt* a landing."

Vivian said, "That's all I ask of you." She let him know, "You can do it."

"We are about to find out."

He cut his power and began a gradual descent toward the village, which was now visible in the distance.

If he let his imagination go, and if he excluded the surrounding jungle, the fields of Shoan could be upstate New York where he first learned to fly as a young man. His mother had said flying was dangerous and urged him to pursue something safer, like writing.

"I am glad to see you smiling."

"I used to write for my high school newspaper and the hometown weekly. I majored in journalism in college. My mother wanted me to have a safe job."

She smiled and said, "I've read only one article that you wrote. Are you any good?"

"My mother thinks so."

"I lost my parents when I was twelve. A plane crash."

"Sorry."

"Maybe I should have picked a better moment to say that."

Purcell didn't know how many moments they actually had left, but he said, "We have a lot to tell each other in Rome."

She unpinned the Saint Christopher medal from the fabric over the windshield and stuck it on his shirt. "Christopher saved a child from a river, and though he was a big and strong man, the surprising weight of the small child almost made him stumble and fall into the raging water, but he would not let go of the child—and when they reached safety, the child revealed to him that he was Jesus, who carried the weight of the world."

"I know the feeling."

He eased the throttle back and continued their descent.

Chapter 44

Purcell looked for an open pasture among the hundreds of acres of orchards and planted fields. He thought he needed about a thousand feet of unobstructed, mostly level terrain, but stone and wooden fences separated many of the fields, and trees grew in most of the pastures.

Purcell wanted to do a wheels-down landing, but if the ground was too wet, rocky, or potholed, he might have to do a belly landing, though he had the rocket pod to contend with.

Most importantly, he had too much fuel on board—about half a tank—and he couldn't risk staying in the air to burn it off. He instructed Vivian and Henry to clear the aircraft quickly after it came to a stop.

He circled around the periphery of the fields, and he could see a few people near the village looking up at him. Hopefully, Gann was one of them.

Vivian asked, "Do you see a place to land?"

"Only one. That pasture ahead."

Mercado asked, "Is that long enough?"

"I'll make it long enough."

The pasture was slightly sloped, and he decided to land upslope so that the land came up to meet the Navion, and the aircraft would slow sooner uphill and hopefully come to a stop before he ran out of pasture.

He lined up the aircraft with the pasture, which looked to be about a thousand feet long. He now noticed there was a stone fence at the end of the rise, but no trees or water holes.

He had no idea what the winds were doing, but it didn't matter; this was the landing strip, and upslope was the direction.

Purcell lowered his landing gear and flaps and pulled back on the throttle. His airspeed was barely sixty miles per hour, and he estimated his altitude at five hundred feet, then four, three... He looked out at the approaching pasture of short brown grass. The goats had scattered, but now he could see rocks and sinkholes. "Hold on."

He cut the power back to idle, pulled the nose up, and the Navion touched down hard and bounced high, then down again and up again across the rocky pasture. He shut down the engine and applied the brakes. Up ahead he could see the stone fence. He worked the rudder, making the aircraft fishtail, and he began to slow, but the stone fence was less than a hundred yards away, then fifty yards.

"Frank..."

"Brace!"

He kicked the rudder hard, causing the Navion to go into a sideways skid. He expected the landing gear to collapse, but the old bird was built well and the gear held as the wheels traveled sideways across the grassy pasture. The Navion came to a jolting, rocking halt less than twenty feet from the stone fence.

Vivian said, "Beautiful."

Mercado said, "Good one, old boy."

Everyone grabbed their canvas bags that held the

maps, camera, and film, as Purcell slid the canopy open and scrambled onto the wing. Vivian followed quickly and jumped to the ground, followed by Mercado. Purcell joined them and they put some distance between themselves and the Navion in case it decided to burst into flames.

Purcell stood looking at Signore Bocaccio's aircraft, which landed a bit better than it flew. Vivian unpinned the Saint Christopher medal from Purcell's shirt, kissed it, then shoved it in his top pocket.

He heard a noise behind him and turned to see a Land Rover coming toward them. The vehicle stopped a distance away and the door opened. Colonel Gann, wearing a white *shamma* and sandals, came out of the driver's side and walked toward them. He called out, "Was that a landing, or were you shot down?"

Mercado replied in the same spirit of British lunacy, "Just dropping in to say hello."

Gann smiled as he continued toward them. "Just in time for tea."

Gann's hair was now very short, Purcell noticed, and jet black, and he'd lost his red mustache somewhere, and also lost his riding crop if he'd had one. Also gone was his prison pallor, replaced by a nice tan.

Gann walked up to Purcell. "Good landing, actually. Frightened the goats a bit, but they'll get over it."

"So will I."

Gann flashed his toothy smile, then took Vivian's hand. "Lovely as always."

"You look good in a shamma."

"Don't tell." He took Mercado's hand. "Is Gondar closed today?"

"It is to us."

"Well, you must have a good story to tell. But first meet my friend." He waved at the Land Rover, and the passenger-side door opened.

A young woman wearing a green *shamma* came out of the vehicle, and they all followed Gann as he walked toward the lady.

Gann announced, "This is Miriam."

She nodded her head.

Purcell looked at her. She was about early thirties, maybe younger, with short curly black hair. Her features were distinctly Semitic, though her skin was very dark, and her eyes were a deep brown. All in all, she was a beautiful woman.

Gann introduced his friends who'd dropped in unexpectedly, and she took each person's hand and said, "Welcome."

Gann didn't say this was his girlfriend, but it was, and that explained a few things. Always *cherchez la femme*, Purcell knew.

Gann asked his visitors, "Are you being pursued?"

Purcell replied, "Possibly by air."

"All right then...we will bury the aircraft in palm fronds." He looked at Miriam, who said in good English, "I will see to that."

Gann let them know, "Miriam is...well, in charge here." He explained, "She's a princess of the royal blood."

Purcell had had a few experiences with Jewish princesses, but he understood that this was different.

Mercado said to Princess Miriam, "We are sorry to intrude, your highness."

"Please, I am just Miriam."

Mercado bowed his head in acknowledgment.

Purcell reminded everyone, "Sir Edmund actually invited us."

Gann replied, "I did, didn't I? Glad you understood that. Well, here you are. So let's be off." He opened the door of the Land Rover for his princess, and said to everyone, "If the aircraft doesn't blow up, your luggage will be along shortly."

Purcell, Mercado, and Vivian squeezed into the rear of the Land Rover. Gann got behind the wheel and turned toward the village, saying, "I'm afraid Shoan will look a bit deserted, as you may have noticed when you flew by a few days ago. Most everyone has gone to Israel. Just a dozen or so left, and they'll be heading off soon."

No one responded to that, and Gann put his hand on Miriam's shoulder and said, "But they'll all be back. You'll see. A year or two."

Miriam didn't reply.

They entered the small village of about fifty stucco houses, and except for the tin roofs and unpaved streets, Purcell thought he could be back in Berini. No church, however, but he did see the building on the small square that he'd seen from the air, and indeed it was the synagogue, with a Star of David painted in blue over the door.

The square was deserted, and so was the narrow street they turned down, which ended at the edge of the village. Purcell saw the large house he'd also seen from the air, which turned out to be the princess's palace.

Gann stopped the vehicle under a stand of tall palms and said, "Here we are."

Everyone got out and Gann opened a small wooden door in the plain, windowless façade. Miriam entered, then Gann waved his guests in.

It wasn't that palatial, Purcell saw, but the white-washed walls were clean and bright, and the floor was laid with red tile. Niches in the walls held ceramic jars filled with tropical flowers. They followed Miriam and Gann through an open arch into a paved courtyard where the round pool that Purcell had seen from the air sat among date palms. Black African violets grew beneath the palms, and bougainvillea climbed the walls of the other wings of the house.

Gann indicated a grouping of teak chairs and they sat.

A female servant appeared and Miriam said something to her and she left, then Miriam said to her guests, "I can offer you only fruit drinks and some bread."

Purcell informed her, "We have about a hundred pounds of coffee beans in the aircraft. Please consider that our houseguest gift."

Miriam smiled, turned to Gann, and said something in Amharic.

Gann, too, smiled, and Purcell had the feeling that Colonel Gann had briefed the princess about his friends.

Vivian said, "This is a beautiful house."

"Thank you."

Purcell went straight to the obvious question and asked Gann, "So, how did you two meet?"

Gann replied, "I was a friend of Miriam's father back in '41. Met him in Gondar after we kicked out the Italians." He explained, "The Falashas own most of the weaving mills and silver shops in Gondar, and the bloody Fascists took everything from them because they are Jews, and arrested anyone who made a fuss about it. I found Sahle in a prison, half dead, and gave him a bit of bread and a cup of gin. Put him right in no time." He continued, "Well, Sahle and I became friends, and before I left in '43, I came to Shoan to see the birth of his daughter." He looked lovingly at Miriam. "She is as beautiful as her mother."

Vivian smiled and asked Miriam, "Are your parents...here?"

"They have passed on."

Gann said, "Miriam has an older brother, David, who unfortunately went to Gondar on business a few months ago, and has not returned." He added, "He is said to be alive in prison." He added, "Getachu has him."

The servant returned with a tray of fruit, bread, and ceramic cups that held purple juice. Everyone took a cup and the servant set the tray on a table. Miriam spoke with the woman, then said to her guests, "The aircraft is being hidden, and your luggage has arrived." She also assured Mr. Purcell that the coffee beans were with the luggage, and coffee would be served later.

Gann raised his cup and said, "Welcome to Shoan."

They all drank the tart juice, which turned out to be fizzy and fermented.

Gann said, "You must tell me everything."

Purcell replied, "Henry is good at telling everything."

Mercado started with their separate arrivals in Addis, and his finding Signore Bocaccio and his aircraft. Gann nodded, but he seemed to know some of this, and Purcell was impressed with the Royalist underground, or whatever counterrevolutionaries Gann was in touch with.

Mercado then described their aerial recon, and Vivian's wonderful photography, and remembered to thank Gann for the maps, but forgot to compliment Purcell on his flying. Purcell noted, too, that Henry didn't tell Sir Edmund that he, Henry Mercado, had recently fucked Frank Purcell's girlfriend. But that wasn't conversation for mixed company, though Henry might mention it later to Sir Edmund, man to man.

Purcell looked at Gann, then at Miriam, then at Mercado and Vivian. He hoped he was as lucky when he hit sixty. He thought, too, of Signore Bocaccio with his Ethiopian wife and children. If all went well—which it would not—they'd be in Rome in a few weeks; he, Vivian, Henry, Colonel Gann, Miriam, and the Bocaccio family, sitting in Ristorante Etiopia, drinking wine out of the Holy Grail. That was not going to happen, but it was nice to think it.

Henry was getting to the good part—the part where Frank Purcell shot down an armed Ethiopian Air Force helicopter. Henry said to Purcell, "Perhaps you'd like to tell this, Frank."

Purcell understood that this was a good story for a bar, far away from Ethiopia. But here, it was not a good story. In fact, he had put them all in mortal danger. Though in Ethiopia, that was redundant.

"Frank?"

"Well, I think this chopper was looking for us, and I think our old friend General Getachu had sent him. So the game was up, one way or the other, and we—I—decided to take this guy out."

Gann asked, "Do you have weapons with you?"

"No." He explained about the rocket pod, and his creative use of the smoke markers. He didn't go into detail, but he did say, "I rode in a lot of Hueys in 'Nam, covering the war, and I saw them using smoke rockets." He added, "Looked easy." He also explained, "We were dead anyway. Or worse than dead if we landed in Gondar."

Gann nodded. "Quite right."

Vivian let Gann know, "They fired a machine gun at us. Frank was very brave. I was petrified."

Mercado admitted, "I was a bit anxious myself."

Gann thought about this, then asked, "Did you see any other aircraft?"

Purcell replied, "No."

Gann said, "They're probably looking for you on the way to the French territory."

"We thought about heading there, instead of here. Or Sudan."

"Well, good that you didn't." He informed them, "You wouldn't have made it." He let them know, "The Ethies don't have many jets—just a few Mirages—but they are getting Russian helicopter gunships with Russian pilots, and you would probably have met them on your way to Somalia or Sudan."

Purcell nodded, then said, "Sorry, though, if we've put you in a difficult situation."

It was Miriam who said, "We are already in a difficult situation. You are most welcome here."

"Thank you."

Vivian assured her, "We won't be here long."

Miriam looked at Vivian and said, "You are welcome to stay, and you are welcome to leave for French Somaliland, and we can help you with that journey." She continued, "But I would prefer if you did not go to the place where you wish to go."

Vivian replied, "We have come a long way to find this place." She assured Miriam, "We mean no harm to these monks, or to their religious objects."

"I understand that from Edmund. I understand, too, that you think you have been chosen to find this place. And I respect your beliefs. But I can offer you no assistance with your search."

Purcell asked, "Why not?"

She looked at him and replied, "We here in Shoan have a sacred covenant with the monks of the black monastery."

Purcell reminded her, "You're Jewish. They're Copts."

"That does not matter. We are of the same tradition for two thousand years."

"Right. Well, all we're asking then is a good night's sleep and food to take on our journey."

"I will gladly give you that, but I wish you would reconsider that journey."

"Can't do that."

Miriam didn't reply.

Purcell said, "And we may have to return here at some point."

"You are welcome to do that, but we may not be here when you return."

Purcell looked at Gann and reminded him, "You let us know you were here." He asked, "Why?"

Gann hesitated, then replied, "I would like to go with you." He explained, "I've spoken to Miriam, and she understands that we believe that the object you are looking for is in danger, and it must be taken to a safe place, though she believes the monks themselves could do that."

"Maybe they can." He asked, "But if *we* took it, where would we take it?"

Gann glanced at Mercado, then said, "It's not my decision to make." He let them know, "We need to discuss this."

Purcell pointed out, "We don't have it yet, and to be honest with you, we probably never will. So maybe this is moot."

Vivian said, "When we find it, we will know what to do."

Purcell thought that Henry had undoubtedly promised the Grail to the Vatican, and Gann may have promised it to the British Museum, to take the place of the Ethiopian royal crown the British had snatched and given back. But in either case, the Grail, if it existed, and if they found it, was to be held in custody until Ethiopia was free again. At least that was the promise.

Mercado asked Gann, "What is the situation in the countryside?"

"A bit unsettled." He explained about the counterrevolutionaries, and the Royalist partisans, both of whom he was in touch with. He also said, "The Gallas have mostly gone east where the Eritreans are fighting for independence from Ethiopia. But there are some left to see if the fighting here resumes."

Purcell told him, "We saw some Gallas from the air." He said to Gann, "I meant to ask you—what do they do with all those balls?"

"They eat them, old boy." He further explained, "Not the Christian or Muslim Gallas, of course. But the pagan Gallas." He added, "Gives them courage."

"Right. You'd need a lot of courage to do that."

"Never thought of that." Gann further addressed Mercado's concerns and told them, "The Israelis have smuggled in some firearms for the Falashas, to be sure the exodus goes off without a problem." He reached into an empty urn and retrieved an Uzi submachine gun. "Nice piece of goods." He handed it to Purcell and told them, "We'll take that with us."

Purcell looked at the compact weapon with a magazine longer than the barrel. "This should scare the hell out of those monks."

Gann smiled. "I was thinking more of the Gallas— or anyone else who we may meet in the jungle." He also informed them, "Getachu has sent some units down this way, but they've gotten a bad reception from the Royalist partisans and the anti-Marxist counterrevolutionaries."

"Good." Purcell asked, "Do you have three more Uzis?"

"I'm afraid not." He let them know, "The few men left here need them."

Purcell passed the Uzi to Mercado, who said, "Reminds me of the old British Sten gun," and gave it to Vivian.

Gann said to his guests, "It's a simple weapon, and I'll show you how to use it in the event...I'm not with you."

Miriam looked at her lover, but said nothing.

Mercado asked Gann, "Is Shoan safe?"

"It is to the extent that the Provisional government has agreed to let the Jews leave, unhindered." He added, "So far the exodus has gone well all over the country, though there have been a few incidents, and thus the Uzis."

Purcell asked Gann, "How do you communicate with the Royalists here, and in Addis?"

"I have a shortwave radio. I keep it outside the village, so as not to compromise the people here."

"Can you show it to us?"

"Of course. But my batteries have died, and I'm waiting for replacements." He added, "My Kipling poem to you was my last transmission."

"We would have brought batteries if they'd been left for us at the hotel."

"If you're found with a shortwave battery, you are shot. After being tortured."

"Right." Maps and photographs were maybe explainable. Shortwave radio batteries were as hard to explain as a gun. He'd rather have the gun, which could explain itself.

Gann took the gun from Vivian and said, "We should push off tomorrow." He asked them, "Do you have any idea where you would like to look?"

Purcell replied, "I hoped you—or Miriam—could suggest something."

"I'm afraid I can't, old boy." He said, "I thought perhaps you'd seen something from the air."

"We did. But we don't want to see all those places on the ground."

"Well, we may have to do that." Gann stayed silent for a moment, then glanced at Miriam and said to his guests, "As I mentioned to you in Rome, the people of Shoan have some contact with the monastery. However, those who had this contact are gone."

Purcell looked at Miriam. She told them, "The secret is with the elders who have left, and they took their secret with them."

Gann looked at his guests. "A relationship...a friendship, that has lasted four hundred years, since the monastery was built, is now severed." He told them, "The last meeting took place two weeks ago, and the monks have been told."

Purcell again had the feeling he'd slipped into an alternate universe. He asked Miriam, "When the people who went to this meeting place left, how long were they gone?"

She looked at him but did not reply.

He asked, "Which way did they go?"

She replied, "They went in a different direction each time, and they were never gone for the same number of days."

"Well, that narrows it down."

Vivian said to him, "Frank, you are being rude."

"Sorry." He explained his rudeness. "I just want to find this place and get out of here."

Miriam said to him, and to her other guests, "Let me think about what you have asked."

"Thank you."

Miriam said softly, "This is a difficult time for

everyone. This civilization—Christian and Jewish—has come to an end. But we look to the future, which will be better. We must all leave here, but when we return, we must return as we were, with our customs and traditions, and our covenants unbroken."

Purcell nodded. "I understand."

Vivian said to Miriam, "We are here to do what you are doing. To take with us what cannot be left here. To keep things safe until this nightmare is over."

Miriam replied, "You should let the monks do that." She stood. "I must see to your comforts. I will return shortly."

The gentlemen stood, and the princess left.

Gann said to his guests, "Miriam and I have had this conversation, as you can well imagine, and I assure you, she knows nothing more than she has told you."

Mercado said, "I'm sure she'd have told you if she knew more."

Purcell wondered if Henry really believed that women told their men everything. If he did, he'd be cuckolded every year.

Vivian told Gann, "Tomorrow, we'd like to go to the spa." She explained that this was not a nostalgia trip, but a bone hunting expedition.

Gann replied, "Rather odd custom, don't you think?"

Mercado, former atheist, now a believer working for the Vatican newspaper, explained, "This is very important to the Church of Rome when a person is proposed for sainthood." He further explained, "A mortal remain is considered a first-class relic. A piece of a garment is second-class, other objects—"

"Yes, well, we can stop at the spa and look about for a bone or two." He added, "Short walk. Half a day at most."

Vivian continued, "And we'd like to see the fortress where Father Armano was imprisoned for forty years."

Mercado told Gann, "We spotted incognita from the air and it was, indeed, Prince Theodore's fortress."

"Good recon." He asked Vivian, "Is this part of the sainthood thing?"

She replied, "It is part of Father Armano's story. It is something I need to see."

"I see . . . Well, I'm sure it's on the way to something."

Mercado said, "Most of the suspected locations of the black monastery are a day or two walk from the fortress."

Vivian added, "There may be a clue there."

Gann nodded. "We'll take a look."

They had more fermented fruit juice as they discussed a few items on everyone's agenda. They agreed they'd be gone a week—or less if they found what they were looking for. If not, they would return to Shoan, and as Colonel Gann said, "Regroup, refit, and strike out again."

Vivian asked Gann, "Will anyone be here when we return?"

He didn't reply for a moment, then said, "Everyone will be gone." He told them, "Miriam and I will meet in Jerusalem."

Vivian smiled. "That's very nice."

Mercado, who was again thinking about exit strategy, asked Purcell, "Could you get that aircraft out of here?"

"We could carry it out."

"Why can't you fly it out?"

"It has to take off first, Henry. That's the hard part."

"If you land, you can take off."

"I may have blown the tires. I'll look at it later." He asked, "Where would you like to go?"

"French Somaliland."

Gann interjected, "I think we will need to walk out of here." He assured them, "A number of Royalist partisans have been to Somalia and back. I have a few chaps who will come along."

Miriam returned and announced that dinner would be served in an hour, and she offered to show everyone to their rooms.

They all stood and Miriam led them to an arched loggia, along which were wooden doors. She indicated a door and said, "For Mr. Mercado." Miriam thought she knew the sleeping arrangements and indicated another door. "For Mr. Purcell, and Miss Smith." She added, "I hope we have gotten your luggage correctly placed."

Gann pointed to the end of the loggia and said, "Bath down there." He suggested, "Let's say cocktails in one hour, on the patio."

Purcell, Vivian, and Mercado thanked their hosts, and entered their rooms.

Purcell looked around the small, whitewashed room with a beamed ceiling. There were no windows, but narrow wooden louvers sat high in the wall to let in air and light, and to keep out wildlife and uninvited guests.

There were two gray steel beds against one wall that

looked like they'd come from an institution. Against the opposite wall was a wooden table, on which sat their luggage and an oil lamp. In one corner was a chair, and in another was a washstand with a bowl and pitcher. He said, "Looks like a monk's cell."

"This will look good after a week in the jungle."

"It will look like a palace."

She asked him, "Are you all right with this?"

He didn't reply.

"I can ask for a separate room."

"Let me do that."

"Frank. Look at me."

He looked at her.

"I am sorry, and I love you."

"We'll discuss this in Gondar."

"We are not going to Gondar."

"Right."

She changed the subject and said, "I didn't think Sir Edmund had so much romance in his soul."

Purcell admitted, "I was a bit surprised."

"Love conquers all."

"Any good news?"

"I'm going to find the bath." She left.

He stood there awhile, then decided he needed a bath.

He found the door at the end of the loggia and went inside a roofless enclosure in which was a sunken pool against the far wall. The face of a black stone lion was embedded in the wall, and a stream of water poured from the lion's mouth. Vivian's clothes lay on a stone bench, and Vivian herself was floating full frontal nude in the pool.

He took off his clothes and slipped into the water, which was unheated but warm.

She said to him, "No one would believe a village of Jews in the middle of the Ethiopian jungle." She added, "Or a Roman spa. Or a monastery of Coptic monks."

"Don't forget the Jewish princess."

"Maybe this is a dream."

With a bit of nightmare, for sure, he thought.

She stayed silent awhile, floating with her eyes closed. She said, "We're very close."

"Closer than I thought we'd get."

"Do you think Miriam will help us?"

"She's thinking about it."

Neither of them spoke for a while, then Vivian said, "Thank you for staying with this."

He didn't reply.

"You could have left, and I wouldn't have blamed you."

"It's a good story."

The door opened, and Mercado said, "Oh... sorry..." He asked, "Mind if I join you?" He explained, "I'm a bit rushed for time."

Vivian did not reply, but Purcell said, "You don't need to ask. We're all friends."

Chapter 45

Purcell, Vivian, and Mercado, all fresh from their communal bath, joined the princess and the colonel for cocktails on the patio. Vivian wore her best khaki pants and green T-shirt, and the two gentlemen wore khakis, top and bottom.

The sun was setting and the night had grown pleasantly cool. The purple African sky above the date palms was magnificent, Purcell thought, and if it wasn't for Colonel Gann's Uzi on the table, he could imagine he was someplace else.

Colonel Sir Edmund Gann had gone unnative, and he wore his paramilitary khakis to cocktails, though he'd kept his afternoon sandals.

Princess Miriam wore a purple evening *shamma*, trimmed with lion's mane, the sign of royalty in old Ethiopia.

Cocktails were limited to Boodles gin, a half bottle of which Colonel Gann had been saving for a special occasion, and this was it—which pleased Henry. The gin could be had with or without fruit juice.

The cocktail chatter had mostly to do with the Falasha exodus and the local security situation. Gann explained, "Getachu and his army control the Gondar area and the surrounding Simien Mountains. Here, to the south, which is nearly unpopulated, there are counterrevolutionaries operating in the jungle valleys, as I've said, as well as the remnants of the Royalist forces." He further explained, "These two groups have far different agendas—an elected government on the one hand, and a return to an absolute monarchy on the other." He told them, "I'm trying to get them to pull together to get rid of the Marxists. I explained to both sides how we in Britain have a monarch and an elected parliament. But they're not understanding the concept."

Purcell admitted, "Neither do I."

Cocktails were brief, and they were escorted into the palace, where dinner was served in a room that held a long table which would seat about twenty; suitable for large family meals, except that everyone was gone. The floor, Purcell noticed, was laid with black stone.

The teak table was set simply, though the silverware was real, Purcell noticed, and each piece was decorated with the Lion of Judah. The dishes, too, had the heraldic lion hand-painted on them. The dinner theme, Purcell saw, was lions.

Fading sunlight came through the high louvers, and oil lamps flickered on the table.

On the menu was grilled goat, some sort of root vegetable, and flatbread, with bowls of dates scattered around the table. Fermented fruit juice was poured into bronze goblets that looked like the ones Prince Joshua once owned, and the one that he, Purcell, had overpaid for in Rome.

Two ladies in middle age served the simple meal and kept the fizzy fruit juice flowing. Miriam promised fresh coffee at the end of the meal.

She was an intelligent and interesting lady, Purcell saw, and he could see why the other old goat in the room—Sir Edmund—was taken with her.

Dinner conversation began light, and in answer to Vivian's question, Miriam explained, "Most of the Solomonic line are Christian, of course, but some are Jewish, and some are even Muslim. The line from Solomon and Sheba is well recorded, but over the centuries, the three religions have influenced the faith of some families." She added, "The Jews are not the oldest religion in Ethiopia—the pagans are. If you call that a religion."

Purcell had just learned that the pagan Gallas ate human testicles, but he didn't know how to work that into the dinner conversation—or if he should try.

Purcell also wanted to ask Miriam why, in her early thirties, she was not married yet with ten kids, but to be more subtle and polite, he asked, "So do you have to marry within the Solomonic line?"

She stayed silent for a few seconds, then replied, "I was married at sixteen, to a Christian ras, but we produced no heirs, so my husband divorced me. This is not unusual." She added, "Most of the rasses are now dead, or they have fled, so I have few prospects for marriage." She looked at her boyfriend and said without cracking a smile, "So I have settled for an Englishman."

Everyone got a laugh at that, and Gann said, "Could do worse, you know."

Vivian asked boldly, "Do you two plan to marry?"

Miriam replied, "We have no word for knight, so here they call him Ras Edmund, which makes him acceptable."

Again everyone laughed, but clearly this was a

touchy subject, so the nosy reporters did not ask follow-up questions.

Miriam switched to another touchy subject—her benighted country. "This is an old civilization in the middle stage of history—a medieval anachronism. The Muslims keep harems and slaves. The Christians dispense biblical justice, and men are made eunuchs, and women are sold for sexual purposes. The Jews, too, have engaged in Old Testament punishment. The pagans practice unspeakable rites, including castration and crucifixion. And now the Marxists have introduced a new religion, the religion of atheism, and a new social order, the mass killing of anyone who is associated with the old order."

Purcell needed another drink after that. When he was first here, in September, living at the Hilton in Addis, he had almost no idea what life was like outside the capital, which itself was no treat. Their trip out of Addis to the northern front had opened his eyes a little to what Ethiopia was about. Gann, however, had known this place since 1941, and Mercado even longer. And yet they'd returned, and in Gann's case, he found something compelling about this country—something that drew him to it the way some men are drawn to those places on the map marked "terra incognita—here be dragons." And Signore Bocaccio…he'd forgotten there were better places to do business.

Vivian, like himself, had come here clueless and free-lance, but she had discovered that she was chosen by God to be here, which was better than being chosen by the Associated Press.

And then there was Frank Purcell. He needed to think again about why he was still here.

In his mental absence, the subject had again turned to dark matters. Miriam said, "Mikael Getachu's father worked for my father in Gondar in the weaving shop. My father treated the family well, and paid for Mikael's education at the English missionary school."

Purcell informed everyone, "Getachu's biography says his parents went without food to pay for his education."

Miriam replied, "They went without nothing."

Gann said, "Miriam's brother, David, was actually lured by Getachu to come to Gondar with the promise that Getachu would release two young nieces and a nephew of the family if David would identify and sign over the family's assets to Getachu." Gann added, "Getachu knows he can't violate the ancient sanctity of Shoan, or more importantly the international agreement protecting the Jews during the exodus. But he has sent a message to Miriam saying that if she voluntarily comes to Gondar, then he will release David, and the nieces and nephew." He added, "The children's parents, who are Sahle's sister and brother-in-law, have already been shot."

Purcell looked at Miriam, who seemed stoic enough on the outside, but he could imagine the conflicts and pain inside her.

Gann said, "Getachu's goal all along was to get hold of his princess."

Miriam said bluntly, "He will not have me."

Vivian was looking at her, but said nothing.

Mercado suggested in a quiet voice, "You should leave here as soon as possible."

"I will be the last to leave. That is my duty."

Gann said, "We're hoping for a UN helicopter pickup here next week."

Purcell would have liked them all to be on that helicopter, but he knew that would jeopardize not only the Falashas, but also the UN mission. In fact, just their being here did all of that, plus some. He said, "We are leaving at daybreak, and we won't return until everyone here is safely gone." He also suggested to Gann, "Set fire to the aircraft so it looks like we crashed and burned. Lots of fuel on board."

Mercado did not like that, but he understood it.

Gann assured everyone, "I'll have that done in the morning."

Miriam wanted to know about Purcell, Mercado, and Vivian, and they filled her in on some of the details, though she seemed to know most of this from her boyfriend, Purcell thought, including the fact that they'd had the pleasure of Mikael's company.

She warned them, "He has a long memory and a great capacity for cruelty and revenge. Do not fall into his hands again." She added, "But you know that."

As for Prince David, Miriam had no illusions that Getachu would be treating him well, but she felt or hoped that after she was out of Getachu's reach, and she was in Israel, Getachu would release her brother, and the nieces and nephew, under pressure from the Israelis and the UN, and hopefully under orders from his own superiors in Addis. Purcell thought that was a possibility, but he was sure that David, if he ever did arrive in Israel, would be a broken man. As General Getachu himself had indicated, shooting a man is easy; breaking a man is more fun—especially if the man or woman was an arrogant aristocrat, or an annoying journalist.

Miriam suggested to her guests, "Perhaps you can write about what you have seen here. And perhaps you will mention my brother and my nieces and nephew. That could be helpful for their release."

They all promised they would do that when they left Ethiopia. And they would keep that promise—if they left Ethiopia.

Miriam thanked them, and then painted for them a grim picture of post-revolutionary Ethiopia for their lead story. "The land is laid waste by war, and by locusts and drought, sent by God. Famine has killed too many to count, and millions more hang by a thread. Pestilence is spreading across the land and the people have withdrawn into themselves. Churches are looted and monks lock themselves in their monasteries. All this is punishment by God for what we have allowed the godless men in Addis to do. God is testing us, and we must show him that we remain true to him. Only then will we be saved by God."

No one spoke, and Gann, Purcell thought, looked both embarrassed and proud of his princess. Clearly, there was a great cultural divide between them, but they were both righteous and decent people, and what separated them was not as great as what connected them. Love conquers all, as Vivian said.

Coffee was served with some sort of concoction of goat's milk, honey, and almonds.

Miriam said, "Trade with Gondar and other cities has been greatly reduced since the troubles began. So we have only what we have. But that is more than they have in the places where the drought and the locusts have killed the land." She forced a smile and added, "In any case, we are all going to the land of milk and honey." She asked if anyone had been to Israel, and Mercado and Purcell had, and they painted a bright picture for Miriam that seemed to comport with what her English knight had already told her.

Purcell had encountered a few former aristocrats or landed gentry and former capitalists in the bars of Hong Kong and Singapore, and in the capitals of Western Europe, and most of them were indignant that they'd been innocent victims of some revolution or another. Almost all expressed a sense of loss, and what they all had in common was a stunned disbelief that the world had changed so much, or had gone so mad. Born to rule or born to great wealth, these refined refugees could not understand or accept that the lowest elements of society—the Getachus—were the most recent mutation of social Darwinism, and that the former lords and masters were the dodo birds in the process of natural selection and extinction.

Princess Miriam, Purcell thought, was a nice person, and he was sure that she and her family had never knowingly hurt anyone. In fact, they'd sent Mikael Getachu, and probably other poor children, to school. But the two greatest scapegoats in the history of the world were the nobility and the Jews—and if you were both, you had a serious problem.

Gann switched to another subject and informed everyone, "Obsidian was quarried in these mountains since ancient times and sent down the Nile on barges to Egypt, where it was prized for its strength and its ability to be polished to a high black luster. We've all seen the Egyptian statuary carved from obsidian in museums. It's difficult to work with, and it is rarely seen as a building material, except in floors, such as the one in this room, which could be a thousand years old."

Purcell wasn't sure where this was going, but then Gann said, "The quarries in this area have not been worked for hundreds of years, and they are mostly overgrown and lost to memory. But there are a few that I've identified, and on the theory that this black monastery is built of obsidian—which is so heavy that it can't be transported too far—I think we should have a look around these three ancient quarries which I've identified on a map."

Everyone nodded, except Miriam, who clearly didn't want to participate in any discussion about finding the black monastery.

It occurred to Purcell that, as Vivian said, they were close, and with some luck and brains they could actually be seeing what Father Armano saw forty years ago—high black walls rising out of the jungle in front of them. But was the monastery now deserted? He suspected that it was, especially after the Jewish elders of Shoan told the monks that they were all leaving. Gone, too, would be the Grail, of course. But if he, Vivian, Mercado, and Gann found the monastery, that would be enough for him and maybe for his companions. The journey would be over, and the Grail—as it had a history of doing—would be gone, but safe from the world which had grown evil.

But if they reached the walls of the monastery and a reed basket was lowered...well, forewarned was forearmed.

Dinner was over, and everyone stood. The long night had begun, and at dawn they would begin their quest for fame, fortune, salvation, a good story, a Grail rescue mission, inner peace, or whatever was driving them into the dark interior.

If, indeed, they had been chosen for this journey, then the answer to why they'd been chosen was waiting for them.

PART IV

The Quest

We shall not cease from exploration
And the end of all our exploring
Will be to arrive where we started
And know the place for the first time.

—T. S. Eliot,
Four Quartets 4: Little Gidding

Chapter 46

They rose before dawn and met in the courtyard, where Miriam had coffee, fruit, and bread for them.

They carried their backpacks and equipment, and what was left behind would be burned along with the Navion, to hide any traces that they'd been in the village.

Vivian and Purcell had slept in the same room, but not in the same bed. So they were friends.

The sky was beginning to lighten, and Purcell could see it was going to be a clear day. No one spoke much, because there was little to say that hadn't already been said, and also because there were no words equal to the moment of heading off into the unknown.

Purcell, Vivian, and Henry thanked Miriam for her hospitality and promised to meet again under better circumstances. She seemed sorry to see them go, Purcell thought, but probably relieved, too. She didn't hand them a map to the black monastery, but she did say, "If God wants you to find this place, you will." She also assured them, "Edmund will be your guide in the jungle. Please be his guide in the ways of God."

Henry and Vivian said they would.

They left Colonel Gann to say his own good-bye to his lady, and they went through a back door and into a flower garden.

They had as much food with them as they could carry, which consisted mostly of boiled eggs, bread, dates, and dried meat, all of which Gann assured them was high in nutrition, and would last a week. They each carried two canteens; one of water, one of the purple juice, which Purcell had come to enjoy. Henry had his Moët, of course, and Vivian had her camera. Purcell was in charge of the maps.

Colonel Gann came out into the garden, and it was obvious that his parting had been difficult. Purcell had never known that feeling himself, or if he had, the sense of loss was always made easier by a larger sense of relief.

Purcell looked at Vivian in the dawn light and saw she was looking at him, and probably thinking the same thing: How will we part? Hopefully, as friends.

Colonel Gann gave everyone a five-minute lesson on the Uzi, which indeed was a simple weapon to load and fire. Gann then led them through a fruit orchard and across a pasture toward the thick rain forest that surrounded the fields and village of Shoan.

He knew his way, and within fifteen minutes he'd found the head of a trail that none of them could have found, even in full sunlight. They entered the rain forest, going from human habitation to a world of flora and fauna that had barely been disturbed since the beginning of time.

The trail was narrow, and the jungle growth encroached on all sides. They walked silently, single file, and crouched most of the way. Gann had a machete with him, but he didn't want to use it and leave evidence that the trail had been traveled.

Their first stop, after about ten minutes, was a huge

gnarled tree that was mostly dead, and which Gann said was a baobab. A few paces from the tree was the shortwave radio, wrapped in plastic and covered with palm fronds.

Gann had hoped that the Royalist partisans had delivered new batteries, but the radio was still dead.

He said in a whisper, "This trail will take us to the spa. The road would be faster, but we're more likely to come upon someone on the road—a vehicle, an army patrol, or Gallas on horseback." He also told them, "I know some of these trails, but so do others. We need to remain silent, and we need to listen to the jungle. I will take the point, and Mr. Purcell will take the rear. If anyone hears anything, you will quickly and silently alert everyone, and point to where you've heard the sound. We will then take cover off the trail." He asked, "Any questions?"

"Can I smoke?"

"No."

They continued on, and the trail became more overgrown. They were heading generally north, paralleling the narrow road that they had driven in September. Purcell hadn't much enjoyed driving the creepy road through the dark jungle, and he wasn't enjoying walking through that jungle now.

The ribbon of sky above the narrow trail was getting lighter, and somewhere out there, the sun was shining.

Vivian was walking ahead of Purcell, and now and then she glanced back and gave him a smile, which he returned. It was hard to stay angry when each step could be your last, and when you were just hours or days away from the greatest religious discovery since Moses found the Ten Commandments—which, as it turned out, were in Axum, inside the Ark of the Covenant.

Purcell still didn't believe in any of this, but he would be happy to be proven wrong.

After about an hour, Gann stopped and motioned everyone to the right side of the trail where an outcropping of black obsidian lay among the ground growth between towering trees. They sat on the rock and took a break. Gann and Purcell looked at one of the maps and estimated where they were. Gann said quietly, "The spa will be another two or three hours."

They both studied the map and agreed that their next objective after the spa would be Prince Theodore's fortress, which was about five or six kilometers east of the spa.

Gann said, "The map does not show a trail between the fortress and the spa, and if we can't find one on the ground, and if there is thick underbrush between the trees, as there is here, we will have to cut a trail." He informed them, "That could take more than a day to travel that five kilometers."

Vivian reminded them, "Father Armano walked from the fortress to the spa, and we saw him at about ten at night."

Gann inquired, "What time did he start from the fortress?"

Vivian replied, "I don't know...but we have to assume he started sometime that evening...he could not have traveled far with that wound."

Purcell reminded them, "Getachu said that his artillery bombarded Prince Theodore's fortress—and this is probably how Father Armano got out of his cell."

Gann nodded and said, "That would have been about seven-fifteen." He told them, "I took note of the time, and I wondered what the idiot was shooting at, because he wasn't shooting at me or Prince Joshua's camp."

So, with a little simple math, everyone agreed that Father Armano was freed from his cell—probably by a lucky artillery round—after 7:15 P.M., and he appeared at the spa about three hours later, meaning there was a good and direct trail between the fortress and the spa. All they had to do was find it.

Vivian looked at the rock they were sitting on and asked, "Could this be the rock that Father Armano mentioned?"

Gann replied, "There are many rock outcroppings in this area, and there is nothing remarkable about this one." He suggested, "I think you should forget the rock, the tree, and the stream, which may have had some meaning to the priest, but that meaning is obscure to us."

Vivian did not reply.

They all stood and continued on. It was becoming warmer, and more humid, and the thick, rotting vegetation gave off noxious vapors, which reminded Purcell of the jungles of Southeast Asia. There was a reason that few people lived in the lush tropical rain forests of the world; it was a hostile environment to humans, and a paradise for insects, slithering snakes, and animals with fangs and claws. In fact, he thought, the jungle sucked.

They continued on.

Colonel Gann walked easily, like he did this every

day before breakfast, Purcell thought. And Vivian had youth on her side, but about sixty pounds of gear on her back, and Purcell could see she was dragging a bit. Henry, too, seemed a bit fatigued, and if physical exhaustion is mostly mental, then Henry should be thinking about their last trek when he'd run out of gas at a bad time, which led to a series of events that nearly got them all killed. Henry now wanted to redeem himself, and impress Vivian, of course, or at least not pass out in front of her, and that should keep him moving. If not, he should think about Gallas coming for his balls.

They continued on through the jungle, or rain forest, as Purcell's editors now wanted it called. The insects and birds made a lot of noise, which covered the sound of danger. But as Purcell had learned in Vietnam when traveling with army patrols, if the birds become quiet, they've heard something. It could be you they've heard, or something else.

Purcell considered himself in fairly good shape, despite the cocktails and cigarettes, and this hike, even with all the carried weight, was so far like a walk in the park. But after a week of this, and sleeping on the ground, and the scant rations, he could imagine that they'd all be having some problems. It was obvious why the Gallas rode horses, and why many armies used mules as pack animals. But Colonel Gann had vetoed both for a variety of practical reasons, mostly having to do with noise discipline, and water and forage for the animals. Purcell did not usually defer to anyone in his business, which was why he was freelance and mostly between jobs; but he would defer to Colonel Gann in *his* business, as long as he thought Gann knew what he was doing.

About two hours later, Gann motioned everyone together and said, "The spa is about fifty meters ahead. I will go first and recon." He borrowed Mercado's binoculars, then handed Purcell the Uzi and three extra magazines and said, "You will cover me." He pulled a long-barreled revolver from under his bush jacket and headed down the trail. Purcell motioned Vivian and Mercado to stay put, and followed Gann.

The trail ended at the clearing around the spa, and fifty yards ahead was the side of the white stucco hotel, sitting in the sunlight. Gann was scanning the area around the building, then moved toward it.

Purcell took the Uzi off safety and followed Gann through the tall grass. Gann went around to the front of the hotel, and Purcell kept about twenty yards behind him. Gann climbed the steps and disappeared into the building, and Purcell waited. A few minutes later, Gann reappeared and signaled all clear.

Purcell looked back to the edge of the jungle and saw Mercado and Vivian making their way through the chest-high grass. He motioned them to join him, and together they walked quickly to the front of the spa hotel.

They stood at the base of the steps that they'd climbed with the Jeep and looked at the crumbling ruin.

Vivian said, "We are back."

Purcell looked across the field toward the narrow road they'd driven that night, and he could see the place where he'd crashed the Jeep through the thick wall of high brush that blocked the spa from the road. He looked back at the hotel. He must have seen the dome, he thought, or it registered subconsciously, and that was why he'd suddenly turned off the road.

Vivian saw what Purcell was looking at and said, "Fate, Frank. Don't try to understand it."

Mercado agreed, "I see God's hand in this."

Hard to argue with that, so he didn't.

Vivian walked halfway up the steps, and Mercado and Purcell joined her.

She looked around and asked, "Can you believe this?" She turned to Purcell. "We are back where it began."

Actually, Purcell thought, this all began in the Hilton bar, with Henry inviting him to come with them to the front lines. A simple "No" would have been a good answer. But Henry's invitation was flattering. And Vivian had smiled at him. And he may have had one cocktail more than he needed.

Ego, balls, alcohol, and a restless dick; a sure combination for glory or disaster.

Vivian said, "We will begin here, where Father Armano ended his life. We have been to Berini, and we have been to Rome, and we will follow the priest's footsteps to his prison. And with his help and God's help we will also follow his footsteps to the black monastery, and the Holy Grail."

Vivian took both their hands, and they continued up the steps to the place where Father Armano's fate had intersected with theirs.

Chapter 47

They found Colonel Gann standing in the rubble-filled lobby. It looked the same as when they'd last seen it, except that along the frescoed wall where Purcell had parked the Jeep, and where they had heard Father Armano's story, there were bones and skulls strewn over the marble floor.

Gann said, "Firing squad."

Vivian stared at the skulls and bones, put her hand over her mouth, and said, "Oh my God..."

Purcell moved closer to the execution wall. Some military gear and rotted *shammas* confirmed that this was a mass slaughter of Prince Joshua's soldiers. Jackals and ants had nearly cleaned the bones, but some desiccated brown tissue remained, and dried blood covered the marble floor.

The plaster fresco on the wall was shattered where fusillade after fusillade had cut down the condemned men. Purcell noticed that splashes of blood and perhaps brain stained the remnants of the fresco, as high as ten feet off the floor, adding a grisly touch to the pink bathing nymphs.

Mercado, too, was staring at the scene, and he said, "This is evidence of a war crime."

Purcell, trying not to sound too cynical or unfeeling, replied, "Henry, this country is drowning in blood. What difference does this make?"

"This is inhuman."

"Right." They'd both seen battle deaths, but that was what passed for normal in war. Mass executions, on the other hand, had a special ugliness.

Purcell counted skulls, but stopped at about fifty.

Gann was poking around the lobby, gun in hand.

Vivian had walked away and was standing at the back of the lobby, which opened out onto the courtyard and gardens.

Mercado stared at the corner where they had laid the priest and covered him with a blanket—the now desecrated spot where he and Vivian felt a miracle of sorts had taken place.

Mercado said, as if to himself, "The blood of the martyrs gives nourishment to the church."

Purcell could not completely understand how people like Henry Mercado, and to some extent Vivian, persisted in their belief in a benevolent power. But he'd come to see that there was a special language used to explain the simultaneous existence of God and human depravity. You would need the right words, Purcell thought, evolved over thousands of years, to keep your faith from slipping.

Vivian had unexpectedly returned to the scene, and she had her camera out now. She took a deep breath and shot a few pictures of the grisly carnage. She moved closer to the corner where the priest had lain and died to shoot photographic evidence of both sainthood and mass murder.

Mercado stood close to her, to give her moral support and silent encouragement. It occurred to Purcell that Vivian and Henry might well be better suited to one another than Vivian and Frank could ever be. It bothered him to think that, but that may have been the truth. Henry and Vivian were, in a way, kindred spirits, eternally joined at their souls, whereas he and Vivian were connected only once a night. Well...but there was more there between them.

Gann had joined them and inquired, "I don't suppose any of these bones are that of the priest?"

Vivian replied, "No. We buried him."

"That's right. Well, lead on."

They exited the lobby through the rear and walked quickly across the paved courtyard, with Vivian and Mercado in the lead and Purcell and Gann on the flanks with their weapons at the ready.

Gann pointed out horse droppings, obvious evidence of Gallas, but he assured them that the droppings looked to be months old. Maybe weeks.

Purcell thought back to when they'd first walked through this spa complex without too much concern about Gallas, soldiers, partisans, or armed and desperate outlaws who roamed the countryside. God, indeed, watched over idiots.

Gann was being both security man and tourist, and remarked, "Incredible engineering." He added, "Rather a waste, though."

They found the garden where they'd buried Father Armano. Getachu's soldiers had exhumed the body, and jackals had scattered the bones in the garden and on the paths. The grave itself had caved in and a colony of red ants had taken residence.

Gann seemed pleased for Vivian at all the bones, and Purcell thought Gann was going to pick one up for her and say, "Here we go. Nice one. Let's move on." But in fact he stood patiently and reverently, staring at the grave. Vivian took photographs of the grave and of the scattered bones, while Mercado again stood beside her.

The time had come to pick a bone as a relic of the saint-to-be, and Mercado informed everyone, "The skull is considered the most important mortal relic."

But there was no skull in sight, so that set off a search through the overgrown gardens. Gann let everyone know, "The jackals will often take a bit of their find to their lairs."

Indeed, Purcell had noticed that there were not enough bones to make a complete skeleton. But there were some good-sized bones, including a femur and a pelvis, and he would have pointed this out to Henry and Vivian, but he wasn't sure of the protocol.

Vivian was about to settle for the femur, but then Henry exclaimed, "Here it is!" and retrieved a skull from the underbrush. He held it up, sans jawbone.

Purcell was standing closest to Henry, so he could see that, thankfully, the skull had been picked clean by jackals and red ants, and that the rains and the sun had contributed to the job, though the white bone was stained with red earth.

Vivian hesitated to take a photograph of Henry holding the skull, which might be considered macabre back at the Vatican, so Henry set the skull on the stone bench, then thought better of that, and set it beside the grave. Vivian took six pictures from different angles and elevations. Gann glanced at his watch.

So now, Purcell knew, they needed to take the skull with them, for eventual delivery to Vatican City. Purcell also knew that if he ever made it back to Rome, he would not be with Henry or Vivian when they presented their relic to the proper church authorities. And when they got to Berini, they'd bring photographs.

Vivian had taken a plastic laundry bag from the Hilton, which was in her backpack, and which she could use to hold Father Armano's skull in a safe and sanitary manner. She opened the bag, and Mercado took a last look at the skull, as though hoping it had something to tell him. He deposited the skull in the bag and they crammed it in her backpack.

Next, the priest's bones needed to be reinterred, and Purcell helped Mercado hand-dig the loose earth from the grave, evicting the red ants and other things from the pit. Gann contributed his machete, which they used to loosen the soil. They went down only about two feet because there were just bones to bury now, and not many of them.

They gathered up the bones and carefully placed them in the shallow grave, in no particular order. The three men refilled the grave and Vivian took photographs. Purcell supposed that as with photos taken on an exhausting holiday, say to the Mojave Desert, these scenes would be more appreciated when viewed at home.

The time had come for a prayer and Mercado volunteered. He said, "Earth to earth, ashes to ashes, dust to dust; in sure and certain hope of the Resurrection unto eternal life." He added, "Rest in peace," and made the sign of the cross, and everyone did the same.

Purcell sat on the stone bench, wiped his sweating face, and recalled that Father Armano's death had compelled him into thoughts of his own mortality. But for some reason, seeing and reburying the priest's bones had filled him with a far deeper sense of mortality. The difference between then and now, he understood, was what he'd seen in Getachu's camp, and what he'd just witnessed in the lobby of this haunting ruin. He had already seen firsthand in Southeast Asia that life was cheap, and death was plentiful. But here... here he was looking for something beyond the grave. And he wanted to find it *before* the grave. *In sure and certain hope of the Resurrection unto eternal life.*

Vivian put her hand on his shoulder and asked, "Would you like a bath?"

He stood and smiled. They found the sulphur pool, but Colonel Gann, in the interest of security, and perhaps modesty, forbade any skinny dipping and suggested, "Mr. Purcell and I will stand watch, and Mr. Mercado and Miss Smith will bathe fully clothed. Five minutes, then we will switch."

So they did that, and it felt good to be submerged in the warm water, which was cooler than the hot, humid air. Purcell made eye contact with Vivian, who was sitting on a stone bench next to Mercado, and she winked at him.

After Purcell got out of the pool, Gann gave him the revolver with a box of ammunition, which Purcell stuck in his cargo pocket, and Gann took the Uzi submachine gun, which was a far more deadly weapon.

They made their way to the back end of the spa where a wide, overgrown field stretched a hundred yards out and ended at a wall of jungle growth. They began crossing the field, and as they walked, Vivian said, "This is where Father Armano walked when he came out of the jungle."

She turned and looked back at the white spa. "I wonder what he thought when he saw that? Or did he know it was there?"

Gann reminded everyone, "It was not built when he was imprisoned." He also told them, "The road was also not yet improved, as we saw on the map in the Ethiopian College."

Purcell assured him, "It is not improved now."

"Well, it has deteriorated over the years. But in '36 or '37, the Italian Army widened it, put in drainage ditches, and paved it with gravel and tar, all the way to Gondar. Then they built the mineral spa for their army and administrators in Gondar. That's what I saw when the British Expeditionary Force came through here in '41 on the way to taking Gondar from the Italians."

Mercado said, "So we know that Father Armano was not looking for this spa—or perhaps not even the road."

Purcell said, "For sure not the spa. But he may have remembered the Ethiopian dirt highway from his travels with his battalion, or from the patrol he was on." He added, "He may have been thinking of following the dirt track to Gondar."

Gann again reminded them, "Gondar was still in Ethiopian hands at the time of Father Armano's imprisonment, and his knowledge of the world was frozen at that moment, and remained so until his escape forty years later."

Purcell said, "Right. So where was he going?"

Mercado suggested, "He had no idea where he was going. He was just running. And if he did know of that dirt road he may have intended to go north to Lake Tana where his battalion had made camp forty years ago. Or he could have taken the road south, toward Addis, where the main units of the Italian Army were pushing north to Tana and Gondar." Mercado added, "As Colonel Gann said, his knowledge was frozen in time, and he was acting on what he knew, or thought he knew."

Everyone seemed to agree with that theory, except Vivian, who said, "He was coming to find us."

Purcell knew better than to argue with that, but he couldn't help pointing out again, "The spa was not here in 1936."

Vivian assured him, "That does not matter. We were here."

They continued on and reached the towering tree line, then separated to look for a trailhead. Gann, who seemed to have a knack for finding openings in the jungle, found it.

They gathered at what seemed at first a solid wall of brush, but Gann parted the vegetation and showed them the narrow path that led into the dark interior of the rain forest. He said, "Game trail. But suitable for human use."

Purcell took out his map, and also the photograph that showed the destroyed fortress. He took a compass reading and assured himself and everyone that this trail led almost due east, toward the fortress, though there was no way of knowing if it turned at some point.

They made their way through the brush and onto the

narrow overgrown trail, and began moving through the deep jungle.

Purcell had no doubt that this trail would lead them to the fortress that they'd seen from the air. And from there, there would be many jungle trails converging on the fortress. But Father Armano had picked this one, and Purcell now thought he knew why.

Chapter 48

The game trail had not been traveled by humans in a very long time—except perhaps Father Armano five months ago—and at some point they thought they'd lost the trail. Gann still refused to use his machete, so there were times when they had to get on all fours and crawl through the tunnel of tropical growth.

The five or six kilometers that showed on the map should have taken about two hours to travel, but they'd been walking and crawling close to three hours because of the slow progress.

They'd drunk most of their water and were now into the fruit juice. Sweat covered their bodies and the insects were becoming annoying. Gann had assured them that the lions in this region were nearly extinct, but something big roared in the deep jungle, which made everyone stop and listen. Snakes, however, were plentiful, and Purcell spotted a few in the trees, but none on the ground, so far.

They stopped for a break and Mercado wondered out loud if the trail had gone off in another direction and if they'd missed the fortress.

Purcell assured him, "My compass says we've been heading generally due east."

Gann concurred and added, "It always seems longer on the ground than on the map."

Purcell looked at Vivian, whose white skin was now alarmingly red, and asked her, "How are you doing?"

She nodded her head.

He looked at Mercado, who also seemed flushed. The jungle, Purcell knew, sucked the life out of you. Theoretically, according to a Special Forces guy he'd interviewed in Vietnam, the jungle was not a killing environment, the way a frozen wasteland was. The jungle had water and food, and the climate, though unpleasant, would not kill you if you knew what you were doing. Snakes and animals could kill you, but you could also kill them. Only disease, according to this SF guy, could kill you, and if you got malaria or dengue fever, or some other fucked-up tropical disease, then you were just an unlucky son of a bitch. End of story.

Gann stood and said, "Press on."

The trail seemed to be getting wider, and there was more headroom now, so they were able to walk upright. Within fifteen minutes Gann held up his hand, then he pointed up the trail. He got down and crawled the last ten yards, then raised Mercado's binoculars and scanned to his front.

Gann got up on one knee and motioned everyone forward. The head of the trail was wide enough for everyone to kneel shoulder to shoulder and they looked out across a clearing to Prince Theodore's fortress—a blasted mass of stone and concrete sitting under the noon sun.

Gann was looking through his binoculars again and said, "Don't see any movement." He handed the binoculars to Mercado, who agreed, and he gave the binoculars to Vivian, who said, "It looks so dead." Purcell took the binoculars and focused on a section of collapsed wall that allowed a peek into the fortress. If anyone was in there, they weren't moving around much.

Gann wanted to go in first, with Purcell covering, but Purcell said, "My turn."

Vivian grabbed his arm, but didn't say anything.

Purcell stood and began walking the fifty yards across the clearing to the fortress walls.

There were wooden watchtowers at intervals along the parapets, and he kept an eye on them as he was sure Gann was doing with his binoculars. As he got closer, he could see more clearly through the opening in the wall, and there didn't seem to be anything living within the fortress.

He reached the pile of rubble from the collapsed wall, pulled his revolver, and climbed to the top. Inside the fortress he could see stone and concrete buildings with corrugated steel roofs in various states of ruin. The whole compound seemed to cover about two acres, which was not large for a fortress, but it looked imposing here in the jungle.

He satisfied himself that the place was deserted, and signaled everyone to join him.

Gann, Mercado, and Vivian began crossing the clearing quickly, and Purcell came down from the rubble pile.

He said to them, "No one home. There's an open gate around the corner."

He led them along the wall and they rounded the corner, where large iron gates stood open in the center of a long stone wall.

They passed cautiously through the gates and into

the fortress. In front of them was an open area, a parade ground, where grass now grew. As they moved farther into the compound, they saw bleached white bones and skulls lying in the brown grass. The smell of the dead was barely noticeable after five months, but it still clung to the dusty earth.

Gann looked around and said, "This is what a half-hour artillery barrage will do." He looked at the collapsed section of wall where Purcell had stood atop the rubble, and said, "Gallas probably came through that breach." He added, "Nasty combination of Getachu's modern artillery and primitive, bloodthirsty savages waiting like jackals to get in."

Purcell could imagine the artillery rounds falling into this tight compound, blasting everything to rubble as the sun set. He could also imagine Prince Theodore's soldiers being blown to pieces by the explosion, or ripped apart by shrapnel. And when the barrage ended, there would be a minute or two of deadly silence before the Gallas came screaming over the walls.

Gann, too, was imagining it and said, "The Gallas who got in first on foot would have opened those gates, and the mounted Gallas would have come charging in." He added, "A Galla war cry is something you don't want to hear more than once in your life—in fact, if you hear it once, you will not hear it again."

Purcell saw Mercado looking over his shoulder at the open gates, as though expecting a horde of Gallas to come charging in. Also, Henry's face had gone from ruddy to pale. Henry was remembering Mount Aradam again.

Purcell shifted his attention to the field of bones.

Indeed, it must have been terrifying, he thought, for the soldiers here who had survived the barrage to see Galla horsemen pouring through the open gates with their scimitars raised. Death on horseback.

Gann said, "I don't see any horse bones, so it wasn't much of a fight." He let them know, "Even if your walls are breached and your gates are open, you must maintain discipline and put up a good resistance. Better than being slaughtered like lambs in a pen."

Purcell didn't think that was information he could ever use, but he was glad to see that Colonel Gann was wearing his brass military balls.

Purcell said, "The question is, how did Father Armano survive this slaughter?" He said quickly to Vivian, "Do not say it."

"Well, I will. God spared him."

Purcell was getting a bit impatient with her divine explanations for everything, and he pointed out, "God wasn't looking out for the Coptic Christian soldiers of Prince Theodore." He suggested, "Maybe God is Catholic."

Vivian seemed annoyed and didn't respond.

Mercado said, "It does seem a bit of a miracle that Father Armano escaped this."

Purcell speculated, "It might have something to do with his prison cell. Certainly the Gallas did not spare him." He suggested, "Let's look around."

They walked through the small fortress which held only about twenty buildings, consisting mostly of barracks and storage structures. A large water-collecting cistern had been shattered by an explosion and it was dry. An ammunition bunker had been hit, and the secondary explosions had flattened everything around it. The headquarters was identified by the Lion of Judah painted in fading yellow over an open doorway. They looked inside and saw that whatever had been there had been burned, and a fine layer of ash lay on the floor and on the skeletons of at least a dozen men.

Gann drew everyone's attention to the pubic bones of the men, and pointed out the hack marks, saying, "They use their scimitars to do their nasty business. Sometimes the poor buggers aren't even dead."

Purcell said, "Thanks for that."

They continued on between the shattered structures and came to an almost undamaged building that measured about ten feet on each side. It was the only building whose door was intact and closed. The door was rusted steel and there was a hasp on it, but the lock was gone. At the bottom of the door was a steel pass-through with an open bolt.

Purcell said, "Looks like a prison to me."

Purcell stepped over several disjointed skeletons that lay near the door and pushed on it, but it would not give. Gann joined him and together they put their shoulders to the door, but it was stuck, probably rusted shut.

Vivian suggested using the pass-through at the bottom, and Purcell knelt and pushed on it until it squeaked open.

Vivian, too, knelt and said, "I'll go." No one objected, so she shucked her backpack but kept her camera, and squeezed her slim body into the opening. Her legs and feet disappeared and the door fell shut.

They all waited for her to call out, but there was only silence.

Finally, Purcell banged on the door. "Vivian!"

"Yes . . . come in."

Purcell went first, followed by Mercado and Gann.

They all stood in the middle of the dirt floor and looked around at the small, stone prison cell. The floor was covered with debris, and the roof was gone except for a single sheet of corrugated steel. There was a small opening high up one wall, and under the opening was a cross that had been etched into the stone.

Vivian said, "Forty years . . . my God."

She reached up and touched the cross. "What incredible faith."

Purcell and Gann looked at each another. Mercado said, "Indeed, this man was a saint and a martyr."

Purcell wanted to point out that it was other Christians who'd put the priest here, but he'd exhausted his theological arguments.

Vivian took a dozen photographs of the cell, then suggested they all observe a silent minute of prayer.

They had been mostly silent anyway, and Purcell had no problem with this as long as they could do it standing, which they did.

Vivian said, "Amen."

Purcell said, "This, I think, solves the mystery of how Father Armano escaped the Gallas."

They looked around the sparse cell in case they missed something, like a note scratched in the wall or, Purcell hoped, a map or instructions directing them to the black monastery. He reminded everyone that Getachu's soldiers had been here five months ago, and said, "This place has been picked clean." Purcell suggested, "We should get out of this cell."

Gann agreed. "This is not a good place to be if any-one comes round."

Gann crawled out first with his Uzi, followed by Mercado, Vivian, and Purcell. Gann suggested, "We can take a short lunch break, then move on to our next objective."

They found a shady spot along a wall and sat on the ground. They broke out some bread and dates, but no one seemed to want the dried meat, perhaps because of the smell of death on the bones all around them.

Gann said, "We need to find a stream. Shouldn't be too difficult, but sometimes it is. Don't drink from the ponds. But a wash is all right."

Mercado said, "I saw some berries on the trail. And fruit of some sort."

"Yes, some are good. Some will kill you."

Vivian asked, "Do you know which is which?"

"Not actually." He admitted, "Never could get them right."

Purcell suggested, "Henry can be our taster."

"After you, Frank."

Gann asked Purcell for the area map. He stud-ied it and said, "I see you've got six numbered circles here." He asked, "Are they numbered in order of importance?"

Purcell replied, "Sort of. But not really."

"All right, then...we'll do them geographically." He studied the map again and said, "Unfortunately, I don't see any marked trails, but all of these places are within fifty kilometers of this fort...and there will be trails converging on this fort. We need to find the various trailheads, then decide which one to take." He looked up from the map. "But these six points are not necessarily connected by trails, or by open terrain. So if we have to cut brush and vines, this could take...well, I'm afraid a month. Or more."

"Unless," Mercado pointed out, "we get lucky on the first try."

"Yes, of course. But you understand, old boy, none of these little circles here could be the place we are looking for."

"In fact," Purcell said, "I don't think any of them are."

No one responded to that, and Purcell continued, "As you said, Colonel, there would be a number of trails converging on this fortress, so the question is, why didn't Father Armano take one of the other trails? Why did he choose and continue along that bad game trail? Was his choice pure chance? I don't think so. How would he have ever found that small game trail? Unless he came to this fortress on that trail."

Again, no one responded, then Vivian said, "He was going back to the black monastery—back to the Grail."

"Where else would he want to go?"

Gann said, "By God, that's it."

Mercado, too, agreed. "It was staring us in the face."

Purcell pointed out, "All of our recon was based on a lot of speculation and false assumptions, all of it wrong. Everything we looked at from the air was east of the road. But in fact, if Father Armano was going back to the black monastery, then the monastery is west of the road, and west of the spa."

They all thought about that, and Mercado stated the obvious. "We have no photos...no idea what is west of the road."

"No," Purcell agreed, "we do not. But we have a map that shows part of the area, and we have two points of reference—this fortress and the spa."

Mercado said, "Any two points will make a straight line...but that line does not necessarily give us the third point."

"Right. But we need to go back to the spa, cross the road, and head west."

Mercado thought about that, then said, "So you're suggesting we abandon all we've done and head into a new, unknown area."

"Only if we all believe that Father Armano was walking to the black monastery."

They all thought that over and Gann said, "You also need to believe he remembered the way he came here from the monastery."

Purcell replied, "I believe it was burned in his mind. And when he escaped from here and walked through those open gates, he knew exactly which way to go."

Gann agreed. "I've heard stories of that."

Vivian spoke. "I think we all believe that Father Armano was going to the black monastery, and that he knew the way."

Everyone nodded in agreement.

They packed up and stood. Vivian asked Purcell, "When did you think of this?"

"Halfway here."

"Why didn't you say something?"

"You needed a photo op." He added, "We needed to be here."

She nodded.

They left the ruins of Prince Theodore's fortress by

the gates that Father Armano had entered forty years before and had exited five months ago. They walked across the clearing toward the game trail, which they now saw was marked by a towering and distinctive cedar.

As they walked, Vivian came up beside Purcell and said with a smile, "That was a divine inspiration, Frank. Don't deny it."

He smiled in return. "I like to think of myself as a rational genius." He added, "But I could be wrong about that and about this, too."

"You're not wrong." She also said to him, "Prepare yourself for a miracle."

They'd already had several of those, mostly having to do with flying. He said, "I am open to miracles."

"And while you're at it, open your heart to love."

He didn't respond.

"We could die here in the blink of an eye. So you need to tell me now that you forgive me, and that you love me. Before it's too late."

He stayed silent a few seconds, considering this, then said, "I love you."

"Forgive me."

"I cheated on you before you came to Rome."

"I forgive you."

He took her hand. "All is forgiven."

Chapter 49

They reached the spa in the late afternoon, and though there were hours of daylight left, Gann made the decision to stop for the day, saying, "I don't want any of us to overdo the first day."

Clearly, Purcell thought, Gann was concerned about Henry, and maybe Vivian. He was a good officer. Purcell also pointed out, "We have no idea where we're going after we cross that road, so we should stop and think about it."

"Quite right."

Vivian reminded Gann, "You said Gallas stop here."

"Yes, well, they've mostly gone east, and their horse droppings look rather old. Also, this is a large place, and we will pick a dark corner of it and be quiet during the night." He added, "I have my Uzi, and Mr. Purcell has my service revolver."

They found the bathhouse, which still had fresh spring water flowing into large sunken pools from the mouths of black stone faces embedded in the marble walls—similar to Miriam's bathhouse, Purcell noted, except these faces were not of lions, but Roman gods and goddesses, one of which looked suspiciously like Benito Mussolini.

Gann again marveled at the engineering, saying, "Reminds me a bit of the Roman baths in Bath. Water's still flowing there after two thousand years."

And that, Purcell thought to himself, was the last decent plumbing installed in England.

They drank from the mouths of the gods and goddesses, hoping the water was potable, then filled their canteens. The spring water was cold, but they bathed privately, and washed their clothes.

Not a bad first day, Purcell thought, and in the morning they'd cross the road and strike out into terra incognita.

They reconnoitered the spa complex and found a wing off the main lobby where the guest rooms had been. Gann explained, "This is where the Italian soldiers, administrators, and men of business came from Gondar for the weekend after a long week of exploiting the Ethiopians." He added, "Built mostly by slave labor—captured Ethiopian soldiers. And staffed by young Ethiopian women."

Purcell commented, "Sounds very Roman Empire-ish."

"Indeed. It's in their blood, you know."

Purcell resisted any comments about the British Empire, but Gann said, "At least we brought order, education, and law."

"Thank God you didn't bring your plumbing."

Gann smiled.

They found a guest chamber that looked fairly clean, and went inside the whitewashed room. All the furniture had been carried off, of course, but a chair sat in the corner in an advanced state of rot.

The spa once had electricity, undoubtedly from a generator, and Purcell noticed electrical outlets, and a ceiling fan that hadn't turned in forty years.

The room also had a large arched window that faced

east and would let in the dawn sun. The window had never been glazed, but sagging louver shutters were still fixed to the stone arch. The view from the window was of a garden that had become a miniature jungle, which Gann pointed out as a place to go if anyone came through the door. Conversely, if anyone showed up at the window, they could exit through the door and retreat into the large hotel complex.

They sat on the red tile floor and Purcell broke out the maps. He told Gann, "We've flown over this area west of the road, on our way to and from Gondar, but as you know, we were not doing an aerial recon of this area. From what I remember, however, this is thick jungle, not much different from the area east of the road." He added, "This map seems to confirm that."

Gann glanced at the map. "Yes, this whole area south of Tana is carpeted with dense growth."

Mercado asked him, "Do you remember any of that terrain from when you were here in '41?"

"I'm afraid not. We pushed up from the road and avoided the jungle." He explained, "The Italian Army, too, avoided the jungle and kept mostly to the roads and the towns. When we took Gondar from them, they retreated into the hills and mountains to the north, not to the jungle." He asked Mercado, "Did you experience the pleasure of jungle warfare when you were here?"

Mercado replied, "I was an army war correspondent." He confessed, "I fought mostly in the bars and brothels."

Vivian laughed, Gann smiled, and Purcell was afraid that Henry and Edmund were on the verge of swapping Gondar 1941 war stories, trying to discover if they knew the same bartenders and prostitutes, so he changed the subject and said, "What I do recall from our flyovers was that there was some high terrain to the west of here—what looked like rocky ridgelines coming through the treetops."

Gann nodded. "Two of the three obsidian quarries I've identified from speaking to the people in Shoan are west of here." He informed them, "The villagers still visit the quarries for small pieces of obsidian to use for carvings or house ornamentation."

Vivian asked, "Could you find the quarries?"

"I have a general idea where they are."

Mercado asked, "And you think the black monastery could be in proximity to these quarries?"

Gann replied, "Perhaps." He pointed out, "We don't have much else to go on."

Purcell looked at Gann and asked, "Is it possible that Miriam said something to you, which if you thought about it…?"

Gann considered the unfinished question, then replied, "The villagers who went out to meet the monks would always return with sacks of carved obsidian, which they would take to Gondar for sale." He explained, "Crosses, saints, chalices…occasionally a Star of David, and now and then a carving of Saint George Cathedral in Addis."

Purcell informed him, "Vivian almost bought one of those in Rome."

Gann smiled and said to her, "You should have bought the one with the map etched on the bottom."

"I wish I'd known."

Mercado said, "So what you're saying is that you think the monks carved these objects and gave them to the villagers in exchange for provisions."

"It would seem so." He asked rhetorically, "What else do monks have to do all day?"

Pray and drink, Purcell thought. He said to everyone, "Well, it seems that this quest has taken on some of the aspects of Arthur's knights running around without a map or a clue looking for the Grail Castle."

Gann replied, "They actually found it, you know."

Purcell pointed out, "There are no jungles in England."

Vivian glanced at Purcell and said, "If we are meant to find it, we will find it. If we are not, we will not."

"Right." Purcell asked, "If the monks' sandals and candles have been cut off from Shoan, how long do you think these monks are going to last in the black monastery?"

"Good question," Gann replied. "I believe the monks are fairly self-sufficient in regards to food, though the villagers of Shoan would always bring something that the monks didn't have. Wine, of course, but also grain for bread." He surmised, "I don't think there would be a lot of grain grown in the monastery or surrounding rain forest. So they will soon be needing their daily bread."

Purcell suggested, "I'd think a single loaf would do, and one fish."

Gann smiled.

Mercado asked Gann, "Where do you think these monks come from? I assume they don't reproduce there."

Gann replied, "No, they don't. All gentlemen, as far as I know." He told them, "It's my understanding that the monks are chosen from monasteries all over Ethiopia. They understand that if they go to the black monastery, they will never leave there." He reminded them, "Like the Atang who guards the Ark of the Covenant in Axum." He concluded, "It's a job for life."

Purcell said, "I have two observations about Ethiopia. One is that this place has been caught in a time warp, and the other is that with the emperor gone, they are free-falling into the twentieth century, and not ready for the landing."

"Perhaps."

He asked Gann, "What has drawn you to this place? I mean, aside from your princess."

Gann smiled, then replied, "It gets into your blood."

Purcell looked at Mercado, who said, "It is the most blessed and most cursed land I have ever been in." He added, "It has biblical magnificence, complete with an apocalyptic sense of doom." He concluded, "I hate the place. But I would come back."

"Send me a postcard." Purcell returned to the earlier subject and said, "I think time is running out for the monks of the black monastery. They, unfortunately, can't multiply the loaves and fishes, and history in the form of General Getachu is breathing down their burnooses. I would not be surprised if they are already gone, but if they're not, they will be soon."

Everyone agreed with that, and Mercado said, "I would be content with just finding the black monastery."

Vivian said, "I would not."

They looked at the map in the fading light as they ate some bread and dates, and Gann asked, "Do you know how long the priest was marched from the black monastery to his fortress prison by the soldiers of Prince Theodore?"

Mercado replied, "As I mentioned, the priest did not

comment on it, so I'm assuming it was a day or two's march."

"All right. We now know that the travel time from here to the fortress is at most four hours. Therefore, let's say the monastery is no more than a day's march west of here. In open country, or on a good trail, either of which would be known by the soldiers, that would be...let's say a ten-hour march at a brisk pace of four K an hour, will give us forty K to the monastery."

Vivian reminded them, "The monks brought Father Armano to the soldiers. The soldiers were not at the monastery."

"Quite right. And we don't know where the soldiers were in relation to the monastery. But let's use fifty K total." He drew a half circle on the map, with the center of the radius starting at the spa and ending at the road. "There we are." He asked, "What is that formula to find the area of a circle?"

There was an embarrassed silence, then Mercado said, "If that were a rectangle and not a half circle, it would be five thousand square kilometers...so if we nip off the curved part of the semicircle, it would be about...let's say, four thousand square kilometers...give or take."

"All right." Gann stared at the map. "That's a good amount of territory to be walking."

Purcell suggested, "It's not really the square kilometers that are important. It's the trails and the few clues we have, including maybe the quarries, that will determine where we look."

"Quite right," Gann agreed. "And we can't be sure that the priest was marched for only one day. It could have been two."

Purcell asked Gann, "How long were the villagers actually gone when they left Shoan to go to the meeting place?"

Gann stayed silent, then said, "I have heard it was two days. A day there, and a day to return." He added, "No part of the walk would be made in the dark, so let's say it was a ten-hour walk, an overnight rest, and ten hours back to Shoan."

Purcell produced the adjoining map that showed Shoan, and they tried to extrapolate from these two known locations—the village and the spa—walking times and distances west of the road, to see what intersected or overlapped.

Purcell was concerned that they were once again making false assumptions, misinterpreting clues, and being too clever, but this time, based on his conclusion that Father Armano was heading for the black monastery when they found him at the spa, he felt a bit more confident that they were narrowing it down.

Gann asked an interesting question. "Did the priest comment in any way about the spa? Did he say anything such as, 'What is this?'"

Everyone thought about that, and Mercado said, "Now that you mention it, he did not, which in retrospect seems a bit odd."

Vivian said, "He did say something...that Henry may have been asleep for." She thought a moment, then said, "He asked, 'Dov'è la strada?' Where is the road?"

No one responded, and Vivian continued, "I didn't think anything of it. He seemed to be delirious."

Purcell said, "Well, if nothing else, that confirms he was looking for the road he remembered. The question is, which way was he going to take it? North? South? Or was he just going to cross it and continue west to the monastery?"

Gann said, "We don't know, but we do know that he had come from the monastery to the fortress on a trail that ended at or crossed the road, and that is what we'd like to find tomorrow." He added, "I would put my bet on this trail being either close to here, or farther south, toward Shoan. And I base that on the traveling time of the villagers."

Again, everyone seemed to agree and they all looked at the maps, and Gann penciled in a few more marks.

Purcell suggested they'd done enough mental exercise, and that they should sleep on it. He lit a cigarette and passed around his canteen of fermented fruit juice.

They made small talk about other things and Purcell told Gann about the Navion and Signore Bocaccio, whose Mia was now a heap of burned and twisted metal. Purcell said, "I hope he and his wife had a good meal at the Hilton."

Vivian said, "I feel awful that we couldn't telex him."

"I think he got the message that we were not returning." He asked Gann, "Would two thousand dollars compensate him for the aircraft?"

Gann assured everyone, "People are selling what they can for whatever they can get, and they are fortunate to get any buyers." He added, "Something such as an aircraft has no buyers, and the government would have expropriated it anyway."

Purcell said, "That's what I thought." He assured Vivian, "Signore Bocaccio is happy."

Gann asked Purcell, "How did you learn to fly?"

"Private lessons. I started in high school, in upstate New York. There was an aerodrome there. Lessons were fourteen bucks an hour, and I made fifteen a week working for the weekly newspaper." He added, "Had a buck left over for cheap dates and cheap wine."

Gann smiled. "How many hours did you have to invest in this?"

"The flying or the dates?"

"The flying, old boy."

"Well, twenty dual would allow you to solo. Then twenty solo would allow you to take the test for a license."

"I see. And why didn't you get into something along those lines?"

"Well..." Purcell looked at Vivian and Mercado. "Well, I never actually took the test."

Mercado asked, "Do you mean you don't have a license?"

"Didn't need one here. No one asked."

"Yes, but..."

"I ran out of money." He said, "I'll bet you couldn't tell."

Vivian laughed and said to everyone, "Can't you tell he's joking with us?" She looked at him. "Frank?"

"Right. Just kidding."

Mercado pointed out, "It's moot in any case. We've burned the plane, and we will not be renting another."

"But I'll take you flying in New York."

"No, thank you."

Purcell stood and said to Vivian, "Take a walk with me."

Gann cautioned, "Do not go far, and be back no later than dark. And don't forget your revolver."

"Yes, sir."

Vivian stood and Mercado looked at her. "I don't think this is a wise thing."

"Don't fret, Henry."

Purcell led Vivian into the hallway and back to the lobby, then out to the courtyard. They walked along the colonnade, then down the steps to the gardens.

The sky was deep purple now, with streaks of red and pink, and night birds began to sing. A soft breeze blew down from the mountains and they could smell the tropical flowers.

Purcell said, "I thought we would make love here."

"I know exactly what you are thinking."

"Sometimes I think about a cocktail."

"You're rather basic, you know."

"Thank you."

They continued their walk and Vivian asked him, "Who was it?"

"Who was who...? Oh...in Rome."

"Yes, in Rome."

"Well...I'm not sure who it was. An English lady."

"How did you meet her?"

"In her hotel bar."

"Did you go to her hotel, or yours?"

They were actually the same place, but he could imagine that Vivian would not like to think they'd all used the same bed. He replied, "Hers." He also said, "I thought you had left for good."

"You should have known better. But I understand, and I forgive you."

"Thank you."

"And when we get back to Rome, if I go off shopping,

I hope you don't think I've left you for good, and go off and fuck another lady you've met in the elevator or somewhere."

"Right. That won't happen." He glanced up at the sky. "It's getting dark."

She took his arm and led him around the statue of the two-faced Janus. She said, "For security reasons, we must keep our clothes on, but I suggest you drop your pants."

He liked that suggestion and pulled his pants and underwear down as she knelt in front of him. Vivian said, "We will learn a new Italian word today. Fellatio." She put his now erect penis in her mouth and showed him the meaning of the word.

On the way back to the spa hotel, she said, "There is a romance in classical ruins—something hauntingly beautiful about a great edifice returning to nature."

"Right." He said to her, "We need to find some privacy tomorrow night."

"I don't think that will happen again out in the bush."

"Well . . . let's see."

"I'm embarrassed as it is that Henry and Colonel Gann know what we've been up to."

"I don't think they do."

"I don't think they could have missed hearing your moaning echoing through the colonnade."

"Really?"

They got back to the lobby, which was very dark now. At the far end of the big room lay the bones of the slaughtered men, where Father Armano had also lain dying.

Vivian said to him, "Tomorrow we go to where

Father Armano was going. Do not be cynical—he will show us the way."

"I'm counting on it."

"Do you know what that statue was?"

"The two-faced guy?"

"That was Janus, the Roman god of the New Year—he faces back and forward."

"I get it."

"This is January."

"Right."

"Which reminded me of something. When I was in boarding school, which was English-run, I read a very beautiful passage—something that George VI said in his Christmas message to the English people, in the darkest year of the war. He said to them, 'I said to the man who stood at the gate of the year, Give me a light that I may tread safely into the unknown. And he replied, Go out into the darkness and put your hand into the hand of God. That shall be to you better than light and safer than a known way.'"

"That is very beautiful."

"Put your hand into the hand of God, Frank."

"I'll try."

"You will."

They rejoined the others.

Chapter 50

They rose before dawn and had some bread and boiled eggs as they waited for better light.

The night had been long and uncomfortable, and the jungle sounds had kept them awake. Purcell began to wonder if anything short of the Holy Grail was worth getting eaten by mosquitoes and listening for Gallas.

Vivian seemed cheerful, and that annoyed him.

Gann, too, seemed ready to get moving, but Henry didn't look well, and Purcell was a bit concerned about him. But if Henry complained, Purcell would remind him whose idea this was. Or was this his own idea?

The dawn came and they left the relative comfort of the spa hotel and walked down the steps. They moved quickly across the field and through the brush, then looked up and down the road. Gann said in a whisper, "I will cross first, then one at a time."

Gann crossed the narrow road and knelt in the brush on the far side. Mercado followed, and then Vivian and Purcell brought up the rear.

They beat the bush on the side of the road, looking for an obvious trail—a trail that Father Armano might have taken to his imprisonment forty years ago, and which he may have been looking for again before he died in the spa. *Dov'è la strada*? But even Gann couldn't find an opening in the wall of tangled vegetation that lined the road.

Gann said, "We will walk on the road, though I'd rather not." He instructed them, "The drainage ditch here is partially filled with dirt, as you see, and choked with brush. But we will dive into it if we hear a vehicle, or the sound of hoofbeats."

Especially hoofbeats, Purcell thought.

"We will continue until we've found a trail that will take us into the interior of this rain forest." He said, "I suggest we try south, toward Shoan."

They began their walk south on the old Italian road that Purcell, Mercado, and Vivian had driven from Addis what seemed so long ago. The road, as Purcell recalled, was hard-packed, and he could now see evidence of the tar and gravel that the Italian Army had laid forty years before. But when Father Armano had walked the road—if he had walked it—the Italian engineers had not yet gotten this far. More important, any trails intersecting this road may have been more obvious forty years ago, before this area had become less traveled and less populated.

Gann stepped off the road now and then and smacked the brush with the side of his machete. After half an hour, Purcell said, "We're going to wind up in Shoan soon."

"That will be another two hours, Mr. Purcell."

Up ahead was a huge gnarled tree, and Purcell picked up his pace. He got to the tree and said to his companions, "I am going to do some aerial recon." He took the binoculars from Mercado, dropped his backpack, and shimmied up the wide trunk, then got hold of a branch and pulled himself up.

Gann said, "Watch for snakes, old boy."

Purcell continued to climb the twisted branches and got about forty feet off the ground.

He sat on a bare branch and scanned the area around him with the binoculars. The trees near the road were not tightly spaced, though there was very dense brush between them. As he looked west, he could see the beginning of a great triple-canopy rain forest.

He turned his attention to the road and looked north, toward Tana and Gondar, but he saw no one approaching. The road was probably better traveled before the revolution and civil war, he thought, but now only armed men roamed the countryside, and he didn't want to meet any of them—unless they were friends of Colonel Gann.

Purcell scanned the road to the south, and it was also deserted, though he saw some sort of catlike animals crossing a hundred yards up the road. He watched them go into the bush, then he focused closely on the area where they'd disappeared.

Gann called up softly, "See anything?"

"Maybe." He made sure he knew where the cats had disappeared, then climbed down and jumped onto the road.

Gann asked, "How was your view?"

"Lots of trees out there."

"What type of trees, old boy?"

Purcell described the terrain and suggested to Gann, "You can climb the next tree." He told everyone, "The good news is I saw some sort of...medium-sized cats going into the bush. So maybe there's a game trail."

"Excellent." Gann guessed, "Some sort of lynx, I would think."

Mercado asked, "Are they dangerous?"

Gann replied, "Only if they have something better than my nine-millimeter Uzi."

Purcell led them up the road, and over the drainage ditch, to the ten-foot-high wall of tropical vegetation. He said, "Right about here."

Gann got on all fours, like a cat, and said, "Here is the trailhead." They all crawled through the tangled brush onto a shoulder-wide trail, overhung with branches that formed a natural ceiling above their heads.

The trail itself was clear, and it was obvious that this was a well-used route.

Purcell said, "This could be the trail used by the villagers."

Gann agreed. "Someone is using it on a regular basis."

Vivian asked, "Does anyone but me think that those cats were sent by God to show us this trail?"

Purcell assured her, "Only you, Vivian."

"Well." She smiled. "I don't think that either."

But Purcell thought she did. And maybe this time she was right.

Gann said, "We will travel about twenty feet apart, but always within sight of one another. Maintain sound discipline, no smoking, and alert everyone if you hear something."

Mercado asked, "Where are we going?"

Gann replied, "I don't know, but we'll make good time getting there." He took Purcell's map and looked at it. "Don't see this trail." He said, "We'll see what we see, and we will fly by the seat of our pants." He added, "We're in the right area, and if we read the land correctly, I feel confident we can find at least one of the abandoned stone quarries, which may be a clue to the location of the black monastery."

Purcell was impressed with Colonel Gann's outdoor skills, and he asked him, "Can we live off the land? I mean if the food runs out."

"I don't much fancy jungle pickings, old boy."

"Me neither."

"Let's make certain we can get back to Shoan before the victuals run out." Gann informed them, "If everyone's gone, there will be a food cache there for us."

Purcell said, "If *you're* gone, where would we find that cache?"

"You should look in the stone cisterns which are high up. This is the dry season, and they will be suitable for food storage."

"Which cistern?"

"Don't know, old boy. Each house has one. You'll find the right one."

"Couldn't they have left the food in the palace kitchen?"

"We don't know who will be coming around after the last person has left." He explained, "Goats, chickens, and such will be left behind, and that draws hungry people."

"Well, let's hope the Gallas don't come around."

"More likely soldiers or partisans." He added, "We need to be careful when we enter the village."

Mercado asked, "How will we actually get out of here after we've completed our mission?"

"There is a Royalist partisan point about fifty K west of Shoan, and I can find it without a map. Been there. Chaps there will guide us to the French Somali border, as I mentioned."

Purcell asked, "And if you're not with us to find that place?"

"Dead, you mean?"

"Or just not feeling well."

Gann smiled, then said seriously, "I'd advise you to walk to Gondar. You should be able to blend into the population, though it's a bit tricky with all the Western tourists and businesspeople gone, and the soldiers everywhere. But it's not impossible to do that."

Purcell suggested, "We could pose as journalists."

"There you are."

"What do we do after we blend?"

"You should try to get to Addis by plane, or get someone with a truck to drive you over the Sudan border." He handed the map back to Purcell and asked, "Have we covered everything?"

"We have."

"Miss Smith? Any questions or concerns?"

"No. Let's go."

Gann, in military style, restated their mission objective. "We are looking for two things. One is the place where the Falashas meet the monks. We will look for signs of human presence—food waste, campfires, footprints, and all that. Our primary objective, not completely dependent on the first objective, is to find the black monastery." He reminded them, "From Shoan, which is a few hours' march south of here, give or take, to the meeting place is, as we know, a day's march.

From the meeting place to the monastery is, we believe, or assume, another day's march." He concluded, "If we find the meeting place, then we know we are a day's march to the monastery—though we don't know in which direction." He added, "It's possible, of course, that we don't find the meeting place, but do find the monastery." Gann looked at Purcell, Mercado, and Vivian and asked, "Is that clear?"

Purcell thought it had already been clear why they were in Ethiopia. But to be a good soldier, he said, "Clear."

Mercado nodded.

Vivian said, "A rock, a tree, and a stream. And maybe a cluster of palms."

Gann looked at her. "Yes, all right." He glanced at his watch, then said, "We will let Mr. Purcell take point and I will bring up the rear." He smiled. "Follow those cats."

Purcell began walking up the trail. Somewhere between here and where they wanted to go lay a vast expanse of unknown. And the end of the trail was also unknown. From the unknown, through the unknown, to the unknown. *Put your hand into the hand of God.* It will be all right.

Chapter 51

What started as a hopeful beginning was becoming a long day in the jungle.

The trail remained wide, but it was soon obvious that it was not the only trail; many smaller trails intersected the main one, though none had any signs of recent footprints or hoofprints, or signs of cut vegetation.

Gann stated the obvious. "There seems to be a network of trails in this area."

Purcell had checked his compass as they moved, and they were headed generally west, but also veering south.

Mercado inquired, "What are we actually doing?"

Gann explained, "We are trail walking, following the paths of least resistance to cover as much ground as possible."

Purcell recalled an army ranger once saying to him on patrol, "We don't know where we are or where we're going, but we're making really good time."

Gann and Purcell looked at the map to try to determine where they were, but the Italian Army maps showed no trails under the dense overhanging canopy. And with no landmarks visible on the ground, it was nearly impossible to determine their position on the map. All they had to go by was the compass and their traveling time.

Gann put his finger on the map and said, "I believe we are here."

Purcell asked, "Where is here?"

"Where we are standing. Give or take a kilometer."

"I'm not even sure we're on the right map."

"I believe we are." He said, "All we can do is continue to run the trails."

"Right. But I can see now that we could pass within fifty meters of the monastery and walk right by it." Purcell added, "We can assume the monastery is not directly on a trail."

"That is a good assumption."

Mercado said, "I think we should have stuck to the original plan and checked out what we saw in the photographs east of the road."

Vivian said, "No, I am convinced that Frank was right—Father Armano was headed this way to return to the black monastery."

Mercado did not reply.

Purcell reminded Gann, "You said you thought you could find one of these stone quarries."

"Yes, I did say that. Unfortunately, now that I'm here, I see the difficulties." He added, "No soldier or explorer has ever had a good experience in the jungle."

"And we're not going to be the first."

"We need to just push on, trust our instincts, look for a clue or two, and pray that fortune is with us."

Vivian reminded them, "Also, we are meant to find the monastery."

Gann said, "The good thing is that we are not restricted by time, as we would be with a military objective." He added, "We have all the time we need."

Purcell reminded him, "The monks may be packing their suitcases right now."

"Yes, but the monastery is not going anywhere."

"Right. But we are restricted by our supplies and stamina."

"That is always a problem," Gann conceded.

Vivian said, "Let's move on."

Mercado cautioned, "We need to be sure we can find and reach Shoan before our provisions run out. I say three more days of this, then we need to start back."

Gann agreed. "But by a different route so we can explore new territory."

They moved on and came to a fork in the trail. They explored down both paths, and for no particular reason decided on the left fork.

They continued on, and saw that the trail was getting narrower.

Vivian had taken a few photos, but there was not much to photograph on the tight trails, and she seemed to lose interest in recording their quest to find the Holy Grail. If you've seen one jungle trail, Purcell knew, you've seen them all.

After an hour, Purcell spotted a tall cedar off the trail and made his way through the brush to get to it. He climbed the trunk to the first branch, then climbed branch by branch until he was about thirty feet off the ground. He scanned the terrain with his binoculars and saw that they were a few kilometers away from the higher ground to the west and the triple-canopy jungle he'd seen from the other tree on the road, and seen when he flew to Gondar. The sun would be below the tree line in about an hour.

He climbed down from the tree and made his way back to the trail. He informed them, "Farther west is triple-canopy jungle, and I suggest we head there."

Gann nodded. "That is also where I'm told an old quarry exists."

Mercado pointed out, "We've been traveling the better part of the day, and the villagers apparently traveled one day to the meeting spot, and we are at the end of that time period."

Gann informed him, "Traveling time is not distance, nor vice versa. If you know where you are going, you probably know how to get there by the quickest and most direct route."

Purcell assured everyone, "We can't be lost if we don't know where we're going."

They continued on the trail, which now turned to the south, and they saw no intersecting trails to the west. Gann did not want to do any backtracking, which he said was a waste of time and energy, and also a sign of desperation that would lead to bad morale.

Vivian said, "Avanti."

The sun was below the highest trees and the jungle light took on that strange quality of shadowy darkness before dusk.

They knew they needed to stop for the night, but there was no suitable clearing, so they set up camp on the narrow trail.

Gann posted a guard—Mercado, Vivian, Purcell, and himself—for two hours each, until first light, when they would move on.

They had not found water, and their canteens were nearly empty. Gann said, "Our first goal tomorrow is water. Without water we will have to sample some of these fruits we see, and edible and poisonous often look similar." He smiled. "It's the jungle trying to kill you."

They spent a restless night sleeping on the bare ground of the path, head to toe, listening to the night sounds of the jungle.

The second day was more or less a repeat of the first, but they found a small, vine-choked stream and filled their canteens.

Purcell noticed that the trails seemed to meander, and most of them headed north, south, or east. Every time they picked up a trail to the west, it turned in another direction, as though the god of the jungle did not want them heading west into the higher ground and the great triple-canopy jungle.

Purcell thought that Mercado was starting to drag, and he suggested to Gann that they slow their pace, which Gann did, but then an hour later Gann picked up his pace. Gann, Purcell thought, was driven, but maybe not the way Vivian and Mercado were driven to find the monastery and the Grail; Gann was driven by Rudyard Kipling—something hidden. Go and find it. If they'd told Gann they were looking for a basket-ball court in the jungle, he'd have been as enthused as he was to find the Holy Grail. Well...maybe not that enthused. But this had become a challenge for Colonel Sir Edmund Gann. Also, of course, he wanted to save the Grail from the godless Marxists. Then he could meet his princess in Jerusalem, and have a whiskey at the King David Hotel. Next stop, his club in London, where his friends would have to coax the story out of him. Bottom line, Purcell was glad they had Gann with them, but he was starting to wonder if Gann was with them or if they were with Gann.

As for himself, Purcell sometimes felt he was just along for the ride, though he knew there was more to his motives. Vivian was one reason he was here in this godawful place, and Vivian might also be his second and third reason. He wasn't normally that good a boyfriend. So there were other and more complex reasons for this journey into the literal heart of darkness.

The tropical dusk spread over the rain forest, and they again set up camp on the trail they were on.

Purcell was one of the few war correspondents in Vietnam who had been allowed to travel with a team of the Long Range Reconnaissance Patrol—the Lurps, as they were called. The sergeant of the ten-man team had told him, "Short patrol. Ten days."

Ten days, deep inside enemy territory in a very hostile environment. He was younger then, and the Lurps had every advanced piece of field equipment known to man, plus enough dried rations to last twice as long as the patrol. They also carried the best weapons the army could offer, and they had three radios if the feces hit the fan, as they said.

Here, however, in the jungles of Ethiopia, they were very much on their own, and none of them knew the jungle, except maybe for Gann, and Purcell was beginning to have doubts about that. Also, the goal here was not recon; it was to find the Holy Grail of Holy Grails—*The* Holy Grail—and that was the only reason they were not heading for the French Somaliland border, which in any case was the other way.

*　　*　　*

Days three and four were more trail walking, except now they had made their way west, and the jungle had become triple canopy, and it was hotter, more humid, and darker. The only good difference was that the underbrush had thinned out and they could wander off the claustrophobic trail if they wanted to and walk between the towering trees.

Purcell told Gann, "As I said, the monastery would not be at the end of a trail. It could be that we need to walk off the trail and through the rain forest to find it."

Gann replied, "If that's true, then what we are dealing with is a trackless expanse, in which any direction is possible, but only one direction will lead us to where we wish to go."

"Right. But maybe that's the best way to cover some of these four thousand square kilometers."

Gann suggested a break and they sat and looked at the map, which showed the same sea of green ink as it had last time they looked at it.

Gann was trying to determine what ground they had already covered, and he drew pencil lines on the map, saying, "We've gone in circles a bit, I think."

"In fact, that snake back there looked familiar."

"Hard to tell with snakes, old boy."

Vivian reminded everyone, "A rock, a tree, a stream. And perhaps a cluster of palm trees."

No one had been talking about those possible clues since Vivian mentioned them four days ago, but everyone had been at least alert to what seemed so important back in Addis.

Here in the bush, however, the reality changed, or reality became altered. The mind played tricks, as it does in the desert or at sea. The eye sees, and the ear hears, but the mind interprets. They had been so thirsty the day before that they all kept spotting things that were not there, especially water.

Also, they had not seen any signs of human presence since the first day when they'd found the wide trail. This was a good and bad thing. Humans were the most dangerous animals in the jungle, but the Grail seekers needed to go where other humans—Falashas and monks—had gone to meet. They had not even found evidence of a campfire or a dropped or discarded item made by man.

Henry pointed out, "Father Armano did not walk for four or five days from the monastery to the fortress."

Gann said, "This priest was with soldiers who obviously knew the terrain, and they quick-marched this chap directly to the fortress and into his little cell." He added, "But I am certain we are still within the area that we agreed at the spa would be the most likely territory for this monastery." He further added, "That comports, too, with the travel time of the villagers to the meeting place."

Purcell commented, "I didn't realize how big four thousand square kilometers was."

Mercado also pointed out, "For all we know, the monks picked a meeting place that was very far from their monastery. Maybe three or four days away."

Gann replied, "Well, I hope not."

Purcell said, "Let's stick with the logical theory that the monks do not want to walk more than a day to meet the Falashas." He added, "The monks are carrying *stone* knickknacks, for God's sake."

"Quite right," Gann agreed.

Vivian was not much into theory or speculation, Purcell noticed, and she didn't contribute to the men's attempts to overthink and outthink themselves.

Gann noticed this and said to her, "Should we be waiting for divine inspiration?"

Vivian replied, "You can't wait for it. It comes when it comes." She added, "You can pray for it, though."

"I've done that."

"Try again," she suggested.

As for the other group dynamics, Purcell had noticed that Henry seemed to have lost interest in Vivian—or in impressing her. There is nothing like exhaustion, thirst, hunger, and fear to get the old libido and weenie down, Purcell knew.

He hoped Henry would hold up, and that Vivian would not have to nurse her ex-lover again. But if it happened, that was all right.

They discussed security and possible run-ins with dangerous people.

Gann said, "The Gallas don't much fancy the jungle, and we've seen no hoofprints or horse droppings. The Gallas' home is the desert, and they only drop by places such as this after a battle." He let them know, "The Royalist partisans are operating to the west, and the counterrevolutionaries are mostly in the Simien Mountains around Gondar, so there is no reason for Getachu's soldiers to be here either. He has his hands full elsewhere." He assured them, "We have the jungle all to ourselves."

Purcell reminded him, "We've seen three army Hueys fly over."

"I actually counted four. But these are normal north-south flights from Gondar to Addis, and vice versa." He assured them, "The army has neither the fuel nor the helicopters for reconnaissance."

Purcell reminded him, "They have one less helicopter than they used to have."

"Quite right."

He also reminded Gann, "Yesterday, a helicopter was going east-west."

"Well, as long as they keep going, and don't hover about, then they're not looking for anything."

"I think they're looking for us, Colonel."

"I doubt that. They think you've flown off to Somaliland." He asked, "Why in the world would you stay here after you've shot down an army helicopter?"

"I've been asking myself that very question."

Gann smiled and said, "Well, let's press on."

On day five, Mercado said, "We need to head to Shoan." He reminded everyone, "We are running out of food."

And Henry was running out of gas, Purcell knew. And they were all dehydrated and covered with insect bites and heat sores.

Mercado reminded Gann, "Regroup, refit, and strike out again."

Gann nodded, but not very enthusiastically. He said, "I feel we should push on just a bit more...perhaps to the south, to a line parallel with Shoan. We might have more luck that way." He added, "Then we can head east toward the road, and Shoan."

Mercado had no reply.

Purcell said, "We could be south of Shoan already."

"That's possible."

Mercado pointed out, "If we just head due east, we will intersect with the road."

Gann reminded him, "We can't go due *any* direction, old boy." He pointed out, "This is not the desert or the tundra." He reminded Mercado, "We're in the bush, you know."

Mercado insisted, "We have passed the point of no return in regards to food."

"Not quite yet. But we're close."

"This is how people die."

"Well," Gann agreed, "that is one way. There are others." He belatedly asked Mercado, "How are you feeling, old boy?"

Mercado hesitated, then said, "I can make it back to Shoan."

"Good." Gann also said, "We must be careful not to get injured or ill."

Purcell agreed, "Let's try not to do that." He asked Vivian, "How are you feeling?"

"I'm all right."

Purcell looked into the dark, triple-canopy jungle. "Let's get off the trail and walk between the trees." He took a compass heading to the south.

They left the trail, and headed south through the rain forest. The terrain had looked deceptively open between the trees, but as they traveled it, it became clear that they had to cut brush and vines, and the carpet of undergrowth, that had looked low, was actually knee-high in most places.

After about an hour, they realized they weren't making good progress, and they also realized that by leaving the trail, they'd effectively lost it, and also lost any trail in the trackless expanse. It was like walking through a great columned building, Purcell thought, with a green-vaulted ceiling and a carpet of wait-a-minute vines. Rays of sunlight penetrated the triple canopy in places, and they found themselves unconsciously walking toward the spots of sun-dappled ground cover.

The darkness was getting deeper, and the sun was no longer penetrating into the forest. It was jungle dusk, and they began looking for a place to stop for the night.

Vivian said, "Look. A cluster of palms."

They looked to where she was pointing to the west and they saw the distinctive trunks of palms, with their fronds buried in the surrounding growth.

They made their way to the palms, where the ground was more clear, and they sat with their backs to the palm trunks.

Gann looked up and said, "Doesn't seem to be anything edible up there."

Purcell handed him a cloth bag. "Have a date."

They drank the last of their water and took stock of their food, which they estimated would last one more day.

Gann and Purcell looked at the map and they both agreed they were between twenty and thirty kilometers west of the road, though they couldn't determine if they were north or south of Shoan. And Shoan was another thirty kilometers east of the road.

Gann said, "We are a long day's march to Shoan."
He added, "Unless we run into rough country."

Purcell said, "That was encouraging until 'unless.'"

They all agreed they'd head back to Shoan in the
morning.

Vivian stood and said, "Be right back."

Everyone assumed she'd gone off to relieve herself, but she kept walking, and Purcell was concerned
that she was becoming delirious and had seen another
mirage. He couldn't call out to her because they needed
to be quiet, so he stood and caught up with her.

"Where are you going?"

"I saw a glint."

"Really?"

"Right over here."

He let her lead him farther into the tight undergrowth.

The ground was rising, he noticed, and he recalled
the high, rocky ground he'd seen when he flew over
this area, returning from Gondar.

The undergrowth began to thin, and he felt rocks
beneath his feet.

He was looking where he stepped, and also looking
left and right to be sure no one was there, and Vivian
was ahead of him again. He drew his pistol from his
cargo pocket and stuck it in his belt.

Vivian stopped and said, "There is the rock."

He caught up to her and looked west into the setting
sun. Spread out to their front was a deep depression
in the ground that covered acres of land. There were
a few trees growing in the sunken ground, but it was
mostly open. In the deep, wide depression grew brush,
crawling vines, and tropical flowers, but he could also

see acres of black rock coming through the ground growth. An old stone quarry.

Vivian pointed, "The rock."

On the far side of the abandoned quarry, about a hundred yards away, was a great black monolith—a quarried slab of rock, about twenty feet high and ten feet wide, that had been shaped by human hands, but never transported from here. The late afternoon sun highlighted the black luster on its top edge. Purcell didn't understand how Vivian could have seen it from where they were sitting.

He heard a noise behind him, pushed Vivian down, drew his revolver, and knelt facing the sound.

Gann and Mercado came up the rise and saw them.

Gann said, "There you are. Don't shoot, old boy. We're still friends."

Purcell put the revolver in his cargo pocket and waved them up the slope.

Gann asked, "What have you found?"

"A quarry."

Vivian said, "We have found Father Armano's rock." She pointed.

Mercado and Gann looked across the quarry and Gann said, "Yes, a quarry. Good scouting."

Mercado was staring at the black monolith on the far edge of the rock quarry. He looked at Vivian and asked, "How do you know?"

"Henry, that is the rock."

Gann spotted the carved rock and said, "Let's have a look, shall we?"

The sun slipped below the tall monolith, and a shadow spread across the expanse of the ancient quarry.

Purcell said, "It's not going anywhere. Let's camp here, and we'll take a look in the morning."

Vivian nodded. "I knew it was here, Frank."

Purcell looked at her, then looked downslope from where they'd come. *Impossible.*

She put her hand on his arm. "No, not impossible."

Chapter 52

They awoke before dawn and ate the last of their bread and dates, leaving only some dried goat meat, which Purcell thought would taste like steak when they were near starvation.

Purcell knew they would run out of food before they got to Shoan, but he wasn't sure they would be starting back today. Not with that black monolith staring them in the face. He looked out across the quarry. It was still too dark to see the black slab—but it was there.

They would have to make a decision; should they look next for Father Armano's tree? Then his stream? Purcell was almost certain that Vivian was right—this was *the* rock.

Purcell asked the question on everyone's minds. "Do we press on from that rock, or do we head back to Shoan and return here when we're reprovisioned?"

No one replied, except Vivian, of course. "We did not come this far to turn back."

Purcell reminded her, "We're about to eat the last goat."

"We need only water."

"Easy to say on a stomach full of dates." He asked, "Henry?"

Mercado looked at Vivian. "We continue on."

Gann agreed and said, "We won't starve to death."

He informed them, "Snakes. Easy to lop their venom-ous heads off with a machete." He further informed them, "You squeeze the buggers and get a good half pint of blood into your cup. Meat's not bad, either."

Purcell suggested, "Let's talk about water." He told them, "In the gypsum quarries where I grew up, there was lots of ground water. In fact, it needed to be pumped out."

Gann agreed, "Should be good water down there."

"So," Purcell asked, "are we all agreed that we've found the rock?"

Everyone agreed.

"And that we have to now look for a tree—which could be long gone after forty years?"

Vivian said, "We will find the tree. And the stream. And the black monastery."

"Good." Purcell said, "Father Armano did not let us down." He said to Mercado, "Cool the champagne."

Mercado smiled weakly. The man did not look well since they began this hike in Shoan, a week ago, Purcell thought. In fact, his face was drawn and his eyes looked dark and sunken. Purcell handed Mercado his last piece of bread and said, "Have this."

Mercado shook his head.

Purcell threw the bread on his lap, and Vivian said, "Eat that, Henry." She picked it up and held it to his lips, but he shook his head. "I'm all right."

Vivian put the bread in his backpack.

Purcell and Gann looked at the map in the dim light. Gann said, "I can see nothing on this map that indicates an abandoned quarry, so I'm not quite sure where we are...but I would guess here..." He pointed to the map where the dark green was a little lighter, an indication that the cartographers had noted the more sparse vegetation shown on the aerial photographs.

Gann continued, "The elevation lines indicate that beyond the quarry, the ground becomes lower and sinks into a deep basin, with dense growth."

Purcell said, "Regarding Father Armano's stream, I don't see any streams."

Gann reminded him, "You will only see on the map what could be seen from the aerial photographs." He added, "Which is not much."

Vivian let them know, "I don't care what is on the maps. We need to see what is out *there*." She pointed at the black rock.

"Good point," Purcell agreed. He stood. "Let's go."

Everyone slipped on their backpacks and they began picking their way down the terraced slope of the rock quarry. The black obsidian was slippery in places, and the vines were treacherous on the downslope.

Purcell glanced at Mercado, who seemed to be doing all right downhill.

The rocky floor of the quarry was about twenty feet down, and near the bottom they saw water flowing out of the rocks. They stopped and washed their faces and hands in the cool ground water, and drank it directly from its source, then filled their canteens. They sat on a rock ledge and waited, as Gann suggested, for the water to rehydrate them.

Vivian looked out at the black slab at the far edge of the quarry. The sun had peeked over the trees behind them, and the rays now illuminated the east-facing side of the rock. Vivian pointed. "Look."

They all looked at the twenty-foot-tall slab, and they could now see that the face of it had been etched with a cross.

Vivian said, "We are close."

They all stood, except for Mercado, who was still sitting, looking at the cross on the rock.

Vivian said to him, "Come on, Henry. We're almost home."

He nodded, stood, and smiled for the first time in days.

They continued down to the floor of the quarry, then began making their way across the uneven rock and tangled growth.

Gann said, "By the look of this place, I'd say it has been abandoned for a very long time."

Purcell wondered if this was where the black stone had come from to build the monastery. He assumed it was. Or had they done again what they were good at— making false assumptions, misinterpreting evidence, and tailoring the clues to fit their theories? Maybe not this time. Somewhere inside him, Purcell felt that they had arrived at the threshold of the black monastery.

They reached the opposite side of the quarry and began climbing the terraced rock. It was not a difficult climb, but they all realized they were weaker than they thought.

The black monolith was set back from the edge of the quarry, and they stood looking at it, and at the cross that they could now see had been deeply cut into the stone by a skilled stone carver. It wasn't a Latin cross, Purcell noted, but a Coptic cross.

At the edge of the quarry, they could see freshly

cleaved faces of obsidian, evidence that people had been here to cut small pieces of the stone.

Gann said, "I would guess that this is where the monks get their stone to carve their little doodads."

Purcell agreed. "Better than chipping away at the monastery."

Mercado had wandered off a few feet and said, "Look at this."

They walked to where he was standing, and on the ground was evidence of campfires, and what looked like chicken bones, and eggshells.

It didn't need to be said, but Gann said, "This could be where the Falashas meet the monks, and set up for the night before returning to Shoan."

Everyone agreed with that deduction, and Purcell added, "Shoan then must be a day's walk from here." He also pointed out, "It took us five days to get here."

Gann replied, "It appears we took the long route." He added, "There is obviously a quick and direct route to Shoan. We'll need to find that."

"Right. Meanwhile, I think it's safe to say that the black monastery is a one-day hike from this meeting place."

Mercado asked, "But in which direction?"

Gann replied, "Probably not east, on the way back to Shoan. So perhaps north or south, or farther west."

Vivian had walked off, and she called back to them, "West."

They moved toward where she was standing on an elevation of rock. The area around the quarry was mostly treeless, covered with rock rubble from hundreds of years of quarrying, but surrounding the open area was thick jungle. To the west, where Vivian was looking, stood a dead cedar about a hundred feet away, and about forty feet in height. The towering trunk of the decay-resistant cedar had turned silver-gray, and all the branches had fallen, or been cut off, except for two that stretched out like arms, parallel to the ground, giving the tree the appearance of a giant cross.

Vivian said, "The tree."

Purcell looked at the giant cedar, which could have been there, alive and dead, for hundreds of years.

Gann and Mercado were also staring at the towering tree, and Gann looked back at the monolith and said, "I believe we have two points in a straight line."

Purcell had his compass out, and with his back to the monolith, and facing the tree, he took a compass reading. "A few degrees north of due west."

Vivian said, "Now we need to find the stream."

Purcell replied, "That should be the easiest thing we've done this week." He said to Mercado, "Henry, get the champagne ready."

Mercado smiled.

Purcell gave Vivian a hug, then Vivian hugged Henry, then Colonel Gann. The men shook hands all around.

Everyone's spirits seemed to be revived, and they forgot their fatigue and jungle sores.

Purcell now noticed, about a hundred feet off to the north, a roofless hut built with scraps of the black rock. The hut sat among flowering bushes, and the branches of a tall gum tree hung over the abandoned structure.

Gann said, "A shelter for the nasty overseer, I would bet."

They all walked toward the hut to check it out, and when they got within ten feet of it, a man suddenly appeared in the shadow of the open doorway and stepped quickly out of the hut, followed by another man, then three more.

Purcell counted five men, dressed in jungle fatigues, carrying AK-47 rifles, which were pointed at them.

Vivian let out a stifled scream and grabbed Purcell's arm.

One of the soldiers shouted something in Amharic, and all the soldiers were pointing their automatic rifles at Gann, shouting, and gesturing for him to drop the Uzi.

Gann hesitated, and one of the soldiers fired a deafening burst of rounds over his head.

Gann let the Uzi fall to the ground.

Vivian pressed against Purcell.

Someone else appeared at the door of the hut, and General Getachu stepped out into the morning sunshine. With him was Princess Miriam, whom he pushed to the ground.

Getachu looked at Purcell, Mercado, Gann, and Vivian. "I have been waiting for you."

Chapter 53

Frank Purcell drew a deep breath and tried to take stock of the situation, which didn't need, he admitted, too much interpretation.

His mind registered that there were five soldiers, and a Huey held seven in the cabin. So if that's how Getachu and Miriam had gotten here, there were no more soldiers—unless there were.

Getachu had a holster strapped to his waist, but his pistol wasn't drawn.

Purcell glanced at the Uzi on the ground, about five feet away, between him and Gann. Was it on safety? Probably. Could he get to it before he was cut down by five AK-47s? Probably not.

Purcell glanced at Mercado, who he saw had tears in his eyes. Vivian had her head buried in Purcell's chest now, her back to the soldiers. Gann was looking at Miriam, who had remained on the ground at Getachu's feet, lying facedown in the dirt. He saw that she wore a white *shamma* that was ripped and stained with blood.

Getachu said, "Colonel Gann does not seem happy to see his princess." He stared at Gann. "I was not happy to hear that they released you in Addis. Now you will wish they had shot you there."

Getachu knew not to expect a reply from the insolent Englishman, so he continued, "I paid a brief visit to Shoan, to pay my respects to my princess before the UN people came to take her away."

Getachu looked at Gann, then Purcell. "And what do I find there? I find an aircraft that has been burned. Your aircraft, Mr. Purcell. The very aircraft that my helicopter pilot radioed had fired a rocket at him. And now the helicopter is missing, and presumed lost, with all the men on board." He let Purcell know, "I have concluded my court-martial, and you will be shot." He added, "Within the next five minutes."

Purcell felt the weight of the revolver in his cargo pocket. He was sure the opportunity would come to pull the revolver and shoot Getachu before the five soldiers cut everyone down with their automatic rifles. At least they'd all die knowing that Getachu was dead.

Getachu lit a cigarette and continued what appeared to be a rehearsed speech. "I promised you a cigarette, Mr. Purcell, before I was going to shoot you in my camp. But I am sorry to break this promise. I will promise you, however, a quick bullet in the brain."

Purcell made the same promise to Getachu, but kept that to himself.

Getachu continued, "So the people of Shoan sheltered a murderer. And they also admitted to me that Mr. Mercado and Miss Smith came from that aircraft, and that the princess gave them all shelter. Therefore, Mr. Mercado will share Mr. Purcell's fate, and Miss Smith…" He smiled at her, "Miss Smith—Vivian— will belong to me for a time. Then she will belong to my soldiers." He said something to his men in Amharic and they smiled and looked at Vivian.

Vivian was shaking now and Purcell held her tightly.

Gann was looking at Miriam, but spoke to Getachu. "What did you do in Shoan?"

"Ah! You speak." He said to Gann, "What do you think I did?"

"You will hang for that."

"For what? Because the Gallas attacked the village and killed everyone, and burned it all? What has that to do with me?"

"You bastard."

"Yes, yes, Colonel Gann. Getachu is a bastard. And you are a knight. A knight for hire. A man who sells himself to kill." He said to Gann, "The prostitutes in Saint George Square charge less, and are better at their profession than you."

Gann looked at Getachu. "You are the most incompetent commander I have ever faced."

"Do not provoke me into putting a bullet into your head. I have something special for you to see before you die." He looked at Miriam lying at his feet and kicked her in the side.

Miriam let out a moan, but remained facedown on the ground.

Gann took a step toward her, but the soldiers leveled their rifles at him and he stopped.

Getachu said, "When I was a young man, and when this princess became a woman—about fourteen, I think—I thought of her in that way. Mikael Getachu, the son of a weaver who worked in the shop of their royal highnesses. I told my father of my desire for the princess, and he beat me, of course. But if he were now living, I would say to him—you see? I have got my princess." Getachu put the toe of his boot under

Miriam's *shamma* and pushed it up over her bare buttocks.

He said something to his soldiers in Amharic, and they laughed. He said to Gann, "So we have this lady in common at least."

Gann took a deep breath, and Purcell knew he was thinking of diving for the Uzi, and Purcell said to him, "No."

Gann took another breath, then stood straight, as though he were in parade formation, and said to Getachu, "You are not a soldier. You are an animal."

"Do *not* provoke me. You will die when and how I want you to die. And I will tell you how you will die— by crucifixion, as you watch me having sport with your lady."

Getachu looked at Vivian, then said, "And perhaps I will have sport with you both. Yes. I think I would like seeing you, Miss Smith, and the princess enjoying the company of each other."

Vivian was still clinging to Purcell, her body shaking.

Getachu turned his attention to Mercado, who had stood silently, his eyes closed and his head down. Getachu said to him, "Will you now tell me that you will write nice words about me?"

Mercado did not answer.

Getachu barked, "I am speaking to you! Look at me!"

Mercado raised his head and looked at Getachu.

"I will spare your life, Mr. Mercado. We will do the interviews, and you will write kind words about General Getachu, a man of the people." He looked at Mercado. "Yes?"

Mercado stared at Getachu. "Go fuck yourself."

Getachu seemed surprised at the response. "What do you say?"

"Go fuck yourself."

Getachu put his hand on the butt of his pistol. "What do you say, Mr. Mercado?"

Mercado said something in Amharic, and the five soldiers seemed almost stunned, and leveled their rifles at him.

Getachu waved them off, then said to Mercado, "I had planned a quick death for you, who are of no consequence. But I will rethink that."

Mercado, recalling what Gann had done in Getachu's tent, turned his back on the general.

Getachu looked at Mercado's back, then shifted his attention to his surroundings. He said, "So this is the place where the Falashas and the monks come to meet, and to exchange goods." He looked around again. "I am told this has gone on for several hundred years, which is a very nice thing." He said to his prisoners, "I have heard of this arrangement, and I wished to see this place for myself. And now I am told that this arrangement has ended because the Falashas have gone. So I came here to bring food to the monks, and I have waited for them—and for you, who I hoped would come here." He looked down at Miriam. "She is a stubborn woman, Colonel. But she did reveal to me the location of this place, but not to you, I think, or you would have been here much sooner." He let them know, "I have been waiting for you for six days now, and I had given up hope. But the princess has been kind enough to keep me amused."

Again, Purcell thought that Gann would go for the

Uzi, and he knew that Getachu had left it lying close to Gann to further torment the man.

In fact, Getachu said, "Why is it that none of you brave men will take up that weapon?" He asked, "Is that not a better way to die? Please, gentlemen. Show me your courage."

Purcell moved slightly so that Vivian was blocking Getachu's view of his right arm, and he began to move his hand toward the cargo pocket. He was sure he could kill Getachu, and he hoped that Gann would then dive for the Uzi—or if he didn't, and Purcell was not dead yet, he could go for it himself, and maybe get off a burst. But whatever scenario played out, he, Vivian, Gann, and Mercado would be cut down by bursts of automatic rifle fire. And that was better than what Getachu had planned. He put his hand on Vivian's thigh, close to his cargo pocket.

Getachu also let them know, "When I am finished with you here, I will find the monastery of the monks, which I know is close by, and I will relieve these holy men of their treasure—and perhaps their lives." He said, "Men have died to protect this thing called the Grail, and men have died looking for it—as you will. You have found death."

Purcell could hear Vivian saying softly, "No, no, no ... Frank."

He held her tighter.

Getachu turned his attention to Miriam and pressed his boot into her bare buttocks. She sobbed and said something in Amharic.

Getachu said to her, "Do not be sad, my princess. I will take care of you. Are you sad at losing your English lover? Do you want to speak to him? To tell him that you betrayed him? He will understand. You were in pain. He will understand that pain very shortly. And he will forgive you, because he will understand what pain can do."

Purcell had his hand in his pocket now, and he wrapped his fingers around the butt of the revolver. No one noticed. He hoped he'd live long enough to see Getachu bleeding his life out.

Gann suddenly let out a strange noise, and Purcell glanced at him. Gann had his hands over his face, and he was crying, and his body was shaking. He called out, "Miriam! Miriam!"

She turned her head toward him and said softly, "Edmund... I am sorry..."

Gann reached out his arms to her and took three long steps toward Miriam, and almost reached her, but two soldiers grabbed him and pushed him back. He struggled with them, and kept shouting, "Miriam!"

Purcell understood instantly that Gann was up to something, and Purcell knew this was the moment. He pulled his revolver. Then something suddenly flew through the air and came to rest on the ground, and Purcell saw it was the safety handle of a hand grenade. And he realized what Gann had done.

Getachu was screaming in Amharic at his two men, and he didn't see the grenade in Gann's hand that Gann had pulled from one of the soldier's web belts, and he also didn't see Gann dropping the live grenade on the ground.

The seven-second fuse had been cooking for at least three or four seconds, Purcell knew, and he should have thrown himself and Vivian on the ground and yelled for Mercado to do the same. But he wanted to kill Getachu himself. He pushed Vivian to the ground, facedown, raised the revolver, and pointed it directly at Getachu's heart.

Getachu saw two things in a quick succession— the grenade, and Purcell taking aim at him. His eyes widened.

Purcell fired, and Getachu was knocked back into the stone wall of the hut.

Purcell threw himself on top of Vivian, who was trying to stand, and he yelled at Mercado, "Down!"

The grenade exploded.

The sound was literally deafening, and Purcell's eardrums felt as though they were going to burst. The ground shook under him.

And then there was complete silence. He felt a burning in his right calf where a piece of hot shrapnel had sliced into him. He whispered in Vivian's ear, "Do not move." He told her, "Getachu is dead." But he wasn't sure of that.

He rolled off her quickly and rose unsteadily to one knee, with his revolver pointed toward the hut.

No one was standing.

He stood and drew a deep breath, then took a few steps toward the hut. The air was filled with dust and the smell of burned explosives.

The two soldiers who'd been grappling with Gann were gushing blood from multiple wounds where the burning shrapnel had torn into their bodies.

Gann, too, was a mass of blood, and his khakis were soaked red. He was still breathing, but frothy blood was running from his mouth.

Purcell moved toward the three soldiers who'd been standing near the hut, near Getachu. They hadn't caught the full blast of the grenade, but they were down, bleeding and stunned by the concussion. One of them looked at him.

Purcell raised his revolver and put a bullet into each of their heads.

He moved over to where Miriam lay on the ground. He saw no blood, and thought she'd been low enough to escape the flying shrapnel. He knelt beside her and shook her. "Miriam." Then he saw the wound in the side of her head where a single piece of shrapnel had entered her skull. He felt her throat for a pulse, but there was none. He reached out and pulled her *shamma* over her buttocks.

He stood and looked at Getachu, who was sitting against the wall where he'd been thrown by the impact of the bullet. His face had caught some shrapnel, and one of his eyes was a mass of blood.

Blood also ran out of his mouth from the bullet wound in his chest. His one eye was following Purcell.

Getachu seemed to be trying to speak, and Purcell knelt near him, though he still could not hear. Getachu spit a glob of frothy blood at him.

Purcell wiped the blood from his face, put the revolver to Getachu's good eye, and pulled the trigger.

Purcell stood and turned, and looked at Vivian, whose body was still shaking, though he saw no blood, and she seemed all right.

He looked at where Mercado had been standing, and saw him lying facedown on the ground.

Purcell knelt beside Vivian and put his hand on her shoulder. "Are you all right?"

Her face was buried in her arms, and she gave a small nod.

"Do not move."

He stood and walked to Mercado and knelt beside him. Mercado's backpack had caught a lot of shrapnel, and he had taken shrapnel in his legs and buttocks, and blood was seeping through his khakis. His shirt was also wet, Purcell saw, but not with blood. The champagne bottle had broken. "Henry. How are you, old man?"

No response.

"Henry." He shook him.

Purcell heard and felt a rushing in his ears; his hearing was returning. "Are you all right?"

"I said I've been hit. I've been hit."

Purcell couldn't tell if the wounds were serious, but the blood was not gushing. It came to him that Henry, by turning his back on Getachu, may have saved his own life. He said to Mercado, "Just lie still. You'll be all right. I'll be right back."

He went back to Vivian, knelt beside her, and again put his hand on her shoulder. "Can you stand?"

She nodded, and he helped her to her feet, keeping her back turned to the carnage around the hut. She put her arms around him. "Frank...oh my God..." She began crying, then took a deep breath and asked in a quiet voice, "What happened?"

He told her again, to reassure her, "Getachu is dead."

She tried to turn to look toward the hut, but he held her against him.

He said, "The soldiers are dead. Listen to me—a

hand grenade exploded. Colonel Gann is dead. Miriam is dead."

She let out a long cry, then got herself under control and asked, "Henry...?"

"Henry is...he will be okay." Maybe.

She turned her head to where she'd last seen Henry, and saw him facedown on the ground with blood on his pants. "Henry!" She pulled loose from Purcell and he let her go.

She ran over to Mercado and knelt beside him. "Henry!"

Mercado turned his head toward her and smiled. "Thank God you are all right."

Purcell didn't recall Henry asking him about Vivian, but he supposed Mercado was in shock.

Vivian was caressing his hair and face. "You will be fine. You *are* fine. Just lie still...are you in pain?"

"A bit. Yes." He turned his head toward Purcell. "Am I going to live?"

Purcell knelt opposite Vivian and put his fingers on Henry's throat to feel his pulse, which seemed strong. "How is your breathing?"

"All right..."

He felt Henry's forehead, and it was not cool or clammy. He informed Mercado, "Gann is dead. Miriam is dead."

"No...oh, God...what happened...?"

"Gann got hold of a grenade."

Purcell stood and walked over to one of the soldiers he'd executed. There was a U.S. Army first aid kit on the man's web belt, and he snapped the canvas kit off and carried it to Vivian. He put it in her hand. "There should be a pressure bandage in there, and iodine. Get his clothes off and we'll patch him up."

She nodded and asked Mercado, "Can you sit up?"

She helped him roll onto his back, which seemed to cause him pain, then she pulled him up into a sitting position, took his backpack off, and began unbuttoning his shirt.

Purcell went back to the other two executed soldiers and retrieved their first aid kits, which each held a pressure bandage. He checked the two soldiers who'd taken the full brunt of the grenade blast, but their web gear was as shredded as their bodies, and he saw that one of them had a protruding intestine.

He went back to Gann, and he knelt beside him and felt for a pulse, but there was none. Purcell pushed his eyelids closed and said, "You did good, Colonel."

Henry was naked now, on all fours, and Vivian was dabbing iodine on his legs and butt, which caused him to cry out in pain.

Purcell walked over to them and knelt on the other side of Henry. He counted three shrapnel wounds in his left leg and two in his buttocks. He could see the shrapnel sticking out of one wound and he pulled it out, which made Henry yell in pain. Purcell said, "I think you may be very lucky." He took his penknife from his pocket and said, "This will hurt, but you will remain still and quiet."

He managed to get all but one piece of metal out of Mercado's flesh, and Henry kept relatively still, as Vivian kept talking to him.

He gave Vivian the other two first aid kits. "Bandage the ones that look the worst."

He looked at her kneeling on the other side of Mercado and she looked at him. He said, "Be quick. We need to get out of here."

"Where are we going?"

"You know where we're going."

She nodded, then started opening the first aid kits.

He stood and again surveyed the scene, then lit a cigarette. "My God. Oh my God."

He wanted to bury Colonel Gann and Miriam and not leave them for the jackals, but he didn't see a shovel, and he didn't want to stay here any longer than he had to.

He walked over to Gann and hefted him onto his shoulder, then carried him to Miriam and laid Gann down beside her. He crossed their arms over their chests. Hopefully Getachu's men, looking for their general, would know that someone had respected the bodies, and maybe they'd do the same. Maybe, too, they'd be happy to find their general with a bullet in his brain.

Purcell watched Vivian help Henry into his clothes. Henry seemed all right.

Purcell pulled up his pant leg and looked at his wound. A piece of metal protruded from his calf and he pulled it out.

Shrapnel from an exploding grenade or shell was a random thing, he recalled from his time in Southeast Asia—hot metal shards or pieces of spring-loaded wire, killing and maiming some, leaving others untouched. It really didn't depend too much on where you were standing or lying when it went off—close, far, standing, or prone as Miriam was—it didn't matter. When it was your time, it was your time. When it wasn't, it wasn't. It was Colonel Gann's time, and Miriam's time. It was not Henry Mercado's time. Or Vivian's, or his. Indeed, they had been chosen.

He walked over to them and said, "We are going to the black monastery. We are going to see the Holy Grail."

Chapter 54

Purcell had the Uzi, and he gave Vivian his reloaded pistol, and Henry retrieved one of the AK-47s. They slipped on their backpacks and walked away from the rock quarry, down the slope toward the giant cedar, and continued on toward the wall of tropical growth in front of them.

No one spoke, but then Mercado asked Purcell, "Did you take any food from the soldiers?"

"No."

"We should go back."

Purcell replied, "Put your hand into the hand of God, Henry. That's why we're here."

Mercado stayed silent as they continued on, then said, "Yes...I will."

Vivian said, "We are all in God's hands now."

Purcell did not have to look at his compass to know he was heading due west, with the cedar and the monolith behind him.

There was a worn black rock lying on the ground at the edge of the wall of trees, and beyond the rock he saw a trailhead. They crossed over the black threshold and entered the rain forest. Limbs and vines reached out overhead and immediately blocked out the sunlight.

The land sloped gently down, and the trees became taller, and the canopy became thicker. After a while,

Purcell noticed that the ground was becoming soft and spongy as though they were entering a marsh or a swamp.

The trail was no longer defined by walls of vegetation, but it was discernible if you looked ahead and saw the slight difference in the ground where it had been walked on.

Mercado said, "I don't see a stream."

Purcell did not reply, and neither did Vivian. They continued on.

The ground was definitely spongy now, and Purcell could see changes in the landscape. Huge banyan trees started to appear, as well as swamp cedar and cypress, which he remembered from the swamps of Southeast Asia.

The land was sloping more steeply now, and Purcell guessed they were entering the bottom drainage basin from the Simien Mountains, which he'd noticed in the air and on the map but which they had not thought to consider as a place where the black monastery could be.

In retrospect, he realized that they had been...maybe mesmerized by Father Armano and his story, and the priest had given them information, but not knowledge. He had told them enough to put them on the trail, but not enough to bring them to the end of it. They had to do that on their own. And if indeed they were chosen, then they would be guided on the right path.

Purcell looked around him. The terrain appeared deceptively pleasant and sylvan, but he could now see pools of water filled with marsh fern on both sides of their disappearing path. Marsh gasses rose in misty clouds, and the air was becoming hot and fetid. Wispy strands of gray moss hung from the tree limbs, and he noticed that there were a lot of dead trees, and creeping marshwort ran over the deadwood on the wet ground. Huge, silent black birds sat on bare tree limbs and seemed to be watching them as they passed. He realized that the marsh was much quieter than the jungle, and there were almost no sounds from insects or birds. A sense of foreboding came over him, but he said nothing and they pressed on.

The land seemed to be bottoming out and becoming a true swamp, and Purcell wondered if this was passable. He also wondered if they were going in the right direction. The path had disappeared, but there was a meandering ribbon of spongy higher ground that passed through the swampy expanse of terrain. The mud was sucking at their boots, and Vivian took off her boots and socks and walked barefoot through the muck. Purcell and Mercado did the same.

Vivian noticed now that Purcell had blood on his pant leg, and she asked him, "Did you get hit there?"

"I'm fine."

"Let me see that."

"I've already seen it."

She insisted they stop, and Purcell sat on the trunk of a fallen tree while Vivian knelt in the mud, extended Purcell's leg, and examined his wound.

He said, "It's really okay."

She had an iodine bottle in her pocket and she dabbed some of it on his wound, then sat beside him on the tree trunk.

They looked around at the swamp. Without saying it, they all knew that Father Armano had never mentioned a swamp.

Vivian said to Mercado, "Sit down, Henry."

He sat slowly on the tree trunk and grimaced in pain.

Purcell said, "I think I left a piece of metal in you."

"Indeed you did."

They all smiled, but it was a tired and forced smile. The shock and horror of what had happened was still very much with them, and it was time to say something.

Purcell said to them, "Edmund Gann was a very brave man."

Mercado said, "He was a soldier and a gentleman... a knight."

Vivian said, "I know that he is with Miriam now."

"Indeed he is," Mercado said.

Vivian put her arm around Purcell and squeezed him closer to her. "*You* are a very brave man, Frank Purcell." She told Henry, "He threw himself over me when the hand grenade exploded."

Mercado nodded.

Vivian put her hand on Mercado's shoulder. "What did you say to Getachu in Amharic?"

"The usual—that his mother was a diseased prostitute who should have smothered him at birth."

Vivian said, "A bit rough, Henry." She smiled.

Mercado said, "I hope he is now burning in hell."

No one spoke for a minute, then Mercado asked Vivian, "Do you still have Father Armano's skull?"

"I do."

"Well, we are going to take him where he wanted to go." He stood. "Ready?"

Vivian and Purcell stood, and Vivian assured them, "The stream is ahead of us."

They continued on.

The ground was rising now, and the marshland was again turning to tropical jungle. What looked like a beaten path began to materialize in front of them.

Vivian suddenly stopped and said, "Listen."

They stopped and listened, but neither Purcell nor Mercado could hear anything.

Mercado asked, "What do you hear?"

"Water." She moved to her right and the men followed.

Running down the slope was a small stream, choked with water lilies and vines. It was, Purcell thought, a stream from the hills that emptied into the marsh basin.

Vivian knelt down and put her hand into the flowing water. She turned to Purcell and Mercado, silently inviting them to do the same.

They knelt beside the stream and let the water run over their hands.

Vivian said, "This is the stream. Do we follow it? Or do we follow the path?"

Purcell thought the path and the stream seemed to run parallel, but they might diverge.

Mercado said, "Ruscello. He said it twice. Il Ruscello. The stream."

Vivian nodded and stood. They all stepped, still barefoot, into the cool, shallow water and walked upstream.

Without looking at his watch, Purcell knew they had been walking about five hours, and it was close to noon—a half day's walk from the meeting place of the monks and the Falashas. And it had been mostly due west, even through the meandering path in the swamp. It seemed simple enough, after you've done it, and he tried to imagine Father Armano on his patrol with the sergeant named Giovanni, walking from the black rock—which the priest and the soldiers had no way of knowing was a meeting place of Coptic Christians and Jews. Giovanni had then taken his patrol to the giant cedar, and through the jungle, to the swamp, and to the stream, all of which the sergeant had found by accident on a previous patrol. And they had arrived again at the black monastery—but this time they entered by the reed basket, and only Father Armano came out of there alive.

And when the priest was healed of his wounds—by nature or by faith—he was given over to the Royalist soldiers and taken by the same route, or maybe another route, to his prison in the fortress, and there he remained for nearly forty years. And whatever he had seen in that monastery had sustained him, not only for all those years in his cell, but also for the hours he walked with a mortal wound on his way back to where he had experienced something so remarkable—or miraculous—that he had to return to that place, even as he was dying. He never made it back, but he had made it as far as the ruined spa, which was not even there when he had last been that way. And what he had found in the spa were three people who themselves were trying to find something. Trying to find the war. And Father Armano had asked them—or asked Vivian—*Dov'è la strada?* Where is the road?

Indeed, where is the road? There are many roads.

The jungle became thicker, and the stream became more narrow, and they could see smaller streams feeding into it from the higher ground. They also noticed more clusters of palm trees. None of them doubted that the black monastery was ahead, and that they were walking toward it. It was just a matter of hours, or maybe days, but it was sitting there, still hidden from the eyes of men, still unwelcoming to visitors, yet hopefully ready to receive them with a basket made of reeds.

The sun was setting ahead of them, and the few patches of sunlight were becoming dimmer. It was harder to see more than twenty or thirty feet ahead, but the stream guided them.

The jungle looked somehow different, Purcell thought, and it was more than the changing light that made it seem altered. Purcell noticed date palms and breadfruit trees, and trees that bore fleshy fruit, and other trees that he thought bore nuts, and black African violets covered the ground. This was tended land, a tropical garden such as Purcell had seen in Southeast Asia, barely distinguishable from the untamed jungle. He said, "The monastery is just ahead."

Vivian, who was in the lead now, said, "I know."

The stream bent sharply to their right, and they followed it for a minute, but then Vivian stepped out of the stream and walked between two towering palms.

Purcell and Mercado joined her.

To their front, about thirty feet away, rising above a twenty-foot-high thicket of bamboo, was a black wall.

Vivian stared up at the glossy stone. She said simply, "We are here."

Chapter 55

Purcell had no image in his mind of what the wall would look like, and he saw now that the black stones were the size and shape of brick, laid without mortar, piece by piece, until the wall reached about forty feet, the height of a four-story building.

The sun had sunk lower, and the east side of the monastery where they were standing was in dark shadow, but there was a sheen to the wall, and the bamboo thicket and surrounding palms seemed to be captured in the stone.

None of them seemed to know what to do or say next, but they all understood, Purcell thought, that the road that had taken them here was strewn with betrayals and death—but also with acts of courage and caring, and memories that would last them a lifetime—no matter how short or long that was.

Mercado asked, "Do you think anyone is here?"

Vivian replied, "Let's find out."

They pushed their way through the thicket of bamboo to a narrow path that ran along the base of the wall and they went to their right.

They walked along the wall for about two hundred yards to the corner and turned along the north side, then around to the west, and to the south side of the long wall, then back to where they had started. As

Father Armano had said, the monastery was built in the style of the Dark Ages, without an opening. But sitting on the ground now was a large basket attached to a thick rope.

Purcell was about to ask if they were sure they wanted to climb into the basket, expecting some hesitation or discussion, but Vivian threw her revolver on the ground and stepped into it without a word. Mercado dropped his AK-47 and followed. They both looked at him. Purcell said, "Maybe we want... a potential survivor."

Vivian said to him, "That is your decision, Frank."

Mercado said, "Don't wait for us too long."

Purcell hesitated again, then threw his Uzi on the ground and climbed into the basket, and held on to the rope that Vivian and Mercado were holding.

The basket began to rise.

They didn't bother to look at the top of the wall—there would be no one there.

The basket came to a halt, and they were now able to see the roof of the church that Father Armano had described.

They climbed over the parapet onto a wooden walkway that surrounded the walls, and they looked down into the monastery below. It was as the priest had described—a fountain, gardens, eucalyptus trees, palms, and a pond. The peaked roof of the large church was made of a translucent material, also as the priest described. There seemed to be no one there. But of course, there was.

Again without hesitation or comment, Vivian led the way along the wooden walk until they came to a staircase, which they descended.

They all walked toward the closed doors of the church, which were covered in silver that had obviously been rubbed and polished not too long ago, and they saw the symbols of the early Christians on the doors— lambs, fish, and palms, and in the center of each door was a Coptic cross.

Vivian asked Purcell, "Do you have any weapons?"

"No."

"Then open the door."

Purcell grasped the large ring on the door and pulled. The door opened easily and he went inside, followed by Vivian, then Mercado.

The inside of the large church was simple and almost crude. The walls and floors were of black stone and there was no ornamentation, and Purcell was reminded of the church of San Anselmo in Berini. But unlike San Anselmo, the altar here was a simple and crude table, partially covered by a white cloth, on which sat a Coptic cross. Also unlike San Anselmo, there were no stained glass windows—in fact, no windows at all.

But the sun was still high enough to come through the high ceiling, and a strange, prismatic light came through the translucent roof, casting rainbows over the floors and walls. The colors seemed to dance, and to separate into their primary components—red, green, blue—then blend again into their various hues.

Purcell noticed a door behind the altar, and he walked toward it. Mercado and Vivian followed, and Vivian said in a barely audible voice, "This is the way Father Armano walked."

This door behind the altar was open and Purcell passed through it. He sensed, but could not see, that he was in a large space. As his eyes adjusted to the darkness, he could make out that he was in a long, narrow gallery, and that two rows of stone columns ran the length of the space.

Vivian came up behind him and put her hand on his shoulder. Mercado stood to Vivian's side, and they all stood where Father Armano and the ten men of his patrol had stood forty years before. Unlike Father Armano, Sergeant Giovanni, and the other men, they did not move forward—but neither did they retreat.

At the end of the long gallery they could now see two fluttering candles, but the candlelight was so weak that they could see nothing but the flames, as though the fire radiated no light, but gave light.

They stared at the candles. Vivian said, "It is there." She took their hands and began walking with them between the two rows of thick columns.

As they passed each set of columns, Purcell thought that he should be feeling fear, but a sense of peace took hold of him, and he continued on with Vivian's hand in his.

As they got closer, the two candle flames seemed to give off more light, and he could see that the candles were set toward the middle of a table. As they got even closer, they could all see that it was a very long table, on which was a white cloth that seemed to shine as though it was luminescent.

Behind the table were thirteen high-backed wooden chairs, facing them, and Purcell understood that this was a representation of the table of the Last Supper, with a chair for Jesus and all the apostles, including one for Judas, though that chair was often missing in such representations.

Vivian and Mercado didn't see it at first, because it was small, and the bronze was not polished, but in the center of the table, between the two candles, and opposite the chair of Jesus, was the kiddush cup of the Passover. The Holy Grail.

Vivian stepped close to the table and let go of the men's hands. She stared at the cup. Mercado, too, stared at it, and took a step closer. He said, "It is filled."

Vivian said, "It is beautiful." She turned to Purcell. "Frank?"

He kept staring where they were looking, but he saw nothing.

"Frank?" Vivian seemed concerned. "Do you see it?"

He didn't reply.

Mercado kept staring at the spot. "How do you not see it?"

"There is nothing there."

Vivian again looked at him, then back at the spot between the candles. "Frank...do you feel it?"

"I don't...I can't see anything, Vivian." He looked at her, then at Mercado, realizing they were sharing the same hallucination.

Tears began running down Vivian's face. "Frank... you must see it. Why can't you...?"

He stepped up to the table and reached his hand out between the candles, but there was nothing there.

Vivian said to Purcell, "Do you want to see the cup or do you want to be proven right?"

Purcell stood there, not knowing what to say or what to do. Finally, he said, "I want to see it, and believe it."

Mercado opened Vivian's backpack and he pulled the skull out and quickly unwrapped it.

Purcell said to him, "Henry, what are you doing?"

Vivian replied, "We have brought Father Armano home."

"No, put that back."

But Mercado had set the skull on the table, in the center, facing the seat of Christ, and Christ's cup.

Purcell drew a deep breath and reached for the skull, and he felt something touch the back of his hand. He felt it again, and he looked at his hand, where two drops of red glistened in the candlelight.

He stared at the two red drops that were now running down to his wrist, then he looked past his hand, and sitting on the table was a small bronze goblet that he had not seen before.

He kept staring at it, to be sure it was there, and he said to Vivian and to Mercado, "I can see it."

He held the back of his hand toward Vivian and Mercado and Vivian smiled. Mercado, too, smiled, and said, "We were worried about you, Frank."

Vivian said to him, "I was never worried about you. You just needed to believe in your soul what your heart already knew."

Purcell nodded.

The three of them looked up toward the ceiling, and they all saw the lance, suspended in air, and as they watched, a red drop formed on the tip and fell into the cup.

They heard something behind them and they turned. Coming out of the darkness of the gallery, between the columns, were figures moving toward them. As the figures got closer, they could see that they were men in monks' robes and cowls, walking two by two. The monks came closer, then separated, left and right, and stood in a line behind them, but seemed not to notice them though they were only a few feet away.

The monks all dropped to their knees, facing the long table, then bowed their heads and began praying silently.

Vivian took Purcell and Mercado by the arm and turned them around, facing the table, and they dropped to their knees. Vivian took their hands again and they all bowed their heads.

Vivian said softly, "We have come a long way and we are not afraid."

Purcell didn't know if she was speaking to him, to the monks, or to God. But whatever fear he felt at seeing the monks vanished, and he squeezed her hand. "There is nothing to be afraid of."

Mercado said, "I told you, Frank, we have been chosen."

Vivian said, "We can go home now."

Purcell nodded. He was ready for that journey home.

PART V

Rome, February

Journeys end in lovers meeting.
—William Shakespeare
Twelfth Night, II

Chapter 56

Frank Purcell sat on a bench and lit a cigarette. A cold wind blew down from the Gianicolo—the hill of Janus—and the Vatican gardens were nearly deserted on this overcast afternoon in February.

It was time to leave Rome, but before he left he wanted to see Vivian and Henry.

Henry had suggested dinner at Etiopia, but Purcell had suggested the Vatican park, after Henry left work. This needed to be short, sweet, and non-alcoholic.

It was 5:30, and Henry was late as usual, but Purcell saw Vivian coming down the path. She spotted him, smiled, waved, and quickened her pace.

He stood and they hesitated for a moment, then hugged and did an air kiss.

He said, "I've saved a seat for you."

She smiled and sat, and he sat at the far end of the bench. He put out his cigarette.

She asked, "Can I have one of those?"

"You shouldn't." But he held out his Marlboros and she took one. He leaned toward her and lit it with a match that flickered in the wind.

She inhaled and let out a stream of smoke and breath mist. "It's cold."

"Spring is coming."

They both stayed silent awhile, then realizing they

might never have another moment alone on a park bench, or anywhere, she said, "He needs me."

He didn't reply.

"And you don't."

"I think we've had this conversation."

"If I change my mind, can I come back?"

He was supposed to be tough and say, "No." But he said, "Yes."

"But you'll be taken by then."

Again he didn't reply.

"Can we remain friends?"

"You don't have to ask."

They stayed silent and Purcell looked across the dark, windy park at the Ethiopian College.

Vivian saw where he was looking and said, "I still haven't developed any of the photographs." She asked, "Are you going to write about...our quest?"

He thought that the world did not need to know what he, Vivian, and Mercado knew. Nor did the monks need the world to know. "I think we should all close the book on Ethiopia and move on."

She nodded. "That is our beautiful and sad secret."

"Right."

She asked him, "Would you ever go back?"

"If I found the right photographer."

She laughed, then asked him, "How are your job prospects?"

"Probably better than yours."

She smiled.

"I'm looking for something in the States." He stayed silent a moment and said, "It's been a long time since I've been home."

"Let me know how I can contact you."

"Will do." He glanced at his watch. "Must be a late-breaking story on the Holy Year."

She smiled again and said, "Why don't you come to dinner with us?"

"Thanks, but I really do have to meet someone."

"How long will you be in Rome?"

"I leave tomorrow."

She looked at him.

"I'm going to London tomorrow to meet Colonel Gann's family. He has an ex-wife who was fond of him, and two grown children."

"That's very nice of you."

"The British embassy still has no word on the body."

"He's in heaven, Frank."

"Right." He asked her, "Did Henry get that skull to the right people?"

"He did." She suggested, "Maybe we could meet in Berini."

Purcell didn't know who she meant by "we." He said, "I'll let you know when I'm going."

"I'll be your translator."

He smiled at her. They both stayed silent, then he asked her, "Tell me again why they let us go."

"Because they knew we were chosen."

"So was Father Armano, and he spent forty years in a cell."

"The Falashas are all gone from Shoan, and the monks were leaving the black monastery with the Grail."

"Right." It was more than the monks thinking they were chosen.

He looked again at the Ethiopian College, where a group of monks were entering, and he thought back to the black monastery, which was now abandoned. The monks had packed a dozen donkey carts, and presumably taken the Holy Grail and the Lance of Longinus with them, though Vivian somehow got the impression that the Lance was spectral, and appeared by itself wherever the Grail was.

In any case, the monks had taken them—he, Vivian, and Henry—with them, and when they reached the monastery of Kirkos on Lake Tana, their three uninvited guests were put in a small boat with two oarsmen who rowed them across the lake to the mouth of the Blue Nile. The oarsmen left them, and the boat continued on in the swift current of the river with Purcell at the helm, across the border into Sudan until it reached Khartoum, where the American embassy helped get the three refugee reporters on a flight to Cairo.

Purcell had chosen to stay in Cairo for a few days to visit his apartment and see some people at the AP office. Henry and Vivian had gone on to Rome. And when Purcell had joined them, he discovered, not to his complete surprise, that Henry and Vivian were at the Excelsior together.

As he'd thought, and as he'd always known, Henry and Vivian were better suited for each other. But better is not best, and though he was angry—and hurt—he was also concerned about Vivian. He still liked Henry, but not as much as Henry liked himself. He would have told Vivian this—as a friend—but she might think it was coming from a jealous ex-lover. So he wasn't going to say anything now.

He said to Vivian, "I meant to ask you—what were we chosen for?"

"I've thought about it. I think we were chosen to give some meaning to Father Armano's life. I think God blessed him, and sent him to us so he could die with peace in his heart."

"Okay. But why us?"

She smiled at him. "There must be something special about us."

"There was—we were the only ones around."

"Don't start being cynical again." She asked him, "How can you be cynical after what you saw?"

"I'm not sure what I saw."

"I am."

"I envy you."

"Open your heart, Frank." She reminded him, "If you believe in love, you believe in God." She asked him, "Do you believe in love?"

"You shouldn't have to ask that." He looked at his watch again. "I have to go." He stood. "Tell Henry I said good-bye. And tell him I'll see him next time I'm in Rome."

She stood, too, and they looked at each other.

He thought she was going to suggest that he walk with her along the path, toward Henry's office. But she didn't.

He said to her, "I wish you all the happiness in the world."

"I wish you God's peace and God's love."

"You, too."

"We have a bond that can never be broken."

"We do."

There wasn't much else to say, and he didn't want it to be awkward or emotional, so he said, "Take care," turned, and walked away.

This was the first time his sense of loss was not made easier by a sense of relief. In fact, he felt as though he were walking away from life.

Purcell knew never to look back, but this time something made him look back. She was standing near the bench, watching him.

He took a few more paces, then turned and looked at her again, and she was still looking at him.

He walked back to where she was standing, and she came to meet him.

They stopped a few feet from one another and he saw she had tears in her eyes.

He asked her, "Where's Henry?"

"I told him not to come."

He nodded.

She reminded him, "You said you'd take me back."

He'd thought it was a moot question, but apparently it was not.

She smiled. "Are you taken?"

"No."

"You are now."

He didn't know what to say, so he asked, "Would you like to take a walk?"

She put her arm through his and they walked through the Vatican park.

She reminded him, "You said we'd return to the Capitoline Hill."

"Right." He asked her, "Are your things in my room at the Forum?"

"I'm not that presumptuous." She let him know, "They're in the lobby." She also let him know, "We have been chosen for each other. Believe it."

"I believe it."

Acknowledgments

I'd like to first thank Rolf Zettersten, publisher of Center Street, for taking an early and earnest interest in my idea, pitched in a bar, of me rewriting and him republishing *The Quest*. It's not often that good decisions are made during cocktails, and less often does that idea survive the sober light of day. I am grateful for Rolf's enthusiasm and long friendship.

Rolf assigned a longtime friend of mine, Kate Hartson, as my editor. Kate read the original version of *The Quest* and immediately saw what needed to be done—more sex. Or, more romance. She helped guide my fictitious characters through their relationships and emotional turmoils while nudging the author toward a happy ending. Much gratitude to Kate for all her help and patience as I missed every deadline but the last.

Many thanks to my assistant Patricia Chichester, who loved this book even while we were both bleary-eyed from late nights spent writing, typing, rewriting, and retyping. Patricia's careful and quick work on all aspects of the manuscript, including research and working closely with Kate Hartson, made this book possible.

Thanks, too, to my assistant Dianne Francis, who also burned the midnight oil to keep the office running, and who became Nelson DeMille while I was locked in my writing cell. Thank you, Dianne, for keeping the world at bay.

Another good decision, made over vino at a long lunch, was my joining up with Jennifer Joel and Sloan Harris, literary agents extraordinaire, at International Creative Management Partners. Jenn and I go back many years, and Sloan had not had the pleasure of my company until we met at that fateful lunch. We all clicked, and I'm happy and proud to be represented by true professionals.

No writer should try to read a publishing or movie contract, or try to deal with the U.S. Copyright Office. I have been fortunate to have as a friend and attorney David Westermann, who won't let me sign my name to anything he hasn't read and revised—including his checks. Thanks, Dave, for your good counsel.

When I first wrote *The Quest* in 1975, my childhood friend Thomas Block, who was a young pilot for Allegheny Airlines, helped with the flying scenes. Thirty-eight years later, I asked the still-young US Airways retired Captain Block to take another look at the flying scenes in the book, which he did. He assured me that he had gotten it right the first time, and that the principles of flight had not changed all that much in the past thirty-eight years. I thanked Tom in 1975 for his time and advice, so I don't need to do it again—but I will. Thanks, Tom.

And last, but never least, I thank my young bride, Sandy DeMille, who said to me, when I was having doubts during the rewriting of *The Quest*, "This is some of the best writing you've ever done." That set the standard, and I remembered those words every time I sat down to face a blank page. As Ovid said, "Scribire iussit amor"—Love bade me write.

If I wanted to see assholes all day, I would have become a proctologist. Instead, I watch assholes for my country.

I was parked in a black Chevy Blazer down the street from the Russian Federation mission to the United Nations on East Sixty-Seventh Street in Manhattan, waiting for an asshole named Vasily Petrov to appear. Petrov is a colonel in the Russian Foreign Intelligence Service—the SVR in Russian—which is the equivalent to our CIA, and the successors to the Soviet KGB. Vasily—who we have affectionately code-named Vaseline—has diplomatic status as Deputy Representative to the UN for Human Rights Issues—which is a joke—but his real job is SVR Legal Resident in New York—the equivalent of a CIA station chief. I have had Colonel Petrov under the eye on previous occasions; and though I've never met him, he's reported to be a very dangerous man, and thus an asshole.

I'm John Corey, by the way, former NYPD homicide detective, now working for the federal government as a contract agent. My NYPD career was cut short by three bullets that left me seventy-five percent disabled (twenty-five percent per bullet?) for retirement pay purposes. In fact, there's nothing wrong with me physically, though the mental health exam for this job was a bit of a challenge.

Anyway, sitting next to me behind the wheel was a young lady who I'd worked with before, Tess Faraday. Tess was maybe early thirties, auburn hair, tall, trim, and attractive. Also in the SUV, looking over my shoulder was my wife, Kate Mayfield, who was actually in Washington, but I could feel her presence. If you know what I mean.

Tess asked me, "Do I have time to go to the john, John?"

She thought that was funny. "You have a bladder problem?"

"I shouldn't have had that coffee."

"You had two." Guys on surveillance pee in the container and throw it out the window. I said, "Okay, but be quick."

She exited the vehicle and double-timed it to a Starbucks around the corner on Third Avenue.

Meanwhile, Vasily Petrov could come out of the mission at any time, get into his chauffeur-driven Mercedes S550, and be off.

But I've got three other mobile units plus four agents on legs, so Vasily is covered while I, the team leader, am sitting here while Ms. Faraday is sitting on the potty.

And what do we think Colonel Petrov is up to? We have no idea. But he's up to something. That's why he's here. And that's why I'm here.

In fact, Petrov arrived only about four months ago, and it's the recent arrivals who are sometimes sent on the field with a new game play, and these guys need more watching than the SVR agents who've been stationed here awhile and who are engaged in routine espionage. Watch the new guys.

The Russian UN mission occupies a thirteen-story brick building with a wrought-iron fence in front of it, conveniently located across the street from the Nineteenth Precinct whose surveillance cameras keep an eye on the Russians 24/7. The Russians don't mind being watched by the NYPD because they're also protected from pissed-off demonstrators and people who'd like to plant a bomb outside their front door. FYI, I live five blocks north of here on East Seventy-Second, so I don't have far to walk when I get off duty at four. I could almost taste the Buds in my fridge.

So I sat there, waiting for Vasily Petrov and Tess Faraday. It was a nice day in early September; one of those beautiful, dry, and sunny days you get after the dog days of August. It was a Sunday, a little after 10 A.M., so the streets and sidewalks of New York were relatively quiet. I volunteered for Sunday duty because Mrs. Corey (my wife, not my mother) had taken the Delta shuttle to DC this morning, and I'd rather be working than trying to find something to do on a Sunday. My mother would suggest church, though considering the weather, I should have called in sick and gone to the beach.

Kate was in DC because she's an FBI special agent with the Anti-Terrorist Task Force, headquartered downtown at 26 Federal Plaza. Special Agent Mayfield was recently promoted to Supervisory Special Agent, and her new duties take her to Washington a lot. She sometimes goes with her boss, Special Agent-in-Charge Tom Walsh, who used to be my ATTF boss, too, but I don't work for him or the ATTF any longer. And that's a good thing for both of us. We were not compatible. Walsh, however, likes Kate, and I think the feeling is mutual. I wasn't sure if Walsh was with Kate on this trip because I never ask, and she rarely volunteers the information.

On a less annoying subject, I now work for the Diplomatic Surveillance Group—the DSG. The group is also headquartered at 26 Fed, but with this new job I don't need to be at headquarters much, if at all.

My years in the Mideast section of the Anti-Terrorist Task Force were interesting, but stressful. And according to Kate, I was the cause of much of that stress. Wives see things husbands don't see. Bottom line: I had some issues and run-ins with the Muslim community (and my FBI bosses), which led directly or indirectly to my being asked by my superiors if I'd like to find other employment. Walsh suggested the Diplomatic Surveillance Group, which would keep me (A) out of his sight, (B) out of his office, and (C) out of trouble.

Sounded good. Kate thought so, too. In fact, she got the promotion after I left.

Coincidence?

My Nextel phone is also a two-way radio, and it blinged. Tess's voice said, "John, do you want a doughnut or something?"

"Did you wash your hands?"

Tess laughed. She thinks I'm funny. "What do you want?"

"A chocolate chip cookie."

"Coffee?"

"No." I signed off.

Tess's career goal is to become an FBI special agent, and to do that she has to qualify for appointment under one of five entry programs—accounting, computer science, language, law, or what's called diversified experience. Tess is an attorney and thus qualifies. Most failed lawyers become judges or politicians, but Tess tells me she wants to do something meaningful, whatever that means. Meanwhile, she's working with the Diplomatic Surveillance Group.

Most of the DSG men and women are twenty-year retirees from various law enforcement agencies, so we have mostly experienced people, ex-cops mixed with inexperienced young attorneys like Tess Faraday who see the Diplomatic Surveillance Group as a stepping-stone where they can get some street creds that look good on their FBI app.

Tess got back in the SUV and handed me an over-sized cookie. "My treat."

She had another cup of coffee. Some people never learn.

She was wearing khaki cargo pants, a blue polo shirt, and running shoes, which are necessary if the target goes off on foot. Her pants and shirt were loose enough to hide a gun, but Tess is not authorized to carry a gun.

In fact, all of the Diplomatic Surveillance Group agents are theoretically not authorized to carry guns. But we're not as stupid as the people who make the rules, so almost all the ex-cops carry. In situations like this where I bend the rules, my personal motto is *Better to face twelve jurors than to be carried by six pallbearers.* Therefore, I had my 9mm Glock in a pancake holster in the small of my back, beneath my loose-fitting polo shirt.

So we waited for Vasily to show.

Colonel Petrov lives in a big high-rise in the upscale Riverdale section of the Bronx. This building, which we call the 'plex—short for complex—is owned and wholly occupied by the Russians who work at the UN, and it is a nest of spies. The building itself, located on a high hill, sprouts more antennas than a garbage can full of cockroaches.

The National Security Agency, of course, has a facility nearby and they listen to the Russians who are listening to us, and we all have fun trying to block each other's signals. And round it goes. The only thing that has changed since the days of the Cold War is the encryption codes.

On a less technological level, the game is still played on the ground as it has been forever: Follow that spy. The Diplomatic Surveillance Group also has a confidential off-site facility—what we call the Bat Cave—near the Russian apartment complex; and the DSG team that was watching the 'plex this morning reported that Vasily Petrov had left, and they followed him here to the mission, where my team picked up the surveillance.

The Russians don't usually work in the office on Sundays, so my guess was that Vasily was in transit to someplace else—or that he was going back to the 'plex—and that he'd be coming out shortly and getting into his chauffeur-driven Benz.

Colonel Petrov, according to the intel, is married, but his wife and children have remained in Moscow. This in itself is suspicious because the families of the Russian UN delegation love to live in New York on the government ruble. Or maybe there's an innocent explanation for the husband-wife separation. Like they hate each other.

Tess informed me, "I have two tickets to the Mets doubleheader today." She further informed me, "I'd like to catch at least the last game."

"You can listen to them lose both games on the radio."

"I'll pretend you didn't say that." She reminded me, "We're supposed to be relieved at four."

"You can relieve yourself any time you want."

She didn't reply.

A word about Tess Faraday. Did I say she was tall, slim, and attractive? She also swims and plays paddleball, whatever that is. She's fairly sharp, and intermittently enthusiastic, and I guess she's idealistic, which is why she left her Wall Street law firm to apply to the FBI where the money is not as good.

But money is probably not an issue for Ms. Faraday. She mentioned to me that she was born and raised in Lattingtown, an upscale community on the North Shore of Long Island, also known as the Gold Coast. And by her accent and mannerisms I can deduce that she came from some money and good social standing. People like that who want to serve their country usually go to the State Department or into intelligence work, not the FBI. But I give her credit for what she's doing and I wish her luck.

Also, needless to say, Tess Faraday and John Corey have little in common, though we get along during these days and hours of forced intimacy.

One thing we do have in common is that we're both married. Her husband's name is Grant, and he's some kind of international finance guy, and he travels a lot for his work. I've never met Grant, and I probably never will, but he likes to text and call his wife a lot. I deduce, by Tess's end of the conversation, that Grant is the jealous type, and Tess seems a bit impatient with him. At least when I'm in earshot of the conversation.

Tess inquired, "If Petrov goes mobile, do we stay with him, or do we hand him over to another team?"

"Depends."

"On what?"

"No, I mean you should wear Depends."

One of us thought that was funny.

But to answer Tess's question, if Vasily went mobile, most probably my team would stay with him. He wasn't supposed to travel farther than a twenty-five-mile radius from Columbus Circle without State Department permission, and according to my briefing, he hadn't applied for a weekend travel permit. The Russians rarely did, and when they did, they would apply on a Friday afternoon so that no one at State had time to approve or disapprove their travel plans. And off they'd go, in their cars or by train or bus to someplace outside their allowed radius. Usually the women were just going shopping at some discount mall in Jersey, and the men were screwing around in Atlantic City. But sometimes the SVR or the military intelligence guys—the GRU—were meeting people or looking at things like nuclear reactors that they shouldn't be looking at. That's why we follow them. But we almost never bust them. The FBI, of which the DSG is a part, is famous—or infamous—for watching people and collecting evidence for years. Cops act on evidence. The FBI waits until the suspect dies of old age.

I said to Tess, "Let me know now if you can't stay past four. I'll call for a replacement."

She replied, "I'm yours."

"Wonderful."

"But if we get off at four, I have an extra ticket."

I considered my reply, then said, perhaps unwisely, "I take it Mr. Faraday is out of town."

"He is."

"Why have we not heard from Grant this morning?"

"I told him I was on a very discreet—and quiet—surveillance."

"You're learning."

"I don't need to learn what I already know."

"Right." Escape and evasion. Perhaps Grant had reason to be jealous. You think?

Regarding the nature of our surveillance of Colonel Vasily Petrov, this was actually a nondiscreet surveillance—what we call a bumper lock, meaning we were going to be up Vasily's ass all day. They always spotted a bumper lock surveillance, and sometimes they acknowledged the DSG agents with a hard stare, or if they were pricks, they gave you the Italian arm salute.

Vasily was particularly unfriendly, probably because he was an intel officer, a big wheel in the Motherland, and he found it galling to be on the receiving end of a surveillance. Well, fuck him. Everybody's got a job to do.

Vasily sometimes plays games with the surveillance team, and he's actually given us the slip twice in the last four months or so, which has earned him the name Vaseline. He's never given me the slip, but some other DSG teams lost him. And there's hell to pay when you lose the SVR Resident. And that wasn't going to happen on my watch. I don't lose anyone. Well, I lost my wife once in Bloomingdale's. I can't figure out the logic of a woman's shopping habits. They don't think like us.

Surveillances can be boring, which is why some people try to make it not boring. Two guys together talk about women, and two women together probably talk about guys. A guy and a woman together either have nothing to talk about, or the long hours lead to whatever.

In the last six months, Tess Faraday has been assigned to me about a dozen times, which, with one hundred fifty DSG agents in New York, defies the odds. As the team leader, I could reassign her to another vehicle or to leg surveillance. But I haven't. Why? Because I think she's asking to work with me; and, being a very sensitive man, I don't want to hurt her feelings. And why does she want to work with me? Because she wants to learn from a master. Or something else is going on.

And by the way, I haven't mentioned Tess Faraday to Kate. Kate is not the jealous type, and there's nothing to be jealous about. Also, like Kate, I keep my work problems and associations to myself. Kate doesn't talk about Tom Walsh, and I don't talk about Tess Faraday. Marital ignorance is bliss. Dumb is happy.

Meanwhile, Vasily has been inside the mission for over an hour, but his Mercedes is still outside, so he's going someplace. Probably back to the Bronx. He sometimes runs in Central Park, which is a pain in the ass. Everyone on the team wears running shoes, of course, and I think we're all in good shape, but Vasily is in excellent shape. Older FBI agents have told me that the Soviet KGB guys were mostly lard asses who smoked and drank too much. But these guys from the new Russia were into granola and health clubs. Their boss, bare-chested Putin, sort of set the new standard.

Vasily, being who he is, also has a girlfriend in town, a Russian lady named Svetlana who sings at a few of the Russian nightclubs in Brighton Beach. I caught a glimpse of her once and she looks like she has good lungs.

I did a radio check with my team and everyone was awake.

A soft breeze fluttered the white, blue, and red Russian flag in front of the mission. I remember when the Soviet hammer and sickle flew there. I kind of miss the Cold War. But I think it's back.

My team today consists of four leg agents and four vehicles—my Chevy Blazer, a Ford Explorer, and two Dodge minivans. We usually have one agent in each vehicle, but today we had two. Why? Because the Russians are particularly tricky, and sometimes they travel in groups and scatter like cockroaches, so recently we've been beefing up the surveillance teams. Today I had two DSG agents in the other three vehicles, all former NYPD. I had the only trainee, an FBI wannabe who probably thinks the DSG job sucks. Sometimes I think the same thing.

In the parlance of the FBI, the DSG is called a "quiet end," which really means a dead end.

But I'm okay with that. No office, no adult supervision, and no bullshit. Just follow that asshole. And do not lose that asshole.

A quiet end. But in this business, there is no such thing.

By J. A. Jance

J. A. JANCE

SECOND WATCH

A J.P. BEAUMONT NOVEL

HARPER

An Imprint of HarperCollins*Publishers*

Photograph of Leonard Douglas Davis on p. 367 is courtesy of Thomas C. Barron.

HARPER

An Imprint of HarperCollins*Publishers*
10 East 53rd Street
New York, New York 10022-5299

Copyright © 2013 by J.A. Jance
"Ring in the Dead" copyright © 2013 by J.A. Jance
ISBN 978-0-06-213468-4

First Harper premium printing: May 2014
First William Morrow hardcover printing: September 2013

HarperCollins® and Harper® are registered trademarks of HarperCollins Publishers.

Printed in the United States of America

Visit Harper paperbacks on the World Wide Web at
www.harpercollins.com

10 9 8 7 6 5 4 3 2 1

For Bonnie and Doug and all those
missing years, and for all those other great guys—
the ones who came home and the ones who didn't.
And also for Rhys, one of the ones who did come home.
Thank you.

SECOND WATCH

PROLOGUE

We left the P-2 level of the parking lot at Belltown Terrace ten minutes later than we should have. With Mel Soames at the wheel of her Cayman and with me belted into the passenger seat, we roared out of the garage, down the alley between John and Cedar, and then up Cedar to Second Avenue.

Second is one of those rare Seattle thoroughfares where, if you drive just at or even slightly below the speed limit, you can sail through one green light after another, from the Denny Regrade all the way to the International District. I love Mel dearly, but the problem with her is that she doesn't believe in driving "just under" any speed limit, ever. That's not her style, and certainly not on this cool September morning as we headed for the Swedish Orthopedic Institute, one of the many medical facilities located in a neighborhood Seattle natives routinely call Pill Hill.

Mel was uncharacteristically silent as she drove hell-bent for election through downtown Seattle, zipping through intersections just as the lights changed from yellow to red. I checked to be sure my seat belt was securely fastened and kept my backseat-driving tendencies securely in check. Mel does not respond well to backseat driving.

"Are you okay?" she asked when the red light at Cherry finally brought her to a stop.

The truth is, I wasn't okay. I've been a cop all my adult life. I've been in gunfights and knife fights and even the occasional fistfight. There have been numerous times over the years when I've had my butt hauled off to an ER to be stitched up or worse. What all those inadvertent, spur-of-the-moment ER trips had in common, however, was a total lack of anticipation. Whatever happened happened, and I was on the gurney and on my way. Since I had no way of knowing what was coming, I didn't have any time to be scared to death and filled with dread before the fact. After, maybe, but not before.

This time was different, because this time I had a very good idea of what was coming. Mel was driving me to a scheduled check-in appointment at the Swedish Orthopedic Institute surgical unit Mel and I have come to refer to as the "bone squad." This morning at eight A.M. I was due to meet up with my orthopedic surgeon, Dr. Merritt Auld, and undergo dual knee-replacement surgery. Yes, dual—as in two knees at the same time.

I had been assured over and over that this so-called elective surgery was "no big deal," but the truth is, I had seen the videos. Mel and I had watched them together. I had the distinct impression that Dr. Auld would be more or less amputating both my legs and then bolting them back together with some spare metal parts in between. Let's just say I was petrified.

"I'm fine," I said.

"You are not fine," Mel muttered, "and neither am I." Then she slammed her foot on the gas, swung us into a whiplash left turn, and we charged up Cherry. Given her mood, I didn't comment on her speed or the layer of rubber she had left on the pavement behind us.

I had gimped along for a very long time without admitting to anyone, most of all myself, that my knees were giving me hell. And once I had finally confessed the reality of the situation, Mel had set about moving heaven and earth to see that I did something about it. This morning we were both faced with a heaping helping of "watch out what you ask for."

"You could opt to just do one, you know," she said.

But I knew better, and so did she. When the doctor had asked me which knee was my good knee, I had told him truthfully that they were both bad. The videos had stressed that the success of the surgery was entirely dependent on doing the required postsurgery physical therapy. Since neither of my knees would stand up to doing the necessary PT for the other, Dr. Auld had reluctantly agreed to give me a twofer.

"We'll get through this," I said.

She looked at me and bit her lip.

"Do you want me to drop you at the front door?"

That was a strategy we had used a lot of late. She would drop me off or pick me up from front doors while she hoofed it to and from parking garages.

"No," I said. "I'd rather walk."

I didn't add "with you," because I didn't have to. She knew it. She also knew that by the time we made it from the parking garage to the building, we would have had to stop to rest three times and my forehead would be beaded with sweat.

"Thank you," she said.

While I eased my body out of the passenger seat and straightened into an upright position, she hopped out and grabbed the athletic bag with my stuff in it out of the trunk. Then she came toward me, looking up at me, smiling.

And the thought of losing that smile was what scared me the most. What if I didn't wake back up? Those kinds of things weren't supposed to happen during routine surgeries, but they did. Occasionally there were unexpected complications and the patient died. What if this was one of those times, and this was the last time I would see Mel or hold her hand? What if this was the end of all of it? There were so many things I wanted to say about how much I loved her and how much she meant to me and how, if I didn't make it, I wanted her to be happy for the rest of her life. But did any of those words come out of my mouth? No. Not one.

"It's going to be okay," she said calmly, as though she had heard the storm of misgivings that was circling around in my head. She squeezed my hand and away we went, limping along, the hare patiently keeping pace with the lumbering tortoise.

I don't remember a lot about the check-in process. I do remember there was a line, and my knees made waiting in line a peculiar kind of hell. Mel offered to stand in line for me, but of course I turned her down. She started to argue, but thought better of it. Instead, she took my gym bag and sat in one of the chairs banked against the wall while I answered all the smiling clerk's inane questions and signed the countless forms. Then, after Mel and I waited another ten minutes, a scrubs-clad nurse came to summon us and take us "back."

What followed was the change into the dreaded backless gown; the weigh-in; the blood draw; the blood pressure, temperature, and pulse checks. Mel hung around for all of that. And she was still there when they stuck me on a bed to await the arrival of my anesthesiologist, who came waltzing into the bustling room with a phony smile plastered on his beaming face. He seemed to be having the time of his life. After introducing himself, he asked my name and my date of birth, and then he delivered an incredibly lame stand-up comic routine about sending me off to never-never land.

Gee, thanks, and how would you like a punch in the nose?

After a second wait of who knows how long, they rolled me into another room. This time Dr. Auld was there, and so were a lot of other people. Again they wanted my name and date of birth. It occurred to me that my name and date of birth hadn't changed in the hour and a half during which I had told four other people the same, but that's evidently part of the program now. Or maybe they do it just for the annoyance factor.

At that point, however, Dr. Auld hauled out a Sharpie and drew a bright blue letter on each of my knees—*R* and *L*.

"That's just so we'll keep them straight," he assured me with a jovial smile.

Maybe he expected me to laugh. I didn't. The quip reminded me too much of the kinds of stale toasts delivered by hungover best men at countless wedding receptions, and it was about that funny, too. I guess I just wasn't up to seeing any humor in the situation.

Neither was Mel. I glanced in her direction and saw the icy blue-eyed stare my lovely wife had leveled in the good doctor's direction. Fortunately, Dr. Auld didn't notice.

"Well," he said. "Shall we do this?"

As they started to roll me away, Mel leaned down and kissed me good-bye. "Good luck," she whispered in my ear. "Don't be long. I'll be right here waiting."

I looked into Mel's eyes and was surprised to see two tears well up and then make matching tracks down her surprisingly pale cheeks. Melissa Soames is not the cry-baby type. I wanted to reach up and comfort her and tell her not to worry, but the anesthesiologist had given me something to "take the edge off," and it was certainly working. Before I could say anything at all, Mel was gone, disappearing from view behind my merry band of scrubs-attired escorts as they wheeled me into a waiting elevator.

I closed my eyes then and tried to remember exactly how Mel looked in that moment before the doors slid shut between us. All I could think of as the elevator sank into what felt like the bowels of the earth was how very much I loved her and how much I wanted to believe that when I woke up, she really would be there, waiting.

CHAPTER 1

Except she wasn't. When I opened my eyes again, that was the first thing I noticed. The second one was that I was "feeling no pain," as they say, so the drugs were evidently doing what they were supposed to do.

I was apparently in the recovery room. Nurses in flowery scrubs hovered in the background. I could hear their voices, but they were strangely muted, as if somebody had turned the volume way down. As far as my own ability to speak? Forget it. Someone had pushed my mute button; I couldn't say a single word.

In the foreground, a youngish woman sat on a tall rolling stool at the side of the bed. My initial assumption was that my daughter, Kelly, had arrived from her home in southern Oregon. I had told her not to bother coming all the way from Ashland to Seattle on the occasion of my knee-replacement surgery. In fact, I had issued a fatherly decree to that effect, insisting that Mel and I would be fine on our own. Unfortunately, Kelly is her mother's daughter, which is to say she is also headstrong as hell. Since when did she ever listen to a word I said?

So there Kelly sat as big as life, whether I had wanted her at the hospital or not. She wore a crimson-and-gray WSU sweatshirt. A curtain of long blond hair shielded her face from my view while she studiously filed her nails—nails that were covered with bright red polish.

Having just been through several hours of major surgery, I think I could be forgiven for being a little slow on the uptake, but eventually I realized that none of this added up. Even to my drug-befuddled brain, it didn't make sense.

Kelly and I have had our share of issues over the years. The most serious of those involved her getting pregnant while she was still a senior in high school and running off to Ashland to meet up with and eventually marry her boyfriend, a wannabe actor named Jeremy. Of course, the two of them have been a couple for years, and my son-in-law is now one of the well-established members of the acting company at the Oregon Shakespeare Festival in Ashland, Oregon.

The OSF offers a dozen or so plays a year, playing in repertory for months at a time, and Jeremy Cartwright has certainly paid his dues. After years of learning his trade by playing minor roles as a sword-wielding soldier in one Shakespearian production after another or singing and occasionally tap dancing as a member of the chorus, he finally graduated to speaking roles. This year he was cast as Laertes in *Hamlet* in the Elizabethan theater and, for the first time ever in a leading role, he played Brick in the Festival's retrospective production of *Cat on a Hot Tin Roof* in the Bowmer Theatre. (I thought he did an excellent job, but I may be slightly prejudiced. The visiting theater critic for the *Seattle Times* had a somewhat different opinion.)

It was September, and the season was starting to wind down, but there was no way for Jeremy to get away long enough to come up to Seattle for a visit, no matter how brief, and with Kayla and Kyle, my grandkids, back in school, in fourth and first grade, respectively, it didn't seem like a good time for Kelly to come gallivanting to Seattle with or without them in tow just to hover at my sickbed.

In other words, I was both surprised and not surprised to see Kelly there; but then, gradually, a few other details began to sink into my drug-stupefied consciousness. Kelly would never in a million years show up wearing a WSU shirt. No way! She is a University of Oregon Duck, green and yellow all the way. Woe betide anyone who tries to tell her differently, and she has every right to insist on that!

To my everlasting amazement and with only the barest of financial aid from yours truly, this once marginal student got her BA in psychology from Southern Oregon University, and she's now finishing up with a distance-learning master's in business administration from the U of O in Eugene. She's done all this, on her own and without any parental prompting, while running an at-home day care center and looking after her own two kids. When Kelly turned into a rabid Ducks fan along the way, she got no complaints from me, even though I'm a University of Washington Husky from the get-go.

But the very idea of Kelly Beaumont Cartwright wearing a Cougars sweatshirt? Nope. Believe me, it's not gonna happen.

Then there was the puzzling matter of the very long hair. Kelly's hair used to be about that same length—which is to say more than shoulder length—but it isn't anymore. A year or so ago, she cut it off and donated her shorn locks to a charity that makes wigs for cancer patients. (Karen, Kelly's mother and my ex-wife, died after a long battle with breast cancer, and Kelly remains a dedicated part of the cancer-fighting community. In addition to donating her hair, she sponsors a Relay for Life team and makes certain that both her father and stepfather step up to the plate with cash donations to the cause on a yearly basis.)

As my visitor continued to file her nails with single-minded focus, the polish struck me as odd. In my experience, mothers of young children in general—and my daughter in particular—don't wear nail polish of any kind. Nail enamel and motherhood don't seem to go together, and on the rare occasions when Kelly had indulged in a manicure she had opted for something in the pale pink realm, not this amazingly vivid scarlet, the kind of color Mel seems to favor.

Between the cascade of long blond hair and the bright red nail polish, I was pretty sure my silent visitor wasn't Kelly. If not her, then, I asked myself, who else was likely to show up at my hospital bedside to visit?

Cherisse, maybe?

Cherisse is my daughter-in-law. She has long hair and she does wear nail polish. She and my son, Scott, don't have kids so far, but Cherisse is not a blonde—at least she wasn't the last time I saw her. Besides, if anyone was going to show up unannounced at my hospital bedside, it would be my son, not his wife.

I finally managed to find a semblance of my voice, but

what came out of my mouth sounded croaky, like the throaty grumblings of an overage frog.

"Who are you?" I asked.

In answer, she simply shook her head, causing the cascade of silvery blond hair to ripple across her shoulder. I was starting to feel tired—sleepy. I must have blinked. In that moment, the shimmering blond hair and crimson sweatshirt vanished. In their place I saw a woman who was clearly a nurse.

"Mr. Beaumont. Mr. Beaumont," she said, in a concerned voice that was far too loud. "How are you doing, Mr. Beaumont? It's time to wake up now."

"I've already been awake," I wanted to say, but I didn't. Instead, looking up into a worried face topping a set of colorful scrubs, I wondered when it was that nurses stopped wearing white uniforms and white caps and started doing their jobs wearing clothes that looked more like crazed flower gardens than anything else.

"Okay," I managed, only now my voice was more of a whisper than a croak. "My wife?"

"Right here," Mel answered, appearing in the background, just over the nurse's shoulder. "I'm right here."

She looked haggard and weary. I had spent a long time sleeping; she had spent the same amount of time worrying. Unfortunately, it showed.

"Where did she go?" I asked the nurse, who was busy taking my blood pressure reading.

"Where did who go?" she asked.

"The girl in the sweatshirt."

"What girl?" she asked. "What sweatshirt?"

Taking a cue from me, Mel looked around the recovery room, which consisted of a perimeter of several curtained-off patient cubicles surrounding a central nurses' station. The whole place was a beehive of activity.

"I see nurses and patients," Mel said. "I don't see anyone in a sweatshirt."

"But she was right here," I argued. "A blonde with bright red nail polish a lot like yours. She was wearing a WSU sweatshirt, and she was filing her nails with one of those pointy little nail files."

"A metal one?" Mel asked, frowning. "Those are bad for your nails. I haven't used one of those in years. Do they even still sell them?"

That question was directed at the nurse, who, busy taking my temperature, simply shrugged. "Beats me," she said. "I'm not big on manicures. Never have been."

That's when I got the message. I was under the influence of powerful drugs. The girl in the sweatshirt didn't exist. I had made her up.

"How're you doing, Mr. B.?" Mel asked. Sidling up to the other side of the bed, she called me by her currently favored pet name and planted a kiss on my cheek. "I talked to the doctor. He said you did great. They'll keep you here in the recovery room for an hour or two, until they're sure you're stable, and then they'll transfer you to your room. I called the kids, by the way, and let everybody know that you came through surgery like a champ."

This was all good news, but I didn't feel like a champ. I felt more like a chump.

"Can I get you something to drink?" the nurse asked. "Some water? Some juice?"

I didn't want anything to drink right then because part of me was still looking for the girl. Part of me was still convinced she had been there, but I couldn't imagine who else she might have been. One of Ron Peters's girls, maybe? Heather and Tracy had both gone to WSU. Of the two, I'd always had a special connection with the younger one, Heather. As a kid she was a cute little blond-haired beauty whose blue-eyed grin had kept me in my place, properly wrapped around her little finger. At fifteen, a barely recognizable Heather, one with hennaed hair and numerous piercings, had gone into full-fledged off-the-rails teenage rebellion, complete with your basic bad-to-the-bone boyfriend.

In the aftermath of said boyfriend's death, unlamented by anyone *but* Heather, her father and stepmother had managed to get the grieving girl on track. She had reenrolled in school, graduated from high school, and gone on to a successful college experience. One thing I did know clearly—this was September. That meant that, as far as I knew, Heather was off at school, too, working on a Ph.D. somewhere in the wilds of New Mexico. So, no, my mysterious visitor couldn't very well be Heather Peters, either.

Not taking my disinterested answer about wanting something to drink for a real no, the nurse handed me a glass with water and a straw bent in my direction. "Drink," she said. I took a reluctant sip, but I was still looking around the room; still searching.

Mel is nothing if not observant. "Beau," she said. "Believe me, there's nobody here in a WSU sweatshirt. And on my way here from the lobby, I didn't meet anybody in the elevator or the hallway who was wearing one, either."

"Probably just dreaming," the nurse suggested. "The stuff they use in the OR puts 'em out pretty good, and I've been told that the dreams that go along with the drugs can be pretty convincing."

"It wasn't a dream," I insisted to the nurse. "She was right here just a few minutes ago—right where you're standing now. She was sitting on a stool."

The nurse turned around and made a show of looking over her shoulder. "Sorry," she said. "Was there a stool here? I must have missed it."

But of course there was no stool visible anywhere in the recovery room complex, and no crimson sweatshirt, either.

The nurse turned to Mel. "He's going to be here for an hour or so, and probably drifting in and out of it for most of that time. Why don't you go get yourself a bite to eat? If you leave me your cell phone number, I can let you know when we're moving him to his room."

Allowing herself to be convinced, Mel kissed me again. "I am going to go get something," she said.

"You do that," I managed. "I think I'll just nap for a while."

My eyelids were growing heavy. I could feel myself drifting. The din of recovery room noise retreated, and just that quickly, the blonde was back at my bedside, sitting on a rolling stool that seemed to appear and disappear like magic at the same time she did. The cascade of swinging hair still shielded her face, and she was still filing her nails.

I've had recurring dreams on occasion, but not very often. Most of the time it's the kind of thing where something in the dream, usually something bad, jars me awake. When I go back to sleep, the dream picks up again, sometimes in exactly the same place, but a slightly different starting point can lead to a slightly different outcome.

This dream was just like that. I was still in the bed

in the recovery room, but Mel was gone and so was my nurse. Everyone else in the room was faded and fuzzy, like from the days before high-def appeared. Only the blonde on the stool stood out in clear relief against everything else.

"Who are you?" I asked. "What are you doing here? What do you want?"

She didn't look up. "You said you'd never forget me," she said accusingly, "but you have, haven't you?"

I was more than a little impatient with all the phony game playing. "How can I tell?" I demanded. "You won't even tell me your name."

"My name is Monica," she answered quietly. "Monica Wellington."

Then she lifted her head and turned to face me. Once the hair was swept away, however, I was appalled to see that there was no face at all. Instead, what peered at me over the neck of the crimson sweatshirt was nothing but a skull, topped by a headful of gorgeous long blond hair, parted in the middle.

"You promised my mother that you'd find out who did it," she said. "You never did."

With that she was gone, plunging me into a strange existence where the boundaries between memory and dream blurred somehow, leaving me to relive that long-ago time in every jarring detail.

CHAPTER 2

When it comes to boring, nothing beats second watch on a Sunday afternoon. It's a time when nothing much happens. Good guys and bad guys alike tend to spend their Sunday afternoons at home. On a sunny early spring day, like this one, the good guys might be dragging their wintered-over barbecue grills out of storage and giving them a first-of-the-season tryout. The bad guys would probably be nursing hangovers of one kind or another and planning their next illegal exploit.

Rory MacPherson was at the wheel of our two-year-old police-pursuit Plymouth Fury as we tooled around the streets of Seattle's Central West Precinct. We were supposedly on patrol, but with nothing much happening on those selfsame streets, we were mostly out for a Sunday afternoon drive, yakking as we went.

Mac and I were roughly the same age, but we had come to Seattle PD from entirely different tracks. He was one of those borderline juvenile delinquent types who ended up being given that old-fashioned bit of legal advice: join the army or go to jail. He had chosen the former and had shipped out for Vietnam after (a) knocking up and (b) marrying his high school sweetheart. The army had done as promised and made a man out of him. He'd come home to the "baby killer" chorus and had gone to work for the Seattle Police Department because it was a place where a guy with a high school diploma could make enough money to support a wife and, by then, two kids. He had been there ever since, first as a beat cop and now working patrol, but his long-term goal was to transfer over to the Motorcycle unit.

Mac's wife, Melody, stayed home with the kids. From what I could tell from his one-sided version of events, the two of them constantly squabbled over finances. No matter how much overtime Mac worked, there was never enough money to go around. Melody wanted to go to work. Mac was adamantly opposed. Melody was reading too many books and, according to him, was in danger of turning into one of those scary bra-burning feminists.

From my point of view, letting Melody go out and get a job seemed like a reasonable solution. It's what Karen and I had decided to do. She had been hired as a secretary at the Weyerhaeuser corporate headquarters, but we had both regarded her work there as just a job—as a temporary measure rather than a career—because our ultimate goal, once we finally got around to having kids, had been for Karen to stay home and look after them, and that's what she was doing now.

In that regard, our story was different from Mac and Melody's. The two of us had met in college, where I had snagged Karen away from the clutches of one of my fraternity brothers, a pompous ass named Maxwell

Cole. Due to the advent of the pill, we did *not* get "in trouble" before we got married, but it wasn't for lack of trying. My draft number came up at about the same time I graduated from the University of Washington, so I joined up before I was drafted. Karen was willing to get married before I shipped out; I insisted on waiting.

Once I came home, also to the by-then-routine "baby-killer" chorus, Karen and I did get married. I went to work at Seattle PD, while Karen kept the job at Weyerhaeuser she had gotten while I was in the service. It's possible that Karen had a few bra-burning tendencies of her own, but it didn't seem like that big an issue for either one of us at the time, not back when we were dating. For one thing, we were totally focused on doing things the "right way." We put off having kids long enough to buy the house on Lake Tapps. Now that Scott had just turned one, we were both grateful to be settled.

Yes, I admit that driving from Lake Tapps to downtown Seattle is a long commute. That's one of the reasons I drove a VW bug, for fuel economy, but as far as this former city kid is concerned, being able to raise our kids in the country rather than the city makes the drive and the effort worthwhile.

I was raised in Seattle's Ballard neighborhood, where I was one of the few kids around with a single mother. My mom supported us by working at home as a seamstress. Growing up in poverty was one of the reasons I was determined to raise my own kids with two parents and a certain amount of financial security. I had my eye on being promoted to investigations, preferably Homicide. I had taken the exam, but so far there weren't any openings.

Karen and I had both had lofty and naive ideas about

how her stay-at-home life would work. However, with one baby still in diapers and with another on the way, reality had set in in a very big way. From Karen's point of view, her new noncareer path wasn't at all what it was cracked up to be. She was bored to tears and had begun to drop hints about being sold a bill of goods. The long commute meant that my workdays were longer, too. She wanted something more in her life than all Scotty, all the time. She also wanted me to think about some other kind of job where there wouldn't be shift work. She wanted a job for me that would allow us to establish a more regular schedule, one where I could be home on weekends like other people. The big problem for me with that idea was that I loved what I did.

So that's how me and Mac's second-watch shift was going that Sunday afternoon. We had met up at Bob Murray's Doghouse for a hearty Sunday brunch that consisted of steak and eggs, despite the warning on the menu specifying that the tenderness of the Doghouse's notoriously cheap steaks was "not guaranteed." I believe it's possible—make that likely—that we both had some hair of the dog. Mac had a preshift Bloody Mary and I had a McNaughton's and water in advance of heading into the cop shop in downtown Seattle.

Once we checked our Plymouth Fury out of the motor pool, Mac did the driving, as usual. When we were together, I was more than happy to relinquish the wheel. My solitary commutes back and forth from Lake Tapps gave me plenty of "drive time." During Mac's and my countless hours together in cars, we did more talking than anything else.

Mac and I were both Vietnam vets, but we did *not* talk about the war. What we had seen and done there was still too raw and hurtful to talk about, and what happened to us after we came back home was even more so. As a result we steadfastly avoided any discussion that might take us too close to that painful reality. Instead, we spent lots of time talking about the prospects for the newest baseball team in town, the second coming of the Seattle Rainiers, to have a winning season.

Mac was still provoked that the "old" Seattle Rainiers, transformed into the Seattle Pilots, had joined the American League and boogied off to Milwaukee. I didn't have a strong feeling about any of it, so I just sat back and let Mac rant. Finished with that, he went on to a discussion of his son, Rolly, short for Roland. For Mac it was only a tiny step from discussing Seattle's pro baseball team to his son's future baseball prospects, even though Rolly was seven and doing his first season of T-ball, complicated by the unbelievable fact that Melody had signed up to be the coach of Rolly's team.

My eyes must have glazed over about then. At our house, Karen and I were still up to our armpits in diapers. By the way, when I say the word "we" in regard to diapers, I mean it. I did my share of diaper changing. From where I stood in the process of child rearing, thinking about T-ball or even Little League seemed to be in the very distant future.

What I really wanted right about then was a cigarette break. Mac had quit smoking months earlier. Out of deference to him, I didn't smoke in the patrol car, but at times I really wanted to.

It must have been close to four thirty when a call came in over our two-way radio. Two kids had been meandering around the railroad yard at the base of Magnolia Bluff. Somewhere near the bluff they had found what they thought was an empty oil drum. When they pried off the top, they claimed, they had discovered a dead body inside. I told Dispatch that we were on our way, but Mac didn't exactly put the pedal to the metal.

"I'll bet dollars to doughnuts this is somebody's idea of a great April Fool's joke," he said. "Wanna bet?"

"No bet," I agreed. "Sounds suspicious to me."

We went straight there, not with lights and sirens, but without stopping for coffee along the way, either. We didn't call the medical examiner. We didn't call for the Homicide squad or notify the crime lab because we thought it was a joke. Except it turned out it wasn't a joke at all.

We located the two kids, carrot-topped, freckle-faced twin brothers Frankie and Donnie Dodd, waiting next to a pay phone at the Elliott Bay Marina where they had called 911. They looked to be eleven or twelve years old. The fact that they were both still a little green around the gills made me begin to wonder if maybe Mac and I were wrong about the possibility of this being an April Fool's joke.

"You won't tell our mom, will you?" the kid named Donnie asked warily. "We're not supposed to be down by the tracks. She'll kill us if she finds out."

"Where do you live?" I asked.

"On Twenty-third West," he said, pointing to the top of the bluff. "Up on Magnolia."

"And where does your mother think the two of you are?" I asked.

Frankie, who may have been the ringleader, made a face at his brother, warning Donnie not to answer, but he did anyway.

"She dropped us off at the Cinerama to see *Charlotte's*

Web. We tried to tell her that's a kids' movie, but she didn't listen. So after she drove away, we caught a bus and came back here to look around. We've found some good stuff here—a broken watch, a jackknife, a pair of false teeth."

Nodding, Frankie added his bit. "Halfway up the hill we found a barrel. We thought there might be some kind of treasure in it. That's why we opened it."

"It smelled real bad," Donnie said, holding his nose and finishing his brother's thought. "I thought I was going to puke."

"How do you know a body was inside?" I asked.

"We pushed it away from us. When it rolled the rest of the way down the hill, she fell out. She wasn't wearing any clothes."

"That's why we couldn't tell our mother," Donnie concluded, "and that's when we went to the marina to call for help."

"How about if you show us," Mac suggested.

We let the two kids into the back of the patrol car. They were good kids, and the whole idea of getting into our car excited them. Kids who have had run-ins with cops are not thrilled to be given rides in patrol cars. Following their pointed directions, we followed an access road on the far side of Pier 91. There were no gates, no barriers, just a series of NO TRESPASSING signs that they had obviously ignored, and so did we.

The road intersected with the path the barrel had taken on its downhill plunge. Its route was still clearly visible where a gray, greasy film left a trail through the hillside's carpet of newly sprung springtime weeds and across the dirt track in front of us. What looked like a bright yellow fifty-gallon drum had come to a stop some fifteen yards farther on at the bottom of the steep incline. The torso of a naked female rested half inside and half outside the barrel. The body was covered in a grayish-brown ooze that I couldn't immediately identify. The instantly recognizable odor of death wafted into the air, but there was another underlying odor as well. While my nicotine-dulled nostrils struggled to make olfactory sense of that second odor, Mac beat me to the punch.

"Cooking grease," he explained. "Whoever killed her must have shoved her feet-first into a restaurant-size vat of used grease. Restaurants keep the drums out on their loading docks. Once they're full, they haul them off to the nearest rendering plant."

I nodded. That was it—stale cooking grease. The combination of rotten flesh and rotting food was overwhelming. For a time we both stood in a horrified stupor while I fought down the urge to lose my own lunch and wondered if the victim had been dead or alive when she had been sealed inside her grease-filled prison.

Eventually the urgent cawing of a flock of crows wheeling overhead broke our stricken silence. Their black wings flapped noisily against the early April blue sky. I'm a crossword puzzle kind of guy. That gives me access to a good deal of generally useless information. In this instance, I knew that a flock of crows is called a murder, and this noisy bunch, attracted by what they must have expected to be a sumptuous feast, seemed particularly aptly named.

Mac was the first to stir. "I guess it's not a joke," he

muttered as he started down the hill toward the body. "I'll keep the damn birds away. You call it in."

Mac was a few years my senior in both regular years and in years on the force. He often issued what sounded like orders. Most of the time I simply went along with the program. In this instance, I was more than happy to comply.

I went back over to the car and leaned inside. Donnie and Frankie were watching, wide eyed, from the backseat. "Did you see her?" Donnie asked. At least I think it was Donnie.

"Yes," I said grimly. "We saw her. While I call this in, I want the two of you to stay right where you are. Got it?"

They both nodded numbly. It wasn't as though they had a choice. There was a web of metal screen between the cruiser's front seat and the backseat. The doors locked from the outside, and there were no interior door handles. Frankie and Donnie Dodd weren't under arrest, but they weren't going anywhere without our permission. They sat there in utter silence while I made the call, letting Dispatch know that they needed to summon the M.E. and detectives from Homicide. When I finished, I hopped out of the car and skidded down the steep incline. Mac was already on his way back up.

"I gave up on the damn birds," he muttered. "She's already dead. How much worse can it be?"

"That's all right," I said. "I think I'll go have a look anyway."

"Suit yourself," Mac said with a shrug. "Some people are dogs for punishment."

We had worked together long enough that he knew I wanted a cigarette, but we were both kind enough not to mention it. I waited until I was far enough down the hill to be out of sight before I lit up. I figured out of sight is out of mind and damn the smoke smell later.

Still, smoking was what I was doing when my eyes were inevitably drawn to the body. People passing car wrecks on the highway aren't the only people guilty of rubbernecking. Cops do it, too, and at that time in my career I was enough of a newbie that seeing dead bodies was anything but routine.

I found myself staring at the dead woman—what I could see of her, at least. She lay sprawled facedown on the weedy hillside, half in and half out of the barrel. A tangle of what looked like shoulder-length blond hair spilled out over the ground. A moment later, something red caught my eye, sticking out through the layer of greasy slurry. At first I thought what I was seeing was blood spatter, but that wasn't possible. Clearly the woman had been dead for some time. Once blood is exposed to the air, it oxidizes and goes from red to muddy brown. This was definitely red. Bright red. Scarlet. Inhaling a lungful of smoke, I moved a step or two closer to get a better look.

What I was seeing, of course, was nothing but tiny little patches of bright red nail polish glowing in the sunlight. And that was the single detail that stayed with me from that crime scene—the nail polish. Wanting to look pretty for someone, the victim had gone to the trouble of having a manicure, or else she had given herself one. Had she been going to a dance or a party, maybe? Had she been out on the town for a night of fun?

Whatever it was, when she'd done her nails, she hadn't expected to be dead soon, or that the vivid red nail polish would be the only thing she'd be wearing when someone found her body.

CHAPTER 3

"Jonas! Jonas. You really do need to wake up now."

That's my name—Jonas Piedmont Beaumont—but other than my mother and grandmother, both deceased now, almost no one calls me that—at least no one who actually knows me. I'm J.P., or Beau, or sweetie pie, or Mr. B. as far as Mel is concerned. I'm Dad for my kids and Grandpa for the grandkids. As a consequence, I wasn't exactly eager to wake up and see who was yelling Jonas somewhere near my left ear.

When I opened my eyes, I saw that the person behind the very loud voice was short and very stout. I was no longer at the base of Magnolia Bluff, dealing with a dead body and a crime scene. Instead, I was in a brightly lit hospital room with someone shaking my shoulder insistently.

"There you are!"

I was momentarily confused, but the woman, another nurse in scrubs, soon set me straight.

"This is called the recovery room," she announced

with a smile. "No more sleeping. I brought you some beef broth. Would you like to try it?" She handed me a paper cup filled with steaming liquid, but my nose was still full of the smell of death. My gag reflex cut in, and I almost barfed.

"Oops," the nurse said, taking back the cup. "Looks like it's too soon for that, then. We'll try the broth a little later."

Somewhere along the way I must have fallen asleep again. It was hard to differentiate how much was dream and how much was memory, although I didn't remember any other time when I'd had a dream that came complete with smells. I lay there for a time. While the room bustled around me, I struggled to put the pieces together. I understood that the girl who had appeared to me earlier, the one with the bright red fingernail polish, was Monica Wellington—the Girl in the Barrel—although at the time, the dead girl was a body without a name.

From my hospital bed in 2010, that case from 1973 seemed to be a very long time ago, but all of it was filed away in my memory bank. On that Sunday afternoon, it wasn't my case right then because at the time I had been assigned to Patrol rather than Homicide.

I remembered that I had turned away from the body and stubbed out my half-finished smoke, then pocketed what was left and gone back to the patrol car, where Mac and the two boys were awaiting the arrival of reinforcements. Surprisingly enough, Dr. Howard Baker, King County's newly appointed medical examiner, beat everyone else to the scene.

Even then, Doc Baker arrived at crime scenes reeking of cigar smoke and with a rumpled look that resembled an unmade bed. He always favored gaudy ties and tweedy jackets that never quite buttoned around his ample middle. In later years his hair would go completely white, but back then it was rapidly going from brown to gunmetal gray, and he wore it in a scraggly crew cut. Whole new generations of weather guys have to use hair gel to achieve that kind of spiky look. Doc Baker came by his naturally.

"What have we got?" he asked.

Mac stepped out of the driver's seat to do the honors. "Down there," he said, pointing. "That's where the body is—in that barrel down there. These two kids claim they found the barrel farther up the hill and rolled it down to where it is now."

Before Doc Baker could do anything other than look, Detectives Larry Powell and Watty Watkins showed up. Watty was ten years my senior. He'd been a detective for five years, but his knees were giving out, and he was angling for a desk job. Powell was ambitious. Everybody had him pegged for being on a fast track for assistant chief, but right then they were still equals, and they'd been partners for as long as I had been on the force.

Once Mac had briefed the new arrivals on the situation, Detective Powell took charge. He looked into the car where Donnie and Frankie were still waiting. "Can you show us where you found the barrel?"

Donnie or Frankie nodded. "Okay, then," Powell said, looking down the steep hillside to the spot where the barrel had come to rest. "Mac, you and Watty take the boys up onto the bluff to show you what's presumably the crime scene. I want you to locate it, and that's all. We'll need to process the scene, and I don't want it disturbed by a bunch of people tramping around in it. After that, Watty can take the boys' statements and then drop them off at home. In the meantime, Officer Beaumont, you're with me."

Powell probably picked the Beaumont part off my name badge. Even so, I was still new enough on the job that I was gratified to think one of the Homicide guys knew me by name. As soon as Mac and Watty drove off and we started down the hill, Powell clarified the situation and put me in my place.

"Watty's knees are giving him hell," he muttered. "Climbing up and down something this steep would kill him."

At the time, the idea of my ever having bad knees myself was inconceivable, but if Watty's failing joints gave me a chance to work with Larry Powell, one of Homicide's hotshots, who was I to complain? After all, that was where I hoped I'd be going eventually—to Homicide. When it came time to make the move, having someone like Powell in my corner wouldn't hurt a bit.

So I trotted down the hillside after him, determined to make myself useful. Minutes earlier the circling flock of crows had been the only visible scavengers at the scene. That had changed. The crows were now duking it out with an equally noisy flock of seagulls, but the flies had turned up as well. Somewhere in the fly world, the dinner bell had rung, and the troops had arrived en masse for the promised feast. A black cloud of them had appeared from out of nowhere. They swarmed around the barrel and its spilled contents.

With his evil-smelling stogie gripped between his teeth, Doc Baker waded into the mess to do his preliminary assessment. Once Powell and I came to a standstill behind him, I reached for my half-smoked cigarette. Seeing it, Powell gave a warning shake of his head.

"No smoking," he said.

"What about Doc Baker's cigar?" I asked, regretting the words as soon as I said them.

"Doc Baker's not my problem," Detective Powell said pointedly. "You are."

He reached into his pocket, pulled out a small camera along with several rolls of film, and handed them over. "You're in charge of photos," he added. "Now make yourself useful."

I did as I was told and went about snapping one picture after another.

Eventually the M.E.'s beefy helpers turned up with their gurney. By then it was clear that the only thing in the barrel besides the body was the rest of the grease. The victim was naked. There was no clothing and no identification, so the investigation's first problem was going to be identifying who she was. As the M.E.'s assistants wrestled the dead woman into a body bag for transport, Powell motioned to me.

"Let's work our way up the hill."

Spotting the track was easy enough, even if climbing the hill to follow it was not. The rolling barrel had left a clear path as it careened down the hill. In the process it had torn through thickets of blackberries and left a trail of flattened ferns and broken sprigs of grass along with slick patches of slimy spilled grease. Gravity had worked for the barrel on the steep hillside, but it worked against us. So did the thick tangles of blackberries. If you've ever hiked through blackberry brambles, you know climbing uphill through them isn't exactly a stroll in the park.

The sun was almost gone by the time we finally made it to the spot where Donnie and Frankie had found the barrel hung up on a bramble and pried off the lid. The lid was still there, and so was the stick the two boys claimed they had used to unleash what turned out to be their own private nightmare.

"Poor kids," Detective Powell muttered. "They had no idea what they were letting themselves in for."

By then enough time had passed that it was going on full dark. I was using the flash to take a few more photos when Mac came roaring down the hill with Detective Watkins limping along behind him.

"Are you about done?" Mac asked. "I'm parked up there," he added, pointing toward the top of the bluff.

"Did you see anything important?" Powell asked.

Mac shook his head. "There's a vacant house up there. It looks like the barrel started down the hill right at the end of the driveway."

"Any vehicle tracks?" Powell wanted to know.

Mac shook his head. "No such luck," he answered. "Asphalt."

I looked to Detective Powell for direction. "You two don't have to stick around here," he said. "I've called for lights and generators that should be here soon. In the meantime, I'd like you two to go back up and start canvassing the street. See if anyone noticed any unusual traffic coming or going from the house."

Expecting to be unceremoniously sent back out on patrol, I was glad to be given another job to do. Once we clambered our way to the top of the hill, however, we had a nasty surprise waiting for us. Someone had alerted the media. A clutch of reporters, attracted by the flashes of the camera, stood waiting for us next to the patrol car. Among them was one of my least favorite people in the whole world, a cub reporter named Maxwell Cole.

As I mentioned before, Max and I had been fraternity brothers at the U-Dub. We had not been friends. We became even less so when he showed up at a dance with a very cute girl named Karen. Not only did I snag her away from him at the dance, I married her, too. Talk about adding insult to injury, and Max was still pissed about it. While I was off doing my duty in Vietnam, Max found a way to stay home. He had gone to work for the *Seattle Post-Intelligencer*, where he was now firmly ensconced on the police beat.

"Hey, Beau," he said when he saw me. "What's the deal down there? I understand some neighborhood kids found a dead woman. Can you confirm that?"

He made it sound like we were the best of pals. The other reporters in the group, thinking he had some kind of an in, backed off and gave him the floor. It did my heart good to tell him, along with the rest of his newsie gang, everything I was allowed to say, which was pretty much nothing.

"Sorry," I said. "Can't confirm or deny."

Grimacing, Max went trudging after MacPherson, but Mac already knew there was no love lost between me and the *P-I*'s self-proclaimed ace reporter.

"You heard the man," Mac said. "Mum's the word. Check with the public information office."

We got into our patrol car. Mac took off like a bat out of hell, and nobody bothered trying to follow us. If they had, they wouldn't have had to go far, since we stopped again two blocks up the street, where Amherst Place West intersects with W. Plymouth Street.

"You take that side, I'll take this one," Mac said. "And you could just as well skip the house back there on the corner of Twenty-third. That's where Donnie and Frankie live. Their mother was a screaming banshee when we brought the boys home. She threatened to tear those poor kids limb from limb when she found out they had been down on Pier Ninety-one instead of where she thought they were, safely stowed at a movie."

"She was probably just worried about the boys messing around down by the railroad tracks," I suggested.

Mac gave me a wink and a lip-smacking, lecherous grin. "Maybe so," he said. "But I doubt it."

"What do you mean?"

"I think it had a lot more to do with Watty and me interrupting whatever it was she and her boyfriend were doing when we brought the boys home. From the looks of it, I'd say the two of them were getting it on pretty hot and heavy. The guys from Homicide are the ones making the big bucks. Since they'll most likely have to talk with the boys again, why should we have to deal with a lady tiger?"

Why indeed? With that, Mac and I hit the bricks.

It was close to dinnertime. As expected, the warm April weather had brought out the early-bird outdoor cooks. Smoke from a dozen separate Weber grills filled the evening air on the southern end of Magnolia Bluff. Residents of Seattle recognized this early bit of faux summer, the exact opposite of Indian summer, for what it was. Soon the sunshine and dry weather would be gone, not to return until sometime in early July. The people we dragged in from their backyard activities weren't especially welcoming or eager to talk to us. Other than using up some shoe leather, we gained precious little information in the process.

The house where the barrel's track originated had been vacant for several months, caught up in the midst of a rancorous divorce. One neighbor mentioned that she thought a sale was now pending, even though the real estate sign in the front yard didn't mention that. No one had noticed any unusual activity around the house in the past several days, although the same neighbor, a Mrs. Jerome Fisk, said she thought some of the neighborhood kids had been hanging around in the backyard of the vacant house and using it as a hideout for smoking cigarettes.

"I didn't turn them in for it, though," she told me. "Those poor boys have a tough enough row to hoe. I didn't want to add to their troubles."

"You're saying what exactly?" I asked.

"Their mother, you know," Mrs. Fisk added confidentially. "Amelia Dodd's a bit of a wild thing. Gentlemen callers coming to the house at all hours of the day and night."

"Gentlemen callers? You mean there's no husband in the picture?"

"Not so as you'd notice," Mrs. Fisk replied. "There are probably plenty of husbands in that group of men swarming around the honey pot, but I doubt any of them belong to her."

"You're saying she's a . . . professional?" I asked.

Mrs. Fisk shrugged. "Believe me, she has plenty of special male friends, and she doesn't appear to have any other kind of job, so you tell me. When I see those two boys left to their own devices so much of the time, it breaks my heart."

I know more than a little about what it's like to be raised as a fatherless boy. I looked at the houses on the street. When I was growing up, my mother and I lived in a tiny Ballard-area apartment located over a bakery. Because of the ovens down below, the apartment was warm in the winter without our having to turn on the heat, but it was hot, hot, hot in the summer. I remember very clearly that when clients came to my mother's place for fittings, I was expected to make myself scarce.

Nevertheless, this Magnolia neighborhood was a big step up from the walk-up apartment where I was raised. I suppose there were plenty of people back then, including my own grandfather, who called my mother a "loose" woman because there was no man in our lives and no ring on Mother's finger. Her fiancé, my father, died in a motorcycle wreck soon after she got pregnant and before they had a chance to marry. Defying her father's wishes, Mother refused to give me up for adoption. Instead, she had raised me entirely on her own. At the time I was interviewing Mrs. Fisk I had no idea that one day in the far distant future I would be reunited with long-lost members of my father's family.

At the time, I regarded Mrs. Fisk as a mean-spirited gossip, a little too eager to condemn her attractive young neighbor to anyone who would listen. It seemed likely that any number of old biddies had probably concocted and spread similar stories about my own mother. In many close neighborhoods and small towns, the single mother was, and still is, a target of scrutiny, if not suspicion.

But even if it was true—if working as a lady of the evening turned out to be Frankie and Donnie's mother's only means of support—she must have been successful in her line of work. After all, Magnolia Bluff was one of Seattle's solidly middle-class neighborhoods. If a working gal was able to earn enough money to maintain a house there, she had to be more of a call girl than a streetwalker, one with a well-heeled, generous clientele with maybe a few power brokers added into the mix.

I may have been relatively new to the force, but I was smart enough to figure out that in a pissing match between power brokers and a uniformed cop, I was the one who was going to come up with the short end of the stick.

In other words, Mrs. Fisk's comments combined with what Mac had said earlier about the mother in question made me more than happy to give Frankie and Donnie's house a wide berth. By the time we finished our canvass of the neighborhood and returned to the patrol car, the enticing aroma of grilling burgers had done its trick. It was now long after dinnertime, and we were both famished.

"Dick's?" he said, putting our police-pursuit Fury in gear.

"Amen," I said.

And that's where we headed, for Ballard and the nearest Dick's Drive-In.

When the first Dick's opened in the fifties, it was in Seattle's Wallingford neighborhood. For a kid too young to drive back then, it was close but no cigar. The only way to get there was to drive. I was a junior in high school when the one in Ballard opened, and it was cause for a school-wide celebration. That's where we headed now.

We were parked in the car munching burgers and fries when Mac said, "I wouldn't mind a piece of that."

For a moment I wasn't sure if he was talking about my burger or about the shapely carhop who had just delivered our food. Turns out it was neither.

"I'm talking about Frankie and Donnie's mom," he

explained. "The woman may have been mad as all hell, but she was a dish, all right—blond, stacked, and gorgeous."

That was when I finally got around to telling him what Mrs. Fisk had said about Frankie and Donnie's mom. When I finished, Mac shook his head sadly. "Too bad. She's probably out of my league."

"What's the matter with you?" I said. "You're married."

"That's right," he said. "But I'm not dead, and neither are you."

CHAPTER 4

Somewhere along the way I had fallen back asleep. When I awoke again it seemed like I was still smelling one of Dick's hamburgers, but it turned out Mel was sitting in the chair next to my bed, munching away on a burger of her own.

"Hey, sleepyhead," she said. "When are you gonna wake up? It's time."

It took a moment for me to make the transition from the world as it was in 1973 to the world as it is now, and it was quite a jolt.

"That was weird," I said.

"What was weird?"

There was a lot of stuff in my head right then that I didn't particularly want to discuss with Mel Soames. Generally speaking, we didn't talk about my life with Karen back when the kids were little or about what I referred to as the "good old days." Discussions of those always seemed to introduce a certain level of tension into the conversation.

I suppose I need to clarify this some. I'm not talking about old love affairs here. I'm referring to my carousing days when I'd have a drink or two before going to work without giving it a second thought. That, by the way, is one of the reasons I'm in AA now. So rather than go into any of those gory details with Mel, I glossed them all over.

"I was dreaming about hamburgers," I said, "and here you are eating one."

"Sorry about that. I was hungry, but don't expect me to share, because you're not allowed solid food yet. Jackie will be back in a minute."

"Who's Jackie?"

"Your nurse. She's on a break, but she gave me strict orders before she left. You can have water or you can have broth. That's it."

Right that minute, neither water nor broth was very high on my wish list. In fact, I still had to fight to keep my eyes open.

"Whatever they gave me really knocked me on my butt," I said.

"It's supposed to," Mel told me. "It's called anesthesia."

The same nurse reappeared—the stout one. This time I noticed that her name badge said she was Jackie Morse. That sounded familiar. Wait, Nurse Jackie. Wasn't that a television show of some kind? From what I remembered of the show, that particular Nurse Jackie wasn't exactly a picture of sweetness and light. It turned out this one wasn't, either.

"Okay," she said after checking my vitals one more time, just for the hell of it, "let's give that broth another try."

She handed me a cup with a straw in it. The stuff inside the cup was no longer hot—far from it—but to my surprise, when I swallowed a sip, it actually tasted good.

"We'll wait long enough to check your vitals one more time, Jonas," she said. "If you're still steady as she goes, we'll get you wheeled out of here and up to your room. That way you'll be somebody else's problem."

When people call me by the name of Jonas, I can never quite wrap my head around the idea that I'm the person they're addressing. Of course, in Nurse Jackie's case, when she used the word "we," it wasn't the royal we, by any means. It was the dismissive form of the word, the one favored by grade school teachers talking down their noses to classrooms full of bored kids.

It must have been the better part of another hour before Nurse Jackie finally pronounced that "we" were sufficiently recovered for me to leave the recovery room. As two uniformed attendants wheeled me into the hallway, I felt as though I had finally graduated from one of the levels of Dante's Inferno. They rolled me down the hall, into the elevator, and then up into a room that was bigger than some hotel rooms I've seen. It had windows, a view of other buildings, and room for more than one bed, although only one bed seemed to be called for at the time.

Once in my new digs I was sufficiently awake to be less concerned about Nurse Jackie and far more worried about what was to come. What if my new knees didn't work? What if I fell flat on my face the first time they tried to stand me up? What if I was destined to spend the rest of my life on one of those little scooters that they're always advertising on the boob tube? Mel was right there, of course, but I didn't mention any of those worries to her. Why would I? Instead, I lay in the bed, with Mel dozing off and on in the chair beside me. The only sound in the room was the soft whisper of the bedsore-preventing mattress under me. Other than that, I did my worrying in complete silence.

Fortunately, however, the orthopedic group didn't leave me there stewing and worrying forever. In advance of the surgery, I had read all the "what to expect" booklets my orthopedic surgeon had sent out. Yes, I had read the part about the "recovery team" getting people back on their feet as soon as possible. Somehow I didn't expect it to happen so soon, not the very same day as my surgery, but it did.

A bare three hours after I had been rolled into the new room, I was approached by a band of three waiflike young women, stick figures every one, who announced they were my PT squad and that they were there to get me out of bed and "up and at 'em," as the one who looked to be in charge told me jauntily.

I didn't share their enthusiasm, or their positive mental attitude. My first, unspoken response was a heartfelt "No way!" I was convinced it was much too soon and that the very idea of expecting me to stand up was an invitation to disaster. I'm sure I outweighed all three of them put together. I doubted they'd be able to support my weight. I could see myself falling to the brightly polished floor and smashing the new synthetic joints in my knees, to say nothing of my face, to pieces, but it was three to one—four, counting Mel—and they were not to be dissuaded. With the help of a strategically placed hoist, they pulled me up into a sitting position and then eased my legs over the edge of the bed. Once I was upright, they planted me in front of a walker.

I remember taking a very deep breath. The next

thing I knew, I took my first step and didn't fall down. That's when a very real miracle happened. For the first time in at least ten years or so, I realized that my knees didn't hurt. Of course, I was on plenty of pain meds at the time, but the steady pain that had ground away at me for years, waking and sleeping, simply wasn't there anymore.

With my helpers and Mel cheering me along, I took one small, careful step after another. I didn't walk all that far—out of the room and into the hallway. I went as far as the nurses' station and then back to my room, where they returned me to my bed. The whole excursion left me feeling inordinately proud of myself—as though I'd just run the equivalent of a marathon. Before my head hit the pillow, I was back in never-never land.

Through the years, booze has always been my drug of choice—booze and, a long time ago, cigarettes, too—but I've never been tempted to wander into the world of harder drugs. For one thing, my fear of needles makes it unlikely that I'd ever manage to be a successful IV drug user. But now, for the first time, lost in the dreamland world of medicinal narcotics, I got a taste of their allure.

For one thing, under the influence of the pain meds my dreams were astonishingly vivid and, in some cases, entirely welcome. Regular dreams tend to dissipate the moment I awake, but that was not the case here. The details stayed with me long after the dreamscape itself was gone. For all intents and purposes, it was a trip down memory lane.

Scenes from forty or even fifty years ago danced back through my head in full Technicolor splendor and in almost 3-D detail. In one, I was standing outside a hospital nursery looking down at the sweetly sleeping swaddled baby that was my newborn son, Scott. In another, I was a callow twenty-year-old youth, still a student at the University of Washington, sitting at my mother's hospital bedside and watching the morphine drip as she slowly, ever so slowly, lost her battle with breast cancer.

In others I walked long-ago crime scenes in more or less chronological order with partners both living and dead. In one I stood on the sidelines while medics tried to revive Milton Gurkey when he suffered a fatal heart attack after a violent confrontation with a homicide suspect. In some I was back in the car with Ron Peters, my former partner, when he was a young, gung-ho guy as well as a newly minted vegan. At the time, he hadn't yet taken his nosedive off a highway overpass and wasn't in a wheelchair, and I was still trying to figure out if I could work every day with a partner who wasn't a carnivore. In others, I was partnered with Big Al Lindstrom. In one I was even back in the elephant enclosure in the Woodland Park Zoo.

Eventually, in the dreams, as I had in real life, I found myself working with Sue Danielson. Even in the depths of sleep, my heart filled with dread, knowing that soon I would once again find myself in Sue's living room reliving the horror that had been part of my life from that day to this. Unable to help her, I had watched my partner and a great cop bleed to death on the floor of her own living room, gunned down by her enraged estranged husband. By the time I finally awoke fresh from the all-too-familiar scene of Sue's fallen-officer memorial, I was exhausted, physically and emotionally, and my cheeks were wet with tears.

That was about the time I began questioning whether I was dead or alive. Maybe I had died on the operating table and this trip through dreamland was God's way of having a little joke with me. Maybe He was using pieces of a lifelong jigsaw puzzle to allow my whole life to pass before my eyes in one disjointed scene after another.

But what had jostled me awake this time was the appearance of yet another nurse. This one was a beefy, much-tattooed guy named Keith who came to take my vitals, check my drains, and see if I needed more pain meds.

Why do they do that? People are in hospitals for a reason—to get better from an illness or to recover from surgery. If patients are sleeping peacefully, why wake them up to see if they're all right? Why not let them sleep until they wake up on their own, at which time they can ring the bell and let someone know if more medication is in order? But let's not even go there, because that's not the way hospitals work, and it isn't going to happen.

So after Nurse Keith confirmed that I was still alive, if not kicking, I tossed around for a while. Wide awake, I would have been glad to have Mel's company about then, but when Keith had woken me up, I'd finally insisted that she go home to get some rest. She had been at the hospital all day long and would willingly have stayed longer, but I told her I was in good hands and that she was the one who needed relief. She had issued instructions to all our friends that no one was to show up at the hospital that first day. It comes as no surprise that not a single person had dared disobey Mel's orders.

So there I was, alone and awake, with only the haunting memories elicited by those vivid dreams to keep me occupied. Karen was always a big Simon and Garfunkel fan, and one of her favorite songs by them was

"Sounds of Silence." In this case, the sleeping vision that was planted in my brain was that of the dead body of a naked girl, spilling out of a yellow barrel in the bright afternoon sunlight. Her long blond hair was in a greasy tangle and her fingernails, poking out of the mire, were covered with garish red polish.

Since I didn't have anything else to think about at the moment, I walked myself back through that pivotal case that would eventually pull me out of a patrol car and drop me into a desk in Homicide on the Public Safety Building's fifth floor.

That Sunday afternoon it didn't take long for Larry Powell and Watty Watkins to sort out the identity of the Girl in the Barrel. Her name was Monica Wellington. She was an eighteen-year-old honor student, valedictorian of her high school graduating class at Leavenworth High School, and a recently enrolled freshman at the University of Washington.

On Friday night, she had gone out on what was purported to be a blind date. When she didn't come back to the dorm, her roommates had called her parents in Leavenworth on Saturday to let them know. The parents in turn were the ones who had called in a missing persons report to Seattle PD later on that same day.

Missing persons reports often get short shrift, but Seattle was starting to see a flurry of women going missing, particularly young coeds. We were right on the cusp of what would later be called the Ted Bundy era. If a prostitute or two went missing back then, no one paid a lot of attention, but when female students from solid families, especially girls in good academic standing, went missing, some effort was made to connect the dots. In this case, the dots were connected early on.

By late Sunday afternoon, while we were still tramping around in the blackberry bushes on Magnolia Bluff, Hannah and Eugene Wellington had driven over to Seattle from Leavenworth. They were doing a full-court press on local television news outlets pleading for information about their missing daughter. One of the guys in missing persons, David Larson, who was interviewed by a local reporter and who had seen a photo of the missing coed, happened to hear that Larry and Watty were investigating a possible homicide. David took it upon himself to bring a copy of the photo to the morgue.

By the time Doc Baker got the layer of grease washed off the body, it was clear that the girl in the photo matched the face of the victim. The Wellingtons were staying at a low-cost motel up on Aurora, and Watty was dispatched with the unenviable job of giving them the bad news that an unidentified body had been found and that there was a good chance the victim would turn out to be their daughter. Watty was also tasked with bringing the parents to the morgue to do the ID.

I didn't know about any of this at the time because Mac and I were still too busy chowing down at Dick's, but Watty told me much later that Eugene Wellington, all six feet six of him, wept like a baby, all the way from the motel to the morgue. Once there, he was the one who fainted dead away when it came time to identify the body. It was Hannah, the mother, all five feet two of her, who made the identification and then helped her sobbing, grieving giant of a husband out of the room.

As for Mac and me? We finished out our shift and our burgers and went home.

Back when Karen and I were in the market for our first house, Boeing was going through a world of hurt.

That meant the local real estate market was in the toilet, which is how we'd lucked into and been able to afford our place on Lake Tapps.

The house was one of those Pan Abode manufactured homes, built of cut cedar logs and then put together elsewhere. Ours was one of the early models that had been built in the fifties. The original owner was halfway through a do-it-yourself remodel when he died of a heart attack. His widow blamed the house for doing him in and wanted nothing more to do with it.

That's why we got the place for such a bargain-basement price, but some of the projects that were left unfinished by the previous owner remained unfinished on my watch, too, and that continued to be a big bone of contention between Karen and me. She had one little kid, was pregnant with another, and wanted things done yesterday. I spent all week working and didn't want to spend my days off working on the house.

Lake Tapps is thirty-five miles south of Seattle. On a good day or late at night, I could get from downtown Seattle to the house in about forty minutes. During busy times of the day, the same trip could take an hour or longer. I used that time to decompress—to put the job away.

And that was how I used the drive that night. It was somewhere between the Public Safety Building and home that I finally realized what was wrong with the place where we found the barrel. There was no path there leading up the hill, no reason for the boys to have gone there. From the bottom to the top, the bluff had been covered with blackberry brambles. That realization brought me to a simple question: What had Donnie and Frankie been doing there?

It was an interesting question, but there wasn't much to do about it right then. I was in my VW bug. If I called to talk to Larry or Watty about it, I'd have to make a long-distance call from our home phone. We weren't dead broke, but with only one of us working, we were in a financial situation where pinching pennies was a necessity. Making unnecessary long-distance calls was not considered essential.

Monday and Tuesday were my regular days off. I figured the next time I went to work would be soon enough to broach that topic with the detectives. In the meantime, I did my best to put the Girl in the Barrel out of my head.

Monday was full of doctors' appointments. Karen had a prenatal checkup. Scott needed to see his pediatrician for some vaccination or another. I had a choice: I could stay home by myself all day—never a good option in Karen's book—or I could drive them both from one appointment to the next. So that's what we did. By the time we got back home, Scotty was screaming his head off while Karen and I weren't speaking. I chalked it up to a hormone malfunction and made the best of it. She went off to bed in a huff right after dinner. I poured myself a drink and then settled into my brand-new recliner to watch *Rowan and Martin's Laugh-In* without ever making it to the Monday-night movie.

The next day I spent pretty much on my hands and knees trying to fix an intractable plumbing problem in the house's sole bathroom. By the time Wednesday came around, I was more than happy to go back to work. When I got to roll call, I was surprised that Mac was nowhere to be seen.

"Where's Rory MacPherson?" I asked Sergeant Rayburn when roll call was over. "If Mac's not here, who am I supposed to ride with?"

"Go see Detective Watkins on the fifth floor," he said.

"But where's Mac?" I began.

"Moved over to Motorcycles. Now get your butt upstairs like I told you."

Arguing with Sergeant Rayburn was never a good idea, so I got in the Public Safety Building's disturbingly slow elevators and creaked my way to the fifth floor. It was a maze of gunmetal gray cubicles surrounding a center office where Captain Tommy Tompkins held sway.

The walls to Captain Tompkins's office were made of glass, which, despite the closed door, made everything that went on in there pretty much an open book, hence the moniker the Fishbowl.

In this instance, Detectives Watkins and Powell were sitting like errant schoolboys in the principal's office and being given a dressing-down. After asking a passerby for directions to Watty's cubicle, I scurried off there and hid out. Word of Captain Tompkins's incredibly foul temper had filtered throughout the building, even as far as Patrol. If he was reading someone the riot act, I didn't want to be within range of the captain's notoriously sharp-tongued verbal onslaughts.

When Watty appeared at the door of his cubicle a few minutes later, he took one look at me and shook his head. It was the kind of welcome look people dish out when a new arrival has not only stepped in fresh dog crap but also walked it into the house and onto the carpet.

"Great," he grumbled. "Just what I need this morning—a baby detective, fresh from Patrol, for me to babysit."

I didn't quite get it. Yes, I had taken the exam for detective, and I'd done all right on it, too—my score had been in the midnineties. That counted as a respectable score, even if it wasn't one that made you full of yourself. I had also been told there were currently no openings in Homicide, as in not a single one.

"I don't know who you know or what kind of strings you pulled to make this happen," Watty continued. "And having you dropped like a fifth wheel into an already ongoing homicide case doesn't do anybody any favors. As of right now, you're working days. Be here by eight on the dot. Got it?"

"Yes, sir."

"You'll go home when Detective Powell and I tell you you're done for the day," he continued. "We'll give you a partner to work with when Larry and I say you're ready to have a partner. In the meantime, you'll be doing whatever grunt work we hand you. You will do it cheerfully, with zero complaints, starting by getting me coffee from downstairs—cream and three sugars. And by the time I see you again, I want you to ditch the damned uniform. Understood?"

I replied with another "Yes, sir."

I wanted to tell him that I hadn't pulled any strings— that I had no idea how this had happened, but I didn't say any of that aloud. Instead, I went straight to the locker room and changed out of the uniform and into the jeans and grubby shirt I had worn in the car for my commute to and from Lake Tapps. I took a look at myself in the mirror and knew that outfit wasn't going to pass muster.

Karen and I had established a charge account at a Seattle department store called the Bon Marché. We generally used that account to the limit at Christmastime. I hoped there was enough room back on our line of credit for me to buy a new shirt, a tie, and a pair of slacks. The guys in Homicide all dressed that way, and I figured I should, too, if I was going to fit in.

I raced out through the lobby, caught the first northbound bus on Third Avenue, and made for the Bon at Third and Pine. Since the trip was all inside the Metro's newly established Magic Carpet zone, I didn't have to pay a fare. Once inside the store, I dashed into the men's department, grabbed up what I needed, changed into it in the dressing room, paid the bill, and then went racing for the next free southbound bus.

By the time I returned with Watty's coffee, I was a new man, properly attired in slacks, shirt, tie, and sports jacket, and in my wallet was a receipt for an expenditure that was going to send Karen into a snit the moment the monthly bill arrived in the mail. The fact that I now had a promotion that came with a minuscule pay raise wasn't going to change her mind about my reckless spending spree.

Watty looked me over as he took his coffee, then nodded in grudging approval. "Took you long enough," he said. "Now how about getting to work?"

"Sure thing. What do you need me to do?"

"Go to the motor pool and check out a car. You drive. I'll give you a lesson in doing homicide interviews."

Our first stop was at Seattle Rendering, located in the Columbia City neighborhood. The plant was a sprawling redbrick warehouse in a collection of similar redbrick warehouses. On a wooden loading dock I spotted a dozen yellow fifty-gallon drums that were dead ringers for the one Donnie and Frankie Dodd had found on Magnolia Bluff.

Watty and I made our way up the stairs leading to the loading dock and then let ourselves inside. The smell hit me at once—the odor of stale grease, only this time without the underlying hint of a dead body. A bullnecked man with the name STEVE embroidered on the pocket of his blue coveralls cut us off before we made it three steps inside. He was a huge, rawboned guy with hands as big as platters. He looked as though he could have taken on both Watty and me at the same time without so much as breaking a sweat. His beaky nose had apparently been broken more than once, and he was missing several front teeth. Looking at the guy, I wondered how an opponent had ever managed to get close enough to land even one of those blows.

"You got an appointment?" Steve asked, barring our way.

Watty held up his badge. "We're looking for the owner," he said.

"Name's Harlan Bates. He's back in the office," the guy said. "Follow me and I'll take you there. He don't like strangers wandering around out here unaccompanied."

Harlan's office was at the far back of the building, closed off from the rest of the warehouse by an unpainted plywood partition. Entry to the office was through a flimsy door with a single windowpane in it. As soon as our guide opened the door, a cloud of cigarette smoke flooded out into the warehouse. I hadn't had a cigarette since before my hurried trip to the Bon, and I breathed in the welcome taste of secondhand smoke with no small amount of gratitude.

Harlan Bates appeared to be shorter and wider than Steve, but he shared the same general physique and fa-

cial features. I guessed the two men were either brothers or cousins.

Harlan sat at a scarred wooden desk under a flicker-
ing fluorescent bulb, poring over a handwritten ledger
that was open before him. The desk was as grubby as
the rest of the office. An immense overflowing ashtray
sat stationed at the man's elbow, while a burning cigarette was clamped between his lips.

Harlan gave Watty and me a hard-eyed once-over.
"Who's this, Stevie?" Harlan demanded, speaking
through clenched teeth and without bothering to let go
of his cigarette. "Salesmen of some kind? You know I
don't talk to salesmen before noon."

"We're not salesmen," Watty interjected, holding up
his badge. "We'd like to talk to you about barrel number
1432."

There were two torn and scuzzy metal-and-vinyl
chairs positioned in front of Harlan's battered desk.
Without waiting to be invited, Watty took a seat on one
of them, and I followed suit with the other.

In response, Bates lowered the remains of his unfil-
tered cigarette from his mouth. Leaving a trail of ashes
across both the ledger and the desk, he returned the
smoldering butt to the ashtray and ground it out, spilling more ashes as he did so.

"What do you want to know about it?" he asked.

"Where was it last?"

Shaking his head in obvious irritation, Bates slammed
shut the open ledger. Then, spinning around on his
decrepit wooden chair, he returned the first book to
a dusty shelf behind him and pulled out another. The
second one looked very much like the first. He dropped
it onto the desk and opened it.

Dampening his tobacco-stained fingers with spit, he thumbed through worn, yellowing pages that were covered with neatly handwritten columns. Finally settling on a single page, he pulled on a pair of reading glasses and peered at the page with studied concentration.

"Dragon's Head Restaurant, in the International District," Bates said. "We dropped off drum number 1432 on Tuesday two weeks ago. Chin Lee, the owner, called here yesterday, screaming and cussing me out in Chinese because his drum had gone missing. He thought I was trying to cheat him or something. I had to send my team by to drop off a replacement late last night. Who the hell would steal a drum full of stale grease? I mean, what's the point?"

"And the owner's name is Mr. Lee?" Watty asked.

Harlan Bates nodded.

"Phone number?"

"You speak Chinese?"

Watty shook his head.

"Having a phone number won't do you any good. You need to go by and talk to him in person. Old man Lee doesn't speak English real well. He'll need his wife or one of his kids to translate for him."

It was Watty's turn to nod.

"Do yourself a favor," Bates continued. "Try the Mandarin duck while you're at it. Old man Lee may not speak much English, but when it comes to cooking, the guy's a genius."

"So you have people who drop off and collect the drums?" Watty asked. "How long before you get them back?"

"Depends on how much grease they use and how much they reuse, if you know what I mean. Places like the Dragon's Head are on a two-week cycle. Saving grease is what my mother used to do during the war. She'd take her can of it in to the butcher and get rationing coupons in return. I was little then, but it made a big impression on me. I guess I never got over it, and here we are."

Harlan Bates was maybe ten years older than me. By the time I was old enough to remember anything, rationing coupons from World War II were a part of the distant, unknowable past.

"They fill up the drum, then what?" Watty asked.

"You already met Stevie. He's strong as an ox. He goes out on the route with another guy, my driver. The two of them make sure the drums are sealed shut, then they tip them over, roll them into our truck, and bring them back here for processing while leaving empty ones in place."

"So where was Stevie on Friday night of last week?" Watty asked.

Harlan pulled a cigarette out of the almost empty pack in his pocket. If he'd offered me one, I would have taken it, but he didn't.

"Look," he said, taking the first draw. "You asked me about drum number 1432. I told you about drum number 1432. Now how about if you tell me what this is really all about?"

"Your drum was found at the base of Magnolia Bluff on Sunday evening," Watty explained. "There was a dead girl mixed in with what was left of the grease. According to the M.E., she had been dead for about two days before she was found. The victim was last seen on Friday night when she left her dormitory at the University of Washington to go on a blind date."

"So you're thinking Steve's the blind date?" Harlan Bates said with a harsh laugh. "Good luck with that." He wasn't the least bit upset about the question. In fact, a slow grin was spreading over his jowly face.

"Where was he?" Watty asked again.

"You ever hear the phrase 'queer as a three-dollar bill'?" Harlan asked.

Watty nodded.

"Well, that's Stevie for you. Doesn't look like a pretty boy by any means. And people who think they can push him around for it generally don't try that stunt a second time. But I'll tell you for sure, my cousin Stevie wouldn't be caught dead with a woman, and most especially not a coed from the University of Washington. He barely finished eighth grade."

"I still need to know where he was on Friday."

"Probably at home with my aunt Nelda and her cats, same as he is every night. Her place is over by the airport. He looks after her, but he wouldn't be driving around late at night because he doesn't have a license. Can't read well enough to pass the test. So if you're thinking he'd be out somewhere hanging out with a cute coed type, you've got another think coming."

"What about the driver?"

"His name's Manny Ortega, but I'm telling you, as far as Manny is concerned, it's the same thing."

"What do you mean the same thing?" Watty asked.

"Manny would be at home on Friday night and Saturday night, too, with Aunt Nelda and Stevie. She lives downstairs, they live upstairs."

"Wait, Stevie and Manny are a couple?" Watty asked. Something about his professional Homicide demeanor had slipped. He looked more than a little shocked.

Harlan Bates shrugged. "Whatever turns them on, I suppose. Before those two guys got into AA, they used to have some hellacious fights. Now they're both sober. Except for the occasional lovers' spat, I couldn't ask for a better team."

Watty said nothing. He seemed to be concentrating on closing his notebook and putting away his pen. If there was an interview lesson for me in all this, I doubt it was the one he had intended.

"Anything else, gentlemen?" Harlan Bates asked.

"No," Watty said quietly. "I believe we have everything we need at the moment."

We went outside and got back into the car. Watty hadn't told me where we were going next. I fired up the engine and a filtered Winston and sat there smoking with the car idling while Watty got on the radio. A few minutes later, the clerk in Records read off an address on Twenty-first Avenue South.

"That's where we're going?" I asked.

"Yup," Watty said. "We're going to go ask Harlan's aunt Nelda a few questions before we interview Manny and Stevie."

Tossing my half-smoked cigarette out the window, I turned and reached into the backseat for the ragged *Thomas Guide,* a dog-eared paperback collection of street maps for Seattle and King County that was standard equipment in every vehicle operated by Seattle PD back before the advent of GPS technology.

While we made our way south and west, Watty shook his head in dismay. "Just looking at that guy," he said, "I never would have guessed."

"Me, either," I agreed. "Never in a million years."

CHAPTER 5

The last thing I remembered, I had been lying awake, listening to the whispered murmurs of the mattress and the continuous motion of the passive-movement exercise machine and thinking about that long-ago time. I had no idea I had drifted off to sleep until good old Nurse Keith came hustling in to disturb my slumber yet again. It was still dark outside, but I saw the occasional flash of lightning in the window, accompanied by the low rumble of thunder.

"It's been pouring for over an hour now," he said. "I guess summer's over."

It was mind boggling to be transported across forty years in what seemed like the blink of an eye. In 1973 the very idea of a pair of guys living openly as a couple was enough to give even a seasoned homicide cop like Watty a bit of a pause. Back in those homophobic good old days, as far as most of us were concerned, the word "gay" had meant nothing more nor less daring than "happy."

I also recalled that way back then most nurses had been women. They wore white uniforms and funny white caps with a black bar across the top. Keith's colorful scrubs were a long way from that. First he took my vitals, and then he dealt with the surgical drains on both my incisions. I think he called them "pomegranates," or some other kind of blood red fruit, but that could just be my random access memory being screwed up due to the drugs. I did notice that Keith was wearing what looked like a wedding band, which might or might not mean what it used to mean. However, since he was clearly good at his job, I didn't ask about his personal life. It was none of my business.

I dozed again after Nurse Keith left, and it was probably the continuing rumble of thunder that took me back to that other time and place. When the next guy to come into the room was wearing a set of fatigues, I wasn't even surprised. The fatigues weren't the new desert-style BDUs that showed up sometime in the early eighties, but the old familiar olive green ones that we used back in 'Nam.

My new unexpected visitor walked over to the bedside table and pulled a deck of playing cards out of his pocket. He peeled off four cards and laid them out in front of me, facedown on the table next to my pitcher of water. I knew without looking that if I reached out and turned them over, they would all be aces of spades. I looked up and saw exactly what I expected: a crooked, chip-toothed grin; a handsome face; penetrating blue eyes; short blond hair. It may have been close to fifty years since I'd seen Second Lieutenant Lennie Davis last, but you never forget the face of the first guy who saved your life.

"Hey, asshole," he said, grinning. "You got old."

And you didn't. That's what I wanted to say, but of course I didn't. When you're in the presence of ghosts, even drug-induced ghosts, I don't suppose it's polite to point out that they're dead and you're not.

He turned and glanced around the room. "What's this?" he asked. "And what's wrong with you?"

"They fixed my knees. Replaced them."

He gave me a quizzical arched-eyebrow look that would have passed muster with *Star Trek*'s Mr. Spock.

"With what?"

"Titanium."

"No shit! They can do that now?" He shook his head in pure wonder.

The truth is, these days medical science can do a lot of things that they couldn't back then. A lot of military folks, our wounded warriors, survive injuries that were fatal back in Vietnam. They not only survive, they return to serve again. Not Lieutenant Davis. Not Lennie D.

He walked away from my bed and stood looking out the window where, framed by neighboring buildings, the Space Needle was barely visible in the rain-blurred distance.

"I wanted to come to Seattle for the World's Fair," he said. "By then I was already at West Point. Never made it."

Looking at him standing there, big as life, I felt a lump forming in my throat. He had been a smart guy. The first time I saw Lieutenant Davis, he was sitting outside his tent reading a grubby copy of *The Rise and Fall of the Third Reich*. I was new to C Company, and I wasn't sure that having a bookworm for a platoon leader was necessarily a good idea. It was mid-July and hot as hell in the Pleiku highlands, hot and dusty.

"At ease, soldier," he told me, once I introduced myself. About that time, he caught me looking questioningly at the book. "Ever read it?"

Reading books was always a chore for me. I only read for book reports, never for fun. The idea of spending an afternoon with a tome that looked as though it weighed in at well over a thousand pages wasn't my idea of a good time. I shook my head.

"The bad guys lose eventually," he said, "but it's a hell of a fight to take them down. When we're not out chasing Charlie, reading's about the only thing there is to do here. I'll be done with it this afternoon. I'll be glad to let you give it a try."

From the way he was holding the book, it looked as though he was only two-thirds of the way through. I may have been the new guy in town, but I knew better than to piss off the second lieutenant.

"Sure thing," I said. "I'd like that."

It's amazing to realize that life and death turn on such small exchanges.

"Thank you," I muttered to my hospital visitor. It was difficult to speak because of the lump in my throat.

"For what?"

"For saving my life."

"That was my job," he said. "You were one of my guys. So what have you done with yourself?"

"I wanted to help people," I answered. "I've been a cop, first at Seattle PD and later for the attorney general's office."

"Married?"

I nodded. I didn't say, "Third time's the charm," but that's what I meant.

"I never got to tell her good-bye," he said quietly.

He didn't say who. I knew Lieutenant Davis had been engaged at the time of his death, but that was all I knew. Once he was gone, I wasn't close enough to know all the gory details, and the guys who were close enough—the ones who were still alive—were all too broken up about losing him to talk about it. As far as they were concerned, Lennie D. was the best and the brightest. And if it's true that the good die young, what am I doing still hanging around?

"I knew you had a girl back home," I said.

It was his turn to nod. "Bonnie and I were engaged. I couldn't talk her into marrying me before I shipped out. We were going to get married in Japan on my R and R."

"Sorry," I said.

"Me, too," he said. "I just wish she knew how much."

Just then Mel appeared in the doorway. The moment she did, Lieutenant Davis disappeared. The playing cards on my hospital tray vanished. I hadn't thought I was asleep, but I must have been.

"Talking in your sleep?" Mel asked, entering the room like a fast-moving storm. "How are you feeling? Did you sleep well? Breakfast is on its way. The lady with the trays is two doors down the hall."

Just that fast, she swept away my nighttime's worth of strange visitations.

"I heard your voice as I was coming down the hall," she said, kissing me lightly on the forehead. "I thought the nurse might be in here with you."

"Nope," I said as brightly as I could manage. "Nobody here but us chickens." I wasn't about to tell her

I had been busy having a heart-to-heart conversation with a fifty-year-old Ghost of Christmas Past.

"I'm on my way to work," she continued. "Thought I'd stop by and check in with you before I hit 520."

The Seattle area branch of the attorney general's Special Homicide Investigation Team is located in the Eastgate area of Bellevue, across Lake Washington from our downtown Seattle condo. We used to cross Lake Washington on I-90, a bit south of the 520 bridge. Now, since the state has seen fit to start charging outrageously expensive tolls on 520—the Money-Sucking Bridge, as Mel calls it—traffic on it has dropped remarkably, while traffic on I-90 has gotten terrible. Since we can afford the tolls, we usually opt for less traffic.

"From here I'll take the scenic route," she said. "I'll go through the arboretum."

Nurse Keith came in just then. "Vitals before you get breakfast," he said, slapping the blood pressure cuff around my arm. While he was inflating it, I introduced him to Mel.

Melissa Soames is very easy on the eyes under the worst of circumstances. Dressed as she was for work, she looked downright spectacular, and I did notice that her looks weren't lost on Keith, either. Clearly my previous musings about his possible sexual preferences were totally off the mark.

"What's on the agenda for today?" Mel asked.

She was being a little too cheerful. That meant she was still worried about me, even though she wouldn't come right out and say so.

"Breakfast and then a round of physical therapy," Keith answered. "Jonas here may think he's on vacation, but he's wrong about that. The PT team will see to it that he doesn't just lie around getting his beauty sleep. We'll have him up and out of bed in no time."

"I told Harry I'd be in today," Mel said. "I already know he wants me up in Bellingham, but I could always call him and let him know I need to take another day off."

Harry was Harry Ignatius Ball, Squad B's hopelessly politically incorrect leader. We generally refer to him in public by his preferred moniker, Harry I. Ball, because it's usually good for a laugh, one Harry enjoys more than anyone else. The fact that Mel avoided using that name with Nurse Keith told me she wasn't in a light-hearted mood. I also knew that her asking for the day off wasn't going to work.

The previous week there had been a supposedly "peaceful" rally just outside the Western Washington University campus in Bellingham. Peaceful is a relative term, and this one had devolved into a window-smashing flash mob in which not just one but three WWU students ended up being Tasered by members of the local police department. Naturally, the errant students were claiming police brutality, even though so far the dash cams on the cops' patrol cars seemed to back up the officers' claims that they had considered themselves to be in grave danger at the time.

I'll never understand why kids think it's okay to come to "peaceful demonstrations" armed with baseball bats, but maybe that's just me.

As soon as the police-brutality claim was raised, Bellingham's chief of police, Veronica Hamlin, was on the phone to the attorney general's office down in Olympia, pleading for backup and for an unbiased investigation.

At that point, the police-brutality investigation could have landed with the Washington State Patrol, but Attorney General Ross Connors, as the ultimate boss of both that agency and ours, was the one who made the call to use Special Homicide.

I doubt Chief Hamlin was thrilled when she learned that Squad B, under Harry's leadership, would be the ones handling the investigation into her department and being responsible for pulling her bacon out of the fire—or not. After all, years earlier in her role as assistant chief, Ms. Hamlin had been the prime mover behind Harry's being given his walking papers from that very same department.

Sometimes what goes around really does come around. Of course, Harry wouldn't ever leave some poor street cop hanging out to dry just to get even. He insisted that the investigation be scrupulously unbiased, which is why, as soon as it came up on Friday, Harry had put Mel in charge. She had spent Saturday and Sunday in Bellingham conducting interviews, and had returned to Seattle late Sunday evening so she could be on tap Monday morning for my surgery.

"You know you can't do that," I said. "Harry needs you."

"Veronica Hamlin is a witch," Mel said. "She'd sell those two poor cops down the river in a minute if she didn't think that ultimately it would make her look bad."

"Which is why you need to go to work instead of hanging around here looking after me."

"What's the matter?" Keith asked, grinning at her. "Don't you trust us?"

A lady waltzed into the room carrying my breakfast tray. The food looked better than it tasted. The omelet was rubbery, the orange juice was anything but fresh squeezed, the toast was unbuttered and cold, and the coffee was only remotely related to the high-test stuff we make at home, but I was hungry enough that I ate it all. And I was glad when Mel gave me a breezy good-bye peck on the cheek and then took off rather than sitting there watching me eat.

True to Keith's word, the PT ladies appeared the moment breakfast was over. Once again, they pried me out of bed. Then they put a second hospital gown on backward to cover my backside while we hit the corridor and walked. I wasn't as worried this time, not as much as I had been the day before. I noticed that there were lovely pieces of art lining the wall—something that had escaped my notice the day before. I also noticed that this time the nurses' station didn't seem nearly as far away as it had the first time we went there. I climbed back into bed, proud of myself and thinking that was it for the day.

"Oh no," the therapist told me with a laugh. "Next up is occupational therapy. They'll be here in an hour or so. Those are the people who will teach you to go up and down stairs and get in and out of beds and cars."

Again, I wanted to say, "Already?" I guess it would have been more of a whine than a question, but my ringing cell phone spared me from embarrassing myself.

"How's it hanging?" Harry asked.

I already warned you that the man doesn't have a politically correct bone in his body.

"Better than I expected," I said.

"Thanks for insisting that Mel come in," he said. "I need her bird-dogging the situation in Bellingham. Can't afford to have any screwups on that one. With you out of play, she's the best man for the job. Do you need anything?"

"No," I told him. "I'm fine."

By then call waiting was letting me know I had yet another caller.

"Gotta go, Harry. My son's on the line."

"Hey, Dad," Scott said. "How's it going?"

"I'm fine," I said. "The surgery went well. They've had me up walking twice so far, and the pain's not bad at all."

The lack of pain probably had more to do with the meds they were plugging into my body than it did with the success of the procedure, but I kept quiet about that. Most of the time when people ask how you're doing, they're looking for your basic generic answer. If someone asks you, "How was your root canal?" they most likely don't want chapter and verse. That was the case here, too. Scott wanted to know how I was. He didn't need to know the gory details about the bloody drain bags the medical folk laughingly referred to as "grenades" or about the weirdly vivid dreams that kept taking me down memory lane. Now that I thought about it, I noticed I hadn't mentioned the dreams to Mel, either. Call it a sin of omission.

There were several more telephone calls from well-wishers after Scott's. They came in one after another. By then the meds I had taken earlier were kicking in and I was ready to stop talking. How many times can you say "I'm fine" without sounding curmudgeonly? When the occupational therapist finally showed up with her walker, I was more than ready to leave the phone in my room and do another forced march down the hall. Once that was over, I was happy to go back to bed, where I

did myself the favor of first taking myself out of circula-
tion by pulling the plug on my bedside phone and then
switching off my cell.

I slept for a while before they woke me up for lunch.
At that point I was beginning to feel bored, so I switched
on the TV set. Nothing was on. My iPad was under lock
and key in the closet, so I asked the next nurse who
came to check my vitals to get it out for me.

People who know me well understand that I had to be
dragged kicking and screaming into the computer age,
first protesting the existence of cell phones and then
trying to cling to a typewriter when Seattle PD was
switching over to computers. So the idea that I would
fall in love with my iPad was not exactly a foregone conclusion, but when Kelly and Scott teamed up to give me
one for Father's Day this year, I was hooked. I've even
taken to doing my crossword puzzles on it.

In this instance I wasn't looking for crossword clues.
I wanted to know about whatever happened to Hannah
and Eugene Wellington in the years since their daughter's lifeless body had been found in a barrel of stale
grease at the bottom of Magnolia Bluff. I had met them
at Monica's funeral, and going to her memorial service
in the picturesque town of Leavenworth was one of my
first official detective duties when I moved up to the
fifth floor.

As soon as I googled the words "Eugene Wellington,
Leavenworth, Washington," the first link was to the
man's obituary:

> Eugene Harold Wellington, a lifelong Leaven-
> worth resident, succumbed after a brief illness. For
> many years he and his wife operated the Apple Inn

outside Leavenworth before it was lost to a forest fire. Services are pending with Wiseman Funeral Chapel. Mr. Wellington is survived by his wife of fifty-five years, Hannah; his son, James; and three grandchildren. He was preceded in death by his beloved daughter, Monica.

What rocked me about that was how little there was of it—a whole life summed up in less than a hundred words. I remembered Eugene as a tall, powerfully built man whose rugged six feet six frame seemed crushed by the terrible weight of losing his daughter. At the funeral, just as Watty had told me about the trip to the morgue, Eugene was the one who sobbed inconsolably all through the service, while his tiny wife had sat stoically beside him, like a dry-eyed sparrow poised to take wing.

Letting the iPad drop onto my chest, I lay there recalling every detail of that first grueling week, the beginning of my career in Homicide.

CHAPTER 6

Initially, Karen had been thrilled when I gave her the news of my unexpected promotion to the rank of detective. Her pleasure quickly dimmed when she learned how much money I had spent in my unauthorized shopping spree at the Bon. And she was even less pleased when she found out that, as a detective, I'd still be pulling hours that weren't remotely related to bankers' hours. I'm not sure why, but Karen had somehow assumed that homicides happen and are investigated on a nine-to-five basis, Mondays through Fridays only. Not so.

"We've got a conference on serial killers down in Olympia this weekend," Detective Powell had told me when he stopped by to see me late Wednesday afternoon. "It's all hands on deck because they're bringing in a guy from the FBI to teach the class. We've all signed up and paid to attend, so you're elected to do funeral duty for Monica Wellington."

"What does that mean?"

"It means you show up at the funeral and at any reception following the service. It means you're polite to the family members. You let them know we're sorry for their loss and we're working the case, but while you're there, you keep an eye out for anything that seems off or anyone who seems off, too. You do not let on that you're a greenhorn. You wear a suit and tie. Got it?"

"Got it," I said, wondering all the while how long it would take for my tiny pay raise to make up for the upgrade to suits and ties required by my new status as a detective.

There's a uniform allowance for cops on the street. There's no such thing when you're working in plainclothes out of the fifth floor. At that stage in my life, I didn't actually own a suit, unless you counted the baby blue tux I wore when Karen and I got married. Even if it still fit, the tux wasn't going to cut it for a funeral. But I also knew that if I was going to get a suit and have it altered in time to wear it to a funeral on Saturday, it had to be purchased that very day—before I went home and gave Karen the news. So that's what I did. Fortunately, it turned out there was still enough room left in our Bon charge account to make that work.

By the time I broke the news to Karen that I would be spending all of Saturday driving to and from Leavenworth to attend a funeral followed by a reception, my wife was barely speaking to me. She stuck Scott in my lap, told me she was going to the store, and why didn't I figure out what we were having for dinner for a change. Cooking has never been my strong suit. I rose to the occasion by opening a can of SpaghettiOs, to which I added some frozen hamburger that I had thawed out and fried. When she came back from the store, Karen ate my slightly burnt offering without comment. I could tell she was neither pleased nor amused, although it was the best I could do with Scott screaming bloody murder the whole time I was trying to cook.

Believe me, I already suspected Karen's job of stay-at-home mom wasn't easy, but that evening's meal made it blazingly clear to all concerned.

On Thursday I left the domestic warfare at home and showed up on time and properly dressed, Homicide style, on the fifth floor. Watty directed me to a cubicle near his that gave evidence of having been recently vacated by someone else—clearly someone who smoked, as there was a dusting of cigarette ash everywhere and a faint whiff of smoke still lingering in the air.

"Don't get too comfortable," Watty told me. "Go down to the motor pool and check out a car. I'll meet you out front on Third."

Welcome to the world of being the last guy in. I had already been warned that I was automatically on tap to do the grunt work, and that was fine with me. I knew that was what it would take to learn the ropes. When I showed up in the garage, I more than half expected Phil Molloy, who ran the motor pool, to give me the business about it.

"So you're out of squad cars and into unmarked," he observed. "Who are you working with?"

"They haven't assigned me a partner yet. I'm working a case with Detectives Watkins and Powell."

"You're lucky," Molloy said. "They're both good people."

I sat in the passenger load zone on Third Avenue for the better part of fifteen minutes before Watty finally put in an appearance.

"Where to?" I asked.

"Saints Peter and Paul Catholic School on Magnolia to have a talk with Donnie and Frankie Dodd," Watty replied. "You're the one who brought up the path question yesterday, so it's only fair that you're there when we talk to them. Do you know where Saints Peter and Paul is?"

I shook my head.

"It's on the far side of Magnolia Village," Watty told me. "Just head over the Magnolia Bridge and turn right."

Magnolia Village was the name of the neighborhood's central shopping district.

"We're going to talk to them at their school?" I asked, heading the patrol car in that direction. "Without their mother being there?"

Watty favored me with an owlish look. "Mac and I already tried talking to them with their mother in the room," he replied. "We didn't get anywhere that way, so now we're going to try talking to them alone."

It seemed like a good time to change the subject.

"How much does tuition to a private school cost?" I asked.

"Funny you should ask," Watty replied. "I wondered that myself, and I already checked. It's seven and a half thousand dollars a year per kid."

I whistled. "Fifteen thousand a year? That's a lot of money. How does a single mom afford something like that?"

"Good question," Watty said.

I was still mulling it over when we arrived at the school and parked in a designated visitor parking slot. A sign on the door directed all visitors to report to the office, which we did. Moments later we were in the pres-

ence of Sister Mary Katherine, a tall bony woman in a
severe black skirt and starched white blouse with a black-
and-white veil pinned to short, graying brown hair. She
examined Watty's ID badge thoroughly through gold-
framed glasses before handing it back to him.

"What can I do for you gentlemen?" she asked.

"Detective Beaumont and I are hoping to have a word
with two of your students, Donnie and Frankie Dodd."

Sister Mary Katherine glared briefly at me. It was the
first time I had heard the word "Detective" attached to
my name, but if she had asked to see my badge, I would
have been stumped. The only ID I had still referred to
me as "Officer Beaumont."

I was relieved when she turned back to Watty.

"What about?"

"The boys were instrumental in helping us find a
body over the weekend," Watty said. "I spoke to them
on Sunday, but a few more questions have come up."

Sister Mary Katherine studied us for a moment longer. "On one condition," she said.

"What's that?" Watty wanted to know.

"That I stay in the room while you speak to them.
These are my students, after all," she added. "I won't
have them pushed around."

"Fine," Watty agreed.

With that, Sister Mary Katherine reached for the in-
tercom button on her desk. "Miss Simmons," she said.
"Please ask Donnie and Frankie Dodd to come to the
office."

I noticed she didn't have to specify in which classrooms the boys might be found. I had the sense that this
wasn't the first time the two red-haired brothers had
been summoned to the office—and that it wouldn't be

the last. I expected them to show up together, but they didn't. When the first one arrived, he was already protesting his innocence.

"Whatever it is," he declared, "I didn't do it and neither did Frankie."

"It's all right, Donnie," Sister Mary Katherine said. "You're not in trouble. These two detectives would like to speak to you and your brother for a few minutes."

I was glad the good sister could tell them apart. In a pinch, I wouldn't have been able to.

A minute or so later Frankie slouched into the room. Without a word, he settled onto a chair next to his brother to await whatever was coming. Yes, they had definitely been summoned to the principal's office on more than one occasion.

"Do you remember me from the other day?" Watty asked.

Both boys nodded. Neither of them met Watty's questioning stare.

"What about Detective Beaumont here?" Watty asked.

They both glanced in my direction and then delivered tiny simultaneous nods.

Watty launched straight into the heart of the matter. "I've been going over Detective Beaumont's report. I believe you mentioned you're not supposed to go down onto the pier or onto the railroad tracks. Is that correct?"

Again both boys nodded in unison.

"But you do go there."

"Sometimes," Donnie said.

On Sunday both boys had been equally communicative, but here—perhaps because they were operating under Sister Mary Katherine's steely-eyed stare—

Donnie seemed to have assumed the role of official spokesman.

"And do you always go up and down the same way?" Watty asked.

"I guess," Donnie said.

"So there's, like, a regular path you follow?"

Donnie nodded, more emphatically this time.

"And you were on the path when you found the barrel?"

This time the two boys exchanged glances before Donnie answered. "I think so," he hedged.

"The funny thing is," Watty said, leaning back in his chair, "I spent all day Monday out at the crime scene. There's a path, all right, but it's nowhere near where you found the barrel."

"But we saw it from the path," Frankie put in. "It was right there in plain sight until we pushed it on down the hill."

Watty ignored the interruption and stayed focused on Donnie. "Is that true?" he asked. "Or did you go looking for it because you already knew it was there?"

"We found it when we were coming back from the movie," Donnie said. "That's all. We found it, and then we opened it, and then we called you."

"How did you open it again?"

"We used a stick to pry off the lid," Donnie declared.

"And where did you find the stick?" Watty asked. "Was it just lying there on the hillside?"

"Yes," Donnie answered. "We found the stick right there."

I could see where Watty was going with this. The barrel had been found in a blackberry bramble. The stick the boys claimed they had used to open the barrel had looked to me like a branch from an alder tree, none of which were anywhere in evidence.

"That's not what the marks on the barrel say," Watty told them. "They say you're lying about that."

He just dropped that one into the conversation and let it sit there. The two boys exchanged glances, squirmed uneasily, and said nothing.

"If you know more than you're saying," Sister Mary Katherine said, inserting herself into the interview, "then you need to tell the detectives what it is."

In other words, it was okay to push Sister Mary Katherine's students around if she was the one doing the pushing.

"We used a crowbar," Donnie admitted finally, after a long, uncomfortable pause. "We only said we used the stick."

"Where is the crowbar now?" Watty asked.

"We dropped it in the water down by the pier when we went to use the phone."

"And where did the crowbar come from in the first place?"

"Our mom's garage."

"And how did it get from the garage to the barrel?"

"We took it down the hill on Sunday morning, while Mom was still asleep."

"Which means you already knew the barrel was there," Watty concluded.

This time both Donnie and Frankie nodded.

"How?"

"We saw the guy who dumped it," Frankie said, speaking for the first time. "On Saturday night, we were outside." He paused and gave Sister Mary Katherine a wary look.

"Go on," she ordered.

"We had stolen some of Mom's cigarettes," he said. "The house next door is empty. We were hiding in the backyard, smoking, when a guy drove into the yard in a pickup with a camper shell on top of it. He drove as far as the end of the driveway. He got out of the truck and pushed something out of the back. When he rolled it out onto the ground, we could see it was a barrel."

"What kind of pickup?" Watty asked.

"I don't know," Frankie said.

"It was a Ford," Donnie put in.

"Color?"

"It was sort of dark, but we couldn't tell much about it because it was late at night."

"How late?"

Donnie shrugged. "After midnight. That's why you can't tell our mom. She'd kill us if she knew we were sneaking out of the house when she thought we were in bed."

"And that's why you made up the story of finding the barrel on Sunday?"

Donnie nodded.

Watty settled in closer, giving the two boys a hard look. "This pickup truck you saw. Had you ever seen it around before?"

"Not that I remember."

"Did you see the license plate?"

"No."

I've heard that twins often develop forms of communication that can pass between them in utter silence. I was suddenly under the impression that that was exactly what was going on here. They were both lying about something, but I couldn't figure out what. I think Watty was getting the same message. Ditto Sister Mary Katherine.

"God knows when you're not telling the truth," the good sister remarked.

Both boys flushed beet red. "Please don't tell our mother," Donnie begged. "Please. We'll be in big trouble."

"So when did you take the crowbar from the garage?" Watty asked.

I closed my eyes and envisioned the house they lived in—a small 1940s vintage brick house with a detached single-car garage at the end of a narrow driveway. The house next door was an exact copy. When they were built, they were probably considered affordable housing for GIs returning from World War II.

"Like I said. We did it in the morning, before she woke up." Donnie was back to doing the talking for both of them. "We knew there wouldn't be time to open the barrel before we went to church. That's why we decided to do it later. We told Mom we wanted to see *Charlotte's Web*, even though we didn't. We got in line at the Cinerama, but as soon as she drove away, we caught a bus back to the Magnolia Bridge. That way we knew we'd have plenty of time to open the barrel before we were supposed to get home. The next showing didn't start until four thirty."

"What did you think you'd find when you opened that barrel?" Watty asked.

"Treasure," Donnie said.

"Money." That was from Frankie.

They were two similar answers, but not quite the same. Not identical, as it were, and it made me wonder why. Treasure is something you keep; money is something you spend. What neither of them had anticipated finding in the barrel was what was actually there—the horrifying naked body of a murdered young woman.

"You said this all happened after midnight? Isn't that kind of late for you to be out of the house and unsupervised?"

"It was the weekend," Donnie said. "We didn't have to get up for school."

"Where was your mom?"

Donnie glanced in Sister Mary Katherine's direction. "She was busy," he said.

Remembering what Mrs. Fisk had told me, I could well imagine that the boys' mother had been busy with something other than her sons on a Saturday night.

"And how did you get out of the house without your mother knowing you were gone?"

"We go out through the window in our room," he said.

"I was by your house the other day," I said. "I seem to remember seeing streetlights. Are you sure it was too dark for you to see that truck? After all, if you were close enough to see the barrel get pushed over the edge of the yard, you must have been close enough to see more of the truck than you're telling us."

"I already said," Donnie insisted. "It was a Ford. And it was dark. Maybe it was black, or it could have been blue. And it was real loud."

"Is it possible it belonged to one of your mother's friends?"

"No!" Donnie said heatedly, unconsciously balling his fists. "And don't talk about my mother."

Obviously my comment about his mother's friends had come a little too close to the truth of the matter. I had no doubt that Donnie had, on occasion, resorted to blows in defense of his mother's somewhat questionable honor. The look Sister Mary Katherine leveled at me said that this wasn't news to her, either.

"Is that all?" she asked. Her question was aimed at Detective Watkins, but we both nodded.

"For the time being," Watty replied.

"All right then," she said to the boys. "You may go back to your classrooms. And, Donnie," she added. "You'd better schedule a time to see Father Hennessey."

"You mean, like, for confession?"

Sister Mary Katherine nodded. "What do you think?" she replied.

"Yes, sister," he replied. Then, biting his lip, Donnie followed his brother from the room.

"They may look identical," Sister Mary Katherine observed, watching the two boys hustle from the room. "But there are definitely some differences, especially when it comes to brains. Frankie got held back last year. He's doing fourth grade for the second time. Donnie is in fifth."

"And you know about their mother?" I asked.

"Detective . . ."

"Beaumont," I supplied.

"Detective Beaumont, we're in the business of hating the sin and loving the sinner. Someone is paying for the boys to attend this school in the firm hope that we're preparing them to make better choices with their lives. For all I know, what they witnessed over the weekend may well be part of God's plan for keeping them on the right path. They did call the incident in, didn't they?"

"Yes."

"So they acted responsibly, correct? If it hadn't been for them, the body of that poor girl might never have been found. Right?"

It was my turn to nod. Sister Mary Katherine seemed to have that effect on everyone—striking people dumb and turning them into complacent nodders, Detective Watkins and myself included.

"Being raised without a father, those boys have a hard enough time holding their heads up in polite society, so I'm asking that you give them a break. Their mother has been known to overreact on occasion. As far as I can see, they're not suspects, are they?"

"No, but they might lead us to a suspect," Watty objected. "If they could give us a better description of the vehicle involved . . ."

"If!" Sister Mary Katherine said derisively. "Let me tell you something for certain. If you rile up their mother about their sneaking out of the house and smoking cigarettes, she's liable to take after both of them with a belt, because it's happened before. I don't know if the mother was the one who did the beating or if someone else did, but the point is, unless you want to accept the responsibility for that—for those two boys being beaten to within an inch of their lives—I suggest you leave Donnie and Frankie out of your crime-fighting equation."

"Yes, ma'am," Detective Watkins said, getting up and heading for the door. "Thank you for your help."

His immediate unconditional surrender surprised me, but I waited until we were outside before I said anything.

"What happened in there?" I asked.

"Donnie and Frankie are off-limits," he said tersely. "Either we'll find our killer without their help or we won't find him."

"But—" I began.

"I had a stepfather with a belt once," Watty said. "Been there, done that. If those two boys end up getting into trouble with their mother or with one of her johns, it won't be on my account, or yours, either. End of story."

And that was the end of the story, at least as far as Donnie and Frankie Dodd were concerned. Watty and I never interviewed those kids again, and by the time I was assigned to my new partner, Milton Gurkey, the Dodd family had left town.

Just for the hell of it, I picked up my iPad now and tried googling them. Donald Dodd. Frank Dodd. Nothing came of it. Not a single link.

While I was doing my computer search, time had passed. When Nurse Jackie hustled into the room a few minutes later, I was surprised to realize that it was already late afternoon. The sun was going down outside. I looked toward the window Lieutenant Davis had peered out of, expecting to see the Space Needle rising in the distance. Except it wasn't there. The window was, but the Space Needle wasn't. The window faced east, not west. There was no view of the Space Needle there in real life, only in my dream.

"I'm working this floor today. Now, what's wrong with your phone?" Nurse Jackie wanted to know, jarring me out of my window problem. "Your wife's on the line, and she won't take no for an answer."

Examining the phone on the bedside table, Nurse Jackie quickly discovered it was unplugged. As soon as she rectified that situation, the phone began to ring. She handed it over, and Mel was already talking by the time I lifted the phone to my ear.

"When you didn't answer, I was worried. I was afraid something bad had happened, that there had been some kind of complication."

"Sorry," I muttered guiltily. "No complication. I must

have pulled the plug on the phone without realizing it. What's up?"

"All hell has broken out," Mel replied. "One of the protesters from last week—one who got Tasered—was found unresponsive in his apartment earlier this morning. An ambulance crew was summoned. They tried to get his heart going again, but it didn't work. He was DOA by the time they got him to the hospital. So now it's gone from being voluntary S.H.I.T. squad involvement to compulsory involvement. In other words, I won't be home tonight. Do you want me to call Kelly and see if she can come up from Ashland?"

"Don't call anyone," I told her. "I'm fine. They had me up and walking twice today. The physical therapist says I'm doing great."

"Are you sure?"

"I'm sure. You've got a job to do, now do it."

It was easy to give her a pep talk, but I knew that there was just a tiny hint of jealousy behind my words. Because I was feeling left behind. Mel was out doing what I usually did—what I would have been doing if my knees hadn't betrayed me and put me on the disabled list.

"I'll call you," she said. "Don't unplug your phone again, okay?"

"Okay," I said. "I promise. You take care."

Good to my word, I turned on my cell phone. I had a number of missed calls and six messages. All of the messages were from Kelly, and they all said the same thing: "Call me."

I did. The relief in her voice as she answered pressed my guilt button in a big way. "Sorry," I said. "I was sleeping."

"It's a good thing you called," she groused. "I was

about to throw the kids in the car and head north to see you."

"You don't need to do any such thing. I'm fine, really. They've already had me up and walking around. The nurse is here right now, waiting to take me on another stroll. Right?"

"If you're up for it, I am," Nurse Jackie said.

"Where's Mel?" Kelly asked. "I thought she was going to be at the hospital with you."

Having women fussing and clucking over me tends to get my back up.

"Mel is out working. Somebody has to, you know."

"If you decide you want me to come up, I will."

"I'm fine. I'll be here in the hospital for at least several more days. Mel might want some help after I get home, but for now I've got it covered."

"*We've* got it covered," Nurse Jackie corrected. She was standing with her hands on her hips, tapping her toes with impatience. "Now are we doing that walk or not? If not, I have other patients to see."

"I've got to go," I told Kelly with no small amount of relief. "Duty calls."

CHAPTER 7

After our measured stroll—there's no such thing as racewalking when you're using a walker—I came back to my room to a stream of visitors. Evidently Mel's one-day moratorium had been lifted, and visitors came in droves to see me.

People from work stopped by, including Squad B's secretary, Barbara Galvin, who arrived armed with a box of chocolates, and Harry I. Ball, who came prepared to eat them. Two of the ladies from Belltown Terrace showed up. One of them was a knee-replacement veteran and the other was a knee-replacement candidate, so their visit was really more of a recon expedition than it was a cheerleading session.

So pardon me if I'm not all cheery about having people sitting around on uncomfortable chairs, staring at me while I'm only half dressed and lying in bed, especially when the one person I would have liked to have had there was off in the wilds of Bellingham chasing bad guys.

I was glad when the last of the visitors finally got shooed out and Nurse Jackie showed up for her last set of vitals and meds.

"How are you on pain meds?" she asked as she fastened the blood pressure cuff around my arm.

"Fine," I said.

She glowered at me. "So you're Superman?" she demanded. "You're telling me you don't need any pain meds?"

"They give me weird dreams," I admitted. "I'd like to back off on them some."

"Let me tell you something," she said. "You're not the first tough guy who's been wheeled onto this floor. If you want those fine new knees of yours to work, you need to do the rehab. If you don't take the pain meds, you won't sleep and you won't do the rehab, and if you don't do the rehab . . . In other words, dreams don't kill you, but don't waste my time by not doing the rehab. Get my drift?"

I nodded. Nurse Jackie was about five feet nothing and as round as she was tall, but she had a glare that would have set that long-ago nun, Sister Mary Katherine, back on her heels. I got the message.

"Yes, ma'am," I said. "Give me the damn pills."

She gave them to me, along with my blood thinners and antibiotics and stool softeners, and stood right there watching until I had downed them all.

"Good boy," she said with a grin and a pat on the shoulder before she turned down the lights and hustled out of the room.

I lay there in the semidarkness, still thinking about my earlier visitors and wondering where the drugs would take me that night. It was a little like standing in line at a roller coaster when you already have your ticket and you're just waiting for the attendant to lock you into your car. You more or less know what's coming, but you don't know how bad it's going to be.

It still bothered me that in my dream, Lieutenant Davis had been standing in front of a window view that didn't exist, but since he didn't exist either, it seemed odd to find that odd. What really surprised me was how much his appearance had triggered my memories of that time. Usually I keep them locked away in a tight little box—boxes, actually: a literal one, a cigar box inside a banker's box, and a mental one. It was that one I scrolled through as the hospital corridor went still and silent outside my room.

It was close to fifty years later, but I still had vivid memories of my first day in country. It was hot that Friday afternoon. I had expected hot; it was the jungle, after all. What I hadn't expected was the hot red dust that got into everything. I had some chow and had settled into my bunk when Lieutenant Davis came looking for me. I leaped to attention, but he put me at ease.

"Time for your official welcome to C Company," he said. "I came to give you your cards."

"Cards?" I asked, thinking he was talking about some kind of required ID card that hadn't been made known to me. "What cards?"

He reached into his pocket and pulled out a box of playing cards. Counting out four of them, he handed them over to me. "These," he said.

They were crisply brand new, with no ground-in red dust, but otherwise they were ordinary in every way—with one notable exception.

"These are all the same card," I pointed out, looking

down at a handful of matching aces of spades. "Shouldn't they all be different?"

"Welcome to 'Nam," Lieutenant Davis said. "And to the world of modern warfare. Here in C Company, we're playing head games with Charlie, a form of psychological warfare. He's a superstitious kind of guy, so when we take someone out, we leave a little message—a calling card, if you will—as though the card we left on him had his name on it. Like he was marked for death."

Lieutenant Davis closed the box and put the rest of the deck back in his pocket. "I gave you four," he said. "If you're a good shot and need more, you know where to find them. Oh, and something else."

He reached inside his shirt and pulled out the copy of *The Rise and Fall* I had seen him reading earlier that afternoon. It was frayed and tattered, and the pages were stained reddish brown from the dust. It was also thick—sixteen hundred pages' worth.

"It's not mine," he told me. "I borrowed it from Lieutenant Fowler, one of the other lieutenants. I decided not to finish it this time through. As I said, I already know how it ends, so I told Lieutenant Fowler I was lending it to you. This will give you something to read in your spare time, and when you finish, there'll be a pop quiz."

With that he turned and sauntered away. I was surprised to see what looked like a long sword hanging on his back. I turned to one of the guys in the tent, Corporal Lara.

"Is he serious? He's going to give me a test on this?"

"That's just Lennie D.'s way of keeping us all engaged," Lara assured me. "He'll expect you to read the book, and he'll talk to you about it, but there won't be an actual test."

"And he's serious about the cards?"

"Dead serious," Lara told me. "In fact, he and the other three lieutenants wrote to the card company, and they sent them back packs of cards that are full of nothing but aces of spades. I saw a copy of the letter. They said they were glad to do their part to win the war. And that's what C Company is called—ace of spades."

"So what is he, some kind of card shark?"

"No, Lennie D.'s a West Pointer. A good guy, too. He's been in country a long time—going on seven months. He's a born leader, and he's turned C Company into the best there is. He's been scheduled to go on R and R several times, but they keep putting it off. Heard he's got a girlfriend, a flight attendant, who's supposed to meet up with him in Tokyo. Somebody was saying they might get married while he's there on leave."

I thought about Karen. What if I didn't come home? Would she marry someone else? Would her old boyfriend, Maxwell Cole, the guy I'd stolen her from, come nosing back around? But we had talked it over before I left and we'd both decided we'd be better off waiting until I came home before scheduling a wedding. Now I wasn't so sure.

I held up the book. "He really expects me to read this whole damned thing?"

"The whole damned thing," Corporal Lara agreed. "And believe me, you'll make a better impression on Lennie D. if you do it immediately, if not sooner."

"What's the deal with the knife?"

"It's not a knife," Lara corrected. "It's a Montagnard sword. There's probably a story behind it, but it goes with him everywhere. Everybody else complains about carrying their packs. He carries his pack and the sword, and never gripes about it, either."

That Friday was my first night in camp, fresh from basic training, scared to death, and more than a little jet-lagged, so they gave me time to get settled in. Since I had nothing better to do, I started reading the book that very night on a cot in a four-man tent where it was far too hot to sleep anyway.

I have never been a history buff. Mr. Gleason's American history class at Ballard High School was beyond boring. I sat in the back row and fell asleep at my desk almost every day while he droned on and on from a wooden desk at the front of the classroom. Believe me, I wasn't the only one of my classmates who dozed his way through the Gettysburg Address and the bombing of Hiroshima.

But somehow, *The Rise and Fall* grabbed me, from the very first words, because I could see that this was an evil that had been allowed to grow and fester. When the people who should have been paying attention didn't, the Third Reich had come very close to taking over the world.

Saturday during the day I went out on patrol for the first time, accompanied by Corporal Lara and two other guys, Mike and Moe. Their last names are lost to memory now, but they both hailed from West Virginia, where they had grown up hunting and fishing. Both of them were said to be crack shots. All three of the other guys on patrol that day were younger than I was, but they had all been in the service and in country for several months. The truth is, I was scared as hell, but I tried not to let on. I also figured that since I was going out with some of C Company's most experienced soldiers, I was probably in fairly good hands.

We came back in without any of us having fired a

shot. We were in the chow line when Lieutenant Davis showed up. He made straight for me.

"How'd it go?" he asked.

"There wasn't much happening out there today," I told him.

He grinned. He had a funny, lopsided grin that made you feel comfortable around him—as long as you hadn't screwed up. If you had screwed up, he'd read you the riot act with enough cuss words to turn the air blue, and when he was finished with you, it was clear that whatever mistake you might have made, you wouldn't be making that one again.

I was standing there, holding my plate and my silverware.

"Sit," he said, motioning me toward a table. "Eat. Don't let me stop you."

I sat. He settled down on the camp stool across from me.

"You're from Seattle."

It was a statement, not a question. Obviously he'd been going through my file. "Yes, sir."

"Always wanted to go there," he said. "My girlfriend is living in Florida at the moment, but that's where some of her family lives now—the Seattle area. I'm hoping they'll send me to Fort Lewis, south of there, when I get back stateside."

He paused for a moment and seemed to be examining a mental list of things he wanted to discuss.

"I understand your BA is in Criminal Justice?" he asked.

"That's right," I said with a nod. "I want to be a cop. That's what I'm hoping anyway."

"Do you have a girl waiting for you?"

"Fiancée," I said. "Karen. We decided not to get married until I get home."

"Probably a good idea," he said. "Your paperwork says your name is Jonas. Unusual name. Is that what you go by?"

Jonas is an odd name, unless maybe you're busy curing polio. As a little kid growing up with that none-too-common name, I hated it as soon as I learned to write it. I would have loved to be a Jimmy, or a Johnny, or even a Richard. So Jonas was bad, but once you combined it with my middle name, Piedmont, and tacked a Beaumont on the end, it became that much worse.

Year after year, in grade school and later in high school, I had to do battle with new teachers and explain that the name in their grade books wasn't the name I wanted to be called. I was happy for them to use my initials, J.P., in class, while most of the kids I grew up with called me Beau. The fact that the lieutenant had bothered asking if I had a preference about what people called me made Lennie D. an exception to every possible army rule.

"My friends call me Beau," I said.

"Okay then," Lieutenant Davis said, clapping me on the shoulder. "We're all friends here. Beau it is. How's that book going?"

"Slowly," I said. "I'm not a fast reader."

"Ever hear of Evelyn Wood?"

"Who?"

"It's a class in speed reading. You might look into it sometime. But I'm glad you're reading it. Like I told you yesterday, when you finish, you can give me a report."

"You mean like an actual book report? In writing?"

He looked at me with that funny crooked grin of his.

"Do I look like an English teacher to you? No, when you finish the book, bring it back to me and we'll talk about it. Man to man."

I wanted to ask if he always gave new arrivals reading assignments, but I didn't. He stood up then and sauntered off to talk to someone else.

Other than our first meeting when I arrived at C Company, that was the only conversation I ever had with the man. A few days later things really started heating up in the highlands. By the end of July I had gone from being a green newbie to being an experienced fighter. I actually ended up using one of my aces, but mostly we were too busy staying alive to think about psychological warfare. I never got around to asking for a replacement.

On the morning of August second, A Company came through, hot on the trail of what they thought to be a vulnerable band of North Vietnamese. It turned out to be a well-laid trap. By the time their platoon leaders realized what was happening, it was too late. Within minutes, their lieutenant and their sergeant were both dead, and C Company was summoned to come to their rescue.

We went into the fight with Lieutenant Davis leading the way. I was in the thick of it when something hit me in the chest and knocked me on my butt. When I fell, I must have hit my head on something. By the time I got my wits back, all hell had broken loose. A corpsman found me and dragged me back to camp, where I spent two days in the hospital tent being treated for a concussion and a broken rib. When I came back around, I learned that Lennie D. was dead. He had been hit in the back by shrapnel from a mortar round while trying to drag two injured soldiers to safety.

Lieutenant Davis was awarded a Silver Star and a Purple Heart for his bravery that day, bravery that cost him his life, fighting a war the politicians were busy deciding not to win. He didn't receive an award for saving my life, but he should have, because he did.

I remember something hitting me in the chest during the firefight. It hit me hard enough that it knocked the wind out of me and put me on the ground. I was unconscious for a while. I don't remember the guy who picked me up and helped me back to camp, where the medics were amazed to discover that where there should have been a bloody, gaping wound on my chest there was nothing but some serious bruising. It wasn't until they brought me back my stuff that I found out what had happened. I had been carrying *The Rise and Fall* inside my shirt, the same way Lennie D. had been carrying it when he handed it to me. The jagged pieces of metal that otherwise would have taken my life only made it as far as page 1,562. If William Shirer had taken forty fewer pages to tell his story, or if I had been a faster reader and had already finished the book and returned it, there's no telling what would have happened, but I'm guessing there's a good possibility that I wouldn't be here today.

Once they let me out of the MASH unit, I tracked down Lieutenant Fowler to return his book. "Sorry about the damage," I said.

He didn't say a word. Instead, he grabbed me and hugged me—hugged me for a long time. When he finally turned away, I caught sight of the tears in his eyes. Mine, too. I don't have a doubt that wherever he is, Gary Fowler probably still has the book. As for me? What I have are the pieces of shrapnel that should have killed me. I keep them where I keep the rest of my treasures, in the banker's box that came with me when I decamped from the house in Lake Tapps. It's on the shelf in the storage unit down on the P-1 parking level in Belltown Terrace. Along with those almost lethal pieces of metal, that's where you'll also find my three remaining aces—the ones Lennie D. gave me on my first day in camp.

I suppose that's the real reason I didn't mention the dream about Lieutenant Davis's visit to my hospital room to Mel Soames—because she didn't know any of that story. She had never seen the cards, never seen the shrapnel. Why not? Because some things are just too damned tough to talk about.

As if to bring that realization even closer to home, my cell phone rang just then with Mel's number in the caller ID.

"I just got back to the hotel from the autopsy," she said. "I dialed you as soon as I kicked off my shoes. Then, when I looked at the clock and saw how late it was, I was afraid you'd be sleeping."

"Don't worry," I said. "I wasn't sleeping. I probably slept too much during the day. How'd the autopsy go?"

"When we got the warrant, we found all kinds of drug paraphernalia in the dead guy's apartment. There are no obvious physical wounds, so the M.E. is leaning toward a possible overdose. He's hoping to have the tox screen results back by the day after tomorrow."

"Those usually take a lot longer than that," I observed.

"Yes, when it's business as usual," Mel agreed. "But this isn't business as usual. Ross Connors is pulling strings and providing the funding to get things done ASAP. The situation in Bellingham is already volatile enough. Unfortunately, the media is busy fanning the flames with speculative stories about the guy dying as a result of the Tasering situation."

"Nothing like a little help from our friends in the fourth estate," I observed.

Mel gave a rueful laugh. "Something like that," she said. "How are you doing?"

"The physical therapy people say I'll be running marathons in no time."

She laughed at that, too, but I could hear from the sound of it that she was beyond tired.

"Ross said he'll be in Seattle tomorrow. He says if he can work it into the schedule, he'll stop by to see you."

"That's fine, as long as it doesn't interfere with something on my end. They're keeping me fully booked, you know."

"How's the pain?" she asked. There was real concern in her voice. After all, she was the one who had insisted that I look into the knee replacement. If it didn't work, or if the pain was unmanageable, she was going to blame herself.

"Not that bad," I said. "Not as bad as it was before, and these guys give me drugs. In fact," I added, thinking of Nurse Jackie, "they give me all kinds of hell if I don't take them."

Nurse Keith popped his head into the room. Like Mel, he had fully expected to find me asleep. That way he could have awoken me. From the expression on his face, I think he was disappointed.

"The nurse just showed up," I told Mel. "I need to go."

"Well, shut off your phone," she advised. "That way no one can wake you up if you're sleeping."

In other words, Mel Soames had spent very little time in hospitals. Lucky her.

"Ready for me to check your vitals?" Nurse Keith asked.

I didn't deign to reply. I simply held out my arm.

"You want something to help you sleep?" he asked when he finished. "I can give you something if you want it."

The truth is, I didn't want to lie around thinking about Lieutenant Davis and all those other guys who never came back. Try as I might, I couldn't even come up with the names of the other two guys who died that day. And although I stayed with C Company the rest of the time I was there, without Lennie D. running our show, it wasn't the same. You didn't dare become friends with someone, because they might not make it—like my bunkmate, Corporal Lara. He didn't come home, either.

Yes, the dreams were weird, but right then, being alone with all my memories was even weirder.

"Yes, please," I said. "I'm ready for something that'll help me sleep."

CHAPTER 8

I'm not sure what was in Nurse Keith's sleeping potion, but whatever he gave me worked like a charm. I was a goner within minutes. This time the dream yo-yo took me out of my hospital room and back to 1973. Back to Leavenworth. Back to Monica Wellington's funeral in the town's small, overheated Catholic church.

I picked a pew close to the back of the church so I could keep an eye on whoever came and went, although I wasn't the least bit sure about what I was supposed to be looking for. I had spent the whole drive over reliving the screaming match between Karen and me as I headed out the door, dressed to the nines in my new fifth-floor duds—a three-piece suit, a starched white shirt that still rustled like paper when I moved, and a tie I had succeeded in tying half an inch too short.

"This is how it's going to be for the rest of our lives, isn't it," she had said as I picked up my car keys. "You're going to be gone working every single weekend, and I'm going to be stuck at home by myself. Except I won't be by myself, will I? I'll be taking care of the kids, and you'll be off playing cops and robbers."

I did a slow burn on that one, the whole trip from Lake Tapps to Leavenworth. It didn't feel like playing. Monica Wellington really was dead, and I was one of the people charged with finding out who did it.

I had gotten to the church early enough that I was one of the first people to be admitted to the sanctuary. The front of the church was awash with flowers, in baskets, on stands, and draping an all-white closed casket. As people filed into the church, there was only one I actually recognized on sight. Gail Buchanan had been one of Monica's roommates in McMahon Hall at the University of Washington. The day before I had gone along with Detective Watkins to the U-Dub and had sat in the corner observing the proceedings as he interviewed Gail along with several other dorm residents.

With the other two roommates at class, Gail was the one who had provided the information about Monica's planned blind date on Friday night, although she could give us very little else. In my experience, someone else hoping to play matchmaker arranges blind dates. In this instance, Gail had no idea about the name of the mystery man in question, nor could she shed any light on the identity of who might be the behind-the-scenes operator. For the first time, I wondered if it had really been a blind date or if that was the story Monica had told her roommates.

"She hadn't had that many dates," Gail confided. "She was glad to be going out. I was happy for her. She said they were going to grab a burger and go to a movie."

"Did she say which one?"

That question was more important than it sounded.

We were hoping to find something that would lead us to a boyfriend. Although I hadn't attended Monica's autopsy, I now knew that Monica had been three and a half months pregnant at the time of her death by strangulation. That was something she had evidently not shared with any of her roommates. But finding out who the unnamed date was might well lead us to the father of Monica's baby, and it might also give us a motive for her murder. But Watty made no mention of the pregnancy during the interview. That, he had assured me, was a holdback. No matter what he called it, I had no doubt that the holdback designation was made more out of respect for Monica's parents than for any investigative purpose.

"No," Gail said. "Sorry."

"And she didn't tell you the guy's name or how she happened to hook up with him?"

Gail shook her head. "But there was something odd about the way she dressed."

"What's that?"

"She went to one of those used clothing places on the Ave. and bought herself an old WSU sweatshirt. That's what she was wearing when she left the dorm that night."

"A WSU sweatshirt. So you're thinking whoever she was going out with went to Washington State over in Pullman rather than to the U-Dub?"

"I guess," Gail said.

I was sitting in the corner. I knew I was supposed to act like an unwelcome kid and be seen but not heard, but the whole sweatshirt thing bothered me. I remembered how hot it had been on Sunday, and it didn't seem like Friday of that week had been a whole lot cooler.

"So a long-sleeved shirt, then," Watty confirmed.

"Yes."

"Do you know where she bought it?"

"Her folks don't have a lot of money," Gail told us. "That's one of the ways she stretched her clothing budget—by buying used clothing."

The dorm room had already been thoroughly searched. According to Watty, it had yielded zip. I sat there examining what had once been Monica's study desk. There was a small Rolodex in the upper-right-hand corner, along with an antique jar made of purple glass that held a collection of pens and pencils. A desk-top calendar covered most of the surface of the desk. On it were penciled notes about when papers were due for various classes as well as one that mentioned Monica's parents' wedding anniversary, which had occurred two weeks earlier. But there was no marking on Friday night about a possible date, blind or otherwise. I also noticed that most of the dates that had already passed had small numbers penciled into the corners that ranged from 1.5 to 3.

"What are these numbers for?" I asked, during a pause in Watty's questions. "The ones on her calendar?"

"She's on a work-study program. She uses those to keep track of her hours."

"Where does she work?"

"The alumni office," Gail replied.

I watched as Watty made a note of her answer. If Monica's roommates didn't know about the source of the blind date, maybe someone she worked with could help on that score.

Off to the side of the calendar was a stack of opened envelopes. I thumbed through them. Several were hand addressed to Monica in thin blue ink. The return address of H. Wellington indicated they were notes from Monica's mother, Hannah. No doubt they were filled with news from home. Another contained an unpaid gasoline bill from Phillips 66. The last was a bill from JCPenney. Both had unpaid balances of less than thirty bucks that were due by the end of the month.

Taken together, all of these things—making do with secondhand clothing, working, worrying about papers, paying bills, staying in contact with her folks back home—spoke to me of a serious young woman, working hard to get an education. Everything I was seeing and hearing made Monica sound like the opposite of the typical dumb blonde who goes off to college with no higher ambition than partying and screwing around. But then again, even without the obvious presence of a boyfriend, Monica had managed to get pregnant.

Once the interview with Gail was over, Watty and I grabbed a burger in the cafeteria and then spent the afternoon talking to people in the alumni office where Monica had made herself useful by answering phones, filing, and typing. If anyone there knew something about her scheduled date on Friday night a week earlier, no one let on. The blind date remained as much of a mystery to Monica's coworkers as it had to her roommates.

Now, seated in the small church, I watched as Gail and three other girls settled uneasily into an empty pew three rows ahead of mine. They were subdued and clearly feeling out of place among this gathering of grieving people. That's not unexpected. Young people in general always seem to feel uncomfortable at funerals, which, in their minds, are generally reserved for people much older than they are.

"I'm surprised they came," someone sniffed in my ear.

I turned and looked and was astonished to find Monica Wellington, still in her sweatshirt and jeans, seated next to me. She had a face now, rather than just a skull. The strangulation marks were clearly visible above the collar of her shirt. She was staring at her fellow coeds with clear disapproval.

"They didn't like me much," she added in an exaggerated whisper. "They all thought I was a snob—too studious and too worried about my grades to have a good time."

I glanced around the church. No one else seemed to have noticed that the guest of honor, who was supposed to be stowed in the white casket at the front of the church, had suddenly appeared at my elbow.

"Why are you here?" I demanded.

"I wanted to see who would show up. Looks like a pretty good crowd."

That was true. At the back of the sanctuary, someone had produced a rolling cart of folding chairs and was setting them up in the empty space behind the last pair of pews.

There had been a clot of people blocking the center aisle as they looked for seats. Now the crowd parted silently. Accompanied by someone who appeared to be a funeral home usher, three people made their way forward to the front row. The two men were tall and rangy—clearly father and son. Between them walked a tiny, upright woman. Each man held one of her arms, but it looked to me as though they were taking strength from her rather than the other way around.

"It's breaking my father's heart," Monica murmured.

"He was so proud that I was going to college. I was the first one," she added. "The first one in my family to get to go."

With that she stood up. The next time I saw Monica, she was standing in front of her parents, between them and the casket, staring curiously back at them, while the organist played doleful music in the background. Then, as the priest emerged to take his place at the pulpit, she disappeared.

One moment Monica was there, peering at her parents, and the next moment she was gone. With no obvious passage of time, the service was evidently over and so was the brief graveside memorial. Suddenly I was in the church's basement social hall, standing in a group of well-wishers in a receiving line and waiting for my turn to offer my condolences to the grieving family members. This was a small town where everyone knew everyone else, and those tearful good wishes were often delivered with tightly gripped hugs.

As I came closer to the spot where Hannah Wellington stood in a simple black dress with a damp hanky clutched in one hand, I felt exactly the way Gail Buchanan and the other coeds must have felt—as though I was intruding and needed to find a way to adequately explain my presence.

Hannah reached out a surprisingly cold hand. When she looked up at me, her eyes may have been dry, but the pain and shock were plainly visible.

"Detective Beaumont," I said quickly in response to her unasked question. "Seattle PD. We'll find whoever did this," I added. "I promise."

"No you won't," Monica Wellington whispered fiercely at my elbow, and then she disappeared again.

"Thank you," Hannah told me with no sign that she had heard her dead daughter's disparaging remark. "I'll hold you to that."

The following week my new partner, Detective Milton Gurkey, a guy everyone called Pickles, came back from vacation. He was an old hand and an excellent teacher. If he had heard rumors about my somewhat unorthodox entry into the fifth floor's hallowed halls, he never gave me a moment's worth of grief about it. As long as I kept my head down and did whatever he told me, there wasn't any problem.

The two of us spent the next six weeks working the Wellington homicide in tandem with Detectives Powell and Watkins, and we never made a bit of progress. For one thing, no matter how hard we tried, we failed to uncover the identity of Monica's date that night. These days it's simple. You want to find out who's hanging out with whom? No problem. You track down their Facebook account, their cell phone records, or their e-mail correspondence. You want to know where someone's been? You track down their credit card records. But credit cards were still in their infancy back then, and Monica's Phillips 66 and JCPenney charge cards were no help in tracing her movements. As for stealing a barrel of grease off a restaurant's loading dock? These days, you'd never pull off something like that without being captured on video by any number of security cameras. Back then, security cameras were almost nonexistent.

Through the expenditure of inordinate amounts of shoe leather, Pickles and I finally found the secondhand boutique on the Ave., Encore Duds, where Monica had purchased the WSU sweatshirt. The salesclerk, who was also the owner, remembered the transaction—three dollars in cash—but that was as far as it went. She remembered the girl. She remembered that Monica bought the shirt and nothing else, but she wasn't sure what day of the week it had been—maybe Wednesday or Thursday. And since many of her transactions seemed to be in the three-dollar range, we were never able to pin it down in any more detail.

Lots of homicide cops are all flash and sizzle. Pickles was a plodder. He wanted to cover all the bases and do it right. He taught me to do reports in a methodical, workable way. He was dogged when it came to asking questions, and he was someone who never wanted to give up on a case. Ever.

We followed up on every lead, including going back to the rendering plant and scouring the parking lot for likely looking Ford pickup trucks. Despite Watty's firm warning to the contrary, we went back to Magnolia and attempted to stage a repeat interview with Donnie and Frankie Dodd. Unfortunately, the family had moved, lock, stock, and barrel. There was a FOR RENT sign in the front yard, and the landlord claimed they had left no forwarding address. That time I even ventured so far as visiting Sister Mary Katherine's office at Saints Peter and Paul Catholic School. She told me the boys' mother was remarrying and the newly reconstituted family was moving to a new location. The good sister had no idea where they were going, since the mother had taken a copy of her sons' school records rather than asking that the records be forwarded to their next location.

I was all for tracking them down, but I was new on the job and Pickles was lead. He made the decision that we would let that particular sleeping dog lie because he didn't have a choice, mainly because it turned out that we had far more than enough to do without it.

We made several trips to the rendering plant. We also made several trips to the Dragon's Head, where Mr. Lee's Mandarin duck definitely lived up to its advance billing. It was easy to see that good food, great prices, and proximity to the Public Safety Building weren't the only things that kept the Dragon's Head at the top of the list as far as Seattle PD personnel were concerned. There was also Mr. Lee's constant supply of very fetching waitresses and barmaids, whose job it was to deliver the food and drink.

"Watch yourself," Pickles warned me when one of them served my lunch with a downcast smile that was off the charts as far as flirting was concerned. "There've been more than a couple of those young ladies who ended up involved with or married to cops they met while working at the Dragon's Head."

"But I'm married," I objected.

Pickles laughed ruefully. "So were some of the guys I just told you about," he said. "Once one of these babes sets her cap for you, you won't know what hit you."

So although I didn't mind going to the Dragon's Head, I never became a regular like some of the other guys did. The Doghouse was a lot more my speed.

In the alley behind the restaurant, the most recent yellow grease barrel sat, awaiting pickup. It was on a loading dock that made for ease of handling, coming and going. It would have taken only a matter of a few seconds to tip it over and load it into a truck parked next to the wooden platform. Pickles and I canvassed that dark alley day and night, talking to the homeless people who frequented that space, trying to find anyone who might have seen the barrel in question disappear from its appointed spot on the weekend of Monica Wellington's murder. To no avail. If there was a witness, we never found him.

That summer was the beginning of Ted Bundy's long reign of terror in the Pacific Northwest. Over a period of months, a whole bevy of young women, coeds mostly, disappeared and died, with their bodies found later, dumped in out-of-the-way places. From a physical point of view, if you had placed Monica Wellington's photo in among a montage of Ted Bundy's other victims, she would have fit right in. She was young and good-looking. She wore her blond hair long and straight and parted in the middle.

Bundy's killing spree lasted for months. Even after he was jailed, however, he continued to play cat-and-mouse games with investigators. He confessed to some of his murders but not to others, and he led officers to believe that he was responsible for deaths to which he was never officially linked.

Seattle PD and other law enforcement agencies in Washington spent inordinate amounts of money tracking Ted Bundy. Eventually the brass upstairs called a halt. One afternoon shortly after he was arrested in Utah and started singing like a bird, our Homicide unit was assembled for a special briefing with Assistant Chief of Police Kenneth Adcock.

Chief Adcock was a smooth operator, the exact opposite of Pickles, and I'd heard there had been bad blood between them somewhere back in the old days when they were both working Patrol. Now, with Adcock's meteoric rise through the ranks, those days were far in the past for both of them.

Adcock stood at a podium with a sheaf of typed notes in hand, recounting the names of the victims for whom Bundy had accepted full responsibility. Then he read off five additional names, one of which was Monica Wellington's. Pickles and I had been working the case off and on the whole time. In fact, we were the ones who had found the witness who claimed to have seen Monica and Ted Bundy together at a movie in the U. District on the night she disappeared, but without some kind of reliable physical evidence, we couldn't make a positive connection.

"These cases are not officially closed," Adcock announced. "There's sufficient circumstantial evidence to lead us to conclude that Theodore Bundy was involved, even though he has not yet confessed to any of these other crimes. For those of you who have been actively working these cases, we thank you for your effort, but for now we're done."

Pickles raised his hand. "In other words, you're saying these cases aren't officially closed, but they could just as well be."

Adcock smiled. "That's right," he said. "As in the past, you'll continue to work these cases until something else comes up. I'm expecting that over time, less and less effort will be expended on these particular cases."

"And what are we supposed to say to the families of these victims?" Pickles asked.

"Glad you asked that, Detective Gurkey," Assistant Chief Adcock said, although from the look on his face, anyone within spitting distance of the man could clearly see that wasn't true. "Tell them that we're continuing with the investigations whenever and wherever we have the time, means, and personnel to do so."

Minutes later, as we filed out of the meeting room, I heard Pickles muttering under his breath.

"Damned slimeball!" he exclaimed, slamming into his chair and propelling it into the battered metal desk that passed for furniture in our cubicle. Assistant Chief Adcock was held in low esteem by many of the rank and file, but I was a little surprised by Pickles's outspoken reaction.

"But he said—" I began.

"I *heard* what Kenneth Adcock said," Pickles replied. "But I've been around this joint long enough to understand what he *means*. He's planning on making sure we're busy with new cases every minute of every day. He'll see to it. The other cases will simply succumb to the slow death of neglect. He can say they're open cases until hell freezes over, but if no one is investigating them, they're not open."

I have to give it to Pickles. His prediction proved to be absolutely on the money. When the next new homicide case came up, it was ours. And whenever we thought we might have a moment when we could get back to the Monica Wellington case, something else would come up. Pretty soon her case was so far back on the back burner that no one even remembered it. Until that morning in the hospital with my passive exercise pump going a mile a minute and with the anti-blood-clot mattress whispering away.

Nurse Keith came in. "Up and at 'em, sunshine," he said. "Ready for some breakfast? How'd you sleep?"

"All right," I said aloud, swallowing the rest of the sentence.

That's the part that went like this: "for someone with a guilty conscience."

The sun was just breaking over the building next
door. I could hear the clattering of trays as the breakfast
lady came down the hallway. My eyelids were gummy
with sleep and there was a sour taste in my mouth. It
could have come from the meds I'd taken, but I suspect it had something to do with the bile of that broken
promise, the one I'd made to Hannah Wellington.

CHAPTER 9

When Mel tried to call me that morning, I was busy with the physical therapy girls ("tyrants" would be a better word), who assured me that phone calls could wait, PT couldn't. When it was PT or OT time, my phone was locked in the cabinet along with my iPad.

Since I was a candidate for both, I had already learned that there's a fine line between physical therapy and occupational therapy. From what I could tell, PT seemed primarily focused on increasing the range of motion in both of my new knees. Progress was measured before and after every round in the hospital's minigym, and every millimeter of improvement was noted on my chart. Occupational therapists were aimed more toward improving my post-op living skills—getting up and down stairs, in and out of pretend cars, and in and out of ordinary beds, which, it turns out, are usually much lower—and much softer—than the ones in the hospital.

Back in my room after the latest round, I had retrieved my phone and was sending Mel a text message, apologizing for missing her call, when Ross Connors appeared in my doorway. Ross always looks like he's on his way to a campaign fund-raiser. In this case, that wasn't far from wrong, since he had stopped by on his way to give a noontime speech to some service group or another—Rotarians, maybe?—who were meeting at the WAC, the Washington Athletic Club, in downtown Seattle.

"Did you see Mel on the news?" he asked.

"Which channel?"

"All of them," he said. "The local news has been all over the mess up in Bellingham, and the media is spinning the police-brutality angle. You know how it goes. If it bleeds, it leads."

When I reached for my iPad, Ross gave me a somewhat skeptical and disapproving sniff. The attorney general's idea of electronic communications doesn't extend much beyond using a television remote. He's a guy who runs a whole department of state government without making use of a personal computer, to say nothing of an iPad. I used the hospital's Wi-Fi system to bring up a local television news site. As soon as Mel's face appeared on the screen, I showed the video to Ross Connors. As a card-carrying Luddite, he was nothing short of amazed.

In the meantime, I was watching my lovely wife, looking a lot more tired than usual, as she faced down a mob of microphone-packing reporters backed up by cameramen wielding video equipment.

"As you all know, the deceased, Mr. Reginald Abernathy, was arrested and booked into the Whatcom County Jail on charges of disturbing the peace and resisting arrest. He was released on his own recognizance on Friday afternoon. At the time, he exhibited no apparent ill effects as a result of the Tasering incident that preceded his arrest. After he failed to respond to voice and text messages on Monday, friends went to his residence early Tuesday morning, where he was found to be nonresponsive. We are still awaiting the results from his autopsy."

"The officers clearly used excessive force," one of the reporters commented. "Why haven't they been placed on administrative leave?"

"The decision about placing them on leave is one that belongs to the Bellingham Police Department," Mel replied. "As I said at the beginning of this interview, I'm with the state attorney general's Special Homicide Investigation Team, which has been called in to assist in the investigation. So far we've found no evidence of wrongdoing on the part of the officers."

"So you're saying Mr. Abernathy's death was a homicide?"

"I'm saying our department has been asked to assist Bellingham PD in conducting an outside investigation of what happened. That means we are asking questions and looking for answers. That doesn't mean we came here with a set of preconceived notions. Once we have reached some conclusions, we will advise Bellingham PD of our findings. At that point, they will decide what action, if any, should be taken with regard to the officers involved."

"Do you think their attack on Mr. Abernathy was racially motivated?"

I noticed the tiny twitch in the corner of Mel's mouth before she answered. It's a signal I've seen before, and it often comes just before she lets someone have it with both verbal barrels. When I see that twitch I know enough to duck and run for cover. In this instance she stayed resolutely on message.

"I'm not at all sure that what happened between the two officers and the deceased could be characterized as an attack, and I've seen nothing to indicate that this is a racial matter."

The reporter, however, merely doubled down. "But Mr. Abernathy is black."

"He was also recorded destroying property and attacking police officers," Mel replied. "That's criminal behavior regardless of the color of his skin or theirs."

"Look at the way she handles those reporters," Ross observed. "She could be a politician, you know. Has she ever thought of running for office?"

"Mel?" I said. "Are you kidding? She wouldn't get to first base. She has no interest in telling people what they want to hear, and she'd rather kick ass than kiss it."

Like the reporter, Ross doubled down. "I still think she'd be a real asset in the state legislature."

Knowing I could go back and view the video later, I switched off the iPad, cutting Mel off in midanswer. "How's this thing in Bellingham going to turn out?"

"I'm like everyone else in the law enforcement community," Ross said. "I'm hoping like hell the tox screen shows an overdose. Otherwise those cops are probably toast, and what started out as a small problem in Bellingham will turn into a big one for all of us, with the anti-Taser folks claiming that they're as much deadly force as hollow-point bullets."

Mel will be right there in the middle of it, and I won't, I thought grudgingly.

There's no rule that says I can't be a sore loser. Before the surgery, my knees had gone a long way toward making me feel irrelevant. Now, stuck in a hospital bed, I felt even more so. And Ross Connors's well-intentioned effort of dropping by to cheer me up seemed to be having exactly the opposite effect. But as long as he was there and feeling magnanimous, I decided to pop the question that two nights of drug-induced blasts from the past had engendered.

"I was wondering if you could do me a favor," I said.

"What?" Ross asked. "That's what I'm here for. Whatever you need, you've got it."

"I'd like you to reopen a homicide case."

Ross was the chief law enforcement officer in the state of Washington. Regardless of jurisdiction, if he said a case was reopened, it was.

"Really," he said with a frown. "Which one?"

"A girl named Monica Wellington," I said.

Ross shook his head. "Never heard of her."

Cops and reporters refer to "cold cases." For the family, a case never goes cold. It's a piece of continuing hurt that may no longer be white hot, but that doesn't mean it goes away, either.

"Monica was a University of Washington coed who died in April of 1973. I was part of the team that worked that case, back when I first got promoted to Homicide."

"And it never got solved?"

I shook my head. "It got closed but not solved. Unofficially that case was lumped in with all of Ted Bundy's cases once he was taken down."

"What you're saying is that the homicide wasn't solved to your satisfaction," Connors said. "What about Seattle PD's Cold Case squad? They've been doing good work the last couple of years."

"I'd be willing to bet no one's taken a look at the Wellington case."

"Why?" Ross asked. "Because it might still step on

someone's toes, even though it's close to forty years old? That's sort of a stretch, don't you think?"

"Maybe," I agreed.

"If I were to reopen it, theoretically, I mean," Connors said, "I suppose you're thinking I should assign you to the investigation?"

"I'm familiar with the case," I said. "I knew the people involved. I'm also the guy who made a promise to the victim's mother that we'd get the guy—that he wouldn't get away with it. If it turns out Ted Bundy wasn't responsible, whoever did it has gotten away with it."

"Why the sudden interest?" Ross asked. "What makes you think Ted Bundy didn't do it, and why now?"

I couldn't very well tell him the truth—that the victim herself had dropped by to give me a push in that direction. That seemed like a surefire way to go from being on temporary medical leave to being out the door permanently.

I shrugged. "I guess it's because Monica's killer is the one that got away. Every Homicide cop has one of those. This one is mine."

Ross appeared to accept that statement at face value, but he still wasn't happy. "If it looks like my agency and you in particular are looking into cases that were handled by your old outfit, couldn't that cause some hard feelings?" Connors objected. "For instance, bringing up one of those long-shelved cases might be seen as venturing into Internal Affairs territory. You know how popular those guys are."

"I've never been one to worry about popularity," I replied. "Besides, I've been away from Seattle PD for a long time. The only guy I know who still works there is Assistant Chief Ron Peters, and I can't see how any of this would blow back on him. Monica Wellington's murder happened almost a decade before Ron set foot in the department."

Ross Connors seemed to consider my proposition. "All right, then," he said, heaving himself out of the chair. "Consider it done. I suppose handing a guy like you a case to work on is better than bringing you flowers."

"Infinitely," I agreed.

"And, I suppose, even though you're officially on sick leave, that wouldn't keep you from working on this."

"Have iPad, will travel," I said.

"But speaking of blowback," Ross added, "I don't want any grief from Mel about this."

That made two of us, but I didn't care to put that concern into words.

"Don't worry." I grinned. "At this point, anything that keeps me occupied and out of her hair will be a welcome diversion."

Ross Connors exited the room, leaving me feeling more alert and energized than I had been in weeks. There's nothing like a case to get an old Homicide dog's juices flowing again. I finished my text to Mel, telling her she looked great on TV (a small white lie), then I switched on my iPad and started making a list of the people I'd need to see:

Hannah Wellington, the victim's mother. Since there was no further mention of her after the one in her husband's obituary, I had to assume that Monica's mother was still among the living and, unless I was sadly mistaken, probably still residing in Leavenworth.

Larry Powell, the lead detective in the case. Larry had left Seattle PD prior to the time I did, resigning to look after his wife, who had been diagnosed with ALS. In fact, it was Powell's successor, a guy I couldn't stand, Phil Kramer, who had been the catalyst for my leaving the department as well. I seemed to remember that Larry's wife had died, that he had eventually remarried and was now living somewhere in Arizona.

Watty Watkins. He had left Seattle PD, too, some time after I did. I had no idea where he was living now.

Doc Baker, the guy who did the autopsy, had long since retired. For all I knew he had croaked out, just as Pickles Gurkey had.

Gail Buchanan, the victim's roommate. In the intervening years, she had probably married, maybe even more than once. Tracking her down wouldn't be easy, but it could be done.

Donnie and Frankie Dodd, the kids who had found Monica's body. Whatever had become of those two? I had always wondered if they had known more than they let on. Watty had put interviewing them off-limits, but this many years later, maybe that didn't matter anymore. What if one or the other of them had something he wanted to get off his chest?

Rory MacPherson. Yes, good old Mac, my partner in Patrol from way back then. We had been the first cops on the scene of Monica's homicide, and we had gotten along all right when we worked together, but once the partnership was over, it was like an acrimonious divorce. We went our separate ways, and there had been enough people in Seattle PD that we stayed separate.

For one thing, not hanging out together was one way of putting the lie to the whisper campaign that said both our promotions had come about because (a) we knew someone, or (b) we knew something. I never heard anything specific on the topic, but I always suspected that Mac was probably getting some of the same treatment over in the Motorcycle unit that I was getting up on the fifth floor. If there was a fix, I hadn't done it, and if Mac had indeed pulled some kind of fast one, I didn't want to know about it.

All of that was reason enough for both of us to make our split permanent.

I was lying there, almost asleep again, with the iPad on my chest, when who should appear in my doorway but my son, Scott.

"Hey, Pop," he said. "How's it going?"

Considering everything that had gone before, you can imagine that I was a little flummoxed by his sudden Jack-in-the-box appearance. My initial thought was that I had once again meandered off into dreamland, and Scott's showing up at my bedside made him yet another member of my continuing cavalcade of ghosts of Christmas Past.

"What are you doing here?" I asked, probably sounding grumpier than I meant to.

"You mean I'm not allowed to come by and check on my dear old dad?" he asked with a grin. "You could at least act happy to see me."

"I am happy to see you," I said.

With some difficulty I managed to stifle saying aloud what I was actually thinking, which was: *Are you real or not?* If it turned out he wasn't real, I wasn't going to keep talking to myself. And if he was real? If I asked him the question, then Scott would think I was nuts for sure. No winners for me in either case.

"When did you get in?" I asked.

It seemed like an innocuous enough question, but

Scott looked distinctly uncomfortable. He bit his lip before he answered. "I actually got in yesterday afternoon," he said. "Mel had told everybody that she didn't want you overwhelmed with visitors, so I stayed away."

There was something about that statement that didn't have the ring of truth in it. Scott's a lot like me in that way. He's never been a particularly capable liar. His mother could always see straight through him. So could I, up to a point.

"I'm sure she would have made an exception for you," I said.

Scott nodded. "I suppose so," he agreed sheepishly. "But I wanted to keep it a surprise."

"Okay," I said. "You did it. I'm surprised."

"No, not that I was coming to visit you. The real reason I was coming to Seattle."

"What?"

"I had a job interview."

This was news to me. Of course, I had hoped that eventually one or the other of my kids would come back home to Seattle to live, but I hadn't voiced that opinion. What they chose to do with their lives was none of my business, really. And Scott and Cherisse had seemed so happy living in the Bay Area that it had never crossed my mind that either of them would consider looking for work in Seattle. The PT ladies would have been astonished, but right that minute I felt like leaping out of my hospital bed and dancing a jig on my brand-new titanium knees.

But I've also learned, from watching Mel's very capable handling of my kids, that overreacting to news of any kind—bad or good—is not the best idea. Just in case this wasn't a dream, I was careful to keep my cool.

"So how did the interview go?"

"That's the thing," Scott said. "I got the job, but I'm worried about what you'll think."

"Look," I said. "You and Cherisse have your heads screwed on straight. You get to make your own decisions. Damn the torpedoes. Full speed ahead, and all that crap."

Scott's face brightened. "Really?" he said. "You mean it?"

"Of course I mean it. Now tell me about the job."

"It's in the new TE unit at Seattle PD."

"TE unit?" I repeated, puzzled about this latest bit of alphabet soup jargon. "Never heard of it. I know about IT, but what the hell's TE?"

"Tactical electronics," Scott said. "Drones. Electronic surveillance. Computer surveillance. SWAT team robots. That kind of stuff. I'll have to make it through the academy, but on the other side of that, I'll be a sworn police officer, just like you. For me, being an engineer has always been a means to an end—a way to support my family. Being a cop is what I've always wanted to do."

I would guess my jaw dropped in utter astonishment. When Scotty was little, he used to say he wanted to be a cop. That was a while after he wanted to be a lion tamer and a fireman and before he wanted to be the star of his own rock band. Karen had taken it upon herself to drum all those childish dreams out of his head. Cops and firemen didn't make enough money—his father's paycheck being a prime case in point. Working as a lion tamer was far too dangerous. Ditto for starring in a rock band. All those guys died of drug overdoses. Karen was an outspoken lady with some very definite ideas.

I wasn't privy to most of the private mother/son conversations full of discouraging words that went on between Karen and Scott, but I did get their gist in what Scott parroted back to me about them. I heard about the other things Karen said as well—including the unstinting encouragement she gave him for his academic achievements. From the time he got his first A in first grade arithmetic, his mother told Scotty exactly how smart he was, and she never once let up. I believe that was the beginning of Karen's single-minded crusade to push the kid in the direction of engineering. People who were great at math would be great at engineering. He'd grow up, invent something important, and we'd all be rich. And, by the way, no guns would be involved, nor any lions, either.

While the kids were growing up, there was never any question that Scotty was Karen's fair-haired boy. He did as he was told; he didn't talk back; he minded his manners; he got good grades. His little sister, Kelly, was the exact opposite—a born rebel and a perpetual troublemaker. She was into making mischief from the time she could walk, and once she could talk, she told grandiose fibs with wild abandon—fibs that were often used to get her older brother into trouble.

In their mother's book, Scott could do no wrong, and Kelly could do no right. You can probably already see where this is going. In the scheme of parental finger pointing, Kelly was mine and Scotty was Karen's. No wonder the little girl Karen often referred to snarlingly as "your daughter" wound up as a high school dropout and a seventeen-year-old pregnant runaway.

But in the real world, things don't always turn out the way you expect them to. Scott did what he was told and became an engineer and evidently hated it. Kelly, who didn't do what she was told, got bad grades in school, and marched to the tune of a different drummer, was now doing things very much her own way, including working on that master's degree in business administration.

Had Karen lived to see those two very different outcomes, I doubt she would have believed either one. She would have loved the fact that Kelly was finally getting her education, but she would have been appalled that Scott was turning his back on her lifelong dream of his future as a successful geek in favor of following in his father's law enforcement footsteps.

All those thoughts tumbled through my brain in far less time than it would take to say them aloud. But eventually Scott noticed my uncharacteristic silence.

"Well," he said. "Aren't you going to say something?"

"Are you sure?" I said. "I mean, I thought you had a good job and everything."

"I did have a good job, and I still have it. I'm not stupid, you know. In this job market, I wasn't about to turn in my resignation unless I had the new job nailed down. But Cherisse and I talked it over. The money that came to us from your aunt Hannah made all the difference. Just because I studied engineering doesn't mean I love engineering. And now I can use that to do something I've always wanted to do—be a cop."

And there you have it—a tale of two Hannahs—Monica's mother and my long-lost aunt, Hannah Mencken Greenwald.

Before I was born, my mother evidently attempted to contact my father's family but was turned away by them, as well as by her own father. That's why, on my birth certificate, my last name is listed as Beaumont—my father's hometown in Texas rather than my father's birth name, Mencken.

Earlier in the year Hannah's daughter, my cousin Sally Mathers, had tracked me down and begged me to come to Houston to meet my father's sister in what, she warned, would be only one step short of a deathbed visit. Putting my long-held misgivings about my father's family aside, Mel and I had flown to Texas and met a truly remarkable woman.

In the course of long conversations conducted in Hannah's frothy pink bedroom we had erased a lifetime's worth of absence from both our lives. She told me about her beloved brother, Hank, to whom I bore a spooky resemblance, just as my son, Scott, was a younger mirror image of me. She told me that growing up, Hank had been the black sheep of the family. When he went away to serve in the navy during World War II, she was the only member of the family who had corresponded with him. In his letters, he had told her about the blossoming relationship between him and my mother. After his death, Hannah urged her parents to get in touch with my mother, but Frederick and Hilda Mencken had ignored their daughter's advice. As for Hank's letters? They had been confiscated by his mother and had surfaced again only a few months earlier. That was what had led my cousin to launch a search for my mother. In the process she ended up finding me.

For my part, I told Hannah what I knew about my mother's relationship with my father and how the few months they'd had together must have sustained her because, as far as I knew, she never went looking for another man in her life. I told her about growing up in Seattle, about my mother's unbending determination in raising me alone, and about her dauntless courage in the face of her long losing battle with cancer. Eventually, I also told Hannah about the rest of my family—first about Karen and the kids, then about Anne Corley, and finally about Mel.

Inevitably our discussions came around to the thorny subject of money. It seems the Mencken family had a bundle of it because, as it turns out, there really are oil wells in Texas. I learned that Hannah had been years younger than her older brother. She had still been living at home when my mother, pregnant and unmarried, had contacted Hank's parents, only to be rebuffed for being what they regarded as a gold-digging opportunist. They had wasted no time in sending her packing.

Although Hannah and her daughter had welcomed Mel and me with open arms, I think they thought of me as some kind of poor relation, and they were shocked to discover that we hadn't come to Houston looking for a handout. Far from it. Anne Corley's legacy to me meant that I didn't have to worry about money, ever. And since I was fixed in that regard, Hannah made up her mind to pass what would have been her brother's share of her father's fortune along to Scott and Kelly. I think it was her very generous way of making amends for her parents.

Over the years, I had offered help to the kids from time to time, but parental help is often eyed suspiciously, and in terms of having strings attached, conscious or otherwise, it probably deserves to be. The money my aunt Hannah left to Kelly and Scott when she died came at them from out of the blue and with no strings whatsoever. I knew Kelly and Jeremy were in the process of negotiating the possible purchase of one of Ashland's B and B's. The news about Scott and Cherisse, however, hit me like a bolt of lightning.

"Dad," Scott said eventually, when he tired of waiting for some kind of response. "I guess this means you don't approve."

Out of deference to Karen, I suppose I should have made some kind of halfhearted objection, but I couldn't. And, truth be known, there were plenty of my footsteps I might have preferred he not follow, but becoming a cop wasn't one of them. On that score I was utterly blown away.

"Just the opposite," I said. "I'm floored, yes, but honored, delighted, and very, very proud."

Scott leaned over the bed. I hugged him close, not wanting him to see the hint of moisture in my eyes.

"Where's Cherisse in all this?" I asked.

"She hates California. She's ready to pack and move whenever I say so," Scott returned. "She's got a line on a possible job with a start-up in Redmond. They've been holding a position open for her, but she was waiting to see if I got offered the job at Seattle PD. I called her on my way here. Now that all systems are go, she's probably already called in her acceptance. She'll give her notice today, and I'll give mine tomorrow. Then we'll have a month and a half to pack up, get moved, and find a place to live. The next class at the academy starts November first, and they've reserved a spot for me."

"It sounds like it's all coming together," I said.

Scott grinned happily. "Yes, it is," he said. "Now, I'd best be on my way to the airport. I don't want to miss my plane home. There's too much to do."

Moments later, he was gone, and I was left consider-

ing the tale of two Hannahs. Hannah Mencken Greenwald had given my son and daughter-in-law the where-
withal to live their lives on their own terms. Along with
the money, she had somehow endowed Scott with the
courage to follow his dream. For whatever complicated reasons, that was a life-changing gift my son would
never have accepted from me. It left me far more in
Hannah's debt than I could ever repay, but as morning
drifted into early afternoon, I realized I could pay it forward, or maybe even backward.

For that to happen, all I had to do was keep the promise I had made long ago to that other Hannah. But first I
had to finish my next round of OT.

CHAPTER 10

Late that afternoon, I had another visitor when Assistant Police Chief Ron Peters rolled his wheelchair into my room.

"How are the sick, the lame, and the lazy?" he asked in that heartily cheerful manner that makes the guy in the bed want to get up and smack his effusive visitor in the nose. "Thought I'd stop by and say hello," he continued, "but I can't stay long. Tonight is Amy's night as den mother for Jared's troop of Cub Scouts. My assignment is to take everyone out for pizza afterward."

I did not like hearing that my namesake, Jared Beaumont Peters, was already old enough to be in Cub Scouts. When had that happened? I must not have been paying attention.

It had been years ago that the hospital visiting shoe was on the other foot. Back then Ron was the one lying in a hospital bed and I was the one doing the visiting. Amy, then his nurse and now his second wife, was the person who had pulled him out of his poor-me doldrums and gotten him back on track. She was the one who had encouraged him to go back to Seattle PD, pick up the pieces of his law enforcement career, and roll with them, as it were. The fact that he was now assistant chief for investigations was in no small part due to Amy.

"I guess by now you know," he said.

"Know what?"

"About Scott. We've offered him the job. HR offered it, actually, and I understand he's accepted, assuming he makes it through the academy."

"Wait," I said. "Are you saying you knew all about Scott's job application before I did?"

"Well, duh," Ron said with a grin. "He used me as one of his personal references. I like to think my recommendation carried some weight."

"But no one told me word one about it." I'm sure I sounded aggrieved. I was.

"Scott asked me not to," Ron explained. "He said if he got the job, he wanted it to be a surprise, and if he didn't get it, you wouldn't be disappointed."

"I was surprised, all right," I muttered. I'm sure I sounded surly. I didn't mean to, but I kept getting the feeling that the world was passing me by while I lay there stuck in that hospital bed.

"So what's the deal with the Monica Wellington homicide?" Ron asked, abruptly moving from one subject to the next. "Your boss gave me a heads-up about this a little while ago. Why, after all these years, are you interested in bringing up one of Ted Bundy's old cases? And why should Special Homicide tackle it? You may not have noticed, but I have a great Cold Case squad these days, one that reports directly to me."

In other words, Scott's being hired by Seattle PD

wasn't the only reason Ron Peters had dropped by to see me that afternoon. He had worked his way up to the top of Seattle PD's investigation heap. Now he needed to know if what I was about to do was going to cause him problems. I hadn't taken Ron Peters into consideration when I told Ross my longtime connections with the department wouldn't be a problem. I probably should have.

"Has some new piece of information surfaced that makes you think now would be a good time to take a second look at that case?"

Ron Peters and I had been friends for a lot more years than we'd been partners. In the past, we had always been straight with each other.

"Nothing conclusive," I said, hedging. "Just a gut feeling."

He raised a single eyebrow. "A gut feeling," he repeated. "About a case from almost forty years ago?"

I didn't answer.

"Let me tell you something," he said. "I know what it's like to be the guy in the bed. I was there for a long time, remember?"

I nodded.

"And when you're lying there, you're not thinking about all the things you did right—about the cases you closed and the ball games you won and the good grades you got in college. No, when you're stuck in a bed, you're thinking about all the failures—about all the things that didn't go right."

Much as I didn't want to admit it, Ron's take on the subject was a lot closer to the truth than the song and dance I had given Ross Connors. My drug-induced visitors had definitely been pointing out my failures and shortcomings, of which Monica Wellington's unsolved murder was a glaring example.

"So after Ross Connors called me, I brought up Monica Wellington's homicide. We have all the records digitized these days, so it wasn't like I had to go prowling through some dusty old file somewhere. And guess what I found there? Your name, for one. You were one of the investigators. And I also saw that the file went inactive once the case was closed on Ted Bundy—there was a reference linking the two."

"That link was only in somebody's vivid imagination," I said. "There wasn't any physical evidence with Ted Bundy's name on it connecting the two. No DNA. Nothing."

"Nor to anyone else, either," Ron agreed. "But there was plenty of circumstantial evidence. Once Bundy was arrested, at least two eyewitnesses came forward placing him with Monica on the night she was murdered."

"If he did it, let me prove it," I said.

"He's dead."

"So is she."

"What's the point, then?" Ron asked. "What are you hoping to accomplish?"

"I'm hoping to keep a promise I made to Monica's mother—that I'd find the guy who was responsible."

"Dead or alive."

"Yes," I said.

"All right, then," Ron said. "Here's the deal. I'll give you my full cooperation on this with one condition."

"What's that?"

"That it's a joint investigation. It's got to be Special Homicide and Seattle PD, working together. Everyone knows we're friends. If I give you and Special Homicide carte blanche to rummage through one of our homicide investigations, especially one like the Bundy case, I'll be putting my own head on the chopping block."

"So what are you suggesting?" I asked.

"I'll be assigning Delilah Ainsworth of the Cold Case squad to work with you on this."

I remembered Delilah Ainsworth from when she showed up in Patrol as a fresh-faced and very good-looking recruit right out of the academy. Being a cop named Delilah is bad enough, but the way the woman filled out her Seattle PD uniform back then was down-right biblical—as in Samson and Delilah. At the time, she had seemed far too young to be a cop, and it was impossible for me to imagine that now she was old enough to be a seasoned detective. On the surface the situation with her was a lot like Jared Peters being too young for Cub Scouts. With one big difference—Mel would not be pleased.

"You know better than most how I feel about working with partners," I said, in hopes of changing his mind. "Besides," I added, "Delilah must already have one, and so do I."

"Her partner just took off for six months of maternity leave, and yours happens to be up in Bellingham at the moment, putting out fires," Ron observed. "I'm talking about literal fires, by the way."

"What do you mean?"

"In case you haven't tuned in to the news this afternoon, Bellingham has had a rash of arson-related fires today, with notes left at the scenes claiming that they were protesting police brutality."

The fires had evidently happened after Mel's appearance on the noon news, which I had not yet gone back to finish watching. And this new development explained why Mel hadn't gotten around to texting me back.

"So what's it going to be?" Ron pressed. "Work the case with Detective Ainsworth or not work it at all?"

The idea of a homicide detective taking off for maternity leave was a bit mind-bending. In addition, I suspected Mel wouldn't be happy about my working with anyone who wasn't her. My wife isn't the least bit insecure. Still, I doubt there are many wives who would be thrilled to have their spouses working as partners with someone as—let's just say—well-endowed as Delilah Ainsworth. But I also understood that it was Ron's way or the highway. I could work the case on his terms, with his blessing and with Delilah's help, or I wouldn't work it at all.

"Done," I said.

"All right," he said, brightening. "I'll have Delilah get in touch. As long as you're laid up here, you won't be able to do much in the way of legwork, and once you get out, you won't be cleared for driving, either. But there is one other condition."

"What's that?"

"No publicity. The press isn't what it used to be, but if they somehow get wind that we're looking into one of the cases that was originally attributed to Ted Bundy, all hell will break loose."

"No problemo," I said. "I don't like the press any better than you do."

"Yes," Ron Peters agreed, "I already knew that, but right this minute I have a lot more to lose than you do. I actually need this job, because I still have a kid to put through college."

With that, Ron Peters started to turn his chair and

head for the door. "Hey," I called after him. "I have one more thing to say, too. Thanks for that reference for Scott. I'm sure it helped get him in the door."

"Getting in the door is one thing," Ron observed. "After that, it will be up to him."

Ron left. Dinner came. I was just settling in to some surprisingly good mac and cheese when my phone rang. It was Mel.

"I only have a couple of minutes," she said, sounding harried and rushed. "You won't believe the kind of day I've had. I thought I'd be able to get away and come home tonight, so I could see you, but it's not going to happen."

"My day's been pretty unbelievable, too, but you go first," I told her. "You tell me about your day, and I'll tell you about mine."

It was not a fair trade. By the time I got around to my part of the conversation, my latest dose of pain medication was starting to kick in, and I ended up telling Mel a lot more than I had originally intended.

"Wait a minute," Mel said. "You're telling me that you've gotten Ross Connors to open up a forty-year-old homicide case because you had a dream about the victim? Is that what you're saying, that you dreamed this whole thing up?"

As I said, I've never been a capable liar to begin with, and the drugs made me that much worse.

"Pretty much," I admitted, "although I didn't exactly mention the dream part. I told him it was about my first homicide case—my first unsolved homicide case—and that I needed to close it."

"And Ron Peters is going along with this—assigning this Ainsworth woman to work with you on it?" Mel gave an exasperated sigh. "There's a reason it's called 'sick leave,'" she said. "And this is definitely sick. I'll talk to you tomorrow. Better yet, I'll try to see you tomorrow. I need to come home to get a change of clothes. Maybe I can knock some sense into your head while I'm there. If not your head, then I'll take a crack at Ross Connors's head."

She hung up then. Clearly she was upset with me, but that was all right. I hadn't been entirely straight with Ross Connors or Ron Peters, but I wasn't married to either one of them. I was married to Mel, and that made all the difference.

That night, for the first time since I'd come into the hospital, I slept like a baby, and with no oddball dreams, either. I seem to remember that they woke me up for vitals periodically, but I went straight back to sleep.

Having a clear conscience is a wonderful thing.

CHAPTER 11

Detective Delilah Ainsworth was waiting in my room the next day when I came back from my morning round of PT. She looked utterly spectacular in a fire-engine-red pantsuit with a top underneath that showed more than a hint of cleavage. The hair that I remembered as pretty much blond was now a soft shade of brunette with a tasteful frost job.

She watched in silence as the attendant helped me into bed and relieved me of the walker. Then she stood up on a pair of amazingly high heels—the kind that usually turn up only on TV shows—and tottered over to the bed, a move that put me at eye level with some pretty spectacular scenery. Naturally, she caught me enjoying the view.

"I'll make you a deal," she said. "You don't look at my boobs, I don't look at your knees."

It was the kind of no-BS introduction that Mel would have loved. That was my first hint that if and when my new partner and Mel ever met, they would get along like gangbusters.

"Fair enough," I replied.

"And since neither one of us appears to be built for foot chases and/or physical combat, if we're going to be working together, we'd better count on brains rather than brawn," she added, pulling an iPad out of a large purse with what looked like multicolored Mickey Mouse ears all over it. "Now what's this about?"

I admit it. I was impressed. The women I've known who have risen through the ranks to become detectives have all been capable, competent, and tough. But to be a homicide cop named Delilah isn't an easy call. And to tackle the job while wearing a bright red pantsuit and scarlet nail polish and carrying an immense, brightly colored purse that screams "Disneyland" all over it? That takes balls! Have I mentioned that Mel also happens to adore brightly colored, humongous, and wonderfully expensive purses?

"How much do you know?" I asked.

"Not much at all," Delilah replied. "When I showed up at work this morning, my captain told me to get my ass up here to meet some guy who works Special Homicide for the attorney general's office. It turns out that would be you, although no one actually got around to explaining how or why I'm supposed to be working with someone who's currently flat on his back in a hospital bed."

"Did your captain tell you what case we'd be working?"

"No."

"Did he tell you that Assistant Chief Peters and I used to be partners a long time ago?"

"No, he didn't mention that, either, but I suppose that gives you a little pull inside the department."

"A little," I agreed. "How about the name Ted Bundy? Does that ring a bell?"

"Ted Bundy's name rings everybody's bell," she replied.

"Monica Wellington was murdered in April of 1973. She was from Leavenworth, first kid in her family to go to a four-year college. The autopsy revealed that she was pregnant at the time she was strangled to death, but no boyfriend ever came forward."

"So you're saying the father of the baby could be the doer?" Delilah asked.

I nodded.

"What happened?"

"Nothing. It was the first homicide case I ever worked, and it was never solved, at least not to my satisfaction," I told her. "My first partner and I worked it off and on for the better part of two years. When Ted Bundy was arrested in Utah in 1975, he was linked to the Wellington case by two eyewitnesses who claimed to have seen the two of them together at a movie theater in Seattle the Friday evening Monica was murdered. The problem was, we never found any additional corroborating evidence, and there was never any solid physical evidence—the kind that would stand up in court—that linked Bundy to the Wellington homicide. Even so, eventually the case was deemed closed by the powers that be. Game over."

"Until now," Delilah said.

I nodded.

"So what's the point of reopening a case that has been closed since I was in kindergarten?" Delilah asked. "If we're going to be working this case, I need to know why."

The first rule for getting out of holes is to stop digging. The first rule for being partners is to tell the truth.

This clearly ambitious young woman deserved the truth, at least up to a point, and if she chucked it back in my face, so be it.

"Because the victim told me so," I said. "In a dream. She told me it wasn't solved."

Delilah blinked. "When?" she asked. "While you've been here and under the influence of powerful narcotics?"

She had hit that nail on the head. "Yes," I admitted. "I was under the influence of drugs when she told me that. Still, that doesn't mean it isn't true."

"So are you prone to seeing visions and having hallucinations?" she asked. "I mean, do they happen often?" I caught a tiny hint of sarcasm in her voice.

"No," I declared hotly. "I'm not claiming premonitions, either. This is pure gut instinct—cop gut instinct. Both my memory and my conscience took a direct hit."

I knew that if our situations were reversed, I'd be every bit as skeptical as she was. For obvious reasons, I made no mention of the Lennie D. situation. I told myself it was because that wasn't remotely a police matter. Monica Wellington's murder was. And just in case I haven't mentioned it before now, I may not be an excellent liar, but I'm great when it comes to the fine art of creative rationalization.

"So when you had this little chat with our long-dead victim, why didn't you come right out and ask her?" Delilah said. "I mean, if she'd gone ahead and told you who did it, wouldn't that save everybody a whole lot of time and trouble?"

Delilah's jab was deftly delivered—a polite way of making fun of me and letting me know that she thought I was pretty much full of it.

"At the time, Monica was too busy taking me to task for not keeping a promise to her mother."

"What promise?" Delilah wanted to know.

"To find her daughter's killer," I replied. "The problem is, that's a promise I made at Monica's funeral."

"Which was after the victim was already dead."

"Correct."

"So how did Monica even know about it?"

I shrugged. "You tell me."

"But she didn't say specifically that Ted Bundy did it."

"No," I agreed, "and she didn't say he didn't do it, either."

"In other words, it could go either way?"

I nodded.

"Do this for me," Delilah said. "If this Monica vision happens to show up again, why don't you ask her? If anybody ever finds out why we reopened this case, we're both going to look really stupid."

I knew I was being razzed, so I was careful not to bite.

"Stupid or not, I'd like to be able to tell her mother for sure what happened to her daughter," I answered after a pause. "Either Ted Bundy did it or he didn't. And regardless of what brought the situation to mind, I feel honor bound to pursue it."

That must have been the right answer. We sat there in silence again for the better part of a minute. Finally Detective Ainsworth nodded. Picking up her iPad, she used her index finger to move the slide on the screen that turned it on.

"I guess that means we'd better get started," she said. "Tell me what you know."

The easiest way to do that, of course, was to simply copy the list I had made on my iPad and send it to hers.

We then spent the next hour going over the people on the list, discussing where they might be found these days and what, if anything, they might have to offer this reopened investigation. When we finished, Delilah gave me a searching look.

"Is there any remaining physical evidence?" she asked.

"I'm not sure," I said. "I believe there used to be. Whether it still exists is another question."

"Times have changed since then," Delilah remarked. "Evidence that couldn't yield DNA results back then might be able to now. What about her clothing?"

"As far as I know, it was never found."

"What about Ted Bundy's other victims?" she asked. "Were any of them found in similar circumstances?"

"As in a barrel?"

Delilah nodded.

"No, as far as I know, that would've been a one-off. I'm not aware of similar cases."

"Did you check other jurisdictions?"

"We did," I said, "but back then those kinds of checks were a lot more difficult. You couldn't just click a mouse to look for other cases the way we can now."

Delilah nodded. "That's where I'll start," she said. "I'll look for similar victimology."

With that she stood up and slipped her iPad into her purse. "After that, I'll review the murder book along with whatever physical evidence is still extant. If there's something that might yield current DNA results, I'll see what I can do about getting it tested. I'll also try to get a line on everyone on this list. I'll locate them, but I won't interview them. We should probably do that together. How much longer do you expect to be here?"

In the preceding days my surgeon had stuck his head in the room periodically, but his visits had mostly been done in passing. When it came to real information, the nurses were the most reliable sources.

"They tell me I'm in here for another couple of days. When you do two knees at once, you qualify for extra rehab."

"Great," Delilah observed drily. "I'll try to remember when it's my turn to get in line for new knees. What about driving?" she asked. "How soon will you be able to do that?"

"Not for several weeks, most likely."

Delilah nodded. "All right, then," she said. "Once you're out, I'll be driving and you'll be riding. In the meantime, I'll go to work and I'll try to keep you posted on my progress."

She left then. I had turned down my morning pain pill. Now I was sorry. I rectified that error when they brought me lunch so I could be ready for whatever torture the PT ladies dished out that afternoon. After that I napped for a little while. I like to think it was because I had finally done enough on my part to get the Monica Wellington ball rolling that no dark ghosts from my past made unwelcome appearances that afternoon. There were dreams all right, but the one that stayed with me was of a long-ago Easter egg hunt on the shores of Lake Tapps when Kelly and Scott were little. The kids were cute. The eggs were brightly colored. And it wasn't raining. That's what made it a dream. It's always raining for Easter egg hunts in the spring.

Later in the afternoon I did another session of PT and an additional session of OT, but by then I was really starting to get bored. I made up for lost time and used my iPad to do all the crossword puzzles I had missed that week. Then I ate dinner while watching the local evening news. One of the stories I saw there threw me into a tailspin. It's the kind of story that's been repeated countless times on TV stations all over the country in the last few years. A soldier from Fort Lewis, a twenty-two-year-old private, had been killed by an IED in Afghanistan. Forty years later in another war in another time zone, another kid wasn't coming home from the battlefield the same way Lennie D. hadn't come home.

Reaching for my iPad once more, I went on a virtual trip, one I'd never had the courage to make in real life. I keyed in the words "Vietnam War Memorial." When the Web site for the Vietnam Veterans Memorial Wall opened up, there was a place on the welcome page that allowed you to do a search for specific names. I didn't have much to go on—Lennie D.'s last name, Davis, and the day he died, the day that was seared in my memory: August 2, 1966. It turns out that was all I needed to put in—the last name and the date. Moments later, I had the results:

LEONARD DOUGLAS DAVIS
Army—2LT—O1

Age: 22
Race: Caucasian
Sex: Male
Date of Birth: Sept. 16, 1943
From: BISBEE, AZ
Religion: ROMAN CATHOLIC
Marital Status: Single

Panel 9 E, Line 96

I sat there, staring at the words and trying to make sense of them while swallowing the growing lump in my throat. His first name was Leonard? Of course it was. Nobody names their kid Lennie. And he was from Bisbee, Arizona? If I had ever known that fact about Lennie D., I had somehow forgotten. I know very little about Arizona as a state, but Bisbee I do know. I've been there twice now, working with Sheriff Joanna Brady. And age twenty-two? That was what struck me now. He was so very young. So incredibly young, with a whole lifetime reduced to those few words, blazing accusingly back at me from my iPod screen.

I was still transfixed when I heard the telltale tapping of a pair of high heels coming down the hall.

Most of the people who work in hospitals wear soft-soled shoes. Why wouldn't they? They're on their feet all day. Only visitors wore high heels. Expecting Mel to appear at any moment, I quickly switched off my iPad, swiped away all trace of tears, and tried to get a grip on myself. But the person who swung through my doorway like a whirling dervish wasn't Mel Soames at all. Instead, my arriving visitor was Detective Delilah Ainsworth, a very angry Detective Ainsworth.

"What the hell are you trying to do and what are you getting me into?" she demanded forcefully.

Here I was still flat on my back in bed, where I had been for days. Whatever had happened, as far as I knew I was totally blameless.

"Why?" I asked. "What's wrong?"

"Monica Wellington's homicide has never been turned over to the current Cold Case squad because it was officially marked closed in 1981. The evidence was then transferred to the evidence warehouse, but it isn't there. That means the murder book is missing as well." Delilah threw the words in my direction as though she was convinced that I was somehow personally responsible.

"What do you mean, there's no murder book?" I shot back. "Of course there is. I wrote some of the entries myself. Look again. It's been almost forty years. It's probably just misfiled somewhere."

"That's what I thought, too," Delilah agreed. "That it had been misfiled; I checked the paperwork. I have an entry that shows it leaving the evidence room, but no entry showing it arrived at evidence storage."

"Does the entry say who took it?"

"It's part of that week's routine evidence transfer. It left the 'active' evidence room without ever arriving at 'inactive.' There's no record of it being checked in at the other end, although the other entries listed on the transfer sheet are present and accounted for. If it weren't for that one outgoing transfer entry, you'd think the evidence never existed."

"You're saying someone hijacked it between one place and the other?"

"Someone?" Delilah asked, arching one eyebrow. "How about you?"

"Me?" I echoed. "Are you kidding? I'm the one who started this—the one who sent you looking for the evidence box in the first place. Why would I do that if I had personal knowledge that it was already gone?"

"It's one of the oldest Indian tricks in the book— classic misdirection. You send everyone else looking for something so no one will suspect you're the one who hid it."

"Isn't talking about old Indian tricks racist?"

"There's nothing wrong with using the term if you happen to be an old Indian."

I probably looked surprised. Delilah's light brown hair and hazel eyes didn't look the least bit Indian— Native American, if you will. Although thinking all Indians look alike is probably as racist as thinking all white guys look alike.

"My dad worked for the Bureau of Indian Affairs," Delilah explained. "My mother was Rosebud Sioux. I can crack Indian jokes as much as I want, but don't change the subject. Are you responsible for hiding that stuff or not?"

"Honest Injun?" I asked, trying for cute. It must have been the pain meds kicking in. I don't usually attempt cute, but this time I couldn't resist and Delilah was not amused.

"You are definitely *not* a Rosebud Sioux," she said with a pointed glare. "So tell me the truth. What did you do with the evidence?"

"I didn't do anything with it," I declared. "I was still working Seattle PD Homicide in 1981, so you're right—I would have had access to the evidence room, but not to routine transfers of evidence. But even if I had managed to get rid of the stuff related to this case that long ago, why in God's name would I bring it up now? That makes no sense."

Delilah sighed and then let out her breath. When she spoke again, it was in a somewhat mollified tone. "I suppose you're right," she agreed, "but the point is, somebody did get rid of it. Somebody moved the case from open to closed. I want to know who did that and why, and so do you. So what's our next step? Do we bring this to the attention of Internal Affairs? If you didn't take it, what are the chances one of the other investigators in the case did?" Delilah pulled out her iPad and consulted the list, repeating the names I had given her earlier. "Detectives Gurkey, Watkins, Powell, and you, as well as that other uniformed officer at the crime scene, Rory MacPherson."

"Whoever did it was someone with something to hide," I replied. "And I'd be willing to bet money that it wasn't any of those people."

"Why not?"

"It couldn't have been Pickles. He was already dead. As for the other guys? I worked with Powell and Watty Watkins for years. They were absolutely true blue!"

"What about Rory MacPherson?" she asked.

I couldn't vouch for Mac in quite the same way I could the others. I shrugged and let it go, while Delilah looked thoughtful. "How long between the time of Monica's murder and the time the case was unofficially dropped?"

"She was murdered in April of 1973."

"You remember that for sure?"

"It's the month I made detective," I answered. "Of course I remember. I think Ted Bundy got picked up and started confessing to some of his crimes a couple of years later. Pickles and I worked the Wellington case off and on from the time it happened until Bundy was off the streets."

Delilah was already punching the keyboard on her iPad. "You're right. Nineteen seventy-five," she reported moments later. "That's when Bundy was taken into custody."

"We must have gotten the word to lay off the case sometime after that," I continued.

"I think we can be reasonably certain that Ted Bundy didn't do it," Delilah concluded. "Because, if he had, there'd be no reason for someone to lift the evidence. Whoever's responsible for its disappearance definitely has an ax to grind."

I nodded. "Makes sense to me."

"So back to my other question. Do we go to Internal Affairs or not?"

"I say not," I answered. "We already have permission from Ron Peters to reopen the case, so we should do exactly that. Let's go back over everything and everyone. We'll treat it like a brand-new case."

Nodding, Delilah kicked off her shoes, curled her legs under her in the poorly named "easy" chair next to my bed, and stared at me expectantly.

"Then you'd better tell me everything you remember," she said, her fingers poised over the keyboard on her iPad. "It turns out, you're the closest thing to a murder book we may ever get."

She stayed for the next two hours, typing away industriously with very few comments or interruptions, while I did my best to re-create that long-ago Sunday afternoon on Magnolia Bluff. It wasn't as hard as it might have been otherwise. After all, in the preceding days, and prompted by Monica's dreamscape appearance, I had done a mental blow-by-blow rerun of the whole thing. As I told Delilah the story, I tried to pay attention to any possible discrepancies between what had shown up in the dreams and what I remembered, but by the time all was said and done, the two versions seemed to be in sync.

This time through, I added in everyone and everything else I remembered. I told Delilah about Sister

Mary Katherine, the principal from Frankie and Donnie's school. I filled her in on the guys from the rendering plant where the barrel had come from, although right at that moment, I couldn't recall any of their names. Then I mentioned the lady from the thrift shop where Monica had purchased the WSU sweatshirt she'd been wearing on the night she disappeared.

A late-night call from Mel was what finally put a halt to our conversation. When I answered the phone, I told Delilah in lip-reading pantomime, "It's my wife." Nodding and allowing Mel and me some privacy, Delilah packed her iPad into her Mickey Mouse purse, gave me a brief wave from the doorway, and headed out.

"I take it you're not coming to see me tonight?" I asked.

"No. I'm still in Bellingham. We're having an arson storm up here. Someone just tossed a firebomb at the home of one of the officers who was involved in the Tasering incident. So things are getting worse instead of better."

"Sorry to hear it," I said. "I thought Bellingham was supposed to be a haven of peace and love."

"Not at the moment," Mel replied. "In fact, at this point, everyone's calling for the chief of police to step down. Her officers have lost confidence in her for standing back and letting the original protest get out of hand. So has the public. In the meantime, the dead guy's girlfriend has dropped out of sight. I just put out a BOLO on her. In other words, I'm not coming to Seattle tonight. And at this rate, maybe not tomorrow, either."

I felt another small twinge of jealousy. Mel had a real case. I had an old case based on my having bad dreams. What was wrong with this picture?

"I called Harry to bring him up to speed," Mel continued. "He's going to ask Barbara Galvin to drive up here tomorrow to bring me a change of clothes. I've made arrangements with the doorman at Belltown Terrace to let her into the unit so she can pick them up."

Talk about useless. It was humbling to realize that at this point I couldn't even be counted on to bring Mel spare duds.

I must have fallen very quiet. "Beau," Mel said. "Are you still there?"

"I'm here," I said. "I'm just wishing I could do something to help."

"What you're supposed to do is get better," she replied. "Right this minute, that's your only job."

I'm sure the words were meant to cheer me up and make me feel better. Unfortunately, they had the opposite effect and left me feeling even more inadequate. That's easy enough to do, when the best you're capable of doing is hobbling up and down hospital hallways on a walker with an attendant at your side.

"You take care now," I said. "I've gotta go. The nurse just came in."

That wasn't true. There wasn't any nurse. There was only me. And what I wanted right then wasn't one of the pain meds Nurse Keith handed out. I wanted the old kind of pain med—my former drug of choice.

I wanted a drink in the very worst way. In the old days, I would have simply picked up the phone and called Lars Jenssen, my AA sponsor. Lars was my sponsor before he married my grandmother, Beverly Piedmont, and he's still my sponsor now that Beverly is gone. But he's also verging on ninety-three and a resident in Queen Anne Gardens, an assisted living place on Queen Anne Hill.

These days, he's early to bed and early to rise, and waking him with a phone call a few minutes after midnight wasn't going to do either one of us a favor.

Hoping to drown out the siren song of Demon Rum, I turned off my bedside light and tried to sleep.

CHAPTER 12

It wasn't a good night. I was restless. I had probably overdone it in PT, and my knees hurt. When I finally got around to asking for some pain meds, I was able to sleep, but once again the dreams kicked in. The only good thing to be said about that night's dreams was that I didn't remember them in the morning when I woke up. When I wasn't sleeping, I wrestled with all those thorny issues, and by the time the sun came up the next morning, I had settled on what I was going to do.

After that day's first round of PT and when I was back in bed, I picked up my phone and went looking for the phone number I knew was stored there. Cochise County sheriff Joanna Brady's mobile number was in my contact list along with her direct number at work. It was midmorning by then, and her work number was the one I used, figuring that there was a good chance she'd be at her desk.

"Sheriff Brady," she answered.

She was all business. I happen to know Sheriff Brady

is only a little over five feet tall, five four or so, but she sounds a lot bigger than that on the phone. Although I couldn't see the little dynamo's bright red hair, I could certainly picture it.

"Beaumont here," I said. "From Seattle."

She laughed. "There's only one Beaumont in my life, and I know where you're from," she said. "What's up?"

"Do you happen to know someone who might be related to Leonard Davis?"

"Not that I know of," she said, sounding genuinely puzzled. "Should I? Who is he, and what did he do?"

I could tell from the way she answered that she expected this to be some kind of police matter. I hated to admit it, but this was personal—intensely personal. Suddenly and unaccountably, the damned lump was back in my throat, making it difficult to talk.

"He's a guy who came from Bisbee," I replied. "He died back in 1966. In Vietnam."

There was a small silence. "Oh," Joanna said after a pause. "You must mean Doug Davis. Now that you mention it, I remember Leonard was his given name, but no one around here ever called him that."

"So you knew him?'"

"No, I never met him, but of course I know about him. He's one of our local heroes. Doug was a very smart guy—valedictorian of his class and a top-notch athlete. He went to West Point after high school, then he went to Vietnam, and then he came home in a flag-draped coffin. What a waste!"

I had to agree with her there. "That certainly squares with what I knew about him."

"The old Letterman's Club installed a bronze plaque over at the high school," Joanna continued. "Doug's name is on it, along with the names of the six other guys from Bisbee High who died over there. The Letterman's Club disbanded a few years ago. Now a local Boy Scout troop maintains that area, and they hold a memorial service there every year on Veterans Day. Memorial Day would probably be more appropriate but school's usually out by then, so the campus is closed. I always try to show up for the ceremony, and I encourage as many of my officers who can make it to be there as well. But you still haven't told me why you want to know."

Good point.

"A buddy of mine showed up in town the other day," I said. "He was hoping to get in touch with Doug's family—with his fiancée actually. Would you happen to know if any of his folks still live around there?"

I just barely remembered to use the right name— Doug rather than Lennie D. As for that tired old "buddy of mine" routine? It sounded lame even to me, and I have no doubt that it sounded pretty lame to Joanna as well.

"I don't know anything about a fiancée," she said. "Doug's mother and his younger brother Blaine used to come to the memorials, but they're both gone now. I could maybe check with the paper."

"The paper?" I asked.

"The local newspaper," she answered. "The *Bisbee Bee*. If you can tell me about when he died, it'll save me some time. There might be some kind of mention of his fiancée in his obituary."

I've been a cop for so long that I always think in terms of law enforcement solutions to finding people. Since this was a personal matter, those avenues weren't open to me. Using police access databases for personal searches happens to be against the law. But this solution was so simple that it stunned me.

"Do you want me to check for you?"

"Actually, if you give me the Web site, I can check for myself."

Joanna laughed aloud at that one. "You are off the beam on that one. The *Bee*'s back copies aren't digitized. I believe the University of Arizona is in the process of doing that, but right now, the only access is microfiche. For that you have to be on the premises, in the flesh. Do you have a date for me?"

I knew the date as well as I knew my own name. It was the day Lennie D. died; the day I didn't.

"August 2, 1966," I replied.

"So I'll check the records for early August of 1966," Joanna said. "If that's when Doug died, it probably took some time for the military to make arrangements to get him home."

In the background I could hear the scratching of pen on paper. Sheriff Brady was clearly not an iPad kind of girl—at least not so far.

"And you're looking for information on the fiancée," Joanna continued. "I have to run uptown for a luncheon meeting in a little while. I can probably stop by the paper while I'm there. Will this afternoon be soon enough?"

"Sure," I said. "This afternoon would be great."

Once that was out of the way, I lay back in my bed and focused on the evidence problems Delilah Ainsworth had uncovered at Seattle PD. How was it possible that all the evidence in Monica Wellington's homicide had disappeared into the great beyond? Delilah had most likely never met Watty Watkins or Larry Powell. Their names, along with that of Pickles Gurkey, might still be mentioned around Homicide on occasion, but to most of this latest crop of detectives, including Delilah Ainsworth, they would be names only and relegated to departmental ancient history, sort of like yours truly.

And if Delilah had zero connection with any of those long-lost detectives, she'd have even less to Rory "Mac" MacPherson. After leaving the Patrol division, I knew he had spent years with the Motorcycle unit, including a decade in which he was in charge of Seattle PD's motorcycle drill team. Although he had loved riding motorcycles, they had almost been the death of him. He left the department years before I did, mustering out as a double amputee with a full medical retirement disability after a drunk driver ran a red light and sent both him and his bike flying through the air.

But I did know all those guys, all four of those honorable fellow officers. I knew them up close and personal, the way partners know partners. Of those four, Mac was the only one whose integrity I could conceivably question—the only one who gave me any cause to worry that he might not be a straight-up kind of guy.

As much as I had tried to avoid this issue, there had always been something slightly hinky about the way the two of us had gotten our two separate promotions. One day we had been out on patrol, riding around in a marked car, pulling over the occasional speeder. And then, the next day, we both got the very promotions we had been chasing.

During my first months and years in Homicide, I had faced down the doubters by working like crazy, earning my fifth-floor chops in my own right. I had always assumed that Mac had done the same thing in his unit. But even if I had some personal doubts about the guy's uprightness, I could see that of all the people involved, he was the least likely one to have had anything to do with the disappearing evidence box. The reason was simple— he wasn't a detective. As a member of the Motorcycle unit, Mac would never have had the kind of access to the evidence room that everybody else did.

I was still thinking about that when Delilah called. "Speak of the devil," I said. "What are you up to this fine day?"

Outside my window, I could see that the early-morning fog had burned off, leaving behind one of those gloriously clear early autumn days when the weather in Seattle just can't get any better. Seeing the blue sky overhead made me wish I was in the great outdoors as opposed to being tethered to a hospital room.

"I'm on my way to Sammamish," she said. "I'm going there to talk to Rory MacPherson."

I know about the City of Sammamish. It's out on the Sammamish Plateau, on the far side of Issaquah, on an area of higher ground between Lake Washington and the Cascades. It used to be part of unincorporated King County, but sometime in the last twenty years or so it had supposedly turned into a city. Having never been there, I couldn't swear one way or the other.

"That's where Mac retired to?" I asked. "Sammamish? I had no idea."

"According to Records it is," Delilah said. "I called to make sure he was home, because I didn't want to go driving all the way out there on a wild-goose chase. He asked me what it was about, and I told him we were reopening one of his cases. Can you tell me anything more about him than what we discussed last night?"

I had already told her everything I remembered from

Mac's and my last second-watch ride together all those years ago—the phone call from Frankie and Donnie; finding the girl in the barrel; doing the initial canvass of the neighborhood under the direction of Watty Watkins and Larry Powell. What I hadn't told her about was what had happened two days later.

"I suppose there is one more thing," I admitted reluctantly, "something I probably should have mentioned earlier but didn't."

"What?"

"It turned out that was my last shift as far as Patrol was concerned, and Mac's, too. I had taken the test and applied for Homicide before then. I had also been told there weren't any openings, but when I came back from my days off two days after that shift, I discovered I had been moved out of Patrol and into Homicide. And I wasn't the only one to get a promotion. All of a sudden, Mac was working Motorcycles, which was the exact assignment he had always wanted."

"The idea of both of you being promoted at once sounds too good to be true and maybe slightly more than coincidental," Delilah observed. "Are you thinking there was some kind of cause and effect here?"

"I tried to convince myself otherwise at the time, but maybe there was," I admitted.

"You never asked anyone about it?"

"If you'll pardon the expression, I was low man on the totem pole back then," I told her. "I had the promotion I wanted, and I sure as hell didn't want to rock any boats."

"Didn't want to get kicked back to the gang?" Delilah asked, ignoring my unauthorized Native American gibe. In law enforcement these days, political correctness rules. Working with someone who was half Sioux was making me aware that, without my noticing it, a lot of those potential land-mine phrases had wormed their way into my manner of speaking. Of course, maybe they had always been there; I was simply not paying attention.

"Exactly," I said.

"So you're suggesting I ask him about it now?" she asked.

"I don't see what it could hurt," I agreed. "After all, we're both out of Seattle PD, along with most of the other guys who were working there at the time."

"Including whoever disappeared the evidence?"

"Most likely," I admitted grudgingly.

My surgeon came in about then. Dr. Auld had breezed through my room a couple of times in the days since my surgery, but I hadn't had a chance for a real conversation with the man. Hoping to get cut loose, I didn't want to miss the chance to talk to him now.

"Gotta go now," I said to Delilah. "Talk to you later."

The doctor stripped the sheet off my knees. Staring down at the two matching lines of staples that were all that showed of his handiwork, he nodded his approval.

"How come they call it rounds?" I asked. "Why don't they call it squares?"

It was a meaningless quip, but Dr. Auld answered it quite seriously. "I believe it had its origins at Johns Hopkins, where the hospital was built under a dome. But let's not worry about that, shall we? Let's get you sorted out."

Pulling his own iPad from the pocket of his white jacket, Dr. Auld clicked it a few times and then studied what appeared on the screen. "From your PT reports, you appear to be a star pupil, Mr. Beaumont," he said.

"Great range of motion. No sign of infection. No fever. How's the pain?"

"Manageable," I said. "But I've got a couple of numb spots, one on each leg."

"Nerve damage," he said. "The numb spots may go away or they may be permanent. No way to tell. What's your house like? How many stairs do you have to negotiate?"

"None whatsoever," I replied. "We live in a condo with full elevator service."

"Anyone there with you?"

"My wife, Mel," I replied. "I'm sure you met her the other day, but she's currently out of town. I'm not sure when she'll be back."

"All right, then," he said, slipping his iPad away. "You're making great progress. I might be able to boot you out of here a couple of days early as long as you agree to continue working on your PT at home, but I can't release you without your having someone there to keep an eye on you. What say we revisit this tomorrow? But here's a word of advice. When you do go home, I want you to ease off the pain meds gradually. No going cold turkey. Got it?"

"Got it," I said. With that, Dr. Auld was gone.

By now I was used to the hospital routine. I did my morning OT and had some lunch. After that, however, it was time to talk to my sponsor. Sighing in resignation, I called Lars Jenssen.

Lars spent a lifetime as a halibut fisherman, commuting between Seattle and Alaska's fishing grounds aboard his boat, the *Viking Star.* Despite having been born and raised in Seattle's Ballard neighborhood, Lars speaks English with a thick Norwegian accent that becomes even more pronounced whenever he gets near a telephone.

"Ja sure," he said, when he heard my voice on the phone. "How're ya doing?"

"I almost called you last night."

I could hear a slight shift in his position, as though he was sitting up straighter than he had been before and was paying closer attention.

"So they got you on some of them painkillers?" Lars asked. "The powerful ones?"

"That's right."

"When you're hopped up on them, it's easy to slip back onto the hard stuff," Lars observed. "You need me, you call me, anytime, day or night. I'll grab a taxi and be there."

I knew he would be.

"Thanks, Lars," I said.

"Ya got yourself a good life now, Beau," he said. "Wouldn't want ya to screw it up, that's for sure."

I agreed with him there. "I promise, if the urge comes over me again, I'll call.

"Gotta go," I told him when call waiting buzzed. "I've got another call." I could tell by the number on the screen that it was coming from Joanna Brady's direct line.

"I think I found what you needed," Sheriff Brady said when I answered. "Doug's death was big news here in town when it happened, and there was quite a spread. Listed among his survivors was his fiancée, Bonnie MacLean, of Coconut Grove, Florida. That's all it says about her. No additional information was given."

"What about other relatives there in town?"

"The obituary said Doug had two brothers. I knew

the one who died about ten years ago, a decade or so after Doug's mother, but I have no idea what's become of the second one."

"The information on the virtual wall said Doug Davis was a Roman Catholic," I offered. "Is it possible a local priest would be able to provide more information?"

"Hardly," Joanna replied. "Father Rowan has only been at St. Benedict's a couple of years. I doubt he'd have any connections going back that far. I can keep asking if you'd like," she added, "but you didn't really tell me what this is about."

It took a while for me to answer. It was time to be straight with someone about my search for Lennie D.'s fiancée, and I decided Joanna Brady was it.

"Doug and I served together," I admitted at last. "In Vietnam. He was my commanding officer, my platoon leader, and he saved my life. I'm hoping to track down his fiancée and tell her thank you."

"So you're what earned Doug that Silver Star?" she asked.

"Not exactly," I said. "Those were two other guys. What he did for me was loan me a book. When we got caught in that firefight, the piece of metal that should have killed me outright got buried in the pages of the book instead of in the wall of my chest. If he hadn't given me the book to read, we wouldn't be having this conversation."

"Under the circumstances, I can see why you'd want to reach out to his fiancée," Joanna said. "I'll keep making inquiries around town. If I come up with anything more, I'll let you know."

"Great," I told her. "Thanks."

There was a pause. "Are you all right?" she asked. "You sound funny."

I didn't know how to answer her on that. After all, Lennie D. died more than four decades ago. But she was correct. I was anything but all right. Why was it so difficult for me to talk about this now? What was wrong with me? And why was that damned lump back in my throat?

"I'm fine," I said.

When she hung up, I tried shaking off this latest mood swing by picking up my iPad and googling Bonnie MacLean. Not surprisingly, I found nothing. Not one thing. It was likely that she had married in the intervening years and moved on. That's what people do.

By then it was time for afternoon PT. When that was over, I wanted to talk to Mel, but I didn't call her. I knew she was busy working, and I didn't want to disturb her. She'd get around to calling when she could, but I was beyond bored. I was delighted when my phone rang.

"You son of a bitch!" It took a while for me to recognize Mac MacPherson's voice.

"Top of the day to you, too," I responded mildly.

"What do you mean opening up this can of worms all these years later?" he raged. "Couldn't you just let things be? Is this the thanks I get?"

"Thanks for what?" I asked.

"For keeping my mouth shut all this time," Mac replied. "For making it possible for you to get that early move up to Homicide. But no, instead of letting it rest—instead of letting a closed case stay closed—you had to send that woman out here to nose around."

"Like it or not," I told him, "the Monica Wellington homicide case has been officially reopened. If both of our promotions back then came about because of something related to that, because of some information you withheld at the time? Too bad. Now's the time to come forward, especially if it's some detail that would help us close the case."

"I don't know anything about the Girl in the Barrel," he insisted, "not a damned thing! As for you? Do me a favor and go straight to hell! And the next time either you or that babe with the boobs stops by for a chat, I'm going to have an attorney present!"

I started to ask him why he was so upset, but before I could, he slammed the phone down in my ear. Having a landline phone crammed into a receiver is a lot more of a statement than ending a call on a cell phone.

Delilah had given me her number, and I dialed it. "What the hell did you say to Mac MacPherson?"

I was about to say something about Mac's being on the warpath, but I caught myself.

"I told him we were reopening the Wellington homicide. He claimed to have no knowledge of the case; said that he'd forgotten it completely after all these years. Which was obviously a lie."

"Why do you say that?"

"Because as the interview went on, I noticed that he seemed to become more and more agitated. Eventually he invited me to leave."

"He threw you out?"

"Yes, and none too politely, either."

"Did you give him my number?"

"I gave him both our numbers in case anything occurred to him after I left. Why are you asking?"

"Because he just called here and read me the riot act for bringing the case up and for siccing you on him. He also said that the next time either of us talks to him, he wants to have a lawyer present."

"That's what he told me, too, but why would he law-
yer up unless he has something to hide?" Delilah asked.
"Is it possible we should be treating him as a suspect in
Monica's murder?"

"No," I said. "I don't see how he could have done it.
We were riding patrol together that day when the call
came in. If he had been involved in it, I would have noticed that something was wrong."

"So maybe he has something to do with the missing
evidence," Delilah suggested.

"Maybe," I said. "But from what he said to me, I suspect whatever he's hiding has something to do with our
promotions."

"From all the way back in 1973?" She sounded skeptical.

"Where are you now?" I asked.

"On my way back to the department. Why?"

"Do me a favor. Go up to HR and see if you can find
the records from back then. I want to see who signed off
on the paperwork for those two promotions."

"I wouldn't get my hopes up," Delilah observed.
"What makes you think they'll still have a paper trail
after all this time?"

"I'm sure the paper itself is long gone," I agreed. "But
if the records haven't yet been digitized, they'll still
have them on microfiche."

"How quaint," she said. "That's just how I don't want
to spend the rest of this lovely fall afternoon, scrolling
through microfiche records."

"Somebody has to do it," I said.

"All right," she allowed grudgingly, "but you owe me."

Call waiting buzzed. I could see that Mel was on the
line. "Gotta go," I told Delilah. "I've missed you," I said

to Mel when I switched over to her call. "I was afraid you had forgotten me completely."

"Not completely," Mel agreed. "But close. We've got a suspect in the death of that supposedly peaceful protester, Mr. Abernathy—Reginald Abernathy—Reggie for short."

"A cop?" I asked.

"Luckily for me and for the rest of Bellingham's law enforcement community, the POI isn't a cop," Mel answered. "Her name is Aspen Leonard, and she happens to be Reggie's girlfriend. Was Reggie's girlfriend," Mel corrected.

"That would be the same girlfriend who went to ground?"

"The very one," Mel said. "We've already put out a BOLO on her, but I'm thinking of changing it to an all points."

It made perfect sense to me that Mel and I would talk business first and whisper sweet nothings later.

"What makes you think the girlfriend is responsible?" I asked.

"Thanks to Ross Connors, the tox report came back weeks earlier than it would have otherwise," Mel replied. "It turns out Reggie died of an overdose all right, but it's an overdose of something that isn't one of your usual recreational drugs."

"Which one?" I asked.

"Pentobarbital," Mel answered. "It's currently the big drug of choice for vets doing pet euthanasia. And guess who happens to work in a vet's office, or at least who used to work in a vet's office?"

"The girlfriend?"

"Right you are, and, strangely enough, two vials of

the stuff—enough to do in two eighty- to one-hundred-pound dogs—have evidently gone missing from the veterinarian's locked drug storage. Unfortunately for the late Mr. Abernathy, he was a bit of a lightweight in that department. He tipped the scales at one sixty-two.

"So that's what's going on with me," Mel added. "How about you?"

"Not much," I said, "other than the fact that I was just bitched out on the phone by Mac MacPherson."

"The guy you rode with on Patrol years ago?"

"The very one, and the same guy who was with me when we found Monica Wellington's body."

"What was his beef?"

"I'm not sure. He's all bent out of shape because Delilah Ainsworth and I have reopened that case. I'm worried that there might be more to it."

"What?" Mel asked.

"That there might have been something irregular in the way Mac and I got our promotions back then. At least that's what he hinted at on the phone."

Mel knew better than anyone how much of me is and always has been wrapped up in the job. "That's a biggie," she said. "And how you got the promotion isn't really the point. What's important is what you did for all those years once you got there."

"Yes, but—"

"What do you propose to do about it?"

"For right now I've asked Delilah to look into it. She's on her way to HR at the department to do that very thing right now. I'll let you know how it turns out."

"All right," Mel said. "So turning to another topic. What does the doctor say?"

What Dr. Auld had actually said was that I could

probably go home early if I had someone there to look after me, but I wasn't about to tell Mel that and summon her back home, not when she was involved in running such a high-profile case.

"Same old, same old," I said offhandedly. "He says I'm doing all right in the rehab department and with my range of motion and all that, but he's not ready to cut me loose today. They're taking great care of me here, so don't worry. You concentrate on catching your bad girl, and I'll concentrate on getting out of here."

"Okay," Mel said with a relieved laugh. "That sounds fair."

After Mel hung up, I lay there with the phone on my chest, wondering exactly what Mac had meant. Of course I would have made it to Homicide eventually, but if there had been something crooked about the timing of it . . .

Dinner came. I ate it. I watched TV without a whole lot of interest. It was almost nine when the phone rang again. It was Delilah Ainsworth.

"We've got a problem," she said. "I think it's time to call in Internal Affairs."

"Why? What's wrong?"

"Somebody's screwed around with the microfiche records, too. The ones from April 3, 1973, don't exist. They skip from Monday, April 2, to Wednesday, April 4."

"You're kidding. Who would do that?"

"Like we both said before, someone with something to hide," Delilah said. "And someone with a whole lot of pull. I'm betting money your friend and mine, Mr. Rory MacPherson, knows exactly who that person is. I'm going to go back out there right now to talk to him.

From the way he smelled this morning, he'll probably be in the bag by now. I'm great at getting information from drunks."

"You're going there tonight? I don't think that's a good idea. He sounded like he had gone off the rails."

"I'm going," Delilah said. "You don't think I can just sit on this, do you?"

Delilah Ainsworth was a detective, after all. I couldn't very well expect her to wait around until I could drag my butt out of bed and go with her. But I also remembered how Mac had sounded on the phone—pissed as hell. And if you added booze into the equation . . .

"Take someone with you," I cautioned. "Don't go alone."

"I'm a big girl," Delilah said. "I can take care of myself. I'll call you when I'm finished."

Except she didn't call. My iPad told me that, with traffic, it was an hour's drive from downtown Seattle to Sammamish. I gave her an hour to get there. I gave her another hour to do the interview. And then I gave her another forty-five minutes after that before I tried calling her cell phone. No answer. The phone rang and then went to voice mail.

"You said you'd call," I snarled into the phone. "I'm waiting."

By one o'clock in the morning, I was seriously concerned, and that's when I finally decided to do something about it. Since I needed someone with some pull of his own, I called Assistant Chief Ron Peters.

"What's up?" he mumbled when he finally figured out who had awoken him out of what must have been a sound sleep.

"I'm worried about Detective Ainsworth," I said. "She

left at about nine o'clock or so and was on her way to Sammamish to do an interview with Rory MacPherson. She was supposed to call me as soon as she finished. It's hours later now, and she still hasn't checked in."

"What kind of interview?" I could hear the rustle of bedclothes as he came to attention.

I filled him in as best I could.

"Okay," he said. "I'll get someone on this right away."

After that there was nothing for me to do but wait and worry. I was still awake and more than a little frantic when Ron called again at three in the morning. "Bad news, Beau," he said. "It's a murder/suicide. Mac MacPherson is dead, and so is Detective Ainsworth. I'm on my way to meet up with the chief of police out in Sammamish, then we'll be going together to notify Detective Ainsworth's family."

I was stunned speechless. I remember thinking, *Her family? Does he mean her parents?* Then I remembered that she had worn a simple gold band, no diamond.

"She was married, then?" I asked in a near whisper. "Is there a husband?"

"A husband and two teenage daughters," Ron said. "I'm sorry, Beau, but you can't take this personally."

The hell I couldn't, and I did.

CHAPTER 13

It's no surprise that I didn't sleep at all the rest of the night, and I didn't ask for any pain meds, either. Detective Delilah Ainsworth had died at 11:00 p.m.—at the end of the second watch. No matter what Ron Peters said to the contrary, her death was my fault, pure and simple. I hadn't pulled the trigger. In fact, I had told her specifically not to go see Mac alone, but maybe telling someone like Delilah that she shouldn't do something was tantamount to making sure it happened. As for who had insisted on reopening the Monica Wellington case? That was on me, too. So now a husband had lost his wife and two girls would grow up without a mother. I wasn't just sick at heart. I was furious.

I didn't call Mel. Instead, I spent the night plotting my escape from the hospital. New knees be damned, I wanted to be feet on the ground in the investigation into Delilah's death. In order to do that, I had to be out of the hospital and in a vehicle with someone else at the wheel. In the old days, I would have turned to Lars, but he had finally been forced to give up his car keys. With both Mel and Lars out of the picture, I needed to find someone else.

Belltown Terrace is blessed with round-the-clock doormen. They are founts of knowledge when it comes to things the residents of the building might need— dog walkers, babysitters, plumbers, window washers, best sources of takeout fast food, best shuttle drivers, and best cabdrivers. You name it, doormen know it. My favorite doorman, Bob, comes on duty at eight in the morning. I was on the phone with him at 8:01.

"Why, good morning, Mr. Beaumont," he said cordially. "How are things going in the new knees department?" Bob knew whereof he spoke because he had his own set of titanium knees. It turns out there are lots of those around these days.

"I'm doing fine," I said. "My doc says he's willing to let me come home later today, but I need to have someone there to look out for me for the next few days. The problem is, Mel is currently out of town."

"Yes," he said. "Someone came by to pick up some extra clothing for her yesterday. Is there something I can do to help?"

"You wouldn't happen to have a spare RN running around, would you?" I asked.

Bob thought about that for a minute. "Maybe," he said. "My wife has a friend who's a retired RN, but she occasionally does at-home care for people coming out of the hospital. Is that the kind of help you're looking for?"

"Exactly," I said.

"Her name is Marge Herndon," he said. "The problem is, she's not exactly everybody's cup of tea."

"How's that?"

"She's bossy and opinionated."

"Can she drive?" I asked.

"She does drive," Bob said wryly. "Whether she can drive is another question. Do you want me to give her a call?"

"Please. Tell her I'm offering five hundred a day. The deal is, when the doctor cuts me loose, she agrees to come here to the hospital to pick me up. Then I'd like her to stick around doing whatever needs doing for the next several days—until I no longer need her or until Mel gets back, whichever comes first."

"If I can reach her and if she's interested, what should I do?"

"Have her call me," I said. "Give her this number."

Twenty minutes later, I was watching the local news for any breaking information on the Sammamish situation. I was also halfway through breakfast when the phone rang.

"Mr. Beaumont? Marge Herndon here." Hers was a grating voice, not unlike nails on a blackboard, but I needed someone who was capable a whole lot more than I needed soft, dulcet tones. "Bob said you were recovering from knee replacement, needed some home health assistance, and that I should call if I was interested, and I am. When do you want me to start?"

"As soon as I can get the doctor to let me go. He would have done it yesterday, but I didn't have someone to backstop me. So today, maybe?"

"This is my cell," she said. "Call when you're ready. And one more thing."

"What's that?" I asked.

"Bob tells me your wife is currently out of town. You

need to know that I won't tolerate any nonsense in the hanky-panky department. Understood?"

About that time, any form of hanky-panky was way at the bottom of my to-do list. "Got it," I said. "What about a vehicle? Do you have one?"

"I drive a Honda Accord. Why?"

"I anticipate that we'll be doing some driving," I said. "You can either keep track of your mileage and I can reimburse you for using your vehicle, or you can drive mine."

"Assuming the doctor actually releases you, we'll use mine for today and see how it goes," she said.

That made sense to me. The news team switched to a live feed from Sammamish, and I wanted to hear what was being said. "Sorry," I told her. "I have to go."

As soon as she was gone, I used the remote to turn up the volume. A young news reporter, a blonde who looked more like a high school cheerleader than anything else, stood with microphone in hand. In the background was a suburban-looking house with a ribbon of crime scene tape wrapped around a front porch that came complete with a wheelchair ramp and a wooden swing.

"Until today, the City of Sammamish had never had a murder inside the city limits. That has changed this morning with two people dead overnight in what is being termed an apparent murder/suicide at the home of a still unidentified man here in Sammamish. According to the King County Sheriff's Department, the shooter is reported to be a retired longtime member of the Seattle Police Department. The female victim is believed to be a current officer with Seattle PD. At this point we have no information about what the relationship was between the two, nor do we have any idea about a possible motive.

"The shooting took place last night. A neighbor reported hearing what he thought was a single gunshot, but he was unable to determine where it had come from. Much later there were reports of what was thought to be a second gunshot, but when there was no further sign of any disturbance in the neighborhood, people assumed that the sounds they had heard had either been backfires or someone setting off fireworks.

"Hours later, when no one was able to raise the female officer on her radio, officers in Sammamish were sent to her last known location to do a welfare check. The female officer was found dead in the living room of the home you see behind me. The presumed shooter, said to be a double amputee, was found in the garage of the home where a vehicle had been left running.

"At the time he was found, the second victim, the alleged shooter, was still alive, but he died a short time later of what was most likely carbon monoxide poisoning. He was pronounced dead on arrival at a local hospital. Because the City of Sammamish doesn't have its own Homicide squad, the King County Sheriff's Department is conducting the investigation. We expect to have more details once next of kin notifications have been made. A press conference has been scheduled at the Sammamish City Hall for eleven o'clock this morning."

That's where the live feed ended. Back in the station, the anchors turned to a story about an ongoing teacher's strike. I tried switching to several other stations, but by then they had moved on to weather and sports. When the attendant came to collect my breakfast tray, I asked her to send both the PT and OT teams in early. I didn't want to miss Dr. Auld's possible visit because I was down in the gym walking laps or climbing fake stairs.

Mel didn't call until after I was back in bed. "I'm on my way to Lake Stevens," she said. "We've had a tip that Aspen may be holed up at her mother's place there. The tip came in late last night, but we weren't able to get a warrant until now."

She was on point. I could hear the excitement in her voice. What I wanted to say was, "Don't go. Don't put yourself in jeopardy." But I couldn't say that, and I didn't. She wouldn't have paid any more attention than Delilah Ainsworth had.

"Be careful," I said.

"Absolutely," she agreed. "We're going in with a whole takedown team."

"Is the girlfriend armed?"

Mel paused. "Maybe," she said. "We don't know that for sure, but yes, I'll be careful. How are you?"

How was I? Sick at heart. Beyond frustrated. Mad as hell. All of the above.

"Fine," I said. "I'm fine."

"How'd you sleep?"

"Like a baby," I said. Out of the corner of my eye, I noticed movement by my door as Ron Peters rolled his wheelchair into the room.

"Oops," I told Mel. "Someone's here. Gotta go."

Ron looked as gray and grim as I ever remember seeing him except for maybe when he was in the hospital and coming to terms with the idea that he would most likely never walk again.

"What happened?" I asked.

"As near as we can tell, Detective Ainsworth showed up at Mac MacPherson's house. He let her into the house and then gunned her down just inside the front door, with no advance warning. Took her out with one shot. She never had a chance to draw her weapon. Then he pulled the plug by going out into his garage, turning on the engine in his car, and letting it idle.

"After you called me, when Detective Ainsworth didn't respond to a radio summons, I called Sammamish and asked them to send officers to Rory MacPherson's house to do a welfare check. They told me that Detective Ainsworth's car was parked outside. When they knocked and got no answer, they went inside. They found Detective Ainsworth dead in the living room. MacPherson was in the garage, sitting in his wheelchair with the car engine running. He was unconscious, presumably from carbon monoxide poisoning. They found what is believed to be the weapon used to kill Ainsworth still in his lap."

"Did he leave a note?"

Ron shook his head. "Not that we've found so far. There was a computer in the house. He might have left something on that, but it'll take time to access it. First we have to get a warrant, and then we'll need to work around whatever password protection he had. There was plenty of evidence that MacPherson had been drinking heavily for some time, probably for months on end. According to neighbors, other than going to the store, he had barely left the house since his wife moved out and divorced him a year or so ago. There were piles of garbage bags full of empty booze bottles stacked along one wall of the garage. It looks as though his drink of choice was vodka, and he didn't bother diluting it with mixers.

"So that's what I know," Ron finished. "What can you tell me?"

I told him everything Delilah had told me—that the evidence in the Wellington case had disappeared and that the HR records for April 2, 1973—the day of Mac's and my unanticipated promotions—had been expunged. I also told him about Mac's furious phone call to me after Delilah's initial visit.

When I finished, Ron let his breath out in a long sigh. "Okay, then," he said. "I'm going to have to bring in Internal Affairs. Someone way up in the food chain has something to hide, and I want to get to the bottom of it."

"I'll do what I can to help," I offered.

Ron shook his head. "No," he said. "Other than being interviewed as needed, you won't be involved. As of this moment, you're out of this. Completely."

"You can't order me around, Ron. Remember? I don't work for you, or for Seattle PD, either."

We were both hurting that morning. Ron had done me a huge personal favor by reopening the Wellington homicide. As a result, he had lost an officer, and I had lost yet another partner. An angry look passed between us. There was a moment when our long years of friendship hung in the balance. I couldn't let it come to that, so I decided to reduce the pressure.

"Let's face it," I said. "There's not much I can do, since I'm stuck in this bed. Can you at least tell me where Delilah lived? I'd like to send her family some flowers."

Ron shook his head as though thinking that might not be such a great idea. Still, he pulled out a notebook and read off an address that sounded like it was somewhere near the Woodland Park Zoo. I dutifully copied it into my iPad.

"Her husband's name?"

"Brian. Her daughters are Kimberly and Kristen. They're sophomores in high school."

Just hearing their names spoken aloud wounded me.

Their lives had turned into a nightmare because I'd had a dream about a long-dead girl and had taken that as a sign that I was destined to do something about it. The end result wasn't fair to anyone.

Ron had barely rolled away down the hall when Dr. Auld showed up. This was earlier than he usually came in, so maybe he didn't have any surgeries scheduled for that particular morning.

"Good news," I told him. "My wife is out of town, but I've hired someone—an RN—to come stay with me until I'm back on my feet. If you let me out today, she'll start today."

"By which you mean to say that you'd like to leave today?"

I nodded. I didn't want to seem too eager, but I also wanted to be in Sammamish at city hall in time for that 11:00 A.M. press conference. Yes, the local newspeople would be covering it, but that wasn't to say that they'd be covering all of it, and I didn't want to miss anything important.

"All right," Dr. Auld said agreeably. "I'll send someone in to help you get dressed. By the time your ride gets here, I should have the paperwork out of the way."

I called Marge Herndon the moment he was out of the room. "Okay," I said. "Come get me."

I would find out in the course of the next several days that Marge Herndon had any number of failings, as Bob had so drolly warned me, but being late wasn't one of them. She arrived in my room with a wheelchair in hand before I'd managed to get my clothes out of the locker, to say nothing of on my body.

Marge was a stocky woman with a wide, square face topped by a mop of curly white hair. She looked more like an NFL tackle than she did a member of the caring professions. When I started trying to get dressed, she immediately took over.

"Let me help you with that," she told me brusquely. "Isn't that why you hired me? Besides, it's nothing I haven't seen before."

In no time at all, she had armed herself with the proper release paperwork along with my take-home prescriptions, and we headed out. She wheeled me out the front door with a practiced hand and stopped me next to a waiting Accord, which she had left under the watchful eye of a parking valet.

"I told you I'd be back in ten," she told him. He nodded and gave me a halfhearted shake of his head. I got the message. He was glad I was the one getting in the car with the woman instead of him.

She helped me into the passenger seat and then buckled me in as though I were a toddler incapable of performing such complicated procedures on my own. The wheelchair evidently belonged to her. She stowed that along with my loaner walker in the back, then climbed in behind the wheel.

"Belltown Terrace?" she said.

I had my iPad out. Google said that it would take us twenty-eight minutes to get from the hospital to city hall in Sammamish, longer with traffic.

"No," I said. "Do you know how to get from here to I-90?"

It wasn't the answer she expected. "I-90?" she asked. "Isn't that the wrong direction?"

"It's the right direction for where I want to go this morning, and we've only got about half an hour to get there."

"Look," she said. "You just got out of the hospital. I'm supposed to be taking care of you."

"I hired you to take care of me and to drive me. Now, either go where I'm telling you, or let me out and I'll call a cab. It's up to you. Do you want that five hundred bucks or not?"

She gave me a scathing look and then roared out of the driveway, peeling rubber and leaving the parking valet watching us go and still shaking his head. Marge didn't so much drive her Honda as aim it. She wove through spaces where I was afraid we were going to shred mirrors off the vehicles next to us, but she got us back down the hill and southbound on I-5 with breathtaking speed. I think she was hoping I'd object, but I had spent years with Mel Soames behind the wheel, and between Mel and Marge, there was no contest.

"Where are we going?" she asked as we headed east on I-90.

"The City of Sammamish," I told her. "City hall. There's a news conference starting in half an hour. You get a hundred-dollar bonus if I'm there before it starts. Do you know how to get there?"

"No idea," she said, "but I'm guessing that gadget in your hand has a map on it." She nodded in the direction of my iPad. "I'm also guessing you'll give me directions as we go."

You've heard that old adage about how money talks? In this case, the offer of a hundred-dollar bonus worked like a charm. Other than calling out directions, we didn't exchange another word. When we arrived at the city government complex in Sammamish, the parking lot around the police department was full of media vans and official-looking vehicles. Marge picked out a woman leaving the library a few buildings away and followed her to her car. Then she waited in the parking aisle until the woman had stowed her bag of books and pulled out of the spot.

"Isn't it a long way from here to city hall?" I asked. I had seen the sign on the way past.

"Don't worry," she said. "It won't be any skin off your nose. You'll be the one in the chair; I'll be the one doing the pushing."

Yes, ma'am.

Thanks to all the OT practice at the hospital, we managed the maneuver of getting me out of her car with little difficulty. Once Marge had me in the chair, we set off for city hall with her handling the wheelchair in the same way she did her car—aiming rather than driving. She dove through spaces between people that were far too small, fully expecting them to get out of her way, which they did. Fortunately for all concerned, the people standing in her path looked up, caught the dead-eye expression on Marge's face, and leaped to safety.

"Looks like there's a big crowd over there by the doors," she said, observing the mob scene from a distance. "What makes you think they'll let us in?"

My ticket to ride was there in my hip pocket along with my wallet—my Special Homicide Investigation Team badge and ID. Considering the cross-jurisdictional nature of the case, there was a good chance that someone else from S.H.I.T. Squad B might be in attendance. There was also an equally good chance that they wouldn't be looking for me to be there at all, to say nothing of my showing up in a wheelchair.

The room was essentially an auditorium, and it was standing room only. The stage consisted of a set of five desks that, under normal circumstances, would have been occupied by the mayor and members of the city council. These were not normal circumstances. A lectern spiked with a collection of microphones stood in the middle of the stage, but it was still empty. Marge had kept her part of the bargain, and we had arrived before the press conference started.

"Okay," I said. "I owe you that bonus."

Marge sniffed her approval. Then, instead of shoving me off to one side or the other at the back of the room, she made a beeline for the stage and parked me in the aisle next to the front row of seats. I wasn't thrilled about being in the front row, but there were enough people with cameras hanging around and enough associated camera lighting that my relatively unauthorized presence wasn't as obvious as it might have been otherwise.

Once I was settled, Marge then proceeded to bully the person occupying the next seat over into going somewhere else. Bob was right. Where Marge was concerned, the word "bossy" didn't quite cover it.

One at a time, grim-faced people filed onto the stage and took seats at the desks. Most of them were law enforcement types, in uniform and out, many of whom I knew on a first-name basis. A total stranger, a white-haired guy wearing a custom-tailored suit, assumed his post at the lectern. He turned out to be the mayor.

"This is a very sad day for our community," he announced solemnly. "Not only do we have our first-ever homicide inside the city limits, we have a related suicide as well. Considering the seriousness of the situation and because at least one officer from another jurisdiction is involved, Randy Olmstead, our chief of police, made the decision to ask the King County Sheriff's Department for help in investigating this case. It will be conducted as a joint investigation, but King County will be taking the lead. As a result, the first person we'll be hearing from today is Captain Todd Thornton, the public information officer for the King County Sheriff's Department."

Todd was someone I had interacted with occasionally through the years, and he was a consummate pro. His job was to give the initial picture as well as an overall view of what had happened and was happening now. He would tell the assembled reporters who was dead and how they died. I suspected that enough time had elapsed between the incident and now to allow for next of kin notifications. That meant Todd would also be able to release the names of the victims and offer reassurances to the public about the unlikelihood of additional suspects still being at large.

Todd assumed his position at the bank of microphones and began his standard briefing.

"At approximately ten forty-seven P.M. last night, a shooting occurred in the twenty-six thousand block of Northeast Forty-fifth Street here in Sammamish. The disturbance was reported at the time, but was assumed to be either a backfire or unauthorized use of fireworks. The shooting wasn't confirmed until several hours later when officers went to do a welfare check at that address. Inside the home, officers found one victim, a female, dead from an apparent gunshot wound. A second individual was later located inside a closed garage where a vehicle had been left running. The second victim, a male, was thought to be suffering from carbon monoxide poisoning. He was treated at the scene but was declared dead on arrival at a local hospital. The victims have been identified as Detective Delilah Ainsworth, a homicide detective with Seattle PD, and Rory MacPherson, who received a medical retirement five years ago. He had been a motorcycle officer with the Seattle PD for many years."

This was all standard stuff. And because I already knew most of it, I only half listened to what was being said. Then, however, halfway through Todd's recitation, it suddenly occurred to me that perhaps I wasn't the only person in the room who knew what had been going on and that Delilah had come calling on Mac MacPherson in search of answers about Monica Wellington's murder back in 1973.

If that other person who was in the know was also responsible for the disappearance of the physical evidence in the case, along with the tampering on the HR microfiche records, it stood to reason that he or she was far more than a disinterested bystander in everything that was happening in the Sammamish City Hall. And if that was the case, what were the chances that that very person might well have come to the press conference this morning, wanting to know exactly how the investigation was going and whether there was anything that would point directly to him?

First I fiddled with my iPad and found the proper application. Once I had 360 Panorama tuned up, I leaned over to Marge. "Stand up and punch this button. Then I want you to walk back up the aisle, turning around and around as you go and holding this in front of you like this."

"Right now?" Marge asked.

"Yes."

"Why?"

"I want you to photograph all the people in the room, on both sides of the aisle."

"What happens when the flash goes off?" she asked. "I'll look like an idiot."

"No, you won't," I countered. "There won't be a flash. The camera in the iPad uses available light."

"If you want me to take pictures," she said. "That'll be extra. I didn't sign on to work as your damned photographer!"

I wanted the pictures way more than I wanted to argue. "Done," I said. "Fifty bucks."

Dutifully, Marge accepted the iPad. I showed her how to switch on the application, then she headed up the aisle, strolling along and turning around and around as she went and doing a credible job of pretending to look for someone seated in the audience. By then I think most of the attendees were so focused on what Todd was saying that they didn't notice her pirouetting her way up the aisle. Marge was anything but a lightweight, and her resemblance to the dancing hippos in *Fantasia* was striking.

She didn't come back immediately. From the sharp scent of cigarette smoke surrounding her when Marge returned, I knew she had taken the opportunity to go outside and have a quick drag or two. By the time she gave me back my iPad, Todd had announced that the King County Medical Examiner's Office would conduct the autopsies later in the day. He then went on to field questions from the assembled members of the fourth estate. There were plenty of questions that were greeted with the standard "No comment." Was there any known connection between Detective Ainsworth and Rory MacPherson? No comment. Was either one of them suspected of any wrongdoing? No comment. Was Detective Ainsworth working on a particular case? No comment.

Was there any indication that a third party had been in the home prior to the shooting?

Once again, Todd's answer was a swift "No comment," but there was the smallest tell in one corner of his mouth before he answered the question. I'm not sure how many other people noticed the tiny twitch, but I've spent a lifetime trying to sort out who's telling the truth and who isn't. As far as I was concerned, it was a clear signal that someone else had been in Mac MacPherson's home on the night in question, someone else who wasn't either Mac or Delilah.

I listened carefully to all the speakers who followed Todd and noticed that there was one critical item that went unmentioned by all concerned. This crime was "blue on blue." It was one cop, retired or not, killing another cop. And it wasn't a case of accidental friendly fire, either. From what was said as well as from what went unsaid, a clearer picture of the incident began to emerge. Rory MacPherson had evidently been lying in wait for Delilah. As soon as she set foot in his house, he had gunned her down before rolling his wheelchair out to the garage, where he managed to take his own life.

When Todd Thornton finished, he yielded the lectern to Alan Walsh, one of the gun guys from the Washington State Patrol Crime Lab. He reported that three handguns had been collected from the crime scene. One was a .38 semiautomatic Smith & Wesson that belonged to Detective Ainsworth; another was a Glock 17 that was evidently her backup weapon. Arriving officers had found both of her weapons still in their holsters, and neither of them had been fired recently. The third weapon, a Colt .45, was registered to Mr. MacPherson. That one had been found in the garage in the possession of the second victim and, unlike the others, appeared to have been recently fired.

I listened to everything Alan Walsh said. Obviously he wasn't saying everything he knew. He wouldn't. That wasn't how the press conference game was played. Switching my iPad over to Notes, I set myself reminders to talk to both Thornton and Walsh later, when they didn't have lights, cameras, and microphones aimed in their direction. I knew that what they would say to the press and what they would say to a fellow cop would be two entirely different things. I also made a note to check with the M.E. once the autopsies had been performed. My badge had gotten me into the press conference, and it would get me in to talk to those other folks as well— as long as no one tumbled to the fact that I was currently on medical leave.

My phone rang. I checked caller ID. When I saw it was Mel, I switched it off. If she had heard about Delilah's death, the jig was about to be up. I didn't want to have that conversation in public. In fact, I didn't want to have the conversation at all.

When the press conference wound down, Marge used my chair as a battering ram to get us back up the aisle and out into the parking lot. Her mutters of "Step aside" and "Clear the path" were far more effective in herding people out of her way than her occasional and ostensibly insincere "Sorry."

Out on the sidewalk, it became clear that Marge had every intention of leaving me parked outside the front door while she went to retrieve her car. That wasn't a popular option with me. I had caught sight of Ron Peters in the crowd of uniformed SPD folks. He had told me to stay out of the case on a friend-to-friend basis, but if he found out I was there, I knew he wouldn't hesitate to call my boss.

"I'd rather go straight to the car," I said.

"Of course you would," Marge grumbled. "Maybe it doesn't look like it's uphill, but trust me, it is."

Under protest, she wheeled me back to the car, growling all the way. Once I was belted into the passenger seat, I turned on my iPad while Marge loaded the chair in the back. Unsurprisingly, there was a single irate message from Mel:

> Your phone is off. You're not at the hospital. I heard about Delilah.
> What's going on?

I stowed the iPad without responding.

"I think I'm about due for some pain meds," I said to Marge once she was in the driver's seat. Naturally, my prescriptions were in the trunk along with the chair.

"Tell me something I don't know," she said. "You're supposed to take them with food. Do you want to stop along the way, or do you want to wait until I get you home?"

"Home will be fine," I said.

The truth is, pain meds or not, I was out like a light within a few blocks of leaving the Sammamish City Hall, and I didn't wake up again until Marge parked in front of the garage gate at Belltown Terrace.

"What am I supposed to do with my car?" she asked. "Parking fees in downtown Seattle are higher than a cat's back."

I used the remote on my key ring to let her in. "Parking on the top floor of the garage, P-1, is free on the weekends. During the week use the parking valet. Tell the attendant to give you the daily all-day rate. I'll pay."

Once Marge had negotiated the parking issue, she used my building key to access the elevator. "What floor?" she asked, standing by the controls.

"Penthouse," I said.

"Figures," she returned.

Once inside the unit, if Marge was impressed by her surroundings, she certainly didn't let on. "Where do you want to be?" she asked. "In bed?"

"No," I said. "I've spent the last five days in bed. There's a recliner in the study. That's where I want to be. It has a better view."

She helped me out of the wheelchair and got me into the recliner. I could tell I was way beyond ready for my pain meds. "No pain meds without food," she insisted. "Now what do you want to eat?"

"I'm not sure what we have."

The answer to that was nothing much. Neither Mel nor I are great when it comes to domesticity. I'm a notoriously bad cook and she's not much better. As a result, we generally eat out or order in.

Marge left me alone for a few moments. I was trying to mask the pain by concentrating on the blue waters of Puget Sound out to the west when she returned, bringing with her a tray containing my pills, a glass of water, and two string cheeses.

"This is going to have to do for the time being," she grumbled. "What on earth do you people eat? The only edible things I could find in your kitchen were one moldy English muffin and this."

I accepted the proffered string cheese.

"We're not big on cooking," I said. After eating the cheese, I swallowed the pills, chasing them with water.

"I noticed," Marge replied. "Now if you expect me to take care of you, I'm going to have to feed you. What do you want for dinner?"

"We could order some mac and cheese from El Gaucho," I suggested hopefully. One order of that was usually enough for Mel and me to share for a meal.

"That's what you might do," Marge said. "It's not what I'm going to do. You've had major surgery. You're supposed to have protein, not carbs. Now give me some money and I'll go get some groceries. You're not Jewish—I mean, you don't eat kosher, do you?"

I shook my head. "No," I said. "I'm not Jewish, and I'm not a vegan, either."

"I'm assuming that until your wife comes home, you'll need me to stay over. Where am I supposed to sleep?"

The guest bedroom and bath in our unit belong to Mel. We learned early on in our relationship that sharing a bathroom didn't work. Ditto for closets. There's a pull-down wall bed that can be used for guests in a pinch, but most of the time the bed stays up and Mel uses the room and accompanying bath as her private domain. That's where she dresses, and she has a desk and love seat in there that she sometimes uses for work. I knew without even asking that having her share space with Marge wasn't going to wash. But I also knew that I did need to have someone on hand, or at least nearby, to help me in the meantime.

I extracted my billfold and peeled off a pair of hundreds. "You go get some food," I said. "I'll figure out the sleeping arrangements. And while you're gone, you should go down to P-2 and get the garage clicker out of my car in space 230. That way you'll be able to get your car in and out even when the outside garage door is closed."

"Keys for that?" Marge asked.

"In the master bedroom," I said. "On my dresser."

As soon as Marge left, I was on the phone to Bob, the doorman.

"How's Marge working out for you?" he asked.

"About how you'd expect," I replied. "Is anyone using the guest suite at the moment?"

Years ago, Belltown Terrace had an on-site manager. When that was no longer necessary, the manager's unit was converted into a guest suite that can be rented by the day or week.

Bob chuckled. "That good, eh?" he asked. "But yes, the suite is currently available. Would you like to book it?"

"For the next five days, if that's possible," I said. "By then, either Mel will be back home or else I'll be well enough to look after of myself."

"Done, Mr. Beaumont," he said. "I'll take care of it right away."

By the time I ended the call, the pain meds were doing their magic. After turning my phone off, I drifted off into dreamland. The last thing I remembered was watching a Washington State ferry slip silently away from the Coleman ferry dock and head out across the bright blue waters of Puget Sound.

CHAPTER 14

The next thing I knew, I was dancing—dancing the way I used to before my knees went south. I wasn't doing what passes for dancing these days, but the old-fashioned kind of ballroom dancing. I had been good enough at one time that my partner and I had won a prize in a dancing competition aboard a cruise ship.

The dance was a tango. As I held my partner close, I assumed I was dancing with Mel. But then I noticed that the hair next to my cheek was brown rather than blond. It wasn't until I held the woman at arm's length to spin her around that I saw who it was—Delilah Ainsworth, not Mel. She was wearing a low-cut white floor-length gown, laughing and smiling despite the blood pouring out of the bullet hole in her chest.

"Where's your vest?" I demanded, pulling her back against my body. "Why weren't you wearing a vest?"

She was still laughing when she answered. "It didn't go with my dress."

I awoke with a start. Two hours had passed. The

dream had been so lifelike, so real, that I more than half expected to find blood on my clothing. There wasn't any. The only thing visible on my chest was my cell phone, still where I'd left it, lying under my hand. I could hear the sound of the front door opening with a key, followed by the rustle of bags of groceries being deposited in the kitchen. Soon I was treated to the sound of banging pots and pans accompanied by Marge's tuneless humming.

Knowing it was time to face some music of my own, I turned on my phone. There were a total of five missed calls from Mel. I called her back.

"What the hell?" she demanded. "Where are you? The hospital said you had been released, even though they weren't supposed to let you out without having someone at home to look after you. And why has your phone been turned off? I've been worried sick, but we've made an arrest in the Bellingham case, and I couldn't just walk away."

"You don't need to," I reassured her. "I hired a nurse, a friend of Bob's. She's looking after me."

"Bob who?" Mel wanted to know.

"Bob, the doorman. Her name is Marge Herndon. She brought me home. In fact, she's out in the kitchen cooking right now."

"In our kitchen?" Mel demanded incredulously. "We don't have any food."

"We do now."

That seemed to satisfy her concerns on that score. "Tell me about Detective Ainsworth."

With the bloody dream still dancing in my head, that was harder to do.

"She went back to see Mac MacPherson late last night, to ask more questions about the Monica Wellington cold case. He shot her dead right there in the living room. Then he rolled his wheelchair out to his garage and turned on the engine in the car. He was still alive when they found him, but he didn't make it."

"This isn't your fault," Mel said.

I said nothing, which, between the two of us, was answer enough.

"What are you going to do about it?"

"What can I do about it?" I returned. "I'm off on sick leave, remember?"

"Don't give me that," Mel answered. "You were supposed to stay in rehab for at least another two days. Delilah's death is the reason you're out today, right?"

Right, I thought, but I didn't say it aloud.

"My understanding is that King County is handling the investigation," Mel said. "Delilah was a cop. Believe me, they're not going to leave a stone unturned."

"The problem is," I told her, "when they finally get around to turning over the Monica Wellington stone, they're not going to find anything. The evidence box, including the murder book, has gone missing. It was evidently lost somewhere between the open case evidence locker and closed case evidence storage."

Mel hesitated for a moment before she replied. "It sounds to me as though Seattle PD has a serious problem."

"Along with one very dead homicide detective," I added grimly.

"But you know you can't do anything about this," Mel interjected. "When Internal Affairs asks you about it, you need to tell them what you know, and let them handle it."

"Right," I said.

We both knew she was wasting her breath.

"Okay," she said, backing off. "I'm glad you're home. I'm glad you have someone there to help you. Now I need to go look in on an interrogation."

"Your suspect hasn't asked for an attorney?"

"Not so far, even though we read her her rights when we first picked her up down in Lake Stevens. Fortunately for us, some people are so convinced of how smart they are that they don't believe they need an attorney."

"You got her, didn't you," I said.

"Yes," Mel agreed. "Yes, I did."

"So will this help settle things back down in Bellingham?"

"That remains to be seen. I may be able to come home later tonight, but I'm glad you've got someone there to fill in for me in the meantime. Is this Marge person going to stay there in the unit with you?"

"No. I've made arrangements for her to use the guest unit downstairs. I'll be able to call her if I need something. I didn't think you'd appreciate sharing your space with an outsider."

"Good," Mel said. She sounded relieved. Once she got around to meeting Marge, I was sure she would be even more so.

Our landline phone rang then. Mel and I keep the phone so we can buzz in visitors from the garage or the outside door, but we don't usually answer it. Most of the callers who use that number are doing political polling or trying to sell us something we don't need, most notably aluminum siding. I had meant to tell Marge that if that phone rang, she should let it go to voice mail, but she answered before I had a chance to do so.

"It's for you," Marge said, bringing me the portable

receiver from the counter in the kitchen. "It's Bob. He says two detectives with the King County Sheriff's Department are waiting downstairs and would like to see you if you're up to it."

"I've gotta go," I told Mel. "It sounds like some detectives are here to start turning over stones."

"Let them," Mel advised. "It's not your problem."

But of course it was my problem. If I hadn't started the ball rolling in the first place, Delilah Ainsworth wouldn't be dead.

I hung up my cell phone and took the portable. "Thanks, Bob," I said. "Go ahead and send them up."

When the doorbell rang, Marge answered the ring and gave them a bit of unsolicited advice. "I'm Mr. Beaumont's nurse," she told them in a no-nonsense fashion. "He's recently undergone major surgery, and it's my job to look after him. So you may see him, but I'm fully prepared to send you on your way if you overstay your welcome."

That was all vintage Marge Herndon, but it occurred to me that there were times when having a bossy gatekeeper might be a good thing.

She brought them into the study. Detectives Hugo Monford and Dave Anderson, like most of the doctors I'd met recently—Dr. Auld excepted—seemed incredibly young and still wet behind the ears. I immediately deemed them both much too inexperienced to be handling Delilah Ainsworth's murder. They were somewhere in their early forties, fit, and probably reasonably smart. The problem was, Delilah deserved the best, and I wasn't convinced these two guys were it. Dave, the younger of the two, was completely smitten with the view from my condo.

"What a great view!" he exclaimed in a tone that was half admiration and the other half envy. "How does someone who works as a cop on the street end up in a place like this?" he asked.

"You start by marrying well," I told him. "Then you hire someone really smart to manage your money."

Marge was still standing in the doorway when I gave my reply. She shook her head, rolled her eyes in disapproval, and stalked off.

"Have a seat," I said. "To what do I owe the honor? I'm assuming it has something to do with Detective Ainsworth's death." I had already decided that my best bet would be to play dumb. If I wanted to know what direction the investigation was taking, all I had to do was pay attention to what the investigators were asking. On the other hand, if my presence at the press conference had been duly noted and/or reported on, it wouldn't do to play too dumb.

Monford nodded. He was clearly the lead. "Yes," he said. "We just had a conversation with Seattle PD assistant chief Ron Peters. He mentioned that you and Detective Ainsworth were involved in reopening a cold case from 1973."

"Yes," I said. "The murdered girl was Monica Wellington."

"Was that at your instigation or Detective Ainsworth's?"

I wasn't going to admit that this whole thing had started as a result of a drug-induced dream.

"It was mine," I said. "It was the first case I worked once I was assigned to Homicide at Seattle PD, and the fact that it's never been solved still bothers me. You'll probably have cases like that someday, too. The ones that never get solved and never go away."

Monford nodded. "Was Rory MacPherson involved in that original investigation?"

"Only at the beginning," I said. "We were both still in uniform and riding Patrol together on the day we got the call about the Girl in the Barrel. We knew the victim's name early on, but that's how the media referred to the victim. Monica Wellington's body was stuffed in a barrel used to collect grease from restaurants for transfer to local rendering plants. Once she was stuffed into the barrel of grease it was rolled down the south end of Magnolia Bluff."

Both detectives pulled out notebooks and started taking notes.

"That was Mac's and my last shift together," I continued. "He and I both got our promotions two days later. He went to Motorcycles; I went to Homicide."

"As far as you know then, that was MacPherson's only contact with the case?" Detective Monford confirmed. "His only involvement? He was there with you when that initial call came in, and that was it?"

"As far as I know."

"Who were the other detectives involved in that case?"

I listed them. "Lawrence Powell; Watty Watkins; Milton Gurkey, my first partner; and myself. The first two are retired. Milton Gurkey died twenty-five years ago."

"Why did Detective Ainsworth go to see Rory MacPherson in the first place?"

"We were in the process of reopening the Wellington homicide when Detective Ainsworth discovered that the evidence box had gone missing."

"Did she think MacPherson might be responsible for taking it?"

"Probably," I agreed, "although I told her I didn't see how that was possible. After Mac left Patrol, he worked in the Motorcycle unit. He would have had no reason to have access to the evidence room or to routine evidence transfers. All the same, Delilah wanted to talk to him. We decided that, without the murder book, we'd need to go back to the beginning. We'd need to find and re-interview whatever witnesses were still available, starting with taking statements from both me and from Rory MacPherson. That was what she was doing."

"How did the interview go?"

"Not well. Mac called me right after she left his place, and he was hot. Told me that I had no business bringing this up after all these years. He said that the next time he talked to either one of us, he wanted to have a lawyer present."

"When was that call?"

"I'm not exactly sure—sometime in the afternoon. When you're locked up in a hospital, time seems to run together. I could probably find the exact call time on my incoming calls list."

I reached for my phone, but Monford waved me off. "Don't bother. We can check that later. Our understanding is that Detective Ainsworth went back out to Sammamish again, much later in the evening. Do you have any idea why?"

This was where I didn't want to go, but I had to. After all, it was the second trip out—the one after Delilah's study of the HR microfiche—that had gotten her killed.

"By then she was convinced that the whole thing might have had something to do with our promotions, Mac's and mine, rather than with the homicide case itself," I said. "As I told you earlier, that Sunday afternoon—the day we were called to the Wellington crime scene—was Mac's and my last ride together on Patrol. Delilah went to HR looking for some kind of paper trail about our promotions. After scrolling through the microfiche records, she ascertained that there isn't any—not for my promotion and not for Mac's, either. The microfiche records for that time have been altered. That day's worth of records has been deleted."

"Is that even possible?" Monford asked. "How do you erase a line on a microfiche?"

"I'm not sure," I answered. "If deleting something isn't possible, then we have to assume that the records for that day were never put on microfiche in the first place."

"Let me get this straight," Detective Anderson said, speaking for the first time. "When Detective Ainsworth went to see MacPherson to begin with, it was to interview him because you and she were reopening the Wellington case. That's when he called and was upset with you about that. What did he say exactly?"

"Something about how dare I bring this up again after all this time, and something else about this being the thanks he got for keeping his mouth shut."

"Mouth shut about what?"

"I don't know."

"So then she goes back to Seattle PD and does some research in the HR microfiche. After that she goes back to see MacPherson again, about the promotion thing, only this time she ends up dead."

"Yes," I said.

Anderson gave me an appraising stare. "Did you cheat to get that initial posting to Homicide?" he asked.

"No," I answered. "I did not."

"What about MacPherson to Motorcycles? Did he cheat?"

"Not to my knowledge," I said. "He might have, but these were promotions we had both put in for long before that Sunday afternoon."

"You're the one who called Assistant Chief Peters when Detective Ainsworth didn't return from Sammamish in a timely fashion. Did you have any advance knowledge that she might be walking into a trap?"

"I knew Mac was angry. I advised her not to go alone because he sounded so steamed, drunk maybe. Even though I didn't think it was a good idea, I had no inkling that he would gun her down."

Marge Herndon appeared in the doorway and pointed at her watch. "That's enough for today," she said. "Mr. Beaumont just got out of the hospital this morning. He needs his rest."

"Which is one way of having a pretty airtight alibi," Anderson said with a grin.

I hadn't much liked the guy to begin with, and I liked him even less now. "Yes," I said. "Airtight."

"Is there a chance Detective Ainsworth and Rory MacPherson had some other kind of connection?" Detective Monford asked. "Is it possible that they had some kind of relationship that you had no knowledge of?"

"No," I said. "That's not possible. Delilah was spectacular looking. She was a capable investigator and definitely on her way up. She was also happily married, with a husband and a couple of kids. Mac was a double amputee, a retired has-been—divorced, bitter, and drowning his sorrows in booze. No, Detective Ainsworth and Rory MacPherson did not have a previous relationship or a personal relationship of any kind."

"So what got her killed, then?" Monford asked. "The fact that the Wellington case had been reopened or the HR discrepancy that you just pointed out?"

I thought about that for a moment. "It could be one of those," I answered finally. "Or else it's both."

Marge cleared her throat. "As I said before," she announced in a voice that left no room for argument, "that is enough! You need to go now."

I had long since tired of the whole interview process, and I was more than a little grateful that Marge had shown up to give the two detectives their walking papers. They allowed themselves to be herded out of the room, but not before getting my cell phone number. After slamming the front door shut behind them, Marge disappeared into the kitchen, emerging a few minutes later with a tray laden with my next dose of pills and a plate that contained a grilled pork chop and a mound of broccoli.

"After slaving away in the kitchen," she told me, "I wasn't about to let it sit around and get cold. Eat before you take your pills. You shouldn't drop them into an empty stomach."

"Yes, ma'am," I said.

"And while you're eating I'll go down and get my stuff out of the car. You really want me to stay in that other unit, the one downstairs? I'm sure I'd be fine here."

"No," I said. "If I need you, I'll call. You'll only be an elevator ride away."

With that, Marge stomped off, leaving me to eat in peace. The woman had made good on her threat to serve up protein, and I have to admit, that pork chop was worth the price of admission. It was glorious. Cooked to a turn, and the broccoli was, too. There was still some crispness to it, and it had been slathered with a healthy dose of lemon. I ate every smidgen of it. I might have asked for a second helping, but Marge had yet to return from the move-in process. Instead, I sat there in my recliner, basking like an overfed cat in the late-afternoon sun, drifting as the pain med did its magic. When I awoke again, it was full dark. Marge had obviously come and gone in utter silence. My dinner tray was gone and someone had turned the lamp on next to my chair.

The problem was, I needed to go in the worst way. So what was it going to be? Pick up the phone and call Marge to come upstairs and shepherd me into the bathroom? There was no dignity in that. In the end, I decided to be a man about it. The walker was right there. My cell phone had been sitting on the charger on a side table. After slipping my fully charged phone into my pocket, I wrestled the walker over in front of me, and then used that to lever myself up and out of the recliner. When I finished up in the bathroom, I felt like I could give myself a gold star. Then, silently thanking the OT team for all their efforts on my behalf, I took myself into the bedroom and went to bed. In my own bed. And gave myself full points for that, too.

The effort had worn me out. I slept again for a while, but that's the problem with sleeping too much during the day—you don't sleep enough at night. By one o'clock in the morning, I was wide awake and thinking. Considering everything that had happened, that wasn't a good thing.

CHAPTER 15

I awoke in the wee small hours of Sunday morning—the third watch. That's the time the bars close and the drunks start beating the crap out of one another. No, wait. That was back in the olden days. Now they simply shoot the crap out of one another. If you're down on the street, that is. I wasn't. I was safely tucked in my bed, far above the Denny Regrade's sometimes tumultuous and deadly late-night street scene, but I was fighting my own kind of battle, wrestling with all the woulda, shoulda, coulda's that would have meant Detective Delilah Ainsworth would still be alive.

On weekends especially, cops aren't the only people dealing with the third watch in the world of big-city law enforcement. Medical examiners' offices are usually fully staffed during those hours as well. Knowing how bureaucratic politics work, I figured the person on duty right then—the low woman on the totem pole, as it were, with apologies to Delilah's Native American sensibilities—would be the most recent arrival in the King County M.E.'s office, Dr. Rosemary Mellon.

There was another good reason, besides being a relative newcomer, which made it likely she would be the M.E. working the least desirable shift—Rosemary is a genuine maverick. She's an antibureaucrat bureaucrat. She gives straight answers. She doesn't pull punches. She's not afraid of going around the chain of command. All of those things may have made her less popular with her coworkers, but for those of us out in the field, she was a gold mine. And for those very same reasons, she was top of the list for Special Homicide's favorite M.E. of all time.

In other words, it was no accident that Rosemary's cell phone number was plugged into my phone's contact list, and if she wasn't working? I figured she would have done what shift workers all over the world do when they're trying to sleep. She would have turned her phone off. As Sherlock Holmes would have said, "Elementary."

But of course she wasn't asleep. She answered on the second ring. "Rosemary Mellon."

That was another reason people like her. She isn't pretentious. She doesn't have to go around rubbing people's noses in the fact that she's an MD and other people aren't.

"J. P. Beaumont here," I said.

"I already figured that out. Caller ID told me so. It's been a long night. Do you have a case for me?" I could tell from her voice that the gangbangers had taken the night off and she was bored out of her skull.

"I'm afraid not," I said. "I'm pretty sure the cases I'm calling about are already in the system."

"Why the middle-of-the-night phone call, then?" she asked.

Answering that would be dicey, but it seemed that being straight with Rosemary was the only thing to do.

"When Delilah Ainsworth was killed, she and I were working a cold case together," I said.

"I see," Rosemary said after a pause.

"And back in the day, Mac MacPherson and I rode Patrol together."

There was another long pause. "Which means you've been told to butt out, and you're at home stewing in your own juices and not sleeping worth a damn."

"Something like that," I agreed.

This time there wasn't a pause at all. "Okay," Rosemary said. "Hang on. Let me see what I can do."

She put down the phone. Unlike being put on hold on the regular M.E. landline, I didn't have to listen to scratchy music, interrupted by someone telling me that my call was very important and that it would be answered by the next available person. What I heard instead was blessed silence that ended only when Rosemary picked the phone back up.

"Which one first," she asked, "Ainsworth or MacPherson?"

Both deaths could conceivably be laid at my door, but Delilah's was the one that hurt more. "Ainsworth," I said.

"She was shot at close range and died from a single gunshot to her throat. The bullet severed her spinal cord, exited through her brain stem. Death was instantaneous."

In a way that was good news. At least she hadn't suffered, bleeding out slowly on the floor with no one to help her. The dancing Delilah of my earlier dream had claimed she wasn't wearing a vest. In this case, a vest wouldn't have made any difference. Still, I had to ask.

"Was she wearing a vest?"

"Yes," Rosemary said. "It's listed among her effects."

I closed my eyes and allowed myself a moment of gratitude. So she hadn't done something totally stupid. She had gone to the meeting with Mac properly dressed, armed, and prepared for any contingency. Yet the man had taken her by surprise, even though he was most likely drunk and in a wheelchair. How had that happened?

"Okay," I said. "Tell me about Rory MacPherson."

"This is interesting," Rosemary said.

"What?"

"I was watching the local news a little while ago," she replied. "The media is still reporting this as a homicide/suicide, but that's not going to wash."

"Why not?"

"For one thing, Mr. MacPherson has a contusion over his left ear from a blow to the head that resulted in a fractured skull and subsequent brain swelling. That's why when the medics tried treating him for carbon monoxide poisoning, he didn't respond."

"Wait," I said. "Are you saying he didn't die from carbon monoxide poisoning?"

"That's exactly what I'm saying," Rosemary said. "Carbon monoxide may have been a contributing factor, but the untreated brain injury would have been fatal anyway. His blood alcohol level was point two eight, more than three times the legal limit, and that was several hours after his death. No telling what it was earlier. Probably a good thing he was driving a wheelchair instead of a car."

Ignoring Rosemary's stab at black humor, I felt my heart racing in my chest. Mac hadn't murdered Delilah.

Someone else had killed them both. It was likely that Mac was already unconscious at the time he was rolled into the garage and someone turned on the engine. Unfortunately, the killer's tap on the head had been more serious than he had intended. Instead of simply knocking Mac unconscious, the blow was the ultimate cause of death. As a consequence, the carbon monoxide window dressing hadn't worked.

I took a deep breath. "Tell me about his hands."

"What do you want to know?"

"Any gunshot residue?"

"Yes."

I was thinking out loud. "So whoever shot Delilah then used the same gun, or a different one, to put gun residue on Mac's hands, leaving him as her presumed killer."

"That would be my call."

"And when were the autopsies finished?"

"This afternoon. The first one, Detective Ainsworth's, is date-stamped 2:55 P.M. The second one is 4:46 P.M."

That meant Detectives Monford and Anderson had already known about this before they came to see me later in the afternoon. It also explained Anderson's comment about my having an airtight alibi. And the fact that no one had mentioned that it was now a double homicide to the media meant that they were using that as a holdback. Maybe they didn't want to cause public panic in the previously homicide-safe streets of Sammamish by letting them know that there was now a multiple murderer loose in their fair city. Or maybe there was something else at work.

"Rosemary, thank you," I said. "I owe you big-time on this one."

"You're welcome," she replied. "You and Mel can take me to lunch sometime, but I'm guessing it won't make it any easier for you to sleep tonight."

"No, it won't," I agreed, "but you've given me a lot more to think about."

"By the way," Rosemary added, "what was the case you and Delilah were working, the cold one?"

"Her name was Monica Wellington. She died in 1973. She was a freshman at the University of Washington at the time she was killed. She went out on a date with an unknown individual on a Friday night in late March and turned up dead in a barrel two days later. At the time of her death, Monica was pregnant. That aspect of the case was never made public, but the troubling thing is that no boyfriend ever came forward."

"You're thinking the baby's father might have been involved?"

"It's a good bet, but we never found him. My new partner and I worked the case off and on for a couple of years, but with no new leads it ended up going cold. Sometime in 1981, the homicide was officially deemed closed, although I have no memory of when or how that happened. Seattle PD didn't have a Cold Case squad back then, but regardless of who closed it, I should have thought I would have been notified, since I had been assigned to that case originally. Somehow, though, in the process of transferring the evidence from the evidence locker to the closed case warehouse, it disappeared."

"The whole box?"

"Yes, the whole thing."

"And you're thinking what?"

"That it was taken by someone with something to

hide. That's the premise Delilah Ainsworth and I were working on when she was killed."

"Where did the Wellington homicide happen?" Rosemary asked. "Here in King County?"

"Yes. In Seattle."

"I'll look into it," she volunteered. "See if there's still something here, although with a case that old, I don't hold out much hope."

I didn't, either. I suspected that whoever had removed the physical evidence from Seattle PD would have been thorough about it and would have cleared out any remaining evidence in the M.E.'s office as well. But still, it was another reason to be glad people like Rosemary Mellon existed.

"Thanks," I said. "Let me know if you find anything."

I ended the call and then scrolled through my contact list until I found the number for the gun guys at the Washington State Patrol Crime Lab. They were another department that worked round the clock, and I wasn't disappointed when what sounded like a real newbie answered the phone. That made sense. Newest techs draw the worst shift.

"This is J. P. Beaumont of the Special Homicide Investigation Team," I said. I made some effort in putting on an official tone, hoping that I sounded more like a guy sitting at a desk in the middle of the night than a post-op knee-replacement patient in his bed. "To whom am I speaking?"

"This is Gerald," the guy answered. "Gerald Spaulding. What can I do for you, Mr. Beaumont?"

Most of the folks at the crime lab know me as J.P., so I was right. Gerald was somebody new. Since he didn't know me from Adam, Spaulding should have asked for more identification than just my name, but he didn't. He sounded both young and nervous. I wondered if he was really working, or if he was whiling away the long hours of his shift by playing solitaire.

"I'm calling about the bullets taken from the crime scene in Sammamish earlier today," I told him. "Can you give me any information on where you are with those?"

Using the term "bullets," plural, was a calculated risk. The crime scene guys had no doubt found the bullet that had killed Delilah. What I was wondering was if anyone had gone back to the house to look for a second bullet from the gunshot that had put the gun residue on Mac MacPherson's hands. If I were a betting man, I would have said they'd find it in the garage, buried out of sight in a wall somewhere.

"Just a second," Gerald said. "Let me put you on hold."

It was regular hold, the kind that comes complete with awful music as well as with the intermittent and unavoidable "your call is important" announcements. Eventually, Gerald came back on the line.

"They're both .45 caliber slugs," he said. "We won't be doing the comparison analysis until tomorrow. The second one, the one they dug out of the Sheetrock, came into the lab just a little while ago. From the looks of it, the slug went through the wallboard and also hit a stud. It's pretty distorted."

Bingo! "Where was it?" I asked. "Just out of curiosity."

"In the garage. It was hidden behind one of those rolling tool chests. It must have taken a while to find it because, like I said, it only came in a couple of hours ago. Do you need anything else?"

"No, Gerald," I told him. "That's all I need for now. You've been a big help."

I ended the call, thinking, one killer. Two murders. And both of them were on me.

I was lying there thinking about what the next step should be when I fell asleep. I awoke to find daylight pouring into the room. Marge Herndon was standing beside my bed with her hands on her hips and a scowl on her face.

"What the hell were you thinking?" she demanded. "What part of 'one elevator ride away' don't you understand?"

"I needed to use the bathroom," I said. "The walker was right there. I was able to manage on my own."

"Well, pin a rose on you!" she said. "What the hell do you need me around for then? I suppose you'll just hobble your own self right out to the kitchen and make your own damned breakfast?"

"No," I said. "Really. I'm sorry. I do need you. And that pork chop was magnificent. Thank you."

"Don't think flattery is going to get you anywhere with me," she sniffed. "It won't work. And since you're feeling so chipper, we're going to make use of that brand-new plastic chair in your shower. In case you haven't noticed, it's pretty ripe around here."

I could see that arguing with the woman was futile, so I didn't bother. I allowed her to help me out of bed and into my bathroom. There, she stripped me down in a fiercely businesslike manner that successfully stripped me of any embarrassment as well. As far as she was concerned, this was a job, one she had done countless times before, and that's all it was to her. If I was going to be shy about it, then it was clearly my problem, not hers. Once

I was naked as a jaybird, she wrapped both my knees in an impenetrable sheath of plastic, turned on the water, and told me to sit on the plastic chair and get with the program. I would be lying if I said the hot water and soap didn't feel wonderful. And, although I hate to admit it, so did the plastic chair.

When I was done, Marge was waiting there with walker, towel, and robe in hand. "I found a tracksuit in your closet," she said. "I laid that out for you to wear. It'll be easier to get in and out of than regular clothes. And you need to be ready. By the time you have some breakfast, the visiting physical therapist should be here."

I was going to object, but I didn't. For physical therapy, a tracksuit was probably fine. But for the rest of the day, considering what I had in mind, it would be time for a clean shirt, a regular suit, and a tie.

New knees or not, I was going to make a condolence call on Delilah Ainsworth's husband and daughters, and for that I would need to dress the part. I owed them at least that much.

When Mel called, I was dressed, sitting in my recliner, drinking coffee, and waiting for breakfast, which, from the smell of it and without my having to ask, was going to be all protein all the time. At this point, however, whatever Marge was cooking would, by definition, be exactly right. This was a case of beggars can't be choosers. Marge would fix it. I would eat it. End of story.

"How are things?" Mel wanted to know.

"I'm up, showered, dressed, and waiting for the physical therapist to show up," I said.

"Sounds like this whole Nurse Nora thing is working out pretty well for you?" Mel commented.

I wanted to say that Marge Herndon was the kind of

woman who didn't play well with others and that we got along swimmingly as long as I did precisely as I was told and didn't try to color outside the lines. I knew instinctively, however, that Marge's kind of take-no-prisoners nursing would be right up Mel's alley, so I didn't bother saying any of those things.

"Fine," I said.

"One eyebrow or two?"

"No, really," I said. "It's fine. She's fine. She's out in the kitchen making breakfast right now. When do you think you'll get home?"

"I think the last question disqualified both of your previous 'fines,'" Mel said.

She was right, of course. I said nothing.

"Aspen's arraignment is this morning," she went on.

"On a Sunday?" I was surprised.

"Special circumstances," Mel answered.

"Did you ever get a confession?"

"We certainly did!" I could hear Mel's smile over the phone. "Signed, sealed, and delivered. Her court-appointed attorney will have a fit. I need to be here for the arraignment. After that I have a ton of paperwork to do, but with any kind of luck, I should be home tonight, though I've kept the hotel room in case I can't get away until tomorrow. You can bet I'm taking some comp time next week."

"Good," I said. "I've missed you."

"I've missed you, too. Yesterday was so crazy that we barely had a chance to talk. I've seen the news, but tell me. Have you learned any more about what happened to Delilah Ainsworth?"

And so I told her. Not just what was on the news—which was still reporting it as a homicide/suicide—but what I had learned on my own from Rosemary Mellon and Gerald Spaulding. Mel heard me out in silence.

"Sounds like MacPherson had something on some-body important," Mel said thoughtfully. "And the inves-tigation you and Delilah reopened was about to blow up in that person's face. If those two had to go, what if you're next?"

Mel's concern wasn't far off the mark. That very thought had occurred to me as well.

"The problem with that is, I don't know anything."

"If whoever it is thinks you know something, if he or she believes Delilah had somehow clued you in before she drove out to MacPherson's house in Sammamish, then you're the next logical target anyway, so be careful."

"Belltown Terrace is a secure building," I pointed out.

"Still," she said. "Don't take any chances. And when that physical therapist shows up, be sure you check her ID."

"Will do," I said. "Good suggestion."

Marge appeared just then, with a serving tray in hand. Three eggs, two strips of crisp bacon, two slices of whole wheat toast along with orange juice, more cof-fee, and my morning's ration of pills.

"Have to go," I told Mel. "Breakfast is served."

Marge handed over the tray and then watched to be sure both the food and the pills went down the hatch. "The therapist isn't due here for another half hour," she said. "So while you finish, I'm going to go downstairs and have a smoke. I noticed there aren't any ashtrays, so I'm assuming smoking here is off-limits. There's a sign in my unit that says no smoking, too. I just wish all those nanny-state folks would get off my back. Who needs 'em?"

"There's a spot on the sidewalk," I said helpfully.

"Just outside the garage door. It's Sunday, though, so if you want to get in and out from P-1, you'll need to take the garage door clicker."

Marge gave me a scathing look. "What do you think I am, stupid? I already figured that much out on my own!"

With that, she turned on her heel and left me in peace. While I ate, I tried turning on the television, hoping for a news update on the Sammamish homicides. Unfortunately, it was Sunday morning. There wasn't much news. Once I finished breakfast, I plucked my iPad off the table at my elbow. I was about to go scrolling through some of the local news sites when I remembered the press conference and the panoramic photos Marge had taken.

For someone using a piece of equipment that was totally foreign to her, Marge had done an impressive job. I went up and down each row, one face at a time, looking for someone familiar, someone who shouldn't have been there but was. I saw no one. I was still engrossed in studying the faces and was almost at the back of the audience when Marge returned, bringing the physical therapist along with her. From the clinging odor of cigarette smoke, it was apparent that they had both lit up before coming upstairs.

It turned out that checking the woman's ID wasn't necessary. She was wearing a name badge around her neck—IDA WITHERSPOON—and the badge came complete with a photo ID embedded in it. Ida was Ida and nobody else. We whipped through the exercises in jig time. Then we went down to the sixth floor and took a single turn around the running track. The building covers half a block lengthwise and half a block from side to side, and the running track goes around the outside rim.

It was a cool, foggy September morning, and it felt wonderful to be outside. And yes, my knees still hurt, but they didn't hurt the way they had for months. I could walk. I was getting better. This was going to work.

When we went back inside, Ida administered my range-of-motion test, and smilingly told me that I had passed with flying colors.

"So now what?" Marge asked, once Ida was on her way back to the elevator. "How do you plan to spend the rest of the day?"

"I'm going to need you to help me get dressed in some real clothes," I said. "Then we're going for a ride. We have some errands to run."

One of the items Marge had brought along in her bag of tricks was a thingamajig made of plastic and string that made it possible for me to put on the knee-high compression socks that I was supposed to wear. Using that made putting the damn things on a snap. And then I dressed for work, complete with a bullet-resistant vest, holster, weapon, and a suit and tie.

Marge looked askance at my .38. "Are you sure you need that? Aren't you making a condolence call?"

"I wouldn't be dressed without it," I told her, pausing for one last check in the mirror. "Now, my car or yours?" I asked.

"Definitely mine," she insisted. "I've seen that fancy contraption of yours, and I'm not going anywhere near it."

We left the Belltown Terrace parking garage in her Honda with a fine cloud of cigarette ash floating in the air around us as she drove. My first choice would have been Ballard Blossom, but they're closed on Sundays. We had to make do with an arrangement from a nearby QFC.

I knew flowers would be mostly meaningless in the face of the Ainsworth family's terrible loss, but I couldn't face the idea of turning up on their doorstep empty-handed.

The Ainsworths lived on North Sixty-first Street, just north of the Woodland Park Zoo. The fog had burned off, leaving behind a beautiful fall Sunday afternoon. Consequently, parking places in the neighborhood were clearly at a premium, especially with at least three local media vans parked front and center. Marge jerked to a stop in an almost nonexistent spot outside a small brick bungalow surrounded by an old-fashioned ornamental iron fence. On either side of the gate leading up to the front door, the whole length of fence had been turned into a makeshift memorial that was lined with the usual collection of candles, teddy bears, American flags, and bedraggled grocery store bouquets not much worse than the one in my hand.

"Are you just going to drop yours off here?" Marge asked, nodding at the collection of memorials.

"No," I said. "I'm going to take them to the door."

"You and what army?" she asked.

I could see she was right to be skeptical. The house had a shallow front porch that was two steps up from the walkway. I was sure I could manage the steps just fine on my walker. Holding on to a bouquet of flowers at the same time wasn't going to work, though.

"Do you mind carrying the flowers up to the door for me?" I asked.

"All right," she agreed grudgingly, "but once I hand them over, I'm coming back to the car for a smoke."

That was fine with me. This was going to be a hard enough conversation without having Marge along to serve as a witness.

"And what if one of those reporters asks me about who I am or who you are?"

"Just say I'm a family friend. That will cover it."

I led the way through the gate and up the concrete walkway with Marge following, carrying the flowers. Once we negotiated the steps, I parked the walker in front of the door. Then, after ringing the doorbell, Marge handed me the bouquet and beat a hasty retreat. As I said, it was Sunday. I dreaded the idea that one of Delilah's daughters would answer the door. Instead, her husband did. I didn't have to ask. The man looked a wreck.

"Mr. Ainsworth?" I asked.

Brian nodded numbly. "Are you from the funeral home?"

"No," I said, offering him the bouquet. "My name is Beaumont. Your wife and I were working together on a case at the time of her death. I wanted to stop by and express my condolences."

"It was you?" he demanded. "You're the one she was working that cold case with?"

Still holding out the flowers, I nodded. I figured this was going to go one of two ways. He would either invite me inside or he would punch my lights out. In the end, he accepted the flowers and stepped back from the door, allowing me inside rather than inviting me.

"She said you were in the hospital. That's why she had to go see that guy alone."

I hobbled into the room, found a chair with a pair of sturdy arms, and dropped into it.

"I tried to talk her out of that," I said. "I told her not to go alone. She didn't listen."

"That's Delilah," he said sadly, and then swiped at a

pair of coursing tears that were too close to the surface. "Telling her not to do something just didn't work." He shook his head.

"I wish I'd known that," I said. "Maybe I could have tried something else."

Brian Ainsworth gave a half laugh that morphed into a stifled sob. "What are you doing here?"

"Have you done anything about planning a funeral?"

"Of course. The chaplain from Seattle PD showed up last night, right after the M.E.'s office released the body to the funeral home. He wanted us to wait until next Saturday for the funeral so they could arrange for a big law enforcement presence, and he suggested we hold it at Key Arena in Seattle Center. I told him no. I also nixed the offer of a police escort to take the body from the M.E.'s office to the funeral home. I told him I didn't want to turn Del's death into a media event, although, from the flowers outside, you can see that's already happened. And I didn't want to put my girls through waiting for a whole week to tell their mother good-bye. Their grandmother had to hustle them out the back door to avoid the people outside.

"So the funeral is scheduled for Wednesday afternoon, at our church, Crown Hill Baptist. The sanctuary holds two hundred people max, including a lot of relatives who are coming in from South Dakota. The church isn't big enough to allow for a couple hundred cops to show up. And the parking lot isn't big enough to hold a couple hundred cop cars, either. Like I told the chaplain, I want to keep the service small and relatively private—limited to the people who actually knew Delilah, and the people who loved her. People who served with her and would like to attend are welcome, but I don't want a show of uniforms. I don't want to turn it into a circus." Brian's voice broke, and he stopped talking.

"That's why I'm here," I said. "I want to ask a favor."

"What?" Brian asked.

"I hadn't known your wife long, but we were working together. I respected her, and I'd like to honor her by serving as an honorary pallbearer." I waved in the direction of my walker. "I can't really carry anything with that damned thing, but I want to be there. No matter what you want, the media is going to be there, and I want to let people know that Delilah Ainsworth and I were working together at the time of her death. I want to serve notice to whoever did this that she and I were partners. With any kind of luck, he'll come looking for me next, and I'll be ready."

"What do you mean?" Brian demanded. "How could he? The guy who shot Del is dead."

I had assumed that someone would have been keeping the victim's family apprised of the direction of the investigation. Obviously no one had. With two new knees, it's not easy to insert a foot in your mouth, and it's even harder to get it back out.

"Mr. Ainsworth," I told him, "I have reason to believe that there was someone else in Rory MacPherson's home that night, someone who murdered both your wife and Mac MacPherson."

"If someone else was at the house, how come nobody told me that?" Brian demanded. "Detectives Monford and Anderson never mentioned a word about it, not last night and not this morning, either."

"I shouldn't have mentioned it, either," I said. "Now that I have, I need to ask you to keep it quiet."

"Why wouldn't the detectives tell me?"

"Monford and Anderson are capable enough cops," I told him, "and this is what homicide detectives do. They hold back information. In this case, I'm sure they don't want the killer to realize that they might be onto him. If he's convinced he's home free, he might make a mistake. The cops working the case are doing just that—working the case. For me, it's different, Mr. Ainsworth. It's personal. I'm hoping that by announcing my presence at the funeral, we'll actually be able to draw the killer out. I want the guy to come looking for me, if for no other reason than to be able to take him down."

Brian Ainsworth thought about that for a time and then he nodded. "All right," he said. "If you want to be an honorary pallbearer, you've got it. When the funeral director comes, I'll put your name in the program. Do you have any idea where Crown Hill Baptist is?"

"I grew up in Ballard," I told him. "I'm sure it's not that hard to find."

"You should probably be at the church by about one or so."

Someone else rang the doorbell. "That's probably the funeral director now," Brian said. "He said he'd be here today."

I stood up and offered my hand. "I'm so sorry for your loss."

"Thank you," Brian murmured.

I might have said more or mentioned that I had lost not one but two wives, but that didn't seem appropriate. Instead, I made my way to the front door to show myself out. The guy standing there, with his finger poised to press the doorbell again, screamed funeral director from the top of his perfectly coiffed head to the tips of his highly polished shoes.

"Mr. Ainsworth?" he asked as I came out.

"No," I said, stepping around him on my way to the steps. "Mr. Ainsworth is just inside."

CHAPTER 16

I have no doubt Marge was smoking up a storm in the car the whole time I was inside the house. When I got back into the Accord, it reeked. The ashtray that had been full to overflowing before I left the car was even worse now, but I was glad Marge hadn't dumped it out in front of the flowers and flags lining Brian Ainsworth's front yard. I rolled down my window to let some of the smoke dissipate but also unleashed another mini dust storm of ash. Luckily for Marge my years in AA have left me a lot more tolerant toward smokers than a lot of Seattleites would be.

"Where to?" Marge wanted to know.

Between the PT and the emotional meeting with Delilah's bereaved husband, I was feeling as though I'd been put through a wringer. For some perverse reason, I said, "Home, James, please, and don't spare the horses."

"I'm your nurse, not your chauffeur," Marge pointed out sourly.

And utterly devoid of humor, I thought.

We sped back down Aurora and whipped into the garage on P-1. Upstairs, I eased myself into the recliner while Marge brought the next set of meds and some more string cheese.

"I'm hoping you don't expect me to spend the rest of the day standing around and watching you snooze in that chair," Marge said. "Is there anything you need me to do?"

It took a minute for me to think of something, but I did. I had left the hospital with two ongoing searches. So far, I had done what I could to locate Delilah Ainsworth's killer, but I had done nothing at all about finding Doug Davis's fiancée.

"Yes," I said. "As a matter of fact, there is something you could do. Down on P-1, next to the elevator, is a door that leads into the storage units. The building key—the one that opens the elevator lobby—opens the first door. The matching unit number key opens the individual storage rooms. I'd like you to go down there and find a box for me. It's a banker's box, and I think it's on one of the lower shelves."

"How will I know which one I'm looking for?"

"I'm pretty sure I wrote 'My Stuff' on the outside."

"How original," Marge observed, but without any further discussion, she grabbed the key ring and set off.

A few minutes later, I had barely dozed off when my phone rang. Caller ID said *Rosemary Mellon, mobile.*

"Hey," I said. "What's up?"

"In the world of tit for tat, I believe you owe me," she answered.

"Why? What have you found?"

"Whoever hijacked your evidence box must not have had enough horses to put in the same fix here. I found some tissue samples hidden away in evidence storage."

"What kind of tissue samples?"

"Two separate kinds—from under Monica's finger-nails and from her fetus, both," Rosemary answered.

"Enough to do DNA testing?"

"I expect so, and I'll be working on that tonight, as soon as I go back to the lab. There was no such thing as DNA profiling in 1981. Given the fact that the tissue samples have been on ice this whole time, I'm thinking I may be able to pull this one out of the hat and identify your killer for you."

"You're right. If you can do that, dinner is definitely on me. Your choice. How long will it take?"

"Five to ten days," Rosemary answered, "that's if the crime lab isn't already overloaded with something else. Which they usually are."

I happened to have two aces in the hole on that score. One was Ron Peters, who had a murdered police detective on his hands, and the other was Attorney General Ross Connors, the same guy who had rushed through the tox screen results for Mel on the dead protester in Bellingham. Between the two, my money was on Ross. The problem was, I wasn't supposed to be working.

"Thanks," I said. "Let me see what I can do to get that testing moved to the head of the line. And in the meantime," I added, thinking of Delilah Ainsworth, "be careful."

"What do you mean?"

"I'm pretty sure working on this case is what got Detective Ainsworth killed," I cautioned.

Rosemary thought about that for a moment. "Well," she said, finally, "as far as I can tell, only two people have any idea I'm working on this. If you promise to keep it quiet, I'll do the same."

"Fair enough," I told her.

Just then I heard the key in the lock and voices in the hallway. Mel and Marge had somehow connected with each other in either the garage or the elevator. From the chatty quality of their animated conversation, they had already managed to become pals. That was potentially bad news for me, but right that moment, between my pain meds kicking in and the news from Rosemary Mellon, I was feeling so euphoric that nothing could rain on my parade.

"So here's the girl who singlehandedly saved the city of Bellingham?"

"I'm the one." Mel grinned as she kissed me hello. "As for you? You look remarkably comfortable."

"I am. It's great to be home."

"You're telling me? My first priority is a visit to my shower. The hotel shower was so low on water flow that I could barely rinse the shampoo out of my hair. And I didn't like the hotel shampoo, either."

She grabbed the oddball collection of luggage and bags that had served her on her TDY stint in Bellingham. Meanwhile, Marge dropped a dusty banker's box at my feet before straightening up and giving me her usual hands-on-hips glare.

"Well," she said, "I suppose now that the missus is home, you'll be giving me my walking papers."

I would have thought so, too. Except the condolence trip to Brian Ainsworth's house had brought me face-to-face with what life would be like until I was once again able to drive myself. Without a driver, I'd be totally dependent on Mel. And even if she took some comp time off work, she'd still have to go to work eventually. Yes, I knew in advance that there were some real drawbacks in having Marge as a combination nurse/driver, but right that minute the good seemed to outweigh the bad even though her skills behind the wheel could be nothing less than hair-raising at times. She would give me some independence of movement that I wouldn't have otherwise.

"If you don't mind, I'd like you to stay on for a while. Long enough for me to be cleared to drive again."

Marge's face brightened considerably. "Really?"

For the first time, it occurred to me that part of Marge's general surliness might have something to do with the fact that she really needed the money.

"Yes," I said. "Really."

"Does fried chicken sound like a good idea for dinner?"

"Sounds good to me," I said. "And I'm sure Mel would agree."

"I'll get started then," she said. "I'll get dinner ready to go on the table, then I'll take off."

While Marge headed for the kitchen, I turned my attention to the box. I knew what was inside—my past, or at least the part of my past that I kept at arm's length most of the time. Most of what I found inside were things I had taken with me when Karen and I divorced. The top layer contained the kind of mementos that parents save forever.

The treasure trove included two Altoid boxes, designated by name, which contained Scott and Kelly's respective collections of baby teeth. One layer was devoted to Scott's scouting experiences—his Cub Scout cap, his Pinewood Derby car, and the sash covered with his collection of Boy Scout badges up to and including his Eagle. There were the two plaster-of-paris plaques containing tiny handprints that had come home from first grade. There were Christmas ornaments that included school pictures of toothless kids. The one of Kelly looked so much like Kayla that at first I wondered if I had somehow slipped one of my granddaughter's photos into the mix.

Kelly's part of the jumble included the programs for the various plays she had participated in both in grade school and in high school. In third grade she'd had a speaking part in a food group skit as a talking carrot. In high school, as a junior, she had done a star turn as the Old Lady in a production of *The Old Lady Shows Her Medals*. After that, I personally had thought she was headed for a university drama program. That, of course, was before she had dropped out of school during her senior year.

The kids' part of my treasure trove took up half the box, and it was separated from the rest by a wall of yearbooks—four years of Ballard High School *Shingle*s. And at the very bottom, in an ancient cigar box, was the rest of the story.

First up was the faded velvet jewelry box that held the ring my father had given my mother. As a sailor during World War II, I'm sure that tiny solitaire diamond was all he could afford, and his unexpected death a few days later meant that the engagement ring was never accompanied by a wedding ring, not until the day I married Anne Corley in Myrtle Edwards Park down on Seattle's waterfront.

Slipping it out of the box, I remembered how graciously Anne Corley had accepted it. Of course, she had been conning me for weeks. At the time she had allowed me to slip the ring on her finger, she must have known the jig was almost up. She had taken the ring without a murmur to seal the deal. When she died, I left the simple gold wedding band on her finger, but I had returned the engagement ring to its box and stowed it, out of sight, in the cigar box. Now, though, I slipped the velvet box into my pocket. Between now and Christmas, maybe I'd be able to find a jeweler who could use that tiny diamond to design a pendant for my granddaughter.

And then, at the very bottom of the cigar box, I found what had caused me to open the banker's box in the first place—three jagged pieces of metal and my three aces of spades. I was holding the pieces of metal in my hands and studying them when Mel emerged from the shower. She was barefoot, wearing a robe, and had her wet hair wrapped in a towel. As I had been unloading the box, I had put the contents on a nearby hassock. She moved those aside and then sat down next to me.

"What are those?" she asked.

"Hold out your hand," I told her. When she did so, I dropped the chunks of metal into her hand. "These are the three pieces of shrapnel that should have killed me on August 2, 1966," I told her. "The only reason they didn't is because of a guy from Bisbee, Arizona. He was our lieutenant. His name was Doug Davis. That's what people in Bisbee called him, but for us in C Company, he was always Lennie D."

Mel's father is retired military. She knew that I had been in Vietnam, but we had never discussed it, not until that afternoon. I told her the whole story—about the aces of spades, and showed her the ones that were still in the cigar box. They had been stored away for all that time, but I knew that if I took them down to the crime lab, a capable latent fingerprint tech could probably still lift one of Lennie D.'s prints off the smooth cardboard surface.

And finally, I told her about Doug's dreamscape appearance.

"So what does this all mean?" Mel asked when I finished.

"I think he wanted me to let Bonnie know how much he loved her."

"Wait," Mel said. "This was only a dream. I mean, that other dream situation has already caused no end of trouble. What if you end up tracking Bonnie MacLean down and she doesn't want to be reminded of what happened back in 1966? She's had a whole lifetime to put it to rest. Why should you bring it all back up?"

"Because it's unfinished business," I said. "Why did Doug show up in my dream now, after all these years? Guilty conscience, most likely, for my not doing what I should have done back then. I came back home, married Karen, and got on with my life. I put the metal pieces away. I put the cards away. What I really should have done at the time was track that poor girl down. I should have thanked her and told her what he did for me. Instead, I buried it. Forgot about it. And I've always been ashamed of that. It's one of the reasons I've never visited the wall in Washington. It's one of the reasons I never show up at any of the reunions."

"What reunions?" Mel asked.

"The Thirty-fifth Infantry has multiwar reunions every year. I've never gone to any of them. I opened the first invitation maybe, but that's about it. Ever since, the envelopes go straight into the round file. If that's not a sign of a guilty conscience, I don't know what is."

Mel was quiet for a long time after I finished. The sun

was going down, turning Puget Sound into a blinding slate of glimmering silver. Mel's hair had dried enough that the towel had slipped off, leaving behind a charming tangle of damp blond tendrils.

"Well then," she said finally, "I suppose we'd better see what we can do to find her."

Mel got up to go finish drying her hair, while I started scooping everything but the shrapnel and the playing cards back into the banker's box. I had the lid back on the box when Marge came into the den.

"All right," she said. "Dinner's in the warming oven." I knew we had a warming oven in the kitchen, but to my knowledge Mel and I had used it only as a handy junk drawer.

"I've laid out your evening pills," Marge added. "I found some egg cups to put them in. The ones that are on the table you should take with dinner. The ones on the counter you should take with food at bedtime. And remember, I really am only an elevator ride away."

With that, Marge left the room, stomping away in her heavy-footed fashion. I called my thanks after her, but she didn't wait around long enough to hear me.

Mel came out minutes later, wearing a pair of pj's I'd given her for her birthday. She paused in the doorway and sniffed the air. "What smells so good?"

"That would be dinner," I told her. "It's in the warming oven. How about if we eat it now while it's fresh?"

Mel reached out a hand to help me up and out of the chair. I think she was a little surprised to see that, with the help of the walker, I was capable of getting myself up and down. I wasn't much help with setting the table, however. While she did that, she asked about my visit with Brian Ainsworth.

"Whoever did it, you're calling them out, aren't you?" Mel said when I told her about my request to be an honorary pallbearer at Delilah's funeral. "What you're saying is that, in a service that won't include the usual fallen-officer police presence, you intend to be front and center."

"That's right. I want Delilah's killer to know that she and I were working the Monica Wellington case together. Whether she died because of Monica's homicide or because of the promotion situation, I want the killer to be under the impression that whatever Delilah knew, I know. Eventually word is going to get out that Delilah's death was a double homicide."

"As soon as that happens, you're hoping he'll come after you."

I nodded.

"Which means I'm going to the funeral, too."

"I hoped you would," I said. "You'll be the eyes in the back of my head."

"I'll be good for more than just eyes," she said.

The food was delicious. We scarfed it down as though we were starving. Over dinner I told Mel about Rosemary Mellon's discovery of what was most likely never-tested physical evidence in the Monica Wellington case.

"She thinks she can get a DNA profile?" Mel asked.

"Yes."

"How long."

"Best-case scenario five to ten days; that's if she can walk it around whatever backlog the crime lab has at the moment."

"Did you call Ross?" Mel asked.

"Not yet," I said. "The Sammamish cases aren't really ours."

"Do you know that for sure?"

"I didn't see anyone from S.H.I.T. at the press conference."

"That doesn't mean anything," Mel allowed. "And just because it's not officially our case doesn't mean Ross couldn't pull strings and grease wheels. Call him. Give him a heads-up. That way, when Rosemary walks her samples over to the crime lab, they'll be looking for them. They won't come as a surprise."

That was one of the things I had come to appreciate about Mel. I always looked at bureaucracy as an insurmountable obstacle. She always looked for ways to make it work.

We were still sitting at a dining room table laden with dirty plates when I took out my phone and called the attorney general.

One of the best things about working for the AG, at least this particular AG, is that Ross gives us access. Everyone who works for Special Homicide has his home number along with his office and cell phone numbers, too. When we need him, we can reach him.

"Hey, Beau," he said. "You still in the hospital? I'm coming to Seattle tomorrow, and I was planning on stopping by."

"They cut me loose," I explained. "I'm at home. So is Mel. If you want to stop by here sometime tomorrow, you're more than welcome."

"She did a great job for us in Bellingham," Ross said. "Harry couldn't be happier. The police chief up there has always been a pain in his butt, and now she owes him big-time. Couldn't be better."

"Mel isn't why I'm calling," I said. "It's about that cold case in Seattle."

The slight hesitation in his voice told me Ross Connors already knew a lot about it. "The one that got the detective killed?" he asked.

"Yes, that's the one. Detective Ainsworth told me that evidence from the Wellington homicide—evidence that should have been there—had been removed from a secure Seattle PD evidence storage facility. She also discovered that some possibly relevant microfiche data, Seattle PD HR data, had been tampered with. The evidence tampering didn't make it as far as the M.E.'s office, however, because earlier this morning, Rosemary Mellon located some tissue samples from back then, samples from the Wellington case. She's going to submit them for DNA profiling. I was hoping to enlist you in doing something to speed the process along."

"To say nothing of paying for it, right?" Connors asked. "You know as well as I do that DNA profiling is expensive, but if what you're telling me is true, shouldn't the cost of any relevant testing be coming out of Seattle PD's Internal Affairs budget instead of mine?"

"That's something else we both know," I countered. "If Internal Affairs is calling the shots and paying the fare, the testing is going to go to the end of the crime lab backlog rather than to the front of it."

"When was this case again?"

"The homicide itself happened in 1973. It's the first case I ever worked for Homicide, and it was never solved. My partner back then, Milton Gurkey, and I worked the case sporadically between then and 1975, when we were told in no uncertain terms that spending any more effort on it was a waste of time and resources. That's when we finally let it go. I don't ever remember getting back to it. Then, without our knowledge, the case was deemed officially closed in 1981."

"You were never notified of that?"

"Never."

"And all of this happened long before any kind of DNA profiling capability," Ross said.

"Yes," I agreed.

"Who closed it?"

"I don't know. Delilah may have discovered something about that. If so, she didn't clue me in."

"But now, Rosemary thinks she can pull something usable off the samples she has?"

"Yes. Whoever was able to manipulate records inside Seattle PD wasn't able to work the same kind of disappearing act inside the M.E.'s office. According to Rosemary, the samples in question have been locked away in cold storage all this time. She's confident that it'll work."

Ross sighed. "All right," he conceded. "I'll call Rosemary and tell her to submit her samples to the crime lab under S.H.I.T.'s name and that she should contact my office on Monday to get an official case number. I'll also call one of the supervisors down there and let him know this is urgent."

"Thanks, Ross," I said. "Solving this case will mean a lot to me."

"I'm a little puzzled about why it came up in the first place. What put it back on the front burner after all this time?"

"I did," I answered. "I guess it's been festering the whole time. Lying around in the hospital for a couple of days brought it to the surface."

That was close enough to the truth to sound plausible, and I let it go at that. It's something my mother used to tell me. Quit while you're ahead.

By the time I was off the phone, Mel had cleared the table, put away the leftovers, and started the dishwasher. Pouring herself a glass of wine from the bottle in the fridge, she made her way to her favorite spot in the unit. For me, the best spot in the house was my recliner, but for Mel it would always be the window seat in the living room with its 180-degree view of Puget Sound, from the grain terminal to Safeco Field. In the far distance, the snow-denuded Olympics stood as a jagged dark dividing line between the fading blue of the water and the darkening evening sky.

"Marge is a good cook," Mel observed as I joined her on the window seat.

"She's also a capable nurse and an adequate driver," I said.

"Does that mean you're keeping her on?"

"For the time being. Having her looking after me and driving me around will give both of us some freedom of action."

Mel leaned her head against my shoulder. "I've had plenty of freedom of action lately. I'm looking for a little togetherness."

"I know," I said, "but once you go back to work, I'll be stuck. I'll go crazy. You've never seen me with cabin fever. It's not a pretty sight."

Mel cuddled closer. "Oh well," she said, "if you're keeping Marge around, I hope you'll be making it worth her while."

"Don't worry," I said. "I don't think you'll be hearing any complaints on that score."

We sat on the window seat together while she told

me about the mess she had encountered in Bellingham. The problem was, I had been up too much that day and I had also overdone it. I could tell that sitting there with my legs hanging down wasn't a good idea because my ankles were swelling inside my knee-high compression socks. Once Mel finished her wine, I took the last of my pills and we went to bed. Mel was lying beside me reading when I closed my eyes and went to sleep.

I didn't dream about Monica Wellington that night, but if I had, I think she would have been smiling.

CHAPTER 17

The next day was Monday. One of the perks about working for Special Homicide is that it really is primarily a nine-to-five gig. There are exceptions to that, as Mel's recent sojourn in Bellingham clearly showed, but that's more the exception than the rule. We work complicated cases where we're called into situations to serve as backup investigators rather than primary ones.

In other words, we generally work Monday through Friday. That was why, when I spoke to him the night before, Ross had assured me that he'd get the case number updated on Monday. There's a good reason for the delay. Ross is a good guy, but he's not a cop. He's a politician and a bureaucrat, in addition to being a complete technophobe. It's only recently that his longtime secretary, Katie Dunn, has been able to convince him that answering e-mail on his own wouldn't kill him.

And so, although Ross is the captain of the ship and calls the shots, Katie is the experienced executive officer who keeps things working behind the scenes, and

Katie is anything *but* a technophobe. I suspected that after our conversation, Ross had most likely called Katie and told her to assign a S.H.I.T. squad case number to the Monica Wellington homicide. He may have gone so far as to leave a message for her, but I'm willing to bet any amount of money that he didn't send a text.

And because Katie is a truly dedicated public servant, I didn't doubt that as soon as she received the message requesting a case number she immediately logged on to the AG's secure server and assigned one. I didn't call Katie at home to ask if she had done so. Instead, while Mel was out on her early-morning run, I called Rosemary Mellon. It was only a little past seven, early enough that I was relatively sure Rosemary wouldn't have already hit the sack after her shift ended at six.

"How's it going?" Rosemary asked.

I was up, had gotten myself dressed, and was comfortably ensconced in my recliner with a cup of coffee when I made the call. "Not bad," I said. "How are things with you?"

"You must have pulled some strings," Rosemary told me. "I had the case number in my hands by nine o'clock last night, and I was able to drive the specimens over to the crime lab as I was leaving work this morning. Not only were they expecting it, they said they'd get right to it."

In other words, Katie Dunn had come through like a champ.

"What's the case number again?" I asked. "I'm sure I could call Katie and get it, but . . ."

Rosemary read it off to me with no hesitation. Being given a case number was like being handed the keys to the kingdom.

I've already told you that I love my iPad, but to do actual work, we're encouraged to use our official S.H.I.T. laptops. I hefted mine off the floor by my chair and was just logging on when Marge and Mel came in together. That was a little disconcerting. It was like the two of them were operating on some mysterious mutual wavelength.

Mel went to shower. Marge, unasked, brought me another cup of coffee. "You got yourself dressed?" she asked suspiciously. "Pressure stockings included?"

"Yes," I said. "That sock applicator is a miracle."

"All right," Marge said grudgingly. "That's good. The missus asked for scrambled eggs for breakfast. The PT lady called and said she isn't coming today, so once you eat and take your meds, you and I will have a go at that running track."

While she was rattling pots and pans in the kitchen, I went back to my computer. I e-mailed myself a copy of the list Delilah Ainsworth and I had constructed—the list that included everyone I could remember who had been involved in the Monica Wellington homicide investigation. Mac MacPherson had been one of the first names on that list. And he was now the first to come off it. I was amending that list with addresses and phone numbers wherever possible when Mel joined me in the den.

"I'm working on an interview list," I told her.

Reading over my shoulder, she scanned through it. "Who's Sister Mary Katherine?"

"She was the principal at Saints Peter and Paul, a Catholic school on Magnolia where Donnie and Frankie Dodd, the two boys who were the closest thing to eyewitnesses, were students."

"They're the kids who pointed you in the direction of the barrel in the first place?"

"Right. The problem is, the school closed in the early nineties. And the Dodd family seems to have disappeared into thin air. I remember they moved away a couple weeks into the investigation, but I have no idea where they went."

Marge called from the kitchen, announcing that breakfast was served.

In preparation for going in for surgery, Mel and I had put together a shopping list of what we thought we'd need. Since I'd been using the walker Marge had brought along to the hospital, the new one was sitting in the bedroom, pristinely unused. Thinking that canes were somehow more civilized and dignified than a walker, we had also purchased a pair of very colorful metal ones. Those I had stowed in the corner behind my chair. When it was time to go eat, I surprised everyone, including myself, by walking from the den to the dining room with my two canes.

Rather than being happy about the situation and giving me attaboy points, Marge put both hands on her hips and scowled at me. "Did Ida Witherspoon say you were ready to graduate from the walker to canes?"

"No," I told her. "I said I was ready."

She shook her head. "Be that as it may, you'd better believe that when it's time to do the running track, we'll be using the walker."

I didn't argue the point then or later, after breakfast, when it was time to head downstairs. Using the canes to get from the den to the dining room was one thing. Doing much more than that wouldn't have worked. The irony of making my way halfway around a "running track" on a walker wasn't lost on me, but by the time we finished that single partial trip I was glad to have that instead of the canes. Note to self: Marge was right today; I was wrong.

When Marge and I came back into the unit, I told her that I thought Mel and I could manage on our own for the rest of the day and that she should consider taking the remainder of the day off. I found Mel sitting cross-legged on the window seat working away at her computer.

"Find anything?" I asked.

"Yes," she said. "Sister Mary Katherine Donnelly is retired and living in a convent in Las Cruces, New Mexico."

"How did you find that out?"

"Saints Peter and Paul Catholic School may have closed in the early nineties, but alumni from there have a very active Web site. When I put in the names for Frank and Donald Dodd, I got cross-referenced to Francis and Donald Clark. Donald is listed as deceased. According to this, Francis, Frank, currently lives in Yakima."

I thought about that for a moment, trying to remember the details of the two interviews with the redheaded twin boys, first that day in the patrol car and again later, at school, with Sister Katherine hovering in the background. In both instances, one of the boys—Donnie, I believed—had done most of the talking.

"Like I said, they left town a couple weeks into the investigation," I said. "My understanding at the time was that their mother was remarrying. From the name change, I would guess that their stepfather adopted them. If Donald is deceased, does it say what he died of, or when?"

"I'm looking for a death certificate right now," Mel said. I waited in silence, letting her do her search.

"Wait," she said. "Here. This has to be him: 'Donald Curtis Dodd Clark, born in Seattle on December 14, 1961. Died February 12, 1999. Cause of death: multiple injuries sustained in a two-car accident.'" There was another pause, and more typing. "Okay," Mel said, "the other driver in the accident was cited for DUI. According to the obituary, Donald's survivors are listed as his mother and stepfather, Amelia and Howard R. Clark of Yakima, and his twin brother, Francis, along with several nieces and nephews."

I started to say something, but Mel held up her hand. "Wait," she said. "Let me check something else."

Again I waited. Mel is great at doing computer searches, and I was happy to leave this to her. "Okay," she said several minutes later, "this is interesting."

"What?"

"I just checked the birth certificate records. Donald and Francis Dodd were born to Amelia Dodd at Providence Hospital in Seattle. The father is listed as unknown."

That was surprising. But then, given Amelia's supposed occupation, maybe not. Still, I remembered the home. It hadn't been really upscale, but the place had been neat and clean—not a slum by any means. And, at the time, the boys had been attending a private school rather than a public one, and tuition there didn't come cheap.

"It's interesting all right," I agreed, "but is it interesting enough to go hightailing it over Snoqualmie Pass to chat up the surviving brother? What about the mother?"

"Amelia Ann Dodd Clark was born in Yakima General

Hospital on March 24, 1941. Died of natural causes, again in Yakima, on July 5, 2002." There was a pause. "Here's the obituary. 'Ms. Clark, well-known throughout the Yakima area for her efforts on behalf of underprivileged children, died at her home surrounded by loved ones on July 5, 2002, after a long battle with diabetes. She is survived by her loving husband of twenty-nine years, Howard B. Clark, and by her surviving son, Francis. Her beloved son Donald preceded Ms. Clark in death. Services are pending. The family suggests that donations be made to Amelia's Fund in care of Tri-City Bank.'"

"So there you have it," I said. "The hooker with the heart of gold gets out of the life, marries someone from out of town, and goes on to live with him for decades and, in the process, becomes a beloved and upstanding member of the community. Who says happily ever after doesn't happen?"

Mel gave me a scathing look. "Just because there's no father listed on the birth certificate, you're assuming that the mother was a hooker?"

"That was the general impression," I said. "In fact, one of the neighbors, a Mrs. Fisk, told us as much at the time."

I had forgotten to add Mrs. Fisk's name to my list earlier, but I did so then.

"Sounds like gossip to me," Mel declared. "Meanspirited gossip." With that, Mel slammed shut her computer and went in search of more coffee.

I could tell at once that I had stepped in something, although I wasn't sure just what. I suppose that there are times when sisterhood is *still* powerful. By impugning Amelia Dodd Clark's reputation, I had somehow offended Mel, thereby making it less than likely that Mel could be persuaded to accompany me (make that drive me) on a day trip across the Cascades to Yakima to track down Frankie Dodd Clark. If I hadn't just put my foot in my mouth, I might have been able to make the case for taking in some autumn leaves along the way. I knew that ruse wasn't going to cut it now.

Left to my own devices, I went back to my list and started making calls, starting with Larry Powell.

Lawrence Powell was still a detective when I first landed in Seattle PD's Homicide unit, but during most of the years I worked there, he was the captain in Homicide and also the guy in charge. I called his listed number in Saddlebrooke, Arizona, a place Google Maps told me was somewhere north of Tucson. The woman who answered the phone said to me, "Hang on." Then, speaking to someone else she added, "Sweetie, it's for you."

Larry Powell had been Captain Powell for so long that I had a tough time wrapping my mind around the idea of him being anybody's "sweetie," but when he came on the phone, I recognized his rich baritone at once.

"Who's calling?" he asked.

"It's J.P.," I said. "Beau."

"How the hell are you?"

"Great," I said. "How about you?"

"Can't complain," he said, "although my golf score's gone to crap. What are you up to? Still hanging out with Ross's S.H.I.T. squad?"

There's something about law enforcement. It's a tight-knit community. You may leave it, but it stays with you wherever you go. The people you once worked with pay attention to where their fellow officers go and what they do.

"Yup," I said. "I'm still there. What do you hear from Watty these days?"

"Not much. He moved to South Carolina. Told me he needed to stretch his pension. He said between pinching his pennies in Mexico or South Carolina, he picked the latter since he never learned to speak Spanish. I doubt he's learned Southern, either, but that's beside the point. He says that because he's a senior he can pay off his property taxes by working in some office or another. I wish they'd start a program like that here."

"You got a number for him?"

"Sure," Larry said. "But what's this all about—Mac MacPherson taking out that female detective?"

As I said, it's a tight-knit community. Word had traveled fast.

"Yes," I said. "As a matter of fact it is. How did you find out about it?"

"I just got off the phone with Melody, Mac's ex-wife. She's really broken up over what happened. She can't believe that even dead drunk, he'd do something like that. It's pretty hard for me to believe it, too."

"You mean you've stayed in touch with her?"

"With Melody? Sure. She was a close friend of my first wife, Marcia, and they stayed in touch after we left Seattle. Melody's father had ALS, so she knew firsthand what Marcia and I were going through. After Marcia died, Melody was supportive of my getting on with my life, and now she and Joanie, my second wife, are good friends, too. In fact, when she was feeling lower than a snake's vest pocket after the divorce was finalized, we invited her to come down and stay with us for a couple of weeks."

"Did she ask for the divorce or did he?" I asked.

"Melody's the one who filed," Larry said, "and who could blame her? She stuck with the man through a lot when other women might have turned tail and run. She was with him all through the aftermath of that terrible accident, the one where he lost his legs. What she couldn't stand later, and what finally drove her away, was the idea of having to sit around helplessly and watch while he drank himself to death."

"I should probably give Melody a call," I said, "but I don't have a number."

Larry gave it to me without a moment's hesitation, and threw in their son's number for good measure.

"So what's the deal?" Larry asked, his tone turning serious. "Melody said the woman who died . . ."

"Detective Ainsworth," I supplied.

"Yes, Ainsworth," Larry said. "I knew Delilah briefly. She was still working Patrol back when I was there. Melody said this was all about reopening some cold case or other."

"Yes," I said. "The Monica Wellington homicide."

"Oh, yes," Larry said at once. "The Girl in the Barrel. We never did solve that one."

"That's the problem," I said. "Delilah and I were in the process of reopening what we thought was a cold case when we learned that it had been marked closed in 1981. She also discovered that all the evidence from that case has gone missing. So here's a head's-up. Seattle PD's Internal Affairs Division is going to be all over this, and I'm guessing you'll be hearing from them sooner or later."

"Sounds like it," he agreed.

"So here's the question, Larry," I said. "Who was in charge of Seattle PD Homicide in 1981?"

"I was," he replied without a moment's hesitation.

"Did you mark the case closed?"

"Of course I didn't!" He sounded indignant; offended. "I just told you. We never solved the case of the Girl in the Barrel. Is that why you're calling me? You think I marked it closed to improve our numbers?"

"No," I answered. "I'm not saying you did it, but I'm wondering who else could have. Who can you think of who would have gone over your head and made a call like that?"

"It would have to have been someone from upstairs," Larry said gloomily. "Someone with a hell of a lot more brass than I had at the time, and probably someone way above my pay grade, but none of this makes any sense. Why would Mac shoot someone for simply reopening that case? It's not like he was ever a suspect."

"In the long run, it may not have had anything to do with Monica Wellington."

"What then?"

"Mac and I were still working Patrol on the day we found the Girl in the Barrel. Two days later, when I came back, I had been moved up to Homicide and Mac had been moved over to the Motorcycle unit. Both of those moves meant a bump up the promotion ladder. So the question is, who signed off on those promotions?"

"I have no idea," Larry answered. "I remember we were all a little surprised when you got dropped on our heads with no warning and, as a consequence, with no partner, but I can tell you for sure that it wasn't me. I was still a detective at that point. Even so, it shouldn't be too hard to find out. All you have to do is go to HR and have them track down the microfiche."

"That's exactly what Delilah Ainsworth did," I told

him, "and it didn't work. The microfiche has been tampered with. That one day has been X-ed out of the record, as in completely removed. Our two promotions, along with whatever else happened on that day, have gone missing. I suspect that the records for that day were never put into the microfiche in the first place."

"You're saying you think the records were physically removed before being transferred to film?"

"That's what Delilah was going to ask Mac about when she was killed. I know that because she called and told me that's what she was on her way to do."

"But why would Mac pull something like this?" Larry asked. "I mean, after all these years, what could it matter if one person signed off on the paperwork or another did?"

And that's when I knew for sure that the holdback was still holding. Melody MacPherson still had no idea that her husband hadn't murdered Delilah Ainsworth. Neither did Larry Powell. Just because I had blown Detectives Monford and Anderson's cover with Brian Ainsworth didn't mean I had to make the same mistake with Larry Powell.

"It's hard to understand when someone goes completely off the rails like that," I said.

Yes, I was hiding out in old-fashioned basic platitudes, but in some situations platitudes are the only things that work.

"I'll say," Larry agreed.

"So you don't really hear much from Watty these days?" I asked casually.

"We get a card every Christmas, but that's about it."

Thank God for Christmas cards. I pulled up my list and typed "South Carolina" after Watty Watkins's name.

"You got a town to go with that?"

"Aiken, I think," he said. "I'll check the list. If that's wrong, I'll give you a call back."

I was just finishing up the phone call with Larry Powell when Mel emerged from her bedroom/study. Barefoot, she padded past my recliner, dropped a yellow sticky note on the armrest, and went on her way. She had written someone's name on the paper—Glenn Madden—along with a telephone number that was clearly somewhere outside Washington state.

The name and phone number didn't mean much, but the very existence of the note imparted a larger message. Whatever I had said or done earlier was forgiven. That's one of the wonderful things about Mel Soames. It's not that she doesn't get angry occasionally. It's impossible for two people to be married and not have the occasional snit fit that comes out of left field and knocks you on your butt. The difference between Mel and some of the other women I've known through the years, and most especially my first wife, is this: Mel gets over it. And so do I. We acknowledge what happened, and then we move on. Neither one of us sits around waiting for some kind of half-baked apology; there are no rounds of silent treatment that linger from one week to the next. Maybe that's what it means to be married to a grown-up.

"Who's this?" I asked, once the call ended.

"That's the name of the guy who's currently in charge of the Cacti reunions," she answered. "I got his contact information off the Internet."

Cacti. The 35th Infantry. Vietnam. Lennie D. I hadn't asked Mel for help on that, but she had given it, and I was smart enough not to turn it down. Instead, I pulled out my phone and dialed the number.

"Madden residence," said the woman who answered. She said it in a way that indicated she was used to handling phone calls from relative strangers.

"My name is J. P. Beaumont," I said. "I was in the Thirty-fifth Infantry. I understand Glenn Madden's been instrumental in putting together the reunions. Would it be possible to speak with him?"

"He's actually in Pittsburgh. There was a reunion this weekend. I don't expect him back here in Colorado Springs until late tomorrow evening. Did you not receive your invitation?"

"I did," I said lamely. "I must have mislaid it."

"Would you like me to have him call you?"

"Sure," I said. "It's nothing urgent. If the convention is going on, he no doubt has his hands full."

"The reunion is over. Today is a board meeting."

I gave her my name and number so she could write it down. As soon as I thanked her and ended the call, I turned to Mel, who had abandoned the living room window seat in favor of the other easy chair, which is to say the chair that isn't a recliner, in the den. She immediately reached over and handed me another sticky note. That one said "Sister Mary Katherine Donnelly." On it was another phone number.

"New Mexico?" I asked.

Mel nodded.

"You said it's a convent." I glanced at my watch. It was midafternoon. "Should I call?"

Mel shrugged. "What's the worst that can happen?" she said. "If they're not accepting phone calls, they'll most likely have voice mail."

But there wasn't a recording. When I asked for Sister Mary Katherine, whoever had answered the phone at

Santa Teresa's said simply, "One moment, please." The receiver, obviously part of an old landline set, clattered noisily onto a counter. There was a long pause. I could make out the sound of women's voices murmuring in the background. Eventually someone answered.

I remembered the steely-eyed woman with her gold-framed glasses and her no-nonsense attitude. I estimated that she must have been somewhere in her fifties when I last saw her. That meant she was somewhere in her nineties now. She sounded just as firm and uncompromising as she had back then.

"Who's calling, please?" she asked.

"My name is Beaumont," I said. "J. P. Beaumont. I was a Seattle PD Homicide detective the last time I spoke to you, in the spring of 1973. Two of your students were witnesses in a case I was working on, and I was hoping you could give me some help."

"I recall that unfortunate situation very well. The boys, the Evil Twins, as I'm afraid we sometimes called them, had discovered the body of a homicide victim and called it in to the authorities. I seem to remember that you came to the school to interview them along with another detective."

I can only hope that when I hit that age, I have even half that much grasp on what happened forty years or so in the past.

"Yes," I said. "That's correct, and Frankie and Donnie Dodd were the boys in question."

"Believe me, the two of them were a real handful," Sister Mary Katherine said. "They were always getting into some kind of mischief. Still, they weren't bad boys, and I was sorry when their mother pulled them out of school. I've always wondered what became of them."

"I believe their mother remarried," I replied. "It looks as though they were adopted by their new stepfather. Donnie died a decade ago as the result of an automobile accident. Frankie still lives and works in Yakima. That was where his mother was from originally and where she and her husband made a life for themselves after she left Seattle."

"Well," Sister Mary Katherine said briskly. "Since it sounds as though you know a lot more about them than I do, why are you calling me?"

I didn't want to make the same kind of blunder with her that I had made with Mel a little earlier, so I tried to tread lightly.

"As I recall, their mother lived alone. I don't remember her having any kind of job, but the family lived in a nice enough house and the boys attended Saints Peter and Paul school. Tuition there couldn't have been cheap. I'm just curious as to whether you have any clue about how a single mom managed all that back then. Were they allowed to go there on a scholarship of some kind?"

I heard the sudden reticence in Sister Mary Katherine's voice the moment she replied, "I don't see why that should be any concern of yours, especially after all this time."

Sister Mary Katherine's sharp response was the verbal equivalent of a solid rap on the knuckle with a ruler, and my hackles went up.

"It was just that the boys were the closest thing we had to eyewitnesses to what had happened to our victim," I said. "Not to the actual crime itself, of course, but to the disposal of the body. Now that we're reopening the case, I was simply wondering if there was anything more to it than that."

"Francis and Donald Dodd were never scholarship students," Sister Mary Katherine declared. "Their school fees were paid in full."

"By whom?"

"That's entirely confidential," she said firmly. "If one of the family members chooses to tell you, that's up to them. You certainly won't hear it from me. Good day, Mr. Beaumont."

The phone banged down in my ear. It would have been easy to be upset, but I wasn't. I realized that something important had just happened. For reasons I had yet to understand, I knew I was on the right track.

I looked over at Mel. "We need to go to Yakima."

There was no need to attempt the "go see the autumn leaves" routine. This was business.

"I'll go get the car keys," she said. "Do you need to take any more medication before we go?"

"Yes," I said. "That's probably a good idea. And don't forget the string cheese."

CHAPTER 18

Mel drove us from Seattle to Yakima, about a hundred and forty miles to the east and over the Cascade Mountains, without actually breaking the sound barrier and without getting a speeding ticket, either. I suppose the leaves were turning as we drove across Snoqualmie Pass, but the truth is, we were hunkered down and talking. We've both put in a lot of years in the world of law enforcement, but the idea of coming face-to-face with the possibility of crooks in the cop shop still has the power to shock and dismay. That had to be what this was. Whoever had tampered with the evidence and the microfiche had to be a cop, and one who was a long way up the food chain.

We were over the pass and driving past Easton when my phone rang. "Mr. Beaumont?" a stranger's voice asked. "This is Glenn Madden. My wife said you called."

I could hear the sounds of voices and laughter in the background. Obviously Madden hadn't waited until he got home from the board meeting to give me a call.

"Thanks for getting back to me so soon," I said. "I didn't mean that you should drop everything to call me."

Madden laughed. "When one of our guys calls, I jump right on it," he said. "Especially if it's someone who hasn't been in touch before. Usually there's a good reason for their calling right then, and if there's some kind of crisis—"

"No crisis," I said quickly. "Not at all. I was in the Thirty-fifth in Vietnam," I said. "I'm trying to get in touch with the fiancée of one of the guys I served with, a guy who died. It's something I should have done a long time ago, but I never did. Now that so many years have passed, I hope it's not too late, but since they weren't married, I'm not even sure you can help me—"

"Hang on," he said. "Let me open up my database."

"Really, if you're still at the convention . . ."

"No, this is fine. Give me the name."

"Second Lieutenant Leonard D. Davis," I said. "From Bisbee, Arizona. He died on August 2, 1966."

I could hear computer keys clicking in the background. "Oh, yes," he said. "Where do you live?"

"Seattle," I replied.

"The fiancée's married name is Bonnie Abney," Madden said. "And you're in luck. She lives somewhere in your neck of the woods, on an island called Whidbey. Do you know where that is?"

By then I had my iPad out and was typing a note of my own. "Yes, I know where Whidbey Island is, but do you mind spelling her name?"

He did so, and I typed it in.

"I remember her well," Madden said.

That stopped me. For a moment I wondered if somehow this Madden guy had been in our outfit. He went on to explain without my having to ask.

"One of Second Lieutenant Davis's friends from West Point, and someone who served with him, encouraged Ms. Abney to come to one of our conventions several years ago. She was the first woman to speak at one of them; she made quite an impression. Out of courtesy to her, though, I'd rather not give out her contact information. I'll be glad to pass along yours to her instead. I hope you don't mind. With things like this, there's always a chance that she'd rather not go there."

"Of course," I said. "That makes perfect sense. You already have my name and number, so feel free to give her those."

"Can I tell her what this is about?"

"Yes," I said. "Please tell her that Second Lieutenant Davis saved my life, and that I have a few mementos I'd like to pass along to her. If she's interested, that is. I don't want to apply any undue pressure."

"Right," Madden said. "We'll put the ball in her court and see what she does with it."

"Thanks for getting back to me so fast," I said. "I really appreciate it."

"No problem," he said. "Your name's in my database, but I see that you haven't attended any of our gatherings."

"I'll think about it," I said. "Don't give up on me."

He ended the call.

"So you found her?" Mel asked.

I nodded. "She lives on Whidbey. Madden is going to send my information to her rather than the other way around."

Mel nodded. "Sounds reasonable to me."

We drove on in silence for the space of several miles before she asked, "What mementos?"

"The ones I showed you," I said.

I reached into my pocket and retrieved the items I had stowed there after Marge brought the box up from the storage unit—three aces of spades and three chunks of what should have been lethal shrapnel. I had taken them out of my pocket and left them on the dresser last night, and had put them back in my pocket that morning when I dressed to go downstairs to the running track.

Mel glanced at what I was holding in my hand and then turned her eyes back to the highway.

"I thought you said he gave you four aces of spades," she said.

"He did," I said quietly. "I used one."

And that was the real reason I didn't go to reunions. As a cop, I've had to shoot people, but they have always been bad people. This was different. It was my fifth day in Pleiku, and my second day on patrol. I saw the guy, took my shot, dropped him, and left my calling card.

Nobody had invented video games in 1966, but that's how it had seemed at first, like it was all some kind of game. Except it wasn't. That other guy, the one I killed—the one on whose bloodied chest I left my own playing card—was a soldier the same as I was. He was out on patrol, doing his job, doing what his government had told him to do. And wherever his family was, he never went back there—back home to his parents or his wife or his sweetheart or his kids.

It stopped being a game for me the moment I dropped that card. I never used another, although I could have, and I never asked for a replacement. And after Lennie D. died, I don't think anyone else did, either. From then on it was definitely not a game. It hurt too much and was far too deadly.

Another ten miles at least must have passed before Mel spoke again. "Do you think she'll want them?" she asked.

"I don't know," I said.

"And what will you do with them if she doesn't?" Mel asked. "Put them back downstairs in the storage unit?"

"I'm not sure," I said, but even then, I was thinking about that wall in Washington and about how I had heard that people sometimes left things there as a remembrance to the fallen.

"I'm sure you'll figure it out," Mel said, reaching over and patting the numb spot on my thigh. "We'll figure it out together."

CHAPTER 19

The thing about pain meds is that they work. I dozed off then and didn't wake up again until we were driving through a residential area in Yakima. Mel had located Frankie Dodd Clark's address on Douglas Drive before we left home. Given Glenn Madden's call about Doug Davis on the way there, the irony of going to that particular address wasn't lost on me.

Douglas Drive turned out to be a neighborhood of upscale brick rambler-type homes with plenty of grassy yards separating one house from another. At a glance it was easy to tell that Frankie Clark had done all right for himself. The door to the two-car garage was open, revealing the presence of two cars—a relatively new white four-wheel-drive Silverado pickup and a spanking-new silver Taurus with dealer plates still pasted in the window. At a time when not many people were plunking down money to buy new cars off the lot, I thought that was telling.

Mel and I had agreed in advance that ours would be a surprise visit with no advance warning. She pulled up behind the two cars and stopped directly behind both of them. Then she came around to my side of the car and handed me the two canes. Using the canes made me feel a little less gimpy. Once on the front porch, she rang the bell, then pulled out her badge and ID.

A young girl with her blond hair in two old-fashioned braids answered the door. She looked to be not much older than her father had been the first time Mac and I met him that Sunday afternoon.

"I'm Special Investigator Mel Soames and this is my partner, Inspector Beaumont," Mel told the little girl. "Is your father here?"

Somewhere in the background I could hear the sound of a baseball game broadcast. It was September, and it was looking like the Mariners had a chance of making it to the World Series.

"Hey, Daddy," she shouted into the house. "Some cops are here to see you."

Frankie Dodd Clark came to the door wearing a pair of blue cutoffs, a Seattle Mariners T-shirt, a pair of flip-flops, and a very concerned look on his face. He was a tall, rangy man—well built and well muscled, with a prematurely receding hairline. His once bright red hair—what he had left of it—was more of a burnished copper now. Other than hair color, I saw very little resemblance between him and the reticent kid I remembered from Sister Mary Katherine's office.

"Is something wrong?" he asked, stopping in the doorway and not inviting us to step inside.

"No," I said. "Not at all. We're with the Special Homicide Investigation Team. My partner, Ms. Soames, and I would like to ask you a few questions about a cold case we're working on."

Frank frowned. "Is this about my brother?" he asked.

"No," I answered. "Nothing to do with your brother. It's about a homicide that happened years ago in Seattle. My partner then, Detective Watkins, and I interviewed you and Donnie about it at the time."

In homicide investigations, timing is everything. The pauses between the time a question is asked and the time the answer is given are sometimes more telling than the answers themselves. This time, not only was the pause far too long, but so was the glance Frankie shot back over his shoulder, as though he was making sure his family members were out of earshot.

At that point, in most interviews, we'd either be sent packing or be invited inside. In this case neither happened. Instead, Frank stepped out on the porch and pulled the door shut behind him.

"This is about the woman in the barrel?" he asked. He had been so young at the time that the young woman who had been a "girl" to us had been a "woman" to him.

"Yes," I said. "That's the one."

"What do you want to know?"

"We're having difficulty locating the records from then," I said. "What can you tell us?"

He closed his eyes for a long moment before he answered. "It was late at night. My brother, Donnie, and I were outside, doing something we weren't supposed to be doing, and we saw this guy drive a pickup into the yard next door."

"You're sure it was a guy?"

Frank nodded. "He pushed a barrel out of the back of the pickup and rolled it down the hill. Then he drove off. The next day Donnie and I went looking for the barrel. When we opened it, that's when we found the dead woman, stuck in there with a bunch of greasy stuff." He paused, looked at me, shuddered, and then shrugged his shoulders.

"That's it," he added. "That's all I remember."

It was such a blatant lie that I wanted to poke him with my cane, just to let him know I knew, but I didn't.

"My partner at the time and I came to school to talk to you about it. As I recall, your brother did most of the talking."

"My brother's dead," Frank offered.

"But why was that?" I asked, ignoring his comment. "Why did you leave it up to him to do the talking for both of you? Or was it always like that? He was sort of the ringleader and you just went along with the program?"

"Why are you asking me about this now?" Frank demanded. "We were just kids back then. You can't possibly think we were the ones who killed her. That's crazy."

"What we think is that you're hiding something," Mel said softly. "What?"

The wary look Frank turned in her direction told me that Mel had nailed it. He really was hiding something.

He shook his head. "I don't want to talk about this. As far as my kids are concerned, Howard Clark is the only grandfather they've ever known. I don't want to have to explain all of that other stuff."

"What other stuff?" Mel asked. "Are you saying your stepfather is responsible for what happened to that girl?"

Frank suddenly drew himself up so that he looked a good three inches taller. "Absolutely not!" he declared hotly. "He wasn't even in the picture then. At least, if he was, Donnie and I didn't know it. When he asked Mom to marry him a couple of weeks later, it was all news to us. As for coming back over here to live? That was fine with us, too."

"So what aren't you telling us?" Mel asked. "I'm guessing there's something you and your brother knew that you didn't tell anyone at the time."

Mel is great when it comes to talking softly and carrying a big stick. Her tone of voice was gentle but utterly firm. Nothing about her allowed for any wiggle room. I suspect Sister Mary Katherine would have approved.

Frank looked her full in the face and then his eyes slid away. "We were scared," he said.

"Scared of what?" I asked.

"Not of what," he answered despairingly. All the fight had gone out of him. "Of who. I saw the face of the man who was driving the truck, the guy who dumped the barrel. I recognized him. He told us if we ever told, he'd come after us, and we believed him. I still do."

"Who was it?" I asked.

"A cop."

We already knew that much. I wanted to shake the guy and knock some sense into him. "What was his name?" I insisted.

"I don't know. We never knew his name. He was our father's bodyguard."

"Wait. I thought you said your father wasn't involved."

"Howard Clark is my stepfather," Frank Dodd declared. "He's my adoptive father and the only one I've ever known. The other guy was a rich guy, a sperm donor only. Oh, he paid the rent for the house where we lived. And he paid for food and for us to go to school. But I understand now that he only came by for what people these days call booty calls. Paying for us to go to school was his way of getting his regular rolls in the hay.

Donnie and I were a means to that end. He also expected us to be properly grateful, to not talk back, and to do
exactly what he said. If we didn't, the belt came out."

I didn't like how this was going. It was like stepping
on what you thought was firm ground and feeling the
slippage as it gave way to seeping quicksand. Some guy
who could ride around town with a Seattle cop serving
as his bodyguard was a guy whose name we probably
didn't want to know.

"We need a name," Mel said softly. "Please."

Frank took a deep, shuddering breath. "Daniel Don-
Leavy," he said, with his voice barely a whisper. "Daniel
McCoy DonLeavy."

I'm sure my jaw dropped. "As in Mayor Daniel Don-
Leavy?"

Mayor DonLeavy had arrived on Seattle's political
scene in the late sixties with a program for cleaning
house in city government, for cutting waste and corrup-
tion, for shaping up the police department. Ironically,
DonLeavy had done so with enough shady dealings on
his part that by the late seventies the former mayor and
a number of his "kitchen cabinet" had not only been in-
dicted, but had also been sent to the slammer.

Frank Clark nodded. "That's the one," he said. Then,
motioning toward a wooden swing on the porch, he
added, "It's a long story. Care to have a seat?"

By then I had been leaning on my canes for what
seemed like forever. I gratefully accepted. Mel and I sat
together on the swing while Frank took a seat on the
front step.

"My mother and Howard Clark were high school
sweethearts," he explained. "They went together during their first two years of college. Then, something

happened and they broke up. At that point, my mother dropped out of college and went to work as a cocktail waitress at Vito's. I suppose you know where that is?"

I nodded.

For decades Vito's, a combination bar/restaurant, had been the in place for the in-crowd's wheeling and dealing in Seattle. That's where the top-tier guys from the cop shop had gone to mingle with the politicos and the well-heeled attorneys, while the guys lower down on the food chain had tended to gather in joints in the International District where the food was cheaper and the atmosphere wasn't quite as alive with political infighting.

"That's where she met DonLeavy?"

It was Frank's turn to nod. "The old story. He was married. Once she got pregnant with my brother and me, he tried to talk her into giving us up, but she wouldn't. And she wouldn't agree to an abortion, either, mostly because they were both good Catholics—well, maybe not exactly good. Anyway, DonLeavy ended up setting her up with a place to live. He gave her money to live on and food to eat. And that's just the way things were. He took care of us. Paid for us to go to that school. He also beat the crap out of us if he thought we were out of line."

"Did you know the man was your father?" I asked.

Frank shook his head.

"Not really," he said. "Our mother told us he was just a friend, but it turns out she had a lot of friends."

Frank Clark drew imaginary quotation marks around the word. It was an admission that didn't require any more detail than that. The gesture told me that Donnie and Frankie had known what their mother was back then, and that old story didn't need rehashing now.

"According to our mother," Frank continued, "the guy was like our uncle—our uncle Dan. The other guys came and went from time to time, but Uncle Dan was different. He showed up on a regular basis, always with a driver who hung around outside while Dan was inside the house visiting."

His fingers drew another set of invisible quotation marks around the word "visiting." I took that to mean that the boys had known what was going on. They had understood.

"A driver and a bodyguard, then?" Mel asked.

Frank nodded. "Donnie and I figured out the bodyguard was some kind of cop, even before that night, the night he showed up at the house next door with the barrel in the back of his truck. When he turned around after pushing the barrel down the hill, he saw us. We were hiding under the back porch, but he saw us anyway. He pulled a gun on us and ordered us to come out from under the porch. That's when he told us that if we ever told anyone that he had been there that night or if we ever talked to anyone about Uncle Dan or him, we were done and so was our mother."

"So he threatened you, and you believed him?" Mel asked.

Frank nodded. "We were kids. He was holding a gun. Of course we believed him."

"But you still went down and looked at the barrel," I said. "Why?"

"It was a dare," Frank said sadly. "One of Donnie's famous double dares."

"When you found there was a body in the barrel, you still called it in. Why?"

"If the guy could do something like that to her—to

the woman in the barrel—we were afraid he could do the same thing to our mom or to us. We thought the cops would figure out who had done it on their own—that you would figure it out," he added, casting an accusatory glance in my direction. "Donnie and I didn't dare try to help much. We were too scared."

"This guy you thought was a cop. Did you ever see him again?" I asked.

Frank nodded. "He was there at the house that Sunday evening."

"The day you found the barrel?"

Frank nodded again.

"What happened?"

"He came to the house and talked to Mom. I don't know what he told her, but I know she was upset and crying after he left. Five days later, Howard Clark showed up at our house. Within a matter of weeks, he and Mom got married—by a justice of the peace—and we moved back here."

"What about DonLeavy?" I asked.

"I never saw him again. I didn't know the whole story—that he was our biological father—until our mother was in the hospital. When she realized she was dying, she decided it was time to tell me the truth. I'm not sure why. It didn't make any difference.

"She said that at the time we were leaving Seattle, someone was threatening to tell DonLeavy's wife about us. She was sure there was going to be a terrible scandal. Mom had burned her bridges with her own family years earlier. She was desperate. She called Howard Clark to ask for his advice and that's when he came riding to the rescue. He brought us back over here. He took care of Mom and of Donnie and me, too.

As far as I'm concerned, he's the only father I've ever needed or wanted.

"After Mom died, I went on the Internet to find out what I could. That's when I discovered that Daniel DonLeavy has been dead for fifteen years. His widow is still around, but I don't feel right showing up and saying, 'Surprise, guess who I am?' So I haven't done that, and I have no intention of doing so, either."

The three of us were sitting there in silence when the front door opened and a woman stuck her head out. She looked worried. "Is everything all right?" she asked.

"It's okay," Frank said quickly. "Just some old stuff from when we lived in Seattle."

She nodded and disappeared back inside.

"My wife," he explained. "She knows about all this. My kids don't. As far as they're concerned, Howard Clark is their grandpa. Why screw that up?"

Why indeed?

"So what do you want from me?" he asked. "Why are you here?"

"A few days ago a decision was made to reopen the Monica Wellington homicide," I said. "As soon as we did so, we discovered some irregularities in the handling of the evidence in that case. Since then, Seattle PD homicide detective Delilah Ainsworth, the investigator who was assigned to work that case, has been murdered, and so has the guy who was my partner back at the time of the original homicide."

"The guy who came to the school to interview us?"

"No, Mac MacPherson. On that Sunday Mac and I were still working patrol, and we were the ones who took the call when you and Donnie reported finding the barrel. We're the ones who picked the two of you up down by the waterfront before you took us back to the barrel."

"Two more people are dead?" Frank asked.

I nodded. "Because of the mishandling of the evidence, we have reason to believe that the person we're looking for is also a police officer. Based on what you've told us, I think we're all looking for the same guy—the one who threatened you. Can you tell us his name?"

Frank shook his head. "No idea," he said. "When our mother had company, she made sure Donnie and I didn't hang around. All I can remember is that he was a big guy, with dark hair. That's all—that and the gun in his hand. That's something I'll never forget. I wish I knew more, but I don't."

I used the canes to lever myself upright. "You've already been a big help," I told him. "If the guy we're looking for was assigned to Mayor DonLeavy, we'll be able to find his name."

"Is all this going to have to come out?" Frank asked. "My mother turned her life around. She and Howard have been pillars of this community for years. They've been good parents. I'd hate to think that their names would have to be dragged through the mud . . ."

"Mr. Clark," I said. "I'd like you to take a moment to think about the dead girl's family—about Monica Wellington's family."

"What about them?"

"There's a good chance that the guy who killed her is the same guy who victimized you and your brother. Probably even your mother as well."

"So?"

"This is a guy who has gotten away with murder for the better part of four decades while you're still afraid

of him and while Monica's family is still waiting for answers. If there was a chance that your testimony would
put this guy away for murdering Monica Wellington all
those years ago, what do you think your mother would
want you to do? What would both your parents—the
real people here in Yakima who raised you—want you
to do?"

"No question," Frank said. "They'd want me to come
forward."

I nodded. "That's what I thought. If there's any way
we can do this without calling on you for help, we will.
But if you're our last hope, we'll be back."

"All right," Frank said, but he didn't sound entirely
convinced.

"One last question," I said. "How old were you when
your mother and Howard got back together—ten or
so?"

"Eleven," Frank answered.

"And in all the intervening years, there had never
been any connection between them?"

"Not as far as I know. After Mom and Howard broke
up, he evidently married someone else, but that marriage ended in divorce or maybe an annulment. I'm not
sure which. All I know is, one day, the week after all this
happened, the doorbell rang and here was this guy I'd
never seen before standing there on the front porch. 'I'm
looking for Amelia Dodd,' he said. 'Tell her Howard's
here. I've come to take her home.'"

"And that's all there was to it?"

"As far as I know. They took up together as though
the years they'd been apart had never happened," Frank
said. "Howard treated my mother like gold. She couldn't
have been happier."

"She had you and Donnie to thank for that," I said.

Frank looked puzzled. "I don't understand."

"Think about it," I said. "When you and your brother did the right thing by calling in the report, you also called the killer's bluff, but he probably didn't let it go at that."

Frank frowned. "What do you mean?"

"Yes, he had threatened you, but he wasn't sure you'd keep your end of the bargain. I'm betting he put the screws to your mother, too. He backed her far enough into a corner that she had to go looking for help. Luckily for all of you that Howard Clark is the guy she called."

Frank seemed stunned. "That never occurred to me," he said. "Never."

"Well, it makes perfect sense to me. And if we need your help, we'll have it, right?"

"Right," Frank agreed. "Whatever you need me to do, I'll do."

CHAPTER 20

Mel and I didn't say another word until we were back in her Cayman and headed for Seattle. "You didn't exactly go easy on him," she said.

"If we need his help, I wanted to know we could count on it."

"What do we do now?" she asked. "Take another spin through HR?"

Sometimes I forget that Mel is a relative newcomer on the Seattle scene. She doesn't have the local history drummed into her head the way I do.

"No need," I said. "We've got a whole lot better source for information than that."

I already had my phone out and was speed-dialing Ross Connors's home number. Long before Ross became the Washington state attorney general, long before he became the King County prosecutor, he had been fresh out of law school and had gone to work as a lowly newbie in the same prosecutor's office he would one day use to pole-vault himself to statewide office.

Ross had already made something of a name for himself in the prosecutor's office by the time I signed on with Seattle PD. I remembered clearly enough that Ross and DonLeavy had always been on opposite sides of the political divide and that Ross had made some of his prosecutorial bones by bringing down members of former Mayor DonLeavy's tarnished administration. I had no doubt that Ross Connors would know who did what to whom back then. He might even be able to supply a few important whys.

When Ross came on the line, I could hear the same television background noise that had been playing at Frank Clark's house. It was a year when Mariners fans were coming out of the woodwork.

"Hey, Beau," he said. "What's up?"

"Who's ahead?" I asked.

"Mariners are up one in the bottom of the eighth. What's going on with you?"

"I'd like to take you back a couple of years and ask a few questions."

"Don't know how much I'll remember, but ask away."

"What's the first word that comes to mind when I mention the name Daniel DonLeavy?"

"Scumbag," Ross replied without having to pause for reflection. "Crook. Got what he deserved. Why? What do you want to know?"

"Mel and I are working on a lead in the Monica Wellington case. We've got a witness who says there was a cop involved, maybe someone from Seattle PD who might have been assigned to chauffeur Mayor Daniel DonLeavy around town, functioning as your basic driver/bodyguard. Do you have any idea who that might have been?"

"Nobody was assigned to the mayor as a bodyguard," Ross said at once. "Certainly not on an official basis, but if you want to know who would have been chumming around with him back then, I know exactly who that would have been—Kenny Adcock."

"You mean the guy who ended up as chief of police? You mean that Kenny Adcock?"

What I didn't say aloud but what I was remembering was being in that conference room with Pickles Gurkey all those years ago and being told to back off on the Monica Wellington case because it was a lost cause. And who was the guy who had told us that? None other than Kenneth Adcock. I couldn't help it. My adrenaline kicked in. We were finally getting somewhere. We were on the right track.

"One and the same," Ross replied. "He and Dan Don-Leavy went to O'Dea together, and the two of them were always great pals. Played football together. Drank together. Screwed around together. Played the horses. Rose through the ranks together—Kenny at Seattle PD and DonLeavy on the city council. By the time Don-Leavy was mayor and Adcock was chief of police, they were a pair to be reckoned with. I kept hoping that when we took DonLeavy down, we'd be able to find something to tie Adcock into his dirty dealings, too. Unfortunately, if there ever was a smoking gun to link Adcock to DonLeavy's shenanigans, we never found it."

"Mel and I may have one now," I said. "We have a witness who claims the guy driving DonLeavy around is the same guy who dumped that barrel with Monica Wellington's body in it down Magnolia Bluff all those years ago."

"That's great," Ross said. "Unfortunately, you'll never make it stick."

"Why not?"

"Because Kenneth Adcock is dead!" Ross exclaimed.

"He died in a deep-sea diving accident somewhere off the Bahamas back in the early eighties, a couple of years after he retired."

I had been so sure we were getting somewhere with the case that Ross's statement took my breath away.

"Kenneth Adcock is dead?" I repeated. "You say it happened in the early eighties? How come I don't remember anything about it?"

"He and Faye were off on a second honeymoon," Ross explained. "He had drawn up a will that specified his not wanting any kind of funeral. He said he wanted to be cremated and have his ashes scattered at sea. Since it would have cost a fortune to bring the body home, that's what Faye did. He was buried at sea."

"It must have been kept a long way under the radar," I suggested. "I don't remember it at all."

Of course, back then, I was doing a lot of drinking and it's possible that any number of things passed under my personal radar without my taking any notice.

"I seem to recall that it wasn't given a lot of press," Ross agreed. "That was partly due to the family's wishes, but I have to believe Seattle PD was on the same page as far as that was concerned. DonLeavy was still in prison, and given Kenny's connections to the previous administration, I suspect Seattle PD was more than happy that there was so little fuss. Not having to stage a fallen-officer memorial would have let them off the hook in a big way."

"So what's his wife's name again? Did you say Faye?"

"Yes. As near as I can remember, Faye was her name. She was his second wife as opposed to his starter wife, and it was a mixed marriage, too. Of course, Anglo/ Asian marriages raised a lot more eyebrows back then than they do now. As I recall, Faye was a tiny little thing, but a real looker."

"If Adcock died that long ago, has his widow remarried?"

"No idea, although I wouldn't be surprised to learn she has. I think there was a son."

"Do you know his name?"

"Nope, he'd probably be in his late fifties by now. I think he was one of those early tech guys who ended up being one of the first or second groups of Microsofties. He's probably worth millions."

"I'm sure his father would be proud," I said.

"Anything else?" Ross asked. "I'd like to get back to my game."

The phone had been on speaker. I looked at Mel. "Do you have any questions?"

"Not at the moment," she said. Then she shouted, "Go Mariners."

Ross laughed, and we ended the call. "What do you think?" I asked.

Mel shook her head. "The whole thing is giving me a headache. We don't know for sure that Kenneth Adcock was the guy driving Mayor DonLeavy to and from his assignations with Frank Clark's mother. So that's probably something we should do right away—put together a photo montage that includes pictures of both the mayor himself and of Kenneth Adcock."

I opened my iPad and typed in a note.

"Did I understand Ross to say that Adcock was chief of police for a while?"

"Not for very long," I answered. "He was too political, and once DonLeavy was gone, people were gunning for him. He put in his twenty and left. What I do remember about him for sure is that he's the guy who told Pickles Gurkey and me to back off on the Monica Wellington case. He's the one who pressed the pedal to the metal on the theory that Ted Bundy was responsible for her murder."

"One he himself may have committed," Mel mused.

I nodded. I almost called what Adcock had done an "old Indian trick." Then, thinking about Delilah, I didn't.

"As chief, he would have had access to the evidence room. He might also have been able to tamper with the microfiche process," Mel theorized. "I'm guessing the evidence has been gone that long—that it disappeared about the same time the Wellington case was deemed closed, but that doesn't explain who killed Mac MacPherson and Delilah Ainsworth."

I nodded. I had arrived at the same conclusion. "So if Adcock is long dead, who still has an ax to grind in all this? How could she or he possibly know that the case was being reopened, and why would that be a threat?"

"Who all would know at Seattle PD?" Mel asked.

"Ron Peters," I answered. "He's the one who put Detective Ainsworth on the case. The other Seattle PD people involved would be whoever was working in the evidence room when Delilah went looking for the evidence and whoever helped her locate the right microfiche file."

"We're talking about clerical staff here," Mel objected. "Delilah was a homicide investigator. There's no way she'd go spilling the beans to them about what she was working on. I can't imagine that she'd be standing around there blabbing about going out to question Mac MacPherson to someone like that."

I could see where Mel was going as she finished her thought.

"But she had already been to see Mac once," I commented. "We know that because he called me and raised hell about it."

"So that's the question, then, isn't it," Mel said. "Who else did he call besides you?"

It made such perfect sense, I was surprised I hadn't seen it before. I had been so busy trying to figure out who it was in Seattle PD who had been ratting us out on the investigation that it never occurred to me that it might have been one of the victims himself, Mac MacPherson.

By then I was already scrolling through my notes looking for a phone number for King County Homicide detective Hugo Monford.

"Monford," he said when he picked up.

I could hear a TV set blaring in the background, but this sounded more like *Monday Night Football* than baseball. With Delilah Ainsworth dead, I would have been a lot happier thinking he was out busting his balls looking for her killer, but maybe that's just me.

"J. P. Beaumont here," I told him, striving to keep my tone pleasant and nonconfrontational. "You and your partner came by to see me the other day."

My days seemed to be running together. I wasn't sure if it was the previous day or the day before that.

"What can I do for you?" Monford said.

"Have you ordered up Rory MacPherson's phone records yet?"

"We need a warrant for that, and we'll most likely have one in hand tomorrow. But really, Mr. Beaumont, this is our case, and if I feel you're interfering with it in any way, I will be lodging a formal complaint."

Let's see. The King County sheriff up against the Washington State attorney general? That kind of one-on-one might be fun to watch, but it wouldn't be any-where near a fair fight.

"Nice talking to you, Detective Monford," I said. "Enjoy the game." By that I meant both of them—the game he was watching and the one I was about to start.

I redialed Ross Connors's number. "Mel just had a brainstorm," I told him. "How hard would it be for you to get a warrant to open up Mac MacPherson's phone records?"

"The dead guy's phone records?" he said. "That shouldn't be hard. Why?"

"Because we need them. I just got off the phone with Detective Monford of the King County Sheriff's Department. He thinks he'll have a warrant to get the phone records tomorrow. I'd like them a little sooner than that if at all possible."

"You think it's going to help point the finger at Ken Adcock?"

"Since he's dead, I don't see how that's possible," I said. "But there is a connection. Back when Monica Wellington's body was found, Adcock threatened two little kids. He told them that if they let on to anyone about seeing him with the barrel, something bad was going to happen to them or to their mother. One way or another, I think this all comes back to that."

"Then your wish is my command," Ross said. "I al-ways wanted to nail that jerk. Now that the ball game is over, I'll get on it right away."

"Who won?" I asked.

"Who do you think?" he said glumly. "It sure as hell wasn't the Mariners."

CHAPTER 21

The state of Washington is divided into two parts, the wet side and the dry side. As you drive east, you drop down from the Cascades into something very close to desert. It had been sunny but chilly in Yakima while we were there, but it started raining as we were coming back across Snoqualmie Pass. A heavy downpour of rain mixed with hail succeeded in slowing Mel down to something just under the speed limit.

We mostly didn't talk while she drove. I was too busy thinking about Monica Wellington. If Kenneth Adcock had been involved in what happened to her, how had we missed that? Yes, we had gone looking unsuccessfully for that mysterious boyfriend and the supposed blind date, but none of the interviews with Monica's roommates had even hinted that she might have been involved with an older man, and especially not with a cop.

Mel had evidently been doing some thinking of her own. "I think we should talk to Mr. Clark."

"Why?" I asked. "What are you thinking?"

"Remember what you told me earlier about Amelia's possibly being a hooker? What if you weren't wrong about that? Sweet young girl from a small farming town goes to the big city and takes up with the wrong crowd. What if the same kind of thing happened to Monica Wellington?"

"You think maybe she ended up on a similar path?"

"It happens," Mel said grimly. "Those fresh-faced small-town girls can be worth a lot in the open market. And if one of them happened to get pregnant and was about to blow the whistle on a guy on his way up in Seattle PD, it would have been in lots of people's best interests to take her out."

"And you're thinking Howard Clark might have known more of the nitty-gritty on that than Frankie would?"

Mel nodded. "Consider this. If you knew you were on your deathbed, how much of the truth about your life would you tell Kelly and Scott, and how much would you leave out?"

I opened my iPad and went searching for a phone number for Howard Clark. His listed number wasn't hard to find, and he answered the phone on the third ring. "Clark residence," he said.

"I'm sorry to interrupt your evening," I told him. "My name is J. P. Beaumont and I'm with the . . ."

"I know all about you," he interrupted. "Frankie called and told me you had stopped by. He said something about bringing up all that bad stuff from years ago. I don't know why you have to do that after all this time."

"A girl was murdered back then," I answered, "and two more people who were involved in that investigation have died this week. We're operating on the assumption that the two new deaths are related to that old one, and since your late wife was evidently acquainted with at least some of the people involved, I was wondering if there was anything you could add to what your stepson already told us."

"Frankie's my son," Howard corrected. "I adopted him. He's mine, so don't go calling him my stepson."

"Sorry."

"As for the murder?" Howard continued without any further prompting from me. "I'm well aware of it. Amelia called me about it the night it happened, or at least the night the body was found. She was scared to death. She said the boys—Donnie and Frankie—had seen something they shouldn't have, and she was afraid something awful was going to happen to them."

"She turned to you for help?" I asked.

"I know, I know," Howard said. "That probably sounds strange to you. At the time, we'd been apart for over a dozen years. Even so, she must have known that deep down, if she was ever in real trouble, she could count on me. You see, it was my fault Amelia and I broke up in the first place. I was an arrogant jerk back then. I broke up with Amelia because I thought I could do better. It turns out I was wrong, of course. My first marriage was a disaster, and that was long over before Mimi called me that night, asking for help."

"You knew her situation?" I asked. "About the boys and about her somewhat questionable living arrangements?"

"You mean did I know some guy had knocked her up and that she was a kept woman?" Howard asked. "Of course I did. Not to begin with, of course, but she told me eventually. And once she clued me in as to who the boys' father was and let me know that the guy who had threatened them was a police officer, I knew I had to do something to get all of them out of there.

"Mimi and I talked on the phone for hours that night and off and on for the next several days with me begging her to come home and marry me. When cops showed up at school to interview the boys behind Mimi's back, that was the last straw. She figured they were probably working for the guy who had made the threats, and she suspected that they would report straight back to him, word for word, whatever Donnie and Frankie had said in the interview."

I wanted to say that wasn't true—that we hadn't done anything of the kind. But without knowing it, we probably had. Kenneth Adcock hadn't been chief of police back then, but as assistant chief, he would have had access to everything any of us wrote in the murder book. He would have known exactly how the investigation was going at any given moment. And it worked. No doubt he had kept tabs on everything from day one. Eventually the case had gone cold at his instigation, and then, with some additional encouragement from him, it had disappeared entirely.

"I'm afraid the boys' mother was probably right about that," I admitted. "The man in question was in a position of authority inside the department, although I can assure you, none of the investigators at the time had any inkling of his involvement."

"How do you know that?" Howard asked.

"Because I was there," I said. "Because I was one of the detectives on the case, and I can assure you that Kenneth Adcock's name never came up."

I heard a catch in Howard Clark's voice when he

spoke again. "Yes," he said. "That's the name she told me. I promised her that I'd never do anything that would jeopardize the boys' safety, so I've made it a point to stay completely out of it, but what about now? If you're bringing this up now because there's no statute of limitations on homicide, what if there's no statute of limitations on Adcock's threats, either? What if he comes after Frankie even after all this time?"

"He can't," I answered simply. "Kenneth Adcock is dead. He died in a diving accident years ago."

"Oh," Howard said. "I'm glad to hear it. Well, not glad so much as relieved. I wish Mimi had known he was dead. It would have been a blessing for her, because she always worried about it. Once I got her out of there and home to Yakima, we turned our backs on all of it. I adopted the boys. DonLeavy's name wasn't on the birth certificate, so he didn't need to abandon his parental rights, and he never paid another dime of child support."

"DonLeavy wasn't concerned she'd blow the whistle on him?"

"I suppose he could have been, of course," Howard conceded, "and we considered it at the time, but asking him for any kind of help would have meant putting the boys back into that situation and in harm's way. That simply wasn't an option. Besides, I was fully capable of providing for them, and I was happy to do so."

"We're wondering if there's a chance Amelia was somehow acquainted with the girl who was murdered, Monica Wellington. Did her name ever come up in any of the conversations you had with your wife, either at the time or later?"

"Of course the girl's name came up," Howard said, his voice hardening. "The man who had killed her had threatened Amelia and her boys. Naturally she was mentioned by name."

"You never thought about reporting it to the police?"

"So that's it? Are you trying to turn Frankie and me into some kind of accessory after the fact? Good luck with that. My wife was terrified, and if you had a rogue cop operating in your department, she wasn't wrong."

"I have to agree with you there, Mr. Clark," I said. "As I said before, Amelia wasn't wrong on that score. Not at all."

"So the boys' reporting the body was one turning point," Mel said, once I ended the call. "But when you and the other detective showed up to interview Donnie and Frankie at the school, you provided another one. So maybe you didn't solve Monica's murder at the time, but it sounds as though you helped pave the way for Howard Clark and Amelia Dodd to get back together. That fact probably provided a stability and a quality of life for Amelia and her two sons that they never would have had if they had stayed in Seattle."

"That's one of the things I like about you," I told her. "You can always find the silver lining."

The rain had let up by the time we made it back across Lake Washington to downtown Seattle. The gated door on the parking garage closes at six, and it was now after eight. I was glad to be back in Belltown Terrace. I was tired. I was only a couple of days out of the hospital. I knew I had done too much, had been up or sitting up in one position far too long. My ankles were swelling inside the compression stockings, and the damaged nerves in my legs were on fire.

When we got out of the car on P-2, I was grateful that Mel had thought to bring the walker along as well as the canes. I was more than ready for the walker and for something sturdy to lean on.

"Are you all right?" she asked as we rode up in the elevator.

"I'm okay," I said. "And that would be several notches under fine."

She nodded. "Why don't you pop another pain pill and crawl back into bed for a while. In the meantime, I'll figure out something to have for dinner."

I wasn't feeling well enough at that point to argue.

We made it to the top floor. I led the way out of the elevator, leaning on the walker, while Mel came behind, carrying the canes. I slipped the key out of my pocket, unlocked the door, and opened it. As soon as I did so, I unleashed a cloud of cigarette smoke.

I was immediately pissed off. Marge! No doubt the woman had let herself into the unit in our absence and was busy smoking up the joint. I wanted to say something like "Who said you could smoke in here?" but I didn't. I stifled it. Instead, shaking my head, I limped farther into the room, making space in the entryway so Mel could follow me. As she did so, the wind slammed the door shut behind both of us. Oddly enough, the entire unit seemed to be swathed in darkness.

Without pausing to wonder about any of it, I flipped on the entryway light switch and was moving forward into the room when Marge Herndon said, "Look out. She's got a gun."

Those are chilling, mind-numbing words. I shouldn't have been moving fast enough to come to a screeching halt, but halt I did. Two women, both of them seated on the window seat, were silhouetted against the darkening sky. The larger one was Marge. The woman next to her was much smaller. I couldn't see her well, but I had no doubt she was the one holding the gun.

"Who are you?" I demanded. "What's going on? What do you want?"

The sun had almost completely set. The storm was over. The bank of leftover gray storm clouds on the horizon had burned blood red as day turned to night.

As my eyes adjusted to the changed lighting, I was finally able to see the gun. It was something small enough to fit inside the woman's tiny hand. Small as it was, however, it was aimed directly at Marge Herndon's ample chest. At that range there could be no doubt the shot would be lethal.

"I assume you both have weapons and backup weapons," the gun holder said. Her voice was chillingly cold. Every word dripped with malice.

"Place them on the dining room table. All of them. If you try anything—anything at all—this woman will die."

I already had Delilah Ainsworth's death on my conscience. I didn't need Marge Herndon's name added to that terrible toll.

Mel and I were standing on the far side of the table. I caught her eye. "Do it," I whispered.

She nodded.

Without another word, we began divesting ourselves of our weapons, one by one. "Why only three?" the woman asked when we finished.

"Because I just had dual knee-replacement surgery," I said. "That's why I need a walker. It's why I need a nurse. I can't wear my ankle holster right now."

That was a lie, but I didn't tell her that.

"You still haven't told us who you are, what you're doing here in our living room, or what you want."

"Come in and sit down," she offered. "I came here to talk. The gun is my insurance that you'll listen to what I have to say."

Mel and I edged our way through the dining room and across the living room, where we perched warily on chairs that faced the expanse of window over Puget Sound. The wall is made up of several different sections of double-paned glass. The three middle sections are stationary. On either side of those there are two much narrower windows that open and close with crank handles that allow for cross ventilation. Both of those were wide open. Rather than taking Marge's cigarette smoke outside, a chill breeze off the water was blowing it back into the room.

The surge of fight-or-flight adrenaline that was speeding through my body had dulled the pain in my legs, but the cold air from the windows blew right through me. Now that we were closer, even in the darkened room, the tiny woman's Asian features came into focus. She was so small that her legs didn't stretch from the cushion on the window seat all the way to the floor. To my knowledge I had never met Faye Adcock before, but I knew that's who she was—who she had to be.

"Could we please close the windows?" I asked. "It's cold in here."

Marge made as if to do as I asked. Faye Adcock shook her head. "Leave them open," she ordered.

Without a word, Marge subsided back onto the cushion.

"What do you want?"

"I'm going to tell you a story."

"What story?" I asked. "About how you murdered Delilah Ainsworth and tried to pin the blame on Mac MacPherson?"

Faye Adcock must have been well into her seventies, but she didn't look it. Her slim figure was swathed in a dark-colored tracksuit. Her raven hair was pulled back in a neat bun. Only the sagging skin on her neck betrayed her age.

Her dark eyes met and held mine in a fathomless stare, and then she raised one eyebrow. "Since you already know that one, I don't need to tell it to you. You never should have reopened that case."

"Which story, then?" I asked, trying to keep my tone bemused and mocking. "What else would you have that could possibly be better than that one?"

"My husband was a cheat," she said venomously. "I should have known that since he cheated on his first wife with me. But then he cheated on me with that girl, that slut, and he knocked her up."

I was gratified to see that she didn't bother with introductions. Obviously she was giving Mel and me credit for having connected some of the dots.

"You're saying Kenneth cheated with Monica Wellington and got her pregnant? How did they meet?"

"Does it matter?" she scoffed. "Does a wife ever know how a husband meets his mistress? I met him when he came into the restaurant for lunch—for Mr. Lee's cashew chicken. I don't think his wife had a clue, and I have no idea how he met Monica."

"Wait," I said. "You mean you worked at the Dragon's Head?" I asked.

She laughed outright at that. "So you hadn't put everything together, had you?" she said.

I said nothing.

"She came to him, told him she was pregnant, and wanted to know what he was going to do about it. He was just starting to make his way up the ladder in Se- attle PD. The scandal would have spoiled everything. So he strangled her, and that was it."

She said it so matter-of-factly that it took my breath away.

"Except that wasn't really it, was it?" I offered.

"No," she said. "He needed to get rid of the body. I was the one who came up with the grease barrel. I knew where it was. Once we got the body loaded into that, he said he knew of a place in town where he could un- load the body and no one would ever be the wiser. But of course, he was wrong about that. Those shitty little boys saw him do it. He warned them that they should be quiet, but of course they couldn't keep it to themselves. Later that Sunday, he went to see the mother, hoping to talk some sense into her head. As he was walking out, who do you suppose he should meet but good old Mac MacPherson. Kenny said he probably came by hoping his uniform would qualify him for a freebie with the boys' mother."

That made sense to me. Mac had always fancied him- self as something of a ladies' man. Reality to the con- trary, Mac believed he was downright irresistible.

"Mac, of course, being Mac," Faye continued, "im- mediately leaped to the wrong conclusion. He thought Kenny was sleeping around with the boys' mother. He threatened to spill the beans and tell the world that Kenny, the mayor's handpicked guy, was carrying on with a hooker. That wasn't even close to the truth, but Kenny knew that if Mac started spouting that story, we were done for."

"Because everything else would have come out?" I asked.

Faye nodded. "We were afraid that if people found out about the existence of the mayor's little side dish, there would be too many people asking all kinds of questions, and before long someone would make a connection back to the dead girl."

"So what happened?"

Faye shrugged. "So they struck a deal, and Mac promised to forget he saw Kenny at the woman's house."

"In exchange for what?" I asked the question even though I already knew the answer.

"Mac got the promotion he wanted, and so did his partner." She paused and looked at me. "I believe that was you, right? So I guess you were in on it, too."

"I wasn't in on it!" I growled. "I had no idea."

"You were that stupid?"

I thought back to how much I had wanted that promotion—how much I had wanted to be a detective and how hard I had worked to put all the rumors about my promotion to bed, even though, in my heart of hearts, I had somehow suspected they were true.

"No," I said, at last. "It wasn't because I was stupid. It was because I was naive."

She shrugged. "It doesn't really matter, does it? You both got what you wanted, and all Mac had to do was keep his mouth shut. I worried about that," Faye continued. "I was afraid we couldn't trust him. Kenny said he'd be fine, and he was for a long while. I thought it had all blown over, but then last week, Mac wasn't fine. When he found out that you and that Ainsworth woman were reopening the case, he went nuts. He called me and raised hell. He tried to blackmail me. He said we both knew that he had concealed possible evidence in that homicide years ago. He figured that since his silence had been good enough for him to get promoted back then, maybe I'd be willing to make it worth his while for him to continue keeping quiet now. My late husband was a good cop. If this had all come out now, it would have destroyed Kenny's reputation at a time when he was no longer able to defend himself. I couldn't have that."

"Of course you couldn't," I agreed soothingly. "So that's when you made up your mind to get rid of him?"

"I had to," Faye said. "Even though Kenny left me in pretty good shape financially, once blackmail gets started, there's never any end to it."

"So you ended it for him," I said. "You went there planning to kill him."

"When I went there, I thought I could talk some sense into him. When that didn't work, I decided that if I could get him drunk enough, I could leave him in the garage with the car running and people would think he had committed suicide. I was just getting ready to leave when the doorbell rang and that woman showed up. I thought whoever it was would go away when no one answered, but the door was unlocked, and she let herself in. She called out her name as she opened the door. I was standing right on the other side of it, and I knew what I had to do. I let her have it."

"Just like that?"

"Just like that."

"What is it you want now?"

"I wanted to be able to live out my life in peace, but as you can see, that isn't going to happen, so now it's really over—all of it."

With that, Faye Adcock seemed to pull back onto the window seat. Sitting there trying to frame a response, I had no idea of her intentions. Even if I had, I'm not sure I would have tried to stop her. As she stood up, I took advantage of that slight distraction to reach down and try to retrieve the Glock from my ankle holster. I had my hand on it and was about to draw it when Faye made her move, darting toward the end of the window seat.

Lithe as a cat, she slithered through a window opening that would have been far too small for any ordinary-size adult to slip through. She stood there for a moment, poised on the ledge and clinging to the metal frame, and then she was gone, falling in absolute silence from a height of twenty-two stories.

The first sound that shattered that ungodly silence was Marge Herndon's horrified scream. Next came an awful crash of metal as Faye's plummeting body slammed into a vehicle far below. That was followed immediately by the urgent bleating of a car alarm.

The sound reinforced what my mind had already grasped. It was over. Faye Adcock was no more, and Monica Wellington's long-unsolved homicide was finally closed.

CHAPTER 22

For most of the time that I was growing up and for a long time afterward, my mother and I were estranged from my mother's parents. This was due primarily to my grandfather's general curmudgeonliness, a trait I do my best not to emulate.

During those years, my grandmother, Beverly, went behind her disapproving husband's back and dutifully kept scrapbooks of all the times she was able to cull anything about me from the newspapers, from Cub Scout postings in the *Queen Anne News* to high school sports articles. Once I became a detective at Seattle PD, whenever one of my homicide cases made it into the pages of the *Seattle Post-Intelligencer* or the *Seattle Times*, Beverly made sure those articles were also clipped and pasted into the mix. I was more than middle aged when I found her precious scrapbooks and realized that she had spent all those years caring about me in silence and following my life from afar. That, more than anything, finally helped put to rest all those long-simmering family-feud issues. Beverly loved me. I loved her. All was forgiven.

But my grandmother stopped cutting and pasting long before the news world went digital, and she would have been astonished by the full-length photo of me that was splashed on the front pages of both the digital and paper editions of the *Seattle Times* on the morning of September twenty-first.

For one thing, it was in full color. I'm not sure how the photographer, listed as R. Tobin, got to the scene so fast. He or she must have arrived close to the same time Mel and I did, and all we had to do was ride down in the Belltown Terrace elevator from the penthouse to the lobby and then walk half a block.

As a result, Mel and I were the first official law enforcement presence on the scene of Faye Adcock's suicide. The photo in the paper shows me, standing silhouetted in a wash of blazing headlights, attempting to direct traffic around the scene of the incident. I was using my walker as I stomped around the scene, but for some reason the walker doesn't show in the image. And somehow, too, in all the noisy hubbub, the photographer neglected to catch my name. As far as I'm concerned, that's just as well.

Fortunately, no one on the ground was injured, although they very easily could have been. Faye's nosedive had plunged her headfirst onto the hood of a parked car. From there she had bounced into traffic. A second vehicle, in trying to avoid hitting her, ended up plowing into yet a third, thus setting off a chain reaction. Traffic at the intersection of First Avenue and Broad came to a complete halt and stayed that way for the better part of the night.

I was in the process of being interviewed by two newly arrived uniformed officers when Marge Herndon made her presence known.

"He lives here," she said, pointing at the building. "You have his name. I'm his nurse and I'm telling you that he has to go back inside. If anyone needs to talk to him, tell them to talk to the building's doorman, and he'll send them up."

With that, Marge grabbed my elbow and pointed me and my walker back up the sidewalk along Broad, toward both the lobby and the elevator. I knew she was right, of course. I was way over the limit on both energy and pain, and I went along with the program without so much as a single whimper. Mel, on the other hand, stayed where she was, talking to arriving officers and taking care of business.

"I'm sorry," I muttered to Marge in the elevator. "I certainly never intended to involve you in something like this."

She waved off my apology as though it were a bothersome gnat.

"How long has it been since you've had a pain pill?" Marge demanded.

"Too long," I admitted.

"Then I guess I'd better rustle up something to eat— scrambled eggs, most likely," she added. "As I told you before, you can't take those pills on an empty stomach."

I was only too grateful to be ordered around. She herded me over to the window seat where I was able to stretch out flat while Marge bustled around bringing me pillows for both my head and under my knees as well as a very welcome duvet. When the duvet settled over me, I realized how cold I was. Marge must have come to the same conclusion, but when she reached for the crank to close the window, I stopped her.

"Who opened the windows?" I asked. "Did you do it or did she?"

"She did," Marge said.

"All right, then," I said. "Let's make sure that hers are the only fingerprints the CSI techs find on that handle. When the detectives come up here, we need to be able to show them exactly how she got out. If you're cold, go ahead and turn up the thermostat."

"Turning up the heat with the windows open will cost a fortune," Marge objected.

"It's okay," I told her. "For this one night, I can afford it. But tell me. How did she get in here in the first place?"

"I was outside, having a smoke. You know, on the sidewalk next to the garage wall, like you told me to. But it was raining. I was getting wet. I was about to let myself into the garage through the gate with the clicker when she came jogging up the sidewalk. She was wet, too. She said she lived in the building and had forgotten her key. Would I mind letting her in. After all, she was just a little bit of a thing. She looked perfectly harmless."

I didn't take Marge to task and tell her that was the oldest trick in the book and a surefire way to make a secure building totally not secure.

"Once we got into the elevator," Marge continued, "I used my building key to run it. When I turned around to ask which floor she wanted, that's when I first saw the gun. She must have had it hidden in her pocket. She said we were going wherever you lived. All the way up in the elevator, I kept hoping someone else would get on with us, but no one did."

"How long was she here?"

"Not that long," Marge said. "She held the gun on me the whole time. It must have been heavy because part of the time she kept it in her lap. It seemed like it was forever. I needed to pee so badly, I was afraid I was going to wet my pants, but I'd be damned if I'd ask that little bitch for permission. She wanted a cigarette, so I lit smokes for both of us. Sorry about that. I hope you don't mind."

Considering what might have happened to Marge Herndon in the course of the confrontation, having a little lingering cigarette smoke in the unit seemed like a small price to pay. Besides, the frigid wind leaking into the room had mostly cleared it out.

Marge left me alone and went to the kitchen. I have to give the woman that much credit. She knew her way around our cooktop.

"So she's the one who killed those people out in Sammamish?" she called to me from the kitchen.

"I guess," I answered. "What I don't understand is how she knew to come here."

"That's easy," Marge replied. "She told me she followed us when we left the press conference in Sammamish. She was there, too. She said that as soon as she saw you there, she knew who you were."

My iPad was lying next to me on the window seat. I picked it up, switched it on, and opened the panoramic photo gallery. Sure enough, one of the series of panoramic shots had captured Faye Adcock, sitting on the aisle in the very last row. So I was right after all. The killer had come to the press conference. I had found her without realizing it. Once she recognized me, she must have understood the danger I posed to her getting away with what she'd done.

I was still thinking about that when I fell asleep with the iPad flat on my chest.

Mel woke me up a few minutes later. "Do you want to eat here or at the table?"

I was glad to be off my feet. "Here, please," I said.

Mel returned a few minutes later carrying a TV tray. On it was a plate of bacon and scrambled eggs, along with a glass of juice and an eggcup containing a multicolored collection of pills. I sat up and Mel helped me maneuver the tray around my legs. I could see that my ankles were still mad at me. Since Marge wasn't looking, I took the pills first thing. As I was lifting the first forkful of scrambled eggs to my mouth, Mel returned to the window seat with her own tray of food.

"Did they find her gun?" I asked.

Mel shook her head. "Not yet. I told them about it, and I'm sure they will. The uniforms are out in force, doing an inch-by-inch search. It's probably under one of the damaged vehicles, and some of those are going to have to be towed away."

"This is going to be hard to explain," I said, glancing at the still-open windows. Marge had cranked up the heat, however, and the room wasn't as cold as it had been.

Mel laughed. "Not as hard as it could be," she said. "Here, listen to this." She pulled her iPhone out of her pocket, put it down on my tray, and pressed a button. Soon I was hearing Faye Adcock's voice as well as my own.

I was dumbfounded. "Are you kidding? You recorded the whole thing?"

"Every bit of it," Mel said with a grin. "The problem is, it's audio only. I couldn't get video because the phone was in my pocket."

"Even so," I said, "a recording like that won't stand up in court."

Mel shrugged her shoulders. "Doesn't need to, but it'll work as a deathbed confession. I think there's a lot more latitude with those."

We listened in silence to the whole thing until Marge's horrified scream and the wailing of the automobile alarm announced that Faye Adcock had made her exit, stage left. It was actually stage right, but let's not be picky.

Mel switched off the phone and put it away. "Are you going to go talk to Monica's mother?"

"Tomorrow," I said. "If you don't mind driving."

"No problem," Mel said. "I just talked to Harry. He told me to take the whole week off. I'm yours for the duration."

We had finished eating and had cleared out both the dishes and the TV trays when two Seattle homicide detectives—guys I didn't recognize—showed up. And since Mel had run up the flag to the King County Sheriff's Department, Detectives Monford and Anderson were hot on the Seattle PD investigators' heels.

As expected, the four detectives began the process by interviewing Marge Herndon, Mel, and me on an individual basis. That was the only way to keep one eyewitness's testimony from muddying someone else's. King County detectives Monford and Anderson accompanied Marge back downstairs to the guest unit and interviewed her there. Seattle PD Homicide detective Taylor Derickson took Mel into the den and closed the doors behind them. I stayed on the window seat, still wrapped in the duvet while Seattle Homicide's Detective Bonnie Hill did the interview honors.

Detective Hill was a poised and intense young woman. I could tell this was personal for her, and I thought I knew why. While she was setting her recording device, I got the drop on her before she ever lobbed a single question in my direction.

"You knew Detective Ainsworth?" I asked.

Biting her lip and fighting back tears, she nodded. "We came through the academy together."

"I'm so sorry," I said. "So let's get this right."

In order to make sense of the thing, I had to go back to the very beginning, starting with waking up in my hospital bed determined to reopen a cold case. I expected Detective Hill to object to that. Instead, she accepted my version of events at face value, and while she was letting the recorder do its job, she was also making quick but careful notes the whole time. In a funny way, she reminded me of Pickles Gurkey, and I suspected her case closure ratio would have a lot to do with her clear determination to cover all the bases.

I told her, to the best of my memory, about the interactions I had had with Delilah prior to her second fateful trip to see Mac MacPherson. I told her about the missing evidence and about the sabotaged human resources microfiche. I told her about being worried when Delilah didn't call me back in a timely fashion and about my summoning Assistant Chief Peters into the fray.

"You know Assistant Chief Peters?" she asked.

"We used to be partners."

In the world of homicide cops, those five words speak volumes. She nodded, and I continued.

When I told Detective Hill about leaving the hospital and making an uninvited visit to the press conference, I switched on my iPad and showed her the photo of Faye Adcock sitting in the back of the room.

"That's her," I said, pointing to Faye's face in the crowd. "I was looking for someone from Seattle PD who maybe shouldn't have been there. I didn't recognize Faye Adcock because, as far as I know, I had never seen her before today."

I went on from there, explaining how Faye had followed Marge's vehicle home from the press conference, how she had duped Marge in order to gain entry to the building, and finally about what was said in those few minutes prior to Faye's fatal plunge. We had finished that part of the interview when the phone rang.

Mel answered and then opened the glass doors between the den and the living room. "That was the doorman," she said. "Ron Peters is on his way up."

That news apparently made a good impression on Detective Hill. I saw her brief nod, but she didn't shut down the recording.

"Did Ms. Adcock say anything to you about the missing evidence or the HR discrepancy?" she asked.

"Not to me," I told her. "She might have had the motive, but I doubt she had the opportunity. My guess would be that her husband took care of that part of the problem before he left the department."

"When was that again?"

"In 1981."

"Were they already digitizing records that early?" Detective Hill asked.

"Definitely not," I said. "I think the physical records themselves disappeared long before the microfiche record was created."

The doorbell rang. Mel hurried out of the den to answer it. Ron rolled into the living room, Mel at his side and with her hand in his.

"Thank God you're both all right!" he exclaimed. He parked his chair next to where I was sitting. Making my knees and his chair maneuver together for a hug wasn't easy, but we managed.

"Has someone notified Faye's son?" I asked.

Ron nodded. "Officers are on their way to his home right now."

A few minutes later, Detectives Monford and Anderson showed up, having finished with their debriefing of Marge Herndon.

Hugo Monford looked at Mel. "I understand you have an audio recording of the incident?"

Mel nodded. "Do you want to hear it now?"

Ron Peters, dressed in his uniform, was clearly the top-ranking officer in attendance. When he nodded his assent, Mel turned on the recording and played it. The roomful of detectives listened in stunned, multijurisdictional silence while Faye Adcock's own voice cleared three of their current cases—two homicides and a suicide—and Monica Wellington's cold case as well. The other cases, even Delilah's, may have belonged to them. Monica Wellington's was all mine.

When the recording ended, Ron nodded toward the still-open windows. The heat pump was doing a great job of keeping up, but the room was still chilly.

"Faye Adcock opened the windows?"

I nodded. "I made sure no one else has touched them."

Ron turned to Detective Hill and issued an order. "I want someone from CSI up here right away to dust for prints on that handle. And let them know they are not to make a mess on the window seat!"

In due time CSI techs came and went, and eventually the windows got closed. The detectives left in a group, with Monford and Anderson headed for Brian Ainsworth's home in Ballard to bring him up-to-date on this latest development. At last Mel, Ron, and I were the only ones left.

"Do you want me to send officers over to Leavenworth tomorrow to talk to Monica Wellington's family?"

I shook my head. "Thanks for the offer, but no. Mel has the day off. She says she'll drive me. It was my case. I need to be the one to give Hannah Wellington the news."

"What about the situation with Delilah's family?" he added. "I understand that her funeral is scheduled for Wednesday and that her husband has specifically requested that there be no fallen-officer trappings to her service?"

"That's correct," I said. "Brian Ainsworth said that people Delilah worked with are welcome to show up, but he'd prefer that they did so in civilian clothing rather than in uniform. I asked to serve as an honorary pallbearer in hopes of calling out the killer. It turns out that's no longer necessary, but that's what I'll be doing all the same."

Ron Peters glanced questioningly at my nearby walker. "Are you sure you're up for that?"

"As I said, I'll be honorary only," I assured him. "I'll be carrying all the blame. Somebody else will have to do the physical lifting."

Ron was too good a friend to try telling me it wasn't my fault. We both knew better.

CHAPTER 23

I slept like a brick that night. It could have been because no one came in to check my vitals. It could have been because the bedroom got so warm in the process of heating the open-windowed living room that it was simply toasty in there. It could have been because I had seriously overdone it in the course of the day. It could have been because Monica Wellington's homicide was finally put to rest. It could have been because Mel was in bed beside me. Or it could have been all of the above.

Whatever the reason, I slept. When I awoke feeling surprisingly rested in the morning, I found myself with a severe craving for something like pancakes or waffles, swimming in a lake of maple syrup.

Marge came into the bedroom, handed me a cup of coffee, and immediately disabused me of the notion that I could choose my own menu. Pancakes and waffles were deemed to contain far too many carbs and not enough protein. Besides, she was already making sausage and eggs.

Mel came back down the hall from her bathroom. She was dressed, made up, and ready to rumble. "It's about time you woke up," she said. "PT in half an hour."

I put off showering until after PT. Instead, I dressed myself in an appropriate set of sweats and used the canes to take myself into the dining room for breakfast.

Marge observed my arrival at the dining room table with a grudging nod of approval. "Not bad," she said, "especially considering you're just one week out."

I accepted her comment as high praise and tucked into my sausage and eggs. I prefer my eggs over easy. Marge's eggs of choice were definitely over hard, but the eggs appeared fully cooked, as if by magic, and I did not complain. Instead, I expressed sincere thanks and ate as directed.

"I talked to Ron while I was getting dressed," Mel said. "Seattle PD has hammered out an agreement with King County and Sammamish that says they won't be releasing any details until midafternoon. That gives us time to get to Leavenworth and talk to Monica's mother before the media bombshell drops."

I knew Ron Peters had probably had to talk like a Dutch uncle in order to make that happen, and I was grateful for that, too. "We'll head out as soon as I finish PT."

There's nothing like waking up alive the day after being held at gunpoint to induce a permanent attitude of gratitude.

During PT I noticed that, with Ida Witherspoon's help, taking one turn around the running track wasn't nearly as challenging as it had been the day before. And I'm happy to report that my range of motion had improved by a tiny margin as well.

After Ida left, I showered—on my own this time—and got dressed. I chose a charcoal gray suit, a plain white shirt, and a subdued blue-and-gray-striped tie. When it comes time to talk to a grieving family member, it's best to look the part.

Mel came into the bedroom and watched in amazement as I used the strange sock-applying gadget to put on my compression stockings. My ankles were still a little swollen from the previous day's long car ride, but they weren't nearly as bad as they had been.

"Canes or walker?" Mel asked as we started out of the unit.

"Both," I said, "just to be on the safe side."

I walked out to the elevator using the canes, but I was glad to know she was dragging the walker along just in case.

This time I opted to ride in the far roomier Mercedes. When we drove out of the underground parking lot, it was into the bright sunlight of a crisp autumn day. As we drove across Lake Washington on 520, the water, mirroring the sky, was a deep shade of blue. We drove up 405 to Woodinville and then out to Highway 2. We were both subdued and we didn't talk much. Notifying families is serious business, and I was worried about what I would say. I hoped that reopening Hannah Wellington's decades-old wound might also offer some measure of comfort.

We had no difficulty in finding Hannah's cozy home—little more than a cottage—on Benton Street, two blocks north of the highway. I hadn't called ahead, so she wasn't expecting us.

We found her dressed in a pair of child-size Oshkosh overalls, raking leaves inside her minuscule front yard.

The last time I'd seen her, both in real life and in the dream, she had worn her hair long and straight. It was white now, and braided into plaits that wrapped around her head like a crown. She was as straight and upright as ever. I guess the best way to put it would be unbowed. Whatever life had thrown at her, this was a woman who had borne up under it with determination and grace.

Hannah quit raking when the car stopped out front. She stripped off her gloves and stood waiting while Mel came around to the passenger side to help me out of the car. With a wary glance at the somewhat bumpy terrain, I opted for the safety of the walker over the supposedly more decorative canes.

"I'm not sure you remember me, Mrs. Wellington," I said, as we made our slow way up the grass-covered walkway. "My name is J. P. Beaumont. This is my partner, Mel Soames."

There wasn't so much as a moment's hesitation on Hannah's part.

"You were much younger then, but you're the detective who came to Monica's funeral," she said at once. "I heard from detectives working the case off and on for a few years, but it's been so long now that I thought surely you had all forgotten about me completely."

"No, ma'am," I said. "We haven't forgotten about you, and we haven't forgotten your daughter. We have some news for you today. Do you mind if we go inside?"

She put down the rake and turned to lead us inside. The living room was small and neat and furnished with frayed furniture that was longer on comfort than it was on style.

The walls were peppered with a collection of photos, and I took some time to survey them. The older pic-

tures were of a girl and a boy together. From the looks
of the hairdos and clothing, I pegged those as most likely being of Monica and her brother. There were what
were clearly high school photos of both of them as well
as a collection of a new generation of Wellington grandchildren, many of them featuring photos with Santa and
elves.

I was relieved to see that life hadn't come to a complete stop for Hannah Wellington after her daughter's
death. Monica's life had ended but the family had gone
on without her. There were new people added into the
mix—new children; new holiday traditions; new graduation photos; new wedding pictures. These were all
things Monica never knew and could never be a part of.

Hannah followed us into the living room and motioned us onto the couch. Then she took a seat in a rocking chair. It was only by rocking forward in it that Hannah's feet touched the floor. That hit me hard. She and
Faye Adcock had to be almost the same size.

"What news?" Hannah asked. She wasn't looking for
niceties; she didn't need anyone softening the blow.

"We believe we've found your daughter's killer," I
said quietly. "The problem is, the man who did it died
years ago, and his widow committed suicide last night."

Hannah's face was utterly devoid of expression as I
delivered the news. "Tell me, then," she urged quietly.
"Tell me all of it."

I told almost the same story I had told Detective Hill
the night before. Hannah heard me out without comment and without shedding a single tear. I didn't hold
that against her. I don't believe she didn't cry because
she didn't care. I think it was because she had cared too
much for far too long.

When I finally finished my painful recitation, I settled back on the sofa and the three of us sat in silence for the better part of a minute.

"That's it, then?" Hannah said at last.

I nodded.

"I always thought that knowing who did it would somehow make me feel better," Hannah murmured. "It doesn't, you know."

I wanted to say, "Closure isn't everything it's cracked up to be," but I didn't. I nodded, and the silence thickened around us once more.

"And this woman claimed Monica was having an affair with her husband?"

"That's what she said."

Hannah hadn't taken her eyes off me the whole time I was speaking. Now she let her glance stray in Mel's direction.

"You're a police officer, too?" she asked. "He said you were his partner."

"I'm a special investigator," Mel answered. "So we are partners, but we're also husband and wife."

"That's what Monica wanted to be eventually," Hannah offered. "A cop. Her father wouldn't have approved, of course, so she didn't start out with criminal justice as her major her freshman year, but she probably would have changed over to it eventually."

That one hurt. Monica had been my case. How was it that I had missed finding out she had wanted to be a cop? I felt my ears redden at the scope of my singular failure. I had been new on the job, but I should have done more. Pickles Gurkey and I should have done more.

I wanted to say I was sorry, but Hannah was still talking.

"Monica was always such a good girl," she said. "She was someone who played by the rules because she thought the rules were important. I can't imagine her having sexual relations with a married man. I just can't."

Of course we all knew that Monica had been pregnant at the time of her death. That meant that somewhere along the way she had turned away from playing by any number of rules. When it comes to that, parents are always the last to know.

Leaving that painful topic behind, Hannah turned away from Mel and looked at me again, squarely. I could barely stand to meet her gaze.

"So when will all this come out?" she asked. "When will the news reporters learn about the woman who committed suicide and her connection to Monica's case?"

"Later this afternoon, most likely," I said.

"I suppose they'll be talking about Monica's death then, too?"

"I would imagine," I offered. "Someone may very well want to interview you about it. We wanted to give you some warning in advance of the media onslaught."

She looked down at her grubby overalls and the tiny work boots. "I suppose I'd better go change my clothes, then," she said. "I should put on something a little more respectable."

Mel and I took that as a sign of dismissal. We stood up to take our leave.

"Oh, my goodness!" Hannah exclaimed. "I've completely forgotten my manners. I didn't even offer you something to drink."

"We don't need anything, Mrs. Wellington," Mel said, holding out her hand. "Nothing at all. And I hope you understand that we're both terribly sorry for your loss."

Hannah gave us a tremulous smile. It was as though that one small gesture of sympathy on Mel's part had somehow cracked through her reserve.

"Yes," she said softly. "The hurt of losing a child never goes away. I always keep a candle burning at the church in Monica's memory. Once I get out of these clothes and into something decent, I'll go over to the cemetery and put one on her grave as well. I've always been grateful for that, by the way, that at least her body was found so we had something to bury."

"You had two young boys to thank for that," I said. "They made the call at no small cost to themselves."

"I don't believe I remember that," Hannah said with a frown. "Who were they? What were their names?"

"Two brothers, Donnie and Frankie," I said. "One of them is dead now. He died in a car accident several years ago. We interviewed the other one, Frankie, yesterday afternoon."

Hannah nodded. "Donnie and Frankie," she said. "Very well, then. I'll light a candle for each of them as well."

We left the house. Mel must have understood how drained I was because once we were in the car, she immediately suggested that we stop for lunch before heading back to Seattle.

We drove around town for a couple of miles, soaking up the faux Bavarian atmosphere before settling in for burgers and fries at a local brew house. Once the waitress put our baskets of food in front of us, I opted for another pain pill.

"I don't think I've ever been to a notification where the mother didn't cry," Mel said, as she swallowed a bite of French fry.

I had to agree. "Me, neither," I said.

"And out of everything you told her, the only thing she objected to was the idea that her daughter had been carrying on with a married man. I suppose that's to be expected, though," Mel added. "I'm sure my mother thought I was a virgin on my wedding night. You and I both know that wasn't true either time."

It was a joke, a tiny attempt at humor in the face of a very grim errand, but I couldn't laugh it off. There was something about Hannah's reaction that still niggled at me, too. Something about it wasn't quite right, but I couldn't put my finger on it.

We had finished our burgers and were getting ready to return to the car when I finally figured out what was wrong.

"Why did she do it?" I said.

"Probably just horny," Mel said.

"No, I'm not talking about Monica," I said. "That's not what's bothering me. What set Faye Adcock off?"

"She said it was because you were reopening the case, and Mac MacPherson was threatening to blackmail her."

"Why didn't she just call his bluff? It wasn't like she could be charged with committing Monica's murder."

"Right," Mel agreed. "The most she could be charged with was being an accessory after the fact, but that might be a stretch."

"So what did she have to lose?"

And then suddenly, with a click, I knew. I knew as surely as if someone had flipped a switch and sent a surge of electricity pulsing through my body. Faye hadn't murdered two people in cold blood and then committed suicide to keep from having to pay some kind of phony blackmail attempt from Mac MacPherson. Everything she had done, including flinging herself to her death, had been done to protect someone else.

According to Occam's razor, the right answer is always the simplest answer, the one requiring the fewest assumptions. In this case that could mean only one thing.

"We have to get back to Seattle," I said, pushing away from the table. "We need to talk to Faye Adcock's son."

CHAPTER 24

I called Ross Connors while Mel drove. "Hey," he said. "All hail the conquering heroes."

"I wish."

"What do you mean?" Ross seemed genuinely surprised. "Everybody I've talked to today, including Harry I. Ball, is singing your praises, saying that you walked out of surgery and started solving cases, including one very cold one, before they even took your stitches out."

"Staples," I said. "They use staples these days instead of stitches. And whatever you're hearing about that cold case may not be quite right. I'm hoping you haven't pulled back on the crime lab doing that DNA testing for us, have you?"

"I meant to," Ross said, "but I had a meeting with a legislative committee this morning, and I hadn't gotten around to it."

"Don't," I said. "In fact, if anything, give it a little prod in the butt."

"Why?" Ross asked. "What's up?"

"Mel and I drove over to Leavenworth this morning to talk to Monica Wellington's mother. Something she said got us thinking that maybe Faye Adcock was covering for someone."

"How could she be?" Ross asked. "And why? Since her husband was the killer and since he's dead . . ."

"*If* her husband was the killer," I corrected, "I'm thinking Kenneth Adcock and his wife were both covering for the same guy—their son."

The phone went so quiet I thought for a moment that Ross had hung up on me.

"Hear me out," I said. "Ken Adcock left Seattle PD in 1981, shortly after the Wellington case was designated closed, something that was done without Captain Larry Powell's knowledge or approval. We have no idea when the evidence box disappeared, but as chief of police, Adcock would certainly have had access to that and to the HR records as well. But he didn't have access to the M.E.'s office, and he had no way of knowing that at some time in the distant future, DNA would be the damning tool it is today."

"Even if we still had the physical evidence, was there anything to link the son—whatever his name is—to the dead girl?" Ross asked.

"Nothing," I answered.

"So even with the DNA evidence, there wouldn't be anything to compare it to."

"Until now," I said.

"What do you mean?"

"You get a fire lit under that DNA testing," I urged. "Mel and I are going to go get the crime lab something to compare it with."

"How can you? You don't have a warrant. You don't have probable cause."

"No," I said. "Maybe not, but we're old and tricky."

"What does that mean?"

"We'll let you know."

"What trick?" Mel asked when I ended the call to Ross.

"Give me a minute," I said. "I'm working on it."

The next person I dialed was Ron Peters, who, unsurprisingly on a Tuesday afternoon, was in his office and taking calls.

"What can I do for you?"

"Mel and I are on our way back from Leavenworth and want to be back in the loop. What can you tell us?"

"Once the tow trucks showed up, officers were able to locate Faye Adcock's weapon," Ron said. "I know Mel mentioned something about that."

"What about her vehicle?"

"A parking enforcement officer found it parked illegally near the Battery Street Tunnel. Her Kia Sportage has been towed to the Big Boy Towing impound lot in Lake City."

I knew from years past that Big Boy was one of the preferred towing companies that plied the streets of Seattle. I also knew the exact location of their impound lot. "We're waiting on a warrant to search it," he finished.

"So things are under control at that end?" I asked.

"Pretty much. All we need now is for everyone to get the paper-trail end of this pulled together—*i*'s dotted and *t*'s crossed. I'll need something in writing from both of you as well."

"You'll have it," I said. "Tomorrow morning if not sooner."

"Oh," Ron added. "Tell Mel that the IT techs downloaded what they needed from her phone, so she can get that back today or tomorrow, too. And speaking of phones, Mac's phone records are on their way over."

Mel hadn't been happy—in fact, she had been pissed as hell—when a CSI tech had collected her telephone in order to examine the authenticity of her recording of the events surrounding Faye Adcock's death.

"She'll be pleased to hear that," I said. "The poor girl feels naked without it. There's one more thing I need."

"What's that?"

"We thought it might be a good idea if we dropped by Faye Adcock's son's place to express our condolences. What's his name again?"

"I'm not sure that's such a great idea," Ron replied dubiously. "But his name is Kenneth James Adcock, and he lives on the east side somewhere. Used to be Kenneth Junior but my understanding is that the junior bit goes away when the old man dies."

While Ron was still musing about that, I used my iPad and my Special Homicide access code to log on to Washington's DMV database. Before Ron Peters and I said good-bye, I had located Kenneth James Adcock's home address on a street in Bellevue called 132nd Avenue North.

"So are you going to tell me or not?" Mel asked. I could hear the impatience in her voice.

"I know you don't have your iPhone, but do you still have your stylus?"

Mel Soames is one tough cookie, and she may have cleaned more than one bad guy's clock, but when it comes to manicures, she is definitely a girly-girl. In case you haven't tried using an iPhone of late, long fingernails and the touch screen pad are not necessarily compatible. To that end, Mel had bought a whole collection of stylus gizmos, brightly colored metal pencil-looking things topped with rounded rubbery tips that work on the touch screen.

Did I mention she's bought several of them? That's because they tend to get lost.

"There might be one in the bottom of my purse," she said. "I think I saw one the other day when I was up in Bellingham and looking for my room key at the hotel." She shoved her purse in my direction. "Have a look," she said.

Let's just say I do not like dredging things out of women's purses. When I was growing up, my mother's purse was absolutely off-limits, which accounts for my long-held phobia. This time, though, if we could make this plan work, digging through Mel's purse might be worth it.

"You still haven't told me," she grumbled as I scrounged through her belongings—several tubes of lipstick, mascara, a compact, an empty tissue container, an assortment of pens and pencils, a container of Splenda, and not one but three separate hotel keys, only one of which was from Bellingham.

"Got it!" I announced at last, holding the stylus up in triumph. It was a shiny bright red, and that was the only reason I had managed to glimpse it in the dark depths of the deep black purse. "Now we're in business."

Moments later I was back on the phone, this time to Todd Hatcher down in Olympia. Todd, who hails from Arizona originally, got pulled into Ross Connors's orbit and into Special Homicide when he was working on his doctorate in forensic economics. His study on the rising costs of an aging prison population had turned Ross into a devoted fan.

So yes, Todd knows his way around the world of economics, but it's due to his uncanny abilities with computers that Ross keeps him on retainer. My best trick with electronic devices is to make them roll over and play dead—or, rather, *be* dead. Todd is able to get them to do handstands and tap dance.

"Hey, Todd," I said, "I need some help."

"What kind of help?"

"I need you to create a bogus form for me, one that can show up on my iPad in—what's it called again?—a PD something."

"You mean a PDF?" Todd offered helpfully.

"Yes, that's the one. I need one that can be signed directly on my iPad."

"I can do that, but what's this bogus form supposed to say?" Todd asked.

"A vehicle belonging to a suicide victim named Faye Adcock has been towed to the Big Boy Towing lot in Lake City. I need to have something with my name on it that I can have her son sign acknowledging that he's being notified, on behalf of Seattle PD, about the location of his deceased mother's vehicle."

"What kind of vehicle?"

"A Kia Sportage. You should be able to get the details on her and on the vehicle itself from the DMV."

"Okeydokey," Todd said. "I'll get right on this. I love writing fiction. You want me to e-mail you the form when I finish it?"

"Please."

"How long do I have?"

"I haven't put the son's address into the GPS, but I'm guessing about an hour and a half."

"You've got it," Todd said.

So did Mel. When I ended the call she was smiling.

"Ken Adcock signs with the stylus. The crime lab grabs his DNA from that, and we're off to the races."

"That's right. No warrant. No muss. No fuss."

"And without having to send him a bogus envelope to lick and return," Mel added. "Isn't technology great!"

Todd was good to his word. My e-mail dinged with his incoming message before we even made it to Wood-inville. His e-mail came with an attachment as well as with directions for opening and duplicating it that would allow for the attachment to be used in an interactive fashion.

When I opened the PDF, I was pleased with Todd's concoction—a simple but very realistic form, stating that an illegally parked vehicle belonging to the deceased, Faye Lee Adcock, had been towed by Seattle PD to the following location, and asking for the signature of the next of kin to acknowledge that they had been told the location of said vehicle. The form came complete with all the proper legal-sounding bells and whistles, including the Kia's VIN. At the bottom, there was a place for the recipient to sign and date, a spot underneath that for him to print both his name and his e-mail address, and a place for me to countersign as well.

As my granddaughter Kayla used to say, easy peasy.

"You do realize," Mel admonished, "that both the stylus and the iPad will have to go in an evidence bag?"

That was the downside of this whole operation. "Well," I said with a grin, "I guess we'll just have to be old-fashioned and be your basic one iPad/one iPhone family for the duration."

"Not for long," she said. "We're getting my iPhone back today!"

By the time we hit I-405, I had programmed Ken

Adcock's address into the GPS. Afternoon traffic was just starting to build up when we turned off at the 70th Street exit and made our way over to 132nd. We drove through a thickly forested area of the city called Bridle Trails, where the lots are what they call "horse acres" or larger, complete with backyard stables and riding trails.

Eventually the GPS directed us off 132nd and into a long driveway that swept uphill to Ken Adcock's looming mansion. The rambling edifice took up most of what was plainly a huge lot with no sign of stables or horses. It reeked of the wealth that grew as well as trees in the Northwest's silicon forest.

The house looked smug and opulent, and just seeing it there made me suddenly furious. I had no doubt that eventually the DNA would tell the tale. Kenneth Adcock the younger had murdered a sweet, innocent girl who had inconveniently become pregnant with his child. With cover-up help from both his parents, Adcock had continued to go to school and live the good life, amassing a reasonably sized fortune in the process. And what did Monica Wellington have to show for her life? A headstone in a Leavenworth cemetery and a mother who, almost forty years later, kept candles burning in her daughter's memory.

Life isn't fair.

The paved circular driveway that wound around a lushly flowing fountain was filled with the cars of sympathetic well-wishers who had evidently arrived en masse to express their condolences about Faye Adcock's tragic death. A pair of swinging ornamental gates had been left open to allow for all the comings and goings. As far as Mel and I were concerned, things were getting better and better.

Fortunately, my Mercedes, even though it wasn't a brand-new model, fit in with all the other spendy vehicles that included at least one chauffeur-driven Bentley. If we'd shown up in that esteemed company driving a beat-up, unmarked patrol car, I have no doubt someone would have immediately emerged from the house and sent us packing. As Cousin Vinny learned all those years ago, it's a good idea to blend.

Before getting out of the vehicle, Mel took great pains to wipe both the iPad screen and the stylus. Then, with the cover flapped shut over both the iPad and the stylus, she carried those while I wrestled my body and my two Technicolor canes out of the car. Slowly I made my way up the smoothly paved driveway and onto the massive porch. The front door was open to accommodate the stream of visitors. We could have walked inside, but without a warrant it was best to stay on the porch.

The woman who came to the door in answer to the doorbell, clearly a caterer's assistant, invited us inside.

"No, thank you," I said cordially. "We know this is a difficult time, and we don't want to intrude, but we do need to have a word with Mr. Adcock."

Nodding, she disappeared.

When Ken Adcock appeared in the entryway a few minutes later, I felt as though I were seeing a ghost. The man was definitely his father's son in size and build, but his face was a mixture of both his mother and his father. He had his father's square jawline and his mother's fathomless dark eyes.

"I understand you wanted to see me?" he asked.

Reaching into my pocket, I pulled out my badge and ID. I worried that Adcock might somehow connect my name with the location of his mother's fatal leap, but he'd had enough interactions with cops that day that he didn't give either of them a second glance.

"You still haven't said what you want."

"Sorry to bother you at a time like this, and we're so sorry for your loss," I said in my most conciliatory fashion.

"What's this about?" he asked brusquely. His voice said it all. Yes, his mother was dead. That made Mel's and my presence a necessary annoyance.

"Your mother's vehicle," I answered.

"What about it?" he said. "My understanding is that it's been towed to a lot somewhere over in Lake City."

"Yes," I said. "That would be Big Boy Towing. Did the people who gave you that information have you sign a receipt?"

Ken frowned. "No," he said. "They didn't. Were they supposed to?"

"That's why we're following up," I explained. "In situations like this, it's best not to leave anything to chance."

"So where's the paper?" he asked impatiently. "Give me whatever it is I'm supposed to sign. I need to get back to my guests."

As if to underscore the statement, another vehicle was just then nosing its way up the drive. Without a hitch, Mel held out the iPad and flipped open the cover, revealing the stylus. Switching on the iPad, she opened it to the proper document, and then she passed the device over to Adcock. In the process she managed to do a well-faked stumble that almost knocked both the stylus and the iPad out of his hands. In juggling to keep from dropping the iPad and the stylus, Adcock managed to put his fingerprints, and hopefully some DNA, all over them.

"So sorry," Mel said with an apologetic smile. "It's the canes. I can't get used to having a gimp for a partner. I keep tripping over the damned things."

As the new arrivals emerged from their vehicle—a bright red Volvo—and came toward the porch, Adcock hurriedly scribbled his signature, the date, printed the required information at the bottom and then handed it back to Mel.

"Are you going to send me a copy of that?" he demanded.

"Yes, of course," Mel said with her sweetest smile as she took hold of the very tip end of the stylus. "That's why we needed your e-mail address. Once we get back to the office, we'll forward you a copy."

As the new guests arrived, Adcock dismissed us and turned to greet them. He didn't see Mel slip both the stylus and the iPad into a waiting evidence bag, and he didn't see the wink she sent in my direction, either.

As far as I was concerned, her wink said it all—mission accomplished!

CHAPTER 25

Obviously I didn't jump up and down and click my heels as we headed back to the car, but I felt like it.

"Where to now?" she asked, once we were in the car and she was fastening her seat belt. "The crime lab?"

"You got it."

Mel nudged our way around the fountain and back out onto 132nd. "You realize this is going to take time, don't you? It's not like having a cheek-swab sample. They may have to use PCR to make it work."

"I don't care how long it takes," I said. "If we're right, he's gotten away with Monica's murder all this time. As far as he's concerned, everyone at Seattle PD is totally buying the idea that Monica was Adcock Senior's lover and that Faye's death is about blackmail. As long as Junior has no clue that you and I are onto him, he's got no reason to run."

"Because he thinks he's got everything sacked and bagged."

"Exactly."

It was full-on traffic now. Because we were at the top end of Bellevue, we went across the 520 Bridge. It was stop-and-go the whole way, from the time we exited 405 until we were midspan. Maybe I wouldn't mind paying the tolls so much if they had actually done something to ease traffic congestion. But they haven't. If anything, it's worse.

We were on I-5 headed south when my phone rang. "Hello," Marge Herndon said. "Remember me? Where are you?"

"We just got back from Leavenworth," I said.

"I didn't get out anything for dinner," Marge said. "But there was no point in standing around all day doing nothing. I've mopped, vacuumed, dusted, and cleaned the bathrooms and kitchen. I'm also calling to tell you I'm taking the rest of the evening off!"

The truth is, Mel and I spend so much time together, coming and going as we please, that I don't think it had occurred to either one of us that we needed to report in to Marge.

"Thank you, Marge," I said. "We didn't mean to leave you hanging."

"I'm not hanging any longer," she said. "I'll see you in the morning."

She didn't add "or else," but I'm sure I heard those two words out there in the ether.

"I guess we missed curfew?" Mel asked with a grin.

I nodded.

"Great," Mel said. "We'll go to El Gaucho for dinner. You can call for a reservation while I run in and out of the crime lab."

That's what we did. After the crime lab stop, we went by Seattle PD and picked up Mel's cell phone as well. Before my knees got really bad, Mel and I would walk the few blocks from Belltown Terrace to El Gaucho. Lately, though, the valet parkers had grown accustomed to our showing up in either Mel's car or mine, and they're careful to leave whichever vehicle we arrive in close at hand.

Walking into the velvety darkness of that particular restaurant with Mel at my side always raises my spirits. I know the food will be good and the conversation will be better.

In the time since Mel had been back, we'd done very little talking about her sojourn in Bellingham. Now, with her sipping a glass of wine and me easing into an O'Doul's, she told me all about it. She was finishing up when she came to the part of the story that scared the hell out of me.

"The sense around town is that Police Chief Hamlin never should have let the protest situation get as out of hand as it did," Mel said thoughtfully.

"So?"

"There's a real movement afoot in the city council to demand her resignation. Several people let me know that if that happens, they think I should apply for the job."

My heart gave a lurch inside my chest. I love living in Seattle. I love living in Belltown Terrace, but maybe that's just me. After all, isn't "whither thou goest" a big part of being married?

"What do you think?" I asked.

She grinned at me. "Bellingham is a nice enough place to visit, but I don't think I want to live there. Besides, I don't think either one of us would be very happy with you stuck in the background as Mr. Mel Soames."

"But if you wanted it . . ."

"I just told you what I want," she said. "I like where we live. I like our life together."

"Good," I said. "I'm with you."

We finished our dinner. For someone who was still out on medical leave, I thought I had put in a pretty good day's work. I didn't care how long it took to nail Kenneth Adcock just as long as we did nail him.

We were back in the unit and I had sunk into the comfort of my recliner when my phone rang. The number wasn't a familiar one, and neither was the tentative voice that replied to my answer.

"Jonas?" she said. "Is this Jonas Beaumont?"

"Yes."

"My name is Bonnie Abney," she said. "I don't believe you know me. Years ago, I was Doug Davis's fiancée. Glenn Madden suggested I might want to give you a call. I take it you knew him? Not Glenn, I mean. That you knew Douglas."

With those few words it all came flooding back, washing over me in a kaleidoscope of color and unholy noise. In that single instant I was transported back to the sights and sounds and smells of war: the clatter of gunfire; the stench of blood and smoke; the screams of the wounded. It was August second of 1966, and I was back in the middle of the firefight.

I had been given a sacred charge to find her, and now that I had, I was speechless. I had no idea what to say. Words failed me.

"Yes," I said finally, after a long pause. "Doug Davis was the platoon leader, my second lieutenant, and he saved my life that day. I should have told you about it a long time ago, but somehow I never got around to doing it, and I'm not sure you're even interested at this point."

"Glenn said you live in Seattle," Bonnie said. "I live in Coupeville on Whidbey Island. If you wanted to come out here tomorrow, maybe we could go have coffee somewhere," she offered.

"Not tomorrow," I said quickly. "I'm involved in a funeral tomorrow. Also, I recently had knee-replacement surgery, so I wouldn't be able to drive there on my own. My wife, Mel, would need to come with me."

The relief in Bonnie's voice was readily apparent. She must have thought I was trying to hook up with her. The news that I had a wife and that she would be with me put the situation in a whole different light. She gave me her address and I jotted it down.

"Why don't we do this on Thursday, then? Maybe you could come here for lunch."

"How far is it to Coupeville?"

"It's only about eighty miles, depending on where you are in Seattle, but it's close to three hours of driving."

"Lunch won't work," I said. "I have a standing appointment for physical therapy in the morning. We won't be able to leave until after that."

"Let's make it either a late lunch or an early dinner," Bonnie said. "I'll fix a salad that I can put out whenever you get here."

"Fair enough," I told her. "We'll be there sometime Thursday afternoon."

Mel came into the room carrying my evening pills and water just as I ended the call.

"We'll be where on Thursday afternoon?" she asked.

"Coupeville on Whidbey Island," I said. "That was Bonnie Abney, Lieutenant Davis's fiancée. She invited us to lunch."

"I've never been to Whidbey Island," Mel said. "How far is it?"

"Eighty miles, give or take."

"Jeez Louise," Mel said. "We're going to turn into regular tourists."

It was only nine o'clock or so when I headed off to bed. I was whipped. I wasn't carrying car keys, but when I emptied my pockets onto the dresser, out came my badge and ID wallet along with the other things that I was keeping there—the three aces of spades and the hunks of shrapnel. I stared at them for a moment when I put them down. Was giving them to Bonnie Abney the right thing to do or the wrong thing? If she had married someone else, I doubted her husband would care to have mementos of a previous fiancé lying around the house.

Tired as I was that night, I didn't sleep very well. Hearing Bonnie Abney's voice had given me something else to worry about. Maybe that was just as well. Otherwise I would have been agonizing about Delilah Ainsworth, Monica Wellington, and Kenneth Adcock. It's possible that thinking about Bonnie was a blessing in disguise.

On Wednesday I focused on Delilah Ainsworth. It was her day, all of it. Everyone at the various cop shops had gotten the memo. No one showed up in uniform, but that didn't keep them from showing up anyway. The church was full to overflowing. In the front of the church, massed around the casket, was a riot of floral bouquets. The service was simple enough. They talked about Delilah's being a good mother and a good wife. No one talked about her being a good cop, but some things go without saying. After all, that was why she was dead.

I walked down the aisle on my canes, just behind the pallbearers carrying the casket, and stood to one side as they loaded it into the hearse. Brian Ainsworth had specifically requested that there not be dozens of cop cars lined up to follow the hearse from the church to the cemetery, and there weren't. But there were plenty of out-of-uniform police officers on either side of the street, standing at attention and holding small American flags as the procession went by. And there were plenty of civilian cars parked along the street, waiting to join the funeral procession.

After the graveside service, Mel and I were making for the car when Brian Ainsworth caught up with us.

"Thank you," he said.

I had managed to get through the whole service without making a fool of myself, but hearing those words from him caught me off guard. After all, wasn't it my bright idea to reopen the Wellington case that had gotten Delilah killed?

"I'm not sure—" I began, but Brian overrode my comment.

"You maybe didn't put Del's killer in jail, but you found her," Brian told me. "She won't be hurting anyone else, and my family won't have to live through the pain of a trial."

It would have been nice to tell him right then that Mel and I were on the trail of Monica's killer, too, which would mean Delilah hadn't died in vain. I could have told him that, but I didn't dare. I didn't want even the slightest hint to leak out that we were after someone else. I didn't want Kenneth James Adcock to know we were onto him until we were ready to take him down.

"You're welcome," I said, blinking back tears. "It was the least I could do."

We made a brief appearance at the reception in the

church's basement social hall, and then Mel and I went home. Marge had pulled together a selection of cold cuts. Those combined with slices of steak left over from the previous night's dinner were probably better than any postfuneral buffet fare we would have found at the reception.

On Thursday morning we were up early. Ida Witherspoon was there to do her stuff. This time we did one and a half times around the running track. I was starting to get the hang of it. There was a soft rain falling, a light drizzle. Not enough to get really wet, and not enough to stay completely dry, either.

By eleven or so, Mel and I were in the car and on I-5, headed north toward Anacortes, Deception Pass, and eventually Whidbey Island.

"I don't understand why we couldn't just catch a ferry," Mel said.

"Sorry," I said. "The vagaries of the Washington State Ferry system are more than I can understand at times. We just have to drive."

"You don't look happy about this," she added. "The words 'invitation to a beheading' come to mind. You were in better spirits on Monday on our way to Leavenworth."

"On Monday we were going to help Hannah Wellington close an old wound. Today I'm afraid we're going to reopen one for Bonnie Abney."

Had Mel been any other kind of wife, she might have taken that moment to point out that finding Bonnie Abney was something I myself had set out to do and that I had only myself to blame. She didn't have to point it out. I was busy blaming myself without the need of any outside assistance.

By the time we were approaching Coupeville, the weather was starting to clear. The morning drizzle had dried out and the sun was breaking through the cloud cover. The GPS warned us that it would not be able to provide turn-by-turn directions. We had backstopped that with a downloaded MapQuest document that did, but in the end, taking that precaution wasn't necessary. We drove straight to the right street. Once we reached the proper address we turned onto a narrow lane that wound through the woods. After several turns we found ourselves in a clearing on a bluff overlooking the slate blue water of Penn Cove. The cozy house was covered with weathered shingles that were punctuated by picture windows. The flagstone porch out front was lined on two sides by massive baskets of slightly faded summer petunias.

I had opened the car door and was struggling to get my canes organized when an immense black-and-white dog, barking his head off, bounded out of the house. A tallish blond woman wearing black slacks and a bright red sweater followed the huge dog into the yard.

"That's Crackerjack," she explained, pointing at the hundred or so pounds of gamboling black fluffy fur. "He's a Bernese mountain dog, and I'm Bonnie. You must be Jonas."

Her information from the guy running the reunions had come from my military records, where I was inevitably listed by my given name.

"Most people call me Beau," I said.

By then, Mel had come around to my side of the car and had thrust her hands deep into Crackerjack's wondrously thick coat. "And this is Melissa Soames, my wife," I added. "Most people call her Mel."

"Welcome," Bonnie said. "I'm glad the weather cleared up enough to enjoy the view. Do come in."

We followed her into the house. It was the kind of comfortable place that makes a visitor feel instantly at home. Light streamed through six triangular skylights that also gave view to the tall pines and cedars that soared above the house. Windows across the front offered panoramic views of the cove with its sailboats and the lush pastures of the Three Sisters Cattle Company far across on the opposite bank. In the rustic living room a wood fire crackled in the fireplace and on the mantel above it sat two small velvet-covered jewel boxes. I didn't have to open them to know what would be inside—Lennie D.'s medals, his Purple Heart, his Silver Star.

Standing before them, I instantly recalled the play Kelly had starred in while in high school—*The Old Lady Shows Her Medals*. It's the story of an old London charwoman during World War II. When her coworkers start bragging about their sons' heroic exploits on the battlefield, the childless old woman pretends to have a son of her own by plucking the name of someone else's son from news reports and laying claim to his battlefield accomplishments. Eventually the soldier gets wind of the old woman's subterfuge. He comes to town and gives her hell about it. Later, though, when he dies in battle, he sees to it that his medals are sent to her.

At the time, seeing my daughter playing the part of the old charwoman, grieving over the loss of her pretend son, had left me breathless. I had sat in a dead-silent auditorium along with the rest of the audience, too stunned with emotion to applaud. Now, all these years later, with those two boxes sitting on the mantel in front of me, I was shocked to realize that the old woman in the play, the one who had seemed so ancient back then, must have been about the same age Bonnie Abney and I were now.

"I don't usually keep the boxes out in plain sight," Bonnie said, crossing the room to stand beside me. "I brought them out today to show them to you."

We stood there looking. She didn't touch the boxes, and neither did I.

Nodding wordlessly and searching for a way to move away from the boxes and all they meant, I glanced around the rest of the room. On a wall to one side of the fireplace was a portrait, and I stood transfixed once more, gazing up a pencil sketch of a young Lennie D. I saw again the same confident eyes and crooked smile, a handsome young guy resplendent in his West Point uniform.

Bonnie's eyes followed mine. "I had that done for Doug's mother the year he was killed," she explained. "It hung in her living room for many years, and it was returned to me when she passed away some years ago."

"It's him," I said with a lump in my throat. "It's absolutely him."

She nodded. "The flag from the coffin went to his mother," she said. "It was in one of those ceremonial glass boxes, and I would have liked to have it, but somehow it disappeared."

"And his West Point sword?" I asked.

"That went to one of his younger brothers, Blaine."

That hurt. Hannah Wellington had her candles. Bonnie Abney had her medals, but she didn't have either the sword or the flag.

We stood there in silence. After a moment Bonnie took a deep breath and seemed to recall her position as hostess. "Won't you sit down?" she urged, pointing me toward an easy chair. "What can I get you? Coffee, tea, some wine—white or red?"

Mel sat down on a nearby couch. Crackerjack had evidently decided she was the best thing since the invention of kibble, and he was seated directly in front of her, soaking up 100 percent of her attention, and although he was seated on the floor and she was on the couch, I noticed they were almost eye to eye.

"If he's too much, I can always send him into the other room," Bonnie offered.

"Oh, no," Mel said. "He's gorgeous. I love him."

"It's a good thing you're wearing black pants," Bonnie told her. "He sheds like crazy. Now, what to drink?"

Mel and I both asked for coffee. I had spent the whole trip trying to decide if I should let her broach the subject or if I should. Ultimately I had determined that sooner was better. If it all went south from there, Bonnie could go ahead and hand us our walking papers without having to go through the trouble of serving us lunch.

With that in mind, once Bonnie disappeared into the kitchen to fetch the coffee, I reached into my pocket and pulled out those six items that seemed to be burning a hole in my pocket. When Bonnie returned to the living room, she was carrying a tray laden with mugs of coffee, cream, and sugar. By then my peace offerings were spread out on the coffee table in front of me.

Bonnie looked at them, but she said nothing as she set down the tray. After passing mugs to Mel and me, Bonnie turned her full attention to the items lying there, waiting for her. She picked them up one at a time, first the hunks of metal and then the playing cards. Holding them nestled gently between her hands, she sank down onto the couch next to Mel.

"Tell me," she said, looking at me. "Please."

And so I did—all of it, starting with my very first meeting with Lennie D. after I arrived in camp and his giving me the cards and the book. I told her everything I could remember about the firefight that had cost Doug Davis his life. She listened with rapt attention. I was an eyewitness. I had been there. When I explained how the book Lieutenant Davis had given me—the one I carried with me into battle—had saved my life, she began to cry. She didn't sob. Silent tears slipped down her cheeks and dripped unnoticed onto the sweater she was wearing.

"And these are the cards he gave you?" she asked when I finished.

"The very ones," I said.

She held them to her cheek briefly, as though some trace of Lennie D.'s touch might still linger on the smooth surface.

"They told me about you when I went to the Cacti reunion," she said quietly.

That one stunned me. "They did?"

"Yes, they told me the story of the guy who didn't die because he had borrowed one of Doug's books. I never imagined that I'd have the chance to meet you and speak to someone else who was there when it happened. And I actually saw the book, by the way—*The Rise and Fall,* with three jagged holes burned almost all the way through it. Gary Fowler brought it to the reunion and showed it to me. He was the one who told me the story."

"Lieutenant Davis was a good man," I declared. "The best. He was brave. He was loyal. He cussed like a sailor, but he was also kind and generous, and it was his kindness in lending me that book that saved my life. I wanted you to know that. I wanted to be able to tell you so in person."

"But why now?" she asked. "Why after all this time?"

"I had surgery on my knees," I said. "And while I was under the influence of the painkillers, I had a dream about . . ." I had to pause for a moment to compose myself and to remember to call Lennie D. by the name Bonnie Abney used. "About Douglas," I concluded finally. "The dream reminded me that I had never come to see you; that I had never said thank you or told you how sorry I was then and still am for your terrible loss."

Bonnie didn't say anything for a few moments. Instead, she used the back of her hand to wipe away the tears.

"So what have you done with your life, Beau?"

It was the same question the dream Lennie D. had asked me, and Bonnie was asking for the same reason. Her Douglas had died. I had lived. She wanted to know what had I done with my side of that bargain.

"I joined Seattle PD after I got out of the service. I spent most of my career there working as a homicide detective. Since then I've worked for the attorney general's office."

"We both do," Mel put in. "We're assigned to the Special Homicide Investigation Team. Sometimes we work new cases, sometimes we work old cases. That's where we met."

"So you've been together a long time?" Bonnie asked.

"Not long at all," Mel said. "It took us a while to get it right."

Mel and I had both finished our coffee by then. Bonnie's cup sat untouched and cold on the coffee table, but she seemed to decide that the time had come to serve our late lunch.

"I'll go put the food on the table," she said. "I made a chicken salad, and this morning I baked some sourdough bread from a ninety-year-old starter my sister brought down from Alaska. That's where my family came from originally."

She got up then. When Mel went to see if there was something she could do to help, Crackerjack proved fickle and turned his considerable attention and charm on me. His coat was amazingly smooth and soft and brushed to a glossy high sheen. As he stared into my face, I was glad to think that Bonnie had the dog's solid presence in this comfortable but solitary place.

When lunch was served, we sat in the dining room, again overlooking the water. The wind had come up. Even from this distance we could see whitecaps churning. "It was still this morning," Bonnie said, "still enough that I went kayaking with some neighbors. Douglas would have loved it."

Just that quickly, she slipped away down memory lane, telling us about the blind date in Florida that had brought them together—a soldier about to head for Vietnam and a young flight attendant; how they had walked and talked until the wee hours of the morning; how he had walked her to her airline's operations department in Miami when it came time for her to board a flight to Rio; how he had shipped off to Ranger school for six weeks, leaving her to wonder why she hadn't heard from him when, in truth, no calls or letters were allowed.

The story took a turn then. He had shown up, fresh out of Ranger school and wanting to visit with her before going home to Bisbee, Arizona, to see his family for Christmas. For the next several weeks, before he shipped out for Vietnam, they traveled together. It wasn't a matter of them falling in love, because that had already happened for both of them.

During their idyllic time together, they managed to grab a few more days together in Hawaii. Then he left for Vietnam and was gone. She told of going to Bisbee and waiting in the desert for the train that brought Doug's body home for burial. Of going to the wake and meeting a young Hispanic man who'd told Bonnie that one cold morning over that last Christmas vacation he had encountered Doug in downtown Bisbee. Doug had handed him his jacket and then walked home in a cotton shirt because he was going to Vietnam and wouldn't need a jacket.

After that Bonnie told us about her life after Douglas—about working and eventually marrying. But that marriage had never quite worked as well as either she or her now former husband would have liked. She had been promoted to director of training at the airline, written a book, become a management consultant, and created her own company, one that specialized in executive training all over the globe. And now, after years of living and working on the road, she had retired to this little haven of a house on Whidbey Island.

I listened to her story with an ache in my heart, because I, of all people, understood. She had had her Douglas Davis; I had had my Anne Corley. The cases were so similar that it took my breath away. Anne had arrived in my life in a whirl of passion that had taken us both by surprise and turned our worlds upside down. The same thing had happened to Bonnie and Doug. Both Doug and Anne had shot through Bonnie's and my separate lives like a pair of brilliant comets, and when the two of them were gone, Bonnie and I were left with our worlds in pieces, our hopes shattered, and our dreams in ashes.

It took me years to grow beyond the legend of Anne Corley so I could find love and comfort in the presence of someone else. It wasn't until I found Mel that I was truly able to put what happened to me back then with Anne in the past.

Maybe that wouldn't happen for Bonnie—maybe the legend of Doug Davis was more than she could ever put behind her—but as I listened to her story, I finally understood what I was doing there in her living room, why I had come. It was my job to listen and to be there because I was the one person in the whole world who could listen to Bonnie's heartbreaking story and truly understand.

Mel and I stayed for hours longer than we expected to. We had dessert back in the living room. I took my next batch of pills with a dose of carb-heavy red velvet cake. Marge Herndon would have been appalled.

As we were gathering up to leave, Bonnie asked me if I wanted the cards back. "No," I told her. "They're yours now, along with the shrapnel."

Nodding, she picked them up, carried them over to the fireplace, and put them on the mantel next to the jewel boxes. She had put them in a place of honor, and I was moved beyond words.

By the time Bonnie and Crackerjack walked Mel and me back out to the car, it was almost dark. My hand was on the door handle when Bonnie reached up and gave me a hug.

"Thanks for listening," she said. "I haven't told anyone that story in a very long time. It's such ancient history and most people don't care to hear it."

"That's what friends are for," I said. "It doesn't matter if they're old friends or new friends. They're the kind of people who will listen as long as you need them to because, sometimes, telling the story and having someone listen is the only way to figure out how to move on."

Bonnie turned to Mel then, and enveloped her in a hug, too. "I'm happy for you," she said. "I'm happy for you both."

Then, with Crackerjack at her side, she turned and walked back into her solitary house. I watched her go. Watched her turn off the porch light after she closed the door.

The sky was dark overhead. Only one star—I'm not sure which one—was visible in the distance. Logically, I know that Lennie D. and that star have no connection whatsoever, but somehow, when I spoke, I believed they were both listening.

"I did it," I said. "I hope I measured up."

CHAPTER 26

In the world of scripted television shows, everything gets wrapped up in an hour of prime time—forty-two minutes of story and the rest of commercials, often for drugs where the announcers spend far more time listing dozens of dire side effects than they do singing the praises of the medication's supposed benefits.

Life isn't like that. DNA PCR takes time. It isn't an instant process, but it's not like I didn't have one or two things to occupy my time while I waited to see if the Washington State Patrol Crime Lab could deliver the goods.

I had been up doing more than I should have been doing for a number of days. Marge Herndon was quick to point out that I was able to function that way because I was still taking far more pain medication than I realized. Soon after we got back from Whidbey, she set off on a program to wean me away from them, and that was no picnic.

For one thing, as I went through withdrawal from

narcotics, I found that it would have been all too easy to once again fall prey to booze. On that score, I went to meetings and spent plenty of quality time with my sponsor. Even when Ida Witherspoon's mandatory visits ended, I continued to do the PT, sometimes doing two and three turns around the running track at a crack, first with the walker, then two canes, then one, and, finally, on my own.

Marge finished her stint as my drill sergeant and went back home to her own place in Shoreline. In some ways, Mel and I were glad to see her go, but in terms of having food magically appear at mealtimes, we both agreed that we missed having her annoying presence bustling around the place.

Kelly flew up from Ashland to visit. She spent two nights in the visitor's suite Marge had just abandoned. And I made arrangements to book it again when Scott and Cherisse were due to arrive in town and would need a place to stay while they closed on their new house in Burien.

By then my knees were making so much progress that I was amazed. When I went to see Dr. Auld to have my staples taken out, I walked into the treatment room carrying both of the canes. That put a smile on his face. "Hey," he told me. "I do good work, don't I?"

He told me the numb spots I was feeling on my legs might or might not go away eventually, but he pronounced me a great patient. I left his office feeling as though I had been given a gold star right along with my new knees.

And all the while, in the background, while I was waiting, I was also working. While my original iPad was still being held hostage in the crime lab, I had gotten a replacement, and I used that to learn everything there was to know about the second Kenneth James Adcock.

It turned out he wasn't one of the earliest Microsofties, but he was close. He was a smart kid who had graduated from WSU with a degree in electronics engineering by the time he was twenty. He had gone on to get a master's and a Ph.D. from UCLA before going to work for Microsoft in the early eighties.

Retired with a bundle of stock and money while still in his forties, Adcock and his wife, Yvette, were known for their philanthropic efforts in the Pacific Northwest in general and in Bellevue and Seattle in particular. There were no blemishes on Kenneth's record—no arrests, no speeding tickets, not even so much as a parking infraction. On the surface, at least, he appeared to be a totally upright, law-abiding guy—a politically active, churchgoing model citizen.

Almost a month passed. I had more or less given up all hope of getting the answers I needed when the phone rang bright and early one morning. When I answered, Ross Connors was on the line.

"Are you sitting down?" he asked. "If you're not, you should be, because I wouldn't want those new knees of yours to go splat."

"Why?" I returned. "What's up?"

"The crime lab just called. They've got a match. Or rather, two of them."

My heart started hammering in my chest. "What do you mean, two?" I asked.

"The DNA off your iPad matches the M.E.'s defensive fingernail scrapings. Adcock's your guy!"

"Amen," I breathed. "But I thought you said two matches."

"I did. The DNA expert assures me that Kenneth James Adcock Junior was the father of Monica Wellington's unborn child. How do you like them apples?"

It was what I had expected all along. It had to be. That was why Faye Adcock had been willing to commit not one but two murders and then leap to her death besides. She had been protecting the one thing she had left in the world—her son and all he stood for.

"I talked to the prosecutor's office about this," Ross continued. "Even with the DNA evidence, he's not ready to swear out an arrest warrant. He wants more. He wanted to know if anyone ever looked into the kid's involvement back during the time of the initial investigation."

"We didn't," I said. "I can tell you that his name never came up, not once."

"It has now," Ross said. "As of now, I'm putting some of my S.H.I.T people—Mel included—on the case. I know it was a long time ago, but someone out there might know something, might still remember something. It's just a matter of finding those people and jogging their memories."

Ross is a smart man, and he was right. With Mel keeping me apprised of how things were going, I stayed on the sidelines while my fellow investigators combed through Kenneth Adcock's high school chums and acquaintances. It didn't take long to discover someone who remembered a rowdy party where a bunch of guys from WSU had gone over to Leavenworth one snowy December weekend and had used the Christmas lighting ceremony as an excuse to get hammered. Several of them remembered that Kenneth had been smitten with one of the young local girls. Yes, things had gotten pretty hot and heavy. No, no one remembered her name. They had never seen her again, but when they were shown Monica's senior yearbook photo, three of the guys on that trip agreed that that was most likely the girl.

These days, if someone falls for someone else, there's an instant trail of the budding romance in Facebook postings, texts, or tweets. In 1973 there was no such thing. There was no way to connect the dots between Monica's coming to the lonely realization that she was most likely pregnant as a result of that unexpected coupling and her equally lonely decisions about what, if anything, she should do about it.

There were no hidden diary entries to tell us if what had happened between them had been consensual or if it had in fact been date rape. Had she contacted Kenneth in Pullman? Had she contacted his parents? Who knows, but by now I was convinced that one Friday evening in late March Monica left her University of Washington dorm for the last time, wearing that WSU sweatshirt, and that Kenneth James Adcock Junior was the guy who was going to be her "blind date" that night—her date and her killer.

I was still officially on medical leave on the day it was time to go pick up Adcock, but they let me be a part of it anyway. It was a Friday afternoon, late in October, when we drove up to the Adcock mansion in the wilds of Bellevue. It was raining. The streets were slick with fallen leaves. Puddles of water had backed up around leaf-clogged storm drains.

Even though I had recently been given permission to drive, Mel was at the wheel and I was in the passenger seat with the arrest warrant in my pocket. We were in

Mel's Cayman, caravanning with two detectives from Seattle PD's Cold Case squad in their own unmarked car. They would be the officers taking Adcock into custody.

We all knew this was a big deal. You don't pick up a murderer with those kinds of connections without running a certain amount of risk. Not life-and-death risk. I didn't figure Adcock would come out of his house shooting. I knew it was more likely that he would immediately try to see to it that anyone connected to the case was committing career suicide.

I went along for the ride because if that's what happened, I wanted to be his natural target.

We had thought on the way there that we might have some trouble getting in through the gates, but it turned out Adcock was a sociable kind of guy. He and his wife were having a Day of the Dead party and the front porch was strewn with brightly lit jack-o'-lanterns and weirdly posed skeletons. Considering the relatively recent death of his mother, that seemed like an odd choice, but maybe the party had been scheduled before Faye Adcock staged her very dramatic exit.

The gates to Kenneth Adcock's mansion were wide open, and we drove right in.

When we got out of the cars, we could hear mariachis playing somewhere in the background. I have no doubt that deep inside that spacious mansion a uniformed bartender was busy handing out margaritas, but Mel and I were bringing our own particular element to the Day of the Dead, one Kenneth Adcock most likely wasn't anticipating. Somebody else had brought the tequila. We were bringing the worm.

We rang the bell. Again, the person who came to the door was part of a catering staff, and again I asked to speak to Mr. Adcock. When he came to the door this time, he looked at me blankly, the way you do when you see someone you think you should know but can't quite place.

"Yes?" he said, questioningly.

"Mr. Adcock, I'm Special Investigator J. P. Beaumont with the Special Homicide Investigation Team. This is my partner, Mel Soames. We have a warrant for your arrest. Please turn around and place your hands on your head."

"Wait. What's this all about?"

"You're under arrest for the murder of Monica Wellington."

He looked at me for a very long moment. In the background, I heard a woman's anxious voice. "What is it, Kenny? What's going on?"

Kenneth shook his head. "Call Winston," he said over his shoulder as we led him away. "Tell him I'm being arrested. I need my attorney."

When I closed the cuffs around his wrists, the sound of the locking mechanism was music to my ears.

CHAPTER 27

I wish I could say it felt triumphant that Saturday morning when Mel and I went back to Leavenworth to tell Hannah Wellington that we had solved her daughter's murder for real this time, but it didn't. It felt like too little, too late. Kenneth Adcock would have the best legal representation money could buy. By the time the judicial wrangling was over, it would be a miracle if he served any prison time.

Still, as we drove back to Seattle, it seemed as though I had done all the things I had been charged to do by the people who had emerged from my past and thrust themselves into my drug-fueled present. A sudden snowstorm hit as we headed down Stevens Pass. Driving into it and trying to see the road through a snow-obscured windshield, I suddenly realized that there was something else I should do, not because I had to but because I wanted to and because I was the only person who could.

The next day, Sunday, I made several phone calls.

Only when I had the arrangements in place did I call
Bonnie Abney.

"What are you doing on November eleventh?" I
asked her.

"November eleventh?" she said. "I don't know. Why?"

"Mel and I would like you to meet us at Boeing Field
at eight o'clock that morning. We have a surprise for
you. We're going to take a little trip."

"What kind of trip?"

"I'm not telling, but dress warmly. It'll probably be cold."

"All right," she said. "But before I say yes, I'll have to
see if I can board Crackerjack. On such short notice that
might not be easy."

"Don't bother boarding him," I said. "He's welcome
to come along."

That was how three humans and one very large
black-and-white dog flew out of Boeing Field bright and
early on Veterans Day.

"Have you figured out where we're going?" I asked.

"Bisbee?" she asked.

"That's right."

"But why?"

"I'm not telling. You'll see when we get there."

We landed in Tucson a scant two and a half hours
later. We'd had a catered breakfast on the plane, so we
didn't need to stop for lunch.

Instead, we got into our waiting rental SUV and
drove straight to Bisbee, where we spent some time
driving around and doing sightseeing. Bonnie pointed
out the house Doug had grown up in and had us drive
past the ballpark where he had played both football and
baseball and the Catholic church where he had served
as an altar boy.

We stopped by Evergreen Cemetery. That's where I discovered that one of Doug's two younger brothers, Blaine, was also laid to rest there. Bonnie explained that he had come home from his service in Vietnam as one of the "walking wounded." He had died in 2002. I left the cemetery shaken by the terrible price that one family had paid in the course of a misguided war.

Last but not least, we drove by all of the schools Doug had attended. We arrived at the last one of those, the one she referred to as the "new" high school, at exactly three o'clock, which, according to my schedule, was right on time.

Joanna Brady had told me that was when they usually held the memorial ceremony—right after school got out, so teachers and students could attend if they chose to do so.

It wasn't until Bonnie saw the crowd of people assembled in the parking lot—the uniformed band standing at attention, the cops and Boy Scouts also in uniform and standing at attention—that she finally realized this wasn't just an ordinary trip down memory lane.

I had called my friend Joanna Brady, and, as promised, she had pulled out all the stops. She had put together the largest Veterans Day gathering Bisbee, Arizona, had seen in many a year, including the appearance of a military band from Fort Huachuca. Joanna had told me to come to where the flagpoles stood in front of the school office and that the memorial to the Bisbee boys lost in Vietnam was nearby.

Mel stopped the SUV long enough for Bonnie, Crackerjack, and me to step out of the car. Then she drove away. Spotting a small lectern set up on a raised stage, I led the way there with Bonnie leaning on my arm and Crackerjack following sedately at her heel.

Once we reached the stage, I led her up on it and seated her on a chair someone had thoughtfully provided. Two months after my knee-replacement surgery, I was able to negotiate the three steps leading up to the stage with no difficulty and no assistance. Under my breath, I breathed a silent thank-you to the doctors and nurses and OT ladies who had made that possible.

I turned back to the audience in time to see Mel slip into an empty chair in the second row, next to Sheriff Brady. Not knowing what else to do, I stayed where I was, standing next to Bonnie on one side while Crackerjack guarded the other.

Eventually, a man who referred to himself as the mayor stepped to the microphone and called the event to order. He introduced a woman minister whose name was Marianne something, who opened the proceedings with a short invocation. The prayer was followed by the recitation of the Pledge of Allegiance and a stirring rendition of "The Star-Spangled Banner" sung by a young uniformed soldier with the band playing the accompaniment.

When the last strains of the national anthem died away, Sheriff Brady came forward, stepped up to the microphone, and introduced me. Then, with my new knees knocking behind the lectern, it was my turn to speak.

I had told the story to Mel and to Bonnie Abney in the privacy of Bonnie's living room, but that chilly afternoon, under a cloudy sky and in the face of a blustery wind that threatened rain, I told my story in public for the very first time. I don't see myself as any kind of orator, but when you have an important story to tell, the words you need seem to come of their own accord.

I wanted the people in Doug Davis's hometown to know the real story about one of the young men whose names were carved in that stone. They knew him as Doug, but I told them about Lennie D. I told them about the four aces and about how he was the lieutenant who did the best job of bringing the scared newbies into the platoon. I told them how he had earned his Silver Star and Purple Heart by showing extraordinary bravery during second watch on the afternoon of August 2, 1966. I wanted the townspeople to know that he had given his life in the service of his country and out of loyalty to what he called "his guys." I wanted them to know that I was one of those guys and that he had saved my life as well.

Finally I told them about my own Purple Heart, also earned on August 2, 1966. That's the one I keep hidden away in the cigar box because I have never felt I really earned it.

When I finished speaking I stepped away from the microphone to a round of subdued but respectful applause while a local priest took my place at the lectern. Slowly and with all due respect, he read aloud the names of the seven men listed on the monument—Leonard Doug Davis, Richard Allen Thursby, Leonard Carabeo, Richard Lynn Embrey, Robert Nathan Fiesler, Willard Wesley Lehman, and Calvin Russell Segar.

I had come to Bisbee in order to pay my respects to Lennie D., but I was glad the others were remembered and honored as well. They all deserved it.

After reading the names, the priest gave a short benediction, and then someone played "Taps." The bugle echoed clear as a bell across that cold parking lot while a team of uniformed Boy Scouts carefully lowered the flag and folded it. As they did so, I realized that it wasn't a new flag, one that had been taken out of its box and flown for the first time on that occasion. No, it was an old flag, one that had flown for months or maybe even years on that very flagpole. The colors had faded some in the hot desert sun, and the seams were slightly frayed from flapping in the wind. That struck me as right, somehow. This was Doug's flag, Lennie D.'s flag. It had flown over the school he loved in the town he loved.

When the well-seasoned flag was folded and tucked into its proper triangle, one of the Boy Scouts, a kid wearing a newly minted Eagle badge, stepped up onto the podium and offered it to Bonnie, just as I had requested. As far as she was concerned, the gesture was completely unexpected. She shot me a questioning glance. I gave her a slight, confirming nod.

"Thank you," she whispered. Then, reaching out, she gathered the flag into her arms and clutched it to her breast. There were tears on her face by then and on mine as well. Doug's mother's flag had been lost. It was high time Bonnie Abney had another.

After the ceremony ended, we drifted up the breezeway to the cafeteria, where some of the mothers from the Boy Scout troop had put together a reception complete with homemade cookies served with weak coffee and genuine Hawaiian punch. Crackerjack went with us into the cafeteria, and no one objected to his doggy presence.

I stayed close by and eavesdropped on the people who came to pay their respects to Bonnie. Some of them were strangers to her because they were parents and brothers and wives of the other men whose names were on the monument down by the flagpole. One by one, they exchanged greetings and hugs. One woman pressed a jagged-edged photo into Bonnie's hand.

"From our Latin Club," she murmured. As the woman melted back into the crowd, I caught a glimpse of the photo over Bonnie's shoulder. It was Lennie D., Doug, wearing a Roman toga and with a garland on his head.

Another guy handed her a gold pin shaped as a football. "I played football with Doug," he said. "This is one of the varsity pins that went on our Letterman sweaters. I thought you might like to have it."

Bonnie looked at the pin and then slipped it into her pocket.

An older woman approached Bonnie and whispered something in her ear. The look that crossed Bonnie's face was indecipherable, but then she turned to me and handed me Crackerjack's lead. "I'll be right back," she said.

She hurried away from me, walking out of the room and disappearing from sight behind the cafeteria. I caught Mel's eye. "Is she all right?" Mel mouthed.

All I could do was shrug in answer, because I didn't know. Bonnie was gone only a few minutes. When she came back into the cafeteria, there was a smile on her face, as though she knew a secret to which no one else was privy. She was actually glowing.

We left shortly after that because we had a plane waiting and needed to get back to Tucson.

"I went outside to see Jack," she explained as we settled into the car. "I wondered if he'd come, and he did."

"Who's Jack?" Mel asked.

"Doug's younger brother. He's troubled. He has a small house outside town, but he lives a vagabondish life. He doesn't come out in public much, but I was glad to see him. One of their mother's friends tracked him down and let him know I'd be here. He stopped by to say hello, but he didn't want to come inside."

I wondered about Jack but I didn't say anything. He sounded like someone with serious issues, and I wondered how much of that had to do with losing both his older brothers.

It was dark as we drove back through town. Bonnie asked us to take the main drag rather than the highway. Tombstone Canyon, the road, winds through Tombstone Canyon, the place, through the businesses of downtown Bisbee and the residential areas above that.

Bisbee is built just over the crest of a mountain pass that Bonnie referred to as "the Divide." When we merged back onto the highway, I watched in the mirror as she turned and stared out the rear window at the lights of the town receding into the distance. Once we entered the Mule Mountain Tunnel, the lights disappeared completely, as though someone had flicked off a switch. It was only when Bonnie turned to face forward again that I noticed she was still cradling the flag.

Bonnie caught my eye in the mirror. "I'm glad you didn't tell me where we were going," she said. "I might not have come. It hurt so much when they brought Douglas home to bury him that it eclipsed everything else. I could barely believe it was happening. This hurt, too, but in a different way. The other time they brought Douglas home. This time you brought me home, Beau. You and the people who came reminded me of how much I loved him and of how much he loved me. Thank you."

That's when I realized that I had done exactly what Lennie D. had asked of me.

"You're welcome," I said. "Believe me, it was the least I could do."

AUTHOR'S NOTE

Second Watch is a work of fiction. Some of the people in this book are real and their names are used by permission, although many of the events depicted about them are fictitious as well. The one true part of this book is that the names of Bisbee's Vietnam dead, the ones engraved on the memorial on the Bisbee High School campus, are all too real: Leonard Douglas Davis, Richard Allen Thursby, Leonard Carabeo, Richard Lynn Embrey, Robert Nathan Fiesler, Willard Wesley Lehman, and Calvin Russell Segar.

It is in memory of their lives, their service, and their sacrifice that I dedicate this book.

THE STORY BEHIND *SECOND WATCH*

Leonard Douglas Davis
1943–1966

Every story has a beginning.

For me, this one started in Mr. Guerra's Latin 2 class at Bisbee High School, in Bisbee, Arizona, in 1959. I was a sophomore, as were most of the other kids in the class. The one exception to that was an upperclassman named Doug Davis.

I was the scrawny awkward girl, the one with glasses and a fair amount of brains, sitting in the third seat in the row of desks next to the window. Doug sat in the third seat in the middle row. If I was the wallflower, he was the star, literally the big man on campus.

Doug was an outstanding student. He was smart, tall, good-looking, and an excellent all-around athlete. He wore a Letterman's sweater loaded with all the accompanying paraphernalia—the pins and stripes—that showed which years he had played on varsity teams and in which of several sports. He had a ready smile and an easygoing way about him that was endearing to fellow students and teachers alike.

Doug was a junior then, and why he was in class with a bunch of sophomores remains a mystery to this day. But I remember him arriving in the classroom early every day and then standing beside his desk waiting for the teacher to show up. He moved from foot to foot with certain impatient grace, like a restless, spirited racehorse ready to charge out of the starting gate. As soon as the teacher called the class to order, Doug was on task. His homework was always done and done right. He always knew the answers. He put the entire class on notice that he was there to learn. He wasn't mean or arrogant about it; he was simply focused.

It turns out that Latin 2 was the only class I shared with Doug. My talents didn't carry over to the kinds of advanced math and science classes in which he excelled. But in that one class we had in common, Doug was the yardstick by which I measured my own efforts. When

Mr. Guerra allowed some of us to do an extra-credit paper to help improve our grades, mine came back with a life-changing notation written on it in bright red pencil: "A+/Research worthy of a college student." I was a high school sophomore, but that was the first time anyone had ever hinted to me that I might be college material. That was a milestone for me. In case you're wondering what kind of a grade Doug got on *his* paper, don't bother. He already had straight A's in the class. He didn't need any extra credit.

I was a bookish young woman, and I know that Doug and I were often the only two students prowling the stacks looking for books after Mrs. Phillippi threw open the school's library doors before class in the morning. Doug was a voracious reader, and so was I. I mostly read novels. I believe he was one of the only kids in the school who checked out and read all the volumes from Edward Gibbon's *The History of the Decline and Fall of the Roman Empire.*

The guy was a hunk. It's beyond doubt that I had a crush on him at the time. Since he was clearly out of my league, I simply admired him from afar and let it go at that. When Doug's class graduated from Bisbee High in 1961, he was the valedictorian. I know I attended the graduation ceremony because I was in the school band, playing endless repetitions of "Pomp and Circumstance" while members of the class marched to their places under the bright field lights shining over the infield in Bisbee's Warren Ballpark. I'm sure I heard Doug's valedictory address; unfortunately I don't recall any of it.

Once Doug graduated, he disappeared from my frame of reference. I had no idea that he had gone on to

West Point or that from there, after attending Ranger school in 1965, he had shipped out for Vietnam.

My life went on. I, too, graduated from Bisbee High School. With the help of a scholarship, I became the first person in my family to attend and graduate from a four-year college. I had always wanted to be a writer. In 1964, when I sought admission to the Creative Writing program at the University of Arizona, the professor in charge wouldn't let me enroll because I was a girl. "Girls become teachers or nurses," he told me. "Boys become writers."

That's why, when I graduated from the U of A in May of 1966, it was with a degree in secondary education with a major in English and a minor in history. By the end of that summer, I was hired as a beginning English teacher at Pueblo High School in Tucson. Sometime early that fall, I received a letter from my mother telling me that Doug Davis had been killed in Vietnam.

This was long before the advent of the Internet or Facebook or Twitter or any of the many other devices that allow us to stay in touch with one another. By the time my mother's letter arrived, the funeral had already taken place. I was not a close friend of Doug's. No one thought to notify me in a more timely fashion, and my mother sent the information along as an interesting scrap of news from home the way she always did—in her own sweet time.

Tucson is only a hundred miles from Bisbee. If I had known about the funeral before it happened, I would have made an effort to be there for it. The upshot was, of course, that since I didn't know, I wasn't there. I suspect that a shard of guilt over my unwitting absence stayed with me through the years—a splinter in my heart that periodically festered and came to the surface.

The first instance of that occurred in the early eighties, shortly after I moved to Seattle. A cardboard replica of the Vietnam War Memorial came to town and was put on display at Seattle Center. My children and I were living downtown then. One afternoon, I took my two grade-school-age kids to Seattle Center to see it. Doug's name was the only one I looked up, shedding tears as I did so, explaining to my puzzled children that Doug was someone I knew from Bisbee, a soldier, who had died in a war. It was only then, in looking up his name, that I learned Douglas was his middle name. His first name was Leonard, but no one in Bisbee ever called him that. Back home he was simply Doug—Doug Davis.

Time passed. Despite the opinion of that Creative Writing professor about girls' inability to write, I nonetheless managed to do so. I wrote nine Beaumont books as original paperbacks. When my first hardback, *Hour of the Hunter,* was published, my first publisher-sponsored book tour took me to Washington, DC. One afternoon, between events, I asked my media escort to take me to the Vietnam Memorial. It's the only "tourist" thing I've ever done on a book tour before or since. While I was there, walking past that long expanse of black granite with all those thousands of names carved into it, again there was only one name that I searched out and touched—Doug's.

More time passed. I wrote more Beaumonts and the first Joanna Brady book, *Desert Heat.* For years the grand opening signings for my books were held at the Doghouse Restaurant in downtown Seattle. By the time Joanna # 2, *Tombstone Courage,* went on sale in 1995, the Doghouse had closed, so we had the grand opening at a Doghouse wannabe, a short-lived place called the Puppy Club. I was seated at the signing table when a woman came up to me, introduced herself as Merrilee MacLean, and asked, "Have you ever been to Bisbee, Arizona?"

"I was raised in Bisbee, Arizona," I told her.

Merrilee followed up with another question. "Did you ever know someone named Doug Davis?"

"Of course I knew Doug Davis!"

For the next several minutes, Merrilee told me about her sister, Bonnie Abney, who at the time was living in Florida. Bonnie had been engaged to marry Doug when he died. According to the sister, Bonnie had been a flight attendant back then. She'd had a bag packed to go to Japan for Doug's R and R, at which time they planned to be married. Instead, at age twenty-two, he came home to Bisbee in a flag-draped casket. Bonnie was twenty-six when she waited alone, in a car parked by a lonely railroad siding in the middle of the Arizona desert. Nearby, two Davis family friends sat in another parked car. Eventually a speeding freight train hove into view. First it slowed; finally it stopped. The door on one of the cars was rolled open, allowing attendants from Dugan's Funeral Chapel to unload Doug's casket from the train and into a waiting hearse.

According to Merrilee, some months before the *Tombstone Courage* signing, Bonnie had read *Desert Heat*. In it, a drug cartel's hit man guns down Joanna's husband, Andy. In the aftermath of Andy's death, there's a moving funeral scene that takes place in Bisbee's Evergreen Cemetery, the same cemetery in which Doug is buried.

As soon as Bonnie read that scene, she was convinced

there had to be some connection between whoever wrote the book and her beloved Douglas. For months afterward she carried that eventually very tattered paperback volume around in her purse because she couldn't let go of the idea of that connection, and of course, she was absolutely right. There was a very real tie between Doug Davis and the woman who wrote the book—that gangly girl from Mr. Guerra's Latin 2 class.

Bonnie's family hailed from Alaska originally, but many of her relatives had settled in the Seattle area. The next time she came to town to visit, she and I got together for lunch. I went armed with my collection of Bisbee High School yearbooks, my *Cuprites*.

Our meeting was supposed to be lunch only, but we huddled over those books for a good three hours. Bonnie knew some of Doug's classmates from West Point, but she knew almost nothing about his high school years. The photos from the yearbooks filled in some of those blanks. We saw Doug in his various sports uniforms; Doug as valedictorian of his class; Doug in a toga for the Latin Club's annual toga party; Doug in the National Honor Society. And as we examined those photos, a lasting friendship was formed. Bonnie Abney and I have been friends ever since.

During lunch she told me a little about how she met Doug on a blind date in Florida in the fall of 1965, after he graduated from West Point and before he went to Ranger school. She told how their short time together was inadvertently extended by the arrival of Hurricane Betsy. She told how lost and alone she had felt after he died. She told me of her marriage to someone else some six years later—a relationship that was not as successful as it had promised to be.

Bonnie's days with Doug have remained a treasured time in her life. I understand that. As a writer, I saw that happen with Beau in the aftermath of his torrid romance with Anne Corley. She shot through his life like a shooting star and then was gone as suddenly as she came. While after lots of years and many books Beau eventually found happiness with Mel Soames, Anne will always remain an indelible and important part of his life.

After our lunch together, Bonnie and I stayed in touch with Christmas cards and periodic short visits. After a career with the airlines, first as a flight attendant and later as director of training, she went on to write a book on management. Later she opened and ran her own management consulting agency, one that trained executives for major companies all over the globe. A few years ago she left Florida behind and retired to a place in the Pacific Northwest on Whidbey Island.

In the meantime, I was writing books, one after another. It was invisible to me, but between one Beaumont book and the next, a certain period of time would have elapsed both in fiction and in real life. Not only was I getting older, so was J.P. Last summer, as I prepared to write Beaumont #21, my son suggested that since Beau was getting a bit long in the tooth, perhaps it was time for me to consider writing a Beaumont prequel.

People often ask me where I get my ideas. They come from things people say to me and from things I read. According to my husband, ideas come into my head, where they undergo a kind of "Waring blender" transformation. When they come back out, leaking through my fingertips into the keyboard on the computer, the stories are different from how they went in.

The other thing about writing books is that they take more thinking than they do typing—approximately six hundred hours of the former and three hundred hours of the latter.

About six months ago now, I sat in my comfy writing chair in front of a burning gas log, wondering what on earth I was going to put into the next Beau book. In twenty previous books, written over a period of thirty years, Beau had evolved into a somewhat curmudgeonly old cuss, a guy with a pair of chronically bad knees, a somewhat younger wife, and a full panoply of coworkers, friends, and relations. The idea of seeing Beau at a younger age had some appeal, so I went back to *Until Proven Guilty,* Beaumont #1, and started reviewing his history.

I was halfway through that book, reading about his experiences with his dying mother, when I came upon the word "Vietnam." It was almost as if someone had flipped a switch in my head. Had Doug Davis lived and had Beaumont been real, the two of them would have been about the same age. They would have served in the same war. What was there to keep me from blending fact and fiction and having the two of them meet in Vietnam?

That very evening I wrote an e-mail to Bonnie Abney, telling her about my idea and asking for her help. She wrote back the next day, signing on for the project. The result of our collaboration is woven into the fabric of Beaumont #21, *Second Watch.*

Over the course of the next several months, Bonnie was kind enough to share with me the details of her life back then and of her life now. She allowed me access to some of the letters she received after Doug's death.

The sympathy notes came from fellow officers, some of whom had been classmates of Doug's at West Point, as well as from guys with whom he served in Vietnam. In the process, I began to gain some insight into the young man Doug Davis became after I lost sight of him.

As I first learned in Seattle Center, in the army, his given name, Leonard, held sway. The men he served with knew him not as Doug but as Lennie D. They told stories of his days in the 35th Infantry; about how he spent his spare time playing poker, writing letters, and reading. Several of them mentioned that one of his favorite books, one he read over and over from beginning to end, was William Shirer's *The Rise and Fall of the Third Reich*. Their notes revealed instances of his innate kindness and of his natural ability to lead his men. He was known for taking raw recruits and molding them into capable soldiers in a platoon that was considered one of the best. He was a smart and dedicated leader who was able to spout off plenty of colorful language when a dressing-down was required. Soldiers who found themselves taking heat from Lennie D. for some infraction or other never made the same mistake twice.

Through that correspondence, I learned about how Doug and three other officers from C Company, while sitting around a card table in their quarters and playing poker one day, heard a news report about how the Vietcong were supposedly a very superstitious lot, especially when it came to seeing the playing card the ace of spades.

The four second lieutenants embarked on a psychological warfare program in which they made a practice of leaving an ace of spades calling card with the body of every dead VC soldier. The problem with that, of course, was that each deck of cards contained only one ace of spades, and when it came to playing poker, fifty-one-card decks didn't really measure up. Eventually one of the four wrote to the card manufacturing company asking for help. The letter was forwarded to a company executive who had lost a son in World War II. The man was only too happy to oblige.

Within days, C Company had an ever-ready supply of decks of cards containing nothing *but* aces of spades. At first those special decks were shipped postage paid, only to C Company. As word spread, however, so did the program, as the card company continued to ship decks of aces of spades to other soldiers serving anywhere in the war zone. Remnants of that ace of spades tradition continue in the U.S. military to this day, including the Ace of Spades squadron based at Fairchild Air Force Base.

Doing research is the easy part of creating a book. Writing it means work.

Eventually, with all the Doug Davis material pulled into a master file, it was time for me to start the actual writing. In *Second Watch* we first meet Beau and his wife, Mel, as they head for Swedish Orthopedic Institute in Seattle, where Beau is scheduled to have dual knee-replacement surgery. While in the hospital and under the influence of powerful narcotics, he encounters a whole series of dreams that offer glimpses of his past. Through the dreams, Beau encounters and reviews former cases.

One of those, the first case he handled after his promotion to the homicide squad at Seattle PD, deals with the still-unsolved murder of a young girl, a University of Washington coed who was murdered in 1973. While

Beau is under the influence of postsurgical medications, Monica Wellington, the long-dead victim, wanders through a series of vivid dreams intent on giving him a piece of her mind. Monica may be dead, but she's disappointed with the fact that J. P. Beaumont failed to keep the promise he made to her mother long ago to bring the killer to justice. Jarred by his dream-prompted recollections and still laid up in the hospital, Beau determines to revisit Monica's case in hopes that new forensic technology may provide new answers.

By the end of August, the writing process for me was well under way. Eighty or so pages into the manuscript, in another drug-fueled dream sequence, a guy in Vietnam War vintage fatigues walks into Beau's hospital room, pulls out a deck of cards, and lays four aces of spades out on the bedside table.

The dreamscape Lennie D. is Doug Davis as Beau remembers him from their initial encounters in the latter part of July of 1966 when Beau first arrived in Vietnam and only days before the August 2 firefight that took Doug's life and earned him a Silver Star and a Purple Heart. I could remember Doug's engaging grin and his slouching stance from Mr. Guerra's classroom, but the other details that I wrote into the scene were drawn from my correspondence with Bonnie and with Lennie D.'s friends and fellow officers. I knew from Bonnie that he had chipped a front tooth in an automobile accident in Texas three weeks before his deployment, and that he had planned on having the tooth fixed once he was back home in the States.

The hospital scene finds Beau and Doug chatting together as though only days rather than nearly half a century had passed between meetings. As I wrote the dialogue, I found myself shedding real tears for the Doug Davis I had known and lost so very long ago. When the apparition Doug charges Beau with finding the unnamed woman to whom Doug was engaged at the time of his death, someone Beau knew nothing about, it struck me as an unlikely mission to be assigned to an ailing homicide cop so many years after the fact.

One of the things that puzzled me as the story continued was Beau's reticence to discuss the situation with anyone else, including his wife, Mel; his boss, Ross Connors; his son, Scott; or his best friend, Ron Peters. I couldn't understand why he was so closed-mouthed about it.

Sometimes, when I don't understand something that's going on with one of my characters, the only way for me to find answers is to keep writing, and that's what I did. During Beau's second encounter with his commanding officer in Vietnam, Lennie D. lends Beau a book to read, a sixteen-hundred-page copy of *The Rise and Fall of the Third Reich*. Not only does he lend Beau the book, he also urges him to read it, with a grinning warning that there will be a pop quiz once he finishes.

Days later, during the lethal firefight in which Lennie D. is killed, J. P. Beaumont's life is spared because the pages of that book, carried inside his shirt, were between him and the three pieces of shrapnel that would otherwise have taken his life. Beau credits the fact that he is still alive to Lennie D.'s kindness in lending him that book.

So why wasn't he talking about it? I still didn't understand.

By then it was early September and time for Bill and me to make our annual pilgrimage down to Ashland,

Oregon, to see the plays at the Oregon Shakespeare Festival. On the way back, I had agreed to do a book-signing event at the library in Lincoln City.

After the presentation, when most of the signing crowd had disappeared, a young Marine made his way over to my table and sat down in front of me. He told me his name was Rhys and explained that he had just come back from a three-mile run on the sandy beach as part of his rehab while he recovered from dual knee-replacement surgery. Having just written about Beau's dual knee replacement, I saw this as quite a coincidence, but when I looked at Rhys, he struck me as being far too young to need two new knees. That was before he told me about them.

I'm not sure if the incident occurred in Afghanistan or Iraq, but when Rhys was caught in a firefight, a copy of my book *Devil's Claw*, the first book of mine he ever read, happened to be between his knees and the bullets. The pages of the book absorbed enough of the impact that doctors were able to replace his knees rather than having to amputate both legs.

The story was so much like the scenario with Beau in my fictional work that it was jaw-dropping! I have yet to see the actual bullet-ridden book, but Rhys tells me he still has it and that when he locates it, he intends to show it to me.

Fueled by that story, I came home from Lincoln City determined to finish the book. As I continued writing and as Beau embarked on his mission for Lennie D., that of finding Doug's missing fiancée, what was going on became increasingly clear to me. Beau was walking around carrying a burden of guilt due to the fact that after he came home from the war, he had made no effort to reach out to Bonnie—to find her and comfort her in her loss.

Obviously that's not the whole story of *Second Watch*, but it's an integral part of it. As first Doug and then Bonnie came to life on the pages of the manuscript, I realized that I was living their love story with them, not as part of it, but as a caring observer, as someone who understood what they had shared and what they had lost. It was inspiring to see that all these years later, Bonnie is as true to her Douglas—she's the only one who calls him that—as she was on the day they met in the fall of 1965.

It's a heartbreaking story. It's a loving story. It's a story I'm honored to tell.

I wanted the world to know about Doug, the guy his army pals called Lennie D. I wanted people to know that he was one of the many unsung heroes of that terrible war, a guy who earned his Silver Star and his Purple Heart trying to save others. He was only one of the 58,000 who died. After Doug was gone, his younger brother, Blaine, who was my age, signed up and served in Vietnam as well. Blaine came home from the war as one of the walking wounded. The price their mother, Bena Cook, paid for her two brave sons is incalculable. The tragedy, of course, is that there are so many other families out there who paid similar prices with their own terrible losses, ones that often went ignored and have been swept under our country's carpet of forgetfulness.

In the process of honoring Doug and Bonnie, I ended up honoring the other six boys from Bisbee as well. All seven of their names are on a bronze plaque affixed to a slab of granite in front of Bisbee High School. They're the ones from our small town who went away to war and didn't make it home alive.

Bonnie and I worked together to get every snippet of Lennie D.'s subplot story straight. Last week we finished the manuscript, and I sent it to my editor in New York. This past weekend, one of the guys who was deployed to Vietnam with Doug, but who served in a different unit, sent an e-mail to Bonnie having heard of our efforts through another vet. He shared his memories of Doug and his sense of guilt for not reaching out to the family or to Bonnie in all these years.

This colleague's way of dealing with the tragedy of Doug's loss is almost a mirror image of J. P. Beaumont's. I was struck by the validation of Beau's feelings and actions, feelings and actions that puzzled me when I was writing them weeks earlier. Along with his e-mail, he sent a photo of Doug, one taken on July 31, 1966, only two days before he died. That photo is the one you see at the top of this story. The guy in the photo was the one I knew, all right, the antsy student standing in the center row of the Latin 2 class waiting for the bell to ring. I knew about the chipped tooth, but it was only in the photo that I saw it for the first time.

Through our efforts, we learned that Doug's West Point sword, once thought lost, was bequeathed by Doug's brother to the son of one of Doug's good friends, because that son is Doug's namesake.

I hope *Second Watch* does justice to Doug's memory and honors Bonnie for her enduring love as well as for her terrible loss. My readers are the ones who will make that final determination, and I'm sure they'll let me know. I hope that my personal gratitude for all those men and women who served, the ones who came back as well as the ones who didn't, shines through this story. I hope it encourages some of them to talk about their

own wartime experiences and bring out their own medals. They were heroes. We should have a chance to say
thank you. And if they neglected to reach out to someone in the past, it is not too late. That goes for the guys
from the Vietnam War, and for the ones from more recent wars as well, Rhys Emery included.

It is my fondest hope that sometime in the next few
months, some veteran reading this book, somebody
around Beau's age, maybe, or perhaps someone much
younger, will realize that he, too, failed to reach out
in a timely fashion to grieving loved ones who lost
someone. I hope Beau's story will resonate with him
enough that he will pick up his courage and find his
way to their doorsteps or to their telephones or to
their e-mail accounts and let them know that he is
sorry for their loss. Even though it may seem like a
long time ago to the rest of the world, I know that
those fathers and mothers, sweethearts and wives and
children are still grieving. They are still mourning
their losses, and it helps to know that they are not
alone and not forgotten.

Because it turns out, it's never too late to say you're
sorry.

Take another look at the photo. That grinning young
man you see there is the guy from Bisbee, the one from
my Latin 2 Class—Doug Davis, aka Lennie D., aka
Douglas. He was and is all of those people. This is the
photo that was taken in the Pleiku Highlands more than
forty years ago. It came to Bonnie from out of the blue all
this time later, just this past weekend, as a direct result of
our collaboration on this book. I can tell you for certain
that she regards being given that photo as a real blessing.

And so do I.

J. P. Beaumont may be an old homicide hand now, but back when he was a rookie working with his first partner, Milton Gurkey—a.k.a. Pickles—things took a turn for the worse ...

One day, at the end of Beaumont and Pickles's shift, a stop at the Doghouse restaurant quickly turns deadly.

Not feeling well, Pickles steps out into the parking lot for a breath of fresh air and stumbles into a crime in progress. He is found unconscious after a heart attack, with a dead woman on the ground nearby and the murder weapon in his hand.

With Pickles under investigation from Internal Affairs, it's up to Beaumont, the new kid on the block, to find out the truth.

Keep reading to join Beaumont as he works to clear his friend's reputation in the novella "Ring in the Dead."

It was New Year's Eve. Back when I was drinking, New Year's Eve was always a good excuse to tie one on, but now those bad old days were far in the past. Mel was out getting a late-breaking mani-pedi in advance of our surprise (to her) date to walk three blocks up First Avenue for an intimate dinner for two at El Gaucho. Our penthouse condo allows a great view of the Space Needle, three blocks away. That means, at midnight, we'd have ringside seats from the shelter of our bedroom balcony for the Needle's New Year's fireworks display. The weather still hadn't made up its mind if midnight revelers would be greeted by a light sprinkle or pouring rain. It was certain, however, that at least it wouldn't be snowing.

My wife, Mel Soames, and I both work for the Attorney General's Special Homicide Investigation Team, affectionately dubbed S.H.I.T. Yes, I know. The name is a running joke and has been for a very long time, but we've grown to like it over the years. In the brave new world of no-overtime, we both had plenty of comp time available to us, and we had chosen to take it over the holidays, including before and after Christmas. Use it or lose it, as they say.

So I was sitting in my den in solitary splendor, reviewing my life and times and considering a possible list of New Year's resolutions, when the phone rang—the landline, not my cell. Not only do we have a landline, we still have a listed number for it, although it's not one that comes readily to mind since that phone isn't the one I use on a daily basis.

The idea behind keeping a listed number is simple. Being in the directory makes it possible for the people I want to find me—fellow Beaver alums from Ballard High School, for example—to find me. As for the people I don't want finding me? For those—for the ones who want to sell me aluminum siding for my high-rise condo, I answer the phone with an icy, salesman-repelling voice that works equally as well on them and on others, like people making political robo-dials for their favorite candidates and the guys trying to convince me to sign up for the policemen's ball—which is a scam, by the way. For the most part, the spam-type calls come through with the originating number blocked. Those always go unanswered, and if they leave a message, those don't get picked up, either.

This particular call came with a caller ID name: Richard Nolan, and a 503 phone number that meant it was from somewhere in Oregon. Even so, I answered using my pissed-off, ditch-the-sales-pitch voice.

"Detective Beaumont?" a woman's voice asked.

I haven't been Detective Beaumont for years now—ever since I left Seattle PD. It doesn't mean, however, that I'm no longer that other person.

"I used to be," I said. "Who's asking?"

"My name's Anne Marie Nolan," she said. "I live in Portland, Oregon. Milton Gurkey was my father."

That took my breath away, and it also took me back. When I got promoted to Homicide from Patrol, Milton Gurkey, aka Pickles, was my first partner. We worked together for five years, starting in the spring of 1973. In fact, only months earlier, I had spent time dealing with our first case, which, prior to that, had gone unresolved for almost four decades. Pickles died in 1978. I had long since lost track of his widow, Anna.

"Pickles's daughter?" I replied. "Great to hear from you."

There was a distinct pause on the phone. "No matter how many times I hear it, I can never get used to the idea that that's what you guys all called my dad— Pickles. It seems disrespectful, somehow."

"Sorry," I mumbled. "I didn't mean any disrespect. For the guys who called him that, it was almost a term of endearment. How's your mother, by the way?"

Anne Marie sighed. "Mother passed away a month ago. She was in hospice up here in Seattle when news about that old Wellington case was in the papers. I read the articles to her. She was glad to know that somebody finally solved it. She said that was a case that haunted Daddy until the day he died."

"I'm sorry to hear about your mother," I said. "I wish I had known."

"You and my dad were partners a long time ago," Anne Marie said. "Mom remarried twice after Daddy died. The first guy was a loser who didn't hang around long. The second one, Dan, was great. He died two years ago. Mom took his name, Lawson, when they married, so it's not surprising that you wouldn't have gotten word about her death."

Anne Marie had given me a graceful out. Still, I couldn't help feeling remiss, as if I had been deliberately neglectful. A part of me was glad Anna Gurkey—clearly Anne Marie was her mother's namesake—had known about our finally solving the long cold Monica Wellington case before she died. That case was a loose end left hanging that Pickles and I had dragged around between us the whole time we worked together. Obviously, in the intervening years since Pickles's funeral, Anna Gurkey's life had continued just as mine had, with some good and some bad. Hers was over now, and I regretted that I hadn't made any effort to see her before she died.

"Anyway," Anne Marie continued, resuming her story, "I was here for several weeks while Mom was in hospice. Once she was gone, I had to go home and get caught up on things in Portland. That's where we . . ." She paused, seemed to catch herself, before going on with the story. "That's where I live now," she corrected. "I just left everything in Mother's house as is because I was at the end of my rope. I had expended every bit of energy I could muster, and I simply couldn't face sorting through all that crap by myself. I'm an only child, you see. At the time she died, Mom was still living in the house she and Daddy bought when they first got married, the one I was raised in.

"My mother wasn't a hoarder by any means," Anne Marie said, rushing on, "but she didn't throw much away. So I've spent all of Christmas vacation up here sorting through the house, getting ready for an estate sale that I'm planning on holding when the weather clears up in the spring. I'm on my way back to Portland now. I want to be back home before all the drunks hit the streets. The thing is, I found something down in the basement in a cedar chest that I thought you might want to see. I don't know where you are in the city, but I'd be happy to drop it off on my way south."

Pickles and Anna had lived at the north end of Ballard in an area called Blue Ridge. Depending on which route Anne Marie was going to take, she'd be within blocks of my Belltown Terrace condo on her way to I-5 and back out of town.

"I'm at Second and Broad," I said. "In downtown Seattle. You're welcome to stop by to visit."

"I was going to head out right away," she said. "I really don't have much time."

"How about at least stopping long enough for a cup of coffee, then?" I suggested.

"You're sure it's no trouble?"

"We have a machine. It's just a matter of pushing the button."

"All right then," she agreed.

"The building has a doorman," I told her. "Just pull up out front in the passenger loading zone. I'll come down, meet you, guide you into the parking garage, and let you into the elevator. You can't get into it from the garage without a key."

Once I put down the phone, I stood up and looked around. In the old days the room would have been awash in newspapers, including at least one section folded open to the crossword puzzle page. These days I do the crosswords on my iPad. I closed it up and put it away. Then, leaving the den and my comfortable recliner behind, I went out into the living room, closing the French doors behind me.

Since all the kids had been home for the holidays, the living room and dining room were still decorated for Christmas,. My daughter, Kelly, and son-in-law, Jeremy, had come up from southern Oregon with their two kids. My son, Scott, and his wife, Cherisse, had recently moved back to Seattle from the Bay Area, so we'd had an over-the-top Christmas celebration. Because we'd hired a friend, an interior designer, to come in and do the holiday decorating, the place looked spectacular. I hoped when it came time to put the decorations away, we'd manage to fit all of them back into our storeroom down in the building's basement.

On my way through the kitchen, I made sure the coffee machine was freshly supplied with water and beans. Then I went downstairs to the lobby to wait. I was sitting there, chatting with Bob, the doorman, when a woman in an aging Honda pulled up outside and honked. I went out through the front entrance to meet her. With the wind blowing and a driving rain falling, I was glad to have the building's protective canopy overhead as I hurried over to the car. She opened the passenger-side window.

"I'm Beau," I told her. "If you don't mind, I'll ride along and show you where to park."

There was a pause with me standing in the rain while she heaved a stack of assorted junk from the front seat to the back. That's what happens when you spend most of your driving time in a car all by yourself. The passenger seat morphs into a traveling storage locker.

Once Anne Marie had cleared the seat, I climbed in. By then I was wet, not quite through, but close enough. I directed her around the building on John, into the garage, and over to where the valet parking attendant stood waiting.

"Just leave your keys with him," I instructed.

"Where do I pay?" she asked.

"Don't worry about it," I told her. "I'll have him put it on my tab. They automatically bill me for guest parking at the end of the month."

I used my building key first to enter the elevator lobby, next to call the elevator, and finally to make it work. Once I had done so and punched the PH button, I caught the questioning look Anne Marie sent in my direction.

"Yes," I said in answer to her unasked question. "My wife, Mel, and I live in the penthouse."

It's a long elevator ride. About the time we passed the sixth floor, Anne Marie said, "I always thought your name was Jonas."

When Pickles and I first started working together, he had insisted on calling me by my given name, even though I much preferred being called Beau or J. P. He had come around eventually, but his family must not have gotten the memo.

"I don't much like my given name," I said. "Never have."

After that we fell silent until the elevator door slid open. The penthouse floor of Belltown Terrace is made up of only two units. I showed her to ours, opening and holding the door to let her inside. The attention of first-time visitors is always drawn straight through the dining room to the expanse of windows at the far end of the living room. The glass goes from the upholstered window seat to the crown molding on the ceiling and offers an unobstructed view of Puget Sound on the west and the grain terminal, Seattle Center, and Lower Queen Anne Hill on the north. In the middle of the north-facing windows sat our nine-foot Christmas tree glittering with its astonishing array of lights and decorations.

As I said, most of the time the views through those windows are spectacular with the generally snow-capped Olympic Mountains looming in the far distance. Today, however, in the lashing downpour, the view amounted to little more than variations on a theme of gray on gray. The point where pewter-colored clouds met the gunmetal gray water was somewhere beyond a heavy curtain of rain as a fast-moving storm cell came on shore.

"Sorry about the view," I said. "It's usually a little better than this."

I hoped the quip might help lighten my visitor's mood. It didn't. Her face had been set in a grim expression when I first climbed into her vehicle, and that didn't change. Instead, she stopped in the middle of the room and sent a second accusatory stare in my direction.

"If you were a cop, how did you get all this?"

I shrugged. "What can I say?" I quipped. "I married well."

That was the truth. Owning a penthouse suite in Belltown Terrace would never have been possible without the legacy left to me by my second wife,

Anne Corley. But my offhand comment about that did nothing to lighten Anne Marie's mood or change her disapproving expression either. She simply turned away and made a beeline for the window seat.

Anne Marie was a relatively tall woman, five-ten or so, squarely built, somewhere in her early fifties. Her graying hair was pulled back in a severe bun, and there was a distinctive hardness about her features that I thought I recognized. Between the time when I'd seen her last—as a teenager at her father's funeral—and now, the woman had done some hard living, and there was nothing in her demeanor to suggest that this was some kind of cheerful holiday visit.

Once Anne Marie sat down, I noticed that instead of putting her purse on the cushion beside her, she kept it on her lap, clutched tightly in her arms like a shield. I wasn't sure if she was holding on to it because it contained something precious or if she was using it as a barrier to help keep me at bay. I also noticed a light band of pale skin on her ring finger that intimated the relatively recent removal of a wedding ring.

If the poor woman's mother had just died and if her marriage was coming to an end at the same time, it was no wonder that Anne Marie Gurkey Nolan was a woman under emotional siege. I didn't comment on that deduction aloud, but I tried to take it into consideration as our conversation continued.

"What do you take in your coffee?" I asked.

"Nothing," she said. "Just black."

"Strong or not?" I asked. "My wife gave me a fancy coffee machine for Christmas. It makes individual cups of coffee, and we can adjust the strength for each one by turning the bean control lighter or darker."

"Strong, please," she said. "It's a long drive."

"I don't envy you making that drive in this weather," I commented as I walked away.

She nodded but said nothing.

I was aware of her watching me through the pass-through while I was in the kitchen, gathering coffee mugs; waiting for the beans to grind and the coffee to brew. I couldn't help wondering what this was all about. When I brought the coffee into the living room, she took the mug from the tray with one hand, but she still didn't relinquish her grip on the purse.

Since Anne Marie was clearly so ill at ease, I made no attempt to join her on the window seat. Instead, I sat in one of the armchairs facing her. Hoping to make things better for her, I bumbled along, doing my best to carry on some semblance of polite conversation. In that regard, I was missing Mel in the worst way. She can always smooth out the kinds of difficult situations that turn me into a conversational train wreck.

"I'm so sorry to hear about your mother," I said regretfully. "I'm afraid I lost track of her after your father died."

"I'm not surprised," Anne Marie replied. "Once Daddy was gone, Mother didn't want to have anything to do with Seattle PD."

"Had she been ill long?"

Anne Marie took a tentative sip of coffee and shook her head. "She had a bout with breast cancer several years ago, but she responded well to the treatment. Her doctors said she was in remission. When she got sick again, we thought at first that the breast cancer had returned. It turns out it was a different kind of cancer altogether—pancreatic—and there was nothing anybody could do."

"Losing your mother is always tough," I said.

Anne Marie gave me a challenging look, as though she suspected I had no real understanding of her situation. I could have told her that I had lost my own mother to cancer when I was in my early twenties and much younger than she was now, but I didn't. Still hoping to be a good host, I tried changing the subject, only to land squarely on yet another painful topic.

"I guess the last time I saw you was at your father's funeral."

Anne Marie nodded. "I was only a sophomore in college when Daddy died. I've always hated funerals," she added. "Mother did, too. She told me she wanted to be cremated, and she stated in writing that she didn't want any kind of service. She probably did that for my sake because she knew how much funerals bother me."

My bouncing unerringly from one loaded topic to another didn't do much for putting Anne Marie at ease. Still, it must have worked up to a point, because after a brief pause she pressed forward with the real purpose of her visit.

She straightened her shoulders and took a deep breath before saying, "Mother always blamed you for Daddy's death. So did I."

I was hard-pressed to summon a suitable response for that. I remembered the day Pickles Gurkey died like it was yesterday—in the middle of the afternoon on a rainy Monday. Pickles and I had just placed a homicide suspect under arrest. The guy had turned violent on us, and it had taken both Pickles and me to subdue him. The suspect was in cuffs and safely in the back of the car, when Pickles had suddenly staggered and fallen. At first I thought he'd been punched in the gut or something during the fight, but I soon realized the situation was far worse than that. He'd already had one heart attack by then, and here we were five years later with the same thing happening When I realized this was a second attack—and a massive one at that—I immediately called for help. Seattle's Medic 1 was Johnny-on-the spot just as they had been the first time around. On this occasion, however, there was nothing they could do; nothing anybody could do.

"I'm sorry," I said. "I did everything I could . . ."

Anne Marie waved aside my attempted apology. "I'm not talking about what you did that day," she said brusquely. "Not when Daddy had his second heart attack. Mother and I blamed you because he went back to work after the first one."

What can you say to something like that? Pickles was a grown man, and grown men get to make their own decisions. We were partners, but I didn't make him come back to work. He wanted to. He insisted on it, in fact, but that was all ancient history. That first had happened back in 1973, almost forty years ago. Even if it had been my fault, what was the point in Anne Marie's bringing it up now? Since I had nothing more to say, I kept quiet. For the better part of a minute an uneasy silence filled the room.

"I'm in a twelve-step program," she explained finally. "Narcotics Anonymous. Do you know anything about them?"

I smiled at that. "Unfortunately I have more than a passing acquaintance as far as twelve steps go," I said. "I'm more into AA than NA, if you know the drill."

Anne Marie nodded. "So I suppose this is what you'd call an eighth step call."

The eighth step in AA and NA is all about making amends to the people we may have harmed. At that moment, I couldn't imagine any reason why Anne Marie Gurkey Nolan would possibly need to make amends to me, but then she continued.

"I did the same thing," she said. "Like Mom, I blamed you. As far as we were concerned, you were the reason Daddy died because you were also the reason he stayed on the job. This week, I found this and discovered we were wrong."

She opened her purse and pulled out a manila envelope. When she handed it over, I could tell from the heft of it that the envelope contained several sheets of paper.

"What is it?" I asked.

"These are some of Daddy's papers. He always said that after he retired, he was going to write a book. Since he never retired, he never completed the book, either, but on his days off, he was always down in the basement, pounding away on an old Smith Corona typewriter. This is the chapter he wrote about you. I thought you might want to see it.

"It was while I was reading this that I finally realized you weren't the reason Daddy kept working. He did it because he was worried about money and about what would happen to Mother if he died. It turns out he had been working a case where some old guy murdered his ailing wife and then took his own life for the same reason—because he didn't think there would be enough money to take care of his widow after he was gone. Daddy wanted to work as long as he could so he could be sure Mother and I wouldn't be left stranded."

I vaguely remembered the case Anne Marie had mentioned, but at that very moment I couldn't recall the exact details or even the names of either victim. What I did remember was that case was the first combination murder-suicide I ever worked. Unfortunately it wasn't the last.

A few minutes later, Anne Marie finished her coffee and abruptly took her leave. After showing her out, I returned to the window seat in the living room, with a brand-new cup of coffee in hand. That's when I finally opened the envelope and removed the yellowing stack of onionskin paper. The keys on the typewriter Pickles had used had been worn and/or broken. Some of the letters in the old-fashioned font had empty spots in them. The ribbon had most likely been far beyond its recommended usage limits as well. The result was something so faded and blurry that it was almost impossible to read.

I expected the piece would focus on the murder-suicide Anne Marie had mentioned earlier. To my surprise, it began with the day Pickles and I first became partners.

It was a big shock to my system to come back from my wife's family reunion in Wisconsin to find out that a new partner had been dropped in my lap. As soon as I clocked in, Captain Tompkins dragged me into the Fishbowl, the glass-plated Public Safety Building's fifth-floor office from which he rules his fiefdom, Seattle PD's Homicide Unit, with a bull-nosed attitude and an iron fist. The powers-that-be are trying to discourage smoking inside the building, but Tommy isn't taking that edict lying down. He smokes thick, evil-smelling cigars that stink to the high heavens. For my money, pipe smoke isn't nearly as bad, but Tommy says pipes are too damned prissy. Prissy is one thing Captain Tompkins is not.

Because he smokes constantly and usually keeps the door to the Fishbowl tightly closed, stepping inside his office is like walking into the kind of smoke-filled room where political wheeling and dealing supposedly gets done. Come to think of it, as far as his office is concerned, that's not as far off the beam as you might think.

As soon as I took a seat in front of Tommy's desk, he slid a file folder across the surface in my direction. There was enough force behind his shove that the file spun off the edge of the desk, spilling the contents and sending loose papers flying six ways to Sunday.

"What's this?" I asked, leaning down to retrieve the scattered bits and pieces. I didn't look at the file folder itself again until I straightened up and had stuffed everything back inside. That's when I saw the name on the outside: Beaumont, Jonas Piedmont.

"Your new partner," Tommy said, leaning back in his chair and blowing a series of smoke rings into the air.

He's a hefty kind of guy, with a wide, flushed face and a bulging, vein-marked nose that hints of too much booze. Sit-

ting there with his jacket off and his tie open at the base of a thick neck, he gazed at me appraisingly through a pair of beady eyes. Looking at him, you might think he'd be clumsy and slow on his feet. You'd be wrong. After years of working for the man, I'm smart enough not to make that mistake. Guys who do don't last long.

"What's this about a new partner?" I asked. "What happened to Eddy?"

Tommy blew another smoke ring and jerked his head to one side. "Guess he finally gathered up enough brown-nosing points to get kicked upstairs," he answered.

Eddy Burnside had been my partner for three years. We got along all right, I guess, but there was no love lost between us, and Eddy's brown-nosing was the least of it. I didn't trust the guy any further than I could throw him, which, in my mind, made him a perfect candidate to move up the ladder. Get him the hell off the streets. If he's upstairs making policy, at least he won't be out in public getting people killed. So even though Eddy was your basic dud for a partner, being stuck with a brand-new detective to wean off his mama's tits and potty-train isn't exactly my idea of a good time, either.

"What the hell kind of a name is Jonas?" I asked.

Calling out someone on account of his name puts me on pretty thin ice. Milton is the name my mother gave me. It's a good biblical name, after all, so I don't have a quarrel with it. Milton may be the name on my badge, but that's not what people call me. I don't know what my father's people were called in the old country, but when they came through Ellis Island, the last name got changed to Gurkey. That word bears only the smallest resemblance to the word "gherkin," one of those little sour pickles my mother and grandmother used to make. But Gurkey and gherkin sounded enough alike that the kids at school and later the guys at the police academy dubbed me Pickles. My family never called me that, but at school and work, that's who I've always been—Pickles Gurkey.

In other words, between me and this Jonas guy, I didn't have a lot of room to talk.

I took a few seconds and scanned through some of the papers in the folder. This Beaumont guy's job application said he was a U-Dub graduate who had done a stint in the military. That probably meant a tour of duty in Vietnam.

"You're sticking me with a college Joe?" I demanded. "Criminal justice? Are you kidding? What does a pack of college professors know about criminals or justice, either one?"

Captain Tompkins listened to my rant and said nothing.

"That's just what I need," I continued. "Some smart-assed kid who probably thinks that, since he's got a degree behind his name, he can run circles around someone like me. All I've got to brag about is my diploma from Garfield High School. Thanks a whole helluva lot. How'd I get so lucky?"

Tommy blew another cloud of smoke before he answered. "He's not brand-new," he assured me. "Beaumont spent a couple of years on Patrol before they shipped him up here last week. Since you were out of town, he's been working with Larry Powell and Watty Watkins on that dead girl they found over on Magnolia."

"The Girl in the Barrel?" I asked.

The kid who delivers our home newspaper lives next door. Rather than turning our subscription off while we were out of town on vacation, Anna and I had him hold our papers. When we got home from Wisconsin on Friday night, the kid had brought them over, and we'd both gone through the stack.

Anna cut out all the coupons she wanted, and I read all the news, just to bring myself back up to speed.

Doing a balancing act to keep from dribbling ashes all over his desk, Tommy managed to park his stogie on the edge of a large marble ashtray that was already overfilled with cigar butts and ashes. I'm sure the cleaning people love dealing with his mess every night.

"That's the one," he said. "As for how you got him? You're the only guy on the fifth floor without a living/breathing partner at the moment. That means your number's up, like it or lump it."

If Tommy had wanted to, I knew he could have moved people around so I wouldn't have been stuck with the new guy, but there was no point in arguing. If I couldn't get Tompkins to change his mind about assigning the new guy to me, maybe I could figure out a way to change the new guy's mind about wanting to be a detective. That was the simplest way to fix the problem—convince the new detective that what he wanted more than anything was to be an ex-detective.

"So where is he?" I asked.

"Probably in your cubicle, writing up his first report. Everybody else was tied up with that serial killer workshop this past weekend, so Beaumont ended up going to the girl's funeral up in Leavenworth."

"He went to the funeral by himself?" I asked. "Who was the genius who decided that was a good idea? Shouldn't an experienced detective have handled it?"

Tommy shrugged. "Didn't have a choice. Everybody else had paid to go to the FBI workshop. I figured, how bad could it be? But you might want to look over his paper before he hands it in."

"Great," I sputtered. "Now I'm supposed to haul out a red pencil and correct his spelling and grammar?"

"That's right," Tommy said with wink and a knowing smirk. "If I were you, I'd make sure his report is one hundred percent perfect. Doing it over a time or two or three will be great practice for him, and marking him down will be good for whatever's ailing you at the moment. Go give him hell."

Dismissed, I left the smoky haze of the Fishbowl, doing a slow burn. Next to Larry Powell and Watty, I was one of the most senior guys on the squad. It made no sense to stick me with a newbie who would do nothing but hold me back. Rather than go straight to my cubicle, I beat a path to Larry and Watty's.

"Gee, thanks," I said, standing in the entrance to their five-foot-by-five-foot cell. Which brings me to something else that provokes me to no end. How come prisoners get more room in their cells than we do in our offices? What's fair about that?

"For what?" Larry asked.

"For giving me the new guy."

"He's not brand-new," Larry advised. "We've had to hold his hand for the better part of a week before you came back, so quit your gritching. Besides, you were new once, too."

"Sure you were," Watty said with a grin. "Back when Noah was building that ark, or maybe was it even earlier, back when dinosaurs still roamed the earth?"

"Funny," I grumbled. "So how did he go about getting moved up from Patrol? The last I heard, the word was out that there weren't any openings in Homicide."

"There weren't until Eddy got promoted," Watty said, "but I've heard some talk from other people about this, too. Beaumont's former partner from Patrol, Rory MacPherson, was angling to get into Motorcycles. Beaumont wanted Homicide. A week ago Sunday, the two of them took a dead body call. The next thing you know, voilà! Like magic, they both get the promotions they wanted."

"In other words, something stinks to the high heavens. Are you telling me my new partner is also some bigwig's fair-haired boy?"

"Can't say for sure, but it could be," Larry Powell allowed.

"Sure as hell doesn't make me like him any better."

Unable to delay the inevitable any longer, I stomped off and headed for my lair. As I approached my little corner of Homicide, I heard the sound of someone pounding the hell out of our old Underwood. My mother did me a whale of a favor by insisting I take touch typing in high school. When it comes to writing reports, being able to use all my fingers is a huge help. Obviously this guy's mother hadn't been that smart. Jonas Beaumont was your basic two-fingered typist, plugging away one slow letter key at a time. When I paused in the entrance, he was frowning at the form in the machine with such purpose and concentration that he didn't see me standing there. I noticed right off that he was sitting in the wrong chair.

"I'm Detective Gurkey, your new partner," I announced by way of introduction. "The desk you're using happens to be mine."

He glanced up at me in surprise. "They told me to use this cubicle," he said. "This is the desk that was empty."

"Maybe so," I told him, "but that was Eddy's desk. He was senior, and he had the window. Eddy's gone now. I'm senior. You're junior. I get the window."

Admittedly, the view from the window is crap. Still, a window is a window. It's a status symbol kind of thing.

"Sorry," he mumbled. "Just let me finish this."

"No," I replied. "I don't think you understand. Like I said, I'm senior. You're junior. That means I don't stand around in the hallway waiting while you get your act together, clear your lazy butt out of my chair, and clean your collection of crap off

my desk. Once your stuff is gone, I move into this one. Just because Watty held your hand and treated you with kid gloves all last week doesn't mean I'm going to. Got it?"

"Got it," he answered promptly, pushing his chair away from the desk. "Right away."

I knew I was being a first-class jerk, but that was the whole idea. I wanted the guy gone, and making him miserable was the fastest way to get that job accomplished. I stood there tapping my foot with impatience while he gathered up his coat from the chair and emptied everything he had carefully loaded into Eddy's empty desk drawers back out onto the top of the desk. After that I took my own sweet time about moving my stuff from one desk to the other. I could tell he was steaming about it while he had to wait, but I didn't let on that I noticed. After all, this was one pissing match I was determined to win.

I left him cooling his heels until I was almost done sorting, then I sent him for coffee. "Two creams, three sugars, and no lectures," I told him. "I get nutritional advice from my wife. I don't need any from you. And if you want coffee for yourself, you'd better get it now. Once we start hitting the bricks, we won't be stopping for coffee and doughnuts. This is Homicide, Jonah; it's not Patrol."

The Jonah bit was a deliberate tweak, and he lunged for the bait.

"Jonas," he corrected. "The name's Jonas, but my friends call me either J. P. or Beau."

"I'm your partner not your friend," I told him. "That means Jonas it is for the foreseeable future."

"Right," he muttered. Then he stalked off to get coffee.

While he was gone, I took it upon myself to read and edit his report. By the time he got back, I had used a red pen to good effect, marking it up like crazy. It turned out Tommy

Tompkins was right. Correcting Detective Beaumont's work made me feel better. When Jonas came back with the coffees, I handed him the form.

"Not good enough," I told him. "Not nearly good enough, especially considering you're a hotshot college graduate. Take another crack at this while I find out what we're supposed to be doing today."

I left him there working on that and went looking for the murder book on the Girl in the Barrel. Tommy had told me that until Jonas and I caught a new case of our own, we'd be doubling up with Larry and Watty Watkins on their ongoing case. I spent some time reviewing the murder book entries. The body of the victim, a girl named Monica Wellington, had been found on Sunday afternoon a week and a day earlier. Beaumont and his Patrol partner, Rory MacPherson, had responded to the 911 call. In the intervening days, Larry and Watty, with Beaumont along for the ride, had done a whole series of initial interviews. The autopsy had revealed that the victim was pregnant at the time of her death, but so far no boyfriend had surfaced.

By the time I'd scanned through the murder book, Jonas had finished the second go-down on his report. He ripped it out of the typewriter, handed it over, and then stood behind me, watching over my shoulder, as I read through it. Unfortunately, there wasn't a damned thing wrong with it.

"I suppose this'll do," I told him dismissively. "Now go down to Motor Pool and get us a car. It's time to hit the road."

And we did, driving all over hell and gone with him at the wheel, doing follow-up interviews with all the people who had been spoken to earlier. Follow-ups aren't fun, by the way. Initial interviews are the real meat and potatoes of the job. The only thing fun about follow-ups is catching people in the lies that they made up on the run the first time around.

Turns out we found nothing—not a damned thing. I was hoping to pull off some little piece of investigative magic to garner some respect and put the new guy in his place, but that didn't happen. Nobody did a Perry Mason–style confession in our presence. We didn't discover some amazing bit of missing evidence. In fact, we never did solve that particular case. We worked it off and on for a couple of years and finally got shunted away from it entirely.

All this is to say, it wasn't a great start for a partnership. In fact, I'd call it downright grim. I kept the pressure on him, expecting him to go crying to whoever it was who had pulled the strings to move him to Homicide, but that didn't happen, either. He was a smart enough guy who tended to go off half-cocked on occasion.

If he was the hare, I was the tortoise. Jonas had good instincts but he was impatient and wanted to sidestep rules and procedures. I pounded down that tendency every chance I could—made him go through channels, across desks, and up the chain of command. The truth is that with enough practice, he started to get pretty good at it.

I could tell early on that he hit the sauce too much. He and his wife had a couple of little kids at home, and I think they squabbled a lot. I don't mean that the kids squabbled—Jonas and his wife did. I know her name but it's slipped my mind at the moment. It's that old familiar story—the young cop works too hard and can't put the job away when he gets home. Meanwhile the wife is stuck handling everything on the home front. In other words, I understood it, because those were issues Anna and I had put to bed a long time ago, but like I told him that first day, I didn't want any advice on nutrition from him, and I figured he didn't need any marital counseling from me. Fair is fair.

We worked together for several months before the night in

early July when everything changed and when our working together morphed from an enforced assignment into a real partnership.

It was an odd week, with the Fourth of July celebration falling on a Wednesday. Jonas and I were at the range doing target practice when we got a call out on the sad case of what, pending autopsies, was being considered murder-suicide. The previous Wednesday, an old guy over in Ballard, a ninety-three-year-old named Farley Woodfield, who had just been given a dire cancer diagnosis, went home from his doctor's office, grabbed his gun, loaded it, and then took out his bedridden wife, the woman for whom he was the primary caregiver. After shooting her dead, he had turned the weapon on himself. Several days after the shootings, the Woodfields' mailman had stepped onto their front porch to deliver a package and had noticed what he termed a "foul odor."

The word "foul" doesn't cover it. Like I said, it was July. The house had been closed up tight. I had been feeling punk over the weekend with something that felt like maybe a summer cold or a case of the flu. I wasn't sick enough to stay home from work, but I can tell you that being called to that ugly crime scene didn't help whatever was ailing me. We found Farley's note on the kitchen table: "With me gone, there goes the pension. Jenny will have nothing to live on and no one to look after her. I can't do that to her. I won't. Sorry for the mess."

He was right about the mess part. It was god-awful. Seeing the crime scene and the note made it clear what had happened, but when you're a homicide detective, that doesn't mean you just fill in the boxes on the report form and call it a job. Once the bodies were transported, Jonas and I spent the day canvassing the neighborhood, talking to people who had lived next to the old couple. From one of the neighbors, we learned that there was a daughter who lived in St. Louis, but there had been some kind of family estrangement, and the daughter had been out of her parents' lives for years.

As for the neighbors? None of them had paid the least bit of attention to the newspapers piling up on the front porch. None of them had noticed that Farley wasn't out puttering in his yard or that the grass he always kept immaculately trimmed with an old-fashioned push mower was getting too long to cut. By the end of the day, I was mad as hell at the neighbors, because I could see that the old guy had a point. With the couple's only child out of the picture, and if Farley wasn't going to be there to look after his wife, who was going to do it? Nobody, that's who!

We had taken the Woodfield call about eleven o'clock in the morning, and it was almost eight o'clock that night when we headed back downtown to file our reports. As usual, Jonas was at the wheel. We were driving east on Denny. When I suggested we take a detour past the Doghouse to grab a bite to eat, he didn't voice any objections. Instead of heading down Second Avenue, he stayed on Denny until we got to Seventh.

The Doghouse is a Seattle institution, started in the thirties by a friend of mine named Bob Murray. It used to be on Denny, but in the early fifties, when the city opened the Battery Street Tunnel to take traffic from the Alaskan Way Viaduct onto Aurora Avenue North, the change in driving patterns adversely affected the restaurant's business. Undaunted, Bob pulled up stakes and moved the joint a few blocks away to a building on Seventh at Battery. The Doghouse has been there ever since. It's one of those places that's open twenty-four hours a day and where you can get breakfast at any hour of the day or night.

It's no surprise that cops go there. In the preceding months,

Jonas and I had been to the Doghouse together on plenty of occasions, grabbing one of the booths that lined the sides of the main dining room. This time, though, when Bob tried to lead us to a booth, I could see we were headed for Lulu McCaffey's station. That's when I called a halt.

Lulu was one of those know-it-all waitresses who was older than dirt. One of the original servers who had made the transition from the "old" Doghouse to the "new" one twenty years earlier, she always acted like she owned the place. Unfortunately and more to the point, this opinionated battle-axe also bore a strong resemblance to my recently departed mother-in-law.

Years ago, I had made the mistake of wising off in front of Lulu. She got even with me by spilling a whole glass of ice water down the front of my menu and into my lap. Ever since, I avoided her station whenever possible. This day in particular, I wasn't prepared to deal with any of her guff, so I asked Bob if we could be seated in the back room.

It turns out that as far as the Doghouse was concerned, Jonas was a back room virgin. There are plenty of restaurant back rooms in Seattle—at the Doghouse, Rosellini's, Vito's, and the Dragon's Head. It's no surprise that many of the people who congregate in those back rooms and play the occasional game of poker are local cops and elected officials who want to keep up appearances as far as the voting public is concerned.

The back room is where Bob delivered us, safely out of Lulu's territory and firing range.

We both ordered burgers.

While we were busy, I had more or less forgotten that I wasn't feeling up to snuff, but sitting still, drinking iced tea, and waiting for our food, it started coming back. The worse I felt, the more I kept remembering everything about that ugly crime scene in Ballard. Farley Woodfield was evidently a World War I vet. There was a framed photo montage hanging over the fireplace. It included several photos of him—a sweet-faced young kid—posing manfully in his brand-new doughboy uniform. The faded cloth matting around the photos was decorated with a collection of miscellaneous pieces that included faded battle ribbons, tarnished medals, and a distinctive sergeant's chevron.

Just thinking about it hit me hard. Here was a poor guy who had given up his youth to go to war and serve his country. Now, seventy years later, he had been left to his own devices with no one to help him or to watch his back.

Our food came. Jonas dove into his; I pushed mine away.

"What's wrong?" he asked.

"Nothing," I said, because I didn't want to talk about what I was thinking. "I need to take a piss is all."

I left the table and the back room, but despite what I'd said, I didn't head for the rest room. I wanted to clear my head, so I went outside and walked around the parking lot for a few minutes. I was thinking about the old guy and wondering what I'd do if I was in his position. If I were gone, would my pension be enough for Anna to be able to get by? If something went wrong with her health, would our daughter come through and take care of her if I wasn't able to do it?

Somewhere along the way, I realized that my arm was hurting—aching like crazy. I kept wondering how I had managed to hurt it that badly without noticing anything had happened. It was hot as hell outside. Even though it was close to nine at night, it wasn't dark outside yet, and it sure as hell wasn't cool. Pretty soon I started feeling light-headed. I went over and stood by the building so I could lean against the wall. That's when all hell broke loose. Two guys came charging out of the restaurant and through the parking lot with Lulu chasing after them, screaming like a banshee.

"You come back here!" she screeched, waving a small piece of paper in the air. "You think you can just walk out on your check, you worthless turds? You think your food's coming out of my paycheck?"

The problem was, as soon as Lulu screamed at them, the two men stopped running and turned on her. At that point, I don't think any of them had seen me, but I saw them. The one guy grabbed Lulu by the arm and swung her around, sending her crashing head first into the trunk of a parked car. That's when things went into slow motion for me. It looked like the other guy was closing in on her. Pushing off from the wall, I drew my Smith & Wesson.

"Okay, you guys," I ordered. "I'm a police officer. Let her go. Get your hands in the air."

Surprised, they all three turned to gawk at me. That's when my body just stopped working, starting with my arm and fingers. The gun fell to the ground and went spinning uselessly away from me across the pavement. I couldn't move and I couldn't breathe because of the crushing pain in my chest. Even while it was happening, I realized I had to be having a heart attack. I had my wits about me enough that I took a step or two back toward the building so that if I fell, I could slide down the wall instead of falling flat on my face or whacking the back of my head on the pavement.

I remember seeing the three other people in the parking lot, standing there frozen in time, staring at me. The one guy was still hanging on to Lulu's arm. Lulu's mouth was open, like she was still screaming although I no longer heard any sound. Her face was red with fury. I more than half expected her to turn around and plant her fist in her attacker's face, but then he dropped out of sight and disappeared from my line of vision for a moment. A second or so later the look on Lulu's face changed. Her eyes widened. In that moment the expression on her face went from utter fury to abject fear. A gun must have gone off then although I don't remember hearing that, either. I saw the blood spray out behind her, saw Lulu stagger backward a step or two, then I blacked out.

When I came to, Jonas was squatting beside me and yelling in my ear. "Pickles! Can you hear me? The ambulance is on its way. What the hell happened?"

He didn't need to tell me about the ambulance. With my hearing back, I could hear the approaching sirens. They were already, in the background, muffled in a load of cotton, but coming closer fast.

"Two guys," I managed. "Lulu. Is she . . . ?"

Jonas shook his head. "She didn't make it," he said. "She's dead. What the hell happened here?"

He reached down then. Putting a pen through the trigger guard of my .38, he carefully pulled the weapon out of my lap and laid it aside, just beyond my reach. I remember wondering: How the hell did my gun get there? But then I figured it out. The guy who shot Lulu must have put it there. A dead woman, my weapon, and my fingerprints. I was screwed.

"There were two guys," I said, gasping around the awful pain in my chest. "They must have taken off. You've got to find them."

"Were they on foot or in a car?"

"On foot, I think. Didn't see a car."

That's the thing. The gun was there in my lap. The assailants were long gone. Jonas knew I hated Lulu's guts, and yet he never doubted me, not for an instant.

"Okay," he said. "Will do, but first I've got to talk to Bob Murray."

A Medic 1 guy appeared over Jonas's shoulder and bodily booted him out of the way. The last thing I remember, as the attendants loaded me onto a gurney, was Jonas striding purposefully back into the restaurant, notebook in hand.

I had other things to think about that night—like living or dying.

I stopped reading for a moment, thrown back into that terrible parking lot scene at the Doghouse.

As suddenly as if it were yesterday, it all came crashing back. As soon as Bob Murray told me shots had been fired, I charged out the restaurant's back door, with him at my heels. Out in the parking lot the smell of burned cordite still lingered in the hot, still air. I found Lulu McCaffey's bloody body lying sprawled on the pavement between cars. A green bit of paper that I recognized as the check from someone's table was still clutched in her hand. I checked her pulse first. Finding none and thinking my partner had been shot, too, I turned to Pickles. By then, Bob Murray had raced back inside to call 911.

Pickles was a few feet away from Lulu, slouched against the building. Kneeling next to him, I looked for a wound of some kind, but there wasn't any. Whatever had happened to Pickles, he hadn't been shot. But I did find his gun and I could tell it had been recently fired. He kept trying to talk to me, but all I could make out from his mumble was that there had been two guys and they had taken off on foot.

I knew that if Pickles had taken a potshot at the two

fleeing bad guys, there was going to be hell to pay, and I didn't want my fingerprints anywhere on the gun. I used a pen to ease his Smith & Wesson out of his lap and set it down on the pavement. He kept trying to talk to me, but most of what he said was too garbled to understand. Eventually the Medic 1 guys showed up. At the time, Seattle had bragging rights because Medic 1's still relatively new presence in the city had made Seattle the best place in the world to have a heart attack. By the time the ambulance showed up, I was pretty sure that's what we were up against—a heart attack.

As soon as the EMTs took over, I heard the sounds of arriving patrol cars converging on the area. I grabbed an evidence bag from the back of our unmarked car, deposited the gun in that, pocketed both, and hurried back into the restaurant. From the way Pickles looked, I was convinced he was a goner. If his death occurred while he was interrupting someone in the process of committing a crime, that meant that whoever had gunned down Lulu McCaffey would be guilty of two counts of homicide—both his and hers—rather than just one.

Bob Murray was a smart guy. He had come to the same conclusions I had—that the two guys who had skipped out on paying their tab had committed cold-blooded murder in his parking lot. Using chairs from the dining room, he had cordoned off both Lulu's station and the booth where the dine-and-dash bad guys had been sitting. Although the rest of the restaurant had somehow managed to return to some semblance of business as usual, Bob had made sure that none of the tables in Lulu's section had been cleared. He was personally standing guard to see to it that no one ventured anywhere near them.

"Did you see the two guys?" I asked him. "Can you give me any kind of description to pass along to the guys on patrol?"

Bob shook his head. "I was in the kitchen when they came in. Lulu seated them and served them, so she's really the only employee who saw them." He handed me a piece of paper. On it were scribbled several names and phone numbers, written in several distinctly separate styles of handwriting.

"Who are these?" I asked.

"They're the people who were seated at nearby tables," he told me. "I had them write down their names and phone numbers in case you need to get back to them."

"Any of them still here?"

Bob nodded, but his customary grin was missing in action. "All of them," he answered. "I sent them to the bar and told them to have one on me while they wait."

See there? I told you Bob Murray was a smart guy.

I glanced over at the booth. "Nobody's touched it?"

"Nope," he said. "And I aim to keep it that way."

"Great," I said. "When the detectives get here, be sure they get prints off everything. It's hard to find a suspect from an unknown print like that, but once we get the bad guys, having their prints in the system will help put them at the scene of the crime."

"You got it," Bob told me. "I'll see to it."

In the bar, the organ that usually filled the place with sing-along music far into the night was notably silent. The organist was there, but he was sitting alone at the bar quietly having a beer. With Lulu's body still in the parking lot, it wasn't at all surprising that nobody felt like singing. In the darkened room, seated against the far wall at four separate tables, were the other eight people who had been seated in Lulu's station at the time all hell broke loose. Still shocked by what had happened, they huddled together in a subdued group, nursing their drinks and their fear.

Milton Gurkey was my partner. Whether Pickles lived or died, I understood this wouldn't be my case to investigate. Someone else would be doing in-depth interviews of all the potential witnesses, including talking to the poor people currently sheltering in the bar of the Doghouse. All I wanted from them right that moment was a general description of the two suspects—something I could give to the guys out on the streets in patrol cars so officers in the area could be on the lookout for them.

What I ended up with was certainly vague enough. Two guys: one about six feet tall, the other a little shorter. The taller of the two was light-complected with dirty blond hair and maybe/maybe not a mustache. He was wearing yellow and brown plaid Bermuda shorts, a white T-shirt, and tennis shoes with no socks. The other guy, five-ten or so, was both shorter and heavier. He had olive skin—maybe Hispanic. He wore jeans, tennis shoes, and a blue plaid shirt. In other words, neither of these guys were fashion plates, but with the seasonably hot weather, their costumes wouldn't give them away, either, not the way sweatshirts or parkas would have.

By the time I went back outside, the response to

the incident made for mayhem on the street. Although the ambulance had already taken off, there were still fire trucks and plenty of patrol cars, marked and unmarked, in attendance. I tracked down the patrol sergeant and gave him what I had gleaned as far as descriptions were concerned. Having done what I could, I drove to Harborview Hospital, where I planted myself in the waiting room of the ER and waited for word on whether or not Pickles Gurkey was going to make it.

I was there when a sergeant from Patrol brought Anna Gurkey to the hospital and dropped her off. Previously, I had never met the woman, but I knew who she was when she walked up to the admitting desk and asked the clerk about her husband, Milton Gurkey. Whatever was going on with the patient right then, he wasn't being allowed visitors. Having been given that information, Anna retreated to one of the straight-backed chairs lining the room. As soon as she was seated, I went up and introduced myself.

Anna Gurkey looked liked she might have stepped out of the movie version of *The Sound of Music*. She reminded me of the homely woman who keeps bobbing and nodding to the sounds of applause when her group is given its second place award in the talent contest. In other words, Anna wasn't a beauty-queen showstopper. She had a broad face with rough, reddish skin. Her dingy, graying hair was pulled back in a straggly bun. Anna's basic plain-Jane looks were worsened by the reality of where she was and what had happened. She looked the way family members found in ER waiting rooms always look—haggard, terrified, and shell-shocked.

"You're Jonas?" she asked when she heard my name. "Were you there? What happened? The officer who brought me here couldn't tell me a thing."

Wouldn't tell was more likely than couldn't tell, but I was under no such constraints. I told her what I knew. That we'd been working; that we'd stopped off at the Doghouse for a dinner break; that Pickles had excused himself to make a pit stop. After that, for reasons I didn't understand, it had all gone to hell, with Pickles caught up in a shootout in the parking lot.

I had finished telling the story when a doctor emerged from behind closed doors. He sought out Anna, spoke with her in a low, grave voice, and then took her back through the swinging doors with him into the treatment rooms. Anna walked away from me without so much as a backward glance. Considering the seriousness of the situation, I didn't blame her. I waited around awhile longer. When no one came out to give me an update, I finally gave up. On my way home, I stopped by the department to write up my report. That's when I learned that even with the help of timely eyewitness information, Pickles's two assailants had disappeared without a trace.

It was far later than it should have been when I finally drove into the garage at our place on Lake Tapps. The kids were already in bed, and so was Karen. I poured myself a McNaughton's—probably more than one—and sat there waiting for sleep to come. I worried about whether Pickles would make it, but I have to say, not once that day—not one single time—

did it ever occur to me that Pickles was the one who shot Lulu McCaffey, but of course, that was just me. I was his partner. What did I know?

When I got to work the following morning, the world had changed. Captain Tompkins called me into his office, where he gave me the welcome news that Pickles was still alive. He was gravely ill and still in Intensive Care, but he was resting comfortably and his condition was listed as stable.

In other words, as far as his health was concerned, Pickles was in better shape than could have been expected. As far as his career was concerned, however, he was not. It turned out that the slug the medical examiner had pulled out of Lulu McCaffey's body had come from Pickles's gun.

As of now, Internal Affairs was on the case. In spades.

The captain sent me straight upstairs to IA, where I spent the next three hours being interviewed by the IA investigator assigned to the case. Lieutenant Gary Tatum was a guy with attitude who was used to throwing his weight around and having people dodge out of the way. We detested each other on sight. I wanted to tell him what Pickles had told me about two guys running away. Tatum didn't want to hear it. He was far more interested in what I knew about the "well-known" feud between Pickles and the dead waitress. I told him about Pickles's water-in-the-crotch experience with Lulu McCaffey, not because I thought it was funny but because it was the truth.

Lieutenant Tatum listened to my version of the story and then nodded. "I've heard that one before."

He said it in a bored fashion—as though he hadn't needed to hear it again from me. "But as I understand it, that was a long time ago—a couple of years anyway. There has to be something more recent than that—something more serious—for them to get in this kind of beef."

"There wasn't any beef," I explained. "Detective Gurkey went to take a leak. I'm not sure why he went outside, but he was there when whatever went down went down. He may have been in the parking lot when Lulu was shot, but that doesn't mean he did it."

Tatum gave me his phony Cheshire cat grin complete with an offhand head shake that implied he wasn't buying a word I said and that he thought I was a complete idiot.

"Detective Gurkey's prints are on the gun," Tatum told me. "His are the only prints on the murder weapon. As far as I'm concerned, that means he pulled the trigger. He's also got shot residue on his hands."

"We were at the range yesterday morning," I countered. "We were doing target practice. You can check with them to verify that."

"Oh, we'll be verifying that story, all right," Tatum assured me. "In the meantime, as long as Detective Gurkey is under investigation, you need to know that you're under investigation as well."

"Why?" I demanded. "What did I do? I was sitting there eating my hamburger and minding my own business when the shots were fired. I don't understand why you're investigating me."

"You know the drill," Tatum said with a shrug. "It's the old what-did-you-know-and-when-did-you-know-it routine. I've told Captain Tompkins to keep you sidelined for the next little while. I wouldn't mind that much if I were you. I got a look at the next week's weather forecast. It's going to be hot as Hades outside. You'll be way better off cooling your heels at a desk job than you will be out tracking bad guys on sidewalks hot enough to fry eggs."

I didn't dignify that statement with a response. Instead, I asked, "What about the two runners—the guys who skipped out on paying their tab, the ones Lulu came outside chasing. What about them? Are you even looking for them?"

"Detective Beaumont," Tatum said with a grim smile. "I don't believe you understand. This matter is not yours to investigate. Internal Affairs is handling it. What we do or do not do is none of your concern. Am I making myself clear?"

The threat was there and so was the message: Stay the hell out of the way or get run over and risk your career in the process.

"Detective Gurkey did not kill that woman," I declared.

Tatum smiled again. "That remains to be seen, doesn't it."

We sat there for a length of time, doing a stare down. "May I go?" I said finally.

"Of course," he said. "Just so long as we understand one another."

We did that! I rode the elevator down to the fifth floor in a cloud of outrage, where I soon discovered I was not alone. Every detective in Homicide was pissed. They all figured like I did that Pickles was getting a bum rap. He was within months of being able to pull the plug and get a pension. If IA somehow made a homicide charge stick against him, he would be out on the street with nothing.

Pickles remained hospitalized for the next ten days. Captain Tompkins found me some inane busywork checking inventories in the Evidence Room. That's what I was doing a week later, when I made it a point to track down the McCaffey murder case file. Among the items in evidence I located the piece of paper—the blank order form—Bob Murray had used to write down the names of potential witnesses in the case. A quick check in the murder book revealed that not one of those folks had been singled out for additional in-terviews beyond my brief questioning of them in the bar at the Doghouse the day the shooting happened. Unbelievable! Pickles Gurkey was being railroaded fair and square.

It was almost time to go home. I had stopped by Pickles and my cubby on my way out. Pickles's desk was awash in cards and flowers and balloons. I was sit-ting there wondering if I should drag all that stuff up to the hospital before I went home, when my phone rang.

"Hey," Bob Murray said. "I've been calling and calling. How come you never answer your phone?"

"Because I haven't been at my desk," I said curtly. "Did you ever think of leaving a message?"

"Is it true Internal Affairs is out to get Milton?" Bob asked.

Police departments are a lot like families. We can say whatever we like about other people inside the organization, but outsiders aren't allowed the same privilege. I wasn't about to badmouth Lieutenant Tatum or what he was doing.

"Internal Affairs is handling the investigation," I said evenly.

"Yes, I know, and you can take it from me that Lieutenant Gary Tatum is an arrogant asshole," Bob Murray responded. "He came in here for a steak once and sent it back to the kitchen because he said it was too tough to eat. I wouldn't give him the time of day."

That made me laugh outright. The Doghouse menu says right there in black and white that the tenderness of steaks can't be guaranteed.

"So he thought you were what, the Canlis?" I asked.

"Do you want to be cute or do you want me to talk to you?" Bob growled.

"Talk to me," I said. "What have you got?"

"I was talking to my produce guy the other day," he told me. "He says the same thing that happened to Lulu has been happening to a lot of people in different restaurants all over town. Two guys come in, order, eat, and then do the old dine-and-dash bit. One minute they're there. The next minute they're gone without a trace and their bill is still on the table. Nobody ever sees 'em drive off in a vehicle. They just disappear into thin air."

"A tall guy and a short guy?" I asked.

"From what he told me, the tall guy is always there—the one with the light-colored hair. The problem is, he doesn't always seem to hang out with the same guy."

"So the second guy varies?"

"That's my understanding," Bob said.

"Has the produce guy talked to Lieutenant Tatum?"

"Not to my knowledge," Murray said. "Listen, this is my produce guy. I'm the one he talks to."

"And these other dine-and-dash incidents," I said. "Has anyone ever reported it?"

"Probably not. Guys like me don't want to get involved in all that police report crap, and we don't want the names of our restaurants showing up in local police blotters that may be sent along to the media. They figure it's like shoplifting—it's all part of the cost of doing business."

"It is shoplifting," I corrected. "What they're lifting is your food."

"Yes, but the amounts are small enough that it doesn't make sense to make a huge issue of it. Lulu, may she rest in peace, was a hothead, and she always raised absolute hell about it. That's how come she chased those guys out into the parking lot, acting like the price of their meal was going to come out of her hide. I've never once dinged one of my servers because somebody skipped. It's not the waitress's fault if the customer turns out to be a dick, pardon the expression. Why should they take a hit for it?"

Lots of people call detectives dicks. I try not to take it personally.

"Would your produce guy talk to me?" I asked.

"In a heartbeat," Bob Murray said. "Be here tomorrow morning at ten, and I'll see to it."

The next morning at ten o'clock sharp, I entered the Doghouse for the first time since the shooting.

The booth where the two killers had sat that fateful afternoon had an OCCUPIED sign on it even though the only thing there was a collection of wilting bouquets, their bedraggled flowers dripping dead petals. Around that small sad memorial, the rest of the Doghouse bustled with business as usual.

Bob Murray met me at the host station and escorted me to a seat at the far end of the counter. "As soon as Alfonso gets here, I'll send him your way."

I was halfway through a plate of ham and eggs when a smallish Mexican man slipped quietly onto the stool beside me.

"You the detective?" he asked.

I held out my hand. "J. P. Beaumont," I said. "And you are?"

"Alfonso Romero of Al's Produce," he said. "I'm Al."

It made sense. In Seattle's white-bread business districts, a Hispanic vegetable delivery guy could pass himself off as white or at least as Italian by plastering the name Al on his truck, and the only people that ruse fooled were the people who needed to be fooled.

"Bob says I should talk to you," he said. "About the skips."

"You think it's a pattern?" I asked.

The waitress brought him coffee and a platter of breakfast that included bacon, eggs over easy, crisp hash browns, whole wheat toast, coffee, and orange juice. It must have been a standing order that was put in place the moment he turned up because Romero hadn't been there nearly long enough for even the fastest short-order cook to deliver a breakfast like that in such a timely fashion.

Romero nodded. "Five different restaurants that I know about, including this one, but those are only the ones I work with. There are a lot of restaurants out there and a lot of produce guys just like me."

"Do you know some of them?" I asked. "Your competition, I mean."

Romero shrugged. "Of course I know them," he said. "We get our stuff from the same suppliers; we're out on the docks, loading our lettuce and tomatoes at the same time before we head out on our routes."

"Would these other drivers know if the same thing was happening at other restaurants?"

"Sure," Romero said. "Owners talk. Waitresses talk. They're all in the same business, and everybody knows what everybody else is doing."

"If I showed up on the dock at the same time, would the drivers talk to me?"

Alfonso thought about that for a moment before he answered. "Maybe," he said. "But only if I asked 'em."

Which is how, the next morning, I found myself on the loading dock of a huge warehouse off Rainer Avenue at O-dark-thirty in the morning. Having Bob Murray vouch for me was good enough for Alfonso, and having Alfonso making the introductions was good enough for the other drivers. They all knew that Lulu McCaffey had been murdered, and they were eager to help. By the time I left the dock and headed into the department, I was as excited as a kid on his way to see Santa Claus because I knew I was on to something.

There was a pattern here, and over and over it was the same thing. Two guys—customers who have never been there before—show up in a restaurant, order, eat, don't pay, and go. According to the drivers, it happened mostly in the evenings, just at rush hour, at restaurants all over the city—from north to south, east to west, but never the same restaurant twice. I took down the drivers' names and phone numbers. I asked them to keep checking. Back at the department, I had a decision to make. I knew from the scuttlebutt that Lieutenant Tatum was waiting for Pickles to recover enough to be let out of the hospital, at which point he intended to make an arrest and formally charge him in the death of Lulu McCaffey.

If I had thought Tatum was a square shooter, I would have gone straight upstairs with what I had found from Alfonso and the other drivers, but he wasn't, and I didn't.

Cops patronize restaurants. We go to restaurants at every hour of the day and night, so it wasn't necessary to launch an official investigation in order to launch an investigation. I just had to get word out to the beat cops and to the guys on patrol and to the detectives riding around in their unmarked cars that the restaurants in Seattle were suffering from an epidemic of check skippers, and that we needed to be good neighbors and help our friends in the restaurant business find these guys.

That was a cover-your-ass subterfuge, of course. I'm guessing most everybody understood that we were working behind the scenes to give Pickles a helping hand, and they came through. As the produce guys ran their routes and as the cops talked to their contacts, a trickle of information started coming in.

The details came in on Post-it notes left on my desk while I was laboring in the Evidence Room; in messages left on my office voice mail; and in some instances, with guys I knew, in phone calls to the house at Lake Tapps.

I finally stapled an oversized map of Seattle to the wallboard in the garage at Lake Tapps and began inserting little plastic beaded straight pins into the map wherever I had a report about another dine-and-dash incident. As the collection of pins grew, it wasn't hard to see the pattern. They ranged all over town, with a gaping hole in the center of the city, from the north end of Columbia City on the south, to Capitol Hill on the east. The Doghouse was the only restaurant with any proximity to downtown.

Everybody on the fifth floor knew what was up, but no one breathed a word of it to Tatum. Instead, we gathered in the break room or in cubicles and talked about it. One of the detectives, who was married to a departmental sketch artist, took her to see the witnesses who had been at the Doghouse the day of the McCaffey shooting and to some of the other restaurants that had been victimized by the check-skipping team. Over time we developed credible composite sketches of the two guys from the Doghouse. Once we had those in hand, we made sure the guys from Patrol had copies with them in their cars; we made sure the beat guys had them, too.

It sounds like this was all straightforward, but it wasn't. For one thing, it was an investigation that wasn't supposed to be happening and had to be invisible. For another, almost everyone had other cases—

official cases—that they were supposed to be working. Continuing to toil in the vineyards of the Evidence Room, I was one of two exceptions to that rule. The other one was Pickles Gurkey, who was now officially on administrative leave. Once he got out of the hospital, he was placed under arrest, and then allowed free on bond to await trial after his family posted his immense bail.

I had visited with him in the hospital only once, after he was out of Intensive Care. He told me what he remembered from the crime scene—that he had dropped his gun when the heart attack hit, but that he was sure he hadn't pulled the trigger. Clearly Lieutenant Tatum wasn't buying his story and neither was the King County prosecutor. I wanted to tell him that the guys from Homicide were working the problem and that we hadn't forgotten him, but I didn't dare. And I never went back to the hospital to see him again. I figured if Tatum got wind that there had been any kind of continuing contact between us, he'd be all over me.

They say luck follows the guy who does the work. In that regard we were bound to get lucky eventually. I was down in the Evidence Room one afternoon when the clerk hunted me down and said someone was waiting outside to talk to me. The guy in the hall was a uniformed officer named Richard Vega. He was holding a copy of one of the Doghouse composites—the one of the taller man with the light-colored hair.

"I've seen this guy," he said, waving the sketch in my direction. "My sergeant sent me to Homicide to talk to you, and the clerk up there sent me down here."

"Where have you seen him?" I asked.

"Hanging out down around Pioneer Square," Vega said. "I'm thinking maybe he works somewhere around there."

I thought about the doughnut hole in my circle of pins. Pioneer Square would be well inside it. So maybe, if the guy lived or worked nearby, maybe he didn't want to crap in his own bed or victimize establishments where he might want to be regarded as a regular paying customer.

I knew just where to go. A few years earlier, a Chinese family had bought up a local deli named Bakeman's. The joint was known all over the downtown area and were doing land-office business selling sandwiches made from fresh turkeys that were roasted on the premises every night.

In regard to restaurant food, pundits often say, "You can get quick, cheap, or good. Pick any two." As far as that was concerned, Bakeman's was in a class by itself because they excelled in all three—quick, cheap, and good! And since they were in the 100 block of Cherry, just down the street from the Public Safety Building, plenty of cops went there for lunch on a daily basis.

Bakeman's was one of the places without a beaded pin on my map, so I rushed there immediately, with a mimeographed copy of the tall guy's composite sketch in hand. It was early, right at the beginning of the lunch rush. The young Asian guy at the cash register took my order: white turkey meat with cranberry sauce on white bread. Mayo and mustard, hold the lettuce and tomato. I handed over my money. When the clerk gave me back my change, he was already eyeing the next customer. That's when I held up the sketch.

"You know this guy?" I asked.

"It's lunch," he replied. "Gotta keep the line moving."

"Have you ever seen him?" I repeated.

He glowered at me. "I'm serving lunch here. I got customers."

I held up my badge next to the sketch. The clerk sighed and shook his head. "You guys," he said wearily in a tone that said he thought all cops were royal pains in the ass.

"Do you know him?" I insisted.

He nodded. "White meat turkey on white, mayo, mustard, cranberry sauce. Almost like you, only he takes lettuce."

"Do you know his name?"

"I don't know names. I know orders. Works construction. Dirty clothes. Who's next?"

"So he comes in after working all day, orders white turkey on white. When does he come in? What time?"

"Afternoons. Before we close. Around two or so. Next?"

"Any day in particular?"

"You want to talk more, order another sandwich."

"Done." I said. "Give me the same as before, both of them to go."

"You didn't say to go for the first one."

"I didn't know I was getting two sandwiches then, either. Now I want them both to go. But tell me, does he come in on a certain day?"

The clerk looked as though he was ready to leap

across the counter and strangle me. Instead he glowered at the servers who were putting my sandwiches together. "Both of those turkeys on white are to go," he shouted, and then he glared back at me. "Tuesdays maybe?" he said. "Sometimes Wednesdays, but not every week. Takes his sandwiches to go. Puts them in a lunch pail."

My heart skipped with joy because this happened to be Tuesday.

I gave the clerk my money. He handed me my change. "Next?"

From the way he shouted, I knew better than to press my luck. Without asking any more questions, I took my sandwiches and left. Giddy with excitement, I practically floated back up Cherry to the Public Safety Building, where I rode straight up to the fifth floor, dodged past Captain Tompkins's Fishbowl, and ducked into the cubicle shared by Detectives Powell and Watkins. They were both in. They looked up in surprise when I entered. Surprise turned to welcome when they caught a whiff of the turkey sandwiches.

By two o'clock that afternoon, the three of us had set up shop. Worried that the two guys might have seen me in the Doghouse the day Pickles and I were there at the same time, I stayed across the street, tucked into the shady alcove of a building that let me watch the door to Bakeman's while using the excuse of smoking a cigarette to hang around outside. Watty, who wasn't as fast on his feet as Larry Powell was, stayed in an unmarked car parked at the bottom of Cherry, while Larry went inside and ate a leisurely bowl of soup. I had also contacted Officer Vega and asked him to hang around at the corner of First and Cherry. I was worried that if the suspect was on foot and headed westbound on the eastbound street, Watty wouldn't be able to follow in his vehicle.

At 2:20 I saw the suspect, trudging up Cherry from First carrying a heavy-duty lunch pail. He certainly looked like the guy in the sketch. He was dressed in grimy clothes and appeared to have put in a hard day of manual labor. I watched him walk past the spot where Watty was waiting at the curb. By the time he turned into Bakeman's, my heart was pounding in my chest. There was nothing to do now but wait.

I checked my watch. The crowd inside the restaurant had died down. With no line, it would take only a couple of minutes for him to order his sandwich, pay, pick up his food, and leave. At 2:26 he appeared again. He stood for a moment at the top of the worn marble steps, then he stepped down, turned right, and headed back down to First. He walked past Watty's vehicle, which was parked at the curb, all right, but it was also pointed in the wrong direction on the one-way street.

I slipped out of my hidey-hole and made my way down the hill. When I got to the corner of First, I waved off Vega. After that, it was up to me. When I turned right onto First, I could see the suspect half a block ahead of me walking uphill. Two blocks later, he turned into a run-down building called the Hargrave Hotel.

In theater circles, SRO means standing room only, and that's considered to be a good thing. In hotel-speak, SRO means single room occupancy, and it's generally not such a good thing. The Hargrave was a flea-bitten flophouse straight out of Roger Miller's "King of the Road." It might have been a lot swankier in an earlier era. Now, though, it was four stories of misery, with ten shoddy rooms, two grim toilets, and one moldy shower per floor. Bring your own towel.

I waited outside until I saw Mr. Lunch Pail get into the creaky elevator and close the brass folding gate behind him. By then, Watty had managed to make it around the block. After flagging him down, I stepped into the building lobby, where a grubby, pockmarked marble countertop served as a front desk. Behind it sat a balding man with a green plastic see-through visor perched on his head.

He looked up at me as I entered. "If you're selling something," he told me, "we ain't buying."

I held up my badge and my composite sketch. As soon as he saw the drawing, the desk clerk glanced reflexively toward the elevator. The dial above the elevator showed that the car had stopped on floor three. Clearly this was a one-elevator building.

"Who's this?" I asked.

"You got a warrant?"

"Not at the moment," I returned mildly, "but I'm wondering how this place would measure up if somebody happened to schedule a surprise inspection from the Health Department?" When he didn't reply, I pressed my advantage. "Who?" I insisted.

"Benjamin Smith."

"How long has he been here?"

The clerk shrugged. "A couple of months, I guess. Pays his rent right on time every week."

"Where does he work?"

"He's a laborer down at that new stadium they're building. The Kingdome, I think it's called. What do you want him for?"

"Girl trouble," I said quickly. "As in underage. Might be better for your relationship with the Health Department if he didn't know that anybody had come by asking about him."

Visor Man nodded vigorously. "My lips are sealed," he said.

I ducked back outside. By then, Larry had caught up and was waiting in the front seat of the car with Watty. I climbed into the back. "The clerk says our guy's name is Benjamin Smith. That may or may not be an alias."

"So if he is our guy," Larry said, "what do we do now? Even if we can get his prints and connect him to the Doghouse crime scene, that still won't be enough to let Pickles off the hook. It'll be his word against Smith's word. Might be enough for reasonable doubt, but I'm not sure. We need to find a way to corroborate Pickles's version of the story."

I thought about that. Presumably there had been three people present when Lulu McCaffey was gunned down. We had found two of them. Now we needed to locate the third. The blond guy was the one who had usually shown up in the establishments marked by the bead pattern on the map in my garage. When it had become clear that the light-haired guy was doing dine-and-dash with a collection of different pals, I had given up carrying the short guy's sketch and focused instead on the tall one. Now I had a hunch.

"Do either of you have that other Doghouse composite?" I asked.

"I think so," Watty said. "Hand me the notebook there on the backseat." I gave it to him. He rummaged through it for several long minutes before finally handing me what I wanted.

"Wait here," I said. "And open the door so I can get out."

With the new sketch in hand, I hurried back into the lobby. When the desk clerk looked up and saw me, he gave a disgusted sigh. "You again," he said.

I held up the drawing. "Have you ever seen this guy?"

"Sure," he said. "That's Fred—Fred Beman. Everybody called him Cowboy Fred."

"Does he live here, too?" I asked.

"Used to. Left sometime in July."

"Do you know where he went?"

"He's in Walla Walla," the clerk said. "Went back home to the family farm. At least, that's what he said he was going to do when he left here. With these guys, you can never tell how much is truth and how much is fiction."

"Did he leave a forwarding address?"

The clerk turned away from me and pulled a long, narrow file box out of the bottom drawer of a file cabinet behind him. Inside the box was a collection of three-by-five cards. After thumbing through them, he pulled out one and handed it to me. All that was on it was a phone number and a P.O. box number in Walla Walla.

It wasn't much, but it was a start.

Detectives Watkins and Powell and I went straight back to the department and looked up Frederick Beman. There were two Frederick Bemans listed. The composite sketch was surprisingly close to the younger one's Department of Licensing photo. His driving record included three DUIs. He'd had a pickup once, but that had been totaled during one of the DUI incidents. The DMV showed no current vehicles listed in his name, although there were several listed for his father, Frederick Beman, Sr., who owned a horse ranch somewhere outside Walla Walla.

"Looks like we're going to Walla Walla," Larry Powell said.

"When?" I asked.

"Right now."

I glanced at my watch. It was after four in the afternoon. "How are we going to do that?"

"We're going to drive," Larry said. "We'll take turns. You go check out a car. Make sure it has a full tank of gas. I'll clear it with the captain."

That's exactly what I did. While the guys at Motor Pool were gassing up the car, I called Karen and told her I wouldn't be home. Since she was stuck there alone with a toddler and a colicky baby, she was not happy to hear that I was off on a cross-state adventure, but there wasn't much she could do about it. Captain Tompkins wasn't thrilled, either, especially with having three members of his Homicide Unit tied up in what he termed a "wild-goose chase," but he relented finally, too. Larry convinced him that this was basically my lead, but that I was too green to chase after it alone. So off we went, all three of us.

Walla Walla is a long way from Seattle—two hundred and fifty miles, give or take. With me sitting in the backseat, I'm sure people who saw us thought I was a crook being hauled off to jail somewhere. We took turns driving. By the time we got into Walla Walla, it was too late to do much of anything but get a room and wait for morning. We opted for one room with two double beds. Not the best arrangement, but bunking with Watty beat sleeping on the floor or out in the car. The next morning, over coffee, we were all complaining about how everyone else snored, so I guess it was pretty even-Steven on that score.

After breakfast we found our way to Beman Arabians. There was a main house and several immense barns with an office complex at the near end of one of them. There were also a number of outbuildings that looked as though they were occupied by workers of one stripe or another. When we asked for Fred Beman, we were directed to the office, where we found a handsome, white-haired, older gentleman seated behind a messy desk. When he stood up and stepped out from behind the desk to greet us, he looked for the all the world as if he had simply emerged, cowboy boots and all, from one of those old Gene Autry movies I loved so much when I was a kid. One look at him was enough to tell us that this might be Fred Beman, but not the one we wanted.

Larry Powell held up his badge. "We're looking for Fred Beman, a younger Fred Beman."

The old man stared at the badge for a moment, then looked back at Larry. "That would be Fred Junior, my son. What's he done now?"

"We're actually interested in a friend of his," Larry said. "A friend from Seattle."

Beman shook his head. "Don't know nothin' about any of those. When Freddie came skedaddlin' back home this summer and begged me to give him another chance, I figured he was in some kind of hot water or other. He's out back shovelin' shit. I told him if he wanted to get back in my good graces and into the family business, he'd be startin' from the bottom."

With that Fred Senior led the way out of his office and into the barn. It was pungent with the smell of horses and hay. We found Fred Junior in one of the stalls, pitchfork in hand. He must have taken after his mother because he didn't look anything like his dad. He didn't smell like his dad, either. His father carried a thick cloud of Old Spice with him wherever he went. The air around Junior reeked of perspiration flavored with something else—vodka most likely. Anyone who thinks vodka doesn't smell hasn't spent any time around a serious drunk. Fred Junior may not have been driving at the moment, but he was most definitely still drinking.

"Someone to see you, Freddie," the old man said, then he turned on the worn heels of his cowboy boots and walked away. It was clear from his posture that whatever problem we represented was his son's problem, and he would have to deal with it on his own.

Fred Junior leaned on the handle of the pitchfork. "What's this about?"

I held up my badge. "It's about your friend Benjamin," I said.

A wary look crossed Fred's face. I had learned at the academy that an assailant with a knife can cut down a guy with a gun before there's time to pull the trigger. I calculated that the wicked metal tines on the long-handled pitchfork could poke holes in my guts faster than any handheld knife. I was glad I had Watty and Larry Powell there for backup if need be. The problem was, I wanted this guy alive and talking, far more than I wanted him dead.

"What about him?" Fred said.

"He's been telling us some interesting stories," I said casually. "He told us you shot a woman a few weeks ago—shot her in cold blood in the parking lot of the Doghouse Restaurant in Seattle."

The only light in the barn came from the open stall doors along the side of the building and from a few grimy windows up near the roof. Still, even in the relative gloom of the barn, I saw the color drain from his face. The muscles in his jaw clenched.

"I never," he said. "I was there, but I never shot her. I told him, 'Hey, man. I've got the money. Let's just pay the woman.' But Benjy's crazy. He picked up the gun and fired away."

"Maybe you'd like to put down that pitchfork and give us a statement," I suggested.

For a long moment, nobody moved while Fred Junior stood there and considered what he would do. It was quiet enough in the barn that you could have heard a pin drop. Somewhere within hearing distance a fly buzzed.

Finally Fred spoke again. "Can you get me a deal?" he asked.

I shook my head. "I can't promise any deals," I said, "but if you'll help us, I'll do what I can to help you."

It was lame, but it was the best I could do under the circumstances, and it probably wouldn't have worked if Fred Beman hadn't been ready to turn himself in. He didn't need a deal. All you had to do was look at him to see that his conscience was eating him alive. He had run home to Daddy after what happened at the Doghouse. He was half dead from a combination of too much booze and too little sleep. I could tell from the haunted look in his eyes that wherever he went and no matter how much he tried to drink himself into oblivion, Fred could find no escape. Lulu McCaffey in her black uniform and little white apron was still lying there on the hot, dirty pavement, as dead as could be.

"Put down the pitchfork, please," I said quietly. "Place your hands on your head."

There was another long pause. I hadn't drawn my weapon, but I had heard the subtle snap of leather as both Larry and Watty drew theirs. As I said, it was deathly quiet in that barn. I think we were all holding our breaths. When Fred finally moved, it was only to lean over and carefully lower the pitchfork to the floor. Without a word, Watty stepped forward and cuffed him. I read him his rights. By then, Fred was crying his eyes out.

"I couldn't believe it when it happened," he sobbed. "It was just supposed to be fun. He shot her down like she was an animal or something."

We were cops from out of town and were a long way outside our jurisdiction. We also hadn't reported our arrival to any of the local authorities. As a consequence, we needed to get out of Dodge. And since

Fred seemed willing enough to talk, we wanted that to happen before he got all lawyered up. Fortunately, Larry Powell had planned ahead. He had brought a battery-powered cassette tape recorder with him. Once the four of us were settled in the car with me riding in back with Fred, we turned on Larry's recorder, read Fred Beman his rights again, and announced into the tape who all was present in the vehicle. Then we began the long drive back to Seattle, listening to his story as we went.

It turned out that skipping out on checks in restaurants was Benjamin Smith's hobby. He did it all the time, whether he had money in his pocket to pay for his dinner or not. He traveled around town on bus passes. That's why he often timed his dine-and-dash events to happen during rush hour when there were plenty of people out and about and lots of buses on the streets. That's how he managed to disappear so readily—by blending in with the crowd.

Gradually, when Fred got a grip on himself, we had him go over the story again, and recount exactly what had happened in the Doghouse parking lot. His story matched Pickles's in every detail, including the fact that none of the three of them—Lulu, Benjamin, or Fred—had seen Pickles Gurkey in the parking lot prior to the moment when he had attempted to intervene in the fight between Lulu and Benjamin. They had stopped their altercation long enough to see him standing there, holding a drawn weapon, and announcing he was a cop. Then he had simply dropped the gun, staggered backward, and fallen against the building.

"I don't know if the guy was drunk or what," Fred continued. "Benjy reached down and picked up the gun. The woman had stopped yelling by then because she was all worried about the guy who had just fallen over. I think she realized at the last moment that Benjy had a gun, but by then it was too late for her to get away. As soon as Benjy shot her, he wiped the gun off with his shirt, put it in the guy's hand, and then dropped it in his lap. The guy on the ground was so out of it, I doubt he had any idea what had just happened. After that, we took off, ran like hell over to Denny, and hopped a bus up to Capitol Hill. Benjy said not to worry, that he was sure both the woman and the cop were dead. Benjy was convinced people would think the cop had done it and that no one would ever find us, but you have," he finished. "You did."

"It turns out Medic 1 showed up in time, and Detective Gurkey didn't die," I told him. "In fact, he's the whole reason we're here today. He's being charged with murder in the death of Lulu McCaffey. He's about to go down for what you did. Our job is to make sure that doesn't happen."

"You still don't understand," Fred insisted. "I'm telling you, I didn't do it. I'm not the one who shot her. Benjy did."

"And then what?"

"And then I had to get out of Seattle. I called my dad and asked if I could come home. Again. He said he'd give me a place to stay and food to eat, but I had to work for it, just like his other hands. And that's what I did."

I looked at my watch. Watty glanced in the rearview mirror and caught me doing it. "Don't worry," he said. "We'll be there in time."

We drove straight back to Seattle. We dropped by Seattle PD long enough to put Fred Beman in an interrogation room, and then we headed for the Hargrove Hotel. In case Benjamin Smith made a run for it, we stationed two uniformed officers at First and Madison. Watty was parked in a car facing northbound at First and Columbia. Larry Powell and I waited inside the scuzzy lobby of the Hargrave, seated on a pair of swaybacked, cracked leather chairs. The clerk seemed distinctly unhappy to see us. As the moments ticked by, I worried that he might have spilled the beans and Benjamin Smith had already skipped town.

Instead, Benjy—I liked thinking of him that way— showed up right on time, at twenty minutes to three, sauntering along, swinging his lunch pail like he didn't have a care in the world. It was Wednesday. There was no telling if he'd stopped at Bakeman's on his way home. As soon as he pushed open the brass and glass door and started for the elevator, I stood up to head him off.

"Mr. Smith," I said, barring his way and holding my badge up to his face. "Detective Beaumont with Seattle PD. If you don't mind, I'd like to have a word."

I was deliberately in his face, and the man did exactly what I hoped he'd do. He took a swing at me with the lunch pail. Since that's what I was expecting, I blocked it easily. When you need an excuse to take someone into custody, there's nothing like resisting in front of a collection of witnesses to give you a warrantless reason to lock some guy up in a jail cell for the next few hours. On the way to Benjy's interrogation room, I made sure he got a look at Fred, anxious and despairing, sitting in his.

"What's he doing here?" Benjy asked, nodding in Fred's direction.

"What do you think he's doing?" I said. "Mr. Beman is singing like a bird. How do you think we found you?"

Mel came in about then, smiling and waving her freshly manicured, scarlet nails in my face as she kissed me hello. "What were you reading?" she asked, looking down at the scatter of yellowing onionskin paper I had dropped onto the carpet in front of the window seat. I had let the pages fall as I read them. After I had finished reading, I had simply let them be as I sat there recalling that long-ago history.

"It's something Pickles Gurkey wrote before he died," I explained.

"Your old partner?"

I nodded. "His widow, Anna, died a few weeks ago. His daughter, Anne Marie, was cleaning out her mother's house and found this. She dropped it off because she thought I'd want to read it."

"Did you?" Mel asked. "Read it, I mean."

I nodded again.

"May I?"

"Sure," I said. "Help yourself."

So Mel gathered up the pages, settled comfortably on the window seat next to me, and started to read.

The storm had long since ended. The clouds had rolled eastward. Outside the sky was a fragile blue, and so was the water out in the sound, but it was getting on toward evening.

I waited quietly until Mel finished reading. Fortunately she's a very fast reader.

"So what happened?" she asked, straightening the sheets of paper and handing them back to me in a neat stack.

"We found the bad guys eventually," I said. "The one who turned state's evidence got off with two years for involuntary manslaughter. The shooter, Benjamin Smith, got fifteen years at Monroe for second-degree homicide, which ended up turning into a life sentence."

"How did that happen?"

"Benjy was an arrogant asshole. That's why he thought it was great fun to dodge out of restaurants without paying his bills. As far as he was concerned, the whole thing was nothing but a lark. Unfortunately for him, prison has a way of cutting arrogance down to size. Another inmate stuck a shiv into him. He died ten months into his fifteen-year sentence."

"The other guy at the restaurant shooting?" Mel asked.

"Fred Beman served his sentence, straightened out his life, and now he's back home in Walla Walla helping his father run his horse farm."

"What about Pickles?"

"I was there in the courtroom the day the prosecutor dropped all charges against him. He turned around, grabbed my hand, shook it like crazy, and said, 'Thanks, Beau. Thanks a lot.'"

"What about the Jonas bit. Did he ever call you that again?" Mel asked.

"Never. Not once. We worked together for the next five years, and he never called me anything but Beau."

Mel frowned, looking at the papers in her hand.

"Isn't Pickles the guy who ended up dying of another heart attack?" Mel asked.

"Right," I said. "That was Pickles. The second one was five years later."

"So if you saved him from a murder charge, I don't get why his family blamed you when he died of a second heart attack that long after the first."

"They thought he was working to make it up to me—that he owed me somehow—for keeping him out of jail, but it turns out, that wasn't it at all. It was the case."

"What case?"

"The Woodfield case, the one we got called out on that day."

"The old guy who killed his wife and then turned the gun on himself?"

"That's the one. From that day on, I remember whenever we'd go somewhere for lunch or dinner, Pickles would spend most of the time sitting there doing arithmetic on paper napkins or in his notebook, trying to figure out if Anna would be better off if he died while he was still on the job so she'd get a lump sum payment or if she'd end up with more money if she was the joint survivor on his pension."

"Which one would have been better?" Mel asked.

"Pickles opted to work," I said with a shrug. "Anna probably got a little more money when he died, twenty or thirty thousand more is all. The problem is, she spent the rest of her life mad at him for choosing to work instead of choosing to stay home with her. To her dying day she was convinced that was all my fault."

"Sounds like they both got the short end of the stick," Mel observed.

I looked at her. Mel was beautiful. She loved me, and I loved her. Yes, Pickles Gurkey may have thought he owed me something for saving his bacon on that murder charge, but it turned out that, as of today, I owed him for something even more important.

"Let's not make the same mistake Pickles did," I said. "Whatever time we have, let's not miss it. Let's spend it together."

Mel smiled back at me and held out her hand. "Deal," she said.

We shook on it.

"So what are we doing for New Year's Eve?" she asked. "Are we going out or staying home?"

I glanced at my watch. The afternoon had disappeared on me. It was almost five o'clock.

"Going out," I said. "Let's go put on our Sunday-go-to-meeting clothes and see what El Gaucho is serving for their blue plate special."

"They don't have a blue plate special," Mel pointed out. "They never have."

"Right," I said. "And it doesn't matter if they do or don't because if there's one lesson Pickles Gurkey taught me today, it's this: Don't worry about the money. Spend the time."

Hours later, when it came time for midnight, we

were standing on the balcony of our penthouse when the first volley of fireworks went off from the top of the Space Needle. Mel was holding her flute of real champagne. I had my glass of faux.

On the balcony below ours, someone had turned up their sound system, and "Auld Lang Syne" was blasting out of their speakers at full volume, loud enough to cover the rock and roll coming at us from Seattle Center.

Mel reached over and clinked her glass gently into mine. "Happy New Year," she said.

I nodded. "Thank you," I said. "And to you, and to time spent together."

The fireworks were still blasting skyward when the song from the unit below ended in the familiar refrain, "We'll take a cup o' kindness yet, for auld lang syne."

Maybe I'm just getting sentimental, but a lump caught in my throat. I wiped a stray tear from my eye.

Mel shot me a concerned look. "What?" she asked. "What's going on?"

"Just remembering," I said. Then I raised my glass again. "Here's to Pickles Gurkey," I said. "May he rest in peace."